Three by Tey

Murder Revisited Series

Three by Tey

MISS PYM DISPOSES
THE FRANCHISE AFFAIR
BRAT FARRAR

by Josephine Tey

With an Introduction by JAMES SANDOE

New York THE MACMILLAN COMPANY *1955*

A Murder Revisited Classic

Introduction

Elizabeth MacKintosh chose to live her public life under two pseudonyms. As "Gordon Daviot" she wrote novels, a biography and a number of plays among which the best remembered is presumably "Richard of Bordeaux" (1933). It afforded Sir John Gielgud his first conspicuous popular success as he attests so warmly in his autobiography, "Early Stages" (1939), and the touching remembrance of "Gordon" which serves as preface to the recent collection of her plays.

Indeed it was as Gordon Daviot and as early as 1929 that Miss MacKintosh made her first appearance as a detective story writer. In that year appeared "The Man in the Queue," recently reprinted and anticipating fully in texture and in interest its seven successors. Inspector Alan Grant is apparent here (the ingratiating Williams at his side then as later) and Miss MacKintosh catches up in the net of her plot the same rich, acutely observed diversity of characters—clergymen and bookies, actors and stockbrokers—one remembers from all of the tales.

But plays were Gordon Daviot's larger concern for a number of years. Until, indeed, "Daviot" all but disappeared from lists of forthcoming publications and "Josephine Tey" made her first appearance with "A Shilling for Candles: The Story of a Crime" in 1936.

Here Miss Tey, with a characteristic minimum of violence, admits a corpse (drowned?) in the opening pages, turns at once to an investigation of the unfortunate business and to a singularly warming retrospective evocation of the victim. Her manner is leisurely but always telling because she is capable of keeping us quite as much absorbed in Grant's encounter with a grubby

Canterbury tobacconist or the coltish Miss Erica's private investigations as with climaxes and revelations.

Any reader unwary enough to mistake this leisure for slowness or the digressions for padding is probably a bird who reads digests of Dickens and Dostoevski or chews up a hamburger because roast beef takes longer to cook. Certainly Miss Tey does not stint her readers. There is a richness of delineation even among the minor players (Dora Siggins in "To Love and Be Wise," for instance) that is particularly contenting. There is savour too in the setting and in the characters' responses to it. This is most integrally apparent in "Brat Farrar" but it is present in all of them.

Then of course there is Grant, the least insistently genteel of detectives (a cousin of E. C. R. Lorac's Inspector Macdonald, one would guess) and the most satisfyingly human even in the private adversities which enter the latest novels. One has only to recall some of Grant's older contemporaries (Lord Peter Wimsey, Mr. Campion, Roderick Alleyn) in a *crise de nerfs* to measure the accomplishment.

Grant himself was absent from the third of the mysteries, "Miss Pym Disposes" * (1947), the earliest of the three novels which make up this volume. For a mystery it is made up of most unpromising stuffs: the students and staff of a girls' physical education college, observed by a visiting "popular psychologist," wound in an all but plotless succession of incident which has as its apparent climax the nomination of one of the girls for "the Arlinghurst job." Save for one premonitory brush there is no mystery, much less murder, until the novel has run four-fifths of its course. The fact of murder thereafter is, to be sure, the more shocking on that account.

But meanwhile, and observing through Miss Pym's alert, sardonic-compassionate perceptions, we have been altered (as she is) from perhaps casual observers to fierce advocates. This is due only in part to Miss Pym herself, admirable companion though she is. It is the consequence of meeting a lively and provoking company from the coolly gaudy Nut Tart to the shifty Miss Rouse. In a day when one opens the first page of a detective story to be blasted at

---

* Although readers may puzzle at three references to an "Alan" (with an Adam's apple) whom Miss Pym remembers nearly accepting years earlier.

once by a tommygun, the skill of sustaining human interest in itself seems as rich as it is certainly rare.*

· II ·

Insisting first that eight mysteries is all too few, one may from affection engage with some spirit in choosing favorites among them, very much as one does among the films of Alec Guinness. A filmgoer susceptible of total recall at mere mention of "The Lavender Hill Mob" may still retain a special devotion for the quiet perfection of Mr. Guinness' Herbert Pocket in "Great Expectations." Another, unable to shake the livid immediacy of Fagin (who had always seemed a safe sort of caricature before), will perhaps have a special leap of contentment in recalling the singular expressiveness of the Captain's abandon to dance in the North African nightclub.

This is not, I think, irrelevant since for me at least Mr. Guinness and Miss Tey have that special capacity for engaging one's affections, catching them up as a friend does and not just as a passing acquaintance.

None of the novels takes any faster or firmer hold on one than "The Franchise Affair" (1948) where in a few pages at the outset Miss Tey realizes Robert Blair (genteel, comfortable, sheltered and just a little restive) and poises him for adventure.

"The Franchise Affair" owes its idea to the eighteenth century case of Elizabeth Canning (called here "Betty Kane" in acknowledgment). Sir John Gielgud recalls that Miss MacKintosh "was distressed by her inability to write original plots, especially when, on two occasions, she was unfairly accused of plagiarism." It was a baseless fear as any of you who know the Canning case will see.

---

* Sustaining it, too, with considerably more toughness of mind than the self-pitying bullyboys who have tried to succeed the detached Hammett and the passionate Chandler with their tommyguns. It is Sir John Gielgud again who recalls of Miss MacKintosh: "Her sudden death . . . was a great surprise and shock to all her friends in London. I learned afterwards that she had known herself to be mortally ill for nearly a year, and had resolutely avoided seeing anyone she knew. This gallant behaviour was typical of her and curiously touching, if a little inhuman too."

It is also the most positive confirmation for the values which illuminate her novels and one reason why Miss Tey and Mr. Chandler have a good deal more in common than either of them would with Mr. Spillane.

She has indeed taken its central situation but transformed it so in time and place and realized it with such fresh and telling immediacy, that it is, in fact, entirely her own.

Here too, of course, physical violence all but vanishes (as it does in very rare examples of the *genre:* Dorothy Sayers' "Gaudy Night" for one) and the puzzle is spun from the dilemma in which the accused mother and daughter find themselves and the appalling difficulty (if indeed they *are* innocent, after all) of making their innocence compulsively plain. It is an astonishing accomplishment and remains past rereadings as one of the most richly (and repeatedly) exciting detective stories I know anything about.

Grant, present peripherally in "The Franchise Affair," is absent from "Brat Farrar" (1949) which is the story of an impostor. Some mystery attaches to the imposition and to its reception but the excitement here is essentially the excitement of watching a tightrope performer with the assurance that he must fall and the desire that he shan't be hurt.

Miss Tey prepares us for Brat by evoking Latchetts, its family and its rich countryside. The evocation is loving and affecting. Brat himself is an uncommon impostor caught past reluctance into a game which must then be played with fastidiousness and even with honor. He has a very genuine charm and his precarious adventure involves the reader early and firmly and then holds on tightly to the explosive conclusion. But "Brat Farrar" is still more a romance than a story of crime, although its romance is no matter of holding hands (much less leaping into beds). It is an expression of devotion to English tradition and the English countryside. Its setting is contemporary but its effect is nostalgic and fetching.

·   III   ·

In "To Love and Be Wise" (1950) Miss Tey employed her boldest deceit and did her most skilful juggling, underscoring her clues and indeed making the very quality of the mystery its principal clue and a gigantic one. To be sure the size of the deceit astonished some readers into protest but a rereading convinces me that, granting one rather large problem not convincingly solved, it is an exceptional and (especially upon a rereading) notably rewarding piece of work.

Orfordshire is its setting and, more particularly, Salcott St. Mary, invaded by a noisy lot of artists seeking a quiet country retreat. Miss Tey's sketches here come closer to caricature than most of her characterizations and lose no pungency by Grant's quiet but penetrating observation as he seeks for evidence about the vanished American photographer, Leslie Searle.

"To Love and Be Wise" was succeeded by the most astonishing detective story of them all, "The Daughter of Time" (1951), an account of Grant's search (from a hospital bed) for the truth about Richard III, the venomous, hunchback monster whose firm place among history's villains is countered so oddly by the sensitive face apparent in a contemporary portrait.

Grant's first doubt, succeeded by others, makes a marvellously exciting narrative evolved once again from what, superficially, are unpromising stuffs. Miss Tey was not, of course, the first to champion Richard Plantagenet, but the terms in which she realizes the processes of scholarly detection here are memorably infectious.*

Grant appears last in that latest of the novels "The Singing Sands" (1952), published posthumously. Again he is sick but here rather in mind than body and the novel is as much an account of his rehabilitation in the Scottish highlands as it is an account of the search for a murderer. On both scores it is absorbing and here, as in the other tales, there are particular delights which return warmingly to mind, among them the scenes of fishing in Highland streams with young Pat and the pungent sequence (complete with *ceilidh*) on Cladda in the Hebrides.

Eight tales there are, all of them (if diversely) contenting for all that Miss Tey was not an innovator. She did not, as Hammett did, give detective fiction a new idiom, nor can she, like Mrs. Christie, be praised for a remarkable sequence of dazzling plots.

* This may be measured best in the novel itself, of course, but interestingly too against the text of "Dickon" ("Plays" by Gordon Daviot: London, 1953, v. 1) in which most of the same historical materials are used in a different fashion and supplemented by some pages of notes on the Richard of fact and the Richard of a carefully nurtured Tudor fiction. It is difficult to say (especially just after encountering again the vividness of the novel) how the play would hold its stage, not least because it lacks by chronological necessity the excitements of the metamorphosis which the novel performs so teasingly.

For that matter, although she succeeded more compellingly than some of her most distinguished peers in evoking character compulsively (and better than some of the most distinguished among them in that her characters never for an instant become pretentious), one cannot comprehend any one of these eight tales by recalling its characters or its plot. And this is because each is more than either and more than the sum of both. It is perhaps the infusion into all of them of a singularly delicate and humorous perception that fixes them in remembrance as cheeringly as a friend, a warm hearth, and a bracing glass on a snowy day.

—JAMES SANDOE

Miss Pym Disposes

・ I ・

A BELL clanged. Brazen, insistent, maddening.

Through the quiet corridors came the din of it, making hideous the peace of the morning. From each of the yawning windows of the little quadrangle the noise poured out on to the still, sunlit garden where the grass was grey yet with dew.

Little Miss Pym stirred, opened one doubtful grey eye, and reached blindly for her watch. There was no watch. She opened the other eye. There seemed to be no bedside table either. No, of course not; now she remembered. There *was* no bedside table; as she had found last night. Her watch had had of necessity to be put under her pillow. She fumbled for it. Good heavens, what a row that bell was making! Obscene. There seemed to be no watch under the pillow. But it must be there! She lifted the pillow bodily, revealing only one small sheer-linen handkerchief in a saucy pattern of blue-and-white. She dropped the pillow and peered down between the bed and the wall. Yes, there was something that looked like a watch. By lying flat on her front and inserting an arm she could just reach it. Carefully she brought it up, lightly caught between the tips of first and second fingers. If she dropped it now she would have to get out of bed and crawl under for it. She turned on her back with a sigh of relief, holding the watch triumphantly above her.

Half-past five, said the watch.

Half-past five!

Miss Pym stopped breathing and stared in unbelieving fascination. No, really, did any college, however physical and hearty, begin the day at *half-past five!* Anything was possible, of course, in a community which had use for neither bedside tables nor bedside lamps, but—half-past five! She put the watch to her small pink ear. It ticked faithfully. She squinted round her pillow at the garden which was visible from the window behind her bed. Yes,

I

it certainly was early; the world had that unmoving just-an-apparition look of early morning. Well, well!

Henrietta had said last night, standing large and majestical in the doorway: "Sleep well. The students enjoyed your lecture, my dear. I shall see you in the morning;" but had not seen fit to mention half-past-five bells.

Oh, well. It wasn't her funeral, thank goodness. Once upon a time she too had lived a life regulated by bells, but that was long ago. Nearly twenty years ago. When a bell rang in Miss Pym's life now it was because she had put a delicately varnished finger-tip on the bell-push. As the clamour died into a complaining whimper and then into silence, she turned over to face the wall, burrowing happily into her pillow. Not her funeral. Dew on the grass, and all that, was for youth: shining resplendent youth; and they could have it. She was having another two hours' sleep.

Very childlike she looked with her round pink face, her neat little button of a nose, and her brown hair rolled in flat invisible-pinned curls all over her head. They had cost her a spiritual struggle last night, those curls. She had been very tired after the train journey, and meeting Henrietta again, and the lecture; and her weaker self had pointed out that she would in all probability be leaving after lunch on the morrow, that her permanent wave was only two months old, and that her hair might very well be left unpinned for one night. But, partly to spite her weaker self with whom she waged a constant and bitter war, partly so that she might do Henrietta justice, she had seen to it that fourteen pins were pressed to their nightly duty. She was remembering her strong-mindedness now (it helped to cancel out any twinge of conscience about her self-indulgence this morning) and marvelling at the survival of that desire to live up to Henrietta. At school, she, the little fourth-form rabbit, had admired the sixth-form Henrietta extravagantly. Henrietta was the born Head Girl. Her talent lay exclusively in seeing that other people employed theirs. That was why, although she had left school to train in secretarial work, she was now Principal of a college of physical culture; a subject of which she knew nothing at all. She had forgotten all about Lucy Pym, just as Lucy had forgotten about her, until Miss Pym had written The Book.

That is how Lucy herself thought of it. The Book.

She was still a little surprised about The Book herself. Her mission in life had been to teach schoolgirls to speak French. But after four years of that her remaining parent had died, leaving her two hundred and fifty pounds a year, and Lucy had dried her eyes with one hand and given in her resignation with the other. The Headmistress had pointed out with envy and all uncharitableness that investments were variable things, and that two hundred and fifty didn't leave much margin for a civilised and cultured existence such as people in Lucy's position were expected to live. But Lucy had resigned all the same, and had taken a very civilised and cultured flat far enough from Camden Town to be nearly Regents Park. She provided the necessary margin by giving French lessons now and then when gas bills were imminent, and spent all her spare time reading books on psychology.

She read her first book on psychology out of curiosity, because it seemed to her an interesting sort of thing; and she read all the rest to see if they were just as silly. By the time she had read thirty-seven books on the subject, she had evolved ideas of her own on psychology; at variance, of course, with all thirty-seven volumes read to date. In fact, the thirty-seven volumes seemed to her so idiotic and made her so angry that she sat down there and then and wrote reams of refutal. Since one cannot talk about psychology in anything but jargon, there being no English for most of it, the reams of refutal read very learnedly indeed. Not that that would have impressed anyone if Miss Pym had not used the back of a discarded sheet (her typing was not very professional) on which to write:

Dear Mr Stallard,

I should be *so* grateful if you would not use your wireless after eleven at night. I find it *so* distracting.

Yours sincerely

Lucy Pym.

Mr Stallard, whom she did not know (his name was on the card outside his door on the floor below) arrived in person that evening. He was holding her letter open in his hand, which seemed to Lucy very grim indeed, and she swallowed several times before she could make any coherent sound at all. But Mr Stallard wasn't

3

angry about the wireless. He was a publishers' reader, it seemed, and was interested in what she had unconsciously sent him on the back of the paper.

Now in normal times a publisher would have rung for brandy at the mere suggestion of publishing a book on psychology. But the previous year the British public had shaken the publishing world by tiring suddenly of fiction, and developing an interest in abstruse subjects, such as the distance of Sirius from the earth, and the inward meaning of primitive dances in Bechuanaland. Publishers were falling over themselves, therefore, in their effort to supply this strange new thirst for knowledge, and Miss Pym found herself welcomed with open arms. That is to say, she was taken to lunch by the senior partner, and given an agreement to sign. This alone was a piece of luck, but Providence so ordained it that not only had the British public tired of fiction, but the intellectuals had tired of Freud and Company. They were longing for Some New Thing. And Lucy proved to be it. So Lucy woke one morning to find herself not only famous, but a best-seller. She was so shocked that she went out and had three cups of black coffee and sat in the Park looking straight in front of her for the rest of the morning.

She had been a best-seller for several months, and had become quite used to lecturing on "her subject" to learned societies, when Henrietta's letter had come; reminding her of their schooldays together and asking her to come and stay for a while and address the students. Lucy was a little wearied of addressing people, and the image of Henrietta had grown dim with the years. She was about to write a polite refusal, when she remembered the day on which the fourth form had discovered her christened name to be Laetitia; a shame that Lucy had spent her life concealing. The fourth form had excelled themselves, and Lucy had been wondering whether her mother would mind very much about her suicide, and deciding that anyhow she had brought it on herself by giving her daughter such a high-falutin name. And then Henrietta had waded into the humourists, literally and meta-phorically. Her blistering comment had withered humour at the root, so that the word Laetitia had never been heard again, and Lucy had gone home and enjoyed jam roly-poly instead of throwing herself in the river. Lucy sat in her civilised and cultured living-room, and felt the old passionate gratitude to Henrietta run over her in waves. She wrote and said that she would be delighted to stay a night with Henrietta (her native caution was not entirely obliterated by her gratitude) and would with pleasure talk on psychology to her students.

The pleasure had been considerable, she thought, pushing up a hump of sheet to shut out the full brilliance of the daylight. Quite the nicest audience she had ever had. Rows of shining heads, making the bare lecture-room look like a garden. And good hearty applause. After weeks of the polite pattering of learned societies it was pleasant to hear the percussion of hollowed palm on hollowed palm. And their questions had been quite intelligent. Somehow, although psychology was a subject on their timetable, as shown in the common-room, she had not expected intellectual appreciation from young women who presumably spent their days doing things with their muscles. Only a few, of course, had asked questions; so there was still a chance that the rest were morons.

Oh well, tonight she would sleep in her own charming bed, and all this would seem like a dream. Henrietta had pressed her to stay for some days, and for a little she had toyed with the idea. But supper had shaken her. Beans and milk pudding seemed an uninspired sort of meal for a summer evening. Very sustaining and nourishing and all that, she didn't doubt. But not a meal one wanted to repeat. The staff table, Henrietta had said, always had the same food that the students had; and Lucy had hoped that that remark didn't mean that she had looked doubtfully upon the beans. She had tried to look very bright and pleased about the beans; but perhaps it hadn't been a success.

"Tommy! Tom-*mee!* Oh, Tommy, darling, waken up. I'm *des*perate!"

Miss Pym shot into wakefulness. The despairing cries seemed to be in her room. Then she realised that the second window of her room gave on to the courtyard; that the courtyard was small, and conversation from room to room through the gaping windows a natural method of communication. She lay trying to quiet her thumping heart, peering down over the folds of sheet to where, beyond the hump of her toes, the foreshortened oblong of the window framed a small piece of distant wall. But her bed lay in the angle of the room, one window to her right in the wall behind her, and the courtyard window to her left beyond the foot of her bed, and all that was visible from her pillow through the tall thin strip of brightness was half of an open window far down the courtyard.

"Tom-*mee! Tom-mee!*"

A dark head appeared in the window Miss Pym could see.

"For God's sake, someone," said the head, "throw something at Thomas and stop Dakers' row."

"Oh, Greengage, darling, you *are* an unsympathetic beast. I've bust my garter, and I don't know *what* to do. And Tommy took my *only* safety-pin yesterday to pick the winkles with at Tuppence-ha'penny's party. She simply *must* let me have it back before—*Tommy!* Oh, *Tommy!*"

"Hey, shut up, will you," said a new voice, in a lowered tone, and there was a pause. A pause, Lucy felt, full of sign language.

"And what does all that semaphoring mean?" asked the dark head.

"Shut up, I tell you. *She's* there!" This in desperate *sotto voce.*

"Who is?"

"The Pym woman."

"What *rubbish*, darling,"—it was the Dakers voice again, high and unsubdued; the happy voice of a world's darling—"she's sleeping in the front of the house with the rest of the mighty. *Do* you think *she* would have a spare safety-pin if I was to ask her?"

"She looks zipp-fastener to me," a new voice said.

"Oh, will you be quiet! I tell you, she's in Bentley's room!"

There was a real silence this time. Lucy saw the dark head turn sharply towards her window.

"How do you know?" someone asked.

"Jolly told me last night when she was giving me late supper." Miss Joliffe was the housekeeper, Lucy remembered, and appreciated the nickname for so grim a piece of humanity.

"Gawd's truth!" said the "zipp-fastener" voice, with feeling.

Into the silence came a bell. The same urgent clamour that had wakened them. The dark head disappeared at the first sound of it, and Dakers' voice above the row could be heard wailing her desperation like a lost thing. Social gaffes were relegated to their proper unimportance, as the business of the day overwhelmed them. A great wave of sound rose up to meet the sound of the bell. Doors were banged, feet drummed in the corridor, voices called, someone remembered that Thomas was still asleep, and a tattoo was beaten on her locked door when objects flung at her from surrounding windows had failed to waken her, and then there was the sound of running feet on the gravel path that crossed the courtyard grass. And gradually there were more feet on the gravel and fewer on the stairs, and the babble of voices swelled to a climax and faded. When the noises had grown faint with distance or died into lecture-room silence, a single pair of feet pattered in flight across the gravel, a voice saying: "Damn, damn, damn, damn, damn—" at each footfall. The Thomas who slept, apparently.

Miss Pym felt sympathetic to the unknown Thomas. Bed was a charming place at any time, but if one was so sleepy that neither riotous bell-ringing nor the wails of a colleague made any impression, then getting up must be torture. Welsh, too, probably. All Thomases were Welsh. Celts hated getting up. Poor Thomas. Poor, poor Thomas. She would like to find poor Thomas a job where she would never have to get up before afternoon.

Sleep ran over her in waves, drawing her deeper and deeper under. She wondered if "looking zipp-fastener" was a compliment. Being a safety-pin person couldn't be thought exactly admirable, so perhaps—

She fell asleep.

· 2 ·

SHE was being beaten with knouts by two six-foot cossacks because she persisted in using the old-fashioned safety-pin when progress decreed a zipp-fastener, and the blood had begun to trickle down her back when she woke to the fact that the only thing that was being assaulted was her hearing. The bell was ringing again. She said something that was neither civilised nor cultured, and sat up. No, definitely, not a minute after lunch

7

would she stay. There was a 2.41 from Larborough, and on that 2.41 she would be; her goodbyes said, her duty to friendship done, and her soul filled with the beatitude of escape. She would treat herself to a half-pound box of chocolates on the station platform as a sort of outward congratulation. It would show on the bathroom scales at the end of the week, but who cared?

The thought of the scales reminded her of the civilised and cultured necessity of having a bath. Henrietta had been sorry about its being so far to the staff bathrooms; she had been sorry altogether to put a guest into the student block, but Fröken Gustavsen's mother from Sweden was occupying the only staff guestroom, and was going to stay for some weeks until she had seen and criticised the result of her daughter's work when the annual Demonstration would take place at the beginning of the month. Lucy doubted very much whether her bump of locality—a hollow according to her friends—was good enough to take her back to that bathroom. It would be awful to go prowling along those bright empty corridors, arriving perhaps at lecture-rooms unawares. And still more awful to ask in a crowded corridor of up-since-dawners where one could perform one's belated ablutions.

Lucy's mind always worked like that. It wasn't sufficient for it to visualise one horror; it must visualise the opposite one too. She sat so long considering the rival horrors, and enjoying the sensation of doing nothing, that still another bell rang and still another wave of drumming feet and calling voices rose up and swamped the quiet of the morning. Lucy looked at her watch. It was half-past seven.

She had just decided to be uncivilised and uncultured and "go in her mook" as her daily woman called it—after all, what was this immersion in water but a modern fad, and if Charles the Second could afford to smell a little high, who was she, a mere commoner, to girn at missing a bath?—when there was a knock on her door. Rescue was at hand. Oh, joy, oh, glory, her marooned condition was at an end.

"Come in," she called in the glad tones of a Crusoe welcoming a landing party. Of course Henrietta would come to say goodmorning. How silly of her not to have thought of that. She was

8

still at heart the little rabbit who didn't expect Henrietta to bother about her. Really, she must cultivate a habit of mind more suitable to a Celebrity. Perhaps if she were to do her hair differently, or say over something twenty times a day after the manner of Coué —"Come in!"

But it was not Henrietta. It was a goddess.

A goddess with golden hair, a bright blue linen tunic, sea-blue eyes, and the most enviable pair of legs. Lucy always noticed other women's legs, her own being a sad disappointment to her.

"Oh, I'm sorry," said the goddess. "I forgot that you might not be up. In college we keep such odd hours."

Lucy thought that it was nice of this heavenly being to take the blame for her sloth.

"I do apologise for interrupting your dressing." The blue eye came to rest on a mule which was lying in the middle of the floor, and stayed there as if fascinated. It was a pale blue satin mule; very feminine, very thriftless, very feathery. A most undeniable piece of nonsense.

"I'm afraid it *is* rather silly," Lucy said.

"If you only knew, Miss Pym, what it is to see an object that is not strictly utilitarian!" And then, as if recalled to her business by the very temptation of straying from it: "My name is Nash. I'm the Head Senior. And I came to say that the Senior students would be very honoured if you would come to tea with them tomorrow. On Sundays we take our tea out into the garden. It is a Senior privilege. And it really is very pleasant out there on a summer afternoon, and we really are looking forward to having you." She smiled with eager benevolence on Miss Pym.

Lucy explained that she would not be there tomorrow; that she was departing this afternoon.

"Oh, no!" protested the Nash girl; and the genuine feeling in her tone caused Lucy a rush of warmth to the heart. "No, Miss Pym, you mustn't! You really mustn't. You have no idea what a god-send you are to us. It's so seldom that anyone—anyone interesting comes to stay. This place is rather like a convent. We are all so hard-worked that we have no time to think of an outside world; and this is the last term for us Seniors, and everything is very grim and claustrophobic—Final Exams, and the Demonstra-

9

tion, and being found posts, and what not—and we are all feeling like death, and our last scrap of sense of proportion is gone. And then *you* come, a piece of the outside, a civilised being—" She paused; half laughing, half serious. "You *can't* desert us."

"But you have an outside lecturer *every* Friday," Lucy pointed out. It was the first time in her life she had been a god-send to anyone, and she was determined to take the assertion with a grain of salt. She didn't at all like the gratified feeling that was sniffing round the edge of her emotions.

Miss Nash explained with clarity, point, and no small bitterness that the last three lecturers had been: an octogenarian on Assyrian inscriptions, a Czech on Central Europe, and a bonesetter on scoliosis.

"What is scoliosis?" asked Lucy.

"Curvature of the spine. And if you think that any of them brought sweetness and light into the College atmosphere, you are wrong. These lectures are supposed to keep us in touch with the world, but if I must be both frank and indiscreet"—she was obviously enjoying being both—"the frock you wore last night did us more good than all the lectures we have ever heard."

Lucy had spent a really shocking sum on that garment when first her book became a best-seller, and it still remained her favourite; she had worn it to impress Henrietta. The gratified feeling came a little nearer.

But not near enough to destroy her common sense. She could still remember the beans. And the lack of bedside lamps. And the lack of any bells to summon service. And the everlasting bells that rang to summon others. No, on the 2.41 from Larborough she would be, though every student of the Leys Physical Training College lay down in her path and wept aloud. She murmured something about engagements—leaving it to be inferred that her diary bulged with pressing and desirable appointments—and suggested that Miss Nash might, meanwhile, direct her to the Staff bathrooms. "I didn't want to go prowling through the corridors, and I couldn't find a bell to ring."

Miss Nash, having sympathised with her about the lack of service—"Eliza really should have remembered that there are no bells in the rooms here and come to call you; she's the Staff housemaid"—suggested that, if Miss Pym didn't mind using the students' baths, they were much nearer. "They are cubicles, of course; I mean, they have walls only part of the way; and the floor is a sort of greenish concrete where the Staff have turquoise mosaic with a tasteful design in dolphins, but the water is the same."

Miss Pym was delighted to use the students' bathroom, and as she gathered her bathing things together the unoccupied half of her mind was busy with Miss Nash's lack of any studentlike reverence for the Staff. It reminded her of something. And presently she remembered what it reminded her of. Mary Barharrow. The rest of Mary Barharrow's form had been meek and admiring young labourers in the field of irregular French verbs, but Mary Barharrow, though diligent and amiable, had treated her French mistress as an equal; and that was because Mary Barharrow's father was "nearly a millionaire." Miss Pym concluded that in the "outside"—strange how one already used Klondyke terms about College—Miss Nash, who had so markedly Mary Barharrow's charming air of social ease and equality, had also a father very like Mary Barharrow's. She was to learn later that it was the first thing that anyone remarked on when Nash's name was mentioned. "Pamela Nash's people are very rich, you know. They have a butler." They never failed to mention the butler. To the daughters of struggling doctors, lawyers, dentists, business men and farmers, he was as exotic as a negro slave.

"Shouldn't you be at some class or other?" asked Miss Pym, as the quietness of the sunlit corridors proclaimed an absorption elsewhere. "I take it that if you are wakened at half-past five you work before breakfast."

"Oh, yes. In the summer we have two periods before breakfast, one active and one passive. Tennis practice and kinesiology, or something like that."

"What is kin—whatever-it-is?"

"Kinesiology?" Miss Nash considered for a moment the best way of imparting knowledge to the ignorant, and then spoke in imaginary quotation. "I take down a jug with a handle from a high shelf; describe the muscle-work involved." And as Miss Pym's nod showed that she had understood: "But in winter we get up like anyone else at half-past seven. As for this particular

11

period, it is normally used for taking outside certificates—Public Health, and Red Cross, and what not. But since we have finished with these we are allowed to use it as a prep. hour for our final exams, which begin next week. We have very little prep. time so we are glad of it."

"Aren't you free after tea, or thereabouts?"

Miss Nash looked amused. "Oh, no. There is afternoon clinic from four o'clock till six; outside patients, you know. Everything from flat feet to broken thighs. And from half-past six to eight there is dancing. Ballet, not folk. We have folk in the morning; it ranks as exercise not art. And supper doesn't finish much before half-past eight, so we are very sleepy before we begin our prep. and it is usually a fight between our sleepiness and our ignorance."

As they turned into the long corridor leading to the stairs, they overtook a small scuttling figure clutching under one arm the head and thorax of a skeleton and the pelvis and legs under the other arm.

"What are you doing with George, Morris?" asked Miss Nash as they drew level.

"Oh, *please* don't stop me, Beau," panted the startled Junior, hitching her grotesque burden more firmly on to her right hip and continuing to scuttle in front of them, "and *please* forget that you saw me. I mean that you saw George. I meant to waken early and put him back in the lecture-room before the half-past five bell went, but I just slept."

"Have you been up all night with George?"

"No, only till about two. I—"

"And how did you manage about lights?"

"I pinned my travelling rug over the window, of course," said the Junior, in the testy tones of one explaining the obvious.

"A nice atmosphere on a June evening!"

"It was hellish," said Miss Morris, simply. "But it really *is* the only way I can swot up my insertions, so *please*, Beau, just forget that you saw me. I'll get him back before the Staff come down to breakfast."

"You'll never do it, you know. You're bound to meet someone or other."

"Oh, please don't discourage me. I'm terrified enough now. And

12

I really don't know if I can remember how to hook up his middle."
She preceded them down the stairs, and disappeared into the front
of the house.

"Positively Through-the-Looking-Glass," commented Miss
Pym, watching her go. "I always thought insertion was something
to do with needlework."

"Insertions? They're the exact place on a bone where a muscle
is attached to it. It's much easier to do it with the skeleton in
front of you, than with just a book. That is why Morris abducted
George." She expelled a breath of indulgent laughter. "Very
enterprising of her. I stole odd bones from the drawers in the
lecture-room when I was a Junior, but I never thought of taking
George. It's the dreadful cloud that hangs over a Junior's life,
you know. Final Anatomy. It really *is* a Final. You're supposed
to know all about the body before you begin practising on it,
so Final Anatomy is a Junior exam, not a Senior one like the
other finals. The bathrooms are along here. When I was a Junior
the long grass at the edge of the cricket field was simply stiff on
Sundays with hidden Juniors hugging their Gray. It is strictly
forbidden to take books out of College, and on Sundays we are
supposed to go all social and go out to tea, or to church, or to
the country. But no Junior in the summer term ever did anything
on a Sunday except find a quiet spot for herself and Gray. It was
quite a business getting Gray out of College. Do you know Gray?
About the size of those old family Bibles that rested on the parlour
table. There was actually a rumour once that half the girls at
Leys were pregnant, but it turned out that it was only the odd
silhouette that everyone made with Gray stuffed up the front of
their Sunday bests."

Miss Nash stooped to the taps and sent a roar of water rushing
into the bath. "When everyone in College bathes three or four
times a day, in the matter of minutes, you have to have a Niagara
of a tap," she explained above the row. "I'm afraid you are going
to be very late for breakfast." And as Miss Pym looked dismayed
and oddly small-girlish at the prospect: "Let me bring up something for you on a tray. No, it won't be any trouble, I'd love to
do it. There isn't any need for a guest to appear at eight o'clock
breakfast, anyhow. You'd much better have it in peace in your

13

room." She paused with her hand on the door. "And do change your mind about staying. It really would give us pleasure. More pleasure than you can imagine."

She smiled and was gone.

Lucy lay in the warm soft water and thought happily of her breakfast. How pleasant not to have to make conversation among all those chattering voices. How imaginative and kind of that charming girl to carry a tray to her. Perhaps after all it would be nice to spend a day or two among these young—

She nearly leaped from her bath as a bell began its maniacal yelling not a dozen yards from where she lay. That settled it. She sat up and soaped herself. Not a minute later than the 2.41 from Larborough, not one minute later.

As the bell—presumably a five-minute warning before the gong at eight o'clock—died into silence, there was a wild rush in the corridor, the two doors to her left were flung open, and as the water cascaded into the baths a high familiar voice was heard shrieking: "Oh, darling, I'm going to be *so* late for breakfast, but I'm in a *muck sweat*, my dear. I know I should have sat down quietly and done the composition of plasma, of which I know *ab*-solutely *noth*-ing, my dear, and Final Phys. is on Tuesday. But it *is* such a lovely morning— Now what *have* I done with my *soap*?"

Lucy's jaw slowly dropped as it was borne in upon her that in a community which began the day at half-past five and ended it at eight in the evening, there were still individuals who had the vitality to work themselves into a muck sweat when they need not.

"Oh, Donnie, *darling*, I've left my soap behind. Do throw me over yours!"

"You'll have to wait till I've soaped myself," said a placid voice that was in marked contrast to Dakers' high emphasis.

"Well, my angel, *do* be *quick*. I've been late twice this week, and Miss Hodge looked dis*tinct*ly *odd* the last time. I say, Donnie, you *couldn't* by any chance take my 'adipose' patient at twelve o'clock clinic, could you?"

"No, I couldn't."

"She really isn't so heavy as she looks, you know. You have only to—"

"I have a patient of my own."

"Yes, but only the little boy with the ankle. Lucas could take him along with her 'tortis colli' girl—"

"No."

"No, I was afraid you wouldn't. Oh, dear, I don't know *when* I'm going to do that plasma. As for the coats of the stomach, they simply *baffle* me, my dear. I don't really believe there are four, anyhow. It's just a conspiracy. Miss Lux says look at tripe, but I don't see that tripe proves anything."

"Soap coming up."

"Oh, *thank* you, darling. You've saved my life. What a nice *smell*, my dear. *Very* expensive." In the momentary silence of soaping she became aware that the bath on her right was occupied. "Who is next door, Donnie?"

"Don't know. Gage, probably."

"Is that you, Greengage?"

"No," said Lucy, startled, "it's Miss Pym." And hoped it wasn't as prim as it sounded.

"No, but really, who is it?"

"Miss Pym."

"It's a very good imitation, whoever you are."

"It's Littlejohn," suggested the placid voice. "She does imitations."

Miss Pym fell back on a defeated silence.

There was the hurr-oosh of a body lifted suddenly from the water, the spat of a wet foot placed firmly on the edge of the bath, eight wet finger-tips appeared on the edge of the partition, and a face peered over it. It was a long pale face, like an amiable pony's, with the straight fair hair above it screwed up into a knob with a hasty hairpin. An oddly endearing face. Even in that crowded moment, Lucy understood suddenly how Dakers had managed to reach her final term at Leys without being knocked on the head by exasperated colleagues.

First horror, then a wild flush together with a dawning amusement, invaded the face above the partition. It disappeared abruptly. A despairing wail rose from beyond.

"Oh, Miss *Pym!* Oh, *dear* Miss Pym! I *do* apologise. I *abase* myself. It didn't occur to me even to *think* it might be you—"

15

Lucy could not help feeling that she was enjoying her own enormity.

"I *hope* you're not offended. Not *terribly*, I mean. We are so used to people's skins that—that—"

Lucy understood that she was trying to say that the gaffe was less important in these surroundings than it would have been elsewhere, and since she herself had been decently soaping a big toe at the operative moment, she had no feelings on the subject. She said kindly that it was entirely her own fault for occupying a student's bathroom, and that Miss Dakers was not to worry about it for a moment.

"You know my *name*?"

"Yes. You woke me in the dawn this morning yelling for a safety-pin."

"Oh, *catastrophe*! Now I shall *never* be able to look you in the face!"

"I expect Miss Pym is taking the first train back to London," said the voice in the further bath, in a now-look-what-you've-done tone.

"That is O'Donnell next door," said Dakers. "She's from Ireland."

"Ulster," said O'Donnell, without heat.

"How d'you do, Miss O'Donnell."

"You must think this is a mad-house, Miss Pym. But don't judge us by Dakers, please. Some of us are quite grown up. And some of us are even civilised. When you come to tea tomorrow you will see."

Before Miss Pym could say that she was not coming to tea, a low murmur began to invade the cubicles, rising rapidly into the deep roar of a gong. Into the tumult Dakers' banshee wail rose like the voice of a sea-gull in a storm. She was going to be *so* late. And she was *so* grateful for the soap, which had saved her life. And *where* was the girdle of her tunic? And if dear Miss Pym would promise to overlook her failings up to date, she would yet show her that she was a sensible female and a civilised adult. And they were *all* looking forward so much to that tea tomorrow.

With a rush and a bang the students fled, leaving Miss Pym alone with the dying pulse of the gong and the throaty protest of bath water running away.

AT 2.41, when the afternoon fast train to London was pulling out of Larborough prompt to the minute, Miss Pym sat under the cedar on the lawn wondering whether she was a fool, and not much caring anyhow. It was very pleasant there in the sun-lit garden. It was also very quiet, since Saturday afternoon was, it appeared, match afternoon, and College *en masse* was down at the cricket field playing Coombe, a rival establishment from the other side of the County. If they had nothing else, these young creatures, they had versatility. It was a far cry from the lining of the stomach to the placing of a cricket field, but they seemingly took it in their stride. Henrietta, coming into her bed-room after breakfast, had said that if she stayed over the week-end she would at least find it a new experience. "They are a very varied and lively crowd, and the work is very interesting." And Henrietta had certainly been right. There was no moment when some new facet of this odd existence was not being presented to her. She had sat through luncheon at the Staff table, eating unidentifiable dishes that were "balanced" to a dietetic marvel, and making the closer acquaintance of the Staff. Henrietta sat in lonely state at the top of the table and gobbled her food in an abstracted silence. But Miss Lux was talkative. Miss Lux—angular, plain, and clever—was Mistress of Theory, and as be-fitted a lecturer on theory had not only ideas but opinions. Miss Wragg, on the other hand, the Junior Gymnast—big, bounc-ing, young, and pink—had apparently no ideas at all and her only opinions were reflections of Madame Lefevre's. Madame Lefevre, the ballet mistress, spoke seldom, but when she did it was in a voice like dark brown velvet and no one interrupted her. At the bottom of the table, with her mother by her side, sat Fröken Gustavsen, the Senior Gymnast, who talked not at all.

It was to Fröken Gustavsen that Lucy found her eyes going during that lunch. There was a sly amusement in the handsome Swede's clear pale eyes that Lucy found irresistible. The heavy

Miss Hodge, the clever Miss Lux, the dumb Miss Wragg, the elegant Madame Lefevre—what did they all look like through the eyes of a tall pale enigma from Sweden?

Now, having spent lunch wondering about a Swede, she was waiting the advent of a South American. "Desterro doesn't play games," Henrietta had said, "so I'll send her to keep you company this afternoon." Lucy had not wanted anyone to keep her company—she was used to her own company and liked it—but the thought of a South American at an English college of physical training teased her. And when Nash, running into her after lunch, had said: "I'm afraid you're going to be deserted this afternoon, if you don't care for cricket," another Senior passing in the crush had said: "It's all right, Beau, The Nut Tart is going to look after her." "Oh, good," Beau had said, apparently so accustomed to the nickname that it had ceased to have either meaning or oddity for her.

But Lucy looked forward to meeting a Nut Tart, and sitting in the sunlit garden digesting the dietetic marvels she pondered the name. "Nut" was Brazil, perhaps. It was also the modern slang for "dippy" or "daft," she believed. But "tart"? Surely not!

A Junior, running past her on the way to the bicycle shed, flashed her a smile, and she remembered that they had met in the corridor that morning. "Did you get George back safely?" she called after her.

"Yes, thank you," beamed little Miss Morris, pausing to dance on one toe, "but I think I'm in a different sort of trouble now. You see, I had my arm round George's waist, sort of steadying him after hanging him up, when Miss Lux came in. I'll never be able to explain away that, I'm afraid."

"Life is difficult," agreed Lucy.

"However, I think I really do know my insertions now," called little Miss Morris, speeding away over the grass.

Nice children, thought Miss Pym. Nice, clean, healthy children. It was really very pleasant here. That smudge on the horizon was the smoke of Larborough. There would be another smudge like that over London. It was much better to sit here where the air was bright with sun and heavy with roses, and be given friendly

18

smiles by friendly young creatures. She pushed her plump little feet a little further away from her, approved the Georgian bulk of the "old house" that glowed in the sunlight across the lawn, regretted the modern brick wings that made a "Mary Ann" back to it, but supposed that as modern blocks go the Leys ensemble was pleasant enough. Charmingly proportioned lecture-rooms in the "old house," and neat modern little bedrooms in the wings. An ideal arrangement. And the ugly bulk of the gymnasium decently hidden behind all. Before she went away on Monday she must see the Seniors go through their gym. There would be a double pleasure in that for her. The pleasure of watching experts trained to the last fine hair of perfection, and the ineffable pleasure of knowing that never, never as long as she lived, would she herself have to climb a rib-stall again.

Round the corner of the house, as she gazed, came a figure in a flowered silk dress and a plain, wide-brimmed shady hat. It was a slim, graceful figure; and watching it come Lucy realised that she had unconsciously pictured the South American plump and over-ripe. She also realised where the "tart" came from, and smiled. The outdoor frocks of the austere young students of Leys would not be flowered; neither would they be cut so revealingly; and never, oh never, would their hats be broad-brimmed and shady.

"Good afternoon, Miss Pym. I am Teresa Desterro. I am so sorry that I missed your lecture last night. I had a class in Larborough." Desterro took off her hat with a leisurely and studied grace, and dropped to the grass by Lucy's side in one continuous smooth movement. Everything about her was smooth and fluid: her voice, her drawling speech, her body, her movements, her dark hair, her honey-brown eyes.

"A class?"

"A dancing class; for shop girls. So earnest; so precise; so very bad. They will give me a box of chocolates next week because it is the last class of the season, and because they like me, and because it is after all the custom; and I shall feel like a crook. It is false pretences. No one could teach them to dance."

"I expect they enjoy themselves. Is it usual? I mean, for students to take outside classes?"

"But we all do, of course. That is how we get practice. At schools, and convents, and clubs, and that sort of thing. You do not care for cricket?"

Lucy, rousing herself to this swift change of subject, explained that cricket was only possible to her in the company of a bag of cherries. "How is it that you don't play?"

"I don't play *any* games. To run about after a little ball is supremely ridiculous. I came here for the dancing. It is a very good dancing college."

But surely, Lucy said, there were ballet schools in London of an infinitely higher standard than anything obtainable at a college of physical training.

"Oh, for that one has to begin young, and to have a métier. Me, I have no métier, only a liking."

"And will you teach, then, when you go back to—Brazil, is it?"

"Oh, no; I shall get married," said Miss Desterro simply. "I came to England because I had an unhappy love affair. He was r-r-ravishing, but qu-ite unsuitable. So I came to England to get over it."

"Is your mother English, perhaps?"

"No, my mother is French. My grandmother is English. I adore the English. Up to here"—she lifted a graceful hand, wrist properly leading, and laid it edge-wise across her neck—"they are full of romance, and from there up, plain horse sense. I went to my grandmother, and I cried all over her best silk chairs, and I said "What shall I do? What shall I do?" About my lover, you understand. And she said: "You can blow your nose and get out of the country." So I said I would go to Paris and live in a garret and paint pictures of an eye and a seashell sitting on a plate. But she said: "You will not. You will go to England and sweat a bit." So, as I always listen to my grandmother, and since I like dancing and am very good at it, I came here. To Leys. They looked a little sideways on me at first when I said I wanted just to dance—"

This is what Lucy had been wondering. How did this charming "nut" find a welcome in this earnest English college, this starting-place of careers?

"—but one of the students had broken down in the middle of her training—they often do, and do you wonder?—and that left a vacant place in the scheme, which was not so nice, so they said: 'Oh, well, let this crazy woman from Brazil have Kenyon's room and allow her to come to the classes. It will not do any harm and it will keep the books straight.' "

"So you began as a Senior?"

"For dancing, yes. I was already a dancer, you understand. But I took Anatomy with the Juniors. I find bones interesting. And to other lectures I went as I pleased. I have listened to all subjects. All but plumbing. I find plumbing indecent."

Miss Pym took "plumbing" to be Hygiene. "And have you enjoyed it all?"

"It has been a li-beral education. They are very naive, the English girls. They are like little boys of nine." Noticing the unbelieving smile on Miss Pym's face: there was nothing naive about Beau Nash. "Or little girls of eleven. They have 'raves.' You know what a 'rave' is?" Miss Pym nodded. "They swoon if Madame Lefevre says a kind word to them. I swoon, too, but it is from surprise. They save up their money to buy flowers for Fröken, who thinks of nothing but a Naval Officer in Sweden."

"How do you know that?" asked Lucy, surprised.

"He is on her table. In her room. His photograph, I mean. And she is Continental. She does not have 'raves'."

"The Germans do," Lucy pointed out. "They are famous for it."

"An ill-balanced people," said Desterro, dismissing the Teutonic race. "The Swedes are not like that."

"All the same, I expect she likes the little offerings of flowers."

"She does not, of course, throw them out of the window. But I notice she likes better the ones who do not bring her offerings."

"Oh? There *are* some who do not have 'raves,' then?"

"Oh, yes. A few. The Scots, for instance. We have two." She might have been talking of rabbits. "They are too busy quarrelling to have any spare emotions."

"Quarrelling? But I thought the Scots stuck together the world over."

"Not if they belong to different winds."

"*Winds?*"

21

"It is a matter of climate. We see it very much in Brazil. A wind that goes 'a-a-a-ah' " [she opened her red mouth and expelled a soft insinuating breath] "makes one kind of person. But a wind that goes 's-s-s-s-ss' " [she shot the breath viciously out through her teeth] "makes another person altogether. In Brazil it is altitude, in Scotland it is West Coast and East Coast. I observed it in the Easter holidays, and so understood about the Scots. Campbell has a wind that goes 'a-a-a-ah,' and so she is lazy, and tells lies, and has much charm that is all of it quite synthetic. Stewart has a wind that goes 's-s-s-s-ss,' so she is honest, and hardworking, and has a formidable conscience."

Miss Pym laughed. "According to you, the east coast of Scotland must be populated entirely by saints."

"There is also some personal reason for the quarrel, I understand. Something about abused hospitality."

"You mean that one went home with the other for holidays and—misbehaved?" Visions of vamped lovers, stolen spoons, and cigarette burns on the furniture, ran through Lucy's too vivid imagination.

"Oh, no. It happened more than two hundred years ago. In the deep snow, and there was a massacre." Desterro did full justice to the word "massacre".

At this Lucy really laughed. To think that the Campbells were still engaged in living down Glencoe! A narrow-minded race, the Celts.

She sat so long considering the Celts that The Nut Tart turned to look up at her. "Have you come to use us as specimens, Miss Pym?"

Lucy explained that she and Miss Hodge were old friends and that her visit was a holiday one. "In any case," she said, kindly, "I doubt whether as a specimen a Physical Training Student is likely to be psychologically interesting."

"No? Why?"

"Oh, too normal and too nice. Too much of a type."

A faint amusement crossed Desterro's face; the first expression it had shown so far. Unexpectedly, this stung Lucy; as if she too had been found guilty of being naive.

"You don't agree?"

"I am trying to think of someone—some Senior—who is normal. It is not easy."

"Oh, come!"

"You know how they live here. How they work. It would be difficult to go through their years of training here and be quite normal in their last term."

"Do you suggest that Miss Nash is not normal?"

"Oh, Beau. She is a strong-minded creature, and so has suffered less, perhaps. But would you call her friendship for Innes quite normal? *Nice,* of course," Desterro added hastily, "quite irreproachable. But normal, no. That David and Jonathan relationship. It is a very happy one, no doubt, but it"—Desterro waved her arm to summon an appropriate word—"it *excludes* so much. The Disciples are the same, only there are four of them."

"The Disciples?"

"Mathews, Waymark, Lucus, and Littlejohn. They have come up the College together because of their names. And now, believe me, my dear Miss Pym, they *think* together. They have the four rooms in the roof"—she tilted her head to the four dormer windows in the roof of the wing—"and if you ask any one of them to lend you a pin she says: 'We have not got one'."

"Well, there is Miss Dakers. What would you say was wrong with Miss Dakers?"

"Arrested development," said Miss Desterro dryly.

"Nonsense!" said Lucy, determined to assert herself. "A happy, simple, uncomplicated human being, enjoying herself and the world. *Quite* normal."

The Nut Tart smiled suddenly, and her smile was frank and unstudied. "Very well, Miss Pym, I give you Dakers. But I remind you that it is their last term, this. And so everything is e-norrrmously exaggerated. Everyone is just the least little bit insane. No, it is true, I promise you. If a student is frightened by nature, then she is a thousand times more frightened this term. If she is ambitious, then her ambition becomes a passion. *And* so on." She sat up to deliver herself of her summing-up. "It is not a normal life they lead. You cannot expect them to be normal."

4

"You cannot expect them to be normal," repeated Miss Pym to herself, sitting in the same place on Sunday afternoon and looking at the crowd of happy and excessively normal young faces clustered below her on the grass. Her eye ran over them with pleasure. If none of them was distinguished, at least none of them was mean. Nor was there any trace of morbidity, nor even of exhaustion, in their sunburnt alertness. These were the survivors of a gruelling course—that was admitted even by Henrietta—and it seemed to Miss Pym that the rigours might perhaps have been justified if the residue were of such excellence.

She was amused to note that the Disciples, by much living together, had begun to look vaguely alike—as husband and wife often do, however different their features. They all seemed to have the same round face with the same expression of pleased expectancy; it was only later that one noticed differences of build and colouring.

She was also amused to observe that the Thomas who slept was most undeniably Welsh; a small, dark aborigine. And that O'Donnell, who had now materialised from a voice in the bath, was equally unmistakably an Irishwoman; the long lashes, the fine skin, the wide grey eyes. The two Scots—separated by the furthest possible distance that still allowed them to be part of the group—were less obvious. Stewart was the red-haired girl cutting up cake from one of the plates that lay about on the grass. ("It's from Crowford's," she was saying, in a pleasant Edinburgh voice, "so you poor creatures who know nothing but Buzzards will have a treat for a change!") Campbell, propped against the bole of the cedar, and consuming bread-and-butter with slow absorption, had pink cheeks and brown hair and a vague prettiness.

Apart from Hasselt, who was the girl with the flat, calm,

early-Primitive face and who was South African, the rest of the Seniors were, as Queen Elizabeth said, "mere English."

The only face that approached distinction, as opposed to good looks, was that of Mary Innes, Beau Nash's Jonathan. This pleased Miss Pym in an odd fashion. It was fitting, she felt, that Beau should have chosen for friend someone who had quality as well as looks. Not that Innes was particularly good-looking. Her eyebrows, low over her eyes, gave her face an intensity, a brood-ing expression, that robbed her fine bones of the beauty they might have had. Unlike Beau, who was animated and smiled easily, she was quiet and so far Miss Pym had not seen her smile, although they had had what amounted in the milieu to a lengthy conversation. That was last night, when Miss Pym was undress-ing after having spent the evening in the company of the Staff. There had come a knock on her door, and Beau had said: "I just came to see if you had everything you want. And to introduce you to your next-door neighbour, Mary Innes. Any time you want to be rescued, Innes will see to it." And Beau had said good-night and gone away, leaving Innes to finish the interview. Lucy had found her attractive and very intelligent, but just a shade disconcerting. She did not bother to smile if she was not amused, and though friendly and at her ease made no effort to be entertain-ing. In the academic and literary circles that Lucy had recently frequented this would not have been remarkable, but in the gay over-accented college world it had the effect almost of a rebuff. Almost. There was certainly nothing of rebuff in Innes's interest in her book—the Book—and in herself.

Looking at her now, sitting in the cedar shade, Lucy wondered if it were just that Mary Innes did not find life very amusing. Lucy had long prided herself on her analysis of facial character-istics, and was beginning nowadays to bet rather heavily on them. She had never, for instance, come across eyebrows beginning low over the nose and ending high up at the outer end without finding that their owner had a scheming, conniving mind. And someone— Jan Gordon, was it?—had observed that of the crowd round a park orator it was the long-nosed people who stayed to listen and the short-nosed people who walked away. So now, looking at Mary Innes's level eyebrows and firm mouth, she wondered whether the concentration of purpose they showed had forbidden any compensating laughter. It was in some way not a contemporary face at all. It was—was what?

An illustration from a history book? A portrait in a gallery?

Not, anyhow, the face of a games mistress at a girls' school. Definitely not. It was round faces like Mary Innes's that history was built.

Of all the faces turning to her so constantly and turning away with chatter and badinage, only two were not immediately likeable. One was Campbell's; too pliant, too soft-mouthed, too ready to be all things to all men. The other belonged to a girl called Rouse; and was freckled, and tight-lipped, and watchful.

Rouse had come late to the tea-party, and her advent had caused an odd momentary silence. Lucy was reminded of the sudden stillness that falls on chattering birds when a hawk hovers. But there was nothing deliberate about the silence; no malice. It was as if they had paused in their talk to note her arrival, but had none of them cared sufficiently to welcome her into their own particular group.

"I'm afraid I'm late," she had said. And in the momentary quiet Lucy had caught the monosyllabic comment: "Swot!", and had concluded that Miss Rouse had not been able to drag herself away from her text-books. Nash had introduced her, and she had dropped to the grass with the rest, and the interrupted conversations flowed on. Lucy, always sympathetic to the odd-man-out, had caught herself being sorry for the latecomer; but a further inspection of Miss Rouse's North Country features had convinced her that she was wasting good emotion. If Campbell, pink and pretty, was too pliant to be likeable, then Rouse was her complement. Nothing but a bull-dozer, Lucy felt, would make an impression on Miss Rouse.

"Miss Pym, you haven't had any of *my* cake," said Dakers, who, quite unabashed, had appropriated Lucy as an old acquaintance, and was now sitting propped against her chair, her legs straight out in front of her like a doll's.

"Which is yours?" asked Lucy, eyeing the various tuck-box products, which stood out from the college bread-and-butter and "Sunday" buns like Creed suits at a country fair.

Dakers' contribution, it seemed, was the chocolate sandwich

26

with the butter icing. Lucy decided that for friendship's sake (and a little for greed) she would forget her weight this once.

"Do you always bring your own cakes to Sunday tea?"

"Oh, no, this is in *your* honour."

Nash, sitting on her other side, laughed. "What you see before you, Miss Pym, is a collection of skeletons out of cupboards. There is no physical training student who is not a Secret Eater."

"There has been *no* moment in my *whole* college career, my dears, when I wasn't *sick* with hunger. Only *shame* makes me stop eating at breakfast, and half an hour afterwards I'm hungry enough to eat the horse in the gym."

"That is why our only crime is—" Rouse was beginning, when Stewart kicked her so hard in the back that she almost fell forward.

"We have spread our dreams under your feet," mocked Nash, covering Rouse's broken sentence. "And a fine rich carpet of carbohydrate they are, to be sure."

"We also had a *solemn* conclave as to whether we ought to *dress* for you," said Dakers, cutting up chocolate sandwich for the others and unaware that there had been any gaffe in the offing. "But we decided that you didn't look very particular." As this raised a laugh, she added hastily, "In the very *nicest* sense, I mean. We thought you would like us as we are."

They were wearing all sorts of garments; as the taste of the wearer or the need of the moment dictated. Some were in shorts, some in blue linen games tunics, some in washing-silk dresses of suitably pastel shades. There were no flowered silks; Desterro was taking tea with the nuns of a convent in Larborough.

"Besides," said Gage, who looked like a Dutch doll and who was the dark head that appeared at a courtyard window at five-thirty yesterday morning and prayed someone to throw something at Thomas and so put a period to the wails of Dakers, "besides, much as we would like to do you honour, Miss Pym, every moment counts with our finals so oppressively near. Even a quick-change artist like a P.T. Senior needs five full minutes to achieve Sunday-bests, and by accepting us in our rags you have contributed"—she paused to count the gathering and do some mental arithmetic—"you have contributed one hour and twenty minutes to the sum of human knowledge."

"You can subtract *my* five minutes from that, my dear," said

Dakers, licking a protuberant piece of butter-icing into safety with an expert tongue. "I've spent the *whole* afternoon doing the cortex of the brain, and the only result is a firm conviction that I personally haven't *got* a cortex."

"You must have a cortex," said Campbell, the literal-minded Scot, in a Glasgow drawl like syrup sliding from a spoon. But no one took any notice of this contribution to the obvious.

"Personally," said O'Donnell, "I think the vilest part of physiology are the villi. Imagine drawing cross-sections of something that has seven different parts and is less than a twentieth of an inch high!"

"But do you have to know the human structure in such detail?" asked Lucy.

"On Tuesday morning we do," said the Thomas who slept. "After that we can forget it for the rest of our lives."

Lucy, remembering the Monday morning visit to the gymnasium which she had promised herself, wondered if physical work ceased during Final Examinations week. Oh, no, they assured her. Not with the Dem. only a fortnight ahead. The Demonstration, she was given to understand, ranked only a short head behind Final Examinations as a hazard.

"All our parents come," said one of the Disciples, "and—"

"The parents of all of us, she means," put in a fellow Disciple.

"—and people from rival colleges, and all the—"

"All the civic swells of Larborough," put in a third. It seemed that when one Disciple burst into speech the others followed automatically.

"And all the County big-wigs," finished the fourth.

"It's murder," said the first, summing it up for them.

"I *like* the Dem.," said Rouse. And again that odd silence fell.

Not inimical. Merely detached. Their eyes went to her, and came away again, expressionlessly. No one commented on what she had said. Their indifference left her marooned in the moment.

"I think it's fun to show people what we can do," she added, a hint of defence in her tone.

They let that pass too. Never before had Lucy met that

negative English silence in its full perfection; in its full cruelty. Her own edges began to curl up in sympathy.

But Rouse was less easily shrivelled. She was eyeing the plates before her, and putting out her hand for something to eat. "Is there any tea left in the pot?" she asked.

Nash bent forward to the big brown pot, and Stewart took up the talk from where the Disciples had left it.

"What really *is* murder is waiting to see what you pull out of the Post lottery."

"Post?" said Lucy. "You mean jobs? But why a lottery? You know what you apply for, surely?"

"Very few of us need to apply," Nash explained, pouring very black tea. "There are usually enough applications from schools to go round. Places that have had Leys gymnasts before just write to Miss Hodge when they have a vacancy and ask her to recommend someone. If it happens to be a very senior or responsible post, she may offer it to some Old Student who wants a change. But normally the vacancies are filled from Leaving Students."

"And a very fine bargain they get," said a Disciple.

"No one works so hard as a First-Poster does," said a second.

"For less money," supplemented a third.

"Or with a better grace," said a fourth.

"So you see," Stewart said, "the most agonising moment of the whole term is when you are summoned to Miss Hodge's room and told what your fate is going to be."

"Or when your train is pulling out of Larborough and you haven't been summoned at all!" suggested Thomas, who evidently had visions of being engulfed, jobless, by her native mountains again.

Nash sat back on her heels and smiled at Lucy. "It is not nearly as grim as it sounds. Quite a few of us are provided for already and so are not in the competition at all. Hasselt, for instance, is going back to South Africa to work there. And the Disciples *en masse* have chosen medical work."

"We are going to start a clinic in Manchester," explained one.

"A very rheumaticky place."

"Full of deformities."

"And brass"—supplemented the other three automatically.

Nash smiled benevolently on them. "And I am going back to my old school as Games Coach. And the Nut—and Desterro, of course, doesn't want a post. So there aren't so many of us to find places for."

"I won't even be qualified if I don't go back to the liver pretty soon," Thomas said, her beady brown eyes blinking in the sun. "What a way to spend a summer evening."

They shifted their positions lazily, as if in protest, and fell to chatter again. But the reminder pricked them, and one by one they began to gather up their belongings and depart, trailing slowly across the sunlit grass like disconsolate children. Until presently Lucy found herself alone with the smell of the roses, and the murmur of insects, and the hot shimmer of the sunlit garden.

For half an hour she sat, in great beatitude, watching the slow shadow of the tree creep out from her feet. Then Desterro came back from Larborough; strolling slowly up the drive with a Rue de la Paix elegance that was odd after Lucy's hour of tumbled youth at tea. She saw Miss Pym, and changed her direction.

"Well," she said, "did you have a profitable afternoon?"

"I wasn't looking for profit," said Lucy, faintly tart. "It was one of the happiest afternoons I have ever spent."

The Nut Tart stood contemplating her.

"I think you are a *very* nice person," she said irrelevantly, and moved away, leisurely, to the house.

And Lucy suddenly felt very young, and didn't like the feeling at all. How dared a chit in a flowered frock make her feel inexperienced and foolish!

She rose abruptly and went to find Henrietta and be reminded that she was Lucy Pym, who had written The Book, and lectured to learned societies, and had her name in *Who's Who*, and was a recognised authority on the working of the Human Mind.

5

"WHAT is the college crime?" she asked Henrietta, as they went upstairs after supper. They had paused by the big fan-lighted window on the landing to look down on the little quadrangle, letting the others precede them up to the drawing-room.

"Using the gymnasium as a short cut to the field-path," Henrietta said promptly.

"No, I mean real crime."

Henrietta turned to look at her sharply. After a moment she said: "My dear Lucy, when a human being works as hard as these girls do, it has neither the spare interest to devise a crime nor the energy to undertake it. What made you think of that subject?"

"Something someone said at tea this afternoon. About their 'only crime.' It was something to do with being perpetually hungry."

"Oh, that!" Henrietta's brow cleared. "Food pilfering. Yes, we do now and then have that. In any community of this size there is always someone whose power of resisting temptation is small."

"Food from the kitchen, you mean?"

"No, food from the students' own rooms. It is a Junior crime, and usually disappears spontaneously. It is not a sign of vice, you know. Merely of a weak will. A student who would not dream of taking money or a trinket can't resist a piece of cake. Especially if it is sweet cake. They use up so much energy that their bodies are crying out for sugar; and though there is no limit to what they may eat at table they are for ever hungry."

"Yes, they do work very hard. What proportion of any one set finishes the course, would you say?"

"Of this lot"—Henrietta nodded down to where a group of Seniors were strolling out across the courtyard to the lawn—"eighty per cent are finishing. That is about average. Those who fall by the wayside do it in their first term, or perhaps their second."

"But not all, surely. There must be accidents in a life like this."

"Oh, yes, there are accidents." Henrietta turned and began to climb the further flight.

"That girl whose place Teresa Desterro took, was it an accident that overtook her?"

"No," said Henrietta shortly, "she had a breakdown."

Lucy, climbing the shallow steps in the wake of her friend's broad beam, recognised the tone. It was the tone in which Henrietta, the head-girl, used to say: "And see that no goloshes are left lying about the cloakroom floor." It did not permit of further discussion.

Henrietta, it was to be understood, did not like to think of her beloved College as a Moloch. College was a bright gateway to the future for deserving youth; and if one or two found the gateway a hazard rather than an opening, then it was unfortunate but no reflection on the builders of the gateway.

"Like a convent," Nash had said yesterday morning. "No time to think of an outside world." That was true. She had watched a day's routine go by. She had also seen the Students' two daily papers lying unopened in the common-room last night as they went in to supper. But a nunnery, if it was a narrow world, was also a placid one. Uncompetitive. Assured. There was nothing of the nunnery about this over-anxious, wildly strenuous life. Only the self-absorption was the same; the narrowness.

And yet *was* it so narrow, she wondered, considering the gathering in the drawing-room? If this were any other kind of college that gathering would have been homogeneous. If it were a college of science the gathering would consist of scientists; if it were a college of divinity, of theologians. But in this long charming room, with its good "pieces" and its chintzes, with its tall windows pushed up so that the warm evening flowed in through them full of grass and roses, in this one room many worlds met. Madame Lefevre, reclining in thin elegance on a hard Empire sofa and smoking a yellow cigarette in a green holder, represented a world theatrical; a world of grease-paint, art, and

32

artifice. Miss Lux, sitting upright in a hard chair, represented the academical world; the world of universities, text-books, and discussion. Young Miss Wragg, busy pouring out coffee, was the world of sport; a physical, competitive, unthinking world. And the evening's guest Dr Enid Knight, one of the "visiting" Staff, stood for the medical world. The foreign world was not present: Sigrid Gustavsen had retired with her mother, who spoke no English, to her own room where they could chatter together in Swedish.

All these worlds had gone to make the finished article that was a Leaving Student; it was at least not the training that was narrow.

"And what do you think of our students, Miss Pym, now that you have had a whole afternoon with them?" Madame Lefevre asked, turning the battery of her enormous dark eyes on Lucy.

A dam-silly question, thought Lucy; and wondered how a good respectable middle-class English couple had produced anything so like the original serpent as Madame Lefevre. "I think," she said, glad to be able to be honest, "that there is not one of them who is not an advertisement for Leys." And she saw Henrietta's heavy face light up. College was Henrietta's world. She lived and moved and had her being in the affairs of Leys; it was her father, mother, lover, and child.

"They *are* a nice lot," agreed Doreen Wragg happily, not yet far removed from her own student days and regarding her pupils with cameraderie.

"They are as the beasts that perish," said Miss Lux incisively. "They think that Botticelli is a variety of spaghetti." She inspected with deep gloom the coffee that Miss Wragg handed to her. "If it comes to that, they don't know what spaghetti is. It's not long since Dakers stood up in the middle of a Dietetics lecture and accused me of destroying her illusions."

"It surprises me to know that anything about Miss Dakers is destructible," observed Madame Lefevre, in her brown velvet drawl.

"What illusion had you destroyed?" the young doctor asked from the window-seat.

"I had just informed them that spaghetti and its relations were

33

made from a paste of flour. That shattered for ever, apparently, Dakers' picture of Italy."

"How had she pictured it?"

"Fields of waving macaroni, so she said."

Henrietta turned from putting two lumps of sugar in a very small cup of coffee (*How* nice, thought Lucy wistfully, to have a figure like a sack of flour and not to mind!) and said: "At least they are free from crime."

"Crime?" they said, puzzled.

"Miss Pym has just been enquiring about the incidence of crime at Leys. That is what it is to be a psychologist."

Before Lucy could protest against this version of her simple search for knowledge, Madame Lefevre said: "Well, let us oblige her. Let us turn out the rag-bag of our shameful past. What crime have we had?"

"Farthing was had up last Christmas term for riding her bike without lights," volunteered Miss Wragg.

"Crime," said Madame Lefevre. "Crime. Not petty misdemeanours."

"If you mean a plain wrong-un, there was that dreadful creature who was man-crazy and used to spend Saturday evenings hanging round the barrack gate in Larborough."

"Yes," said Miss Lux, remembering. "What became of *her* when we tossed her out, does anyone know?"

"She is doing the catering at a Seamen's Refuge in Plymouth," Henrietta said, and opened her eyes when they laughed. "I don't know what is funny about that. The only real crime we have had in ten years, as you very well know, was the watches affair. And even that," she added, jealous for her beloved institution, "was a fixation rather than plain theft. She took nothing but watches, and she made no use of them. Kept them all in a drawer of her bureau, quite openly. Nine, there were. A fixation, of course."

"By precedent, I suppose she is now with the Goldsmiths and Silversmiths," said Madame Lefevre.

"I don't know," said Henrietta, seriously. "I think her people kept her at home. They were quite well-to-do."

"Well, Miss Pym, the incidence appears to be point-something

per cent." Madame Lefevre waved a thin brow
an unsensational crowd."

"Too normal by half," Miss Wragg volunteered
of scandal would be nice now and again. A nice
hand-stands and upward circlings."

"I should like to see some hand-stands and upward
Lucy said. "Would it be all right if I came and w
Seniors tomorrow morning?"

But of course she must see the Seniors, Henrietta said. They
were busy with their Demonstration programme, so it would
be a private Demonstration all for herself. "They are one of
the best sets we ever had," she said.

"Can I have first go of the gym. when the Seniors are doing
their Final Phys. on Tuesday?" Miss Wragg asked; and they
began to discuss time-tables.

Miss Pym moved over to the window-seat and joined Dr
Knight.

"Are you responsible for the cross-section of something called
the villi?" she asked.

"Oh, no; physiology is an ordinary college subject: Catherine
Lux takes that."

"Then what do you lecture on?"

"Oh, different things at different stages. Public Health. The
so-called 'social' diseases. The even more so-called Facts of
Life. Your subject."

"Psychology?"

"Yes. Public Health is my job, but psychology is my specialty.
I liked your book so much. So common-sensical. I admired that.
It is so easy to be high-falutin about an abstract subject."

Lucy flushed a little. There is no praise so gratifying as that
of a colleague.

"And of course I am the College medical advisor," Dr Knight
went on, looking amused. "A sinecure if ever there was one.
They are a disgustingly healthy crowd."

"But—" Lucy began. It is the outsider, Desterro (she was
thinking), who insists on their abnormality. If it is true, then
surely this trained observer, also from the outside, must be
aware of it.

35

have accidents, of course," the doctor said, misunder-
... ding Lucy's 'but'. "Their life is a long series of minor accidents
—bruises, and sprains, and dislocated fingers, and what not—
but it is very rarely that anything serious happens. Bentley has
been the only instance in my time—the girl whose room you have.
She broke a leg, and won't be back till next term."

"But—it is a strenuous training, a gruelling life; do they never
break down under it?"

"Yes. That's not unknown. The last term is particularly trying.
A concentration of horrors from the student's point of view.
Crit. classes, and—"

"Crit. classes?"

"Yes. They each have to take a gym. and a dancing class in
the presence of the united Staff and their own set, and are
judged according to the show they make. Nerve-shattering.
These are all over, the crit. classes; but there are still the Finals,
and the Demonstration, and being given jobs, and the actual
parting from student life, and what not. Yes, it is a strain for them,
poor dears. But they are amazingly resilient. No one who wasn't
would have survived so long. Let me get you some more coffee.
I'm going to have some."

She took Lucy's cup and went away to the table; and Lucy
leaned back in the folds of the curtain and looked at the garden.
The sun had set, and the outlines were growing blurred; there was
the first hint of dew in the soft air that blew up against her face.
Somewhere on the other side of the house (in the students'
common-room?) a piano was being played and a girl was singing.
It was a charming voice: effortless and pure, without professional
tricks and without fashionable dealing in quarter-tones. The
song, moreover, was a ballad; old-fashioned and sentimental,
but devoid of self-pity and posing. A frank young voice and a
frank old song. It shocked Lucy to realise how long it was
since she had heard any voice raised in song that was not a
product of valves and batteries. In London at this moment the
exhausted air was loud with radios; but here, in this cool, scented
garden, a girl was singing for the love of it.

I have been too long in London, she thought; I must have a

change. Find a hotel on the South Coast, perhaps. Or go abroad. One forgets that the world is young.

"Who is singing?" she asked, as her cup was handed to her again.

"Stewart, I think," Dr Knight said, not interested. "Miss Pym, you can save my life if you like to."

Lucy said that to save a doctor's life would give her immense satisfaction.

"I want to go to a medical conference in London," Dr Knight said in a conspiratorial undertone. "It is on Thursday, but that is the day of my psychology lecture. Miss Hodge thinks I am for ever going to conferences, so I can't possibly beg off again. But if you were to take that lecture for me, everything would be grand."

"But I am going back to London myself tomorrow after lunch."

"No!" said Dr Knight, much dashed. "Do you have to?"

"Oddly enough, I was just thinking how much I should hate going back."

"Then don't go. Stay on for a day or two, and save my life. Do, Miss Pym."

"And what would Henrietta think of the substitution?"

"That, of course, is sheer affectation, and you ought to be ashamed of yourself. *I'm* not a best-seller, *I'm* not a celebrity, *I'm* not the author of the latest text-book on the subject—"

Lucy made a small gesture acknowledging her fault, but her eyes were on the garden. Why *should* she go back to London yet? What was there to take her back? Nothing and nobody. For the first time that fine, independent, cushioned, celebrated life of hers looked just a little bleak. A little narrow and inhuman. Could it be? Was there, perhaps, a lack of warmth in that existence she had been so content with? Not a lack of human contact, certainly. She had her fill of human contact. But it was a very all-of-a-piece contact, now that she thought of it. Except for Mrs Montmorency from one of the suburbs of Manchester, who was her daily help, and her Aunt Celia down in Walberswick who sometimes had her for weekends, and the tradespeople, she never talked to anyone who wasn't somehow

37

connected with the publishing or the academic worlds. And though all the ladies and gentlemen belonging to these two worlds were, of course, both intelligent and amusing, there was no denying that their interests were limited. You couldn't, for instance, talk to one and the same person about Social Security, hill-billy songs, and what won the 3.30. They each had their "subject." And their subject, she found to her cost, was only too likely to be royalties. Lucy herself had only the vaguest idea about royalties; especially her own, and could never keep her end up in this sort of conversation.

Besides, none of them was *young*.

At least, not young as these children here were young. Young in years a few of her acquaintances might be, but they were already bowed down with the weight of the world's wrongs and their own importance. It was nice to meet a morning-of-the-world youngness for a change.

And it was nice to be liked.

There was no good in trying to diddle herself about why she wanted to stay a little longer; why she was seriously prepared to forgo the delights of civilisation that had seemed so desirable—so imperatively desirable—only yesterday morning. It *was nice* to be liked.

In the last few years she had been ignored, envied, admired, kow-towed to, and cultivated; but warm, personal liking was something she had not had since the Lower Fourth said goodbye to her, with a home-made pen-wiper and a speech by Gladys Someone-or-other, shortly after her legacy. To stay in this atmosphere of youth, of liking, of warmth, she was willing to overlook for a space the bells, the beans, and the bathrooms.

"Knight," said young Miss Wragg, raising her voice from the conversation behind them, "did the Disciples ask you about giving them an introduction to some doctor or other in Manchester?"

"Oh, yes, they asked me. In concert. I said yes, of course. As a matter of fact, I was glad to; I think they will be a great success."

"Individually, the Disciples are null and void," Miss Lux said. "But collectively they have a quadruple ruthlessness that will be very useful in Lancashire. It is the only occasion I have ever come across when nothing multiplied by four became something like six-and-a-half. If nobody wants the *Sunday Times* I shall take it to bed with me."

No one apparently wanted it. It had been lying unopened in the drawing-room after lunch when Lucy had been the first to look at it, and as far as she had noticed no one except Miss Lux had picked it up since.

"This set of Seniors are planting themselves out very nicely. Almost without our help," Madame Lefevre said. "There will be less heart-burning than usual." She did not sound very sorry about the heart-burning; just sardonic.

"It continually surprises me," said Miss Hodge, not at all sardonic, "how each year the students slip into their appropriate places in the world's work. The openings come up as the students are ready to fill them. Almost like—like two pieces of the same machine. So surprising and so satisfactory. I don't think we have had a misfit in all my years at Leys. I had a letter from the Cordwainers School, by the way; in Edinburgh, you know. Mulcaster is getting married and they want someone in her place. You will remember Mulcaster, Marie?" She turned to Madame Lefevre who, except for Henrietta, was the Oldest Inhabitant—and who, incidentally, had been christened plain Mary.

"Of course I remember her. A lump without leaven," said Madame, who judged everyone by their capacity to execute *rondes de jambes*.

"A nice girl," Henrietta said placidly. "I think Cordwainers will be a very good place for Sheena Stewart."

"Have you told her about it?" Miss Wragg asked.

"No, oh, no; I always like to sleep on things."

"Hatch them out, you mean," Madame said. "You must have heard about Cordwainers before lunch-time yesterday because that was the last post, and it is only now we hear about it."

"It was not very important," Henrietta said defensively; and then added with what was nearly a simper: "But I *have* heard rumours of a 'plum,' a really wonderful chance for someone."

"Tell us," they said.

But Henrietta said no; that no official notice had come, that

39

no official notice or application might come at all, and until it did it was better not to talk about it. But she still looked pleased and mysterious.

"Well, I'm going to bed," Miss Lux said, picking up the *Times* and turning her back on Henrietta's elephantine coyness. "You are not going before lunch tomorrow, are you, Miss Pym?"

"Well," said Lucy, pitchforked of a sudden into decision, "I wondered if I might stay on for a day or two? You did ask me to, you know," she reminded Henrietta. "It has been so nice— So interesting to watch a world so different—And it is so lovely here, so—" Oh, dear, why must she sound so idiotic. Would she never learn to behave like Lucy Pym the Celebrity?

But her stammerings were swamped in the loud wave of their approval. Lucy was touched to note a gleam of pleasure even on the face of Miss Lux.

"Stay on till Thursday and take my Senior Psychology lecture, and let me go to a conference in London," Dr Knight suggested, as if it had just occurred to her.

"Oh, I don't know whether—" began Lucy, all artistic doubt, and looked at Henrietta.

"Dr Knight is always running away to conferences," Miss Hodge said, disapproving but without heat. "But of course we would be delighted and honoured, Lucy, if you agreed to give the students a second lecture."

"I should like to. It would be nice to feel myself a temporary member of the Staff, instead of a mere guest. I should like to very much." She turned in rising to wink at Dr Knight, who was squeezing her arm in a rapture of gratitude. "And now I think I must get back to the student wing."

She said goodnight and went out with Miss Lux.

Lux eyed her sideways as they moved together to the back of the house, but Lucy, catching the glance, thought that there was a friendly gleam in that ice-grey eye.

"Do you really like this menagerie?" Lux asked. "Or are you just looking for things to stick on cardboard with pins?"

That was what The Nut Tart had asked yesterday afternoon. Have you come looking for specimens? Well, she would make the same answer and see what Lux's reaction would be.

"Oh, I'm staying because I like it. A college of Physical Train-ing wouldn't be a very good place to look for the abnormal, anyhow, would it." She made it a statement, not a question; and waited.

"Why not?" asked Miss Lux. "Sweating oneself into a coma may stultify the reason but it doesn't destroy the emotions."

"Doesn't it?" Lucy said, surprised. "If I were dog-tired I'm certain I wouldn't have any feelings about anything but going to sleep quickly."

"Going to sleep dead tired is all right; normal, and pleasant, and safe. It is when one wakens up dead tired that the trouble begins."

"What trouble?"

"The hypothetical trouble of this discussion," Lux said, smoothly.

"And is wakening up dead tired a common thing, would you say?"

"Well, I'm not their medical adviser so I can't run round with a stethoscope and fond inquiries, but I should say that five Seniors out of six in their last term are so tired that each morning is a mild nightmare. It is when one is as tired as that that one's emo-tional state ceases to be normal. A tiny obstacle becomes an Everest in the path; a careless comment becomes a grievance to be nursed; a small disappointment is all of a sudden a suicidal affair."

There swam up in Lucy's mind a vision of that circle of faces at tea-time. Brown, laughing, happy faces; careless and for the most part notably confident. Where in that relaxed and healthy crowd had there been the least hint of strain, of bad temper? Nowhere. They had moaned over their hard lot certainly, but it was a humourous and detached complaint.

Tired they might be; in fact tired they certainly were—it would be a miracle if they were not; but tired to the point of abnormality, no. Lucy could not believe it.

"This is my room," Lux said, and paused. "Have you some-thing to read? I don't suppose you brought anything if you meant to go back yesterday. Can I lend you something?"

She opened the door, exhibiting a neat bed-sitting-room of

41

which the sole decorations were one engraving, one photograph, and an entire wainscotting of books. From next-door came the babble of Swedish chat.

"Poor Fröken," Lux said unexpectedly, as Lucy cocked an ear. "She has been so homesick. It must be wonderful to be able to talk family gossip in one's own tongue again." And then, seeing Lucy's eyes on the photograph: "My young sister."

"She is very lovely," Lucy said; and hoped instantly that there had been no hint of surprise in her tone.

"Yes." Lux was drawing the curtains. "I hate moths. Do you? She was born when I was in my teens, and I have practically brought her up. She is in her third year at Medical school." She came and stood for a moment looking at the photograph with Lucy. "Well, what can I give you to read? Anything from Runyon to Proust."

Lucy took *The Young Visiters*. It was a long time since she had read it last, but she found that she was smiling at the very sight of it. A sort of reflex action; quite involuntary. And when she looked up she found that Lux was smiling too.

"Well, that is one thing I shall never do," Lucy said regretfully.
"What?"

"Write a book that makes all the world smile."

"Not all the world," Lux said, her smile broadening. "I had a cousin who stopped half-way through. When I asked her why, she said: 'So *unlikely*'."

So Lucy went smiling away towards bed, glad that she was not going to catch that train tomorrow, and thinking about the plain Miss Lux who loved a beautiful sister and liked absurdity. As she turned into the long corridor of the E-wing she saw Beau Nash standing at the angle of the stairs at the far end, in the act of lifting a hand-bell to shoulder height, and in another second the wild yelling of it filled the wing. She stood where she was, her hands over her ears, while Beau laughed at her and swung the evil thing with a will. Lovely, she was, standing there with that instrument of torture in her hands.

"Is ringing the 'bedroom' bell the Head Girl's duty?" Lucy asked, as Beau at last ceased to swing.

"No, the Seniors take week-about; it just happens to be my

week. Being well down the list alphabetically I don't have more than one week each term." She looked at Miss Pym and lowered her voice in mock-confidence. "I pretend to be glad about that —everyone thinks it a frightful bore to have to watch the clock— but I *love* making a row."

Yes, thought Lucy; no nerves and a body brimming with health; of course she would love the row. And then, almost automatically, wondered if it was not the row that she liked but the feeling of power in her hands. But no, she dismissed that thought; Nash was the one that life had been easy for; the one who had, all her life, had only to ask, or take, in order to have. She had no need of vicarious satisfactions; her life was one long satisfaction. She liked the wild clamour of the bell; that was all.

"Anyhow," Nash said, falling into step with her, "it isn't the 'bedroom bell.' It's 'Lights Out'."

"I had no idea it was so late. Does that apply to me?"

"Of course not. Olympus does as it likes."

"Even a boarded-out Olympus?"

"Here is your hovel," Nash said, switching on the light and standing aside to let Lucy enter the bright little cell, so gay and antiseptic in the unshaded brilliance. After the subtleties of the summer evening and the grace of the Georgian drawing-room, it was like an illustration from one of the glossier American magazines. "I am glad I happened to see you because I have a confession to make. I won't be bringing your breakfast tomorrow."

"Oh, that is all right," Lucy was beginning, "I ought to get up in any case—"

"No, I don't mean that. Of *course* not. It is just that young Morris asked if she might do it—she is one of the Juniors—and—"

"The abductor of George?"

"Oh, yes, I forgot you were there. Yes, that one. And she seemed to think that her life would not be complete unless she had brought up your breakfast on your last morning, so I said that as long as she didn't ask for your autograph or otherwise make a nuisance of herself, she could. I hope you don't mind. She is a nice child, and it would really give her pleasure."

Lucy, who didn't mind if her breakfast was brought by a wall-eyed and homicidal negro so long as she could eat the

43

leathery toast in peace and quiet, said she was grateful to young Morris, and anyhow it wasn't going to be her last morning. She was going to stay on and take a lecture on Thursday.

"You *are*! Oh, that's wonderful. I'm so glad. Everyone will be glad. You are so *good* for us."

"A medicine?" Lucy wrinkled her nose in protest.

"No, a tonic."

"Somebody's Syrup," Lucy said; but she was pleased.

So pleased that even pushing little hairpins into their appointed places did not bore her with the customary frenzy of boredom. She creamed her face and considered it, unadorned and greasy in the bright hard light, with unaccustomed tolerance. There was no doubt that being a little on the plump side kept the lines away; if you had to have a face like a scone it was at least comforting that it was a smooth scone. And, now she came to think of it, one was given the looks that were appropriate; if she had Garbo's nose she would have to dress up to it, and if she had Miss Lux's cheek-bones she would have to live up to them. Lucy had never been able to live up to anything. Not even The Book.

Remembering in time that there was no bedside light—students were discouraged from working in bed—she switched the light off and crossed to pull aside the curtains of the window looking out on the courtyard. She stood there by the wide-open window, smelling the cool scented night. A great stillness had settled on Leys. The chatter, the bells, the laughter, the wild protests, the drumming of feet, the rush of bath water, the coming and going, had crystallised into this great silent bulk, a deeper darkness in the quiet dark.

"Miss Pym."

The whisper came from one of the windows opposite.

Could they see her, then? No, of course not. Someone had heard the small noise of her curtains being drawn back.

"Miss Pym, we are so glad you are staying."

So much for the college grape-vine! Not fifteen minutes since Nash said goodnight, but already the news was in the opposite wing.

44

Before she could answer, a chorus of whispers came from the unseen windows round the little quadrangle. Yes, Miss Pym. We are glad. Glad, Miss Pym. Yes. Yes. Glad, Miss Pym.

"Goodnight, everyone," Lucy said.

Goodnight, they said. Goodnight. So glad. Goodnight.

She wound her watch and pulled up a chair to put it on— *the* chair, rather: there was only one—so that there should be no burrowing under pillows for it in the morning; and thought how odd it was that only yesterday morning she could not wait to get out of this place.

And perhaps it was because no self-respecting psychologist would have anything to do with a thing so outmoded as Premonition that no small helpful imp from the Unexplainable was there to whisper in her drowsy ear: "Go away from here. Go away while the going is good. Go away. Away from here."

· 6 ·

THE chairs scraped on the parquet floor as the students rose from their kneeling position, and turned to wait while the Staff filed out of morning prayers. Lucy, having become "temporary Staff," had made the gesture of attending this 8.45 ceremony as an off-set to the un-staff-like indulgence of breakfast in bed; and she had spent the last few minutes considering the collective legs of College as spread before her in kneeling rows and marvelling at their individuality. Dress was uniform at this hour of the morning, and heads were bowed in dutiful hands, but a pair of legs were as easy to identify as a face, she found. There they were: stubborn legs, frivolous legs, neat legs, dull legs, doubtful legs—already she needed only a turn of calf and piece of ankle to say: Dakers, or Innes, or Rouse, or Beau, as the case might be. Those elegant ones at the end of the first row were The Nut Tart. Did the nuns not mind that their protégé should listen to Anglican prayers, then? And those rather stick-like ones were Campbell, and those—

"Amen," said Henrietta, with unction.

45

"Amen," murmured the students of Leys, and rose to their feet with the scraping of chairs. And Lucy filed out with the Staff.

"Come in and wait while I arrange this morning's post," Henrietta said, "and then I'll go over to the gymnasium with you," and she led the way into her own sitting-room, where a meek little part-time secretary was waiting for instructions. Lucy sat down on the window seat with the *Telegraph*, and listened with only half an ear to the professional conversation that followed. Mrs So-and-so had written to ask the date of the Demonstration, Mrs Someone-else wanted to know whether there was a hotel near-by where she and her husband could stay when they came to see their daughter perform, the receipt for the butcher must be looked out and presented to his disbelieving eye, the special lecturer for the last Friday of term had cried off, three Prospective Parents wanted prospectuses.

"All quite straightforward, I think," Henrietta said.

"Yes," agreed the meek little secretary. "I'll get on with them at once. There was a letter from Arlinghurst. It doesn't seem to be here."

"No," Henrietta said. "That can be answered later in the week."

Arlinghurst, Lucy's mind said. Arlinghurst. The school for girls, of course. A sort of female Eton. "I was at Arlinghurst," they said, and that settled it. She took her attention from the *Telegraph* leader for a moment and thought that if the "plum" that Henrietta had been waiting for was Arlinghurst then indeed it was going to create more than the usual stir among the interested Seniors. She was on the point of asking whether Arlinghurst was in fact the "plum," but was stopped partly by the presence of the meek little secretary but more immediately by the expression on Henrietta's face. Henrietta—there was no denying it—Henrietta had a wary, a sort of guilty, look. The look of a person who is Up To Something.

Oh, well, thought Lucy, if she is merely hugging her lovely secret to herself, let her. I shan't spoil it for her. She followed her friend down the long corridor that ran the length of the wing, and out to the covered way that continued the corridor to the gymnasium. The gymnasium lay parallel to the house and

46

to the right-angled wing, so that from the air the buildings made a complete letter E; the three horizontal strokes being "old house," the right-angled wing, and the gymnasium; the vertical stroke being the connecting wing and the covered way.

The door to which the covered way led was open, and from inside the gymnasium came the sounds of unco-ordinated activity; voices, laughter, thudding feet. Henrietta paused by the open door and pointed through to the door on the other side, now closed. "*That* is the college crime," she said. "Crossing the gymnasium to the field-path instead of using the appointed covered way round the building. That is why we have had to lock it up. One wouldn't think that a few extra steps would mean much to students who took so many in the day, but there was no argument or threat which would stop them using the short-cut through. So we removed the temptation altogether."

She turned from the open door and led the way to the other end of the building, where a small porch held the stairway to the gallery. As they climbed the stairs Henrietta paused to point to a piece of mechanism on a low trolley, which filled the well of the staircase. "That," she said, "is the most famous College character of all. That is our vacuum cleaner; known from here to New Zealand as The Abhorrence."

"Why abhorrent?" Lucy asked.

"It used to be Nature's Abhorrence, but it became shortened to The Abhorrence. You remember the tag one is taught at school: Nature abhors a vacuum." She looked a moment longer at the monstrous object, caressing it with her eyes. "It cost us a deplorable sum, The Abhorrence, but it was money well spent. However well the gymnasium was cleaned in the old days, there was always a residue of dust, which was beaten into the air by the students' feet and sucked up, of course, by the students' respiratory passages; and the result was catarrh. Not universal, of course, but there never was a time, summer or winter, when some student or other was not having a bout of catarrh. It was Dr Knight's predecessor who suggested that it might be invisible dust that was responsible, and she was right. Since we squandered that immense sum on The Abhorrence there has been no more catarrh. And of course," she added happily, "it was a saving in

47

the end since it is Giddy the gardener's job to vacuum the gymnasium now, and we don't have to pay cleaners."

Lucy stopped as they reached the top of the stairs, and looked over the railings into the well again. "I don't think I like it. It is very well named, it seems to me. There is something obscene about it."

"It is unbelievably powerful. And very easy to work. It takes Giddy only about twenty minutes every morning, and when he has finished there is, as he says himself, 'nothing left but the fixtures.' He is very proud of The Abhorrence. He grooms it as if it were an animal." Henrietta opened the door at the top of the stairs and they entered the gallery.

A gymnasium as a building does not permit of architecture. It is purely functional. It is an oblong box, lit by windows which are either in the roof or high up the walls. The gymnasium at Leys had windows where the walls met the roof, which is not a beautiful arrangement; but through their far-away panes at no hour of any day could direct sunlight blind a student's eyes, and so cause an accident. The great oblong box of a building was filled with the reflected radiance of a summer morning; golden and soft. Across the floor were scattered the Senior students, limbering up, practising, criticising, and in a few happy instances playing the fool.

"Do they mind an audience?" Lucy asked as they sat down.

"They are very used to one. Hardly a day goes by without a visitor of some kind."

"What is under the gallery? What is it they watch all the time?"

"Themselves," said Henrietta succinctly. "The whole wall below the gallery is one long mirror."

Lucy admired the impersonal interest on the faces of the students as they watched their reflected performances. To be able to view one's physical entity with such critical detachment was surely no bad thing.

"It is one of the griefs of my life," the dutch-doll Gage was saying, looking at her up-stretched arms, "that my arms have that kink at the elbow."

"If you listened to that Friday-friend and used your will-power,

48

you'd have them straight by now," Stewart observed, not pausing in her own contortions.

"Probably bent back the other way," Beau Nash mocked, from a doubled-up position at the rib-stalls.

Lucy deduced that a Friday-friend was the "interest" lecturer who appeared on Friday evenings; and wondered idly whether that particular one had called his subject "faith" or "mind-over-matter"; was it Lourdes or was it Coué?

Hasselt, the South African with the flat Primitive face, was clutching Innes's ankles in the air while Innes stood on her hands. "*Reeeee*-ly on thee *arrrrms*, Mees Innes," Hasselt was saying, in a would-be Swedish accent that was evidently a quotation from Fröken; and Innes laughed and collapsed. Looking at them, flushed and smiling (this, she thought, is the first time I have seen Mary Innes smile) Lucy felt again how out-of-place these two faces were. Hasselt's belonged above a Madonna-blue robe, with a tiny landscape of hills and castles and roads somewhere at her left ear. And Innes's to a portrait on some ancestral staircase—seventeenth century, perhaps? No, too gay, too adaptable, too arched-of-eye-brow. Sixteenth-century, rather. Withdrawn, uncompromising, unforgiving; the-stake-or-nothing.

Away by herself in a far corner was Rouse, painstakingly stretching her ham-strings by walking her palms up to her feet. She couldn't really *need* to stretch her ham-strings, not after years of continued stretching, so presumably this was merely a north-country example of "makking siccar." There was no fooling about for Miss Rouse; life was real, life was earnest; life was long ham-strings and a good post in the offing. Lucy wished she liked Miss Rouse better, and looked round for Dakers as a sort of antidote. But there was no tow-head and cheerful pony-face among the collection.

And then, suddenly, the desultory noise and the chatter faded. No one had come in by the open door at the far end, but there was beyond doubt a Presence in the place. Lucy could feel it coming up through the gallery floor at her feet. She remembered that there was a door at the foot of the stairway; where The Abhorrence stood. Someone had come in down there.

There was no audible word of command, but the students, who a moment before had been scattered over the floor like beads from a broken string, were now, as if by magic, standing in a still, waiting line.

Fröken Gustavsen walked out from under the gallery, and surveyed them.

"Unt wvere ees Mees Dakers?" she asked in a cool small voice. But even as she said it a flustered Dakers ran in through the open door, and stopped short as she saw the picture that waited her.

"Oh, *catastrophe!*" she wailed, and darted to the gap that some-one had accommodatingly left for her. "Oh, I *am* sorry, Fröken. *Abyssmally* sorry. It was just that—"

"Ees eet proposed to be laate at the Demonstraation?" asked Fröken, with almost scientific interest.

"Oh, *no,* of *course* not, Fröken. It was just that—"

"We know. We know. Something was lost, or broke. Eef eet wass possible to come to thees plaace naakid, Mees Dakers would still find something to lose or break. Attention!"

They came to attention, and were motionless except for their quick breathing.

"Eef Mees Thomas were to pull een her stow-mach the line would be improved, I theenk."

Thomas obliged instantly.

"Unt Mees Appleyard shows too much cheen."

The plump little girl with the red cheeks pulled her chin further into her neck. "So!"

They right-turned into file, covered, and marched in single file down the gymnasium; their feet falling so lightly on the hard wood floor that they were almost inaudible.

"Quieter, quieter. Lightly, lightly!"

Was it possible?

But it was possible, apparently. Still more quietly fell those long-trained feet, until it was unbelievable that a collection of solid young females weighing individually anything up to ten stones were marching, marching, round the hall.

Lucy slid an eye round to Henrietta; and almost instantly switched it away again. The fond pride on Henrietta's large pale countenance was startling, almost painful, to see; and for a little

50

Lucy forgot the students below and thought about Henrietta. Henrietta of the sack-line figure and the conscientious soul. Henrietta who had had elderly parents, no sisters, and the instincts of a mother hen. No one had ever lain awake at night over Henrietta; or walked back and fore in the darkness outside her house; or even, perhaps, sent her flowers. (Which reminded her to wonder where Alan was nowadays; there had been several weeks, one spring, when she had thought quite seriously of accepting Alan, in spite of his Adam's apple. It would be nice, she had thought, to be cherished for a change. What had stopped her was the realisation that the cherishing would have to be mutual. That she would inevitably have to mend socks, for instance. She didn't like feet. Even Alan's.) Henrietta had been apparently doomed to a dull if worthy life. But it had not turned out like that. If the expression on her unguarded face had been any criterion, Henrietta had built for herself a life that was full, rich, and satisfying. She had said, in her first re-union gossip with Lucy, that when she took over Leys a decade ago it had been a small and not very popular college, and that she and Leys had flourished together; that she was, in fact, a partner now as well as Principal, and a partner in a flourishing concern. But until she had surprised that look on Henrietta's face, Lucy had not realised how much her old friend identified herself with her work. That College was her world, she knew; Henrietta talked of little else. But absorption in a business was one thing, and the emotion on Henrietta's face was quite another.

She was roused from her speculations by the sound of apparatus being dragged out. The students had stopped arching themselves into bows at the rib-stalls, puffed out like figureheads on a ship, and were now bringing out the booms. Lucy's shins ached with remembered pain; how often had she barked her bones against that unyielding piece of wood; certainly one of the compensations of middle-age was not having to do uncomfortable things.

The wooden upright was now standing in the middle of the floor, and the two booms were fitted into its grooved sides and hoisted as high as hands could reach. The iron pins with wooden handles shot home through their appointed holes in the upright to hold the booms up, and there was the instrument of torture ready. Not that it was shin-barking time yet; that would come later. Just now it was only "travelling." Two by two, one at each end, the students proceeded along the boom, hanging by their hands, monkey-wise. First sideways, then backwards, and lastly with a rotary movement, like a travelling top. All this was done with monotonous perfection until it was Rouse's turn to rotate. Rouse had bent her knees for the spring to the boom, and then dropped her hands and looked at her instructor with a kind of panic on her tight, freckled face.

"Oh, Fröken," she said, "I'm not going to be able to do it."

"*Nonsense*, Mees Rouse," Fröken said, encouraging but not surprised (this was apparently a repetition of some previous scene), "you have done eet perfectly since you were a Junior. You do it now of course."

In a strained silence Rouse sprang to the boom and began her progress along it. For half its length she performed with professional expertness, and then for no apparent reason her hand missed the boom as she turned, and her body swung away, suspended by her other hand. She made an effort to recover herself, pulling up with her sustaining hand, but the rhythm had broken and she dropped to her feet.

"I knew it," she said. "I'm going to be like Kenyon, Fröken. Just like Kenyon."

"*Mees* Rouse; you are not going to be like *anyone*. It is knack, that. And for a moment you haf lost the knack, that is all. You will try again."

Rouse sprang once more to the boom above her head.

"*No!*" said the Swede with emphasis; and Rouse came back to the ground looking inquiring.

"*Not* saying: Oh, dear, I cannot do eet. But saying: This I do often, with ease, and now al*so*. So!"

Twice more Rouse tried, and failed.

"Ve-ry well, Mees Rouse. That will do. One half of the boom will be put up last thing at night, as it is now, and you will come een the morning early and practise, until the knack has come back."

"Poor Rouse," Lucy said, as the booms were being reversed for balance exercises, flat side up instead of rounded.

"Yes, such a pity," Henrietta said. "One of our most brilliant students."

"Brilliant?" said Lucy, surprised. It was not an adjective she would have applied to Rouse.

"In physical work, anyhow. Most brilliant. She finds written work a difficulty, but makes up for it by hard work. A model student, and a great credit to Leys. Such a pity about this little nervous development. Over-anxiety, of course. It happens sometimes. Usually over something quite simple, strangely enough."

"What did she mean by 'being like Kenyon'? That is the girl whose place Teresa Desterro took, isn't it?"

"Yes. How clever of you to remember. That was a case in point. Kenyon suddenly decided that she could not balance. She had always had abnormally good balance, and there was no reason why she should lose it. But she began by being wobbly, took to jumping off in the middle of an exercise, and ended by being unable to get up from sitting position on the boom. She sat there and clung to the boom like a frightened child. Sat there and cried."

"Some inner insufficiency."

"Of course. It was not the balance that she was frightened of. But we had to send her home. We are hoping that she will come back to finish her training when she has had a long rest. She was very happy here."

Was she? thought Lucy. So happy that she broke down. What had reduced the girl who was good at balance to a crying and shivering piece of misery, clutching at the boom?

She watched with a new interest the progress of the balancing that had been poor Kenyon's Waterloo. Two by two the students somersaulted upwards on to the high boom, turned to a sitting position sideways, and then slowly stood up on the narrow ledge. Slowly one leg lifted, the muscles rippling in the light, the arms performed their appointed evolution. The faces were calm, intent. The bodies obedient, sure, and accustomed. When the exercise was finished they sank until they were sitting on their heels, upright and easy, put forward blind hands to seize the boom, descended to sideways sitting once more, and from there to a forward somersault and so the ground again.

53

No one fluffed or failed. The perfection was unblemished. Even Fröken found no word to say. Lucy found that she had been holding her breath. She sat back and relaxed and breathed deeply.

"That was lovely. At school the balance was much lower, wasn't it, and so it was not exciting."

Henrietta looked pleased. "Sometimes I come in just to see the balance and nothing else. So many people like the more spectacular items. The vaulting and so on. But I find the quiet control of the balance very satisfying."

The vaulting, when it came, was spectacular enough. The obstacles were, to Lucy's eyes, horrific; and she looked with uncomprehending wonder at the delighted faces of the students. They *liked* this. They liked launching themselves into nothingness, flying through the air to problematical landings, twisting and somersaulting. The restraint that had characterised their attitude up to now had vanished; there was verve in their every movement, a sort of laughter; living was good and this was a physical expression of their joy in living. Amazed, she watched the Rouse who had stumbled and failed over the simple boom exercise, performing hair-raising feats of perfection that must require the maximum of courage, control, and "knack." (Henrietta had been right, her physical performance was brilliant. She was also, no doubt, a brilliant games player; her timing was excellent. But still that "brilliant" stuck in Lucy's throat. "Brilliant" meant someone like Beau; an all-round fineness; body, mind, and spirit.)

"*Mees* Dakers! Take the left hand off at *wons*. Is eet *mountaineering* you are?"

"I didn't mean to leave it so long, Fröken. Really I didn't."

"That is understood. It is the not meaning to that ees rrreprehensible. Come again, after Mees Mathews."

Dakers came again, and this time managed to make her rebellious hand release its grip at the appropriate moment.

"Ha!" she said, delighted with her own success.

"Ha indeed," agreed Fröken, a smile breaking. "Co-ordination. All is co-ordination."

"They like Fröken, don't they," Lucy said to Henrietta, as the students tidied away the implements of their trade.

"They like all the Staff," Henrietta said, with a faint return of her head-girl tone. "It is not advisable to keep a mistress who is unpopular, however good she may be. On the other hand it is desirable that they should be just a little in awe of their preceptors." She smiled in her senior-clergy-making-a-joke manner; Henrietta did not make jokes easily. "In their different ways, Fröken, Miss Lux, and Madame Lefevre all inspire a healthy awe."

"Madame Lefevre? If I were a student, I don't think it would be awe that would knock my knees together, but sheer terror."

"Oh, Marie is quite human when you know her. She likes being one of the College legends."

Marie and The Abhorrence, thought Lucy; two College legends. Each with identical qualities; terrible and fascinating.

The students were standing in file, breathing deeply as they raised their arms and lowered them. Their fifty minutes of concentrated activity had come to an end, and there they were: flushed, triumphant, fulfilled.

Henrietta rose to go, and as she turned to follow Lucy found that Fröken's mother had been sitting behind them in the gallery. She was a plump little woman with her hair in a bun at the back, and reminded Lucy of Mrs. Noah, as portrayed by the makers of toy Arks. Lucy bowed and smiled that extra-wide-for-foreigners smile that one uses to bridge the gap of silence, and then, remembering that although this little woman spoke no English she might speak German, she tried a phrase, and the little woman's face lit up.

"To speak with you, Fräulein, is such pleasure that I will even speak German to do it," she said. "My daughter tells me that you are very distinguished."

Lucy said that she had had a success, which was not the same thing as being distinguished unfortunately; and expressed her admiration for the work she had just witnessed. Henrietta who had taken Classics instead of Modern Languages at school, washed her hands of this exchange of civilities, and preceded them down the stairs. As Lucy and Fru Gustavsen came out into the sunlight the students were emerging from the door at the other end, running or dawdling across the covered-way to the house. Last of the group came Rouse, and Lucy could not help suspecting

55

that her emergence was timed to coincide with the passing of Henrietta. There was no need for her to linger a yard or two behind the others like that; she must see out of the tail of her eye that Henrietta was bearing down on her. In similar circumstances Lucy would have bolted, but Rouse was lingering. She liked Miss Rouse even less than usual.

Henrietta overtook the girl and paused to speak to her; and as Lucy and her companion passed them Lucy saw the expression on the tight freckled face turned up to receive the Principal's words of wisdom, and remembered what they had called that at school. "Being smarmy." And laying it on with a trowel, too, she thought with vulgar satisfaction.

"And I've always liked freckles, too," she said regretfully.

"*Bitte?*"

But this was not a subject that could be done justice to in German. The Significance of Freckles. She could see it: a thick tome full of portmanteau words and portentousness. No, it would need French to do it justice. Some distilled essence of amiable cynicism. Some pretty little blasting phrase.

"Is this your first visit to England?" she asked; and instead of entering the house with the others they strolled together through the garden towards the front of the house.

Yes, this was Fru Gustavsen's first visit to England, and it amazed her that a people who created gardens like this should also create the buildings in them. "Not this, of course," she said, "this old house is very pleasant. It is of a period that was good, yes? But what one sees from train and taxi; after Sweden it is horrible. Please do not think that I am Russian about things. It is—"

"Russian?"

"Yes. Naive, and ignorant, and sure that no one can do anything as well as my own country can do it. It is just that I am used to modern houses that are good to look at."

Lucy said that she might as well get over the subject of our cooking while she was at it.

"Ach, no," said the little woman surprisingly, "it is not so, that. My daughter has told me. Here in College it is according to regime"—Lucy thought that "according to regime" was tact of

56

the most delicate—"and so is not typical. Nor in the hotels is it typical, my daughter says. But she has stayed in private houses in holiday time, and the dishes of the country, she says, are delicious. Not everything she liked. Not everyone likes our raw herring, after all. But the joint roasted in the oven, and the apple tart with cream, and the cold ham very pink and tender, all that is most admirable. Most admirable."

So, walking through the summer garden Lucy found herself expatiating on herrings fried in oatmeal, and parkins, and Devonshire splits, and hot-pot, and collops, and other regional delicacies. She concealed the existence of the pork pie, which she privately considered a barbarism.

As they turned the corner of the house towards the front door, they passed the windows of a lecture-room where the Seniors were already engaged in listening to Miss Lux. The windows were pushed up from the bottom as far as they would go, so that the room was visible in all its details, and Lucy cast an idle glance at the assembled profiles presented to her.

She had looked away before she realised that these were not the faces she had seen only ten minutes ago. She looked back again, startled. Gone was the excitement, the flush of exercise, the satisfaction of achievement. Gone for the moment was even the youth. The faces were tired and spiritless.

Not all of them, of course. Hasselt still had her air of calm well-being. And Beau Nash's face had still its bright indestructible good-looks. But the majority looked sunken; indescribably weary. Mary Innes, seated nearest the window, had a marked line from nostrils to chin; a line that had no business there for thirty years yet.

A little saddened and uncomfortable, as one is at the unexpected discovery of an unhappiness in the middle of delight, Lucy turned her head away, and her last glimpse as she walked past was the face of Miss Rouse. And the expression on the face of Miss Rouse surprised her. It reminded her of Walberswick.

Now why Walberswick?

The wary freckled countenance of Miss Rouse had nothing in common with that formidable grande dame who was Lucy's aunt.

57

Certainly not.

Then why—but stop! It wasn't her aunt; it was her aunt's cat. The expression on that north-country face in the lecture-room was the expression on the face of Philadelphia when she had had cream instead of milk in her saucer. And there was only one word for that expression. The word smug.

Lucy felt, not unreasonably, that someone who had just failed to perform a routine exercise had no right to be looking smug. And the last faint lingering inclination to be sorry for Miss Rouse died in her.

~~~~~~

· 7 ·

"Miss Pym," said The Nut Tart, materialising at Lucy's elbow, "let us run away together."

It was Wednesday morning, and College was sunk in the thick silence of Final Examinations. Lucy was leaning over a five-barred gate behind the gymnasium, staring at a field of buttercups. It was here at the end of the Leys garden that the country began; the real country, free of the last tentacles of Larborough, unraped and unlittered. The field sloped to a stream, beyond which was the cricket field; and beyond that into the far distance stretched the unbroken pattern of hedge and tree and pasture; yellow, and white, and green; asleep in the morning sunshine.

Lucy took her eyes with difficulty from the shimmering yellow of the buttercups that had been mesmerising her, and wondered how many flowered silk frocks the Brazilian possessed. Here was yet another one, shaming the English subtleties with its brilliance.

"Where do you propose that we run to?" she asked.

"Let's go to the village."

"Is there a village?"

"There is always a village in England; it is that kind of country. But more especially there is Bidlington. You can see the weather thing of the church steeple just over those trees there."

"It looks a long way," said Lucy, who was no great walker and was greatly content where she was; it was a long time since

58

she had had a field of buttercups to look at and all time to do it in. "Is it much of a place?"

"Oh yes. It is a two-pub village," Desterro said, as one quoting a calibre. "Besides, it has everything a village in England should have. Queen Elizabeth slept there, and Charles the Second hid there; and Crusaders are buried in the church—there is one just like the manager of our ranch in Brazil—and all the cottages are obtainable on postcards at the shop; and it appears in books, the village does—"

"Guide books, you mean?"

"No, no. It has an author who specialised in it, you understand. I read one of his books when I came first to Leys. *Rain Over The Sky* it was called. All breasts and incest. And it has the Bidlington Martyrs—that is six men who threw stones at the police station last century some time and got put in jail. Imagine a country that remembers a thing like that! In my country they use knives—when they can't afford revolvers—and we smother the corpses with flowers, and cry a lot, and forget all about it next week."

"Well—"

"We can have some coffee at The Teapot."

"A little Hibernian, surely?"

But that was too much for even an intelligent stranger to these shores. "It is *real* coffee, I may tell you. It both smells and tastes. Oh, come on, Miss Pym. It is a small fifteen minutes away, and it is not yet ten o'clock. And there is nothing to do in this place until we are summoned to eat beans at one o'clock."

"Are you not taking any of the examinations?" Lucy asked, passing meekly through the gate that was held open for her.

"Anatomy I shall take, I think. Just, as you say, for the hell of it. I have taken all the lectures, so it will be fun to find out how much I know. It is worth knowing anatomy. It is a great labour, of course; it is a subject in which imagination is not appreciated, but it is worth learning."

"I suppose so. One wouldn't feel a fool in an emergency."

"Emergency?" said Desterro, whose mind had apparently not been running along these lines. "Oh, yes, I see. But what I meant

59

is that it is a subject that does not get out of date. Now *your* subject, if you will forgive me, Miss Pym, is continually getting out of date, no? To listen to it is charming, but to work at it would be very foolish. An idea today may be nonsense tomorrow, but a clavicle is a clavicle for all time. You see?"

Lucy saw, and envied such economy of effort.

"So tomorrow, when the Juniors take their Final Anatomy, I take it too. It is a respect-worthy thing; my grandmother would approve of it. But today they are busy about conundrums, and so me, I walk to Bidlington with the charming Miss Pym and we have coffee."

"Conundrums?"

The Nut Tart fished a folded paper from the minute pocket of her frock and read from it: "If the ball is over the touch line but has not reached the ground and a player standing inside hits or catches the ball and brings it into the court again, what decision would you give?"

In a silence more eloquent than speech she folded up the cyclostyled sheet and put it away again.

"How did you get a copy of their paper if they are still busy on the subject of games?"

"Miss Wragg gave me one. She said it might amuse me. It does."

Down between the yellow field and the may-white hedge the path led them to the stream. They paused by the small bridge to stare at the shadowed water under the willows.

"Over there," Desterro said, pointing at the level ground across the stream, "is the games field. In winter it is deep in mud, and they have bars across their shoes to keep them from slipping in it." Lucy thought that if she were saying: "They wear rings through their noses to add to their attraction" the tone would be identical. "Now we walk down-stream to the next little bridge and get on to the road there. It is not a road; just a lane." She moved in silence down the shaded path, a bright dragon-fly of a creature, graceful and alien; and Lucy was surprised to find that she was capable of so unbroken a quiet.

As they came up on to the road at last she said: "Have you any money, Miss Pym?"

"No," said Lucy, stopping in dismay.

"Neither have I. But it is all right. Miss Nevill will finance us."

"Who is Miss Nevill?"

"The lady who runs the tea-house."

"That is rather unusual, isn't it?"

"Not with me. I am always forgetting my money. But Miss Nevill is charming. Do not feel bad about it, dear Miss Pym, I am in good standing in the village, you will see."

The village was all the Desterro had claimed for it; and so was Miss Nevill. So indeed, was The Teapot. It was one of those tea-shops so much despised by the bread-and-cheese-and-beer school, and so gladly welcomed by a generation of tea-drinkers who remember the fly-blown rooms behind village bakers' shops, the primitive buns with currants like dead insects, the cracked and ill-washed cups, and the black evil tea.

It had all the properties stigmatised by the literary frequenters of village inns: the Indian-tree-pattern china, the dark oak tables, the linen curtains in a Jacobean design, the herbaceous bouquets in unglazed brown jugs; yes, even the arts and crafts in the window. But to Lucy, who in the Alan period had had her share of undusted "snugs," it was quite frankly charming. There was a rich scent of spiced cakes straight from the oven; there was, as well as the long window on the street, a further window that gave on a garden bright with colour; there was peace, and coolness, and welcome.

Miss Nevill, a large lady in a chintz apron, received Desterro as an old and valued acquaintance, and asked if she were "playing hookey, as you say on your side of the Atlantic." The Nut Tart ignored this identification with the back streets of Brooklyn. "This is Miss Pym who writes books about psychology and is our guest at Leys," she said, politely introducing Lucy. "I have told her that here one can drink real coffee, and be in general civilised. We have no money at all, either of us, but we will have a great deal to eat and pay you back later."

This appeared to Miss Nevill to be quite a normal proposition, and she went away to the kitchen to get the coffee with neither surprise nor demur. The place was empty at this hour of the morning, and Lucy wandered round inspecting the old prints and the new crafts—she was pleased to observe that Miss Nevill

61

drew the line at Brummagem brass door-knockers even if there were raffia mats—and then sat down with Desterro at the table looking on to the village street. Before their coffee arrived, they were joined by a middle-aged couple, husband and wife, who drove up in a car as if they were searching for the place. The car was the kind that a provincial doctor might use; low in petrol consumption and in its third or fourth year of wear. But the woman who came round from the further seat with a laughing remark to her husband was not a typical doctor's wife. She was grey, and slim, with long legs and narrow feet in good shoes. Lucy watched her with pleasure. It was not often nowadays that one saw good bones; smartness had taken the place of breeding.

"In *my* country," said Desterro, looking with a considering eye at the woman and with a contemptuous eye on the car, "that woman would have a chauffeur *and a footman*."

It was not often, moreover, that one saw a middle-aged husband and wife so pleased with each other, Lucy thought, as she watched them come in. They had a holiday air. They came in and looked about them expectantly, questioningly.

"Yes, this is it," the woman said. "That is the window on the garden that she talks about, and there is the print of Old London Bridge."

They moved about looking at things, quietly, unselfconsciously, and then took the table at the other window. Lucy was relieved to see that the man was the mate she would have chosen for such a woman; a little saturnine, perhaps, more self-absorbed than the woman; but quite admirable. He reminded her of someone, but she could not think of whom; someone whom she admired. The eyebrows, it was. Dark level brush-marks low over the eyes. His suit was very old, she noticed; well-pressed and kept, but with that much-cleaned air that overtakes a garment in its old age. The woman's suit, a tweed, was frankly shabby, and her stockings were darned—very neatly darned—at the heels. Her hands, too, looked as if they were accustomed to household tasks, and her fine grey hair was washed at home and unwaved. What had she got to look so happy about, this woman who struggled with straitened means? Was it just being on holiday with a husband she loved? Was it that that gave her grey luminous eyes their almost childlike happiness?

Miss Nevill came in with the coffee and a large plate of spiced cakes shining with newness and crisp at the edges. Lucy decided to forget her weight just this once and enjoy herself. This was a decision she made with deplorable frequency.

As she poured the coffee she heard the man say: "Good morning. We have come all the way from the West Country to taste your griddle cakes. Do you think you could make us some, or are you too busy at this hour of the morning?"

"If you are too busy it doesn't matter," said the woman with the hard-worked hands. "We shall have some of the cakes that smell so good."

But Miss Nevill would not be a minute in preparing the griddle cakes. She had no batter standing, she said, so the griddle cakes would not be as wonderful as when the batter was allowed to stand; but she was not often asked for them in summer time.

"No, I expect not. But our daughter at Leys has talked so often of them, and this may be our only chance of tasting them." The woman smiled, half it seemed at the thought of her daughter, half at their own childish desire.

So they were College parents.

Whose? Lucy wondered, watching them over the rim of her coffee cup.

Beau's, perhaps. Oh, no; Beau was rich, of course. Then whose?

She wouldn't mind giving them to Dakers, but there were objections. That tow-head could not be sired by that dark grave man; nor could that adult and intelligent woman have given birth to the through-other piece of nonsense that was Dakers.

And then, quite suddenly, she knew whose eyebrows those were.

Mary Innes's.

They were Mary Innes's parents. And in some odd way they explained Mary Innes. Her gravity; her air of belonging to a century other than this one; her not finding life very amusing. To have standards to live up to, but to have little money to live up to them with, was not a happy combination for a girl burdened with the need to make a success of her training.

Into the silence that had succeeded Miss Nevill's departure, Lucy heard her own voice saying: "Forgive me, but is your name Innes?"

They turned to her, puzzled for a moment; then the woman smiled. "Yes," she said. "Have we met somewhere?"

"No," said poor Lucy, growing a little pink as she always did when her impulsiveness had led her into an unexpected situation. "But I recognised your husband's eyebrows."

"My *eyebrows*," said Mr Innes.

But his wife, quicker-witted, laughed. "Of course," she said. "Mary! Are you from Leys, then? Do you know Mary?" Her face lit and her voice sang as she said it. Do you know Mary? Was it because she was going to see her daughter that she was happy today?

Lucy explained who she was, and introduced Desterro, who was pleased to find that this charming couple knew all about her. "There is very little we don't know about Leys," Mrs Innes said, "even if we have never seen the place."

"Not seen it? Won't you come over and have your coffee with us, by the way?"

"It was too far for us to inspect it before Mary went there. So we decided that we would wait until her training was finished and then come to the Demonstration." Lucy deduced that if fares had not been a problem, Mary Innes's mother would not have had to wait these years before seeing Leys; she would have come if only so that she could picture her daughter in her setting.

"But you are going there now, surely?"

"No. Oddly enough, we are not. We are on our way to Larborough, where my husband—he's a doctor—has to attend a meeting. We *could* go to Leys, of course, but it is the week of the final examinations, and it would only distract Mary to have her parents descending suddenly on her for no reason. It is a little difficult to pass by when we are so near, but we have waited so long that we can wait another ten days or so. What we couldn't resist was turning off the main West road as far as Bidlington. We didn't expect to run into any College people at this hour of the morning, especially in Examination week, and we did want to see the place that Mary had talked so much about."

"We knew that we shouldn't have time on Demonstration Day," Dr Innes said. "There will be so much to see then. A surprisingly varied training, isn't it?"

Lucy agreed, and described her first impression of the staff-room with its varying worlds.

"Yes. We were a little puzzled when Mary chose that for her career—she had never shown any great interest in games, and I had thoughts that she might take a medical training—but she said she wanted a career with a great many facets; and she seems to have found it!"

Lucy remembered the concentration of purpose in those level brows; she had been right in her face-reading; if Mary Innes had an ambition it would not lightly be given up. Really, eyebrows were the most *helpful* things. If psychology ever went out of fashion she would write a book about face-reading. Under another name, of course. Face-reading was not well seen among the intelligentsia.

"She is very beautiful, your daughter," said Desterro unexpectedly. She polished off a large mouthful of spice cake, and then, feeling the surprise in their silence, looked up at them. "Is it not a proper thing in England to compliment parents on their daughter's looks?"

"Oh, yes," Mrs Innes said hastily, "it is not that, it is just that we had not thought of Mary as beautiful. She is nice to look at, of course; at least we think so, but then parents are apt to be fatuous about an only daughter. She—"

"When I came first to this place," Desterro said, reaching out for another cake from the plate (how *did* she keep that figure!), "it was raining, and all the dirty leaves were hanging down from the trees like dead bats and dripping on everyone, and everyone was rushing round College and saying: 'Oh *darling*, how *are* you? Did you have nice hols? Darling, you won't believe it but I left my new hockey stick on *Crewe platform*!' And then I saw a girl who was *not* running about and *not* talking, and who looked a little like my great-grandmother's grandmother who is

65

in the dining-room at the house of my grandmother's great-nephew, so I said: 'It is not after all a barbarism. If it were as it seems to be that girl would not be here. I shall stay.' Is there more coffee, Miss Pym, please? She is not only beautiful, your daughter, she is the only beautiful person at Leys."

"What about Beau Nash?" asked Lucy loyally.

"In England at Christmas time—*very* little milk, Miss Pym, please—the magazines go all gay and give away bright pretty pictures that one can frame and hang above the kitchen mantelpiece to make glad the hearts of the cook and her friends. Very shiny, they are, with—"

"Now that," said Mrs Innes, "is sheer libel! Beau is lovely, quite lovely, and you know it. I forgot that you would know Beau, too," she turned to Lucy, "that you would know them all, in fact. Beau is the only one we know because she came to us for the holidays once; at Easter time when the West is kinder than the rest of England; and Mary went to them once for some weeks in the summer. We admired Beau so much." She looked to her husband for confirmation; he had been too withdrawn.

Dr Innes roused himself—he had the wrung-out look of the overworked G.P. when he sank into repose—and the saturnine face took on a boyish and faintly malicious, if tender, amusement. "It was very odd to see our competent and self-reliant Mary being looked after," he said.

Mrs Innes evidently felt that this was not the contribution she had been looking for, but decided to make the best of it. "Perhaps," she said, as if thinking of it for the first time, "we have always taken Mary's self-reliance so much for granted that she finds it pleasant to be looked after." And to Miss Pym: "It is because they are complementary, I think, that they are such great friends. I am glad about it because we like Beau so much, and because Mary has never made intimate friends easily."

"It is a very strenuous training, isn't it?" Dr Innes said. "I sometimes look at my daughter's notebooks and wonder why they bother with stuff that even a doctor forgets as soon as he leaves medical school."

"The cross-section of the villi," remembered Lucy.

"Yes; that sort of thing. You seem to have picked up a remarkable amount of physical lore in four days."

The crumpets came, and even without the ritual standing of the batter they were worth coming even from the West Country for, supposing that had been true. It was a happy party. Indeed, Lucy felt that the whole room was soaked in happiness; that happiness bathed it like a reflexion from the sunlight outside. Even the doctor's tired face looked content and relaxed. As for Mrs Innes, Lucy had rarely seen such happiness on the face of a woman; merely being in this room that her daughter had used so often was, it seemed, a sort of communion with her, and in a few days' time she would see her in the flesh and share her achievement.

If I had gone back to London, Lucy thought, I would have had no share in this. What would I be doing? Eleven o'clock. Going for a walk in the Park, and deciding how to get out of being guest of honour at some literary dinner. Instead I have this. And all because Dr Knight wanted to go to a medical conference tomorrow. No, because once long ago Henrietta stood up for me at school. It was odd to think that this sun-lit movement in an English June began to take shape thirty years ago in a dark crowded school cloakroom filled with little girls putting on their goloshes. What were first causes, anyhow?

"This has been *very* pleasant," said Mrs Innes, as they stood once more in the village street. "And it is nice to think that we shall meet again so soon. You will still be at Leys when the Demonstration comes off, won't you?"

"I hope so," Lucy said, and wondered if she could cadge a bed from Henrietta for so long.

"And you have both promised, solemnly and on your word of honour, not to tell anyone that you saw us today," Dr Innes said.

"We have," they said, waiting to see their new friends get into their car.

"Do you think I can turn the car in one swoop without hitting the Post Office?" Dr Innes said, consideringly.

"I should hate to make any more Bidlington martyrs," his wife said. "A tiresome breed. On the other hand, what is this life without some risk?"

So Dr Innes encouraged his engine and swung into this risky evolution. The hub of his off front wheel left a faint smudge on the Post Office's virgin white-wash.

"Gervase Innes, his mark," said Mrs Innes, and waved her hand to them. "Till Demonstration Day, and pray for fine weather for it! Au revoir!"

They watched the car grow small up the village street, and turned towards the field path and Leys.

"*Nice* people," Desterro said.

"Charming. Odd to think that we should never have met them if you had not had a craving for good coffee this morning."

"That is the kind of English, let me tell you in confidence, Miss Pym, that make every other nation on earth sick with envy. So quiet, so well-bred, so good to look at. They are poor, too, did you notice? Her blouse is quite washed-out. It used to be blue, the blouse; you could see when she leaned forward and her collar lifted a little. It is wrong that they should be so poor, people like that."

"It must have cost her a lot not to see her daughter when she was so near," Lucy said reflectively.

"Ah, but she has character, that woman. She was right not to come. None of the Seniors has one little particle of interest to spare this week. Take away even one little particle, and *woops!* the whole thing comes crashing down." She plucked an ox-eyed daisy from the bank by the bridge and gave the first giggle Lucy had ever heard from her. "I wonder how my colleagues are getting on with their one-leg-over-the-line puzzles."

Lucy was wondering how she herself would appear in Mary Innes's Sunday letter home. "It will be amusing," Mrs Innes had said, "to get back home and read all about you in Mary's Sunday letter. Something to do with relativity. Like coming back the previous night."

"It was strange that Mary Innes should have reminded you of someone in a portrait," she said to Desterro. "That is how she seemed to me, too."

"Ah yes, my great-grandmother's grandmother." Desterro dropped the daisy on to the surface of the water and watched the stream bear it down under the bridge and away out of sight. "I did not say it to the nice Inneses, but my great-grandmother's grandmother was a little unpopular with her generation."

"Oh? Shy, perhaps. What we call nowadays an inferiority complex."

"I would not know about that. Her husband died too conveniently. It is always sad for a woman when her husband dies too conveniently."

"You mean that she murdered him!" Lucy said, standing stock-still in the summer landscape, appalled.

"Oh, no. There was no *scandal*." Desterro sounded reproving. "It was just that her husband died too conveniently. He drank too much, and was a great gambler, and *not* very attractive. And there was a loose tread at the top of the stairs. A long flight of stairs. And he stepped on it one day when he was drunk. That was all."

"And did she marry again?" Lucy asked, having absorbed this information.

"Oh, no. She was not in love with anyone else. She had her son to bring up, and the estates were safe for him now that there was no one to gamble them away. She was a very good estate manager. That is where my grandmother got her talent from. When my grandmother came out from England to marry my grandfather she had never been further from her own county than Charles Street, West One; and in six months she was running the estate." Desterro sighed with admiration. "They are wonderful, the English."

• 8 •

Miss Pym was invigilating at the Senior Pathology Final, so as to give Miss Lux more time for the correction and marking of previous papers, when Henrietta's meek little secretary tiptoed in and laid the day's letters reverently on the desk in front of her. Miss Pym had been frowning over a copy of the examination paper, and thinking how badly words like *arthritis gonorrhoica* and *suppurative teno-synovitis* went with the clean air of a summer morning after breakfast. *Emphysema* was not so bad; it might be the gardener's name for a flower. A sort of columbine.

And *kyphosis* she could picture as something in the dahlia line. *Myelitis* would be a small creeping plant, very blue, with a tendency to turn pink if not watched. And *tabes dorsalis* was obviously an exotic affair of the tiger lily persuasion, expensive and very faintly obscene.

Chorea. Sclerosis. Pes Varus.

Dear goodness. Did those young things know all that? Differentiate the treatment of something-or-other according to whether it is (a) congenital (b) traumatic (c) hysterical. Well, well. How had she ever erred so far as to feel patronising about these young creatures?

She looked down from her dais with affection on them; all writing away for dear life. The faces were sober but not on the whole anxious. Only Rouse looked worried, and Lucy decided that her face looked better worried than smug, and withheld her sympathy. Dakers was ploughing steadily over the paper with her tongue protruding and an automatic sigh as she came to the end of each line and began a new one. Beau was confident and detached as if she were writing invitations; doubt was something that had never entered her life; neither her present standing nor her future life was in jeopardy. Stewart's face under the bright red hair was pale, but a faint smile played round her mouth; Stewart's future, too, was assured; she was going to The Cordwainers' School, going home to Scotland bringing her sheaves with her, and Lucy was going to the party she was giving in her room on Saturday night to celebrate. ("We don't ask Staff to individual parties, but since you are not quite Staff you could rank as just a friend.") The Four Disciples, spread across the front row, cast each other communal and encouraging glances now and then; this was their own particular subject and obviously what they did not know about it was not worth mentioning; Manchester was going to get its money's worth. Innes, by the window, lifted her head every now and then to look out at the garden, as if seeking refreshment; that it was not inspiration she sought was apparent from her unhurried progress through the questions; she turned to the garden for some spiritual comfort; it was as if she said: "Ah yes, you are still there, Beauty; there is a world outside this lecture-room." Innes was beginning to look as if

70

College might be too much with her. That tired line from nostril to mouth was still there.

Lucy picked up the paper-knife from Miss Lux's neat desk, and considered her post. Three bills, which she need not disturb the holy hush by opening. A receipt. An Annual Report. A large, square, deep-blue, and very stiff and expensive envelope with MILLICENT CRAYE embossed in scarlet across the flap (really there was no end to the self-advertising instinct in actresses) which would be five lines of thanks with a broad nib and out-size capitals for her contribution to the Benevolent Fund. That left only Mrs Montmorency. So into Mrs Montmorency she inserted the paper-knife.

Maddam (wrote Mrs Montmorency),

I as done as you sed an sent the urgent by passel post. Registered. Fred put it into Wigmore Street on is way to work receit enclosed I as packed the blue and the blouses also underclose as per instruxions your pink nitie not having come back from the laundry I as put in the bedge instead hopping this will be all rite.

Maddam, please dont think that I presoom but this is a good thing. It is no life for a woman writin books and not havin no young company please dont think I presoom but I as your welfare at heart you ben one of the nicest ladies I ever worked for Fred says the same. A nice lady like that he says when look at the things thats around not write it isnt please dont think I presoom

yrs respectfully

Mrs Montmorency.

P.S. Wire brush in toe of swede shoe

Lucy spent the next fifteen minutes being touched by Mrs Montmorency's concern for her, being furious with the laundry, and wondering why she paid education rates. It wasn't public schools for everyone that was needed but a great many elementary school classes of not more than a dozen, where the future Mrs Montmorencys could be adequately taken care of in the matter of the Three Rs. Old McLean, their jobbing gardener at home, had left school when he was twelve, but he could write as good a letter as any University acquaintance of hers; and why? Because he came from a small village school with small classes and a good schoolmaster.

And of course because he lived in an age when the Three Rs were more important than Free Milk. They made him literate and left the rest to him. He lived on white-flour scones and stewed tea and died hale and hearty at the age of ninety-two.

She was roused from her musings by Miss Rouse. There was a new expression on Miss Rouse's face, and Lucy didn't like the new expression at all. She had seen Miss Rouse look despairing, smarmy, smug, and worried, but till now she had never seen her look furtive.

Why should she be looking furtive?

She watched her for a moment or two, curiously.

Rouse looked up and caught her gaze and looked quickly away again. Her furtive expression had gone; what had taken its place was one labelled Consciously Carefree. Lucy knew all about that expression. She had not been Form Mistress of the Lower Fourth for nothing. Every eater of illicit sweets wore that expression. So did those who were doing their arithmetic in French lesson.

So did those who were cheating at an examination.

What was it Henrietta had said? "She finds written work difficult."

So.

Emphysema and all those flowery sounding things were too much for Miss Rouse, and so she had provided some aids to memory. The question was what kind of aids and where were they? Not on her knee. The desks were open in front, so that a lap was no safe billet for a crib. And one could hardly write enough pathology on one's finger-nails to be of much help; finger-nails were useful only for formula. The obvious solution would be the notes up the sleeve, with or without an arrangement of elastic, but these girls had no sleeves below the elbow. Then, what? Where? Or was it that she was just having glimpses of O'Donnell's paper in front of her? Or Thomas's to her right?

Lucy went back to her letters for a moment or two, and waited. All schoolmistresses know this gambit. She looked up casually at the Seniors in general and again went back to her letters. When next she looked up it was straight at Rouse. Rouse's head was low over her paper and in her left hand she held a handkerchief. Now even on a handkerchief it is not possible to write anything that is helpful on so large a subject as pathology, nor is it an easy affair to manipulate; on the other hand handkerchiefs were not common objects at Leys, and certainly no one else was clutching one and dabbing a nose occasionally with it. Lucy decided that whatever sources of information Rouse had lay in her left hand. Her desk was at the back on the window side, so that the wall was to her left; whatever she did with her left hand was not overlooked by anyone.

Well, thought Lucy, what does A do?

Walk down the room and demand the handkerchief and find that it is a square piece of white linen, nine inches by nine inches, with the owner's initials properly marked in one corner, and as candid as a good laundry can make it?

Demand the handkerchief and unearth a scandal that will blast the Senior set like a hurricane at their least stable moment?

See that Rouse gets no chance to use her source of information, and say nothing?

The last was certainly the most sensible. She couldn't have obtained very much aid from anything so far; it would be doing no injustice to anyone to make her a present of that small amount.

Lucy left the desk and strolled down the room to the back, where she stood leaning against the wall, Thomas to her right and Rouse to her left. Thomas stopped writing for a moment and looked up at her with a quick smile. But Rouse did not look up. And Lucy watched the hot blood dye her sandy neck a dull red. And presently she put away the handkerchief— and whatever else that hand contained—in her tunic pocket.

Well, she had foiled the machinations of the evil-intended, but she could feel no satisfaction about it. For the first time it occurred to her that what was very naughty and deplorable in the Fourth Form was quite sickening in a Senior Final. She was glad that it was Rouse and not anyone else. Presently she strolled back to her desk on the dais, and as far as she could see Rouse made no further effort to obtain help with her paper. On the contrary, she was very obviously in deep waters. And Lucy was infuriated to find herself feeling sorry for her. Yes, *sorry*. Sorry for *Rouse*. After all, the girl had worked. Worked like a madman, if all reports were true. It was not as if she had been taking an easy way out to save herself effort. It was just that she found acquiring theoretical knowledge difficult almost to the point of impossibility, and had succumbed to temptation in her desperation.

This point of view made Lucy feel much better about it, and she spent the rest of her invigilating time speculating quite undistressedly about the nature of the crib. She would look again at the examination paper, and consider the enormous range of material it covered, and wonder how Rouse had devised anything at once helpful and invisible. She longed to ask her.

The most likely explanation was that there were two or three particular subjects that Rouse was afraid of, and that help with them was scribbled on a piece of paper.

Innes was the first to shuffle the written sheets together and slip the waiting clip over their upper edge. She read through the pages, making a correction now and then, laid the sheaf down on her desk, sat for a few relaxed moments taking in the beauty of the garden, and then rose quietly and came forward to leave her work on the desk in front of Miss Pym.

"Oh, *catastrophe*!" wailed Dakers; "is somebody *finished*? And I have a whole question and a half to do yet!"

"Hush, Miss Dakers," said Lucy, as in duty bound.

Dakers favoured her with a radiant smile, and went back to her steady plodding.

Stewart and Beau Nash followed Innes very shortly; and presently the pile of papers in front of Miss Pym began to grow. With five minutes of the allotted time still to go there were only three students left in the examination room: the little dark Welsh Thomas, who presumably slept too much to be a good "study"; the imperturbable Dakers still plodding steadily; and a flushed and unhappy Rouse, who was plainly making heavy weather of it. With two minutes still to go there was only Rouse;

74

she was looking confused and desperate; making hasty little excursions back and fore through her papers, deleting, amending, and adding.

The distant yelling of the bell put an end to her indecisions and to her chances; whatever she had done must now abide. She shoved her papers hastily together, aware that the bell meant an instant appearance in the gymnasium and that Fröken would not consider the ordeal of an examination paper any excuse for being late, and brought them up to Lucy at the double. Lucy had expected her to avoid her eye, or otherwise to display symptoms of awkwardness or selfconsciousness. But Rouse surprised her by a frank smile and a still franker remark.

"Whoo!" said Rouse, blowing her breath out expressively, "that was a horror." And she ran out to join the rest of her set.

Lucy opened the much-scored offering and looked at it with compunction. She had been imagining things. Rouse had not been cheating after all. Or at least not systematically. That furtive look might have been the guilt of inadequacy, now she came to think of it; or perhaps, at the worst, a hope of hints from her neighbour's paper. And that flush that had dyed her neck was due to her awareness of being suspected; Lucy could remember very well even yet times at school when the very knowledge that her innocent act was capable of sinister interpretation was enough to make her face burn with false guilt. Really, she owed Rouse an apology. She would find some way of making it up to her.

She stacked the papers neatly together, put them in alphabetical order from sheer force of habit, checked their number, and carried them upstairs to Miss Lux's room, glad that it would not be her chore to correct them. There was no one in the room, so she left them on the desk and stood for a moment wondering what to do with the hour before lunch. She toyed with the thought of watching the gymnastics, but decided that she must not allow the performance to become familiar, and consequently devoid of wonder, before Demonstration Day. Having induced Henrietta to keep her until then—Henrietta had not required much inducement, it is true—she was not going to mar her own pleasure in the day by too many tastings beforehand. She went downstairs again, lingering by the tall window on the landing—

how well eighteenth century architects had understood how to build houses; nowadays landings were not things to linger on, but breakneck little corners lit, if at all, by a small circular light like a ship's port-hole—and from there, beyond the courtyard and the opposite wing she could see the elms of the field that led to the stream. She would go and look at the buttercups for a little. There was no better way of wasting a summer hour than staring at a field of buttercups. So down she went, and along the wing, and so out to the covered path to the gymnasium, for beyond the gymnasium were the buttercups.

As she went down the covered way her eye caught a spot of colour in the grass that bordered the path. At first she took it for a flower petal and was going to ignore it, when she noticed that it was square, and certainly not a petal. She turned back and picked it up. It was a tiny address-book in faded red leather. It looked as if it had formed part of the fittings of a handbag; an old-fashioned handbag probably since one did not see leather nor workmanship like that nowadays. Idly, with her thoughts on the femininity of that vanished bag with its miniature fittings—there would of course have been a little tube of scent, and a gold pencil, and one of those ivory tablets to scribble engagements on—she opened it, and read, on a page crowded with writing in a tiny script: "Path. anat. changes as in traumatic. Fibrin in synov. memb. Tissues contr. by fibr. and folds of caps. joined to bone. Anchylosis. Fever."

It meant nothing to Lucy as information but its meaning was obvious. She turned the pages, finding nearly all of them crowded with the same succinct information. Even the X page—devoted by the keepers of address-books to measurements for new curtains or that good story that would do for the W.R.I. speech next Tuesday—even the X page had cryptic remarks about rays. What bowled Lucy over was the comprehensiveness of it; the premeditation. This was no product of a last-minute panic; it was a cold-blooded insurance against failure. By the neatness and method shown in the compiling, it looked as though the entries had been made as each subject was studied. Had the notebook been of a normal size, in fact, it would have been nothing more than a legitimate précis of a subject. But no one making a précis would have chosen a book not much larger than a good-sized postage stamp when an equally portable but normal-sized note-book could be had for a few pence. The use of a book so tiny that a mapping pen had been necessary in order to make the entries legible could have only one explanation.

Lucy knew very well what had happened. Rouse had pulled out her handkerchief as she ran. She had never before carried the little book in a pocket, and her mind was divided urgently between the bad paper she had done and the fear of being late for gymnastics, so there was no care in the pulling out of the handkerchief. And so the little book dropped on to the grass at the edge of the path.

She walked on beyond the gymnasium and through the five-barred gate into the field, but she had no eye for the buttercups. She walked on slowly down the field to the coolness under the willows and the quiet green water. She hung over the rail of the bridge watching the weeds trail and the occasional fish dart, and thought about Rouse. There was no name on the fly-leaf, nor as far as she could see any means of identification in the book itself. Most schools taught script as well as current form in writing nowadays; and script was much less easily recognisable than current writing. A handwriting expert would no doubt be easily able to trace the author, but to what end? There was no evidence that the book had been used for any illegitimate purpose; no evidence even that it had been compiled with any sinister intent—although the presumption was strong. If she handed it over to Henrietta as lost property what would happen? No one would claim it, and Henrietta would be faced with the fact that one of her Seniors had prepared a précis that could be conveniently palmed at an examination.

If nothing was ever said about the book, then Rouse's punishment would be a perpetual and life-long doubt as to what had become of it. Lucy felt that such a punishment fitted the crime admirably. She thumbed the tiny India-paper pages once more, wondered again what Edwardian elegancy had given it birth, and, leaning over, dropped it into the water.

As she walked back to the house she wondered how Rouse had managed the other Final Examinations. Pathology could be no less easy to memorise than Kinesiology or any of the other obscurities studied by the budding P.T.I. How had Rouse, the

77

difficult "study," managed with these? Was the little red leather book only one of five or six? Did one invest in a mapping pen for one subject only? One *could*, she supposed, buy very tiny address books if one searched long enough; though not perhaps so fine or so tiny as the little red one. It may have been the possession of the little red one which first put the thought of insurance against failure into Rouse's mind.

She remembered that the result of the previous examinations would be exhibited on the letter-board by the students' entrance, so instead of walking round to the front of the house as she had meant to she turned in at the quadrangle door. There were several Junior lists pinned to the green baize, and three Senior lists. Lucy read them with interest.

FINAL PHYSIOLOGY

Honours

Mary Innes	93

First Class

Wilhelmina Hasselt	87
Pamela Nash	86
Sheena Stewart	82
Pauline Lucas	79
Janet Gage	79
Barbara Rouse	77

Second Class

Dorothy Litlejohn	74
Beatrice Appleyard	71
Joan Dakers	69
Eileen O'Donnell	68
Margaret Campbell	67
Ruth Waymark	66
Lilian Mathews	65

and the rest, below that mark, mere Passes.

Well, Rouse had scraped into a First by two marks, it seemed. Lucy turned to the next list.

FINAL MEDICALS

First Class

Pauline Lucas	89
Pamela Nash	89
Mary Innes	89
Dorothy Littlejohn	87
Ruth Waymark	85
Wilhelmina Hasselt	82
Sheena Stewart	80
Lilian Mathews	79
Barbara Rouse	79

Second Class

Jenny Burton	73
Janet Gage	72
Eileen O'Donnell	71
Joan Dakers	69

and the rest mere Passes.

And again Rouse managed to scrape a First.

FINAL KINESIOLOGY

Honours

Mary Innes	96

First Class

Pauline Lucas	89
Pamela Nash	88
Sheena Stewart	87
Wilhelmina Hasselt	85
Ruth Waymark	80
Janet Gage	79
Joan Dakers	78
Barbara Rouse	78

Another First! Three Firsts out of three tries. The girl who found written work so difficult? There was surely a strong case for the existence of more little notebooks?

Oh, well; this being Friday, tomorrow would see the end of examinations, and it was not likely that Rouse would, after this morning's experience, bring any extraneous help to the test tomorrow morning. The little book prepared for tomorrow, if it existed, would be still-born.

While she mused over the lists (it was nice to see that Dakers had managed at least one First) Miss Lux arrived with the results of yesterday's Final.

"Thank you for bringing up the Path. papers," she said. "And thank you for invigilating. It helped me to get these done."

She thumbed the drawing-pin into the board and stood back to look at the list.

FINAL HYGIENE

Honours
   Mary Innes 91

First Class
   Pamela Nash 88
   Wilhelmina Hasselt 87
   Sheena Stewart 86
   Pauline Lucas 81
   Barbara Rouse 81

"Barbara Rouse, eighty-one," Lucy said, before she thought.

"Yes, surprising, isn't it?" Miss Lux said placidly. "But she works like a black. She is so brilliant in her physical work that I think it maddens her to be far down any list."

"Innes seems to make a habit of heading the lists."

"Oh, Innes is wasted here."

"Why? The more intelligence one brings to a profession the better surely?"

"Yes, but with an intelligence like Innes's one could head much more thrilling lists than these. It's a waste."

"I somehow don't think that Rouse will get eighty-one for today's paper," Lucy said, as they moved away from the board.

"Why? Was she in difficulties?"

"Bogged down," said Lucy; and hoped that she did not sound too pleased. "*What* a life it is," she added, as the five-minute bell rang, and the dripping Seniors came running in from the gymnasium, ripping off their tunics as they tore into the bath-rooms for a shower before the gong went. "When you think of the leisurely way we acquired knowledge. At university, I mean. If we sat a final examination, the rest of the day would almost certainly be our own to recover in. But these young creatures do it as part of their time-table."

From the bathrooms came cursing and chaos. "Oh, Donnie, you *swine*, that was *my* shower!" "Mark, you brute, get off my foot!" "Oh, no, you don't, my girl; these are *my* tights!" "God, look at my blisters!" "Kick over my shoe, Greengage, the floor's sopping." "*Must* you shoot the cold water round like that, you chump!"

"They like it, you know," Lux said. "In their heart they like the rush and the overwork. It makes them feel important. Very few of them will ever have any legitimate reason for feeling important, and so it is comforting for them to have the image of it at least."

"Cynic," said Lucy.

"No, psychologist." She inclined her head towards the row as they moved away. "It sounds like a free fight, doesn't it? Everyone sounds desperate and furious. But it is all play-acting. In five minutes they will be sitting like good children in the dining-room with not a hair out of place."

And so they were. When the Staff filed in to the top table five minutes later, there were the scramblers of the bathroom, standing dutifully behind their chairs, calm, and combed, and neat, their interest already absorbed by the thought of food. Truly, they *were* children. Whatever heartbreaks they suffered would be forgotten in tomorrow's toy. It was absurd to think of them as harassed adults, trembling on the precipice edge of break-down. They were volatile children; their griefs were loud, and vocal, and transient. For five days now, ever since The Nut Tart had been so knowing under the cedar tree last Saturday afternoon, she had looked for some hint of abnormality, of aberration, of lack of control, and what had she found? One

81

very normal and highly controlled piece of dishonesty; unremarkable except for its neatness.

"Isn't it nice," Henrietta said, helping out something that looked like cheese-and-vegetable pie, "I've got a post in Wales for little Miss Thomas. Near Aberystwyth. I am so delighted."

"A very soporific atmosphere, Wales," Madame Lefevre said, consideringly; blasting Henrietta's whole conception with five gentle words.

"Yes," said Miss Lux, "who is going to keep her awake?"

"It's not who is going to *keep* her awake, it's who is going to wake her in the first place," Wragg said, with a greedy eye on the pie. Wragg was still near enough her College days to be possessed of a large hunger and no gastronomic judgment.

"Wales is her native atmosphere," Henrietta said, repressive, "and I have no doubt she will know how to deal with it. In any case she is not likely to have any great success *outside* Wales; the Welsh are extraordinarily provincial, using the word in its literal sense. I have noticed before how they gravitate back to their own province. It is as well for them to go there in the first place if the chance offers. And luckily, in this case, it has offered very conveniently. The junior gymnast of three. That will suit Miss Thomas very nicely. She has no great initiative, I'm afraid."

"Is Thomas's the only new post?" Wragg asked, falling on the pie.

"No, there was one that I wanted to discuss with you."

Aha, thought Lucy, here comes Arlinghurst at last.

"Ling Abbey wants someone to be wholly responsible for the younger children, and to take dancing as well all through the school. That is to say, the dancing would have to be of a high standard. I wanted to give the post to Miss Dakers—she is very good with small children—but I wanted to know what you thought of her dancing, Marie."

"She is a cow," said Madame.

"She *is* very good with little ones, though," Wragg said.

"A *heavy* cow," said Madame.

"It isn't her personal performance that is important," Henrietta

82

said. "It is her power to inspire performance in others. Does she understand the subject sufficiently, that is the point?"

"Oh, she knows the difference between three-four time and four-four, certainly."

"I saw Dakers teaching the babies at West Larborough their dances for their do last Christmas," Wragg said, "and she was wonderful. I was there to crit. her, and I was so fascinated I forgot to make any notes at all. I think she would be just right for that post."

"Well, Marie."

"I can't imagine why anyone bothers," Madame said. "The dancing at Ling Abbey is quite frightful anyhow."

This Pilatian washing of hands, in spite of its negative quality, seemed positive enough to all concerned. It was apparent that Dakers was going to Ling Abbey. And since Ling Abbey was a good place to be going to—if one had to be going to a school—Lucy was glad for her. She glanced down the room to where, even above this babel, Dakers' high voice could be heard italicising her opinion of the Pathology paper. "I said that a joint went *gummy*, my dear, and I'm certain that's not the *technical* word."

"Shall I warn them both, Miss Hodge?" Wragg asked, later.

(Warn?)

"No, just Miss Thomas today, I think. I shall tell Miss Dakers tomorrow. It is better to spread the excitement out."

As the Staff rose from their table and filed out, Wragg turned to the politely standing and temporarily silent students and said: "Miss Hodge will see Miss Thomas in her office when luncheon is over."

This was apparently a ritual pronouncement, for the buzz broke out almost before the Staff had reached the door. "A post, Tommy!" "Congrats, Tommy." "Hoorah, old Thomas." "Up the Welsh!" "Hope it's a thousand a year, Tom." "Iss nott thatt the lucky thing, now!" "Cheers, Tommy!"

And still no one had mentioned Arlinghurst.

WHEN Lucy first heard Arlinghurst mentioned it was not by any of the Staff but by the students themselves. She had spent Saturday afternoon with Fröken and her mother, helping to finish the Swedish folk costumes which the Juniors would wear for some of the country dances at the Demonstration. It was a lovely day and they had taken the piles of bright primitive colour to the furthest corner of the garden, where they could sit and look over the English countryside. Both cricket and tennis matches were "away" this week, so the garden was deserted, and no toiling figures marred the virgin green of the field beyond the stream. They had sewed in great beatitude, and Fru Gustavsen seemed to have reported well of Lucy to her daughter, for Fröken's reticence had largely vanished, and Lucy was delighted to find that a young woman who had always reminded her of sunlight on snow was the possessor of a rich warm chuckle and a sense of humour to match. (It is true that Lucy's sewing considerably shook Fru Gustavsen's faith in her, but much must be forgiven the English.) Fru Gustavsen had gone back to the subject of food, and had held forth at great length on the virtues of something called "frikadellar"; which, it appeared, was a kind of mince. Lucy (whose cooking consisted of chopping up a few tomatoes in a pan at the last moment, adding whatever was to be cooked, and pouring some cream over the lot) thought it a very lengthy and complicated affair, and decided to have nothing to do with it.

"Are you doing anything tonight?" Fröken had asked. "My mother and I are going into Larborough to the theatre. She has not yet seen an English company. We would be delighted if you would care to come with us."

Lucy explained that tonight she was going to a party in Stewart's room to celebrate her Post. "I understand that Staff don't usually go, but I am not real Staff."

Fröken slid an eye round at her and said: "You ought to be. You are very good for them."

That medicinal phrase again. As if she were a prescription.

"How?"

"Oh, in ways too subtle for my English—and *much* too subtle for the German language. It is, a little, that you wear heels; a little, that you have written a book; a little, that they don't have to be just a tiny bit afraid of you; a little that—oh, a thousand littles. You have come at a good time for them; a time when they need a distraction that is not—distracting. Oh, dear, I wish my English was better."

"You mean, I am a dose of alkali on an acid stomach."

Fröken gave her unexpected chuckle. "Yes, just that. I am sorry you will not be coming to the theatre, but it is a great mark of favour to be invited to a students' party, and you will enjoy it, I think. Everyone will be happy tonight, now that the examinations are over. Once they come back from the match they are free for the week-end. So they will be gay this Saturday. Off the chain," she added, in English.

And off the chain they certainly were. As Lucy came in by the quadrangle door, leaving Fröken and her mother to go round to the front of the house where they lived, a blast of sound rose up round her. The rush of bath water on two floors, the calling of innumerable voices, the drumfire of feet on bare oak stairs, singing, whistling, crooning. Both teams had apparently come back—victorious to judge by the atmosphere—and the place was alive. The place was also excited, and one word was woven like a leit-motif through the babble. Arlinghurst. Arlinghurst. As she walked past the ground-floor bathrooms on her way to the stairs, she heard the first of it. "*Have* you *heard*, my dear! *Arlinghurst!*"

"What?"

"*Arling-hurst!*"

A tap was turned off.

"I can't hear with the blasted water. Where, did you say?"

"Arlinghurst!"

"I don't believe it."

"But yes," said another voice, "it's true."

"It can't be; they don't send First Posters to Arlinghurst."

"No, really it's true. Miss Hodge's sec. told Jolly in confidence and Jolly told her sister in the village and *she* told Miss Nevill at The Teapot, and Miss Nevill talked about it to The Nut Tart when she was there to tea this afternoon with that cousin of hers."

"Is that gigolo here again?"

"I say, *Arlinghurst*! Who would believe it! Whom do you think they'll give it to?"

"Oh, that's easy."

"Yes, Innes of course."

"Lucky Innes."

"Oh, well, she deserves it."

"Just imagine. *Arlinghurst!*"

And on the first floor it was the same; the rushing of bath water, the splashing, the babble, and Arlinghurst.

"But who told you?"

"The Nut Tart."

"Oh, my dear, she's dippy, everyone knows."

"Well, it's a cert for Innes, anyhow, so it's nothing to do with me. I'll probably wind up in the L.C.C."

"She may be dippy, but she's not M.D., and she'd got it pat. She didn't even know what Arlinghurst *was*, so she wasn't making it up. She said: 'Is it a school?' "

"*Is it a school!* My hat!"

"I say, won't The Hodge be just dizzy with pride, my dears!"

"D'you suppose she'll be dizzy enough to give us tart for supper instead of that milk pudding?"

"I expect Jolly made the puddings yesterday and they're all standing waiting in rows on the hatch."

"Oh, well, they can wait as far as I'm concerned. I'm for Larborough."

"Me, too. I say, is Innes there?"

"No, she's finished. She's dressing."

"I say, let's throw Innes a party, all of us, instead of letting her give a little private one. After all, it's—"

"Yes. Let's do that, shall we? After all, it isn't every day that someone gets a post like that, and Innes deserves it, and everyone will be glad about it, and—"

"Yes, let's have a do in the common-room."

"After all, it's a sort of communal honour. A decoration for Leys."

"Arlinghurst! Who'd have believed it?"

"Arlinghurst!"

Lucy wondered if the meek little secretary's indiscretion had been prompted by the knowledge that the news was about to be made public. Even the cautious and secretive Henrietta could not sit on such a piece of information much longer; if for no other reason than that Arlinghurst would be expecting an answer. Lucy supposed that Henrietta had been waiting until the "bad" week was over before providing her sensation; she could not help feeling that it was a very neat piece of timing.

As she walked along the corridor to her cell at the end, she met Innes, buttoning herself into a fresh cotton frock.

"Well," said Lucy, "it seems to have been a successful afternoon."

"The row, you mean?" Innes said. "Yes, we won. But the row is not a war chant. It's a paean of praise that they will never have to live this week again."

Lucy noticed how unconsciously she had used the word "they." She wondered for a moment at the girl's calm. Had she, possibly, not yet heard about the Arlinghurst vacancy? And then, as Innes moved from the dimness of the corridor into the light from Dakers' wide-open door, Lucy saw the radiance on her face. And her own heart turned over in sympathy. *That* was how it felt, was it? Like seeing Heaven opened.

"*You* look happy, anyhow," she said, falling back on bald platitude since there were no words to describe what was shining in Innes's eyes.

"To use a phrase of O'Donnell's, I wouldn't call the king my cousin," Innes said, as they moved apart. "You are coming to Stewart's party, aren't you? That's good. We'll meet again there."

Lucy powdered her nose, and decided to go over to the "old house" and see how the Staff were reacting to the news of Arlinghurst. Perhaps there would still be some tea; she had forgotten all about tea and so apparently had the Gustavsens. She re-arranged the bottle of champagne which was waiting **for**

87

Stewart's party in the ice she had begged from Miss Joliffe, regretted yet once more that the Larborough wine merchant had not been able to supply a better year, but trusted (rightly) that Rheims and all its products were simply "champagne" to a student.

To go over to the "old house" one had to pass both the Seniors' bedrooms and the first floor bathrooms again, and it seemed to Lucy that the orchestration of sound had reached a new pitch of intensity, as more and more students heard the news and passed it on and commented on it above the roar of water, and banging of doors, and the thudding of feet. It was strange to come from that blare of sound and excitement into the quiet, the cream paint and mahogany, the tall windows and space, the waiting peace of the "house." She crossed the wide landing and opened the door of the drawing-room. Here too there was quiet, and she had shut the door behind her and come forward into the room before becoming aware of the exact quality of that quiet. Before realising, in fact, that the quiet was electric, and that she had walked into the middle of a Staff row. A row, moreover, if one was to judge from the faces, of most unholy proportions. Henrietta was standing, flushed and defensive and stubborn, with her back to the fireplace, and the others were staring at her, accusing and angry.

Lucy would have beaten a retreat, but someone had automatically poured out a cup of tea and thrust it at her, and she could hardly put it down again and walk out. Though she would have liked to for more reasons than one. The tea was almost black and quite cold.

No one took any notice of Lucy. Either they accepted her as one of themselves, or they were too absorbed in their quarrel to realise her fully. Their eyes had acknowledged her presence with the same absent acquiescence that greets a ticket collector in a railway carriage; a legitimate intruder but not a partaker in discussion.

"It's monstrous," Madame was saying. "Monstrous!" For the first time within Lucy's experience she had discarded her Récamier pose and was sitting with both slender feet planted firmly on the floor.

88

Miss Lux was standing behind her, her bleak face even bleaker than usual, and two very unusual spots of bright red high on her cheek-bones. Fröken was sitting back in one of the chintz-covered chairs looking contemptuous and sullen. And Wragg, hovering by the window, looked as much confused and embarrassed as angry; as if, having so lately come up from the mortal world, she found this battling of Olympians disconcerting.

"I fail to see anything monstrous about it," Henrietta said with an attempt at her head-girl manner; but even to Lucy's ears it had a synthetic quality. Henrietta was obviously in a spot.

"It is more than monstrous," Madame said, "it is very nearly criminal."

"Marie, don't be absurd."

"Criminal from more than one point of view. You propose to palm off an inferior product on someone who expects the best; and you propose at the same time to lower the credit of Leys so that it will take twenty years to recover it, if it ever recovers. And for what, I ask you? For what? Just to satisfy some whim of your own!"

"I fail to see where the whim comes in," Henrietta snapped, dropping some of her Great Dane dignity at this thrust. "No one here can deny that she is a brilliant student, that she has worked hard and deserved her reward. Even her theoretical work has been consistently good this term."

"Not consistently," said Miss Lux in a voice like water dropping on to a metal pan. "According to the paper I corrected last night, she could not even get a Second in Pathology."

It was here that Lucy stopped wondering what to do with her tea, and pricked up her ears.

"Oh, dear, that is a pity," Henrietta said, genuinely distracted from the main point by this news. "She was doing so well. So much better than I had dared to hope."

"The girl is a moron, and you know it," Madame said.

"But that is nonsense. She is one of the most brilliant students Leys has ever—"

"For God's sake, Henrietta, stop saying that. You know as well as any of us what they mean by brilliant." She flourished a sheet of blue note-paper in her thin brown hand, and holding it at arm's length (she was "getting on" was Madame, and she hated to wear glasses) read aloud. " 'We wondered if, among your leaving students, you had one brilliant enough to fill this place. Someone who would be "Arlinghurst" from the beginning, and so more part of the school and its traditions than a migrant can ever be, and at the same time continue the Leys connection that has been so fortunate for us.' The Leys connection that has been so fortunate! And you propose to end it by sending them Rouse!"

"I don't know why you are all so stubbornly against her. It can be nothing but prejudice. She has been a model student, and no one has ever said a word against her until now. Until I am prepared to give her the rewards of her work. And then you are all suddenly furious. I am entirely at a loss. Fröken! Surely you will bear me out. You can never have had a better pupil than Miss Rouse."

"Mees Rouse is a very good gymnast. She is also, I understand from Mees Wragg, a very fine games player. But when she goes out from thees plaace it will not matter any longer that she can do a handstand better than anyone else and that she ees a good half-back. What will matter then is character. And what Mees Rouse has of character is neither very much nor very admirable."

"Fröken!" Henrietta sounded shocked. "I thought you liked her."

"Did you?" The two cold, disinterested little words said: I am expected to like all my students; if you had known whom I liked or disliked I should be unworthy.

"Well, you *asked* Sigrid, and you've certainly been told," Madame said, delighted. "I could not have put it better myself."

"Perhaps—" began Miss Wragg. "I mean, it *is* for gymnastics they want her. They are separate departments at Arlinghurst: the gym., and the games, and the dancing; one person for each. So perhaps Rouse wouldn't be too bad."

Lucy wondered whether this tentative offering was inspired by Rouse's performance for Miss Wragg's department at half-back, or by a desire to smooth things over and draw the two edges of the yawning gap even a little nearer.

"Doreen, my pet," said Madame, in the tolerant tones that one uses to a half-wit, "what they are looking for is not someone who 'wouldn't be too bad'; what they are looking for is someone so outstanding that she can step straight from College to be one of the three gymnasts at the best girls' school in England. Does that sound to you like Miss Rouse, do you think?"

"No. No, I suppose not. It does sound like Innes, I must admit."

"Quite so. It does sound like Innes. And it is beyond the wit of man why it doesn't sound like Innes to Miss Hodge." She fixed Henrietta with her enormous black eyes, and Henrietta winced.

"I've told you! There is a vacancy at the Wycherley Orthopædic Hospital that would be ideal for Miss Innes. She is excellent at medical work."

"God give me patience! The Wycherley Orthopædic Hospital!"

"Doesn't the unity of the opposition persuade you that you are wrong, Miss Hodge?" It was Miss Lux, incisive even in her anger. "Being a minority of one is not a very strong position."

But that was the wrong thing to say. If Henrietta had ever been open to persuasion, she was by now far past that stage. She reacted to Miss Lux's logic with a spurt of fury.

"My position as a minority may not be very strong, Miss Lux, but my position as Principal of this college is unquestioned, and what you think or do not think of my decisions is immaterial. I took you into my confidence, as I always have, about the disposal of this vacancy. That you do not agree with me is, of course, regrettable, but of no consequence. It is for me to make decisions here, and in this case I have made it. You are free to disapprove, of course; but not to interfere, I am glad to say."

She picked up her cup with a hand that shook, and put it away on the tea-tray, as was her habit; and then made for the door. Lumbering and hurt, like a wounded elephant, thought Lucy.

"Just a minute, Henrietta!" Madame said, her eyes having lighted on Lucy and a spark of amused malice appearing therein. "Let us ask the outsider and the trained psychologist."

"But I am *not* a trained psychologist," said poor Lucy.

"Just let us hear what Miss Pym thinks."

"I don't know what Miss Pym has to do with the vacancies—"

"No, not about the appointment. Just what she thinks of these two students. Come along, Miss Pym. Give us your frank opinion. After a mere week among us you cannot be accused of bias."

"You mean Rouse and Innes?" asked Lucy, playing for time. Henrietta had paused with her hand on the door. "I don't know them, of course; but it certainly surprises me that Miss Hodge should think of giving that appointment to Rouse. I don't think she is at all—in fact I think she would be *quite* the wrong person."

Henrietta, to whom this was apparently the last straw, cast her an *et tu Brute* look and blundered out of the room, with a muttered remark about it being "surprising what a pretty face can do to influence people." Which Lucy took to refer to Innes, not to herself.

In the drawing-room was a very crowded silence.

"I thought I knew all about Henrietta," Madame said at last, reflective and puzzled.

"I thought one could trust her to do justice," Miss Lux said, bitter.

Fröken got to her feet without a word, and still looking contemptuous and sullen, walked out of the room. They watched her go with gloomy approbation; her silence was comment enough.

"It is a pity that this should have happened, when everything was going so well," Wragg said, producing another of her unhelpful offerings. She was like someone running round with blackcurrant lozenges to the victims of an earthquake. "Everyone has been so pleased with their posts, and—"

"Do you think she will come to her senses when she has had time to think it over?" Lux asked Madame.

"She has been thinking it over for nearly a week. Or rather she has had it settled in her mind for nearly a week; so that by now it has become established fact and she will not be able to see it any other way."

"And yet she couldn't have been sure about it—I mean, sure of our reaction—or she would not have kept it to herself until now. Perhaps when she thinks it over—"

"When she thinks it over she will remember that Catherine Lux questioned the Royal Prerogative—"

"But there is a Board in the background. There is no question of Divine Right. There must be someone who can be appealed to against her decision. An injustice like this can't be allowed to happen just because—"

"Of course there is a Board. You met them when you got the job here. You see one of them when she comes to supper on the Friday nights when the lecture happens to be on Yoga, or Theosophy, or Voodoo, or what not. A greedy slug in amber beads and black satin, with the brains of a louse. She thinks Henrietta is wonderful. So do the rest of the Board. And so, let me say it here and now, do I. That is what makes it all so shocking. That Henrietta, the shrewd Henrietta who built this place up from something not much better than a dame's school, should be so blind, so suddenly devoid of the most elementary judgment—it's fantastic. Fantastic!"

"But there must be *something* we can do—"

"My good if tactless Catherine," Madame said rising gracefully to her feet, "all we can do is go to our rooms and pray." She reached for the scarf that even in the hottest weather draped her thin body as she moved from one room to another. "There are also the lesser resorts of aspirin and a hot bath. They may not move the Almighty but they are beneficial to the blood pressure." She floated out of the room; as nearly without substance as a human being can be.

"If Madame can't do anything to influence Miss Hodge, I don't see that anyone else can," Wragg said.

"I certainly can't," Lux said. "I just rub her the wrong way. Even if I didn't, even if I had the charm of Cleopatra and she hung on my every word, how can one reduce a mental astigmatism like that? She is quite honest about it, you see. She is one of the most honest persons I have ever met. She really *sees* the thing like that; she really sees Rouse as everything that is admirable and deserving, and thinks we are prejudiced and oppositious. How can one alter a thing like that?" She stared a moment, blankly, at the bright window, and then picked up her book. "I must go and change, if I can find a free bathroom."

Her going left Lucy alone with Miss Wragg, who obviously wanted to go too but did not know how to make her departure sufficiently graceful.

"It is a mess, isn't it?" she proffered.

93

"Yes, it seems a pity," Lucy said, thinking how inadequately it summed up the situation; she was still stunned by the new aspect presented to her. She became aware that Wragg was still in her out-door clothes. "When did you hear about it?"

"I heard the students talking about it downstairs—when we came in from the match, I mean—and I bolted up here to see if it was true, and I walked straight into it. Into the row, I mean. It *is* a pity; everything was going so well."

"You know that the students take it for granted that Innes will get the post," Lucy said.

"Yes," Wragg sounded sober. "I heard them in the bathrooms. It was a natural thing to think. All of us would take it for granted that Innes would be the one. She is not very good for me—in games, I mean—but she is a good coach. She understands what she is doing. And of course in other things she is brilliant. She really should have been a doctor or something brainy like that. Oh, well, I suppose I must go and get out of these things." She hesitated a moment. "Don't think we do this often, will you, Miss Pym? This is the first time I have seen the Staff het up about anything. We are all such good friends as a rule. That's what makes this such a pity. I wish someone could change Miss Hodge's point of view. But if I know her no one can do that."

~~~~~~

· 10 ·

No ONE can do that, they said; but it was just possible that she, Lucy, might. When the door closed behind Wragg she found herself faced with her own dilemma. She had reason to know that Miss Lux's first view of Henrietta's reaction was much truer than her second. That mental astigmatism that Lux talked about was not great enough to exclude a doubt of her own judgment; Lucy had not forgotten the odd guilty look on Henrietta's face last Monday morning when her secretary had tried to bring up the subject of the Arlinghurst letter. It had been an up-to-something look. Not a Father Christmas up-to-something, either. Quite definitely it was something she was a little ashamed of. Astigmatic

94

enough she might be to find Rouse worthy, but not cock-eyed enough to be unaware that Innes had a prior claim.

And that being so, then it was Lucy's duty to put certain facts before her. It was a great pity about the little red book now dissolving into pulp among the weeds—she had been altogether too impulsive about its disposal—but book or no book, she must brave Henrietta and produce some cogent reasons for her belief that Rouse was not a suitable person to be appointed to Arlinghurst.

It surprised her a little to find that an interview with Henrietta on this footing brought back a school-girl qualm that had no place in the bosom of any adult; least of all one who was a Celebrity. But she was greatly fortified by that remark of Henrietta's about "pretty faces." That was a remark that Henrietta really should not have made.

She got up and put the cup of black, cold tea on the tray; noticing regretfully that they had had almond-fingers for tea; she would have very much liked an almond-finger ten minutes ago, but now she could not have eaten even an éclair. It would not be true to say that she had discovered feet of clay in Henrietta, since she had never made any sort of image in Henrietta's likeness. But she *had* looked up to Henrietta as a person of superior worth to her own, and the habit of mind acquired at school had stayed with her. She was therefore shocked to find her capable of what was at worst cheating, and at the very least a *bêtise*. She wondered what there had been in Rouse to unseat so solid a judgment as Henrietta's. That remark about "pretty faces." That unconsidered, blurted remark. Was there something in that plain, north-country face that had touched a woman so used to good looks in her students? Was there something in the plain, unloved, hardworking, ambitious Rouse that Henrietta identified with herself? Was it like seeing some old struggle of her own? So that she adopted, and championed, and watched over her unconsciously. Her disappointment over Rouse's comparative failure in Pathology had been so keen that it had distracted her even from the urgent quarrel with her Staff.

Or was it just that Rouse had made good use of those admiring

95

—not to say adoring—looks that she had sampled on the covered way the other morning?

No, not that. Henrietta had her faults but silliness was not one of them. She had, moreover, like everyone else in the scholastic world, served a long apprenticeship to adoration, both real and synthetic. Her interest in Rouse might be heightened by Rouse's obvious discipleship, but the origin of that interest was elsewhere. It was most likely that the Henrietta who had been plain, and unloved, and ambitious, had viewed the plain, and unloved, and ambitious young Rouse with a kindliness that was half recognition.

Lucy wondered whether to go to Henrietta at once, or to wait until she simmered down. The snag was that as Henrietta simmered down, so would her own determination to beard Henrietta on the subject. All things considered, and with the memory of previous fiascos, she thought that she had better go now while her feet would still carry her in the proper direction.

There was no immediate answer to her tap at the office door, and for a moment she hoped that Henrietta had retired to her own room upstairs and so reprieved her from her plain duty for a few hours longer. But no; there was her voice bidding her come in, and in went Lucy, feeling horribly like a culprit and furious with herself for being such a rabbit. Henrietta was still flushed and wounded-looking, and if she had not been Henrietta, Lucy would have said that there were tears in her eyes; but that was manifestly impossible. She was very busy about some papers on her desk, but Lucy felt that until she had knocked Henrietta's only activity had been mental.

"Henrietta," she began, "I'm afraid you thought it presumptuous of me to express an opinion about Miss Rouse." (Oh dear, that sounded very pompous!)

"A little uncalled-for," Henrietta said coldly.

Of all the Henrietta phrases! "Uncalled-for!" "But it *was* called for," she pointed out. "That is just what it was. I should never have dreamed of offering my opinion unasked. The point is, that opinion—"

"I don't think we need discuss it, Lucy. It is a small matter, anyhow, and not one to—"

"But it *isn't* a small matter. That is why I've come to see you."

"We pride ourselves in this country, don't we, that everyone has a right to his opinion, and a right to express it. Well, you expressed it—"

"When I was asked to."

"When you were asked to. And all I say is that it was a little tactless of you to take sides in a matter of which you can know very little, if anything at all."

"But that is just it. I *do* know something about it. You think I am just prejudiced against Miss Rouse because she is not very attractive——"

"Not very attractive to *you*, perhaps," amended Henrietta quickly.

"Shall we say not very obviously attractive," Lucy said, annoyed and beginning to feel better. "You think I have judged her merely on her social graces, but that is not so."

"On what else could you judge her? You know nothing of her work."

"I invigilated at one of her examinations."

Lucy observed with satisfaction that this brought Henrietta up short.

There was silence while one could count five.

"And what quality of a student could you possibly test by invigilating at an examination?"

"Her honesty."

"Lucy!" But the tone was not shocked. It was a warning. It meant, if it meant anything: Do-you-know-what-the-punishment-for-slander-is?

"Yes, I said her honesty."

"Are you trying to tell me that you found Miss Rouse—obtaining help during an examination?"

"She did her best. I haven't spent the best years of my life in Fourth-Form circles without knowing the routine. It was at the beginning that I noticed what she was about, and since I didn't want to make a scandal of it I thought the best way was to prevent her from using it."

"Using it? Using what?"

"The little book."

"You mean that you saw a student using a small book at an examination, and *said nothing about it*?"

"No, of course not. It was only afterwards that I knew about the book. All that I knew at the time was that there was something she was trying to refer to. She had a handkerchief in her left hand—although she hadn't a cold, and seemed to have no legitimate use for the thing—and she had that bag-of-sweets-under-the-desk look that you know as well as I do. There wasn't anything under her desk, so I deduced that whatever she had was in her hand with the handkerchief. As I had no proof——"

"Ah! You had no proof."

"No. I had no proof, and I didn't want to upset the whole room by demanding any, so I invigilated from the back of the room, where I was directly behind her, and could see to it that she got no help from anything or anybody."

"But if you did not ask her about the affair, how did you know about a book?"

"I found the book lying by the path to the gymnasium. It was——"

"You mean the book was not in her desk? Not *in the room at all*?"

"No. If it had been in her desk you would have known about it five minutes later. And if I had found such a book in the examination room I would have brought it to you at once."

"Such a book? What kind of book?"

"A tiny address-book filled with Pathology notes."

"An address-book?"

"Yes. A, arthritis—and so on."

"You mean that the book was merely a book of reference compiled by a student in the course of her study?"

"Not 'merely'."

"And *why* not 'merely'?"

"Because the whole thing was not much bigger than an outsize postage stamp."

Lucy waited for this to sink in.

"And what connection is there between this book you found and Miss Rouse?"

"Only that no one else in the room had a bag-of-sweets-under-the-desk expression; in fact, no one else seemed to be particularly worried about the paper. And that Rouse was the last to leave the room."

"What has that to do with it?"

"If the book had been dropped before Rouse came out of the examination room it would almost certainly have been picked up by one of the other students. It was a sort of dahlia red, and was lying very obviously on the grass at the edge of the path.

"Not *on the path*?"

"No," said Lucy, reluctantly. "About half an inch off it."

"So that it could have been passed many times by a crowd of chattering students excited over an examination, and anxious not to be late for their next class?"

"Yes, I suppose it could."

"And was there a name on the book?"

"No."

"No name? No means of identification?"

"Nothing except the script. It was in script, not current form."

"I see." One could see Henrietta bracing herself. "Then you had better bring me the book and we will take the proper steps to have the owner identified."

"I haven't got it," said poor Lucy. "I drowned it."

"You what?"

"I mean, I dropped it into the stream by the games field."

"That was surely a very extraordinary thing to do?" *Was* there a spark of relief in Henrietta's eye?

"Not really. I suppose it was impetuous. But what was I to do with it? It was a précis of Pathology, and the Pathology Final was over and the book had not been used. Whatever had been planned had not been carried out. Why, then, worry you by bringing the book to you? It seemed to me that the best punishment for whoever had compiled the thing was never to know what had become of it. To live the rest of her days with a question at the back of her mind."

" 'Whoever had compiled it.' That describes the situation, doesn't it? There is not one iota of evidence to connect the book with Miss Rouse."

"If there had been evidence, as I said before, I would have

brought it to you. There is only presumption. But the presumption is very strong. A great many people are ruled out altogether."

"Why?"

"Those who don't consider themselves likely to be at a loss don't waste time insuring against it. That is to say, those who are good on the theoretical side are innocent. But you yourself told me that Rouse finds written work extraordinarily difficult."

"So do a great many others."

"Yes. But there is another factor. A great many no doubt find difficulty with theory but don't particularly care as long as they struggle through. But Rouse is brilliant at practical work, and it galls her to be also-ran in examinations. She is ambitious, and a hard-worker. She wants the fruits of her labours, and she is very doubtful of getting them. Hence the little book."

"That, my dear Lucy, is psychological theorising."

"Maybe. But psychological theorising is what Madame asked me to do, in the drawing-room. You thought I had based my opinion on a mere prejudice. I thought you ought to know that I had some better foundation for my theorising." She watched Henrietta's flushed face, and wondered if she might venture into the minefield again, now that she had proved that she was not merely wantonly trespassing. "As one friend to another, Henrietta, I don't understand why you even consider sending Rouse to Arlinghurst when you have someone as suitable as Innes." And she waited for the explosion.

But there was no explosion. Henrietta sat in heavy silence, making a dotted pattern with her pen on the fine clean blotting-paper; a measure of her troubled state, since neither doodling nor wasting paper was a habit of Henrietta's.

"I don't think you know much about Innes," she said at length, in a reasonably friendly tone. "Because she has a brilliant mind and good looks you credit her with all the other virtues. Virtues that she quite definitely does not possess. She has no sense of humour, and she does not make friends easily—two serious disabilities in anyone who plans to live the communal life of a residential school. Her very brilliance is a drawback in that it makes it difficult for her to suffer fools gladly. She has a tendency —quite unconscious, I am sure—to look down her nose at the rest of the world." (Lucy remembered suddenly how, this very afternoon, Innes had automatically used the word "they" in referring to the students. Old Henrietta was shrewd enough.) "In fact, ever since she came here she has left me with the impression that she despises Leys, and is using it only as a means to an end."

"Oh, surely not," Lucy protested mechanically, while her inner self was wondering whether that were indeed so, and whether that accounted for a great deal that had puzzled her about Mary Innes. If being at Leys had indeed been a secret purgatory, a trial endured as a means to an end, that might explain that too-adult reticence, that air of concentration in a person who had no natural need of concentration, that inability to smile.

She remembered, irrelevantly, Desterro's light-hearted account of how she changed her mind and decided to stay at Leys when she saw Innes. It was because Innes was not "of" Leys that Desterro had noticed her on that dreary autumn afternoon, picking her out from the milling crowd as someone from an alien, more adult world.

"But she is very popular with her colleagues," Lucy said aloud.

"Yes, her own set like her well enough. They find her aloofness —intriguing, I think. She is not so popular with children, unfortunately; they find her intimidating. If you looked at her crit. book—the book that the Staff use for reports when they go to outside classes with students—you would find that the word 'antagonistic' appears again and again in describing her attitude."

"Perhaps it is just those eyebrows," Lucy said. She saw that Henrietta, uncomprehending, thought this a mere frivolousness, and added: "Or perhaps like so many people she has an inner doubt about herself, in spite of all appearances to the contrary. That is the usual explanation of antagonism as an attitude."

"I find psychologists' explanations a little too glib," Henrietta said. "If one has not the natural graces to attract friendship, one can at least make an *effort* to be friendly. Miss Rouse does."

(I bet! thought Lucy.)

"It is a great tragedy to lack the natural graces; one is not only denied the ready friendship of one's colleagues but one has to overcome the unreasoning prejudice of those in office. Miss

Rouse has fought hard to overcome her natural disabilities: her slowness of mind and her lack of good looks; she goes more than halfway to meet people and puts herself to great pains to be adaptable and pleasant and—and—and acceptable to people. And with her pupils she succeeds. They like her and look forward to seeing her; her reports from her classes are excellent. But with the Staff in their private capacity she has failed. They see only her personal—unattractiveness, and her efforts to be friendly and adaptable have merely annoyed them." She looked up from her pen-patterns and caught Lucy's expression. "Oh, yes, you thought my preference for Rouse as a candidate was the result of blind prejudice, didn't you? Believe me, I have not brought up Leys to its present position without understanding something of how the human mind works. Rouse has worked hard during her years here and has made a success of them, she is popular with her pupils and sufficiently adaptable to make herself acceptable to her colleagues; she has the friendliness and the adaptability that Innes so conspicuously lacks; and there is no reason why she should not go to Arlinghurst with my warm recommendation."

"Except that she is dishonest."

Henrietta flung the pen down on its tray with a clatter.

"That is a sample of what the unattractive girl has to struggle against," she said, all righteousness and wrath. "You think that one out of a score of girls has tried to cheat at an examination, and you pick on Rouse. Why? Because you don't like her face —or her expression, if one must be accurate."

So it had been no use. Lucy drew her feet under her and prepared to go.

"There is nothing at all to connect the little book you found with any particular student. You just remembered that you hadn't liked the looks of Miss Rouse; and so she was the culprit. The culprit—if there is one; I should be sorry to think that any Senior student of mine would stoop to such a subterfuge —the culprit is probably the prettiest and most innocent member of the set. You should know enough of human nature, as distinct from psychology, to know that."

Lucy was not sure whether it was this last thrust or the

accusation of fastening crime on to plain faces, but she was very angry by the time she reached the door.

"There is just one point, Henrietta," she said, pausing with the door-knob in her hand.

"Yes?"

"Rouse managed to get a First in all her Finals so far."

"Yes."

"That is odd, isn't it."

"Not at all odd. She had worked very hard."

"It's odd, all the same; because on the occasion when someone was prevented from using the little red book she could not even get a Second."

And she closed the door quietly behind her.

"Let her stew over that," she thought.

As she made her way over to the wing her anger gave way to depression. Henrietta was, as Lux said, honest, and that honesty made arguing with her hopeless. Up to a point she was shrewd and clear-minded, and beyond that she suffered from Miss Lux's "astigmatism"; and for mental astigmatism nothing could be done. Henrietta was not consciously cheating, and therefore could not be reasoned, frightened, nor cajoled into a different course. Lucy thought with something like dismay of the party she was to attend presently. How was she going to face a gathering of Seniors, all speculating about Arlinghurst and rejoicing openly over Innes's good luck?

How was she going to face Innes herself, with the radiance in her eyes? The Innes who "wouldn't call the king her cousin."

• 11 •

SUPPER at Leys was the formal meal of the day, with the Seniors in their dancing silks and the rest in supper frocks, but on Saturdays when so many had "Larborough leave" it was a much more casual affair. Students sat where they pleased, and, within the bounds of convention, wore what they pleased. Tonight the atmosphere was even more informal than usual since so many had departed to celebrate the end of Examination Week elsewhere, and still more were planning celebration on the spot after supper. Henrietta did not appear—it was understood that she was having a tray in her room—and Madame Lefevre was absent on concerns of her own. Fröken and her mother were at the theatre in Larborough, so Lucy shared the top table with Miss Lux and Miss Wragg, and found it very pleasant. By tacit consent the burning question of Arlinghurst was not referred to.

"One would think," said Miss Lux, turning over with a fastidious fork the vegetable mysteries on her plate, "that on a night of celebration Miss Joliffe would have provided something more alluring than a scranbag."

"It's *because* it's a celebration night that she doesn't bother," said Wragg, eating heartily. "She knows quite well that there is enough good food waiting upstairs to sink a battleship."

"Not for us, unfortunately. Miss Pym must put something in her pocket for us when she is coming away."

"I bought some cream puffs in Larborough on the way home from the match," Wragg confessed. "We can have our coffee in my room and have a gorge."

Miss Lux looked as if she would have preferred cheese straws, but in spite of her chill incisiveness she was a kind person, so she said: "I take that very kindly of you, so I do."

"I thought you would be going to the theatre, or I would have suggested it before."

"An out-moded convention," said Miss Lux.

"Don't you like the theatre?" asked the surprised Lucy, to whom the theatre was still a part of childhood's magic.

Miss Lux stopped looking with a questioning revulsion at a piece of carrot, and said: "Have you ever considered what you would think of the theatre if you were taken to it for the first time, now, without the referred affection of childhood pantomimes and what not? Would you really find a few dressed-up figures posturing in a lighted box *entertaining*? And the absurd convention of intervals—once devoted to the promenade of toilettes and now perpetuated for the benefit of the bar. What other entertainment would permit of such arbitrary interruption? Does one stop in the middle of a symphony to go and have a drink?"

"But a play is made that way," Lucy protested.

"Yes. As I said; an out-moded convention."

This dashed Lucy a little, not because of her lingering affection for the theatre, but because she had been so wrong about Miss Lux. She would have said that Miss Lux would be a passionate attender of try-out performances in the drearier suburbs of plays devoted to a Cause and Effects.

"Well, I nearly went tonight myself," Wragg said, "just to see Edward Adrian again. I had a terrific rave on him when I was a student. I expect he's a bit passé now. Have you ever seen him?"

"Not on the stage. He used to spend his holidays with us when he was a boy." Miss Lux ran her fork once more through the heap on her plate and decided that there was nothing further worth her attention.

"*Used to spend the holidays!* At your *house?*"

"Yes, he went to school with my brother."

"Good heavens! how absolutely incredible!"

"What is incredible about it?"

"I mean, one just doesn't think of Edward Adrian as being an ordinary person that people *know*. Just a schoolboy like anyone else."

"A very horrid little boy."

"Oh, *no!*"

"A quite revolting little boy. Always watching himself in mirrors. And possessed of a remarkable talent for getting the best of everything that was going." She sounded calm, and clinical, and detached.

"Oh, Catherine, you shatter me."

"No one I have ever met had the same genius for leaving someone else holding the baby as Teddy Adrian."

"He has other kinds of genius though, surely," Lucy ventured.

"He has talent, yes."

"Do you still see him?" asked Wragg, still a little dazzled to be getting first-hand news of Olympus.

"Only by accident. When my brother died we gave up the

house that our parents had had, and there were no more family gatherings."

"And you've never seen him on the stage?"

"Never."

"And you didn't even go a sixpenny bus-ride into Larborough to see him play tonight."

"I did not. I told you, the theatre bores me inexpressibly."

"But it's Shakespeare."

"Very well, it's Shakespeare. I would rather sit at home and read him in the company of Doreen Wragg and her cream puffs. You won't forget to put something in your pocket for us when you leave your feast, will you, Miss Pym? Anything gratefully received by the starving proletariat. Macaroons, Mars bars, blood oranges, left-over sandwiches, squashed sausage rolls—"

"I'll put a hat round," promised Lucy. "I'll pass the hat and quaver: 'Don't forget the Staff'."

But as she lifted the champagne bottle out of its melting ice in her wash-bowl she did not feel so gay about it. This party was going to be an ordeal, there was no denying it. She tied a big bow of ribbon to the neck of the bottle, to make it look festive and to take away any suggestion of "bringing her own liquor"; the result was rather like a duchess in a paper cap, but she didn't think that the simile would occur to the students. She had hesitated over her own toilette, being divided between a rough-and-tumble outfit suitable to a cushions-on-the-floor gathering, and the desire to do her hosts honour. She had paid them the compliment of putting on her "lecture" frock, and doing an extra-careful make-up. If Henrietta had taken away from this party by her vagaries, she, Lucy, would bring all she could to it.

Judging by the noise in other rooms, and the running back and fore with kettles, Stewart's was not the only party in Leys that evening. The corridors smelt strongly of coffee, and waves of laughter and talk rose and died away as doors were opened and shut. Even the Juniors seemed to be entertaining; if they had no Posts to celebrate they had the glory of having their first Final behind them. Lucy remembered that she had not found out from The Nut Tart how she had fared in that

Anatomy Final. ("Today's idea may be nonsense tomorrow, but a clavicle is a clavicle for all time.") When she passed the students' notice-board again she must look for Desterro's name.

She had to knock twice at the door of Number Ten before the sound penetrated, but when a flushed Stewart opened the door and drew her in a sudden shyness fell on the group, so that they got to their feet in polite silence like well-brought-up children.

"We are so glad to have you," Stewart was beginning, when Dakers sighted the bottle and all formality was at an end.

"*Drink!*" she shrieked. "As I live and breathe, *drink!* Oh, Miss Pym you are a *poppet!*"

"I hope that I am not breaking any rules," Lucy said, remembering that there had been an expression in Miss Joliffe's eye that she had still not accounted for, "but it seemed to me an occasion for champagne."

"It's a triple occasion," Stewart said. "Dakers and Thomas are celebrating too. It couldn't be *more* of an occasion. It was lovely of you to think of the champagne."

"It will be sacrilege to drink it out of tooth-glasses," Hasselt said.

"Well, anyhow, we drink it now, as aperitif. A course by itself. Pass up your glasses everyone. Miss Pym, the chair is for you."

A basket chair had been imported and lined with a motley collection of cushions; except for the hard chair at the desk it was the only legitimate seat in the room, the rest of the party having brought their cushions with them and being now disposed about the floor or piled in relaxed heaps like kittens on the bed. Someone had tied a yellow silk handkerchief over the light so that a golden benevolence took the place of the usual hard brightness. The twilight beyond the wide-open window made a pale blue back-cloth that would soon be a dark one. It was like any student party of her own college days, but as a picture it had more brilliance than her own parties had had. Was it just that the colours of the cushions were gayer? That the guests were better physical types, without lank hair, spectacles, and studious pallor?

No, of course it wasn't that. She knew what it was. There was no cigarette smoke.

"O'Donnell isn't here yet," Thomas said, collecting tooth-glasses from the guests and laying them on the cloth that covered the desk.

"I expect she's helping Rouse to put up the boom," a Disciple said.

"She can't be," a second Disciple said, "it's Saturday."

"Even a P.T.I. stops work on a Sunday," said a third.

"Even Rouse," commented the fourth.

"Is Miss Rouse still practising rotatory travelling?" Lucy asked.

"Oh, yes," they said. "She will be, up to the day of the Dem."

"And when does she find time?"

"She goes when she is dressed in the morning. Before first class."

"Six o'clock," said Lucy. "Horrible."

"It's no worse than any other time," they said. "At least one is fresh, and there is no hurry, and you can have the gym. to yourself. Besides, it's the only possible time. The boom has to be put away before first class."

"She doesn't have to go," Stewart said, "the knack has come back. But she is terrified she will lose it again before the Dem."

"I can understand that, my dear," Dakers said. "Think what an *immortal* fool one would feel hanging like a sick monkey from the boom, with all the élite looking on, and Fröken simply *stabbing* one with that eye of hers. My dear, *death* would be a happy release. If Donnie isn't doing her usual chore for Rouse, *where* is she? She's the only one not here."

"Poor Don," Thomas said, "she hasn't got a post yet." Thomas with her junior-of-three in Wales was feeling like a millionaire.

"Don't worry over Don," Hasselt said, "the Irish always fall on their feet."

But Miss Pym was looking round for Innes, and not finding her. Nor was Beau there.

Stewart, seeing her wandering eye, interpreted the question in it and said: "Beau and Innes wanted me to tell you how sorry they were to miss the party, and to hope that you would be their guest at another one before the end of term."

"Beau will be giving one for Innes," Hasselt said. "To celebrate Arlinghurst."

"As a matter of fact, we're *all* giving a party for Innes," a Disciple said.

"A sort of general jamboree," said a second Disciple.

"It's an honour for College, after all," said a third.

"You'll come to that, won't you, Miss Pym," said a fourth, making it a statement rather than a question.

"Nothing would please me more," Lucy said. And then, glad to skate away from such thin ice: "What has happened to Beau and Innes?"

"Beau's people turned up unexpectedly and took them off to the theatre in Larborough," Stewart said.

"That's what it is to own a Rolls," Thomas said, quite without envy. "You just dash around England as the fit takes you. When *my* people want to move they have to yoke up the old grey mare —a brown cob, actually—and trot twenty miles before they reach any place at all."

"Farmers?" Lucy asked, seeing the lonely narrow Welsh road winding through desolation.

"No, my father is a clergyman. But we have to keep a horse to work the place, and we can't have a horse and a car too."

"Oh, well," said a Disciple arranging herself more comfortably on the bed, "who wants to go to the theatre anyhow?"

"Of all the boring ways of spending an evening," said a second.

"Sitting with one's knees in someone's back," said a third.

"With one's eyes glued to opera glasses," said a fourth.

"Why opera glasses?" asked Lucy, surprised to find Miss Lux's attitude repeated in a gathering where sophistication had not yet destroyed a juvenile thirst for entertainment.

"What would you see without them?"

"Little dolls walking about in a box."

"Like something on Brighton pier."

"Except that on Brighton pier you can see the expression on the faces."

They were rather like something from Brighton pier themselves, Lucy thought. A turn. A sort of extended Tweedledum and Tweedledee. They were apparently not moved to speech unless one of their number made a remark; when the others felt called upon to produce corroborative evidence.

"Me, I'm only too glad to put my feet up and do nothing for a change," Hasselt said. "I'm breaking in a new pair of ballet shoes for the Dem. and my blisters are spectacular."

"Miss Hasselt," said Stewart, obviously quoting, "it is a student's business to preserve her body in a state of fitness at all times."

"That may be," said Hasselt, "but I'm not standing in a bus for five miles on a Saturday night to go anywhere, least of all to a theatre."

"Anyhow, it's only Shakespeare, my dears," Dakers said. " 'It is the cause, my soul!' " she burlesqued, clutching at her breast.

"Edward Adrian, though," volunteered Lucy, feeling that her beloved theatre must have one champion.

"Who is Edward Adrian?" Dakers asked, in genuine inquiry.

"He's that weary-looking creature who looks like a moulting eagle," Stewart said, too busy about her hostess's duties to be aware of the reaction on Lucy: that was a horribly vivid summing-up of Edward Adrian, as seen by the unsentimental eyes of modern youth. "We used to be taken to see him when I was at school in Edinburgh."

"And didn't you enjoy it?" Lucy asked, remembering that Stewart's name headed the lists on the notice-board along with Innes's and Beau's, and that mental activity would not be for her the chore that it probably was for some of the others.

"Oh, it was better than sitting in a class-room," Stewart allowed. "But it was all terribly—old-fashioned. Nice to look at, but a bit dreary. I'm a tooth-glass short."

"Mine, I suppose," O'Donnell said, coming in on the words and handing over her glass. "I'm afraid I'm late. I was looking for some shoes that my feet would go into. Forgive these, won't you, Miss Pym," she indicated the bedroom slippers she was wearing. "My feet have died on me."

"Do *you* know who Edward Adrian is?" Lucy asked her.

"Certainly I do," O'Donnell said. "I've had a rave on him ever since I went to see him at the age of twelve in Belfast."

"You seem to be the only person in this room either to know or to admire him."

"Ah, the heathen," said O'Donnell, casting a scornful eye on the gathering—and it seemed to Lucy that O'Donnell was suspiciously bright about the eyes, as if she had been crying. "It's in Larborough I would be this minute, sitting at his feet, if it wasn't practically the end of term and I lacked the price of a seat."

And if, thought Lucy pitying, you hadn't felt that backing out of this party would be put down to your being the only one present not yet to have a post. She liked the girl who had dried her eyes and thought of the bedroom slipper excuse and come gaily to the party that was none of hers.

"Well," said Stewart, busy with the wire of the cork, "now that O'Donnell is here we can open the bottle."

"Good heavens, champagne!" O'Donnell said.

The wine came foaming into the thick blunt tooth-glasses, and they turned to Lucy expectantly.

"To Stewart in Scotland, to Thomas in Wales, to Dakers at Ling Abbey," she said.

They drank that.

"And to all our friends between Capetown and Manchester," Stewart said.

And they drank that too.

"Now, Miss Pym, what will you eat?"

And Lucy settled down happily to enjoy herself. Rouse was not going to be a guest; and she was by some special intervention of Providence in the shape of rich parents in a Rolls-Royce going to be spared the ordeal of sitting opposite an Innes bursting with happiness that had no vestige of foundation.

• 12 •

But by noon on Sunday she was much less happy, and was wishing that she had had the foresight to invent a luncheon engagement in Larborough and so remove herself out of the area of the explosion that was coming. She had always hated explosions, literal and metaphorical; people who blew into paper bags and then burst them had always been regarded by Lucy with a mixture of abhorrence and awe. And the paper bag that was going to be burst after lunch was a particularly nasty affair; an explosion whose reverberations would be endless and unpredictable. At the back of her mind was the faint hope that Henrietta might have changed her mind; that the silent witness of those tell-tale lists on the notice-board might have proved more eloquent than her own poor words. But no amount of encouragement could make this hope anything but embryonic. She remembered only too clearly that a shaking of Henrietta's faith in Rouse would not mean a corresponding access of belief in Innes as a candidate. The best that could be hoped for was that she might write to the Head at Arlinghurst and say that there was no Leaving Student good enough for so exalted a post; and that would do nothing to save Innes from the grief that was coming to her. No, she really should have got herself out of Leys for Sunday lunch and come back when it was all over. Even in Larborough, it was to be supposed, there were people that one might conceivably be going to see. Beyond those over-rich villas of the outskirts with their smooth sanded avenues and their pseudo everything, somewhere between them and the soot of the city there must be a belt of people like herself. Doctors, there must be, for instance. She could have invented a doctor friend—except that doctors were listed in registers. If she had thought in time she could have invited herself to lunch with Dr Knight; after all, Knight owed her something. Or she could have taken sandwiches and just walked out into the landscape and not come home till bed-time.

Now she sat in the window-seat in the drawing-room, waiting for the Staff to assemble there before going down to the dining-room; watching the students come back from church and wondering if she had sufficient courage and resolution to seek out Miss Joliffe even yet and ask for sandwiches; or even just walk out of College with no word said—after all, one didn't starve in the English country even on a Sunday. As Desterro said, there were always villages.

Desterro was the first to come back from church; leisured and fashionable as always. Lucy leant out and said: "Congratulations on your knowledge of the clavicle." For she had looked at the board on the way to bed last night.

"Yes, I surprised myself," said The Nut Tart. "My grandmother will be so pleased. A 'first' sounds so well, don't you think? I boasted about it to my cousin, but he said that was most unseemly. In England one waits to be asked about one's successes."

"Yes," agreed Lucy, sadly, "and the worst of it is so few people ask. The number of lights under bushels in Great Britain is tragic."

"Not Great Britain," amended Desterro. "He says—my cousin —that it is all right north of the river Tweed. That is the river between England and Scotland, you know. You can boast in Dunbar but not in Berwick, Rick says."

"I should like to meet Rick," Lucy said.

"He thinks you are quite adorable, by the way."

"*Me?*"

"I have been telling him about you. We spent all the intervals talking about you."

"Oh you went to the theatre, did you?"

"He went. I was taken."

"Did you not enjoy it, then?" asked Lucy, mentally applauding the young man who made The Nut Tart do anything at all that she did not want to do.

"Oh, it was as they say, 'not too bad.' A little of the grand manner is nice for a change. Ballet would have been better. He is a dancer manqué, that one."

"Edward Adrian?"

"Yes." Her mind seemed to have strayed away. "The English wear all one kind of hat," she said reflectively. "Up at the back and down in front."

With which irrelevance she trailed away round the house, leaving Lucy wondering whether the remark was occasioned by last night's audience or Dakers' advent up the avenue. Dakers' Sunday hat was certainly a mere superior copy of the hat she had worn at school, and under its short brim her pleasant, waggish, pony's face looked more youthful than ever. She took off the hat with a gesture when she saw Miss Pym, and loudly expressed her delight in finding Lucy alive and well after the rigours of the night before. This was the first morning in *all* her college career, it seemed, when she had positively *failed* to eat a fifth slice of bread and marmalade.

"Gluttony is one of the seven deadly sins," she observed, "so I had need of shriving this morning. I went to the Baptist place because it is nearest."

"And do you feel shriven?"

"I *don't* know that I *do*, now you come to mention it. It was all very *conversational*."

Lucy took it that a shamed soul demanded ritual.

"Very friendly, though, I understand."

"Oh, *frightfully*. The clergyman began his sermon by leaning on one elbow and remarking: 'Well, my friends, it's a very fine day.' And everyone shook hands with everyone coming out. And they had some fine warlike hymns," she added, having thought over the Baptist good points. She looked thoughtful for a moment longer and then said: "There are some Portsmouth Brothers on the Larborough road—"

"Plymouth."

"Plymouth what?"

"Plymouth Brethren, I suppose you mean."

"Oh, yes; I know it had something to do with the Navy. And I'm Pompey by inclination. Well, I think I shall sample *them* next Sunday. You don't suppose they're *private*, or anything like that?"

Miss Pym thought not, and Dakers swung her hat in a wide gesture of burlesque farewell and went on round the house.

By ones and twos, and in little groups, the students returned from their compulsory hour out of College. Waving or calling a greeting or merely smiling, as their temperaments were. Even Rouse called a happy "Good morning, Miss Pym!" as she passed. Almost last came Beau and Innes; walking slowly, serene and relaxed. They came to rest beneath the window looking up at her.

"Heathen!" said Beau, smiling at her.

They were sorry they missed the party, they said, but there would be others.

"I shall be giving one myself when the Dem. is over," Beau said. "You'll come to that, won't you?"

"I shall be delighted. How was the theatre?"

"It might have been worse. We sat behind Colin Barry."

"Who is he?"

"The All-England hockey 'half'."

"And I suppose that helped *Othello* a lot."

"It helped the intervals, I assure you."

"Didn't you want to see *Othello*?"

"Not us! We were dying to go to Irma Ireland's new film—*Flaming Barriers*. It sounds very sultry but actually, I believe, it's just a good clean forest fire. But my parents' idea of a night out is the theatre and a box of chocolates for the intervals. We couldn't disappoint the old dears."

"Did *they* like it?"

"Oh, they *loved* it. They spent the whole of supper talking about it."

"You're a fine pair to call anyone 'heathen'," Lucy observed.

"Come to tea with the Seniors this afternoon," Beau said.

Lucy said hastily that she was going out to tea.

Beau eyed her guilty face with something like amusement, but Innes said soberly: "We should have asked you before. You are not going away before the Dem., are you?"

"Not if I can help it."

"Then will you come to tea with the Seniors next Sunday?"

"Thank you. If I am here I should be delighted."

"My lesson in manners," said Beau.

They stood there on the gravel looking up at her, smiling. That was how she always remembered them afterwards. Standing there in the sunlight, easy and graceful; secure in their belief in the world's rightness and in their trust in each other. Untouched by doubt or blemish. Taking it for granted that the warm gravel under their feet was lasting earth, and not the precipice edge of disaster.

It was the five-minute bell that roused them. As they moved away, Miss Lux came into the room behind, looking grimmer than Lucy had ever seen her.

"I can't imagine why I'm here," she said. "If I had thought in time I wouldn't be taking part in this God-forsaken farce at all."

Lucy said that that was exactly what she herself had been thinking.

"I suppose there has been no word of Miss Hodge having a change of heart?"

"Not as far as I know. I'm afraid it isn't likely."

"What a pity we didn't *all* go out to lunch. If Miss Hodge had to call Rouse's name from a completely deserted table, College would at least be aware that we had no part in this travesty."

"If you didn't have to mark yourself 'out' on the slate before eleven, I would go now, but I haven't the nerve."

"Oh well, perhaps we can do something with our expressions to convey that we consider the whole thing just a bad smell."

It's the being there to countenance it she minds, thought Lucy; while I just want to run away from unpleasantness like a child. Not for the first time, she wished she was a more admirable character.

Madame Lefevre came floating in wearing a cocoa-brown silk affair that was shot with a metallic blue in the high-lights; which made her look more than ever like some exotic kind of dragonfly. It was partly those enormous headlamps of eyes, of course; like some close-up of an insect in half-remembered Nature "shorts"; the eyes and the thin brown body, so angular yet so graceful. Madame, having got over her immediate rage, had, it seemed, recovered her detached contempt for the human species, and was regarding the situation with malicious if slightly enjoyable distaste.

"Never having attended a wake," she said, "I look forward with interest to the performance today."

"You are a ghoul," Lux said; but without feeling, as if she were too depressed to care greatly. "Haven't you done anything to alter her mind?"

"Oh, yes, I have wrestled with the Powers of Darkness. Wrestled very mightily. Also very cogently, may I say. With example and precept. Who was it who was condemned to push an enormous stone up a hill for ever? Extraordinary how appropriate these mythological fancies still are. I wonder if a ballet of Punishments would be any good? Sweeping out stables, and so forth. To Bach, perhaps. Though Bach is not very inspirational,

116

choreographically speaking. And a great many people rise up and call one damned, of course, if one uses him."

"Oh, stop it," Lux said. "We are going to connive at an abomination and you speculate about choreography!"

"My good, if too earnest, Catherine, you must learn to take life as it comes, and to withdraw yourself from what you cannot alter. As the Chinese so rightly advise: When rape is inevitable, relax and enjoy it. We connive at an abomination, as you so exquisitely put it. True. But as intelligent human beings we concern ourselves with the by-products of the action. It will be interesting to see how, for instance, the little Innes reacts to the stimulus. Will the shock be a mortal one, will it galvanise her into action, or will it send her into crazy throes of galvanic activity that has no meaning?"

"Damn your metaphors. You are talking nonsense and you know it. It is someone else's rape we are invited to countenance; and as far as I know there is nothing in the history of philosophy, Chinese or otherwise, to recommend that."

"Rape?" said Fröken, coming in followed by her mother. "Who is going to be raped?"

"Innes," Lux said dryly.

"Oh." The twinkle died out of Fröken's eye, leaving it cold and pale. "Yes," she said, reflectively. "Yes."

Fru Gustavsen's round "Mrs Noah" face looked troubled. She looked from one to another, as if hoping for some gleam of assurance, some suggestion that the problem was capable of being resolved. She came over to Lucy in the window-seat, ducked her head in a sharp Good-morning, and said in German:

"You know about this thing the Principal does? My daughter is very angry. Very angry my daughter is. Not since she was a little girl have I seen her so angry. It is very bad what they do? You think so too?"

"Yes, I'm afraid I do."

"Miss Hodge is a very good woman. I admire her very much. But when a good woman makes a mistake it is apt to be much worse than a bad woman's mistake. More colossal. It is a pity."

It was a great pity, Lucy agreed.

The door opened and Henrietta came in, with a nervous Wragg

117

in tow. Henrietta appeared serene, if a little more stately than usual (or than circumstances demanded) but Wragg cast a placatory smile round the gathering as if pleading with them to be all girls together and look on the bright side. Their close-hedged antagonism dismayed her, and she sent an appealing glance at Madame, whose dogsbody she normally was. But Madame's wide sardonic gaze was fixed on Henrietta.

Henrietta wished them all good morning (she had breakfasted in her own room) and she had timed her entrance very neatly, for before her greeting was finished, the murmur of the distant gong made the moment one for action, not conversation.

"It is time for us to go down, I think," Henrietta said, and led the way out.

Madame rolled her eye at Lux in admiration of this piece of generalship, and fell in behind.

"A wake indeed!" Lux said to Lucy as they went downstairs. "It feels more like Fotheringay."

The demure silence waiting them in the dining-room seemed to Lucy's heightened imagination to be charged with expectation, and certainly during the meal College seemed to be more excited than she had ever seen it. The babble of conversation deepened to a roar, so that Henrietta, coming-to between her busy gobbling of the meat course and her expectation of the pudding, sent a message by Wragg to Beau, asking that College should contain themselves.

For a little they were circumspect, but soon they forgot and the talk and laughter rose again.

"They are excited to have Examinations Week over," Henrietta said indulgently, and let them be.

This was her only contribution to conversation—she never did converse while eating—but Wragg served up brave little platitudes at regular intervals, looking from one to the other of the shut faces round the table hopefully, like a terrier which has brought a bone to lay at one's feet. One could almost see her tail wag. Wragg was to be the innocent means of execution, the passive knife in the guillotine, and she felt her position and was tacitly apologising for it. Oh, for Pete's sake, she seemed to be saying, I'm only the Junior Gymnast in this set-up, it's not my fault that I have to tag along in her rear; what do you expect me to do?—tell her to announce the damned thing herself?

Lucy was sorry for her, even while her pious pieces of the obvious made her want to scream. Be quiet, she wanted to say, do be quiet, there is nothing for a situation like this but silence.

At last Henrietta folded up her napkin, looked round the table to make sure that all her Staff had finished eating, and rose. As the Staff rose with her, College came to its feet with an alacrity and a unanimity that was rare. It was apparent that they had been waiting for this moment. Against her will, Lucy turned to look at them; at the rows of bright expectant faces, half-smiling in their eagerness; it did nothing to comfort her that they looked as if at the slightest provocation they would break into a cheer.

As Henrietta turned to the door and the Staff filed after her, Wragg faced the delighted throng and said the words that had been given her to say.

"Miss Hodge will see Miss Rouse in her office when luncheon is over."

~~~~~~

· 13 ·

Lucy could no longer see the faces, but she felt the silence go suddenly blank. Become void and dead. It was the difference between a summer silence full of bird-notes and leaves and wind in the grasses, and the frozen stillness of some Arctic waste. And then, into the dead void just as they reached the door, came the first faint sibilant whisper as they repeated the name.

"Rouse!" they were saying. "Rouse!"

And Lucy, stepping into the warm sunlight, shivered. The sound reminded her of frozen particles being swept over a snow surface by a bitter wind. She even remembered where she had seen and heard those particles: that Easter she had spent on Speyside when they had missed the Grantown bus and they were a long way from home and they had to walk it every foot of the way, under a leaden sky into a bitter wind over a frozen world. She felt a long way from home now, crossing the sunny courtyard to the quadrangle door, and the sky seemed to her as leaden as any Highland one in a March storm. She wished for a moment that she were at home, in her own quiet little sitting-room, settling down for a Sunday afternoon of unbroken peace, untouched by human problems and unhurt by human griefs. She toyed with the idea of inventing an excuse to go when to-morrow morning's post would give her a chance; but she had looked forward like a child to the Demonstration on Friday, and she had now a quite personal interest in what had promised to be for her merely something new in spectacles. She knew all the Seniors personally and a great many of the Juniors; she had talked "Dem." with them, shared their half-fearful anticipation of it, even helped to make their costumes. It was the summit, the triumphant flower, the resounding full-stop of their College careers, and she could not bear to go without seeing it; without being part of it.

She had dropped the rest of the Staff, who were bound for the front of the house, but Wragg, coming behind her to pin a notice on the students' board, mopped her forehead in frank relief and said: "Thank heaven that is over. I think it was the worst thing I have ever had to do. I couldn't eat my lunch with thinking of it." And Lucy remembered that there had indeed been the phenomenon of a large piece of tart unfinished on Miss Wragg's plate.

That was life, that was. Innes had Heaven's door shut in her face, and Wragg couldn't finish her pudding!

No one had yet come out of the dining-room—College appetites being so much larger than Staff ones, their meals lasted at least ten or fifteen minutes longer—so the corridors were still deserted as Lucy went up to her room. She resolved to get away from Leys before the crowd of students overran the countryside. She would go away deep into the green and white and yellow countryside, and smell the may and lie in the grass and feel the world turning on its axis, and remember that it was a very large world, and that College griefs were wild and bitter but soon over and that in the Scale of Things they were undeniably Very Small Beer.

She changed her shoes to something more appropriate to field paths, crossed to the "old house" and ran down the front stairs and out by the front door so as to avoid the students who would now be percolating out of the dining-room. The "old house" was very silent and she deduced that there had been no lingering in the drawing-room after lunch today. She skirted the house and made for the field behind the gymnasium, with vague thoughts of Bidlington and The Teapot stirring in her mind. The hedge of may was a creamy foam on her right and on her left the buttercups were a golden sea. The elms, half-floating in the warm light, were anchored each to its purple shadow, and daisies patterned the short grass under her feet. It was a lovely world, a fine round gracious world, and no day for—Oh, poor Innes! *poor* Innes!—no day for the world to turn over and crush one.

It was when she was debating with herself whether to cross the little bridge, to turn down-stream to Bidlington, or up-stream to the unknown, that she saw Beau. Beau was standing in the middle of the bridge watching the water, but with her green linen dress and bright hair she was so much a part of the sunlight-and-shadow under the willows that Lucy had been unaware that anyone was there. As she came into the shade herself and could see more clearly, Lucy saw that Beau was watching her come, but she gave her no greeting. This was so unlike Beau that Lucy was daunted.

"Hullo," she said, and leaned beside her on the wooden rail. "Isn't it beautiful this afternoon?" *Must* you sound so idiotic? she asked herself.

There was no answer to this, but presently Beau said: "Did you know about this appointment?"

"Yes," said Lucy. "I—I heard the Staff talking about it."

"When?"

"Yesterday."

"Then you knew this morning when you were talking to us."

"Yes. Why?"

"It would have been kind if someone had warned her."

"Warned whom?"

"Innes. It isn't very nice to have your teeth kicked in in public."

She realised that Beau was sick with rage. Never before had she seen her even out of temper, and now she was so angry that she could hardly talk.

"But how could I have done that?" she asked reasonably, dismayed to be taken personally to task for something that she considered none of her business. "It would have been disloyal to mention it before Miss Hodge had announced her decision. For all I knew she might have altered that decision; when I left her it was still possible that she might see things from—" She stopped, realising where she was headed. But Beau too had realised. She turned her head sharply to look at Miss Pym.

"Oh. You argued with her about it. You didn't approve of her choice, then?"

"Of course not." She looked at the angry young face so near her own and decided to be frank. "You might as well know, Beau, that no one approves. The Staff feel about it very much as you do. Miss Hodge is an old friend of mine, and I owe her a great deal, and admire her, but where this appointment is concerned she is 'on her own.' I have been desolated ever since I first heard of it, I would do anything to reverse it, to waken up tomorrow and find that it is just a bad dream; but as to warning anyone—" She lifted her hand in a gesture of helplessness.

Beau had gone back to glaring at the water. "A clever woman like you could have thought of something," she muttered.

The "clever woman" somehow made Beau of a sudden very young and appealing; it was not like the confident and sophisticated Beau to look for help or to think of her very ordinary Pym self as clever. She was after all a child; a child raging and hurt at the wrong that had been done her friend. Lucy had never liked her so well.

"Even a hint," Beau went on, muttering at the water. "Even a suggestion that there might be someone else in the running. *Anything* to warn her. To make the shock less shattering. To put her on her guard, so that she wasn't wide open. It had to be punishment, but it needn't have been a massacre. You could have sacrificed a little scruple in so good a cause, couldn't you?"

Lucy felt, belatedly, that perhaps she might have.

"Where is she?" she asked. "Where is Innes?"

"I don't know. She ran straight out of College before I could catch her up. I know she came this way, but I don't know where she went from here."

"She will take it very badly?"

"Did you expect her to be brave and noble about the hideous mess?" Beau said savagely, and then, instantly: "Oh, I'm sorry. I do beg your pardon. I know you're sorry about it too. I'm just not fit to be spoken to just now."

"Yes, I am sorry," Lucy said. "I admired Innes the first time I saw her, and I think she would have been an enormous success at Arlinghurst."

"Would have been," muttered Beau.

"How did Miss Rouse take the news? Was she surprised, do you think?"

"I didn't wait to see," Beau said shortly. And presently: "I think I shall go up-stream. There is a little thorn wood up there that she is very fond of; she may be there."

"Are you worried about her?" Lucy asked; feeling that if it were merely comforting that Beau planned, Innes would surely prefer solitude at the moment.

"I don't think she is busy committing suicide, if that is what you mean. But of course I am worried about her. A shock like that would be bad for anyone—especially coming now, at the end of term when one is tired. But Innes—Innes has always cared too much about things." She paused to look at the water again. "When we were Juniors and Madame used to blister us with her sarcasm—Madame can be simply unspeakable, you know—the rest of us just came up in weals but Innes was actually flayed; just raw flesh. She never cried, as some of the others did when they'd had too much for one go. She just—just burned up inside. It's bad for you to burn up inside. And once when—" She stopped, and seemed to decide that she had said enough. Either she had been on the verge of an indiscretion or she came to the conclusion that discussing her friend with a comparative stranger, however sympathetic, was not after all the thing to do. "She has no oil on her feathers, Innes," she finished.

She stepped off the bridge and began to walk away up the path by the willows. "If I was rude," she said, pausing just before she disappeared, "do forgive me. I didn't mean to be."

Lucy went on looking at the smooth silent water, wishing passionately that she could recover the little red book which she had consigned so smugly to the brook two days ago, and thinking of the girl who had no "duck's back"—no protective mechanism against the world's weather. The girl who could neither whimper nor laugh; who "burned up inside" instead. She rather hoped that Beau would not find her until the worst was over; she had not run to Beau for sympathy, she had run as far and as fast from human company as she could, and it seemed only fair to let her have the solitude she sought.

It would do Beau no harm at any rate, Lucy thought, to find that the world had its snags and its disappointments; life had been much too easy for Beau. It was a pity that she had to learn at Innes's expense.

She crossed the bridge into the games field, turned her face to open country and took the hedge gaps as they came; hoping that she might not overtake Innes, and determined to turn a blind eye in her direction if she did. But there was no Innes. No one at all moved in the Sunday landscape. Everyone was still digesting roast beef. She was alone with the hedges of may, the pasture, and the blue sky. Presently she came to the edge of a slope, from which she could look across a shallow valley to successive distances, and there she sat with her back against an oak, while the insects hummed in the grass, and the fat white clouds sailed up and passed, and the slow shadow of the tree circled round her feet. Lucy's capacity for doing nothing was almost endless, and had been the despair of both her preceptors and her friends.

It was not until the sun was at hedge level that she roused herself to further decision. The result of her self-communing was a realisation that she could *not* face College supper tonight; she would walk until she found an inn, and in the half-dark she would come back to a College already hushed by the "bedroom" bell. She made a wide circle round, and in half an hour saw in the distance a steeple she recognised, whereupon she jettisoned her thoughts of an inn and wondered if The Teapot was open on Sundays. Even if it wasn't perhaps she could persuade Miss Nevill to stay her pangs with something out of a can. It was after seven before she reached the outskirts of Bidlington, and she looked at the Martyr's Memorial—the only ugly erection in the place—with something of a fellow interest, but the open door of The Teapot restored her. *Dear* Miss Nevill. Dear large clever business-like accommodating Miss Nevill.

She walked into the pleasant room, already shadowed by the opposite cottages, and found it almost empty. A family party occupied the front window, and in the far corner were a young couple who presumably owned the expensive coupé which was backed in at the end of the garden. She thought it clever of Miss Nevill to manage that the room should still look spotless and smell of flowers after the deluge of a Sunday's traffic in June.

She was looking round for a table when a voice said: "Miss Pym!"

Lucy's first instinct was to bolt: she was in no mood for student chat at the moment; and then she noticed that it was The Nut Tart. The Nut Tart was the female half of the couple in the corner. The male half was undoubtedly "my cousin"; the Rick who thought her adorable and who was referred to in College parlance as "that gigolo."

Desterro rose and came over to meet her—she had charming manners on formal occasions—and drew her over to their table. "But this is lovely!" she said. "We were talking of you, and Rick was saying how much he would like to meet you, and here you are. It is magic. This is my cousin, Richard Gillespie. He was christened Riccardo, but he thinks it sounds too like a cinema star."

"Or a band leader," Gillespie said, shaking hands with her and putting her into a chair. His unaccented manner was very English, and did something to counteract his undoubted resemblance to the more Latin types of screen hero. Lucy saw where the "gigolo" came from; the black smooth hair that grew so thick, the eyelashes, the flare of the nostrils, the thin line of dark moustache were all according to the recipe; but nothing else was, it seemed to Lucy. Looks were what he had inherited from some Latin ancestor; but manner, breeding, and character seemed to be ordinary public school. He was considerably older than Desterro —nearly thirty, Lucy reckoned—and looked a pleasant and responsible person.

They had just ordered, it seemed, and Richard went away to the back premises to command another portion of Bidlington rarebit. "It is a cheese affair," Desterro said, "but not those Welsh things you get in London teashops. It is a very rich cheese sauce on very soft buttery toast, and it is flavoured with odd things like nutmeg—I think it is nutmeg—and things like that, and it tastes divine."

Lucy, who was in no state to care what food tasted like, said that it sounded delicious. "Your cousin is English, then?"

"Oh, yes. We are not what you call first cousins," she explained as Richard came back. "The sister of my father's father married his mother's father."

"In simpler words," Richard said, "our grandparents were brother and sister."

"It may be simpler, but it is not explicit," Desterro said, with all the scorn of a Latin for the Saxon indifference to relationships.

"Do you live in Larborough?" Lucy asked Richard.

"No, I work in London, at our head office. But just now I am doing liaison work in Larborough."

In spite of herself Lucy's eye swivelled round to Desterro, busy with a copy of the menu.

"One of our associated firms is here, and I am working with them for a week or two," Rick said smoothly; and laughed at her with his eyes. And then, to put her mind completely at rest: "I came with a chit to Miss Hodge, vouching for my relationship, my respectability, my solvency, my presentability, my orthodoxy—"

"Oh, be quiet, Rick," Desterro said, "it is not my fault that my father is Brazilian and my mother French. What is saffron dough-cake?"

"Teresa is the loveliest person to take out to a meal," Rick said. "She eats like a starved lion. My other women friends spend the whole evening reckoning the calories and imagining what is happening to their waists."

"Your other women friends," his cousin pointed out a trifle astringently, "have not spent twelve months at Leys Physical Training College, being sweated down to vanishing point and fed on vegetable macedoine."

Lucy, remembering the piles of bread wolfed by the students at every meal, thought this an overstatement.

"When I go back to Brazil I shall live like a lady and eat like a civilised person, and it will be time then to consider my calories."

Lucy asked when she was going back.

"I am sailing on the last day of August. That will give me a little of the English summer to enjoy between the last day of College and my going away. I like the English summer. So green, and gentle, and kind. I like everything about the English except their clothes, their winter, and their teeth. Where is Arlinghurst?"

Lucy, who had forgotten Desterro's abrupt hopping from one subject to another, was too surprised by the name to answer immediately and Rick answered for her. "It's the best girls' school in England," he finished, having described the place. "Why?"

"It is the College excitement at the moment. One of our students is going there straight from Leys. One would think she had at least been made a Dame, to listen to them."

"A legitimate reason for excitement, it seems to me," Rick observed. "Not many people get professional plums straight out of college."

"Yes? It really is an honour then, you think?"

"A very great one, I imagine. Isn't it, Miss Pym?"

"Very."

"Oh, well. I am glad of it. It is sad to think of her wasting the years in a girls' school, but if it is an honour for her, then I am glad."

"For whom?" Lucy asked.

"For Innes, of course."

"Were you not at lunch today?" asked Lucy, puzzled.

"No. Rick came with the car and we went over to the Saracen's Head at Beauminster. Why? What has that to do with this school affair?"

"It isn't Innes who is going to Arlinghurst."

"Not Innes! But they all said she was. Everyone said so."

"Yes, that is what everyone expected, but it didn't turn out like that."

"No? Who is going, then?"

"Rouse."

Desterro stared.

127

"Oh, no. No, that I refuse to believe. It is quite simply not possible."

"It is true, I am afraid."

"You mean that—that someone—that they have preferred that *canaille*, that *espèce d'une*—!"

"Teresa!" warned Rick, amused to see her moved for once. Desterro sat silent for a space, communing with herself.

"If I were not a lady," she said at length in clear tones, "I would *spit*!"

The family party looked over, surprised and faintly alarmed. They decided that it was time they were going, and began to collect their things and reckon up what they had had.

"Now look what you have done," Rick said. "Alarmed the lieges."

At this moment the rarebits arrived from the kitchen, with Miss Nevill's large chintz presence behind them; but The Nut Tart, far from being distracted by the savoury food, remembered that it was from Miss Nevill that she had first had news of the Arlinghurst vacancy, and the subject took a fresh lease of life. It was Rick who rescued Lucy from the loathed subject by pointing out that the rarebit was rapidly cooling; Lucy had a strong feeling that he himself cared nothing for the rarebit, but that he had somehow become aware of her tiredness and her distaste for the affair; and she felt warm and grateful to him and on the point of tears.

"After all," pointed out Rick as The Nut Tart at last turned her attention to her food, "I don't know Miss Innes, but if she is as wonderful as you say she is bound to get a very good post, even if it isn't exactly Arlinghurst."

This was the argument with which Lucy had sought to comfort herself all the long afternoon. It was reasonable, logical, and balanced; and as a sort of moral belladonna-plaster it was so much red flannel. Lucy understood why The Nut Tart rejected it with scorn.

"How would *you* like to have *that* preferred to you?" she demanded through a large mouthful of rarebit. "That" was Rouse. "How would you like to believe that they were going to

128

pay you honour, a fine public honour, and then have them slap your face in front of everyone?"

"Having your teeth kicked in," Beau had called it. Their reactions were remarkably similar. The only difference was that Desterro saw the insult, and Beau the injury.

"And we had such a lovely happy morning in this very room the other day with Innes's father and mother," Desterro went on, her fine eyes wandering to the table where they had sat. This, too, Lucy had been remembering. "Such nice people, Rick; I wish you could see them. We were all nice people together: me, and Miss Pym, and the Inneses *père et mère*, and we had an interval of civilisation and some good coffee. It was charming. And now—"

Between them, Lucy and Rick steered her away from the subject; and it was not until they were getting into the car to go back to Leys that she remembered and began to mourn again. But the distance between Bidlington and Leys as covered by Rick's car was so short that she had no time to work herself up before they were at the door. Lucy said goodnight and was going to withdraw tactfully, but The Nut Tart came with her. "Goodnight, Rick," she said, casually. "You are coming on Friday, aren't you?"

"Nothing will stop me," Rick assured her. "Three o'clock, is it?"

"No, half-past two. It is written on your invitation card. The invitation I sent you. For a business person you are not very accurate."

"Oh, well, my business things I naturally keep in files."

"And where do you keep my invitation?"

"On a gold chain between my vest and my heart," Rick said, and went the winner out of that exchange.

"Your cousin is charming," Lucy said, as they went up the steps together.

"You think so? I am very glad. I think so too. He has all the English virtues, and a little spice of something that is not English virtue at all. I am glad he is coming to see me dance on Friday. What makes you smile?"

Lucy, who had been smiling at this typically Desterro view

of her cousin's presence on Friday, hastened to change the subject.

"Shouldn't you be going in by the other door?"

"Oh, yes, but I don't suppose anyone will mind. In a fortnight I shall be free to come up these steps if I like—I shall not like, incidentally—so I might as well use them now. I do not take well to tradesmen's entrances."

Lucy had meant to pay her respects to the Staff before going to her room in the wing, but the hall was so quiet, the air of the house so withdrawn, that she was discouraged and took the line of least resistance. She would see them all in the morning.

The Nut Tart paid at least a token obedience to College rules, and it was apparent from the hush in the wing corridor that the "bedroom" bell must have gone some minutes ago; so they said goodnight at the top of the stairs, and Lucy went away to her room at the far end. As she undressed she found that her ear was waiting for a sound from next door. But there was no sound at all; nor was there any visible light from the window, as she noticed when she drew her own curtains. Had Innes not come back?

She sat for a while wondering whether she should do something about it. If Innes had not come back, Beau would be in need of comfort. And if Innes had come back and was silent, was there perhaps some impersonal piece of kindness, some small service, that she could do to express her sympathy without intrusion?

She switched off her light and drew back the curtains, and sat by the open window looking at the brightly lit squares all round the little quadrangle—it was considered an eccentricity to draw a curtain in this community—watching the separate activities of the now silent and individual students. One was brushing her hair, one sewing something, one putting a bandage on her foot (a Foolish Virgin that one; she was hopping about looking for a pair of scissors instead of having begun with the implement already laid out, like a good masseuse), one wriggling into a pyjama jacket, one swatting a moth.

Two lights went out as she watched. Tomorrow the waking bell would go at half-past five again, and now that examinations were over they need no longer stay awake till the last moment over their note-books.

She heard footsteps come along her own corridor, and got up, thinking they were coming at her. Innes's door opened quietly, and shut. No light was switched on, but she heard the soft movements of someone getting ready for bed. Then bedroom slippers in the corridor, and a knock. No answer.

"It's me: Beau," a voice said; and the door was opened. The murmur of voices as the door closed. The smell of coffee and the faint chink of china.

It was sensible of Beau to meet the situation with food. Whatever demons Innes had wrestled with during the long hours between one o'clock and ten she must now be empty of emotion and ready to eat what was put in front of her. The murmur of voices went on until the "lights out" bell sounded; then the door opened and closed again, and the silence next-door merged into the greater silence that enveloped Leys.

Lucy fell into bed, too tired almost to pull up the covers; angry with Henrietta, sad for Innes, and a little envious of her in that she had a friend like Beau.

She decided to stay awake a little and think of some way in which she could express to poor Innes how great was her own sympathy and how deep her own indignation; and fell instantly asleep.

~~~~~~

· 14 ·

MONDAY was an anticlimax. Lucy came back into a community that had talked itself out on the subject of Arlinghurst. Both Staff and students had had a whole day's leisure in which to spread themselves over the sensation, and by night-time there was nothing more to be said; indeed every possible view had already been repeated *ad nauseam*; so that with the resumption of routine on Monday the affair had already slipped into the background. Since she still had her breakfast brought to her by the devoted Miss Morris, she was not there to see Innes's first public appearance; and by the time she came face to face with the students as a body, at lunch, habit had smoothed over the rough places and College looked much as usual.

Innes's face was composed, but Lucy thought that its normal withdrawn expression had become a shut-down look; whatever emotions she still wrestled with, they were under hatches and battened down. Rouse looked more than ever like Aunt Celia's cat, Philadelphia, and Lucy longed to shut her out-of-doors and let her mew. The only curiosity she had had about the affair was to know how Rouse took that unexpected announcement; she had even gone the length of asking Miss Lux on the way down to lunch.

"What did Rouse look like when she heard the news?"

"Ectoplasm," said Miss Lux.

"Why ectoplasm?" Lucy had asked, puzzled.

"It is the most revolting thing I can think of."

So her curiosity remained unsatisfied. Madame twitted her about her desertion of them yesterday, but no one wanted to harp on the probable reason for it. Already the shadow of the Demonstration, only four days away, loomed large over them all; Arlinghurst was a yesterday's sensation and already a little stale. College was once more into its stride.

Indeed only two small incidents livened the monotony of routine between Monday and Friday.

The first was Miss Hodge's offer to Innes of the post at the Wycherley Orthopaedic Hospital, and Innes's refusal of it. The post was then offered to and gratefully accepted by a much-relieved O'Donnell. ("*Darling*, how *nice!*" Dakers had said. "Now I can sell you my clinic overalls which I shall *never* use again, my dear." And sell them she did; and was so delighted to have good hard cash in her purse so near the end of term that she instantly began to hawk the rest of her belongings round the wing, and was only dissuaded when Stewart asked caustically if the safety-pins were standard equipment.)

The second incident was the arrival of Edward Adrian, thespian. This unlooked-for occurrence took place on Wednesday. Wednesday was swimming afternoon, and all the Juniors and such Seniors as had no afternoon patients were down at the pool. Lucy, who by prayer, counting, and determination, could just get across the bath, took no part in this exercise in spite of warm invitations to come in and be cool. She spent half an hour watching the gambols, and then walked back to the house for tea. She was crossing the hall to the stairs when one of the Disciples —she thought it was Luke, but she was still not quite certain about them—dashed out of the clinic door and said:

"Oh, Miss Pym, would you be an angel and sit on Albert's feet for a moment?"

"Sit on Albert's feet?" repeated Lucy, not quite sure that she had heard aright.

"Yes, or hold them. But it's easier to sit on them. The hole in the strap has given way, and there isn't another that isn't in use." She ushered the dazed Lucy into the quiet of the clinic, where students swathed in unfamiliar white linen superintended their patients' contortions, and indicated a plinth where a boy of eleven or so was lying face down. "You see," she said, holding up a leather strap, "the thing has torn away from the hole, and the hole in front is too tight and the one behind too loose. If you would just hang on to his feet for a moment; if you wouldn't rather sit on them."

Lucy said hastily that she would prefer to hang on.

"All right. This is Miss Pym, Albert. She is going to be the strap for the nonce."

"Hullo, Miss Pym," said Albert, rolling an eye round at her.

Luke—if it was she—seized the boy under the shoulders and yanked him forward till only his legs remained on the plinth. "Now clamp a hand over each ankle and hang on, Miss Pym," she commanded, and Lucy obeyed, thinking how well this breezy bluntness was going to suit Manchester and how extremely heavy a small boy of eleven was when you were trying to keep his ankles down. Her eyes strayed from what Luke was doing to the others, so strange and remote in this new guise. Was there no end to the facets of this odd life? Even the ones she knew well, like Stewart, were different, seen like this. Their movements were slower, and there was a special bright artificially-interested voice that they used to patients. There were no smiles and no chatter; just a bright hospital quiet. "Just a *little* further. *That's* right." "That is looking much better today, isn't it!" "Now, we'll try that once more and then that will be all for today."

Through a gap in Hasselt's overall as she moved, Lucy caught a glimpse of silk, and realised that she was already changed for dancing, there being no interval between finishing her patient and appearing in the gym. Either she had already had tea, or would snatch a cup en route.

While she was thinking of the oddity of this life of dancing silks under hospital clothes, a car passed the window and stopped at the front door. A very fashionable and expensive car of inordinate length and great glossiness, chauffeur-driven. It was so seldom nowadays that one saw anyone but an invalid driven by a chauffeur that she watched with interest to see who might emerge from it.

Beau's mother, perhaps? That was the kind of car that went with a butler, undoubtedly.

But what came out of the car was a youngish man—she could see only his back—in the kind of suit one sees anywhere between St. James's Street and the Duke of York's Steps any time between October and the end of June. What with the chauffeur and the suit Lucy ran through in her mind the available Royalties, but could not find an appropriate one; Royalty drove itself nowadays, anyhow.

"Thank you very much, Miss Pym. You've been an enormous help. Say thank you, Albert."

"Thank you, Miss Pym," Albert said dutifully; and then, catching her eye, winked at her. Lucy winked back, gravely.

At this moment O'Donnell erupted into the room clutching the large sifter of talcum powder that she had been having refilled by Fröken in the further room, and hissed in an excited whisper: "What do you think! *Edward Adrian!* In the car. *Edward Adrian!*"

"Who cares?" Stewart said, relieving her of the sifter. "You were a damned long time getting the talc."

Lucy closed the clinic door behind her and emerged into the hall. O'Donnell had spoken truth. It was Edward Adrian who was standing in the hall. And Miss Lux had also spoken truth. For Edward Adrian was examining himself in the mirror.

As Lucy climbed the stairs she met Miss Lux coming down, and as she turned to the second flight could see their meeting.

"Hullo, Teddy," Miss Lux said, without enthusiasm.

"Catherine!" Adrian said, with the most delighted enthusiasm, going forward to meet her as if about to embrace her. But her cool solitary hand, outstretched in conventional greeting, stopped him.

"What are you doing here? Don't tell me you have developed a 'niece' at Leys."

"Don't be a beast, Cath. I came to see you, of course. Why didn't you tell me you were here? Why didn't you come to see me, so that we could have had a meal together, and a talk about old——"

"Miss Pym," Miss Lux's clear accents came floating up the staircase, "don't run away. I want you to meet a friend of mine."

"But Catherine——" she heard him say in quick low protest.

"It's the *famous* Miss Pym," Miss Lux said, in a you'll-like-that-you-silly-creature tone, "and a great admirer of yours," she added as a final snare.

Does he realise how cruel she is being? she wondered as she waited for them to come up to her, or is his self-satisfaction too great to be pierced by her rating of him?

As they went together into the deserted drawing-room, she remembered suddenly Stewart's description of him as a "weary-looking creature who looked like a moulting eagle" and thought how apt it was. He had good looks of a sort, but although he could not be much older than forty—forty-three or four, perhaps—they already had a preserved air. Without his paints and his pencils and his toupees, he looked tired and worn, and his dark hair was receding. Lucy felt suddenly sorry for him. With the youth and strength and beauty of Desterro's Rick fresh in her mind, she found the spoiled and famous actor somehow pitiful.

He was being charming to her—he knew all about her book; he read all the best-sellers—but with one eye on Miss Lux while she examined what was left of tea, inspected the contents of the tea-pot, and apparently deciding that a little more hot water would meet the case, lit the burner under the tea-kettle again. There was something in that consciousness of Catherine Lux's presence that puzzled Lucy. It wasn't in the part, as she had

135

imagined the part for him. The successful star calling on the humble lecturer at a girls' college should surely show more detachment; more willingness to peacock in front of the stranger, after the manner of actors. He was "doing his act" for her, of course; all his charm was turned full on, and it was a very considerable charm; but it was mere reflex action. All his interest was centred round the cool scraggy woman who rated him at some washy tea. It couldn't be very often, Lucy thought with amusement, that Edward Adrian arrived on any doorstep without trumpets; for nearly twenty years—ever since that first heart-breaking Romeo had brought tears to the eyes of critics sick of the very name of Montague—his comings and goings had been matters of moment, he had moved in a constant small eddy of importance; people ran to do his bidding and waited for his pleasure; they gave him things and asked nothing in return; they gave up things for him and expected no thanks. He was Edward Adrian, household word, two feet high on the bills, national possession.

But he had come out this afternoon to Leys to see Catherine Lux, and his eyes followed her round like an eager dog's. The Catherine whose estimate of him was a little hot water added to the tea-pot. It was all very strange.

"I hope you are doing well in Larborough, Teddy?" Lux asked, with more politeness than interest.

"Oh, yes; fair. Too many schools, but one must put up with that when one plays Shakespeare."

"Don't you like playing to young people?" Lucy asked, remembering that the young people she had met lately had not greatly liked having to listen to him.

"Well—they don't make the best audience in the world, you know. One would prefer adults. And they get cut rates, of course; which doesn't help the takings. But we look on it as an investment," he added with generous tolerance. "They are the future theatre-goers, and must be trained up in the way they should go."

Lucy thought that the training, if judged by results, had been singularly unsuccessful. The way the young went was in a bee-line to something called *Flaming Barriers*. It wasn't even true to say that they "didn't go" to the theatre; it was much more positive than that: they fled from it.

However, this was a polite tea-party and no time for home truth. Lucy asked if he was coming to the Demonstration—at which Miss Lux looked annoyed. He had never heard of a Demonstration and was all eagerness. It was years since he had seen anyone do any more P.T. than putting their toes under the wardrobe and waving their torso about. Dancing? Goodness, was there dancing? But of course he would come. And what was more, they should come back with him to the theatre and have supper with him afterwards.

"I know Catherine hates the theatre, but you could stand it for once, couldn't you, Catherine? It's *Richard III* on Friday night, so you wouldn't have to put up with me in a romantic effort. It isn't a good play, but the production is wonderful, even if it is I who say it that shouldn't."

"A criminal libel on a fine man, a blatant piece of political propaganda, and an extremely silly play," Lux opined.

Adrian smiled broadly, like a schoolboy. "All right, but sit through it and you shall see how good a supper the Midland at Larborough can provide when egged on by a miserable actor. They even have a Johannisberger."

A faint colour showed in Lux's cheek at that.

"You see I remember what you like. Johannisberger, as you once remarked, tastes of flowers, and will take the stink of the theatre out of your nostrils."

"I never said it stank. It creaks."

"Of course it does. It has been on its last legs for quite two hundred years."

"Do you know what it reminds me of? The Coronation Coach. A lumbering anachronism; an absurd convention that we go on making use of because of inherited affection. A gilded relic——"

The kettle boiled, and Miss Lux poured the hot water into the pot.

"Give Miss Pym something to eat, Teddy."

An almost nursery tone, Lucy thought, taking one of the curled-up sandwiches from the plate he offered her. Was that

137

what attracted him? Was it a sort of nostalgia for a world where he was taken for granted? He would not like such a world for long, that was certain, but it was quite possible that he wearied sometimes of the goldfish life he led, and would find a refreshment in the company of someone to whom he was just Teddy Adrian who used to come in the holidays.

She turned to say something to him, and surprised the look in his eyes as he watched Catherine spurning the various eatables. The amusement, the affection, that lit them might be a brother's, but there was something else. A—hopelessness, was it? Something like that. Something, anyhow, that had nothing to do with brotherliness; and that was very odd in a Great Star looking at the plain and ironic Mistress of Theory at Leys.

She looked across at the unconscious Catherine, and for the first time saw her as Edward Adrian saw her. As a woman with the makings of a *belle laide*. In this scholastic world one accepted her "good" clothes, her simple hairdressing, her lack of make-up, as the right and appropriate thing, and took her fine bones and lithe carriage for granted. She was just the plain and clever Miss Lux. But in the theatre world how different she would be! That wide supple mouth, those high cheek bones with the hollow under them, the short straight nose, the good line of the lean jaw —they cried aloud for make-up. From the conventional point of view Lux had the kind of face that, as errand boys say, would "stop a clock"; but from any other view-point it was a face that would stop them eating at the Iris if she walked in at lunch time properly dressed and made-up.

A combination of *belle laide* and someone who knew him "when" was no inconsiderable attraction. For the rest of tea-time Lucy's mind was busy with revision.

As soon as she decently could she retired, leaving them to the tête-à-tête that he had so obviously sought; the tête-à-tête that Miss Lux had done her best to deny him. He pleaded once more for a theatre party on Friday night—his car would be there and the Dem. would be over by six o'clock and College supper would be nothing but an anti-climax, and *Richard III* might be a lot of nonsense but it *was* lovely to look at, he promised them, and the food at the Midland was really wonderful since they had

138

lured the chef away from Bono in Dover Street, and it was a very long time since he had seen Catherine and he had not talked half enough to the clever Miss Pym who had written that wonderful book, and he was dead sick anyhow of the company of actors who talked nothing but theatre and golf, and just to please him they might come—and altogether what with his practised actor's charm and his genuine desire that they should say yes, it was agreed that on Friday night they should go back to Larborough with him, witness his production of *Richard III,* and be rewarded with a good supper and a lift home.

As she crossed to the wing, however, Lucy found herself a little depressed. Yet once more she had been wrong about Miss Lux. Miss Lux was not an unwanted plain woman who found compensation in life by devoting herself to a beautiful younger sister. She was a potentially attractive creature who so little needed compensation that she couldn't be bothered with one of the most successful and handsome men in the world today.

She had been all wrong about Miss Lux. As a psychologist she began to suspect she was a very good teacher of French.

• 15 •

THE only person who was moved by Edward Adrian's incursion into the College world was Madame Lefevre. Madame, as the representative of the theatre world in College, evidently felt that her own share in this visit should have been a larger one. She also gave Miss Lux to understand that she had, in the first place, no right to know Edward Adrian, but that, in the second place, having known him she had no right to keep him to herself. She was comforted by the knowledge that on Friday she would see him in person, and be able to talk to him in his own language, so to speak. He must have felt greatly at sea, she gave them to understand, among the aborigines of Leys Physical Training College.

Lucy, listening to her barbed silkinesses at lunch on Thursday, hoped that she would not ingratiate herself sufficiently with Adrian to be included in the supper party; she was looking forward to Friday night, and she most certainly would not look

139

forward any more if Madame was going to be watching her all evening with those eyes of hers. Perhaps Miss Lux would put a spoke in her wheel in time. It was not Miss Lux's habit to put up with something that was not to her mind.

Still thinking of Madame and Miss Lux and tomorrow night, she turned her eyes absently on the students, and saw Innes's face. And her heart stopped.

It was three days, she supposed, since she had seen Innes for more than a moment in passing; but could three days have done this to a young girl's face? She stared, trying to decide where the change actually lay. Innes was thinner, and very pale, certainly, but it was not that. It was not even the shadows under her eyes and the small hollow at the temple. Not even the expression; she was eating her lunch with her eyes on the plate in apparent calm. And yet the face shocked Lucy. She wondered if the others saw; she wondered that no one had mentioned it. The thing was as subtle and as obvious as the expression on the face of the Mona Lisa; as indefinable and as impossible to ignore.

So that is what it is to "burn up inside," she thought. "It is bad to burn up inside," Beau had said. Verily it must be bad if it ravaged a face like that. How could a face be at the same time calm and—and look like that? How, if it came to that, could one have birds tearing at one's vitals and still keep that calm face?

Her glance went to Beau, at the head of the nearer table, and she caught Beau's anxious look at Innes.

"I hope you gave Mr Adrian an invitation card?" Miss Hodge said to Lux.

"No," said Lux, bored with the subject of Adrian.

"And I hope you have told Miss Joliffe that there will be one more for tea."

"He doesn't eat at tea-time, so I didn't bother."

Oh, stop talking little sillinesses, Lucy wanted to say, and look at Innes. What is happening to her? Look at the girl who was so radiant only last Saturday afternoon. *Look* at her. What does she remind you of? Sitting there so calm and beautiful and all wrong inside. What does she remind you of? One of those brilliant things that grow in the woods, isn't it? One of those apparently perfect things that collapse into dust at a touch because they are hollow inside.

"Innes is not looking well," she said in careful understatement to Lux as they went upstairs.

"She is looking very ill," Lux said bluntly. "And would you wonder?"

"Isn't there something one can do about it?" Lucy asked.

"One could find her the kind of post she deserves," Lux said dryly. "As there is no post available at all, that doesn't seem likely to materialise."

"You mean that she will just have to begin to answer advertisements?"

"Yes. It is only a fortnight to the end of term, and there are not likely to be any more posts in Miss Hodge's gift now. Most places for September are filled by this time. The final irony, isn't it? That the most brilliant student we have had for years is reduced to application-in-own-handwriting-with-five copies-of-testimonials-not-returnable."

It was damnable, Lucy thought; quite damnable.

"She *was* offered a post, so that lets Miss Hodge out."

"But it was a medical one, and she doesn't want that," Lucy said.

"Oh, yes, yes! you don't have to convert me; I'm enlisted already."

Lucy thought of tomorrow, when the parents would come and radiant daughters would show them round, full of the years they had spent here and the new achievement that was theirs. How Innes must have looked forward to that; looked forward to seeing the two people who loved her so well and who had by care and deprivation managed to give her the training she wanted; looked forward to putting Arlinghurst in their laps.

It was bad enough to be a leaving student without a post, but that was a matter susceptible to remedy. What could never be remedied was the injustice of it. It was Lucy's private opinion that injustice was harder to bear than almost any other inflicted ill. She could remember yet the surprised hurt, the helpless rage, the despair that used to consume her when she was young and the victim of an injustice. It was the helpless rage that was worst; it consumed one like a slow fire. There was no outlet, because there was nothing one could do about it. A very destructive emotion indeed. Lucy supposed that she had been like Innes, and lacked a sense of humour. But did the young ever have the detachment necessary for a proper focusing of their own griefs? Of course not. It was not people of forty who went upstairs and hanged themselves because someone had said a wrong word to them at the wrong moment, it was adolescents of fourteen.

Lucy thought she knew the passion of rage and disappointment and hate that was eating Innes up. It was enormously to her credit that she had taken the shock with outward dignity. A different type would have babbled to all and sundry, and collected sympathy like a street singer catching coins in a hat. But not Innes. A sense of humour she might lack—oil on her feathers, as Beau said—but the suffering that lack entailed was her own affair; not to be exhibited to anyone—least of all to people she unconsciously referred to as "them."

Lucy had failed to think of a nice non-committal way of expressing her sympathy; flowers and sweets and all the conventional marks of active friendship were not to be considered, and she had found no substitute; and she was disgusted with herself now to realise that Innes's trouble, even though it was next-door to her all night, had begun to fade into the back-ground for her. She had remembered it each night as Innes came to her room after the "bedroom" bell, and while the small noises next-door reminded her of the girl's existence. She had wondered and fretted about her for a little before falling to sleep. But during the crowded many-faceted days she had come near forgetting her.

Rouse had made no move to give a Post party on Saturday night; but whether this was due to tact, an awareness of College feeling on the subject, or the natural thrift with which, it seemed, she was credited, no one knew. The universal party that had been so triumphantly planned for Innes was no more heard of; a universal party for Rouse was something that was apparently not contemplated.

Although, even allowing for the fact that Lucy had not been present at the height of the excitement when presumably tongues would have wagged with greater freedom, College had been strangely reticent about the Arlinghurst appointment. Even little

Miss Morris, who chattered with a fine lack of inhibition every morning as she planked the tray down, made no reference to it. In this affair Lucy was for College purposes "Staff"; an outsider; perhaps a sharer in blame. She did not like the idea at all.

But what she liked least of all, and now could not get out of her mind, was Innes's barren tomorrow. The tomorrow that she had slaved those years for, the tomorrow that was to have been such a triumph. Lucy longed to provide her with a post at once, instantly, here and now; so that when tomorrow that tired happy woman with the luminous eyes came at last to see her daughter she would not find her empty-handed.

But of course one could not hawk a P.T.I. from door to door like a writing-pad; nor offer her to one's friends like a misfit frock. Goodwill was not enough. And goodwill was practically all she had.

Well, she would use the goodwill and see where it got her. She followed Miss Hodge into her office as the others went upstairs, and said: "Henrietta, can't we *invent* a post for Miss Innes? It seems all wrong that she should be jobless."

"Miss Innes will not be long jobless. And I can't imagine what consolation an imaginary post would be to her meanwhile."

"I didn't say imagine, I said invent; manufacture. There must be dozens of places all up and down the country that are still vacant. Couldn't we bring the job and Innes together somehow without her going through the slow suspense of applying? That waiting, Henrietta. Do you remember what it used to be like? The beautifully written applications and the testimonials that never came back."

"I have already offered Miss Innes a post and she has refused it. I don't know what more I can do. I have no more vacancies to offer."

"No, but you could get in touch with some of those advertised vacancies on her behalf, couldn't you?"

"I? But that would be most irregular. And quite unnecessary. She naturally gives my name as a reference when she applies; and if she were not commendable——"

"But you could—oh, you could ask for particulars of the post since you have a particularly brilliant student——"

143

"You are being absurd, Lucy."

"I know, but I want Innes to be very much sought-after by five o'clock this afternoon."

Miss Hodge, who did not read Kipling—or indeed, acknowledge his existence—stared.

"For a woman who has written such a noteworthy book—Professor Beatock praised it yesterday at the University College tea—you have an extraordinarily impulsive and frivolous mind."

This defeated Lucy, who was well aware of her mental limitations. Punctured, she stood looking at Henrietta's broad back in the window.

"I am greatly afraid," Henrietta said, "that the weather is going to break. The forecast this morning was anything but reassuring, and after so long a spell of perfect summer we are due for a change. It would be a tragedy if it decided to change tomorrow of all days."

A tragedy, would it! My God, you big lumbering silly woman, it is you who have the frivolous mind. I may have a C₃ intelligence and childish impulses but I know tragedy when I see it and it has nothing to do with a lot of people running to save their party frocks or the cucumber sandwiches getting wet. No, by God, it hasn't.

"Yes, it would be a pity, Henrietta," she said meekly, and went away upstairs.

She stood for a little at the landing window watching the thick black clouds massing on the horizon, and hoping evilly that tomorrow they would swamp Leys in one grand Niagara so that the whole place steamed with damp people drying like a laundry. But she noticed almost immediately the heinousness of this, and hastily revised her wish. Tomorrow was their great day, bless them; the day they had sweated for, borne bruises and sarcasm for, been pummelled, broken, and straightened for, hoped, wept, and lived for. It was plain justice that the sun should shine on them.

Besides, it was pretty certain that Mrs Innes had only one pair of "best" shoes.

144

EACH successive day of her stay at Leys saw Lucy a little more wide awake in the mornings. When the monstrous clamour of the 5.30 bell had first hurled her into wakefulness, she had turned on her other side as soon as the noise stopped and had fallen asleep again. But habit was beginning to have its way. Not only did she not fall asleep again after the early waking, but for the last day or two she had been sufficiently conscious to know in some drowsy depths of her that the waking bell was about to ring. On Demonstration morning she made history by wakening before the reveillé.

What woke her was a faint fluttering under the point of her sternum: a feeling that she had not had since she was a child. It was associated with prize-giving days at school. Lucy had always had a prize of sorts. Never anything spectacular, alas—2nd French, 3rd Drawing, 3rd Singing—but she was definitely in the money. Occasionally, too, there was a "piece" to be played —the Rachmaninoff Prelude, for one; not the DA, DA, DA one but the DA-de-de-de; with terrific concentration on the de-de-de —and consequently a new frock. Hence the tremor under the breastbone. And today, all those years afterwards, she had recaptured the sensation. For years any flutterings in that region had been mere indigestion—if indigestion can ever be mere. Now, because she was part of all the young emotion round her, she shared the thrill and the anticipation.

She sat up and looked at the weather. It was blank and grey, with a cool mist that might later lift on a blazing day. She got up and went to the window. The silence was absolute. Nothing stirred in the still greyness but the College cat, picking its way in an annoyed fashion over the dew-wet stones, and shaking each foot in turn as protest against the discomfort. The grass was heavy with dew, and Lucy, who had always had a perverted affection for wet grass, regarded it with satisfaction.

The silence was ripped in two by the bell. The cat, as if suddenly reminded of urgent business, sprang into wild flight. Giddy crunched past on his way to the gymnasium; and presently the faint whine of his vacuum-cleaner could be heard, like some far-distant siren. Groans and yawns and inquiries as to the weather came from the little rooms all round the courtyard, but no one came to a window to look; getting up was an agony to be post-poned to the last moment.

Lucy decided to dress and go out into the dew-grey morning, so cool and damp and beneficent. She would go and see how the buttercups looked without the sun on them. Wet gamboge, probably. She washed sketchily, dressed in the warmest things she had with her, and slinging a coat over her shoulders went out into the silent corridor and down the deserted stairs. She paused by the quadrangle door to read the notices on the students' board; cryptic, esoteric, and plain. "Students are reminded that parents and visitors may be shown over the bedroom wings and the clinic, but not the front of the house." "Juniors are reminded that it is their duty to wait on the guests at tea and so help the domestic staff." And, by itself, in capitals, the simple statement:

DIPLOMAS WILL BE PRESENTED ON
TUESDAY MORNING AT 9 O'CLOCK

As she moved on towards the covered way, Lucy visualised the diploma as an imposing roll of parchment tied up with ribbon, and then remembered that even in the matter of diplomas this place was a law unto itself. Their diploma was a badge to stick in their coat; a little enamel-and-silver affair that, pinned to the left breast of their working garment, would tell all and sundry where they had spent their student years and to what end.

Lucy came out into the covered way and dawdled along it to the gymnasium. Giddy had long since finished his cleaning opera-tions—she had seen him from her window before she left her room contemplating his roses at the far side of the lawn—and it was apparent that Rouse had already performed her morning routine—the faint damp marks of her gym. shoes were visible on the concrete path—so the gymnasium was deserted. Lucy paused as she was about to turn along the path by its side wall, and stepped in at the wide-open door. Just as a race-course is more dramatic before the crowds blur it or an arena before its traffic writes scribbles over it, so the great waiting hall had a fascination for her. The emptiness, the quiet, the green sub-aqueous light, gave it a dignity and a mysteriousness that did not belong to its daytime personality. The single boom that Rouse used swam in the shadows, and the liquid light of the mirrors under the gallery wavered at the far end in vague repetition.

Lucy longed to shout a command so as to hear her voice in this empty space; or to climb a ribstall and see if she could do it without having heart-failure; but she contented herself with gazing. At her age gazing was enough; and it was a thing that she was good at.

Something winked on the floor half-way between her and the boom; something tiny and bright. A nail-head or something, she thought; and then remembered that there were no nail-heads in a gymnasium floor. She moved forward, idly curious, and picked the thing up. It was a small filigree rosette, flat, and made of silvery metal; and as she put it absently into her jersey pocket and turned away to continue her walk, she smiled. If the quiver under her sternum this morning had reminded her of school days, that small metal circle brought back even more clearly the parties of her childhood. Almost before her conscious mind had recognised it for what it was she was back in the atmosphere of crackers-and-jellies and white silk frocks, and was wearing on her feet a pair of bronze leather pumps with elastic that criss-crossed over the ankle and a tiny silver filigree rosette on each toe. Going down the path to the field gate, she took it out again and smiled over it, remembering. She had quite forgotten those bronze pumps; there were black ones too, but all the best people wore bronze ones. She wondered who in College possessed a pair. College wore ballet shoes for dancing, with or without blocked toes; and their gymnasium shoes were welted leather with an elastic instep. She had never seen anyone wear those pumps with the little ornament at the toe.

Perhaps Rouse used them for running down to the gymnasium in the mornings. It was certainly this morning the ornament had been dropped, since The Abhorrence under Giddy's direction was guaranteed to abstract from the gymnasium everything that was not nailed down.

She hung over the gate for a little but it was chilly there and disappointing; the trees were invisible in the mist, the buttercups a mere rust on the grey meadow, and the may hedges looked like dirty snow. She did not want to go back to the house before breakfast, so she walked along to the tennis courts where the Juniors were mending nets—this was odd-job day for everyone, they said, this being the one day in the year when they conserved their energies against a greater demand to come—and with them she stayed, talking and lending a hand, until they went up to College for breakfast. When they marvelled at her early rising little Miss Morris had suggested that she was tired of cold toast in her room, but when she said frankly that she could not sleep for excitement they were gratified by so proper an emotion in an alien breast, and promised that the reality would beggar expectation. She had not seen anything yet, it seemed.

She changed her wet shoes, suffered the friendly gibes of the assembled Staff at her access of energy, and went down with them to breakfast.

It was when she turned to see how Innes was looking this morning that she became aware of a gap in the pattern of bright heads. She did not know the pattern well enough to know who was missing, but there was certainly an empty place at one of the tables. She wondered if Henrietta knew. Henrietta had cast the usual critical eye over the assembly as she sat down, but as the assembly was also at that moment in the act of sitting down the pattern was blurred and any gap not immediately visible.

Hastily, in case Henrietta did not in fact know about that gap, she withdrew her gaze without further investigation. It was none of her wish to call down retribution on the head of any student, however delinquent. Perhaps, of course, someone had just "gone sick"; which would account for the lack of remark where their absence was concerned.

Miss Hodge, having wolfed her fish-cake, laid down her fork and swept the students with her small elephant eye. "Miss Wragg," she said, "ask Miss Nash to speak to me."

Nash got up from her place at the head of the nearest table and presented herself.

"Is it Miss Rouse who is missing from Miss Stewart's table?"

"Yes, Miss Hodge."

"Why has she not come to breakfast?"

"I don't know, Miss Hodge."

"Send one of the Juniors to her room to ask why she is not here."

"Yes, Miss Hodge."

A stolid amiable Junior called Tuttle, who was always having to take the can back, was sent on the mission, and came back to say that Rouse was not in her room; which report Beau bore to the head table.

"Where was Miss Rouse when you saw her last?"

"I can't remember actually seeing her at all, Miss Hodge. We were all over the place this morning doing different things. It wasn't like sitting in class or being in the gym."

"Does anyone," said Henrietta addressing the students as a whole, "know where Miss Rouse is?"

But no one did, apparently.

"Has anyone seen her this morning?"

But no one, now they came to think of it, had seen her.

Henrietta, who had put away two slices of toast while Tuttle was upstairs, said: "Very well, Miss Nash," and Beau went back to her breakfast. Henrietta rolled up her napkin and caught Fröken's eye, but Fröken was already rising from table, her face anxious.

"You and I will go to the gymnasium, Fröken," Henrietta said, and they went out together, the rest of the Staff trailing after them but not following them out to the gymnasium. It was only on the way upstairs to make her bed that it occurred to Lucy to think: "I could have told them that she wasn't in the gymnasium. How silly of me not to think of it." She tidied her room—a task that the students were expected to perform for themselves and which she thought it only fair that she likewise should do for herself—wondering all the time where Rouse could have disappeared to. And why. Could she suddenly have failed

149

again this morning to do that simple boom exercise and been overtaken by a *crise des nerfs*? That was the only explanation that would fit the odd fact of any College student missing a meal; especially breakfast.

She crossed into the "old house" and went down the front stairs and out into the garden. From the office came Henrietta's voice talking rapidly to someone on the telephone, so she did not interrupt her. There was still more than half an hour before Prayers; she would spend it reading her mail in the garden, where the mist was rapidly lifting and a shimmer had come into the atmosphere that had been so dead a grey. She went to her favourite seat at the far edge of the garden overlooking the countryside, and it was not until nine o'clock that she came back. There was no doubt about the weather now: it was going to be a lovely day; Henrietta's "tragedy" was not going to happen.

As she came round the corner of the house an ambulance drove away from the front door down the avenue. She looked at it, puzzled; but decided that in a place like this an ambulance was not the thing of dread that it was to the ordinary civilian. Something to do with the clinic, probably.

In the drawing-room, instead of the full Staff muster demanded by two minutes to nine o'clock, there was only Miss Lux.

"Has Rouse turned up?" Lucy asked.

"Yes."

"Where was she?"

"In the gymnasium, with a fractured skull."

Even in that moment of shock Lucy thought how typical of Lux that succinct sentence was. "But *how?* What happened?"

"The pin that holds up the boom wasn't properly in. When she jumped up to it it came down on her head."

"Good heavens!" Lucy could feel that inert log crash down on her own skull; she had always hated the boom.

"Fröken has just gone away with her in the ambulance to West Larborough."

"That was smart work."

"Yes. West Larborough is not far, and luckily at this hour of the morning the ambulance hadn't gone out, and once it was on the way here there was no traffic to hold it up."

"What dreadful luck for everyone. On Demonstration Day."

"Yes. We tried to keep it from the students but that was hopeless, of course. So all we can do is to minimise it."

"How bad is it, do you think?"

"No one knows. Miss Hodge has wired to her people."

"Weren't they coming to the Dem.?"

"Apparently not. She has no parents; just an aunt and uncle who brought her up. Come to think of it," she added after a moment's silence, "that is what she looked like: a stray." She did not seem to notice that she had used the past tense.

"I suppose it was Rouse's own fault?" Lucy asked.

"Or the student who helped her put up the thing last night."

"Who was that?"

"O'Donnell, it seems. Miss Hodge has sent for her to ask her about it."

At that moment Henrietta herself came in, and all the vague resentments that Lucy had been nursing against her friend in the last few days melted at sight of Henrietta's face. She looked ten years older, and in some odd fashion at least a stone less heavy.

"They have a telephone, it seems," she said, continuing the subject that was the only one in her mind, "so I shall be able to talk to them perhaps before the telegram reaches them. They are getting the trunk call for me now. They should be here before night. I want to be available for the telephone call, so will you take Prayers, Miss Lux. Fröken will not be back in time." Fröken was, as Senior Gymnast, second in rank to Miss Hodge. "Miss Wragg may not be at Prayers; she is getting the gymnasium put to rights. But Madame will be there, and Lucy will back you up."

"But of course," said Lucy. "I wish there was something more that I could do."

There was a tap at the door, and O'Donnell appeared.

"Miss Hodge? You wanted to see me?"

"Oh, in my office, Miss O'Donnell."

"You weren't there, so I—"

"Not that it matters, now that you are here. Tell me: when you put up the boom with Miss Rouse last night—It *was* you who helped her?"

"Yes, Miss Hodge."

"When you put up the boom with her, which end did you take?"

There was a tense moment of silence. It was obvious that O'Donnell did not know which end of the boom had given way and that what she said in the next few seconds would either damn her or save her. But when she spoke it was with a sort of despairing resolution that stamped what she said with truth.

"The wall end, Miss Hodge."

"You put the pin into the upright that is fixed to the wall?"

"Yes."

"And Miss Rouse took care of the upright in the middle of the floor."

"Yes, Miss Hodge."

"You have no doubt as to which end you attended to?"

"No, none at all."

"Why are you so certain?"

"Because I always did do the end by the wall."

"Why was that?"

"Rouse is taller than I am and could shove the boom higher than I could. So I always took the end by the wall so that I could put a foot in the ribstalls when I was putting the pin in."

"I see. Very well. Thank you, Miss O'Donnell, for being so frank."

O'Donnell turned to go, and then turned back.

"Which end came down, Miss Hodge?"

"The middle end," Miss Hodge said, looking with something like affection on the girl, though she had been on the point of letting her go without putting her out of suspense.

A great wave of colour rushed into O'Donnell's normally pale face. "Oh, thank you!" she said, in a whisper, and almost ran out of the room.

"Poor wretch," said Lux. "That was a horrible moment for her."

"It is most unlike Miss Rouse to be careless about apparatus," Henrietta said thoughtfully.

"You are not suggesting that O'Donnell is not telling the truth?"

"No, no. What she said was obviously true. It was the natural thing for her to take the wall end where she would have the help of the ribstalls. But I still cannot see how it happened. Apart from Miss Rouse's natural carefulness, a pin would have to be very badly put in indeed for it to be so far *not* in that it let the boom come down. And the hoisting rope so slack that it let the boom fall nearly three feet!"

"I suppose Giddy couldn't have done something to it accidentally?"

"I don't know what he could have done to it. You can't alter a pin put in at that height without stretching up deliberately to it. It is not as if it were something he might possibly touch with his apparatus. And much as he prides himself on the strength of The Abhorrence there is no suction that will pull a pin out from under a boom."

"No." Lux thought a little. "Vibration is the only kind of force that would alter a pin's position. Some kind of tremor. And there was nothing like that."

"Not inside the gymnasium, certainly. Miss Rouse locked it as usual last night and gave the key to Giddy, and he unlocked it just after first bell this morning."

"Then there is no alternative to the theory that for once Rouse was too casual. She was the last to leave the place and the first to come back to it—you wouldn't get anyone there at that hour of the morning who wasn't under the direst compulsion—so the blame is Rouse's. And let us be thankful for it. It is bad enough as it is, but it would be far worse if someone else had been careless and had to bear the knowledge that she was responsible for—"

The bell rang for Prayers, and downstairs the telephone shrilled in its own hysterical manner.

"Have you marked the place in the Prayer book?" Lux asked.

"Where the blue ribbon is," Miss Hodge said, and hurried out to the telephone.

"Has Fröken not come back?" asked Madame, appearing in the doorway. "Ah, well, let us proceed. Life must go on, if I may coin a phrase. And let us hope that this morning's ration of uplift is not too apposite. Holy Writ has a horrible habit of being apposite."

Not for the first time, Lucy wished Madame Lefevre on a lonely island off Australia.

It was a silent and subdued gathering that awaited them, and Prayers proceeded in an atmosphere of despondency that was foreign and unprecedented. But with the hymn they recovered a little. It was Blake's and had a fine martial swing, and they sang it with a will. So did Lucy.

"Nor shall the sword sleep in my hand," she sang, making the most of it. And stopped suddenly, hit in the wind.

Hit in the wind by a jolt that left her speechless.

She had just remembered something. She had just remembered why she had been so sure that Rouse would not be found in the gymnasium. Rouse's damp footprints had been visible on the concrete path, and so she had taken it for granted that Rouse had already been and gone. But Rouse had not been. Rouse had come later, and had sprung to the insecure boom and had lain there until after breakfast when she was searched for.

Then—whose footprints were they?

~~~~~~

· 17 ·

"STUDENTS," said Miss Hodge, rising in her place after lunch and motioning the rest of the Staff to remain seated, "you are all aware of the unfortunate accident which occurred this morning—entirely through the carelessness of the student concerned. The first thing a gymnast learns is to examine apparatus before she uses it. That a student as responsible and altogether admirable as Miss Rouse should have failed in so simple and fundamental a duty is a warning to you all. That is one point. This is the other. This afternoon we are entertaining guests. There is no secret about what happened this morning—we could not keep it secret even if we wanted to—but I do ask you not to make it a subject of conversation. Our guests are coming here to enjoy themselves; and to know that this morning an accident took place sufficiently serious to send one of our students to hospital would undoubtedly take the edge off their pleasure; if indeed it did not fill them with a quite unnecessary apprehension when watch-

154

ing gymnastics. So if any of you have a desire to dramatise today's happenings, please curb it. It is your business to see that your guests go away happy, without reservations or regrets. I leave the matter to your own good sense."

It had been a morning of adjustment; physical, mental, and spiritual. Fröken had come back from the West Larborough hospital to put a worried lot of Seniors through a routine that would allow for the fact that they were one short. Under her robust calm they took the alterations, and necessity for them, with a fair degree of equanimity; although she reported that at least a third of them shied like nervous colts each time they handled the right-hand front boom, or passed the place where it had fallen. It was going to be a miracle, Fröken said with resignation, if they got through this afternoon's performance without someone or other making a fool of themselves. As soon as Fröken had released them Madame Lefevre took them over for a much lengthier session. Thanks to her physical prowess, Rouse had been part of almost every item on the ballet programme; which meant that almost every item had to undergo either patching or reconstruction. This thankless and wearisome business had lasted until nearly lunch-time, and the echoes of it were still audible. Most of the lunch-table conversation appeared to consist of remarks like: "Is it you I give my right hand to when Stewart passes in front of me?" and Dakers lightened the universal anxiety by being overtaken by one of those sudden silences common to all gatherings, which left her announcing loudly that my *dears*, the last hour had *proved* that one could be in two places at the same time.

The most fundamental adjustment, however, occurred when both Fröken and Madame had finished their respective revisions. It was then that Miss Hodge had sent for Innes and offered her Rouse's place at Arlinghurst. Hospital had confirmed Fröken's diagnosis of a fracture, and there was no chance that Rouse would be able for work until many months had passed. How Innes had taken this no one knew; all that anyone knew was that she had accepted. The appointment, having all the qualities of anti-climax and being overshadowed by an authentic sensation, was taken as a matter of course; and as far as Lucy could see neither Staff nor students gave it a thought. Madame's sardonic: "The Deity disposes," was the solitary comment.

But Lucy was less happy about it. A vague uneasy stirring plagued her like some mental indigestion. The patness of the thing worried her. The accident had happened not only opportunely but at the last available moment. Tomorrow there would have been no need for Rouse to go to the gymnasium and practise; there would have been no boom set up and no pin to be insecurely placed. And there were those damp foot-marks in the early morning. If they were not Rouse's own, whose were they? As Lux had very truly observed, no one could be dragged anywhere near the gymnasium at that hour by anything less compelling than wild horses.

It was possible that they were Rouse's prints and that she had done something else before going into the gymnasium for her few minutes on the boom. Lucy could not swear that the footprints actually went into the building; she could remember no actual print on either of the two steps. She had merely seen the damp marks on the covered way and concluded, without thinking about it at all, that Rouse was ahead of her. The prints may have continued round the building, for all she knew. They may have had nothing to do with the gymnasium at all. Nothing to do with the students, even. It was possible that those heelless impressions, so vague and blurred, were made by a maid-servant's early-morning shoes.

All that was possible. But allied to the steps that were not likely to be Rouse's was the oddity of a small metal ornament lying on a floor that had been swept twenty minutes before by a powerful vacuum-cleaner. An ornament lying directly between the door and the waiting boom. And whatever was conjecture, one thing was certain: the ornament was not lost by Rouse. Not only had she almost certainly not been in the gymnasium this morning before Lucy entered it, but she did not possess a pair of pumps. Lucy knew, because one of her helpful chores today had been to pack poor Rouse's things. Miss Joliffe, whose task it would nominally have been, was overwhelmed by preparations for the afternoon's entertainment, and had passed the duty on to Wragg. Wragg had no student to enlist as substitute, since they were all busy with

Madame, and it was not a duty that could be entrusted to a Junior. So Lucy had willingly taken over the job, glad to find a way to be of use. And her first action in Number Fourteen had been to take Rouse's shoes out of the cupboard and look at them.

The only pair that were not there were her gymnastic shoes, which presumably had been what she wore this morning. But to be sure she summoned O'Donnell when she heard the Seniors come back from the gymnasium and said: "You know Miss Rouse very well, don't you? Would you cast your eye over these shoes and tell me whether they are all she had, before I begin packing them."

O'Donnell considered, and said yes, these were all. "Except her gym. shoes," she added. "She was wearing those."

That seemed to settle it.

"Nothing away being cleaned?"

"No, we clean our own—except for our hockey boots in winter."

Well, that seemed to be that. What Rouse had worn this morning were regulation College gym. shoes. It was not off any shoes of Rouse's that the little filigree rosette had come.

Then from where? Lucy asked herself as she packed Rouse's belongings with a care she never accorded her own. From where?

She was still asking herself that as she changed her dress for the party. She put the rosette into one of the small drawers of the dressing-table-desk affair, and dully looked over her scanty collection of clothes for something that would be suitable to a garden-party afternoon. From her second window, the one looking out on the garden, she could see the Juniors busy with small tables and basket-chairs and tea-umbrellas. Their ant-like running about was producing a gay border of colour round three sides of the lawn. The sun streamed down on them, and the picture in its definition and variety of detail was like a Brueghel gone suddenly gay.

But Lucy, looking down at the picture and remembering how she had looked forward to this occasion, felt sick at heart; and could not bring herself yet to acknowledge why she should be heartsick. Only one thing was clear to her. Tonight she must go to Henrietta with the little rosette. When all the excitement

157

was over and Henrietta had time to be quiet and consider, then the problem—if there was a problem—must be handed over to her. She, Lucy, had been wrong last time when she had tried to save Henrietta suffering by dropping the little red book into the water; this time she must do her duty. The rosette was no concern of hers.

No. It was no concern of hers. Certainly not.

She decided that the blue linen with the narrow red belt was sufficiently Hanover Square to satisfy the most critical of parents from the provinces, brushed the suede shoes with the brush so dutifully included by Mrs Montmorency, and went down to help wherever she could be useful.

By two o'clock the first guests were arriving; going into the office to pay their respects to Miss Hodge, and then being claimed by excited offspring. Fathers prodded doubtfully at odd gadgets in the clinic, mothers prodded the beds in the wing, and horticultural uncles prodded Giddy's roses in the garden. She tried to find distraction in "pairing" the parents she met with the appropriate student. She noticed that she was searching unconsciously for Mr and Mrs Innes and anticipating their meeting with something that was half dread. Why dread? she asked herself. There was nothing in the world to dread, was there? Certainly not. Everything was lovely. Innes had after all got Arlinghurst; the day was after all a triumph for her.

She came on them unexpectedly, round the corner of the sweet-pea hedge; Innes walking between them with her arms through theirs and a light on her face. It was not the radiance that had shone in her eyes a week ago, but it was a good enough substitute. She looked worn but at peace; as if some inner battle was over, the issue settled for good or bad.

"You knew them," she said to Miss Pym, indicating her parents, "and you never told me."

It was like meeting old friends, Lucy thought. It was unbelievable that her only traffic with these people had been across a coffee table for an hour on a summer morning. She seemed to have known them all her life. And she felt that they in their turn felt like that about her. They really were glad to see her again. They remembered things and asked about them, referred to things she had said, and generally behaved as if she not only was of importance in their scheme of things, but was actually part of that scheme. And Lucy, used to the gushing indifference of literary parties, felt her heart warm afresh to them.

Innes left them together and went away to get ready for the gymnastic display that would open the afternoon's programme, and Lucy walked over to the gymnasium with them.

"Mary is looking very ill," her mother said. "Is there anything wrong?"

Lucy hesitated, wondering how much Innes had told them.

"She has told us about the accident, and about falling heir to Arlinghurst. I don't suppose she is very happy at profiting by another student's bad luck, but it can't be just that."

Lucy thought that the more they understood about the affair the better it would be if—well, the better it would be anyhow.

"Everyone took it for granted that she would get the appointment in the first place. I think it was a shock to her when she didn't."

"I see. Yes," said Mrs Innes, slowly; and Lucy felt that more explanation was not necessary; the whole tale of Innes's suffering and fortitude was clear to her mother in that moment.

"I think she might not approve of my having told you that, so—"

"No, we will not mention it," said Innes's mother. "How lovely the garden is looking. Gervase and I struggle along with our patch but only his bits look like the illustration; mine always turn out to be something else. Just look at those little yellow roses."

And so they came to the gymnasium door, and Lucy showed them up the stairs and introduced them to The Abhorrence— with pricking thought of a little metal rosette—and they found their seats in the gallery, and the afternoon had begun.

Lucy had a seat at the end of the front row. From there she looked down with affection on the grave young faces waiting, with such tense resolution, Fröken's word of command. "Don't worry," she had heard a Senior say, "Fröken will see us through," and one could see the faith in their eyes. This was their ordeal, and they came to it shaken, but Fröken would see them through.

She understood now the love that had filled Henrietta's eyes when she had watched with her on that other occasion. Less than a fortnight ago, that was, and already she had a proprietorial interest and pride in them. When the autumn came the very map of England would look different to her because of these two weeks at Leys. Manchester would be the place where the Disciples were, Aberystwyth the place where Thomas was trying to stay awake, Ling the place where Dakers was being good with the babies, and so on. If she felt like that about them after a matter of days, it was not much wonder that Henrietta, who had seen them come untried into their new life, had watched them grow and improve, struggle, fail, and succeed, not much wonder that she looked on them as daughters. Successful daughters.

They had got through their preliminaries, and a little of the strain had gone from their faces; they were beginning to settle down. The applause that marked the end of their free-standing work broke the silence and warmed them and made the affair more human.

"What a charming collection," said a dowager with lorgnettes who was sitting next her (now who owned that? she couldn't be a parent) and turning to her confidentially asked: "Tell me, are they hand-picked?"

"I don't understand," murmured Lucy.

"I mean, are these all the Seniors there are?"

"You mean, are these just the best? Oh, no; that is the whole set."

"Really? Quite wonderful. So attractive, too. Quite amazingly attractive."

Did she think we had given the spotty ones half a crown to take themselves off for the afternoon, wondered Lucy.

But of course the dowager was right. Except for a string of two-year-olds in training, Lucy could think of nothing more attractive to mind and eye than that set of burnished and controlled young creatures busy dragging out the booms below her. The ropes rushed down from their looped position near the roof, the window-ladder came to vertical, and over all three pieces of apparatus the Seniors swarmed in easy mastery. The applause as they put ropes and ladder away and turned the booms for balance was real and loud; the spectacular had its appeal.

Very different the place looked from that mysterious vault of greenish shadows that she had visited this morning. It was golden, and matter-of-fact, and alive; the reflected light from the sunlit roof showering down on the pale wood and making it glow. Seeing once more in her mind's eye that dim empty space with the single waiting boom, she turned to see whose lot it might be to perform her balance on the spot where Rouse had been found. Who had the inner end of the right-hand front boom?

It was Innes.

"Go!" said Fröken; and eight young bodies somersaulted up on to the high booms. They sat there for a moment, and then rose in unison to a standing position, one foot in front of the other, facing each other in pairs at opposite ends of each boom.

Lucy hoped frantically that Innes was not going to faint. She was not merely pale; she was green. Her opposite number, Stewart, made a tentative beginning, but, seeing that Innes was not ready, waited for her. But Innes stood motionless, apparently unable to move a muscle. Stewart cast her a glance of wild appeal. Innes remained paralysed. Some wordless message passed between them, and Stewart went on with her exercise; achieving a perfection very commendable in the circumstances. All Innes's faculties were concentrated on keeping her standing position on the boom long enough to be able to return to the floor with the rest, and not to ruin the whole exercise by collapsing, or by jumping off. The dead silence and the concentration of interest made her failure painfully obvious; and puzzled sympathy settled on her as she stood there. Poor dear, they thought, she was feeling ill. Excitement, no doubt. Positively green, she was. Poor dear, poor dear.

Stewart had finished, and now waited, looking at Innes. Slowly they sank together to the boom, and sat down on it; turned together to lean face-forward on it; and somersaulted forward on to the ground.

And a great burst of applause greeted them. As always, the English were moved by a gallant failure where an easy success left them merely polite. They were expressing at once their sympathy and their admiration. They had understood the strength of purpose that had kept her on the boom, paralysed as she was.

But the sympathy had not touched Innes. Lucy doubted if she actually heard the applause. She was living in some tortured world of her own, far beyond the reach of human consolation. Lucy could hardly bear to look at her.

The bustle of the following items covered up her failure and put an end to drama. Innes took her place with the others and performed with mechanical perfection. When the final vaulting came, indeed, her performance was so remarkable that Lucy wondered if she were trying to break her neck publicly. The same idea, to judge by her expression, had crossed Fröken's mind; but as long as what Innes did was controlled and perfect there was nothing she could do. And everything that Innes did, however breath-taking, was perfect and controlled. Because she seemed not to care, the wildest flights were possible to her. And when the students had finished their final go-as-you-please and stood breathless and beaming, a single file on an empty floor as they had begun, their guests stood up as one man and cheered.

Lucy, being at the end of the row and next the door, was first to leave the hall, and so was in time to see Innes's apology to Fröken.

Fröken paused, and then moved on as if not interested, or not willing to listen.

But as she went she lifted a casual arm and gave Innes a light friendly pat on the shoulder.

~~~~~~

· 18 ·

As THE guests moved out to the garden and the basket-chairs round the lawn, Lucy went with them, and while she was waiting to see if sufficient chairs had been provided before taking one for herself, she was seized upon by Beau, who said: "Miss Pym! There you are! I've been hunting for you. I want you to meet my people."

She turned to a couple who were just sitting down and said: "Look, I've found Miss Pym at last."

Beau's mother was a very lovely woman; as lovely as the best beauty parlours and the most expensive hairdressers could make her—and they had good foundation to work on since when Mrs Nash was twenty she must have looked very like Beau. Even now, in the bright sunlight, she looked no older than thirty-five. She had a good dressmaker too, and bore herself with the easy friendly confidence of a woman who has been a beauty all her life; so used to the effect she had on people that she did not have to consider it at all and so her mind was free to devote itself to the person she happened to be meeting.

Mr Nash was obviously what is called an executive. A fine clear skin, a good tailor, a well-soaped look, and a general aura of mahogany tables with rows of clean blotters round them.

"I should be changing. I must fly," said Beau, and disappeared.

As they sat down together Mrs Nash looked quizzically at Lucy and said: "Well, now that you are here in the flesh, Miss Pym, we can ask you something we are dying to know. We want to know *how you do it?*"

"Do what?"

"Impress Pamela."

"Yes," said Mr Nash, "that is just what we should like to know. All our lives we have been trying to make some impression on Pamela, but we remain just a couple of dear people who happen to be responsible for her existence and have to be humoured now and then."

"Now *you*, it seems, are quite literally something to write home about," Mrs Nash said, and raised an eyebrow and laughed.

"If it is any consolation to you," Lucy offered, "I am greatly impressed by your daughter."

"Pam *is* nice," her mother said. "We love her very much; but I wish we impressed her more. Until you turned up no one has made any impression on Pamela since a Nanny she had at the age of four."

"And that impression was a physical one," Mr Nash volunteered.

"Yes. The only time in her life that she was spanked."

"What happened?" Lucy asked.

"We had to get rid of the Nanny!"

"Didn't you approve of spanking?"

"Oh yes, but Pamela didn't."

"Pam engineered the first sit-down strike in history," Mr Nash said.

"She kept it up for seven days," Mrs Nash said. "Short of going on dressing and forcibly feeding her for the rest of her life, there was nothing to do but get rid of Nanny. A first-rate woman she was, too. We were devastated to lose her."

The music began, and in front of the high screen of the rhododendron thicket appeared the bright colours of the Junior's Swedish folk dresses. Folk-dancing had begun. Lucy sat back and thought, not of Beau's childish aberrations, but of Innes, and the way a black cloud of doubt and foreboding was making a mockery of the bright sunlight.

It was because her mind was so full of Innes that she was startled when she heard Mrs Nash say: "Mary, darling. There you are. How nice to see you again," and turned to see Innes behind them. She was wearing boy's things; the doublet and hose of the fifteenth century; and the hood that hid all her hair and fitted close round her face accentuated the bony structure that was so individual. Now that the eyes were shadowed and sunk a little in their always-deep sockets, the face had something it had not had before: a forbidding look. It was—what was the word?—a "fatal" face. Lucy remembered her very first impression that it was round faces like that that history was built.

"You have been overworking, Mary," Mr Nash said, eyeing her.

"They all have," Lucy said, to take their attention from her.

"Not Pamela," her mother said. "Pam has never worked hard in her life."

No. Everything had been served to Beau on a plate. It was miraculous that she had turned out so charming.

"Did you see me make a fool of myself on the boom?" Innes asked, in a pleasant conversational tone. This surprised Lucy, somehow; she had expected Innes to avoid the subject.

"My dear, we sweated for you," Mrs Nash said. "What happened? Did you turn dizzy?"

"No," said Beau, coming up behind them and slipping an arm into Innes's, "that is just Innes's way of stealing publicity. It is not inferior physical powers, but superior brains the girl has. None of us has the wit to think up a stunt like that."

Beau gave the arm she was holding a small reassuring squeeze. She too was in boy's clothes, and looked radiant; even the quenching of her bright hair had not diminished the glow and vivacity of her beauty.

"That is the last of the Junior's efforts—don't they look gay against that green background?—and now Innes and I and the rest of our put-upon set will entertain you with some English antics, and then you shall have tea to sustain you against the real dancing to come."

And they went away together.

"Ah, well," said Mrs Nash, watching her daughter go, "I suppose it is better than being seized with a desire to reform natives in Darkest Africa or something. But I wish she would have just stayed at home and been one's daughter."

Lucy thought that it was to Mrs Nash's credit that, looking as young as she did, she wanted a daughter at home.

"Pam was always mad on gym. and games," Mr Nash said. "There was no holding her. There never was any holding her, come to that."

"Miss Pym," said The Nut Tart, appearing at Lucy's elbow, "do you mind if Rick sits with you while I go through this rigmarole with the Seniors?" She indicated Gillespie, who was standing behind her clutching a chair, and wearing his habitual expression of grave amusement.

The wide flat hat planked slightly to the back of her head on top of her wimple—Wife of Bath fashion—gave her an air of innocent astonishment that was delightful. Lucy and Rick exchanged a glance of mutual appreciation, and he smiled at her as he sat down on her other side.

"Isn't she lovely in that get-up," he said, watching Desterro disappear behind the rhododendrons.

"I take it that a rigmarole doesn't count as dancing."

"Is she good?"

"I don't know. I have never seen her, but I understand she is."

"I've never even danced ballroom stuff with her. Odd, isn't it. I didn't even know she existed until last Easter. It maddens me to think she has been a whole year in England and I didn't know about it. Three months of odd moments isn't very long to make any effect on a person like Teresa."

"Do you want to make an effect?"

"Yes." The monosyllable was sufficient.

The Seniors, in the guise of the English Middle Ages, ran out on to the lawn, and conversation lapsed. Lucy tried to find distraction in identifying legs and in marvelling over the energy with which those legs ran about after an hour of strenuous exercise. She said to herself: "Look, you have to go to Henrietta with the little rosette tonight. All right. That is settled. There is nothing you can do, either about the going or the result of the going. So put it out of your mind. This is the afternoon you have been looking forward to. It is a lovely sunny day, and everyone is pleased to see you, and you should be having a grand time. So relax. Even if—if anything awful happens about the rosette, it has nothing to do with you. A fortnight ago you didn't know any of these people, and after you go away you will never see any of them again. It can't matter to you what happens or does not happen to them."

All of which excellent advice left her just where she was before. When she saw Miss Joliffe and the maids busy about the tea-table in the rear she was glad to get up and find some use for her hands and some occupation for her mind.

Rick, unexpectedly, came with her. "I'm a push-over for passing plates. It must be the gigolo in me."

Lucy said that he ought to be watching his lady-love's rigmaroles.

"It is the last dance. And if I know anything of my Teresa her appetite will take more appeasing than her vanity, considerable as it is."

He seemed to know his Teresa very well, Lucy thought.

"Are you worried about something, Miss Pym?"

The question took her by surprise.

"Why should you think that?"

166

"I don't know. I just got the impression. Is there anything I can do?"

Lucy remembered how on Sunday evening when she had nearly cried into the Bidlington rarebit he had known about her tiredness and tacitly helped her. She wished that she had met someone as understanding and as young and as beautiful as The Nut Tart's follower when she was twenty, instead of Alan and his Adam's apple and his holey socks.

"I have to do something that is right," she said slowly, "and I'm afraid of the consequences."

"Consequences to you?"

"No. To other people."

"Never mind; do it."

Miss Pym put plates of cakes on a tray. "You see, the proper thing is not necessarily the right thing. Or do I mean the opposite?"

"I'm not sure that I know what you mean at all."

"Well—there are those awful dilemmas about whom would you save. You know. If you knew that by saving a person from the top of a snow slide you would start an avalanche that would destroy a village, would you do it? That sort of thing."

"Of course I would do it."

"You would?"

"The avalanche might bury a village without killing a cat—shall I put some sandwiches on that tray?—so you would be one life to the good."

"You would always do the right thing, and let the consequences take care of themselves?"

"That's about it."

"It is certainly the simplest. In fact I think it's too simple."

"Unless you plan to play God, one has to take the simple way."

"Play God? You've got two lots of tongue sandwiches there, do you know?"

"Unless you are clever enough to 'see before and after' like the Deity, it's best to stick to rules. Wow! The music has stopped and here comes my young woman like a hunting leopard." He watched Desterro come with a smile in his eyes. "Isn't that hat a knock-out!" He looked down at Lucy for a moment. "Do the obvious right thing, Miss Pym, and let God dispose."

"Weren't you watching, Rick?" she heard Desterro ask, and then she and Rick and The Nut Tart were overwhelmed by a wave of Juniors come to do their duty and serve tea. Lucy extricated herself from the crush of white caps and Swedish embroidery, and found herself face to face with Edward Adrian, alone and looking forlorn.

"Miss Pym! You are just the person I wanted to see. Have you heard that—"

A Junior thrust a cup of tea into his hand, and he gave her one of his best smiles which she did not wait to see. At the same moment little Miss Morris, faithful even in the throes of a Dem., came up with tea and a tray of cakes for Lucy.

"Let us sit down, shall we?" Lucy said.

"Have you heard of the frightful thing that has happened?"

"Yes. It isn't very often, I understand, that a serious accident happens. It is just bad luck that it should be Demonstration Day."

"Oh, the accident, yes. But do you know that Catherine says she can't come to Larborough tonight? This has upset things, she says. She must stay here. But that is absurd. Did you ever hear anything more absurd? If there has been some kind of upset that is all the more reason why she should be taken out of herself for a little. I have arranged everything. I even got special flowers for our table tonight. *And* a birthday cake. It's her birthday next Wednesday."

Lucy wondered if any other person within the bounds of Leys knew when Catherine Lux's birthday was.

Lucy did her best to sympathise, but said gently that she saw Miss Lux's point of view. After all, the girl was seriously injured, and it was all very worrying, and it would no doubt seem to her a little callous to go merrymaking in Larborough.

"But it isn't merrymaking! It is just a quiet supper with an old friend. I really can't see why because some student has had an accident she should desert an old friend. You talk to her, Miss Pym. You make her see reason."

Lucy said she would do her best but could offer no hope of success since she rather shared Miss Lux's ideas on the subject.

"You, too! Oh, my God!"

"I know it isn't reasonable. It's even absurd. But neither of us would be happy and the evening would be a disappointment and you don't want that to happen? Couldn't you have us to-morrow night instead?"

"No, I'm catching a train directly the evening performance is over. And of course, it being Saturday, I have a matinée. And anyhow, I'm playing Romeo at night and that wouldn't please Cath at all. It takes her all her time to stand me in *Richard III*. Oh dear, the whole thing is absurd."

"Cheer up," Lucy said. "It stops short of tragedy. You will be coming to Larborough again, and you can meet as often as you like now that you know she is here."

"I shall never get Catherine in that pliant mood again. Never. It was partly your doing, you know. She didn't want to appear too much of a Gorgon in front of you. She was even going to come to see me act. Something she has never done before. I'll never get her back to that point if she doesn't come tonight. Do persuade her, Miss Pym."

Lucy promised to try. "How are you enjoying your afternoon, apart from broken appointments?"

Mr Adrian was enjoying himself vastly, it appeared. He was not sure which to admire most: the students' good looks or their efficiency.

"They have charming manners, too. I have not been asked for an autograph once, all the afternoon."

Lucy looked to see if he was being ironic. But no; the remark was "straight." He really could not conceive any reason for the lack of autograph hunters other than that of good manners. Poor silly baby, she thought, walking all his life through a world he knew nothing about. She wondered if all actors were like that. Perambulating spheres of atmosphere with a little actor safely cocooned at the heart of each. How nice it must be, so cushioned and safe from harsh reality. They weren't really born at all; they were still floating in some pre-natal fluid.

"Who is the girl who fluffed at the balance exercise?"

Was she not going to get away from Innes for two minutes together?

"Her name is Mary Innes. Why?"

"What a wonderful face. Pure Borgia."

"Oh, no!" Lucy said, sharply.

"I've been wondering all the afternoon what she reminded me of. I think it is a portrait of a young man by Giorgione, but which of his young men I wouldn't know. I should have to see them again. Anyhow, it's a wonderful face, so delicate and so strong, so good and so bad. Quite fantastically beautiful. I can't imagine what anything so dramatic is doing at a girls' Physical Training College in the twentieth century."

Well, at least she had the consolation of knowing that someone else saw Innes as she did; exceptional, oddly fine, out of her century, and potentially tragic. She remembered that to Henrietta she was merely a tiresome girl who looked down her nose at people less well endowed with brains.

Lucy wondered what to offer Edward Adrian by way of distraction. She saw coming down the path a floppy satin bow-tie against a dazzling collar and recognized Mr Robb, the elocution master; the only member of the visiting Staff, apart from Dr Knight, that she knew. Mr Robb had been a dashing young actor forty years ago—the most brilliant Lancelot Gobbo of his generation, one understood—and she felt that to hoist Mr Adrian with his own petard would be rather pleasant. But being Lucy her heart softened at the thought of the wasted preparations he had made—the flowers, the cake, the plans for showing off—and she decided to be merciful. She saw O'Donnell, gazing from a discreet distance at her one-time hero, and she beckoned to her. Edward Adrian should have a real, authentic, dyed-in-the-wool fan to cheer him; and he need never know that she was the only one in College.

"Mr Adrian," she said, "this is Eileen O'Donnell, one of your most devoted admirers."

"Oh, Mr Adrian—" she heard O'Donnell begin.

And she left them to it.

WHEN tea was over (and Lucy had been introduced to at least twenty different sets of parents) the drift back from the garden began, and Lucy overtook Miss Lux on the way to the house.

"I'm afraid that I am going to cry off tonight," she said. "I feel a migraine coming."

"That is a pity," Lux said without emotion. "I have cried off too."

"Oh, why?"

"I'm very tired, and upset about Rouse, and I don't feel like going junketing in town."

"You surprise me."

"I surprise you? In what way?"

"I never thought I should live to see Catherine Lux being dishonest with herself."

"Oh. And what am I fooling myself about?"

"If you have a look at your mind you'll find that that's not why you're staying at home."

"No? Why, then?"

"Because you get such pleasure out of telling Edward Adrian where he gets off."

"A deplorable expression."

"Descriptive, though. You simply jumped at the chance of being high and mighty with him, didn't you?"

"I own that breaking the engagement was no effort."

"And a little unkind?"

"A deplorable piece of self-indulgence by a shrew. That's what you're trying to say, isn't it?"

"He is looking forward so much to having you. I can't think why."

"Thanks. I can tell you why. So that he can cry all over me and tell me how he hates acting—which is the breath of life to him."

"Even if he bores you——"

"If! My God!"

"——you can surely put up with him for an hour or so, and not use Rouse's accident as a sort of ace from your sleeve."

"Are you trying to make an honest woman of me, Lucy Pym?"

"That is the general idea. I feel so sorry for him, being left—"

"My—good—woman," Lux said, stabbing a forefinger at Lucy with each word, "*never* be sorry for Edward Adrian. Women spend the best years of their lives being sorry for him, and end by being sorry for it. Of all the self-indulgent, self-deceiving——"

"But he *has* got a Johannisberger."

Lux stopped, and smiled at her.

"I could do with a drink, at that," she said reflectively.

She walked on a little.

"Are you really leaving Teddy high and dry?" she asked.

"Yes."

"All right. You win. I was just being a beast. I'll go. And every time he trots out that line about: 'Oh, Catherine, how weary I am of this artificial life' I shall think with malice: That Pym woman got me into this."

"I can bear it," Lucy said. "Has anyone heard how Rouse is?"

"Miss Hodge has just been on the telephone. She is still unconscious."

Lucy, seeing Henrietta's head through the window of her office—it was known as the office but was in reality the little sitting-room to the left of the front door—went in to compliment her on the success of the afternoon and so take her mind for at least a moment or two off the thing that oppressed it, and Miss Lux walked on. Henrietta seemed glad to see her, and even glad to have repeated to her the platitudes she had been listening to all the afternoon, and Lucy stayed talking to her for some time; so that the gallery was almost filled again when she took her seat to watch the dancing.

Seeing Edward Adrian in one of the gangway seats she paused and said:

"Catherine is coming."

"And you?" he said, looking up.

"No, alas; I am having a migraine at six-thirty sharp."

Whereupon he said: "Miss Pym, I adore you," and kissed her hand.

His next-door neighbour looked startled, and someone behind tittered, but Lucy liked having her hand kissed. What was the good of putting rose-water and glycerine on every night if you didn't have a little return now and then?

She went back to her seat at the end of the front row, and found that the dowager with the lorgnettes had not waited for the dancing; the seat was empty. But just before the lights went down—the hall was curtained and artificially lit—Rick appeared from behind and said: "If you are not keeping that seat for anyone, may I sit there?"

And as he sat down the first dancers appeared.

After the fourth or fifth item Lucy was conscious of a slow disappointment. Used to the technical standards of international ballet, she had not allowed in her mind for the inevitable amateurism of dancing in this milieu. In everything she had seen the students do so far they had been the best of their line in the business; professionals. But it was obviously not possible to give to other subjects the time and energy that they did and still reach a high standard as dancers. Dancing was a whole-time job.

What they did was good, but it was uninspired. On the best amateur level, or a little above. So far the programme had consisted of the national and period dances beloved of all dancing mistresses, and they had been performed with a conscientious accuracy that was admirable but not diverting. Perhaps the need for keeping their minds on the altered track took some of the spontaneity from their work. But on the whole Lucy thought that it was that neither training nor temperament was sufficient. Their audience too lacked spontaneity; the eagerness with which they had watched the gymnastics was lacking. Perhaps they had had too much tea; or perhaps it was that the cinema had brought to their remotest doors a standard of achievement that made them critical. Anyhow their applause was polite rather than enthusiastic.

A piece of Russian bravura roused them for a moment, and they waited hopefully for what might come next. The curtains parted to reveal Desterro, alone. Her arms raised above her head

173

and one slim hip turned to the audience. She was wearing some sort of native dress from her own hemisphere, and the "spot" made the bright colours and the barbaric jewels glitter so that she looked like one of the brilliant birds from her Brazilian forests. Her little feet in their high-heeled shoes tapped impatiently under the full skirt. She began to dance; slowly, almost absent-mindedly, as if she were putting in time. Then it became evident that she was waiting for her lover and that he was late. What his lateness meant to her also became rapidly apparent. By this time the audience were sitting up. From some empty space she conjured a lover. One could almost see the hang-dog look on his swarthy face. She dealt with him: faithfully. By this time the audience were sitting on the edge of their seats. Then, having dealt with him, she began to show off to him; but did he not realise his luck in having a girl like her, a girl who had a waist, an eye, a hip, a mouth, an ankle, a total grace like hers? Was he a boor that he could not see? She therefore showed him; with a wit in every movement that brought smiles to every face in the audience. Lucy turned to look at them; in another minute they would be cooing. It was magic. By the time she began to relent and let her lover have a word in, they were her slaves. And when she walked away with that still invisible but undoubtedly subdued young man, they cheered like children at a Wild West matinée.

Watching her as she took her bow, Lucy remembered how The Nut Tart had chosen Leys because for the proper dancing schools "one must have a métier."

"She was modest about her dancing after all," she said aloud. "She could have been a professional."

"I am glad she didn't," Rick said. "Coming here she has learned to love the English countryside. If she had trained in town she would have met only the international riff-raff that hang around ballet."

And Lucy thought that he was probably right.

There was a distinct drop in temperature when the conscientious students reappeared to continue their numbers. Stewart had a Celtic verve that was refreshing, and Innes had grace and moments of fire, but the moment Desterro came among them even Lucy forgot Innes and all the others. Desterro was enchanting.

At the end she had an ovation all to herself.

And Miss Pym, catching the look on Rick's face, felt a small pang.

It was not enough to have one's hand kissed.

"Nobody told me that Desterro could dance like that," she said to Miss Wragg as they went over to supper together when the guests had at last taken their departure with much starting up of engines and shouted goodbyes.

"Oh, she is Madame's little pet," Wragg said in the unenthusiastic voice of Madame's follower speaking of a creature so far gone in sin that she did not play games. "I think she is stagey, myself. Out of place here, somehow. I honestly think that first dance wasn't quite nice. Did you think that?"

"I thought it delightful."

"Oh, well," Wragg said, resignedly; and added: "She must be good, or Madame wouldn't be so keen on her."

Supper was a quiet meal. Exhaustion, anti-climax, and the recollection (now that they were idle) of this morning's accident, all served to damp the students' spirits and clog their tongues. The Staff, too, were tired after their shocks, exertions, social efforts, and anxieties. Lucy felt that the occasion called for a glass of good wine, and thought with a passing regret of the Johannisberger that Lux was drinking at that moment. Her heart had begun to thud in a horrid way when she thought that in a few moments she must take that little rosette into the office, and tell Henrietta where she found it.

She had still not taken it out of the drawer where she had left it, and after supper she was on the way up to fetch it when she was overtaken by Beau, who slid an arm into hers and said:

"Miss Pym, we are brewing cocoa in the Common Room, the whole shoot of us. Do come and cheer us up. You don't want to go and sit in that morgue upstairs"—the morgue was presumably the drawing-room—"do you? Come and cheer us up."

"I don't feel particularly cheerful myself," Lucy said, thinking with loathing of the cocoa, "but if you put up with my gloom I shall put up with yours."

As they turned towards the Common Room a great wind out of nowhere swept down the corridor through all the wide-open windows, dashing the green branches of the trees outside against one another and tearing the leaves upward so that their backs showed. "The end of the good weather," Lucy said, pausing to listen. She had always hated that restless destroying wind that put paid to the golden times.

"Yes; it's cold too," Beau said. "We've lit a wood fire."

The Common Room was part of the "old house" and had an old brick fireplace; and it certainly looked cheerful with the flame and crackle of a freshly lit fire, the rattle of crockery, the bright dresses of the students lying about in exhausted heaps, and their still brighter bedroom slippers. It was not only O'Donnell who had had recourse to odd footwear tonight; practically everyone was wearing undress shoes of some sort or another. In fact Dakers was lying on a settee with her bare bandaged toes higher than her head. She waved a cheerful hand at Miss Pym, and indicated her feet.

"Haemostosis!" she said. "I bled into my *best* ballet shoes. I suppose no one would like to *buy* a pair of ballet shoes, slightly soiled? No, I was afraid not."

"There's a chair over by the fire, Miss Pym," Beau said, and went to pour out the cocoa. Innes, who was sitting curled up on the hearth superintending a Junior's efforts with a bellows, patted the chair and made her welcome in her usual unsmiling fashion.

"I've cadged the rest of the tea stuff from Miss Joliffe," Hasselt said, coming in with a large plate of mixed left-overs.

"How did you do that?" they asked. "Miss Joliffe never gives away even a smell."

"I promised to send her some peach jam when I got back to South Africa. There isn't really very much though it looks a plateful. The maids had most of it after tea. Hullo, Miss Pym. What did you think of us?"

"I thought you were all wonderful," Lucy said.

"Just like London policemen," Beau said. "Well, you bought that, Hasselt."

Lucy apologised for the cliché, and sought by going into further detail to convince them of her enthusiasm.

"Desterro ran away with the evening, didn't she, though?"

they said; and glanced with friendly envy at the composed figure in the bright wrap sitting upright in the ingle-nook.

"Me, I do only one thing. It is easy to do just one thing well."

And Lucy, like the rest of them, could not decide if the cool little remark was meant to be humble or reproving. On the whole she thought humble.

"That's enough, March, it's going beautifully," Innes said to the Junior, and moved to take the bellows from her. As she moved her feet came out from under her and Lucy saw that she was wearing black pumps.

And the little metal ornament that should have been on the left one was not there.

Oh, *no*, said Lucy's mind. No. No. No.

"That is your cup, Miss Pym, and here is yours, Innes. Have a rather tired macaroon, Miss Pym."

"No, I have some chocolate biscuits for Miss Pym."

"No, she is going to have some Ayrshire shortbread, out of a tin, and *fresh*. None of your pawed-over victuals."

The babble went on round her. She took something off a plate. She answered what was said to her. She even took a sip of the stuff in the cup.

Oh, no. No.

Now that the thing was here—the thing she had been afraid of, so afraid that she would not even formulate it in her mind— now that it was here, made concrete and manifest, she was appalled. It had all suddenly become a nightmare: the bright noisy room with the blackening sky outside where the storm was rushing up, and the missing object. One of those nightmares where something small and irrelevant has a terrifying importance. Where something immediate and urgent must be done about it but one can't think what or why.

Presently she must get up and make polite leavetaking and go to Henrietta with her story and end by saying: "And I know whose shoe it came from. Mary Innes's."

Innes was sitting at her feet, not eating but drinking cocoa thirstily. She had curled her feet under her again, but Lucy had no need for further inspection. Even her faint hope that someone else might be wearing pumps had gone overboard. There was a fine colourful variety of footgear present but not a second pair of pumps.

In any case, no one else had a motive for being in the gymnasium at six o'clock this morning.

"Have some more cocoa," Innes said presently, turning to look at her. But Miss Pym had hardly touched hers.

"Then I must have some more," Innes said, and began to get up.

A very tall thin Junior called Farthing, but known even to the Staff as Tuppence-Ha'penny, came in.

"You're late, Tuppence," someone said. "Come and have a bun." But Farthing stood there, uncertainly.

"What is the matter, Tuppence?" they asked, puzzled by her shocked expression.

"I went to put the flowers in Fröken's room," she said slowly.

"Don't tell us there were some there already?" someone said; and there was a general laugh.

"I heard the Staff talking about Rouse."

"Well, what about her? Is she better?"

"She's dead."

The cup Innes was holding crashed on the hearth. Beau crossed over to her to pick up the pieces.

"Oh, nonsense," they said. "You heard wrong, young Tuppence."

"No, I didn't. They were talking on the landing. She died half an hour ago."

This was succeeded by a dismayed silence.

"I *did* put up the wall end," O'Donnell said loudly, into the silence.

"Of course you did, Don," Stewart said, going to her. "We all know that."

Lucy put down her cup and thought that she had better go upstairs. They let her go with murmured regrets, their happy party in pieces round them.

Upstairs, Lucy found that Miss Hodge had gone to the hospital to receive Rouse's people when they arrived, and that it was she who had telephoned the news. Rouse's people had come, and had taken the blow unemotionally, it seemed.

"I never liked her, God forgive me," said Madame, stretched at full length on the hard sofa; her plea to the Deity for forgiveness had a genuine sound.

"Oh, she was all right," Wragg said, "quite nice when you knew her. And the most marvellous centre-half. This is frightful, isn't it! Now it will be a matter of inquiry, and we'll have police, an inquest, and appalling publicity, and everything."

Yes, police and everything.

She could not do anything about the little rosette tonight. And anyhow she wanted to think about it.

She wanted to get away by herself and think about it.

～～～～～～～～～～～～～～～～～～～～

·   20   ·

BONG! BONG! The clock in that far-away steeple struck again. Two o'clock.

She lay staring into the dark, while the cold rain beat on the ground outside and wild gusts rose every now and then and rioted in anarchy, flinging her curtains out into the room so that they flapped like sails and everything was uncertainty and turmoil.

The rain wept with steady persistence, and her heart wept with it. And in her mind was a turmoil greater than the wind's.

"Do the obvious right thing, and let God dispose," Rick had said. And it had seemed a sensible ruling.

But that was when it had been a hypothetical affair of "causing grievous bodily harm" (that was the phrase, wasn't it?) and now it had ceased to be hypothesis and it wasn't any longer mere bodily harm. It was—was *this*.

It wouldn't be God who would dispose this, in spite of all the comforting tags. It would be the Law. Something written with ink in a statute book. And once that was invoked God Himself could not save a score of innocent persons being crushed under the Juggernaut wheels of its progress.

An eye for an eye and a tooth for a tooth, said the old Mosaic law. And it sounded simple. It sounded just. One saw it against

179

a desert background, as if it involved two people only. It was quite different when one put it in modern words and called it "being hanged by the neck until you are dead."

If she went to Henrietta in the——

If?

Oh, all right, of course she was going.

When she went to Henrietta in the morning, she would be putting in motion a power over which neither she nor anyone else had control; a power that once released would catch up this, that, and the next one from the innocent security of their peaceful lives and fling them into chaos.

She thought of Mrs Innes, happily asleep somewhere in Larborough; bound home tomorrow to wait for the return of the daughter in whom she had her life. But her daughter would not come home—ever.

Neither will Rouse, a voice pointed out.

No, of course not, and Innes must somehow pay for that. She must not be allowed to profit by her crime. But surely, surely there was some way in which payment could be made without making the innocent pay even more bitterly.

What was justice?

To break a woman's heart; to bring ruin and shame on Henrietta and the destruction of all she had built up; to rub out for ever the radiance of Beau, the Beau who was unconditioned to grief. Was that a life for a life? That was three—no, four lives for one.

And one not worth——

Oh, no. That she could not judge. For that one had to "see before and after," as Rick said. A curiously sober mind, Rick had, for a person with a play-boy's face and a Latin lover's charm.

There was Innes moving about again next-door. As far as Lucy knew she had not slept yet either. She was very quiet, but every now and then one heard a movement or the tap in her room ran. Lucy wondered whether the water was to satisfy a thirst or to cool temples that must be throbbing. If she, Lucy, was lying awake with her thoughts running round and round inside her skull like trapped mice, what must Innes be going through? Humourless she might be, unenamoured of the human species she probably was, but insensitive she most certainly was not. Whether it was thwarted ambition, or sheer anger and hate, that had driven her down to the gymnasium through the misty morning, she was not the sort to be able to do what she had done with impunity. It might well be, indeed, that given her temperament it was herself she had destroyed when she tampered with that boom. In the case-histories of crime there were instances of women so callous that they had come to a fresh blooming once the obstacle to their desires was out of the way. But they were not built like Mary Innes. Innes belonged to that other, and rarer, class who found too late that they could not live with themselves any more. The price they had paid was too high.

Perhaps Innes would provide her own punishment.

That, now she came to think of it, was how she had first thought of Innes, on that Sunday afternoon under the cedar. The stake or nothing. A self-destroyer.

That she had destroyed a life that stood in her way was almost incidental.

It had not, in any case, been intended as destruction; Lucy was quite sure of that. That is what made this business of starting the machine so repellent, so unthinkable. All that the insecure pin was meant to achieve was a temporary incapacity. An assurance that Rouse would not go to Arlinghurst in September—and that she would.

Had she had that in mind, Lucy wondered, when she refused the appointment at the Wycherley Orthopaedic Hospital? No, surely not. She was not a planner in cold blood. The thing had been done at the very last moment, in desperation.

At least, it had been *achieved* at the very last moment.

It was possible that its lateness was due to lack of previous opportunity. The way to the gymnasium might never have been clear before; or Rouse may have got there first.

"A Borgia face," Edward Adrian had said, delightedly.

And Teresa's great-grandmother's grandmother, whom she resembled, *she* had planned. And had lived a long, secure, and successful life as a widow, administering rich estates and bringing up a son, without apparently any signs of spiritual suicide.

The wind flung itself into the room, and Innes's window began to rattle. She heard Innes cross the room to it, and presently it stopped.

She wished she could go next-door, now, at this minute, and put her hand down. Show Innes the ace she held and didn't want to play. Together they could work something out.

Together? With the girl who loosened that pin under the boom?

No. With the girl she had talked to in the corridor last Saturday afternoon, so radiant, so full of dignity and wisdom. With the girl who could not sleep tonight. With her mother's daughter.

Whatever she had done, even if she had planned it, the result had been something she had neither planned nor foreseen. The result was catastrophe for her.

And who in the first place had brought that catastrophe?

Henrietta. Henrietta with her mule-like preference for her inferior favourite.

She wondered if Henrietta was sharing Innes's vigil. Henrietta who had come back from West Larborough so strangely thin and old-looking. As if the frame she was strung on had collapsed and the stuffing had shifted. Like a badly stuffed toy after a month in the nursery. That is what Henrietta had looked like.

She had been truly sorry for her friend, bereft of someone she had—loved? Yes, loved, she supposed. Only love could have blinded her to Rouse's defects. Bereft; and afraid for her beloved Leys. She had been truly moved by her suffering. But she could not help the thought that but for Henrietta's own action none of this would have happened.

The operative cause was Innes's vulnerability. But the button that had set the whole tragedy in motion was pressed by Henrietta.

And now she, Lucy, was waiting to press another button which would set in motion machinery even more monstrous. Machinery that would catch up in its gears and meshes, and maim and destroy, the innocent with the guilty. Henrietta perhaps had bought her punishment, but what had the Inneses done to have this horror unloaded on them? This unnameable horror.

Or *had* they contributed? How much had Innes's upbringing been responsible for her lack of resilience? Given that she had been born without "oil on her feathers," had they tried to condition her to the lack? Who could ever say where first causes lay?

Perhaps after all, even through the Law, it was the Deity who disposed. If you were a Christian you took that for granted, of course. You took for granted that nothing ever happened that there was no cause for. That everyone who would be tortured incidentally by Innes's trial for murder had in some way "bought" their punishment. It was a fine comfortable theory, and Lucy wished that she could subscribe to it. But she found it difficult to believe that any deficiency on the part of parents as responsible and as devoted as the Inneses could warrant the bringing down on their heads of a tragedy so unspeakable.

Or perhaps——

She sat up, to consider this new thought.

If God did dispose—as undoubtedly He did in the latter end—then perhaps the disposing was already at work. Had begun to work when it was she and not someone else who found the little rosette. It had not been found by a strong-minded person who would go straight to Henrietta with it as soon as she smelt a rat, and so set the machinery of man-made Law in motion. No. It had been found by a feeble waverer like herself, who could never see less than three sides to any question. Perhaps that made sense.

But she wished very heartily that the Deity had found another instrument. She had always hated responsibility; and a responsibility of this magnitude was something that she could not deal with at all. She wished that she could throw away the little rosette—toss it out of the window now and pretend that she had never seen it. But of course she could not do that. However rabbity and inadequate she was by nature, there was always her other half—the Laetitia half—which stood watching her with critical eyes. She could never get away from that other half of herself. It had sent her into fights with her knees knocking, it had made her speak when she wanted to hold her tongue, it had kept her from lying down when she was too tired to stand up. It would keep her from washing her hands now.

She got up and leaned out into the wet, lashing, noisy night. There was a puddle of rain water on the wood floor inside the window. The cold shock of it on her bare feet was somehow grateful; a physical and understandable discomfort. At least she did not have to mop it up, or wonder about a carpet. All the elements came into this place at their will and everyone took it for granted. One of Innes's few volunteered remarks had been how lovely it had been one morning to waken and find her pillow crusted with snow. That had happened only once, she said, but you could always tell the season by what you found on your pillow in the morning: spiders in the autumn and sycamore seeds in June.

She stayed so long cooling her burning head that her feet grew cold, and she had to wrap them in a jersey to warm them when she got back into bed. That completes it, she thought: cold feet mentally and physically. You're a poor thing, Lucy Pym.

About three o'clock when she was growing sleepy at last, she was shot wide awake by the realisation of what she was proposing to do. She was seriously considering keeping back evidence in a capital charge. Becoming an accessory after the fact. A criminal.

She, respectable, law-abiding Lucy Pym.

How had she got to that point? What could she have been thinking of?

Of course she had no choice in the matter at all. Who disposed or did not dispose was no concern of hers. This was a matter of public inquiry, and she had a duty to do. A duty to civilisation, to the State, to herself. Her private emotions had nothing to do with it. Her views on justice had nothing to do with it. However unequal and wrong-headed the Law might be, she could not suppress evidence.

How in the name of all that was crazy had she ever thought that she could?

Rick was right: she would do the obvious right thing, and let God dispose.

About half-past four she really did fall asleep.

THE morning was bleary and sodden, and Lucy regarded it with distaste. The waking-bell had sounded as usual at five-thirty, although on the morning after the Demonstration there were no classes before breakfast. College might make concessions but it did not discard its habits. She tried to fall asleep again, but reality had come with the daylight, and what had been feverish theory in the dark hours was now chill fact. In an hour or two she would have pressed that button, and altered beyond computing lives of whose existence she was not even aware. Her heart began to thud again.

Oh, dear, why had she ever come to this place!

It was when she had finished dressing and was sticking a few invisible hairpins into appropriate places that she realised that she could not go to Henrietta about the rosette without first going to Innes. She was not sure whether this was a remnant of some childish conception of "playing fair" or whether she was just trying to find a way of breaking the matter that would make her own personal responsibility less absolute.

She went to Innes's door, quickly before the impulse to action should evaporate, and knocked. She had heard Innes come back from her bath and reckoned that by now she must be dressed.

The Innes who opened the door looked tired and heavy-eyed but composed. Now that she was face to face with her Lucy found it difficult to identify her with the Innes of her disturbed thoughts last night.

"Do you mind coming into my room for a moment?" she asked.

Innes hesitated, looked uncertain for a second, and then recovered herself. "Yes, of course," she said; and followed Lucy.

"What a night of rain it was," she said brightly.

It was unlike Innes to bother with remarks about the weather. And it was exceedingly unlike Innes to be bright.

Lucy took the little silver rosette out of her drawer and held it out on her palm for Innes to see.

"Do you know what that is?" she asked.

In a second the brightness had disappeared and Innes's face was hard and wary.

"Where did you get that?" she snapped.

It was only then that Lucy realised how, deep down, she had counted on Innes's reaction being different. How, unconsciously, she had expected Innes to say: "It looks like something off a dancing pump; lots of us have them." Her heart stopped thudding and sank into her stomach.

"I found it on the gymnasium floor very early yesterday morning," she said.

The hard wariness melted into a slow despair.

"And why do you show it to me?" Innes said dully.

"Because I understand that there is only one pair of those old-fashioned pumps in College."

There was silence. Lucy laid the little object down on the table and waited.

"Am I wrong?" she asked at last.

"No."

There was another silence.

"You don't understand, Miss Pym," she said in a burst, "it wasn't meant to be——. I know you'll think I'm just trying to white-wash it, but it was never meant to be—to be the way it turned out. It was because I was so sick about missing Arlinghurst—I practically lost my reason over that for a time—I behaved like an idiot. It got so that I couldn't think of anything in the world but Arlinghurst. And this was just to be a way of—of letting me have a second chance at it. It was never meant to be more than that. You must believe that. You must——"

"But of course I believe it. If I didn't I don't suppose I should be sharing the knowledge of this with you." She indicated the rosette.

After a moment Innes said: "What are you going to do?"

"Oh, dear God, I don't know," said poor Lucy, helpless now that she was face to face with reality. All the crimes she had met with were in slick detective stories where the heroine, how-

186

ever questionable, was invariably innocent, or in case-histories where the crime was safely over with and put away and a matter only for the scalpel. All those subjects of case-history record had had friends and relations whose stunned disbelief must have been very like her own, but the knowledge was neither comfort nor guide to her. This was the kind of thing that happened to other people—happened daily if one could believe the Press—but could not possibly happen to oneself.

How *could* one believe that someone one had laughed and talked with, liked and admired, shared a communal life with, could be responsible for another's death?

She found herself beginning to tell Innes of her sleepless night, of her theories about "disposing," of her reluctance to destroy half a dozen lives because of one person's crime. She was too absorbed in her own problem to notice the dawning hope in Innes's eyes. It was only when she heard herself saying: "Of course you cannot possibly be allowed to profit by Rouse's death," that she realised how far she had already come along the road that she had had no intention of travelling.

But Innes pounced on this. "Oh, but I won't, Miss Pym. And it has nothing to do with your finding the little ornament. I knew last night when I heard that she was dead that I couldn't go to Arlinghurst. I was going to tell Miss Hodge this morning. I was awake too last night. Facing a lot of things. Not only my responsibility for Rouse's death—my inability to take defeat and like it. But—oh, well, a lot of things that wouldn't interest you." She paused a moment, considering Lucy. "Look, Miss Pym, if I were to spend the rest of my life atoning for yesterday morning will you—would you——" She could not put so brazen a suggestion into words, even after Lucy's dissertation on justice.

"Become an accessory after the fact?"

The cold legality of the phrase discouraged Innes.

"No. I suppose it is too much to expect anyone to do. But I *would* atone, you know. It wouldn't be any half-hearted affair. It would be my life for—hers. I would do it gladly."

"I believe you, of course. But how do you plan to atone?"

"I thought of that last night. I began with leper colonies and things like that, but they were rather unreal and didn't make

187

much sense in connection with a Leys training. I have a better idea. I decided that I would work alongside my father. I hadn't planned to do medical work, but I am good at it and there is no orthopaedic clinic in our home town."

"It sounds admirable," Lucy said, "but where is the penance?"

"My one ambition since I was a little girl has been to get away from living in a little market town; coming to Leys was my passport to freedom."

"I see."

"Believe me, Miss Pym, it would be penance. But it wouldn't be a barren one. It wouldn't be just personal flagellation. I would be doing something useful with my life, something that would —would make it good value for exchange."

"Yes, I see."

There was another long silence.

The five-minute bell rang, but for the first time since she came to Leys Lucy was unconscious of a bell.

"Of course you have nothing but my word for it——"

"I would accept your word."

"Thank you."

It seemed too easy a way out, she was thinking. If Innes was to be punished, the living of a dull and useful life hardly seemed a sufficient exaction. She had forfeited Arlinghurst of course; that would cost her something. But would it pay for a death?

What, in any case, would pay for a death? Except a death.

And Innes was offering what she obviously considered a living death. Perhaps after all it was not so poor an exchange.

What she, Lucy, was faced with was the fact that all her deliberations, her self-communing and comparing of arguments, fused at this moment into one single and simple issue: Was she going to condemn to death the girl who was standing in front of her?

It was, after all, as simple as that. If she took that little rosette to Henrietta this morning, Innes would die before the first students came back to Leys in the autumn. If she did not die she would spend her twenties in a living death that would indeed be "barren."

188

Let her spend her years in the prison of her choice, where she could be useful to her fellows.

Certainly she, Lucy Pym, was quite unequal to the task of condemning her.

And that was that.

"I am entirely in your hands," she said slowly to Innes, "because I am quite incapable of sending anyone to the gallows. I know what my plain duty is and I can't do it." Odd, she thought, that I should be in her reverence rather than she in mine.

Innes stared at her, doubtfully.

"You mean——" Her tongue came out and ran along her dry lips. "You mean that you won't tell about the rosette?"

"No. I shall never tell anyone."

Innes went suddenly white.

So white that Lucy realised that this was a phenomenon that she had read about but never seen. "White as a sheet," they said. Well, it was perhaps an unbleached sheet but it certainly was "going white."

Innes put her hand out to the chair by the dressing-table and sat down abruptly. Seeing Lucy's anxious expression she said: "It's all right, I'm not going to faint. I've never fainted in my life. I'll be all right in a minute."

Lucy, who had been antagonised by her self-possession, her ready bargaining—Innes had been far too lucid on the subject, she felt—was seized with something like compunction. Innes had not after all been self-possessed. It had been the old story of emotion clamped down and taking a mean revenge when it found escape.

"Would you like a drink of water?" Lucy said, moving to the wash-basin.

"No, thank you, I'm all right. It's just that for the last twenty-four hours I've been so afraid, and seeing that silver thing on your hand was the last straw, and then suddenly it is all over, you've let me buy a reprieve, and—and——"

Sobs came up in her throat and choked the words. Great rending sobs without a single tear. She put her hands over her mouth to stop them, but they burst through and she covered her face and struggled for composure. It was no use. She put

189

both arms on the desk with her head between them and sobbed her heart out.

And Lucy, looking at her, thought: Another girl would have begun with this. Would have used it as a weapon, a bid for my sympathy. But not Innes. Innes comes self-contained and aloof, offering hostages. Without the breakdown no one would have guessed that she was suffering. Her present abandonment was the measure of her previous torture.

The first low murmur of the gong began in a slow crescendo.

Innes heard it and struggled to her feet. "If you'll forgive me," she said, "I'll go and dash some cold water on myself. That will stop it."

Lucy thought it remarkable that a girl so racked with sobs that she could hardly speak should prescribe for herself with such detachment; as if she were another person from this hysterical individual who had taken possession of her and was making such an exhibition of herself.

"Yes, do," Lucy said.

Innes paused with her hand on the door-knob.

"Some day I'll be able to thank you properly," she said, and disappeared.

Lucy dropped the little silver rosette into her pocket and went down to breakfast.

<hr>

• 22 •

IT WAS a horrible weekend.

The rain poured down. Henrietta went about looking as though she had had a major operation that had not proved a success. Madame was at her worst and not at all helpful, either actually or verbally. Fröken was furious that such a thing should have happened in "her" gymnasium. Wragg was an ever-present Cassandra scattering depressing truisms. Lux was quiet and tired.

Lux had come back from Larborough bearing a small pink candle wrapped in pale green tissue paper. "Teddy said I was to give you this," she said. "I can't think why."

"Oh? From a cake?"

190

"Yes. It's my birthday about now."

"How nice of him to remember."

"Oh, he keeps a birthday diary. It's part of his publicity. It is his secretary's duty to send telegrams to all the appropriate people on the appropriate days."

"Don't you ever give him credit for anything?" Lucy asked.

"Teddy? Not for a real emotion, I don't. I've known him since he was ten, don't forget. He can't fool me for more than five seconds together."

"My hairdresser," Lucy said, "who lectures to me while he is doing my hair, says that one should allow everyone three faults. If one makes that allowance, one finds that the rest is surprisingly nice, he says."

"When you allow for Teddy's three faults there is nothing left, unfortunately."

"Why?"

"Because his three faults are vanity, selfishness, and self-pity. And any one of the three is totally destructive."

"Whew!" said Lucy. "I give up."

But she stuck the silly little candle on her dressing-table, and thought kindly of Edward Adrian.

She wished she could think as kindly of her beloved Beau, who was making things as difficult as possible by being furious with Innes for giving up Arlinghurst. In fact Lucy understood that things had come as near a quarrel between them as was possible between two people so mutually devoted.

"Says she wouldn't be happy in dead men's shoes," said Beau, positively giving off sparks with wrath. "Can you imagine anything more ridiculous? Turning down Arlinghurst as if it were a cup of tea. After nearly dying of chagrin because she didn't get it in the first place. For God's sake, Miss Pym, you talk to her and make her see sense before it is too late. It isn't just Arlinghurst, it's her whole future. Beginning at Arlinghurst means beginning at the top. You talk to her, will you? Talk her out of this absurd notion!"

It seemed to Lucy that she was always being implored to "talk to" people. When she wasn't being a dose of soothing syrup she was being a shot of adrenalin, and when she wasn't being that she was being just a spoonful of alkaline powder for general consumption.

When she wasn't being a *deus ex machina;* a perverter of justice. But she tried not to think of that.

There was nothing she could say to Innes, of course, but other people had said it. Miss Hodge had wrought with her long and faithfully; dismayed by the defection of the girl she had not wanted to appoint in the first place. Now she had no one to send to Arlinghurst; she must write and tell them so and see the appointment go elsewhere. Perhaps when the news of the fatal accident leaked round the academic world Arlinghurst would decide to look elsewhere next time they wanted a gymnast. Accidents shouldn't happen in well conducted gymnasiums; not fatal accidents, anyhow.

That, too, was the police point of view. They had been very nice, the police, very considerate. Very willing to consider the harm that undesirable publicity would do the establishment. But there had to be an inquest, of course. And inquests were painfully public and open to misconstruction. Henrietta's lawyer had seen the local Press and they had promised to play down the affair, but who knew when a clipping might catch the eye of a sub-editor at a temporary loss for a sensation? And then what?

Lucy had wanted to go away before the inquest, to get away from the perpetual reminders of her guilt in the eyes of the Law, but Henrietta had begged her to stay. She had never been able to say no to Henrietta, and this pathetic aged Henrietta was someone whom she could not refuse. So Lucy stayed; doing odd jobs for Henrietta and generally leaving her free to deal with the crowd of extraneous duties that the accident had saddled her with.

But to the inquest she would not go.

She could not sit there with all her load of knowledge and not at some point be tempted to stand up and tell the truth and have the responsibility off her soul.

Who knew what rat the police might smell out? They had come and viewed the gymnasium, and measured things, and reckoned the weight of the boom, and interviewed all and sundry, and consulted the various experts on the subject, and listened and said nothing. They had taken away the pin that had been so fatally insecure; and that may have been mere routine, but who could tell? Who could tell what suspicions they might be entertaining in their large calm breasts and behind their polite expressionless faces?

But as it turned out, a quite unexpected saviour appeared at the inquest. A saviour in the person of Arthur Middleham, tea importer, of 59 West Larborough Road; that is to say, a resident in one of the villas which lined the highroad between West Larborough and the gates of Leys. Mr Middleham knew nothing about College except that it was there, and that the scantily attired young women who flew about the district on bicycles belonged to it. But he had heard about the accident. And it had struck him as odd that a pin in the gymnasium at Leys had moved out of place on the same morning, and presumably about the same time, as a pane of glass had been shaken out of his drawing-room window by a passing convoy of tanks from the works at South Larborough. His theory was, in fact, the same as Miss Lux's; vibration. Only Miss Lux's had been a hit in the dark and of no value. Mr Middleham's was reasonable and backed by three-dimensional evidence: a pane of broken glass.

And as always when someone has given a lead, there were gratuitous followers. (If someone invented a story and wrote to the Press that they had seen a green lion in the sky at 5.30 the previous evening, at least six people would have seen it retrospectively.) An excited woman, hearing Mr Middleham's evidence, got up from the body of the hall and said that her ginger jar that she had had for years had dropped off the little table in her window of its own accord at the same time.

"Where do you live, madam?" the coroner asked, when he had winkled her out of the crowd and installed her as evidence.

She lived in the cottages between Leys and Bidlington, she said. On the highroad? Oh, yes, much too much on the highroad; in the summer the dust was a fair sickener, and when the traffic was them there tanks——. No, she had no cat. No, there had been no one in the room. She had just come in after breakfast and found it on the floor. It had never happened before.

Poor O'Donnell, very nervous but clear and decided, gave

evidence that she had put up the end by the wall and that Rouse had attended to the middle end. "Putting it up" meant hoisting the boom by the pulley rope and pushing the pin under it to keep it up. It was also kept up, to a certain extent, by the rope, the hanging end of which was given a turn round a cleat on the upright. No, they had not tested the apparatus before going.

Fröken, asked about the rope which had not proved a substitute for the pin, said that it had not been wound tightly enough to prevent sagging when the pin was removed. The twisting of the rope round the cleat was an automatic gesture, and no student thought of it as a precautionary measure. It was that, in fact, of course. The metal of the pin might break through some fault, and the rope in that case took the strain. Yes, it was possible that a rope, unaccustomed to a greater strain than the weight of a boom, stretched under the sudden addition of a ten-stone burden, but she thought not. Gymnasium ropes were highly tested and guaranteed. It was much more likely that the twist Miss Rouse gave it had been inadequate.

And that seemed to be all. It was an unfortunate accident. The pin the police had abstracted had been used by all and sundry during the Demonstration, and was no evidence of anything.

It was obviously Death By Misadventure.

Well, that was the end of it, Lucy thought, when she heard the news. She had waited in the drawing-room, looking out at the rainy garden, not able to believe that something would not go wrong. No crime was ever committed without a slip-up somewhere; she had read enough case-histories to know that.

There had been one slip-up already, when that little ornament came loose from a shoe. Who knew what else the police might have unearthed? And now it was over, and Innes was safe. And she knew now that it was for Innes that she had put herself in the Law's reverence. She had thought it was for Innes's mother, for Henrietta, for absolute justice. But in the latter end it was because whatever Innes had done she had not deserved what the Law would do to her. She had been highly tried, and her breaking-point was lower than normal. She lacked some alloy, some good coarse reinforcing stuff, that would have helped her to stand tension without giving way. But she was too fine to throw away.

Lucy noticed with interest the quality of the cheer that

greeted her as she went up to receive her diploma on Wednesday morning. The cheers for the various Seniors varied not only in intensity but in quality. There was laughter, for instance, and affection in the reception they gave Dakers. And Beau got a Head Senior's tribute; the congratulations of her inferiors to a highly popular Senior. But there was something in the cheer that they gave Innes that was remarkable; a warmth of admiration, a sympathy, and a well-wishing, that was accorded to no one else. Lucy wondered if it was merely that her inability to take the Arlinghurst appointment had moved them. Henrietta had said, during that conversation about Rouse and her examination tactics, that Innes was not popular. But there was something more in that cheer than mere popularity. They admired her. It was their tribute to quality.

The giving of diplomas, postponed from Tuesday to Wednesday because of the inquest, was the last event of Lucy's stay at Leys. She had arranged to catch the twelve o'clock train to London. She had been touched during the last few days to receive an endless string of small presents, which were left in her room with written messages attached. She hardly ever returned to her room without finding a new one there. Very few people had given Lucy presents since she grew up, and she still had a child's pleasure in being given something, however small. And these gifts had a spontaneity that was heart-warming; it was no concerted effort, no affair of putting the hat round; they had each given her something as it occurred to them. The Disciples' offering was a large white card which said:

THIS WILL ADMIT
Miss Lucy Pym
TO THE FOUR DISCIPLES CLINIC
AT MANCHESTER
and will provide
A COURSE OF TREATMENTS
Of any kind whatever
At any time whatever.

Dakers had contributed a small untidy parcel, labelled: "To remind you every morning of our first meeting!" which on being opened proved to be one of those flat loofahs for back-scrubbing. It was surely in some other life that she had been peered at over the bathroom partition by that waggish pony's-face. It was certainly not this Lucy Pym who had sat in the bath.

The devoted Miss Morris had made her a little felt purse—Heaven alone knew when the child had found time to fabricate it—and at the other end of the scale of worldly magnificence was Beau's pigskin case, which bore the message: "You will have so many parting gifts that you will need something to put them in," and was stamped with her initials. Even Giddy, with whom she had spent odd half hours talking about rheumatism and rats, had sent up a plant in a pot. She had no idea what it was—it looked fleshy and faintly obscene—but was relieved that it was small. Travelling with a pot plant was not her idea of what was fitting.

Beau had come in between breakfast and Diploma-giving to help her pack, but all the serious packing was done. Whether anything would close once everything was in was another matter.

"I'll come back and sit on them for you before morning clinic," Beau said. "We are free until then. Except for clinic there is nothing much to do until we go home on Friday."

"You'll be sorry to finish at Leys?"

"Dreadfully. I've had a wonderful time. However, summer holidays are a great consolation."

"Innes told me some time ago that you were going to Norway together."

"Yes, we were," Beau said, "but we're not any more."

"Oh."

"Innes has other plans."

It was evident that this relationship was not what it had been.

"Well, I'd better go and see that the Juniors haven't hogged all the best seats at the Diploma Do," she said, and went.

But there was one relationship that showed satisfactory progress.

The Nut Tart knocked at her door and said that she had come to give dear Miss Pym a luck-piece. She came in, looked at the piled cases, and said with her customary frankness: "You are not a very good packer, are you? Neither am I. It is a pedestrian talent."

Lucy, whose luck-pieces in the last few days had ranged from a Woolworth monkey-on-a-stick to a South African halfpenny,

196

waited with some curiosity to see what The Nut Tart's idea of the thing might be.

It was a blue bead.

"It was dug up in Central America a hundred years ago and it is almost as old as the world. It is very lucky."

"But I can't take that from you," Lucy protested.

"Oh, I have a little bracelet of them. It was the bracelet that was dug up. But I have taken out one of the beads for you. There are five left and that is plenty. And I have a piece of news for you. I am not going back to Brazil."

"No?"

"I am going to stay in England and marry Rick."

Lucy said that she was delighted to hear it.

"We shall be married in London in October, and you will be there and you will come to the wedding, no?"

Yes, Lucy would come to the wedding with pleasure.

"I am so glad about it," she said. She needed some contact with happiness after the last few days.

"Yes, it is all very satisfactory. We are cousins but not too near, and it is sensible to keep it in the family. I always thought I should like to marry an Englishman; and of course Rick is a parti. He is senior partner although he is so young. My parents are very pleased. And my grandmother, of course."

"And I take it that you yourself are pleased?" Lucy said, a shade dashed by this matter-of-fact catalogue.

"Oh yes. Rick is the only person in the world except my grandmother who can make me do things I don't want to do. That will be very good for me."

She looked at Lucy's doubtful face, and her great eyes sparkled.

"And of course I like him very much," she said.

When the diplomas had been presented, Lucy had mid-morning coffee with the Staff and said goodbye to them. Since she was leaving in the middle of the morning no one was free to come to the station with her. Henrietta thanked her, with undoubted tears in her eyes this time, for the help she had been. (But not in her wildest imaginings would Henrietta guess how much the help amounted to.) Lucy was to consider Leys as her home any time

197

she wanted to come and stay, or if she ever wanted a lecturer's job again, or if—or if—

And Lucy had to hide the fact that Leys, where she had been so happy, was the one place in the world that she would never come back to. A place that she was going, if her conscience and the shade of Rouse would let her, to blot out of her mind.

The Staff went to their various duties and Lucy went back to her room to finish packing. She had not spoken to Innes since that so-incredible conversation on Saturday morning; had hardly seen her, indeed, except for the moment when she had taken her diploma from Miss Hodge's hands.

Was Innes going to let her go without a word?

But when she came back to her room she found that word on her table. A written word. She opened the envelope and read

Dear Miss Pym,

Here it is in writing. For the rest of my life I shall atone for the thing I can't undo. I pay forfeit gladly. My life for hers.

I am sorry that this has spoiled Leys for you. And I hope that you will not be unhappy about what you have done for me. I promise to make it worth while.

Perhaps, ten years from today, you will come to the West Country and see what I have done with my life. That would give me a date to look forward to. A landmark in a world without them.

Meanwhile, and always, my gratitude—my unspeakable gratitude.

Mary Innes.

"What time did you order the taxi for?" Beau asked, coming in on top of her knock.

"Half-past eleven."

"It's practically that now. Have you everything in that is going in? Hot water bottle? You hadn't one. Umbrella downstairs? You don't possess one. What do you do? Wait in doorways till it's over, or steal the nearest one? I had an aunt who always bought the cheapest she could find and discarded it in the nearest waste-paper-bin when the rain stopped. More money than sense, as my nanny used to say. Well, now. Is that all? Consider well, because once we get those cases shut we'll never get them open again. Nothing left in the drawers? People always leave things stuck at the back of drawers." She opened the small drawers of the table and ran her hands into the back of them. "Half the divorces in the Western Hemisphere start through the subsequent revelations."

She withdrew her right hand, and Lucy saw that she was holding the little silver rosette; left lying at the back of the drawer because Lucy had not been able to make up her mind what to do with it.

Beau turned it over in her fingers.

"That looks like the little button thing off my shoe," she said. "*Your* shoe?"

"Yes. Those black pump things that one wore at dancing class. I hung on to them because they are so lovely when one's feet are tired. Like gloves. I can still wear the shoes I wore when I was fourteen. I always had enormous feet for my age, and believe me it was no consolation to be told that you were going to be tall." Her attention went back to the thing she was holding. "So *this* is where I lost it," she said. "You know, I wondered quite a lot about that." She dropped it into her pocket. "You'll have to sit on this case, I'm afraid. You sit on it and I'll wrestle with the locks."

Automatically Lucy sat on it.

She wondered why she had never noticed before how cold those blue eyes were. Brilliant and cold and shallow.

The bright hair fell over her lap as Beau wrestled with the locks. The locks would do what she wanted, of course. Everything and everyone, always, since the day she was born, had done what she wanted. If they hadn't, she took steps to see that they did. At the age of four, Lucy remembered, she had defeated a whole adult world because her will to have things her way was greater than all the wills combined against her. She had never known frustration.

She could not visualise the possibility of frustration.

If *her* friend had the obvious right to Arlinghurst, then to Arlinghurst she should go.

"There! That's done it. Stand by to sit on the other if I

can't manage it. I see Giddy's given you one of his loathsome little plants. What a bore for you. Perhaps you can exchange it for a bowl at the back door one day."

How soon, Lucy wondered, had Innes begun to suspect? Almost at once? Certainly before the afternoon, when she had turned green on the spot where it had happened.

But she had not been sure until she saw the silver rosette on Lucy's palm, and learned where it had been found.

Poor Innes. Poor Innes, who was paying forfeit.

"*Tax-i!*" yelled a voice along the corridor.

"There's your cab. I'll take your things. No, they're quite light; you forget the training I've had. I wish you weren't going, Miss Pym. We shall miss you so much."

Lucy heard herself saying the obvious things. She even heard herself promising Beau that she might come to them for Christmas, when Beau would be home for her first "working" holidays.

Beau put her into the cab, took a tender farewell of her, and said: "The station" to the driver, and the taxi slid into motion and Beau's face smiled a moment beyond the window, and was gone.

The driver pushed back the glass panel and asked: "London train, lady?" Yes, Lucy said, to London.

And in London she would stay. In London was her own, safe, nice, calm, collected existence, and in future she would be content with it. She would even give up lecturing on psychology.

What did she know about psychology anyhow?

As a psychologist she was a first-rate teacher of French.

She could write a book about character as betrayed by facial characteristics. At least she had been right about that. Mostly.

Eyebrows that sent people to the stake.

Yes, she would write a book about face-reading.

Under another name, of course. Face-reading was not well seen among the intelligentsia.

The Franchise Affair

IT was four o'clock of a spring evening; and Robert Blair was thinking of going home.

The office would not shut until five, of course. But when you are the only Blair, of Blair, Hayward, and Bennet, you go home when you think you will. And when your business is mostly wills, conveyancing, and investments your services are in small demand in the late afternoon. And when you live in Milford, where the last post goes out at 3.45, the day loses whatever momentum it ever had long before four o'clock.

It was not even likely that his telephone would ring. His golfing cronies would by now be somewhere between the fourteenth and the sixteenth hole. No one would ask him to dinner, because in Milford invitations to dinner are still written by hand and sent through the post. And Aunt Lin would not ring up and ask him to call for the fish on his way home, because this was her bi-weekly afternoon at the cinema, and she would at the moment be only twenty minutes gone with feature, so to speak.

So he sat there, in the lazy atmosphere of a spring evening in a little market town, staring at the last patch of sunlight on his desk (the mahogany desk with the brass inlay that his grandfather had scandalised the family by bringing home from Paris) and thought about going home. In the patch of sunlight was his tea-tray; and it was typical of Blair, Hayward, and Bennet that tea was no affair of a japanned tin tray and a kitchen cup. At 3.50 exactly on every working day Miss Tuff bore into his office a lacquer tray covered with a fair white cloth and bearing a cup of tea in blue-patterned china, and, on a plate to match, two biscuits; petit-beurre Mondays, Wednesdays and Fridays, digestive Tuesdays, Thursdays and Saturdays.

Looking at it now, idly, he thought how much it represented the continuity of Blair, Hayward, and Bennet. The china he could remember as long as he could remember anything. The tray had been used when he was very small by the cook at home to take the bread in from the baker, and had been rescued by his young mother and brought to the office to bear the blue-patterned cups. The cloth had come years later with the advent of Miss Tuff. Miss Tuff was a war-time product; the first woman who had ever sat at a desk in a respectable solicitor's in Milford. A whole revolution Miss Tuff was in her single gawky thin earnest person. But the firm had survived the revolution with hardly a jolt, and now, nearly a quarter of a century later, it was inconceivable that thin grey dignified Miss Tuff had ever been a sensation. Indeed her only disturbance of the immemorial routine was the introduction of the tray-cloth. In Miss Tuff's home no meal was ever put straight on to a tray; if it comes to that, no cakes were ever put straight on to a plate; a tray-cloth or a doyley must intervene. So Miss Tuff had looked askance at the bare tray. She had, moreover, considered the lacquered pattern distracting, unappetising, and "queer." So one day she had brought a cloth from home; decent, plain, and white, as befitted something that was to be eaten off. And Robert's father, who had liked the lacquer tray, looked at the clean white cloth and was touched by young Miss Tuff's identification of herself with the firm's interests, and the cloth had stayed, and was now as much a part of the firm's life as the deed-boxes, and the brass plate, and Mr. Heseltine's annual cold.

It was when his eyes rested on the blue plate where the biscuits had been that Robert experienced that odd sensation in his chest again. The sensation had nothing to do with the two digestive biscuits; at least, not physically. It had to do with the inevitability of the biscuit routine; the placid certainty that it would be digestive on a Thursday and petit-beurre on a Monday. Until the last year or so, he had found no fault with certainty or placidity. He had never wanted any other life but this: this quiet friendly life in the place where he had grown up. He still did not want any other. But once or twice lately an odd, alien thought had crossed his mind; irrelevant and unbidden. As nearly as it could be put into words it was: "This is all you are ever going to have." And with the thought would come that moment's constriction in his chest. Almost a panic reaction; like the heart-squeezing that re-membering a dentist appointment would cause in his ten-year-old breast.

2

This annoyed and puzzled Robert; who considered himself a happy and fortunate person, and adult at that. Why should this foreign thought thrust itself on him and cause that dismayed tightening under his ribs? What had his life lacked that a man might be supposed to miss?

A wife?

But he could have married if he had wanted to. At least he supposed he could; there were a great many unattached females in the district, and they showed no signs of disliking him.

A devoted mother?

But what greater devotion could a mother have given him than Aunt Lin provided; dear doting Aunt Lin.

Riches?

What had he ever wanted that he could not buy? And if that wasn't riches he didn't know what was.

An exciting life?

But he had never wanted excitement. No greater excitement, that is, than was provided by a day's hunting or being all-square at the sixteenth.

Then what?

Why the "This is all you are ever going to have" thought?

Perhaps, he thought, sitting staring at the blue plate where the biscuits had been, it was just that Childhood's attitude of something-wonderful-tomorrow persisted subconsciously in a man as long as it was capable of realisation, and it was only after forty, when it became unlikely of fulfilment, that it obtruded itself into conscious thought; a lost piece of childhood crying for attention.

Certainly he, Robert Blair, hoped very heartily that his life would go on being what it was until he died. He had known since his schooldays that he would go into the firm and one day succeed his father; and he had looked with good-natured pity on boys who had no niche in life ready-made for them; who had no Milford, full of friends and memories, waiting for them; no part in English continuity as was provided by Blair, Hayward, and Bennet.

There was no Hayward in the firm nowadays; there had not been one since 1843; but a young sprig of the Bennets was occupying the back room at this moment. Occupying was the operative word, since it was very unlikely that he was doing any work;

3

his chief interest in life being to write poems of an originality so pristine that only Nevil himself could understand them. Robert deplored the poems but condoned the idleness, since he could not forget that when he had occupied that same room he had spent his time practising mashie shots into the leather arm-chair.

The sunlight slipped off the edge of the tray and Robert decided it was time to go. If he went now he could walk home down the High Street before the sunlight was off the east-side pavement; and walking down Milford High Street was still one of the things that gave him conscious pleasure. Not that Milford was a show-place. It could be duplicated a hundred times anywhere south of Trent. But in its unselfconscious fashion it typified the goodness of life in England for the last three hundred years. From the old dwelling-house flush with the pavement that housed Blair, Hayward, and Bennet and had been built in the last years of Charles the Second's reign, the High Street flowed south in a gentle slope—Georgian brick, Elizabethan timber-and-plaster, Victorian stone, Regency stucco—to the Edwardian villas behind their elm trees at the other end. Here and there, among the rose and white and brown, appeared a front of black glass, brazening it out like an overdressed parvenu at a party; but the good manners of the other buildings discounted them. Even the multiple businesses had dealt leniently with Milford. True, the scarlet and gold of an American bazaar flaunted its bright promise down at the south end, and daily offended Miss Truelove who ran the Elizabethan relic opposite as a tea-shop with the aid of her sister's baking and Ann Boleyn's reputation. But the Westminster Bank, with a humility rare since the days of usury, had adapted the Weavers Hall to their needs without so much as a hint of marble; and Soles, the wholesale chemists, had taken the old Wisdom residence and kept its tall surprised-looking front intact.

It was a fine, gay, busy little street, punctuated with pollarded lime trees growing out of the pavement; and Robert Blair loved it.

He had gathered his feet under him preparatory to getting up, when his telephone rang. In other places in the world, one understands, telephones are made to ring in outer offices, where a minion answers the thing and asks your business and says that if you will be good enough to wait just a moment she will "put you

4

thrrrough" and you are then connected with the person you want to speak to. But not in Milford. Nothing like that would be tolerated in Milford. In Milford if you call John Smith on the telephone you expect John Smith to answer in person. So when the telephone rang on that spring evening in Blair, Hayward, and Bennet's it rang on Robert's brass-and-mahogany desk.

Always, afterwards, Robert was to wonder what would have happened if that telephone call had been one minute later. In one minute, sixty worthless seconds, he would have taken his coat from the peg in the hall, popped his head into the opposite room to tell Mr. Heseltine that he was departing for the day stepped out into the pale sunlight and been away down the street. Mr. Heseltine would have answered his telephone when it rang and told the woman that he had gone. And she would have hung up and tried someone else. And all that followed would have had only academic interest for him.

But the telephone rang in time; and Robert put out his hand and picked up the receiver.

"Is that Mr. Blair?" a woman's voice asked; a contralto voice that would normally be a confident one, he felt, but now sounded breathless or hurried. "Oh, I am so glad to have caught you. I was afraid you would have gone for the day. Mr. Blair, you don't know me. My name is Sharpe, Marion Sharpe. I live with my mother at The Franchise. The house out on the Larborough road, you know."

"Yes, I know it," Blair said. He knew Marion Sharpe by sight, as he knew everyone in Milford and the district. A tall, lean, dark woman of forty or so; much given to bright silk kerchiefs which accentuated her gipsy swarthiness. She drove a battered old car, from which she shopped in the mornings while her white-haired old mother sat in the back, upright and delicate and incongruous and somehow silently protesting. In profile old Mrs. Sharpe looked like Whistler's mother; when she turned full-face and you got the impact of her bright, pale, cold, seagull's eye, she looked like a sibyl. An uncomfortable old person.

"You don't know me," the voice went on, "but I have seen you in Milford, and you look a kind person, and I need a lawyer. I mean, I need one now. this minute. The only lawyer we ever have business with is in London—a London firm, I mean—and they are not actually ours. We just inherited them with a legacy. But now I am in trouble and I need legal backing, and I remembered you and thought that you would——"

"If it is your car——" Robert began. "In trouble" in Milford meant one of two things; an affiliation order, or an offence against the traffic laws. Since the case involved Marion Sharpe, it would be the latter; but it made no difference because in neither case was Blair, Hayward, and Bennet likely to be interested. He would pass her on to Carley, the bright lad at the other end of the street, who revelled in court cases and was popularly credited with the capacity to bail the Devil out of hell. ("Bail him out!" someone said, one night at the Rose and Crown. "He'd do more than that. He'd get all our signatures to a guinea testimonial to the Old Sinner.")

"If it is your car——"

"Car?" she said, vaguely; as if in her present world it was difficult to remember what a car was. "Oh, I see. No. Oh, no, it isn't anything like that. It is something much more serious. It's Scotland Yard."

"Scotland Yard!"

To that douce country lawyer and gentleman, Robert Blair, Scotland Yard was as exotic as Xanadu, Hollywood, or parachuting. As a good citizen he was on comfortable terms with the local police, and there his connection with crime ended. The nearest he had ever come to Scotland Yard was to play golf with the local Inspector; a good chap who played a very steady game and occasionally, when it came to the nineteenth, expanded into mild indiscretions about his job.

"I haven't *murdered* anyone, if that is what you are thinking," the voice said hastily.

"The point is: are you *supposed* to have murdered anyone?" Whatever she was supposed to have done this was clearly a case for Carley. He must edge her off on to Carley.

"No; it isn't murder at all. I'm supposed to have kidnapped someone. Or abducted them, or something. I can't explain over the telephone. And anyhow I need someone now, at once, and——"

"But, you know, I don't think it is me you need at all," Robert

6

said. "I know practically nothing about criminal law. My firm is not equipped to deal with a case of that sort. The man you need——"

"I don't want a criminal lawyer. I want a friend. Someone who will stand by me and see that I am not put-upon. I mean, tell me what I need not answer if I don't want to, and that sort of thing. You don't need a training in crime for that, do you?"

"No, but you would be much better served by a firm who were used to police cases. A firm that——"

"What you are trying to tell me is that this is not 'your cup of tea'; that's it, isn't it?"

"No, of course not," Robert said hastily. "I quite honestly feel that you would be wiser——"

"You know what I feel like?" she broke in. "I feel like someone drowning in a river because she can't drag herself up the bank, and instead of giving me a hand you point out that the other bank is much better to crawl out on."

There was a moment's silence.

"But on the contrary," Robert said, "I can provide you with an expert puller-out-of-rivers; a great improvement on my amateur self, I assure you. Benjamin Carley knows more about defending accused persons than anyone between here and——"

"What! That awful little man with the striped suits!" Her deep voice ran up and cracked, and there was another momentary silence. "I am sorry," she said presently in her normal voice. "That was silly. But you see, when I rang you up just now it wasn't because I thought you would be clever about things" ("*Wasn't* it, indeed," thought Robert) "but because I was in trouble and wanted the advice of someone of my own sort. And you looked my sort. Mr. Blair, do please come. I need you *now*. There are people from Scotland Yard here in the house. And if you feel that it isn't something you want to be mixed up in you could always pass it on to someone else afterwards; couldn't you? But there may be nothing after all to be mixed up in. If you would just come out here and 'watch my interests' or whatever you call it, for an hour, it may all pass over. I'm sure there is a mistake somewhere. Couldn't you please do that for me?"

On the whole Robert Blair thought that he could. He was too good-natured to refuse any reasonable appeal—and she had given

7

him a loophole if things grew difficult. And he did not, after all, now he came to think of it, want to throw her to Ben Carley. In spite of her *bêtise* about striped suits he saw her point of view. If you had done something you wanted to get away with, Carley was no doubt God's gift to you; but if you were bewildered and in trouble and innocent, perhaps Carley's brash personality was not likely to be a very present help.

All the same, he wished as he laid down the receiver that the front he presented to the world was a more forbidding one—Calvin or Caliban, he did not care, so long as strange females were discouraged from flinging themselves on his protection when they were in trouble.

What possible kind of trouble could "kidnapping" be, he wondered as he walked round to the garage in Sin Lane for his car? *Was* there such an offence in English law? And whom could she possibly be interested in kidnapping? A child? Some child with "expectations"? In spite of the large house out on the Larborough road they gave the impression of having very little money. Or some child that they considered "ill-used" by its natural guardians? That was possible. The old woman had a fanatic's face, if ever he saw one; and Marion Sharpe herself looked as if the stake would be her natural prop if stakes were not out of fashion. Yes, it was probably some ill-judged piece of philanthropy. Detention "with intent to deprive parent, guardian, etc., of its possession." He wished he remembered more of his *Harris and Wilshere*. He could not remember off-hand whether that was a felony, with penal servitude in the offing, or a mere misdemeanour. "Abduction and Detention" had not sullied the Blair, Hayward, and Bennet files since December 1798, when the squire of Lessows, much flown with seasonable claret, had taken the young Miss Gretton across his saddle-bow from a ball at the Gretton home and ridden away with her through the floods; and there was no doubt at all, of course, as to the squire's motive on that occasion.

Ah, well; they would no doubt be open to reason now that they had been startled by the irruption of Scotland Yard into their plans. He was a little startled by Scotland Yard himself. Was the child so important that it was a matter for Headquarters?

Round in Sin Lane he ran into the usual war but extricated

8

himself. (Etymologists, in case you are interested, say that the "Sin" is merely a corruption of "sand," but the inhabitants of Milford of course know better; before those council houses were built on the low meadows behind the town the lane led direct to the lovers' walk in High Wood.) Across the narrow lane, face to face in perpetual enmity, stood the local livery stable and the town's newest garage. The garage frightened the horses (so said the livery stable), and the livery stable blocked up the lane continually with delivery loads of straw and fodder and what not (so the garage said). Moreover the garage was run by Bill Brough, ex-R.E.M.E., and Stanley Peters, ex-Royal Corps of Signals; and old Matt Ellis, ex-King's Dragoon Guards, looked on them as representatives of a generation which had destroyed the cavalry and an offence to civilisation.

In winter, when he hunted, Robert heard the cavalry side of the story; for the rest of the year he listened to the Royal Corps of Signals while his car was being wiped, oiled, filled, or fetched. Today the Signals wanted to know the difference between libel and slander, and what exactly constituted defamation of character. Was it defamation of character to say that a man was "a tinkerer with tin cans who wouldn't know a nut from an acorn"?

"Don't know, Stan. Have to think over it," Robert said hastily, pressing the starter. He waited while three tired hacks brought back two fat children and a groom from their afternoon ride ("See what I mean?" said Stanley in the background) and then swung the car into the High Street.

Down at the south end of the High Street the shops faded gradually into dwelling houses with doorsteps on the pavement, then to houses set back a pace and with porticos to their doors, and then to villas with trees in their gardens, and then, quite suddenly, to fields and open country.

It was farming country; a land of endless hedged fields and few houses. A rich country, but lonely; one could travel mile after mile without meeting another human being. Quiet and confident and unchanged since the Wars of the Roses, hedged field succeeded hedged field, and skyline faded into skyline, without any break in the pattern. Only the telegraph posts betrayed the century.

9

Away beyond the horizon was Larborough. Larborough was bicycles, small arms, tin-tacks, Cowan's Cranberry Sauce, and a million human souls living cheek by jowl in dirty red brick; and periodically it broke bounds in an atavistic longing for grass and earth. But there was nothing in the Milford country to attract a race who demanded with their grass and earth both views and tea-houses; when Larborough went on holiday it went as one man west to the hills and the sea, and the great stretch of country north and east of it stayed lonely and quiet and unlittered as it had been in the days of the Sun in Splendour. It was "dull"; and by that damnation was saved.

Two miles out on the Larborough road stood the house known as The Franchise; set down by the roadside with the inconsequence of a telephone kiosk. In the last days of the Regency someone had bought the field known as The Franchise, built in the middle of it a flat white house, and then surrounded the whole with a high solid wall of brick with a large double gate, of wall height, in the middle of the road frontage. It had no relation with anything in the countryside. No farm buildings in the background; no side-gates, even, into the surrounding fields. Stables were built in accordance with the period at the back of the house, but they were inside the wall. The place was as irrelevant, as isolated, as a child's toy dropped by the wayside. It had been occupied as long as Robert could remember by an old man; presumably the same old man, but since The Franchise people had always shopped at Ham Green, the village on the Larborough side of them, they had never been seen in Milford. And then Marion Sharpe and her mother had begun to be part of the morning shopping scene in Milford, and it was understood that they had inherited The Franchise when the old man died.

How long had they been there, Robert wondered. Three years? Four years?

That they had not entered Milford socially was nothing to reckon by. Old Mrs. Warren, who had bought the first of the elm-shaded villas at the end of the High Street a small matter of twenty-five years ago in the hope that midland air would be better for her rheumatism than the sea, was still referred to as "that lady from Weymouth." (It was Swanage, incidentally.)

The Sharpes, moreover, might not have sought social contacts. They had an odd air of being self-sufficient. He had seen the daughter once or twice on the golf-course, playing (presumably as a guest) with Dr. Borthwick. She drove a long ball like a man, and used her thin brown wrists like a professional. And that was all Robert knew about her.

As he brought the car to a stop in front of the tall iron gates, he found that two other cars were already there. It needed only one glance at the nearer—so inconspicuous, so well-groomed, so discreet—to identify it. In what other country in this world, he wondered as he got out of his own car, does the police force take pains to be well-mannered and quiet?

His eye lighted on the further car and he saw that it was Hallam's; the local Inspector who played such a steady game on golf-course.

There were three people in the police car: the driver, and, in the back, a middle-aged woman and what seemed to be either a child or a young girl. The driver regarded him with that mild, absent-minded, all-observing police eye, and then withdrew his gaze, but the faces in the back he could not see.

The tall iron gates were shut—Robert could not remember ever seeing them open—and Robert pushed open one heavy half with frank curiosity. The iron lace of the original gates had been lined, in some Victorian desire for privacy, by flat sheets of cast iron; and the wall was too high for anything inside to be visible; so that, except for a distant view of its roof and chimneys, he had never seen The Franchise.

His first feeling was disappointment. It was not the fallen-on-evil-times look of the house—although that was evident; it was the sheer ugliness of it. Either it had been built too late to share in the grace of a graceful period, or the builder had lacked an architect's eye. He had used the idiom of the time, but it had apparently not been native to him. Everything was just a little wrong: the windows the wrong size by half a foot, wrongly placed by not much more; the doorway the wrong width, and the flight of steps the wrong height. The total result was that instead of the bland contentment of its period the house had a hard stare. An antagonistic, questioning stare. As he walked across the courtyard to the unwelcoming door Robert knew what it reminded him of: a dog that has been suddenly wakened from sleep by the advent of a stranger, propped on his forelegs, uncertain for a moment whether to attack or merely bark. It had the same what-are-you-doing-here? expression.

Before he could ring the bell the door was opened; not by a maid but by Marion Sharpe.

"I saw you coming," she said, putting out her hand. "I didn't want you to ring because my mother lies down in the afternoons, and I am hoping that we can get this business over before she wakes up. Then she need never know anything about it. I am more grateful than I can say to you for coming."

Robert murmured something, and noticed that her eyes, which he had expected to be a bright gipsy brown, were actually a grey hazel. She drew him into the hall, and he noticed as he put his hat down on a chest that the rug on the floor was threadbare.

"The Law is in here," she said, pushing open a door and ushering him into a drawing-room. Robert would have liked to talk to her alone for a moment, to orientate himself; but it was too late now to suggest that. This was evidently the way she wanted it.

Sitting on the edge of a bead-work chair was Hallam, looking sheepish. And by the window, entirely at his ease in a very nice piece of Hepplewhite, was Scotland Yard in the person of a youngish spare man in a well-tailored suit.

As they got up, Hallam and Robert nodded to each other.

"You know Inspector Hallam, then?" Marion Sharpe said. "And this is Detective-Inspector Grant, from Headquarters."

Robert noticed the "Headquarters," and wondered. Had she already at some time had dealings with the police, or was it that she just didn't like the slightly sensational sound of "the Yard"?

Grant shook hands, and said:

"I'm glad you've come, Mr. Blair. Not only for Miss Sharpe's sake but for my own."

"Yours?"

"I couldn't very well proceed until Miss Sharpe had some kind of support; friendly support if not legal, but if legal so much the better."

"I see. And what are you charging her with?"

"We are not charging her with anything——" Grant began, but Marion interrupted him.

"I am supposed to have kidnapped and beaten up someone."

"*Beaten up?*" Robert said, staggered.

"Yes," she said, with a kind of relish in enormity. "Beaten her black and blue."

"Her?"

"A girl. She is outside the gate in a car now."

"I think we had better begin at the beginning," Robert said, clutching after the normal.

"Perhaps I had better do the explaining," Grant said, mildly.

"Yes," said Miss Sharpe, "do. After all it is your story."

Robert wondered if Grant were aware of the mockery. He wondered a little, too, at the coolness that could afford mockery with Scotland Yard sitting in one of her best chairs. She had not sounded cool over the telephone; she had sounded driven, half-desperate. Perhaps it was the presence of an ally that had heartened her; or perhaps she had just got her second wind.

"Just before Easter," Grant began, in succinct police-fashion, "a girl called Elisabeth Kane, who lived with her guardians near Aylesbury, went to spend a short holiday with a married aunt in Mainshill, the suburb of Larborough. She went by coach, because the London-Larborough coaches pass through Aylesbury, and also pass through Mainshill before reaching Larborough; so that she could get off the coach in Mainshill and be within a three-minute walk of her aunt's house, instead of having to go into Larborough and come all the way out again as she would have to if she travelled by train. At the end of a week her guardians— a Mr. and Mrs. Wynn—had a postcard from her saying that she was enjoying herself very much and was staying on. They took this to mean staying on for the duration of her school holiday, which would mean another three weeks. When she didn't turn up on the day before she was supposed to go back to school, they took it for granted that she was merely playing truant and wrote to her aunt to send her back. The aunt, instead of going to the nearest call-box or telegraph office, broke it to the Wynns in a letter, that her niece had left on her way back to Aylesbury a fortnight previously. The exchange of letters had taken the best part of another week, so that by the time the guardians went to the police about it the girl had been missing for four weeks. The police took all the usual measures but before they could really get going the girl turned up. She walked into her home near Aylesbury late one night wearing only a dress and shoes, and in a state of complete exhaustion."

"How old is the girl?" Robert asked.

"Fifteen. Nearly sixteen." He waited a moment to see if Robert had further questions, and then went on. (As one counsel to another, thought Robert appreciatively; a manner to match the car that stood so unobtrusively at the gate.) "She said she had been 'kidnapped' in a car, but that was all the information anyone got from her for two days. She lapsed into a semi-conscious condition. When she recovered, about forty-eight hours later, they began to get her story from her."

"They?"

"The Wynns. The police wanted it, of course, but she grew hysterical at any mention of police, so they had to acquire it second-hand. She said that while she was waiting for her return coach at the cross-roads in Mainshill, a car pulled up at the kerb with two women in it. The younger woman, who was driving, asked her if she was waiting for a bus and if they could give her a lift."

"Was the girl alone?"

"Yes."

"Why? Didn't anyone go to see her off?"

"Her uncle was working, and her aunt had gone to be godmother at a christening." Again he paused to let Robert put further questions if he was so minded. "The girl said that she was waiting for the London coach, and they told her that it had already gone by. Since she had arrived at the cross-roads with very little time to spare, and her watch was not a particularly accurate one, she believed this. Indeed, she had begun to be afraid, even before the car stopped, that she had missed the coach. She was distressed about it because it was by then four o'clock, beginning to rain, and growing dark. They were very sympathetic, and suggested that they should give her a lift to a place whose name she did not catch, where she could get a different coach to London in

14

half an hour's time. She accepted this gratefully and got in beside the elder woman in the back of the car."

A picture swam into Robert's mind of old Mrs. Sharpe, upright and intimidating, in her usual place in the back of the car. He glanced at Marion Sharpe, but her face was calm. This was a story she had heard already.

"The rain blurred the windows, and she talked to the older woman about herself as they went along, so that she paid little attention to where they were going. When she at last took notice of her surroundings the evening outside the windows had become quite dark and it seemed to her that they had been travelling for a long time. She said something about its being extraordinarily kind of them to take her so far out of their way, and the younger woman, speaking for the first time, said that as it happened it was not out of their way, and that, on the contrary, she would have time to come in and have a cup of something hot with them before they took her on to her new cross-roads. She was doubtful about this, but the younger woman said it would be of no advantage to wait for twenty minutes in the rain when she could be warm and dry and fed in those same twenty minutes; and she agreed that this seemed sensible. Eventually the younger woman got out, opened what appeared to the girl to be drive gates, and the car was driven up to a house which it was too dark to see. She was taken into a large kitchen——"

"A kitchen?" Robert repeated.

"Yes, a kitchen. The older woman put some cold coffee on the stove to heat while the younger one cut sandwiches. 'Sandwiches without tops,' the girl called them."

"Smorgasbord."

"Yes. While they ate and drank, the younger woman told her that they had no maid at the moment and asked her if she would like to be a maid for them for a little. She said that she wouldn't. They tried persuasion, but she stuck to it that that was not at all the kind of job she would take. Their faces began to grow blurred as she talked, and when they suggested that she might at least come upstairs and see what a nice bedroom she would have if she stayed she was too fuddled in her mind to do anything but follow their suggestion. She remembers going up a first flight with a carpet, and a second flight with what she calls 'something hard' underfoot, and that was all she remembered until she woke in daylight on a truckle bed in a bare little attic. She was wearing only her slip, and there was no sign of the rest of her clothes. The door was locked, and the small round window would not open. In any case——"

"*Round* window!" said Robert, uncomfortably.

But it was Marion who answered him. "Yes," she said, meaningly. "A round window up in the roof."

Since his last thought as he came to her front door a few minutes ago had been how badly placed was the little round window in the roof, there seemed to Robert to be no adequate comment. Grant made his usual pause for courtesy's sake, and went on.

"Presently the younger woman arrived with a bowl of porridge. The girl refused it and demanded her clothes and her release. The woman said that she would eat it when she was hungry enough and went away, leaving the porridge behind. She was alone till evening, when the same woman brought her tea on a tray with fresh cakes and tried to talk her into giving the maid's job a trial. The girl again refused, and for days, according to her story, this alternate coaxing and bullying went on, sometimes by one of the women and sometimes by the other. Then she decided that if she could break the small round window she might be able to crawl out of it on to the roof, which was protected by a parapet, and call the attention of some passerby, or some visiting tradesman, to her plight. Unfortunately, her only implement was a chair, and she had managed only to crack the glass before the younger woman interrupted her, in a great passion. She snatched the chair from the girl and belaboured her with it until she was breathless. She went away, taking the chair with her, and the girl thought that was the end of it. But in a few moments the woman came back with what the girl thinks was a dog whip and beat her until she fainted. Next day the older woman appeared with an armful of bed-linen and said that if she would not work she would at least sew. No sewing, no food. She was too stiff to sew and so had no food. The following day she was threatened with another beating if she did not sew. So she mended some of the linen and was given stew for supper. This arrangement lasted for some time,

16

but if her sewing was bad or insufficient, she was either beaten or deprived of food. Then one evening the older woman brought the usual bowl of stew and went away leaving the door unlocked. The girl waited, thinking it was a trap that would end in another beating; but in the end she ventured on to the landing. There was no sound, and she ran down a flight of uncarpeted stairs. Then down a second flight to the first landing. Now she could hear the two women talking in the kitchen. She crept down the last flight and dashed for the door. It was unlocked and she ran out just as she was into the night."

"In her slip?" Robert asked.

"I forgot to say that the slip had been exchanged for her dress. There was no heating in the attic, and in nothing but a slip she would probably have died."

"If she ever was in an attic," Robert said.

"If, as you say, she ever was in an attic," the Inspector agreed smoothly. And without his customary pause of courtesy went on: "She does not remember much after that. She walked a great distance in the dark, she says. It seemed a highroad but there was no traffic and she met no one. Then, on a main road, some time later, a lorry driver saw her in his headlight and stopped to give her a lift. She was so tired that she fell straight asleep. She woke as she was being set on her feet at the roadside. The lorry driver was laughing at her and saying that she was like a sawdust doll that had lost its stuffing. It seemed to be still night time. The lorry driver said this was where she said she wanted to be put off, and drove away. After a little she recognised the corner. It was less than two miles from her home. She heard a clock strike eleven. And shortly before midnight she arrived home."

～～～～～～～～～～～～～～～～～～～～～～～～～～～～～～

· 2 ·

THERE was a short silence.

"And this is the girl who is sitting in a car outside the gate of The Franchise at this moment?" said Robert.

"Yes."

"I take it that you have reasons for bringing her here."

17

"Yes. When the girl had recovered sufficiently she was induced to tell her story to the police. It was taken down in shorthand as she told it, and she read the typed version and signed it. In that statement there were two things that helped the police a lot. These are the relevant extracts:

'When we had been going for some time we passed a bus that had MILFORD in a lighted sign on it. No, I don't know where Milford is. No, I have never been there.'

"That is one. The other is:

'From the window of the attic I could see a high brick wall with a big iron gate in the middle of it. There was a road on the further side of the wall, because I could see the telegraph posts. No, I couldn't see the traffic on it because the wall was too high. Just the tops of lorry loads sometimes. You couldn't see through the gate because it had sheets of iron on the inside. Inside the gate the carriage way went straight for a little and then divided in two into a circle up to the door. No, it wasn't a garden, just grass. Yes, lawn, I suppose. No, I don't remember any shrubs; just the grass and the paths.'"

Grant shut the little notebook he had been quoting from.

"As far as we know—and the search has been thorough—there is no other house between Larborough and Milford which fulfils the girl's description except The Franchise. The Franchise, more-over, fulfils it in every particular. When the girl saw the wall and the gate today she was sure that this was the place; but she has not so far seen inside the gate, of course. I had first to explain matters to Miss Sharpe, and find out if she was willing to be confronted with the girl. She very rightly suggested that some legal witness should be present."

"Do you wonder that I wanted help in a hurry?" Marion Sharpe said, turning to Robert. "Can you imagine a more nightmare piece of nonsense?"

"The girl's story is certainly the oddest mixture of the factual and the absurd. I know that domestic help is scarce," Robert said, "but would anyone hope to enlist a servant by forcibly detaining her, to say nothing of beating and starving her."

"No normal person, of course," Grant agreed, keeping his eye steadily fixed on Robert's so that it had no tendency to slide over to Marion Sharpe. "But believe me in my first twelve months in the force I had come across a dozen things much more incredible. There is no end to the extravagances of human conduct."

"I agree; but the extravagance is just as likely to be in the girl's conduct. After all, the extravagance begins with her. She is the one who has been missing for——" He paused in question.

"A month," Grant supplied.

"For a month; while there is no suggestion that the household at The Franchise has varied at all from its routine. Would it not be possible for Miss Sharpe to provide an alibi for the day in question?"

"No," Marion Sharpe said. "The day, according to the Inspector, is the 28th of March. That is a long time ago, and our days here vary very little, if at all. It would be quite impossible for us to remember what we were doing on March the 28th—and most unlikely that anyone would remember for us."

"Your maid?" Robert suggested. "Servants have ways of marking their domestic life that is often surprising."

"We have no maid," she said. "We find it difficult to keep one: The Franchise is so isolated."

The moment threatened to become awkward and Robert hastened to break it.

"This girl—— I don't know her name, by the way."

"Elisabeth Kane; known as Betty Kane."

"Oh, yes; you did tell me. I'm sorry. This girl—may we know something about her? I take it that the police have investigated her before accepting so much of her story. Why guardians and not parents, for instance?"

"She is a war orphan. She was evacuated to the Aylesbury district as a small child. She was an only child, and was billeted with the Wynns, who had a boy four years older. About twelve months later both parents were killed, in the same 'incident,' and the

Wynns, who had always wanted a daughter and were very fond of the child, were glad to keep her. She looks on them as her parents, since she can hardly remember the real ones."

"I see. And her record?"

"Excellent. A very quiet girl, by every account. Good at her school work but not brilliant. Has never been in any kind of trouble, in school or out of it. 'Transparently truthful' was the phrase her form mistress used about her."

"When she eventually turned up at her home, after her absence, was there any evidence of the beatings she said she had been given?"

"Oh, yes. Very definitely. The Wynns' own doctor saw her early next morning, and his statement is that she had been very extensively knocked about. Indeed, some of the bruises were still visible much later when she made her statement to us."

"No history of epilepsy?"

"No; we considered that very early in the inquiry. I should like to say that the Wynns are very sensible people. They have been greatly distressed, but they have not tried to dramatise the affair, or allowed the girl to be an object of interest or pity. They have taken the affair admirably."

"And all that remains is for me to take my end of it with the same admirable detachment," Marion Sharpe said.

"You see my position, Miss Sharpe. The girl not only describes the house in which she says she was detained; she describes the two inhabitants—and describes them very accurately. 'A thin, elderly woman with soft white hair and no hat, dressed in black; and a much younger woman, thin and tall and dark like a gipsy, with no hat and a bright silk scarf round her neck.' "

"Oh, yes. I can think of no explanation, but I understand your position. And now I think we had better have the girl in, but before we do I should like to say——"

The door opened noiselessly, and old Mrs. Sharpe appeared on the threshold. The short pieces of white hair round her face stood up on end, as her pillow had left them, and she looked more than ever like a sibyl.

She pushed the door to behind her and surveyed the gathering with a malicious interest.

"Hah!" she said, making a sound like the throaty squawk of a hen. "*Three* strange men!"

"Let me present them, Mother," Marion said, as the three got to their feet.

"This is Mr. Blair, of Blair, Hayward, and Bennet—the firm who have that lovely house at the top of the High Street."

As Robert bowed the old woman fixed him with her seagull's eye.

"Needs re-tiling," she said.

It did, but it was not the greeting he had expected.

It comforted him a little that her greeting to Grant was even more unorthodox. Far from being impressed or agitated by the presence of Scotland Yard in her drawing-room of a spring afternoon, she merely said in her dry voice: "You should not be sitting in that chair; you are much too heavy for it."

When her daughter introduced the local Inspector she cast one glance at him, moved her head an inch, and quite obviously dismissed him from further consideration. This, Hallam, to judge by his expression, found peculiarly shattering.

Grant looked inquiringly at Miss Sharpe.

"I'll tell her," she said. "Mother, the Inspector wants us to see a young girl who is waiting in a car outside the gate. She was missing from her home near Aylesbury for a month, and when she turned up again—in a distressed condition—she said that she had been detained by people who wanted to make a servant of her. They kept her locked up when she refused, and beat and starved her. She described the place and the people minutely, and it so happens that you and I fit the description admirably. So does our house. The suggestion is that she was detained up in our attic with the round window."

"Remarkably interesting," said the old lady, seating herself with deliberation on an Empire sofa. "What did we beat her with?"

"A dog whip, I understand."

"Have we got a dog whip?"

"We have one of those 'lead' things, I think. They make a whip if necessary. But the point is, the Inspector would like us to meet this girl, so that she can say if we are the people who detained her or not."

21

"Have you any objections, Mrs. Sharpe?" Grant asked.

"On the contrary, Inspector. I look forward to the meeting with impatience. It is not every afternoon, I assure you, that I go to my rest a dull old woman and rise a potential monster."

"Then if you will excuse me, I shall bring——"

Hallam made a motion, offering himself as messenger, but Grant shook his head. It was obvious that he wanted to be present when the girl first saw what was beyond the gate.

As the Inspector went out Marion Sharpe explained Blair's presence to her mother. "It was extraordinarily kind of him to come at such short notice and so quickly," she added, and Robert felt again the impact of that bright pale old eye. For his money, old Mrs. Sharpe was quite capable of beating seven different people between breakfast and lunch, any day of the week.

"You have my sympathy, Mr. Blair," she said, unsympathetically.

"Why, Mrs. Sharpe?"

"I take it that Broadmoor is a little out of your line."

"Broadmoor!"

"Criminal lunacy."

"I find it extraordinarily stimulating," Robert said, refusing to be bullied by her.

This drew a flash of appreciation from her; something that was like the shadow of a smile. Robert had the odd feeling that she suddenly liked him; but if so she was making no verbal confession of it. Her dry voice said tartly: "Yes, I expect the distractions of Milford are scarce and mild. My daughter pursues a piece of gutta-percha round the golf course——"

"It is not gutta-percha any more, Mother," her daughter put in.

"But at my age Milford does not provide even that distraction. I am reduced to pouring weedkiller on weeds—a legitimate form of sadism on a par with drowning fleas. Do you drown your fleas, Mr. Blair?"

"No, I squash them. But I have a sister who used to pursue them with a cake of soap."

"Soap?" said Mrs. Sharpe, with genuine interest.

"I understand that she hit them with the soft side and they stuck to it."

"How *very* interesting. A technique I have not met before. I must try that next time."

With his other ear he heard that Marion was being nice to the snubbed Inspector. "You play a very good game, Inspector," she was saying.

He was conscious of the feeling you get near the end of a dream, when waking is just round the corner, that none of the inconsequence really matters because presently you'll be back in the real world.

This was misleading because the real world came through the door with the return of Inspector Grant. Grant came in first, so that he was in a position to see the expressions on all the faces concerned, and held the door open for a police matron and a girl.

Marion Sharpe stood up slowly, as if the better to face anything that might be coming to her, but her mother remained seated on the sofa as one giving an audience, her Victorian back as flat as it had been as a young girl, her hands lying composedly in her lap. Even her wild hair could not detract from the impression that she was mistress of the situation.

The girl was wearing her school coat, and childish low-heeled clumpish black school shoes; and consequently looked younger than Blair had anticipated. She was not very tall, and certainly not pretty. But she had—what was the word?—appeal. Her eyes, a darkish blue, were set wide apart in a face of the type popularly referred to as heart-shaped. Her hair was mouse-coloured, but grew off her forehead in a good line. Below each cheek-bone a slight hollow, a miracle of delicate modelling, gave the face charm and pathos. Her lower lip was full, but the mouth was too small. So were her ears. Too small and too close to her head.

An ordinary sort of girl, after all. Not the sort you would notice in a croc. Not at all the type to be the heroine of a sensation. Robert wondered what she would look like in other clothes.

The girl's glance rested first on the old woman, and then went on to Marion. The glance held neither surprise nor triumph, and not much interest.

"Yes, these are the women," she said.

"You have no doubt about it?" Grant asked her, and added: "It is a very grave accusation, you know."

"No, I have no doubt. How could I?"

"These two ladies are the women who detained you, took your clothes from you, forced you to mend linen, and whipped you?"

"Yes, these are the women."

"A remarkable liar," said old Mrs. Sharpe, in the tone in which one says: "A remarkable likeness."

"You say that we took you into the kitchen for coffee," Marion said.

"Yes, you did."

"Can you describe the kitchen?"

"I didn't pay much attention. It was a big one—with a stone floor, I think—and a row of bells."

"What kind of stove?"

"I didn't notice the stove, but the pan the old woman heated the coffee in was a pale blue enamel one with a dark blue edge and a lot of chips off round the bottom edge."

"I doubt if there is any kitchen in England that hasn't a pan exactly like that," Marion said. "We have three of them."

"Is the girl a virgin?" asked Mrs. Sharpe, in the mildly interested tone of a person inquiring: "Is it a Chanel?"

In the startled pause that this produced Robert was aware of Hallam's scandalised face, the hot blood running up into the girl's, and the fact that there was no protesting "Mother!" from the daughter as he unconsciously, but confidently, expected. He wondered whether her silence was tacit approval, or whether after a lifetime with Mrs. Sharpe she was shock-proof.

Grant said in cold reproof that the matter was irrelevant.

"You think so?" said the old lady. "If I had been missing for a month from my home it is the first thing that my mother would have wanted to know about me. However. Now that the girl has identified us, what do you propose to do? Arrest us?"

"Oh, no. Things are a long way from that at the moment. I want to take Miss Kane to the kitchen and the attic, so that her descriptions of them can be verified. If they are, I report on the case to my superior and he decides in conference what further steps to take."

"I see. A most admirable caution, Inspector." She rose slowly to her feet. "Ah, well, if you will excuse me I shall go back to my interrupted rest."

24

"But don't you want to be present when Miss Kane inspects—to hear the——" blurted Grant, surprised for once out of his composure.

"Oh, dear, no." She smoothed down her black gown with a slight frown. "They split invisible atoms," she remarked testily, "but no one so far has invented a material that does not crease. I have not the faintest doubt," she went on, "that Miss Kane will identify the attic. Indeed I should be surprised beyond belief if she failed to."

She began to move towards the door, and consequently towards the girl; and for the first time the girl's eyes lit with expression. A spasm of alarm crossed her face. The police matron came forward a step, protectively. Mrs. Sharpe continued her unhurried progress and came to rest a yard or so from the girl, so that they were face to face. For a full five seconds there was silence while she examined the girl's face with interest.

"For two people who are on beating terms, we are distressingly ill acquainted," she said at last. "I hope to know you much better before this affair is finished, Miss Kane." She turned to Robert and bowed. "Goodbye, Mr. Blair. I hope you will continue to find us stimulating." And, ignoring the rest of the gathering, she walked out of the door that Hallam held open for her.

There was a distinct feeling of anti-climax now that she was no longer there, and Robert paid her the tribute of a reluctant admiration. It was no small achievement to steal the interest from an outraged heroine.

"You have no objections to letting Miss Kane see the relevant parts of the house, Miss Sharpe?" Grant asked.

"Of course not. But before we go further I should like to say what I was going to say before you brought Miss Kane in. I am glad that Miss Kane is present to hear it now. It is this. I have never to my knowledge seen this girl before. I did not give her a lift anywhere, on any occasion. She was not brought into this house either by me or by my mother, nor was she kept here. I should like that to be clearly understood."

"Very well, Miss Sharpe. It is understood that your attitude is a complete denial of the girl's story."

"A complete denial from beginning to end. And now, will you come and see the kitchen?"

GRANT and the girl accompanied Robert and Marion Sharpe on the inspection of the house, while Hallam and the police matron waited in the drawing-room. As they reached the first-floor landing, after the girl had identified the kitchen, Robert said:

"Miss Kane said that the second flight of stairs was covered in 'something hard,' but the same carpet continues up from the first flight."

"Only to the curve," Marion said. "The bit that 'shows.' Round the corner it is drugget. A Victorian way of economising. Nowadays if you are poor you buy less expensive carpet and use it all the way up. But those were still the days when what the neighbours thought mattered. So the lush stuff went as far as eye could see and no further."

The girl had been right about the third flight, too. The treads of the short flight to the attic were bare.

The all-important attic was a low square little box of a room, with the ceiling slanting abruptly down on three sides in conformity with the slate roof outside. It was lit only by the round window looking out to the front. A short stretch of slates sloped from below the window to the low white parapet. The window was divided into four panes, one of which showed a badly starred crack. It had never been made to open.

The attic was completely bare of furnishing. Unnaturally bare, Robert thought, for so convenient and accessible a store-room.

"There used to be stuff here when we first came," Marion said, as if answering him. "But when we found that we should be without help half the time we got rid of it."

Grant turned to the girl with a questioning air.

"The bed was in that corner," she said, pointing to the corner away from the window. "And next it was the wooden commode. And in this corner behind the door there were three empty travelling-cases—two suitcases and a trunk with a flat top. There was a chair but she took it away after I tried to break the window." She referred to Marion without emotion, as if she were not present. "There is where I tried to break the window."

It seemed to Robert that the crack looked much more than a few weeks old; but there was no denying that the crack was there.

Grant crossed to the far corner and bent to examine the bare floor, but it did not need close examination. Even from where he was standing by the door Robert could see the marks of castors on the floor where the bed had stood.

"There was a bed there," Marion said. "It was one of the things we got rid of."

"What did you do with it?"

"Let me think. Oh, we gave it to the cowman's wife over at Staples Farm. Her eldest boy got too big to share a room with the others any more and she put him up in their loft. We get our dairy stuff from Staples. You can't see it from here but it is only four fields away over the rise."

"Where do you keep your spare trunks, Miss Sharpe? Have you another box-room?"

For the first time Marion hesitated. "We do have a large square trunk with a flat top, but my mother uses it to store things in. When we inherited The Franchise there was a very valuable tallboy in the bedroom my mother has, and we sold it, and used the big trunk instead. With a chintz cover on it. My suitcases I keep in the cupboard on the first-floor landing."

"Miss Kane, do you remember what the cases looked like?"

"Oh, yes. One was a brown leather with those sort-of caps at the corners, and the other was one of those American-looking canvas-covered ones with stripes."

Well, that was definite enough.

Grant examined the room a little longer, studied the view from the window, and then turned to go.

"May we see the suitcases in the cupboard?" he asked Marion.

"Certainly," Marion said, but she seemed unhappy.

On the lower landing she opened the cupboard door and stood back to let the Inspector look. As Robert moved out of their way he caught the unguarded flash of triumph on the girl's face. It so altered her calm, rather childish, face that it shocked him. It was a savage emotion, primitive and cruel. And very startling on the face of a demure schoolgirl who was the pride of her guardians and preceptors.

The cupboard contained shelves bearing household linen, and on the floor four suitcases. Two were expanding ones, one of pressed fibre and one of rawhide; the other two were: a brown cowhide with protected corners, and a square canvas-covered hat-box with a broad band of multi-coloured stripes down the middle.

"Are these the cases?" Grant asked.

"Yes," the girl said. "Those two."

"I am not going to disturb my mother again this afternoon," Marion said, with sudden anger. "I acknowledge that the trunk in her room is large and flat-topped. It has been there without interruption for the last three years."

"Very good, Miss Sharpe. And now the garage, if you please."

Down at the back of the house, where the stables had been converted long ago into garage, the little group stood and surveyed the battered old grey car. Grant read out the girl's untechnical description of it as recorded in her statement. It fitted, but it would fit equally well at least a thousand cars on the roads of Britain today, Blair thought. It was hardly evidence at all. " 'One of the wheels was painted a different shade from the others and didn't look as if it belonged. The different wheel was the one in front on my side as it was standing at the pavement,' " Grant finished.

In silence the four people looked at the darker grey of the near front wheel. There seemed nothing to say.

"Thank you very much, Miss Sharpe," Grant said at length, shutting his notebook and putting it away. "You have been very courteous and helpful and I am grateful to you. I shall be able to get you on the telephone any time in the next few days, I suppose, if I want to talk to you further?"

"Oh, yes, Inspector. We have no intention of going anywhere."

If Grant was aware of her too-ready comprehension he did not show it.

He handed over the girl to the matron and they left without a backward glance. Then he and Hallam took their leave, Hallam still with an air of apologising for trespass.

28

Marion had gone out into the hall with them, leaving Blair in the drawing-room, and when she came back she was carrying a tray with sherry and glasses.

"I don't ask you to stay for dinner," she said, putting down the tray and beginning to pour the wine, "partly because our 'dinner' is usually a very scratch supper and not at all what you are used to. (Did you know that your aunt's meals are famous in Milford? Even I had heard about them.) And partly because—well, because, as my mother said, Broadmoor is a little out of your line, I expect."

"About that," Robert said. "You do realise, don't you, that the girl has an enormous advantage over you. In the matter of evidence, I mean. She is free to describe almost any object she likes as being part of your household. If it happens to be there, that is strong evidence for her. If it happens not to be there, that is not evidence for you; the inference is merely that you have got rid of it. If the suitcases, for instance, had not been there, she could say that you had got rid of them because they had been in the attic and could be described."

"But she did describe them, without ever having seen them."

"She described two suitcases, you mean. If your four suitcases had been a matching set she would have only one chance in perhaps five of being right. But because you happened to have one of each of the common kinds her chances worked out at about even."

He picked up the glass of sherry that she had set down beside him, took a mouthful, and was astonished to find it admirable.

She smiled a little at him and said: "We economise, but not on wine," and he flushed slightly, wondering if his surprise had been as obvious as that.

"But there was the odd wheel of the car. How did she know about that? The whole set-up is extraordinary. How did she know about my mother and me, and what the house looked like? Our gates are never open. Even if she opened them—though what she could be doing on that lonely road I can't imagine—even if she opened them and looked inside she would not know about my mother and me."

"No chance of her having made friends with a maid? Or a gardener?"

29

"We have never had a gardener, because there is nothing but grass. And we have not had a maid for a year. Just a girl from the farm who comes in once a week and does the rough cleaning."

Robert said sympathetically that it was a big house to have on her hands unaided.

"Yes; but two things help. I am not a house-proud woman. And it is still so wonderful to have a home of our own that I am willing to put up with the disadvantages. Old Mr. Crowle was my father's cousin, but we didn't know him at all. My mother and I had always lived in a Kensington boarding-house." One corner of her mouth moved up in a wry smile. "You can imagine how popular Mother was with the residents." The smile faded. "My father died when I was very little. He was one of those optimists who are always going to be rich tomorrow. When he found one day that his speculations had not left even enough for a loaf of bread on the morrow, he committed suicide and left Mother to face things."

Robert felt that this to some extent explained Mrs. Sharpe.

"I was not trained for a profession, so my life has been spent in odd-jobs. Not domestic ones—I loathe domesticity—but helping in those lady-like businesses that abound in Kensington. Lamp-shades, or advising on holidays, or flowers, or bric-à-brac. When old Mr. Crowle died I was working in a tea-shop—one of those morning-coffee gossip shops. Yes, it is a little difficult."

"What is?"

"To imagine me among the tea-cups."

Robert, unused to having his mind read—Aunt Lin was incapable of following anyone's mental processes even when they were explained to her—was disconcerted. But she was not thinking of him.

"We had just begun to feel settled down, and at home, and safe, when this happened."

For the first time since she had asked his help Robert felt the stirring of partisanship. "And all because a slip of a girl needs an alibi," he said. "We must find out more about Betty Kane."

"I can tell you one thing about her. She is over-sexed."

"Is that just feminine intuition?"

"No. I am not very feminine and I have no intuition. But I have never known anyone—man or woman—with that colour of eye who wasn't. That opaque dark blue, like a very faded navy—it's infallible."

Robert smiled at her indulgently. She was very feminine after all.

"And don't feel superior because it happens not to be lawyers' logic," she added. "Have a look round at your own friends, and see."

Before he could stop himself he thought of Gerald Blunt, the Milford scandal. Assuredly Gerald had slate-blue eyes. So had Arthur Wallis, the potman at The White Hart, who was paying three different monetary levies weekly. So had—— Damn the woman, she had no right to make a silly generalisation like that and be right about it.

"It is fascinating to speculate on what she really did during that month," Marion said. "It affords me intense satisfaction that someone beat her black and blue. At least there is one person in this world who has arrived at a correct estimate of her. I hope I meet him someday, so that I may shake his hand."

"Him?"

"With those eyes it is bound to be a 'him'."

"Well," Robert said, preparing to go, "I doubt very much whether Grant has a case that he will want to present in court. It would be the girl's word against yours, with no other backing on either side. Against *you* would be her statement; so detailed, so circumstantial. Against *her* would be the inherent unlikeliness of the story. I don't think he could hope to get a verdict."

"But the thing is there, whether he brings it into court or not. And not only in the files of Scotland Yard. Sooner or later a thing like that begins to be whispered about. It would be no comfort to us not to have the thing cleared up."

"Oh, it will be cleared up, if I have anything to do with it. But I think we wait for a day or two to see what the Yard mean to do about it. They have far better facilities for arriving at the truth than we are ever likely to have."

"Coming from a lawyer, that is a touching tribute to the honesty of the police."

"Believe me, truth may be a virtue, but Scotland Yard discov-

31

ered long ago that it is a business asset. It doesn't pay them to be satisfied with anything less."

"If he *did* bring it to court," she said, coming to the door with him, "and *did* get a verdict, what would that mean for us?"

"I'm not sure whether it would be two years' imprisonment or seven years penal servitude. I told you I was a broken reed where criminal procedure is concerned. But I shall look it up."

"Yes, do," she said. "There's quite a difference."

He decided that he liked her habit of mockery. Especially in the face of a criminal charge.

"Goodbye," she said. "It was kind of you to come. You have been a great comfort to me."

And Robert, remembering how nearly he had thrown her to Ben Carley, blushed to himself as he walked to the gate.

〜〜〜〜〜〜〜〜〜〜〜〜〜〜〜〜〜

· 4 ·

"HAVE you had a busy day, dear?" Aunt Lin asked, opening her table napkin and arranging it across her plump lap.

This was a sentence that made sense but had no meaning. It was as much an overture to dinner as the spreading of her napkin, and the exploratory movement of her right foot as she located the footstool which compensated for her short legs. She expected no answer; or rather, being unaware that she had asked the question, she did not listen to his answer.

Robert looked up the table at her with a more conscious benevolence than usual. After his uncharted step-picking at The Franchise, the serenity of Aunt Lin's presence was very comforting, and he looked with a new awareness at the solid little figure with the short neck and the round pink face and the iron-grey hair that frizzed out from its large hairpins. Linda Bennet led a life of recipes, film stars, god-children, and church bazaars, and found it perfect. Well-being and contentment enveloped her like a cloak. She read the Women's Page of the daily paper (How To Make A Boutonnière From Old Kid Gloves) and nothing else as far as Robert was aware. Occasionally when she tidied away the paper that Robert had left lying about, she would pause to read the headlines and comment on them. ("MAN ENDS EIGHTY-TWO DAY FAST"—Silly creature! "OIL DISCOVERY IN BAHAMAS"—Did I tell you that paraffin is up a penny, dear?) But she gave the impression of never really believing that the world the papers reported did in fact exist. The world for Aunt Lin began with Robert Blair and ended within a ten-mile radius of him.

"What kept you so late tonight, dear?" she asked, having finished her soup.

From long experience Robert recognised this as being in a different category from: "Have you had a busy day, dear?"

"I had to go out to The Franchise—that house on the Larborough road. They wanted some legal advice."

"Those odd people? I didn't know you knew them."

"I didn't. They just wanted my advice."

"I hope they pay you for it, dear. They have no money at all, you know. The father was in some kind of importing business—monkey-nuts or something—and drank himself to death. Left them without a penny, poor things. Old Mrs. Sharpe ran a boarding-house in London to make ends meet, and the daughter was maid-of-all-work. They were just going to be turned into the street with their furniture, when the old man at The Franchise died. So providential!"

"Aunt Lin! Where do you get those stories?"

"But it's true, dear. Perfectly true. I forget who told me—someone who had stayed in the same street in London—but it was first-hand, anyhow. I am not one to pass on idle gossip, as you know. Is it a nice house? I always wondered what was inside that iron gate."

"No, rather ugly. But they have some nice pieces of furniture."

"Not as well kept as ours, I'll be bound," she said, looking complacently at the perfect sideboard and the beautiful chairs ranged against the wall. "The vicar said yesterday that if this house were not so obviously a home it would be a show place." Mention of the clergy seemed to remind her of something. "By the way, will you be extra patient with Christina for the next few days. I think she is going to be 'saved' again."

"Oh, poor Aunt Lin, what a bore for you. But I was afraid of it. There was a 'text' in the saucer of my early-morning tea today. 'Thou God seest me' on a pink scroll, with a tasteful design of Easter lilies in the background. Is she changing her church again, then?"

"Yes. She has discovered that the Methodists are 'whited sepulchres,' it seems, so she is going to those 'Bethel' people above Benson's bakery, and is due to be 'saved' any day now. She has been shouting hymns all the morning."

"But she always does."

"Not 'sword of the Lord' ones. As long as she sticks to 'pearly crowns' or 'streets of gold' I know it is all right. But once she begins on the 'sword of the Lord' I know that it will be my turn to do the baking presently."

"Well, darling, you bake just as well as Christina."

"Oh, no, she doesn't," said Christina, coming in with the meat course. A big soft creature with untidy straight hair and a vague eye. "Only one thing your Aunt Lin makes better than me, Mr. Robert, and that's hot cross buns, and that's only once a year. So there! And if I'm not appreciated in this house, I'll go where I will be."

"Christina, my love!" Robert said, "you know very well that no one could imagine this house without you, and if you left I should follow you to the world's end. For your butter tarts, if for nothing else. Can we have butter tarts tomorrow, by the way?"

"Butter tarts are no food for unrepentant sinners. Besides I don't think I have the butter. But we'll see. Meanwhile, Mr. Robert, you examine your soul and stop casting stones."

Aunt Lin sighed gently as the door closed behind her. "Twenty years," she said meditatively. "You won't remember her when she first came from the orphanage. Fifteen, and so skinny, poor little brat. She ate a whole loaf for her tea, and said she would pray for me all her life. I think she has, you know."

Something like a tear glistened in Miss Bennet's blue eye.

"I hope she postpones the salvation until she has made those butter tarts," said Robert, brutally materialistic. "Did you enjoy your picture?"

"Well, dear, I couldn't forget that he had five wives."

"Who has?"

34

"*Had*, dear. One at a time. Gene Darrow. I must say, those little programmes they give away are very informative but a little disillusioning. He was a student, you see. In the picture, I mean. Very young and romantic. But I kept remembering those five wives, and it spoiled the afternoon for me. So charming to look at too. They say he dangled his third wife out of a fifth-storey window by the wrists, but I don't really believe that. He doesn't look strong enough, for one thing. Looks as if he had chest trouble as a child. That peaky look, and thin wrists. Not strong enough to dangle anyone. Certainly not out of a fifth-storey . . ."

The gentle monologue went on, all through the pudding course; and Robert withdrew his attention and thought about The Franchise. He came to the surface as they rose from table and moved into the sitting-room for coffee.

"It is the most becoming garment, if maids would only realise it," she was saying.

"What is?"

"An apron. She was a maid in the palace, you know, and wore one of those silly little bits of muslin. So becoming. Did those people at The Franchise have a maid, by the way? No? Well, I am not surprised. They starved the last one, you know. Gave her——"

"Oh, Aunt *Lin!*"

"I assure you. For breakfast she got the crusts they cut off the toast. And when they had milk pudding . . ."

Robert did not hear what enormity was born of the milk pudding. In spite of his good dinner he was suddenly tired and depressed. If kind silly Aunt Lin saw no harm in repeating those absurd stories, what would the real gossips of Milford achieve with the stuff of a real scandal?

"And talking of maids—the brown sugar is finished, dear, so you will have to have lump for tonight—talking of maids, the Carleys' little maid has got herself into trouble."

"You mean someone else has got her into trouble."

"Yes. Arthur Wallis, the potman at The White Hart."

"What, Wallis *again!*"

"Yes, it really is getting past a joke, isn't it. I can't think why the man doesn't get married. It would be much cheaper."

But Robert was not listening. He was back in the drawing-room

35

at The Franchise, being gently mocked for his legal intolerance of a generalisation. Back in the shabby room with the unpolished furniture, where things lay about on chairs and no one bothered to tidy them away.

And where, now he came to think of it, no one ran round after him with an ash-tray.

· 5 ·

It was more than a week later that Mr. Heseltine put his thin, small, grey head round Robert's door to say that Inspector Hallam was in the office and would like to see him for a moment.

The room on the opposite side of the hall where Mr. Heseltine lorded it over the clerks was always referred to as "the office," although both Robert's room and the little one behind it used by Nevil Bennet were, in spite of their carpets and their mahogany, plainly offices too. There was an official waiting-room behind "the office," a small room corresponding to young Bennet's, but it had never been popular with the Blair, Hayward, and Bennet clients. Callers stepped into the office to announce themselves and usually stayed there gossiping until such times as Robert was free to see them. The little "waiting-room" had long ago been appropriated by Miss Tuff for writing Robert's letters in, away from the distraction of visitors and from the office-boy's sniffings.

When Mr. Heseltine had gone away to fetch the Inspector, Robert noticed with surprise that he was apprehensive as he had not been apprehensive since in the days of his youth he approached a list of Examination Results pinned on a board. Was his life so placid that a stranger's dilemma should stir it to that extent? Or was it that the Sharpes had been so constantly in his thoughts for the last week that they had ceased to be strangers?

He braced himself for whatever Hallam was going to say; but what emerged from Hallam's careful phrases was that Scotland Yard had let them understand that no proceedings would be taken on the present evidence. Blair noticed the "present evidence" and gauged its meaning accurately. They were not dropping the case —did the Yard ever drop a case?—they were merely sitting quiet.

The thought of Scotland Yard sitting quiet was not a particularly reassuring one in the circumstances.

"I take it that they lacked corroborative evidence," he said.

"They couldn't trace the lorry driver who gave her the lift," Hallam said.

"That wouldn't surprise them."

"No," Hallam agreed, "no driver is going to risk the sack by confessing he gave anyone a lift. Especially a girl. Transport bosses are strict about that. And when it is a case of a girl in trouble of some kind, and when it's the police that are doing the asking, no man in his senses is going to own up to even having seen her." He took the cigarette that Robert offered him. "They needed that lorry driver," he said. "Or someone like him," he added.

"Yes," Robert said, reflectively. "What did you make of her, Hallam?"

"The girl? I don't know. Nice kid. Seemed quite genuine. Might have been one of my own."

This, Blair realised, was a very good sample of what they would be up against if it ever came to a case. To every man of good feeling the girl in the witness box would look like his own daughter. Not because she was a waif, but for the very good reason that she wasn't. The decent school coat, the mousy hair, the unmade-up young face with its appealing hollow below the cheek-bone, the wide-set candid eyes—it was a prosecuting counsel's dream of a victim.

"Just like any other girl of her age," Hallam said, still considering it. "Nothing against her."

"So you don't judge people by the colour of their eyes," Robert said idly, his mind still on the girl.

"Ho! Don't I!" said Hallam surprisingly. "Believe me, there's a particular shade of baby blue that condemns a man, as far as I'm concerned, before he has opened his mouth. Plausible liars every one of them." He paused to pull on his cigarette. "Given to murder, too, come to think of it—though I haven't met many killers."

"You alarm me," Robert said. "In the future I shall give baby-blue eyes a wide berth."

Hallam grinned. "As long as you keep your pocket book shut

you needn't worry. All Baby-Blue's lies are for money. He only murders when he gets too entangled in his lies. The real murderer's mark is not the colour of the eyes but their setting."

"Setting?"

"Yes. They are set differently. The two eyes, I mean. They look as if they belonged to different faces."

"I thought you hadn't met many."

"No, but I've read all the case histories and studied the photographs. I've always been surprised that no book on murder mentions it, it happens so often. The inequality of setting, I mean."

"So it's entirely your own theory."

"The result of my own observation, yes. You ought to have a go at it sometime. Fascinating. I've got to the stage where I look for it now."

"In the street, you mean?"

"No, not quite as bad as that. But in each new murder case. I wait for the photograph and when it comes I think: 'There! What did I tell you!' "

"And when the photograph comes and the eyes are of a mathematical identity?"

"Then it is nearly always what one might call an accidental murder. The kind of murder that might happen to anyone given the circumstances."

"And when you turn up a photograph of the revered vicar of Nether Dumbleton who is being given a presentation by his grateful parishioners to mark his fiftieth year of devoted service, and you note that the setting of his eyes is wildly unequal, what conclusion do you come to?"

"That his wife satisfies him, his children obey him, his stipend is sufficient for his needs, he has no politics, he gets on with the local big-wigs, and he is allowed to have the kind of services he wants. In fact, he has never had the slightest need to murder anyone."

"It seems to me that you are having your cake and eating it very nicely."

"Huh!" Hallam said disgustedly. "Just wasting good police observation on a legal mind. I'd have thought," he added, moving to go, "that a lawyer would be glad of some free tips about judging perfect strangers."

"All you are doing," Robert pointed out, "is corrupting an innocent mind. I shall never be able to inspect a new client from now on without my subconscious registering the colour of his eyes and the symmetry of their setting."

"Well, that's something. It's about time you knew some of the facts of life."

"Thank you for coming to tell me about the 'Franchise' affair," Robert said, returning to sobriety.

"The telephone in this town," Hallam said, "is about as private as the radio."

"Anyhow, thank you. I must let the Sharpes know at once."

As Hallam took his leave, Robert lifted the telephone receiver.

He could not, as Hallam said, talk freely over the telephone, but he would say that he was coming out to see them immediately and that the news was good. That would take the present weight off their minds. It would also—he glanced at his watch—be time for Mrs. Sharpe's daily rest, so perhaps he would have a hope of avoiding the old dragon. And also a hope of a tête-à-tête with Marion Sharpe, of course; though he left that thought unformulated at the back of his mind.

But there was no answer to his call.

With the bored and reluctant aid of the Exchange he rang the number for a solid five minutes, without result. The Sharpes were not at home.

While he was still engaged with the Exchange, Nevil Bennet strolled in clad in his usual outrageous tweed, a pinkish shirt, and a purple tie. Robert, eyeing him over the receiver, wondered for the hundredth time what was going to become of Blair, Hayward, and Bennet when it at last slipped from his good Blair grasp into the hands of this young sprig of the Bennets. That the boy had brains he knew, but brains wouldn't take him far in Milford. Milford expected a man to stop being undergraduate when he reached graduate age. But there was no sign of Nevil's acceptance of the world outside his coterie. He was still actively, if unconsciously, epaté-ing that world. As his clothes bore witness.

It was not that Robert had any desire to see the boy in customary suits of solemn black. His own suit was a grey tweed; and his country clientèle would look doubtfully on "town" clothes. ("That awful little man with the striped suits," Marion Sharpe

39

had said of a town-clad lawyer, in that unguarded moment on the telephone.) But there were tweeds and tweeds, and Nevil Bennet's were the second kind. Quite outrageously the second kind.

"Robert," Nevil said, as Robert gave it up and laid down the receiver, "I've finished the papers on the Calthorpe transfer, and I thought I would run into Larborough this afternoon, if you haven't anything you want me to do."

"Can't you talk to her on the telephone?" Robert asked; Nevil being engaged, in the casual modern fashion, to the Bishop of Larborough's third daughter.

"Oh, it isn't Rosemary. She is in London for a week."

"A protest meeting at the Albert Hall, I suppose," said Robert, who was feeling disgruntled because of his failure to speak to the Sharpes when he was primed with good news for them.

"No, at the Guildhall," Nevil said.

"What is it this time? Vivisection?"

"You are frightfully last-century now and then, Robert," Nevil said, with his air of solemn patience. "No one objects to vivisection nowadays except a few cranks. The protest is against this country's refusal to give shelter to the patriot Kotovich."

"The said patriot is very badly 'wanted' in his own country, I understand."

"By his enemies; yes."

"By the police; for two murders."

"Executions."

"You a disciple of John Knox, Nevil?"

"Good God, no. What has that to do with it?"

"*He* believed in self-appointed executioners. The idea has a little 'gone out' in this country, I understand. Anyhow, if it's a choice between Rosemary's opinion of Kotovich and the opinion of the Special Branch, I'll take the Special Branch."

"The Special Branch only do what the Foreign Office tells them. Everyone knows that. But if I stay and explain the ramifications of the Kotovich affair to you, I shall be late for the film."

"What film?"

"The French film I am going into Larborough to see."

"I suppose you know that most of those French trifles that the British intelligentsia bate their breath about are considered very so-so in their own country? However. Do you think you could pause long enough to drop a note into the letter-box of The Franchise as you go by?"

"I might. I always wanted to see what was inside that wall. Who lives there now?"

"An old woman and her daughter."

"Daughter?" repeated Nevil, automatically pricking his ears.

"Middle-aged daughter."

"Oh. All right, I'll just get my coat."

Robert wrote merely that he had tried to talk to them, that he had to go out on business for an hour or so, but that he would ring them up again when he was free, and that Scotland Yard had no case, as the case stood, and acknowledged the fact.

Nevil swept in with a dreadful raglan affair over his arm, snatched up the letter and disappeared with a "Tell Aunt Lin I may be late. She asked me over to dinner."

Robert donned his own sober grey hat and walked over to the Rose and Crown to meet his client—an old farmer, and the last man in England to suffer from chronic gout. The old man was not yet there, and Robert, usually so placid, so lazily good-natured, was conscious of impatience. The pattern of his life had changed. Up to now it had been an even succession of equal attractions; he had gone from one thing to another without hurry and without emotion. Now there was a focus of interest, and the rest revolved round it.

He sat down on one of the chintz-covered chairs in the lounge and looked at the dog-eared journals lying on the adjacent coffee table. The only current number was *The Watchman*, the weekly review, and he picked it up reluctantly, thinking yet once more how the dry feel of the paper offended his finger tips and its serrated edges set his own teeth on edge. It was the usual collection of protests, poems, and pedantry; the place of honour among the protests being accorded to Nevil's future father-in-law, who spread himself for three-quarters of a column on England's shame in that she refused sanctuary to a fugitive patriot.

The Bishop of Larborough had long ago extended the Christian philosophy to include the belief that the underdog is always right. He was wildly popular with Balkan revolutionaries, British strike

41

committees, and all the old lags in the local penal establishment. (The sole exception to this last being that chronic recidivist, Bandy Brayne, who held the good bishop in vast contempt, and reserved his affection for the Governor; to whom a tear in the eye was just a drop of H_2O, and who unpicked his most heart-breaking tales with a swift, unemotional accuracy.) There was *nothing*, said the old lags affectionately, that the old boy would not believe; you could lay it on with a trowel.

Normally Robert found the Bishop mildly amusing, but today he was merely irritated. He tried two poems, neither of which made sense to him, and flung the thing back on the table.

"England in the wrong again?" asked Ben Carley, pausing by his chair and jerking a head at *The Watchman*.

"Hullo, Carley."

"A Marble Arch for the well-to-do," the little lawyer said, flicking the paper scornfully with a nicotine-stained finger. "Have a drink?"

"Thanks, but I'm waiting for old Mr. Wynyard. He doesn't move a step more than he need, nowadays."

"No, poor old boy. The sins of the fathers. Awful to be suffering for port you never drank! I saw your car outside The Franchise the other day."

"Yes," said Robert, and wondered a little. It was unlike Ben Carley to be blunt. And if he had seen Robert's car he had also seen the police cars.

"If you know them you'll be able to tell me something I always wanted to know about them. Is the rumour true?"

"Rumour?"

"*Are* they witches?"

"Are they supposed to be?" said Robert lightly.

"There's a strong support for the belief in the countryside, I understand," Carley said, his bright black eyes resting for a moment on Robert's with intention, and then going on to wander over the lounge with their habitual quick interrogation.

Robert understood that the little man was offering him, tacitly, information that he thought ought to be useful to him.

"Ah well," Robert said, "since entertainment came into the country with the cinema, God bless it, an end has been put to witch-hunting."

42

"Don't you believe it. Give these midland morons a good excuse and they'll witch-hunt with the best. An inbred crowd of degenerates, if you ask me. Here's your old boy. Well, I'll be seeing you."

It was one of Robert's chief attractions that he was genuinely interested in people and in their troubles, and he listened to old Mr. Wynyard's rambling story with a kindness that won the old man's gratitude—and added, although he was unaware of it, a hundred to the sum that stood against his name in the old farmer's will—but as soon as their business was over he made straight for the hotel telephone.

There were far too many people about, and he decided to use the one in the garage over in Sin Lane. The office would be shut by now, and anyhow it was further away. And if he telephoned from the garage, so his thoughts went as he strode across the street, he would have his car at hand if she—if they asked him to come out and discuss the business further, as they very well might, as they almost certainly would—yes, of course they would want to discuss what they could do to discredit the girl's story, whether there was to be a case or not—he had been so relieved over Hallam's news that he had not yet come round in his mind to considering what——

"Evening, Mr. Blair," Bill Brough said, oozing his large person out of the narrow office door, his round calm face bland and welcoming. "Want your car?"

"No, I want to use your telephone first, if I may."

"Sure. Go ahead."

Stanley, who was under a car, poked his fawn's face out and asked:

"Know anything?"

"Not a thing, Stan. Haven't had a bet for months."

"I'm two pounds down on a cow called Bright Promise. That's what comes of putting your faith in horseflesh. Next time you know something——"

"Next time I have a bet I'll tell you. But it will still be horseflesh."

"As long as it's not a cow——" Stanley said, disappearing under the car again; and Robert moved into the hot bright little office and picked up the receiver.

It was Marion who answered, and her voice sounded warm and glad.

"You can't imagine what a relief your note was to us. Both my mother and I have been picking oakum for the last week. Do they still pick oakum, by the way?"

"I think not. It is something more constructive nowadays, I understand."

"Occupational therapy."

"More or less."

"I can't think of any compulsory sewing that would improve my character."

"They would probably find you something more congenial. It is against modern thought to compel a prisoner to do anything that he doesn't want to."

"That is the first time I have heard you sound tart."

"Was I tart?"

"Pure angostura."

Well, she had reached the subject of drink; perhaps now she would suggest his coming out for sherry before dinner.

"What a charming nephew you have, by the way."

"Nephew?"

"The one who brought the note."

"He is not my nephew," Robert said coldly. Why was it so age-ing to be avuncular? "He is my first cousin once removed. But I am glad you liked him." This would not do; he would have to take the bull by the horns. "I should like to see you sometime to dis-cuss what we can do to straighten things out. To make things safer——" He waited.

"Yes, of course. Perhaps we could look in at your office one morning when we are shopping? What kind of thing could we do, do you think?"

"Some kind of private inquiry, perhaps. I can't very well discuss it over the telephone."

"No, of course you can't. How would it do if we came in on Friday morning? That is our weekly shopping day. Or is Friday a busy day for you?"

"No, Friday would be quite convenient," Robert said, swallow-ing down his disappointment. "About noon?"

44

"Yes, that would do very well. Twelve o'clock the day after tomorrow, at your office. Goodbye, and thank you again for your support and help."

She rang off, firmly and cleanly, without all the usual preliminary twitterings that Robert had come to expect from women.

"Shall I run her out for you," Bill Brough asked as he came out into the dim daylight of the garage.

"What? Oh, the car. No, I shan't need it tonight, thanks."

He set off on his normal evening walk down the High Street, trying hard not to feel snubbed. He had not been anxious to go to The Franchise in the first instance, and had made his reluctance pretty plain; she was quite naturally avoiding a repetition of the circumstances. That he had identified himself with their interests was a mere business affair, to be resolved in an office, impersonally. They would not again involve him further than that.

Ah, well, he thought, flinging himself down in his favourite chair by the wood fire in the sitting-room and opening the evening paper (printed that morning in London), when they came to the office on Friday he could do something to put the affair on a more personal basis. To wipe out the memory of that first unhappy refusal.

The quiet of the old house soothed him. Christina had been closeted in her room for two days, in prayer and meditation, and Aunt Lin was in the kitchen preparing dinner. There was a gay letter from Lettice, his only sister, who had driven a truck for several years of a bloody war, fallen in love with a tall silent Canadian, and was now raising five blond brats in Saskatchewan. "Come out soon, Robin dear," she finished, "before the brats grow up and before the moss grows *right* round you. You know how *bad* Aunt Lin is for you!" He could hear her saying it. She and Aunt Lin had never seen eye to eye.

He was smiling, relaxed and reminiscent, when both his quiet and his peace were shattered by the irruption of Nevil.

"Why didn't you *tell* me she was like that!" Nevil demanded.

"Who?"

"The Sharpe woman! Why didn't you tell me?"

"I didn't expect you would meet her," Robert said. "All you had to do was drop the letter through the door."

45

"There was nothing in the door to drop it through, so I rang, and they had just come back from wherever they were. Anyhow, *she* answered it."

"I thought she slept in the afternoons."

"I don't believe she ever sleeps. She doesn't belong to the human family at all. She is all compact of fire and metal."

"I know she's a very rude old woman but you have to make allowances. She has had a very hard——"

"*Old?* Who are you talking about?"

"Old Mrs. Sharpe, of course."

"I didn't even see old Mrs. Sharpe. I'm talking about Marion."

"Marion Sharpe? And how did you know her name was Marion?"

"She told me. It does suit her, doesn't it? She couldn't be anything but Marion."

"You seem to have become remarkably intimate for a doorstep acquaintance."

"Oh, she gave me tea."

"Tea! I thought you were in a desperate hurry to see a French film."

"I'm never in a desperate hurry to do anything when a woman like Marion Sharpe invites me to tea. Have you noticed her eyes? But of course you have. You're her lawyer. That wonderful shading of grey into hazel. And the way her eyebrows lie above them, like the brush-mark of a painter genius. Winged eyebrows, they are. I made a poem about them on the way home. Do you want to hear it?"

"No," Robert said firmly. "Did you enjoy your film?"

"Oh, I didn't go."

"You didn't *go!*"

"I told you I had tea with Marion instead."

"You mean you have been at The Franchise *the whole afternoon!*"

"I suppose I have," Nevil said dreamily, "but, by God, it didn't seem more than seven minutes."

"And what happened to your thirst for French cinema?"

"But Marion *is* French film. Even you must see that!" Robert winced at the "even you." "Why bother with the shadow, when you can be with the reality? Reality. That is her great quality, isn't it? I've never met anyone as real as Marion is."

"Not even Rosemary?" Robert was in the state known to Aunt Lin as "put out."

"Oh, Rosemary is a darling, and I'm going to marry her, but that is quite a different thing."

"Is it?" said Robert, with deceptive meekness.

"Of course. People don't marry women like Marion Sharpe, any more than they marry winds and clouds. Any more than they marry Joan of Arc. It's positively blasphemous to consider marriage in relation to a woman like that. She spoke very nicely of you, by the way."

"That was kind of her."

The tone was so dry that even Nevil caught the flavour of it.

"Don't you like her?" he asked, pausing to look at his cousin in surprised disbelief.

Robert had ceased for the moment to be kind, lazy, tolerant Robert Blair; he was just a tired man who hadn't yet had his dinner and was suffering from the memory of a frustration and a snubbing.

"As far as I am concerned," he said, "Marion Sharpe is just a skinny woman of forty who lives with a rude old mother in an ugly old house, and needs legal advice on occasion like anyone else."

But even as the words came out he wanted to stop them, as if they were a betrayal of a friend.

"No, probably she *isn't* your cup of tea," Nevil said tolerantly. "You have always preferred them a little stupid, and blond, haven't you." This was said without malice, as one stating a dullish fact.

"I can't imagine why you should think that."

"All the women you nearly married were that type."

"I have never 'nearly married' anyone," Robert said stiffly.

"That's what you think. You'll never know how nearly Molly Manders landed you."

"Molly Manders?" Aunt Lin said, coming in flushed from her

47

cooking and bearing the tray with the sherry. "Such a silly girl. Imagined that you used a baking-board for pancakes. And was always looking at herself in that little pocket mirror of hers."

"Aunt Lin saved you that time, didn't you, Aunt Lin?"

"I don't know what you are talking about, Nevil dear. Do stop prancing about the hearthrug, and put a log on the fire. Did you like your French film, dear?"

"I didn't go. I had tea at The Franchise instead." He shot a glance at Robert, having learned by now that there was more in Robert's reaction than met the eye.

"With those strange people? What did you talk about?"

"Mountains—Maupassant—hens——"

"*Hens,* dear?"

"Yes; the concentrated evil of a hen's face in a close-up."

Aunt Lin looked vague. She turned to Robert, as to terra firma.

"Had I better call, dear, if you are going to know them? Or ask the vicar's wife to call?"

"I don't think I would commit the vicar's wife to anything so irrevocable," Robert said, dryly.

She looked doubtful for a moment, but household cares obliterated the question in her mind. "Don't dawdle too long over your sherry or what I have in the oven will be spoiled. Thank goodness, Christina will be down again tomorrow. At least I hope so; I have never known her salvation take more than two days. And I don't really think that I *will* call on those Franchise people, dear, if it is all the same to you. Apart from being strangers and very odd, they quite frankly terrify me."

Yes; that was a sample of the reaction he might expect where the Sharpes were concerned. Ben Carley had gone out of his way today to let him know that, if there was police trouble at The Franchise, he wouldn't be able to count on an unprejudiced jury. He must take measures for the protection of the Sharpes. When he saw them on Friday he would suggest a private investigation by a paid agent. The police were overworked—had been overworked for a decade and more—and there was just a chance that one man working at his leisure on one trail might be more successful than the orthodox and official investigation had been.

Bᴜᴛ by Friday morning it was too late to take measures for the safety of The Franchise.

Robert had reckoned with the diligence of the police; he had reckoned with the slow spread of whispers; but he had reckoned without the *Ack-Emma*.

The *Ack-Emma* was the latest representative of the tabloid newspaper to enter British journalism from the West. It was run on the principle that two thousand pounds for damages is a cheap price to pay for sales worth half a million. It had blacker head-lines, more sensational pictures, and more indiscreet letterpress than any paper printed so far by British presses. Fleet Street had its own name for it—monosyllabic and unprintable—but no protection against it. The press had always been its own censor, deciding what was and what was not permissible by the principles of its own good sense and good taste. If a "rogue" publication decided not to conform to those principles then there was no power that could make it conform. In ten years the *Ack-Emma* had passed by half a million the daily net sales of the best selling newspaper in the country to date. In any suburban railway carriage seven out of ten people bound for work in the morning were reading an *Ack-Emma*.

And it was the *Ack-Emma* that blew the Franchise affair wide open.

Robert had been out early into the country on that Friday morning to see an old woman who was dying and wanted to alter her will. This was a performance she repeated on an average once every three months and her doctor made no secret of the fact that in his opinion she "would blow out a hundred candles one day without a second puff." But of course a lawyer cannot tell a client who summons him urgently at eight-thirty in the morning not to be silly. So Robert had taken some new will forms, fetched his car from the garage, and driven into the country. In spite of his usual tussle with the old tyrant among the pillows—who could never be brought to understand the elementary fact that you cannot give away *four* shares amounting to one third each—he enjoyed the spring countryside. And he hummed to himself on the way home, looking forward to seeing Marion Sharpe in less than an hour.

He had decided to forgive her for liking Nevil. After all, Nevil had never tried to palm her off on Carley. One must be fair.

He ran the car into the garage, under the noses of the morning lot going out from the livery stable, parked it, and then, remembering that it was past the first of the month, strolled over to the office to pay his bill to Brough, who ran the office side. But it was Stanley who was in the office; thumbing over dockets and invoices with the strong hands that so surprisingly finished off his thin forearms.

"When I was in the Signals," Stanley said, casting him an absent-minded glance, "I used to believe that the Quarter-bloke was a crook, but now I'm not so sure."

"Something missing?" said Robert. "I just looked in to pay my bill. Bill usually has it ready."

"I expect it's somewhere around," Stanley said, still thumbing. "Have a look."

Robert, used to the ways of the office, picked up the loose papers discarded by Stanley, so as to come on the normal tidy strata of Bill's arrangement below. As he lifted the untidy pile he uncovered a girl's face; a newspaper picture of a girl's face. He did not recognise it at once but it reminded him of someone and he paused to look at it.

"Got it!" said Stanley in triumph, extracting a sheet of paper from a clip. He swept the remaining loose papers on the desk into a pile and so laid bare to Robert's gaze the whole front page of that morning's *Ack-Emma*.

Cold with shock, Robert stared at it.

Stanley, turning to take the papers he was holding from his grasp, noticed his absorption and approved it.

"Nice little number, that," he said. "Reminds me of a bint I had in Egypt. Same far-apart eyes. Nice kid she was. Told the most original lies."

50

He went back to his paper-arranging, and Robert went on staring.

THIS IS THE GIRL

said the paper in enormous black letters across the top of the page; and below it, occupying two-thirds of the page, was the girl's photograph. And then, in smaller but still obtrusive type, below:

IS THIS THE HOUSE?

and below it a photograph of The Franchise.

Across the bottom of the page was the legend:

THE GIRL SAYS YES: WHAT DO THE
POLICE SAY?
See inside for the story.

He put out his hand and turned over the page.

Yes; it was all there, except for the Sharpes' name.

He dropped the page, and looked again at that shocking frontispiece. Yesterday The Franchise was a house protected by four high walls; so unobtrusive, so sufficient unto itself, that even Milford did not know what it looked like. Now it was there to be stared at on every bookstall; on every newsagent's counter from Penzance to Pentland. Its flat, forbidding front a foil for the innocence of the face above it.

The girl's photograph was a head-and-shoulders affair, and appeared to be a studio portrait. Her hair had an arranged-for-an-occasion look, and she was wearing what looked like a party frock. Without her school coat she looked—not less innocent, nor older; no. He sought for the word that would express it. She looked less—tabu, was it? The school coat had stopped one thinking of her as a woman, just as a nun's habit would. A whole treatise could probably be written, now he came to think of it, on the protective quality of school coats. Protective in both senses: armour and camouflage. Now that the coat was no longer there, she was feminine instead of merely female.

But it was still a pathetically young face, immature and appeal-

51

ing. The candid brow, the wide-set eyes, the bee-stung lip that gave her mouth the expression of a disappointed child—it made a formidable whole. It would not be only the Bishop of Larborough who would believe a story told by that face.

"May I borrow this paper?" he asked Stanley.

"Take it," Stanley said. "We had it for our elevenses. There's nothing in it."

Robert was surprised. "Didn't you find this interesting?" he asked, indicating the front page.

Stanley cast a glance at the pictured face. "Not except that she reminded me of that bint in Egypt, lies and all."

"So you didn't believe that story she told?"

"What do *you* think!" Stanley said, contemptuous.

"Where do you think the girl was, then, all that time?"

"If I remember what I *think* I remember about the Red Sea sadie, I'd say very definitely—oh, but definitely—on the tiles," Stanley said, and went out to attend to a customer.

Robert picked up the paper and went soberly away. At least one man-in-the-street had not believed the story; but that seemed to be due as much to an old memory as to present cynicism.

And although Stanley had quite obviously read the story without reading the names of the characters concerned, or even the place-names, only ten per cent of readers did that (according to the best Mass Observation); the other ninety per cent would have read every word, and would now be discussing the affair with varying degrees of relish.

At his own office he found that Hallam had been trying to reach him by telephone.

"Shut the door and come in, will you," he said to old Mr. Heseltine, who had caught him with the news on his arrival and was now standing in the door of his room. "And have a look at that."

He reached for the receiver with one hand, and laid the paper under Mr. Heseltine's nose with the other.

The old man touched it with his small-boned fastidious hand, as one seeing a strange exhibit for the first time. "This is the publication one hears so much about," he said. And gave his attention to it, as he would to any strange document.

"We are both in a spot, aren't we!" Hallam said, when they

were connected. And raked his vocabulary for some epithets suitable to the *Ack-Emma*. "As if the police hadn't enough to do without having that rag on their tails!" he finished, being naturally absorbed in the police point of view.

"Have you heard from the Yard?"

"Grant was burning the wires at nine this morning. But there's nothing they can do. Just grin and bear it. The police are always fair game. Nothing you can do, either, if it comes to that."

"Not a thing," Robert said. "We have a fine free press."

Hallam said a few more things about the press. "Do your people know?" he asked.

"I shouldn't think so. I'm quite sure they would never normally see the *Ack-Emma*, and there hasn't been time for some kind soul to send it to them. But they are due here in about ten minutes, and I'll show it to them then."

"If it was ever possible for me to be sorry for that old battle-axe," Hallam said, "it would be at this minute."

"How did the *Ack-Emma* get the story? I thought the parents—the girl's guardians, I mean—were very strongly against that kind of publicity."

"Grant says the girl's brother went off the deep end about the police taking no action and went to the *Ack-Emma* off his own bat. They are strong on the champion act. 'The *Ack-Emma* will see right done!' I once knew one of their crusades run into a third day."

When he hung up Robert thought that if it was a bad break for both sides, it was at least an even break. The police would without doubt redouble their efforts to find corroborative evidence; on the other hand the publication of the girl's photograph meant for the Sharpes a faint hope that somebody, somewhere, would recognise it and say: "This girl could not have been in The Franchise on the date in question because she was at such-and-such a place."

"A shocking story, Mr. Robert," Mr. Heseltine said. "And if I may say so a quite shocking publication. Most offensive."

"That house," Robert said, "is The Franchise, where old Mrs. Sharpe and her daughter live; and where I went the other day, if you remember, to give them some legal advice."

"You mean that these people are our clients?"

"Yes."

"But, Mr. Robert, that is not at all in our line." Robert winced at the dismay in his voice. "That is quite outside our usual—indeed quite beyond our normal—we are not competent——"

"We are competent, I hope, to defend any client against a publication like the *Ack-Emma*," Robert said, coldly.

Mr. Heseltine eyed the screaming rag on the table. He was obviously facing the difficult choice between a criminal clientèle and a disgraceful journal.

"Did you believe the girl's story when you read it?" Robert asked.

"I don't see how she could have made it up," Mr. Heseltine said simply. "It is such a very circumstantial story, isn't it?"

"It is, indeed. But I saw the girl when she was brought to The Franchise to identify it last week—that was the day I went out so hurriedly just after tea—and I don't believe a word she says. Not a word," he added, glad to be able to say it loudly and distinctly to himself and to be sure at last that he believed it.

"But how could she have thought of The Franchise at all, or known all those things, if she wasn't there?"

"I don't know. I haven't the least idea."

"It is a most unlikely place to pick on, surely; a remote, invisible house like that, on a lonely road, in country that people don't visit very much."

"I know. I don't know how the job was worked, but that it *is* a job I am certain. It is a choice not between stories, but between human beings. I am quite certain that the two Sharpes are incapable of insane conduct like that. Whereas I don't believe the girl incapable of telling a story like that. That is what it amounts to." He paused a moment. "And you'll just have to trust my judgment about it, Timmy," he added, using his childhood's name for the old clerk.

Whether it was the "Timmy" or the argument, it was apparent that Mr. Heseltine had no further protest to make.

"You'll be able to see the criminals for yourself," Robert said, "because I hear their voices in the hall now. You might bring them in, will you."

54

Mr. Heseltine went dumbly out on his mission, and Robert turned the newspaper over so that the comparatively innocuous GIRL SMUGGLED ABOARD was all that would meet the visitors' eye.

Mrs. Sharpe, moved by some belated instinct for convention, had donned a hat in honour of the occasion. It was a flattish affair of black satin, and the general effect was that of a doctor of learning. That the effect had not been wasted was obvious by the relieved look on Mr. Heseltine's face. This was quite obviously not the kind of client he had expected; it was, on the other hand, the kind of client he was used to.

"Don't go away," Robert said to him, as he greeted the visitors; and to the others: "I want you to meet the oldest member of the firm, Mr. Heseltine."

It suited Mrs. Sharpe to be gracious; and exceedingly Victoria Regina was old Mrs. Sharpe when she was being gracious. Mr. Heseltine was more than relieved; he capitulated. Robert's first battle was over.

When they were alone Robert noticed that Marion had been waiting to say something.

"An odd thing happened this morning," she said. "We went to the Ann Boleyn place to have coffee—we quite often do—and there were two vacant tables, but when Miss Truelove saw us coming she very hastily tilted the chairs against the tables and said they were reserved. I might have believed her if she hadn't looked so embarrassed. You don't think that rumour has begun to get busy already, do you? That she did that because she has heard some gossip?"

"No," Robert said, sadly, "because she has read this morning's *Ack-Emma*." He turned the newspaper front side up. "I am sorry to have such bad news for you. You'll just have to shut your teeth and take it, as small boys say. I don't suppose you have ever seen this poisonous rag at close quarters. It's a pity that the acquaintance should begin on so personal a basis."

"Oh, no!" Marion said, in passionate protest as her eye fell on the picture of The Franchise.

And then there was unbroken silence while the two women absorbed the contents of the inner page.

55

"I take it," Mrs. Sharpe said at last, "that we have no redress against this sort of thing?"

"None," Robert said. "All the statements are perfectly true. And it is all statement and not comment. Even if it were comment—and I've no doubt the comment will come—there has been no charge so the case is not *sub judice*. They are free to comment if they please."

"The whole thing is one huge implied comment," Marion said. "That the police failed to do their duty. What do they think we did? Bribed them?"

"I think the suggestion is that the humble victim has less pull with the police than the wicked rich."

"Rich," repeated Marion, her voice curdling with bitterness.

"Anyone who has more than six chimneys is rich. Now. If you are not too shocked to think, consider. We *know* that the girl was never at The Franchise, that she could not——" But Marion interrupted him.

"Do *you* know it?" she asked.

"Yes," Robert said.

Her challenging eyes lost their challenge, and her glance dropped.

"Thank you," she said quietly.

"If the girl was never there, how could she have seen the house! . . . She did see it somehow. It is too unlikely for belief that she could be merely repeating a description that someone else gave her. . . . How could she see it? Naturally, I mean."

"You could see it, I suppose, from the top deck of a bus," Marion said. "But there are no double-decker buses on the Milford route. Or from on top of a load of hay. But it is the wrong time of year for hay."

"It may be the wrong time for hay," croaked Mrs. Sharpe, "but there is no season for lorry-loads. I have seen lorries loaded with goods as high as any hay waggon."

"Yes," Marion said. "Suppose the lift the girl got was not in a car, but on a lorry."

"There is only one thing against that. If a girl was given a lift on a lorry she would be in the cabin, even if it meant sitting on someone's knee. They wouldn't perch her up on top of the load.

Especially as it was a rainy evening, you may remember. . . . No one ever came to The Franchise to ask the way, or to sell something, or to mend something—someone that the girl could have been with, even in the background?"

But no; they were both sure that no one had come, within the time the girl had been on holiday.

"Then we take it for granted that what she learned about The Franchise she learned from being high enough on one occasion to see over the wall. We shall probably never know when or how, and we probably could not prove it if we did know. So our whole efforts will have to be devoted, not to proving that she wasn't at The Franchise, but that she *was* somewhere else!"

"And what chance is there of that?" Mrs. Sharpe asked.

"A better chance than before this was published," Robert said, indicating the front page of the *Ack-Emma*. "Indeed it is the one bright spot in the bad business. *We* could not have published the girl's photograph in the hope of information about her whereabouts during that month. But now that *they* have published it— her own people, I mean—the same benefit should come to us. They have broadcast the story—and that is our bad luck; but they have also broadcast the photograph—and if we have any good luck at all someone, somewhere, will observe that the story and the photograph do not fit. That at the material time, as given in the story, the subject of the photograph could not possibly have been in the stated place, because they, personally, know her to have been elsewhere."

Marion's face lost a little of its bleak look, and even Mrs. Sharpe's thin back looked less rigid. What had seemed a disaster might be, after all, the means of their salvation.

"And what can we do in the way of private investigation?" Mrs. Sharpe asked. "You realise, I expect, that we have very little money; and I take it that a private inquiry is a spendthrift business."

"It does usually run away with more than one had bargained for, because it is difficult to budget for. But to begin with I am going, myself, to see the various people involved, and find out, if possible, on what lines any inquiry should be based. Find out what she was *likely* to do."

57

"Will they tell you that?"

"Oh, no. They are probably unaware themselves of her tendencies. But if they talk about her at all a picture must emerge. At least I hope so."

There was a few moments' silence.

"You are extraordinarily kind, Mr. Blair."

Victoria Regina had come back to Mrs. Sharpe's manner, but there was a hint of something else. Almost of surprise; as if kindness was not one of the things she had normally met with in life; nor expected. Her stiffly gracious acknowledgement was as eloquent as if she had said: "You know that we are poor, and that we may never be able to pay you adequately, and we are not at all the kind of people that you would choose to represent, but you are going out of your way to do us the best service in your power, and we are grateful."

"When do you go?" Marion asked.

"Directly after lunch."

"Today!"

"The sooner the better."

"Then we won't keep you," Mrs. Sharpe said, rising. She stood for a moment looking down at the paper where it lay spread on the table. "We enjoyed the privacy of The Franchise a great deal," she said.

When he had seen them out of the door and into their car, he called Nevil into his room and picked up the receiver to talk to Aunt Lin about packing a bag.

"I suppose you don't see the *Ack-Emma* ever?" he asked Nevil.

"I take it that the question is rhetorical," Nevil said.

"Have a look at this morning's. Hullo, Aunt Lin."

"Does someone want to sue them for something? It will be sound money for us, if so. They practically always settle out of court. They have a special fund for the——" Nevil's voice died away. He had seen the front page that was staring up at him from the table.

Robert stole a look at him over the telephone, and observed with satisfaction the naked shock on his cousin's bright young features. The youth of today, he understood, considered themselves shock-proof; it was good to know that, faced with an ordinary slab of real life, they reacted like any other human being.

"Be an angel, Aunt Lin, and pack a bag for me, will you? Just for overnight. . . ."

Nevil had torn the paper open and was now reading the story.

"Just London and back, I expect, but I'm not sure. Anyhow, just the little case; and just the minimum. Not all the things I *might* need, if you love me. Last time there was a bottle of digestive powder weighing nearly a pound, and when in heck did I ever need a digestive powder! . . . All right, then I *will* have ulcers. . . . Yes, I'll be in to lunch in about ten minutes."

"The blasted *swine!*" said the poet and intellectual, falling back in his need on the vernacular.

"Well, what do you make of it?"

"*Make* of it! Of what?"

"The girl's story."

"Does one have to *make* anything of it? An obvious piece of sensationalism by an unbalanced adolescent?"

"And if I told you that the said adolescent is a very calm, ordinary, well-spoken-of school-girl who is anything but sensational?"

"Have you seen her?"

"Yes. That was why I first went to The Franchise last week, to be there when Scotland Yard brought the girl to confront them." Put that in your pipe and smoke it, young Nevil. She may talk hens and Maupassant with you, but it is me she turns to in trouble.

"To be there on their behalf?"

"Certainly."

Nevil relaxed suddenly. "Oh, well; that's all right. For a moment I thought you were against her. Against them. But that's all right. We can join forces to put a spoke in the wheel of this——" he flicked the paper—"this moppet." Robert laughed at this typically Nevil choice of epithet. "What are you going to do about it, Robert?"

Robert told him. "And you will hold the fort while I am gone." He saw that Nevil's attention had gone back to the "moppet." He moved over to join him and together they considered the young face looking so calmly up at them.

"An attractive face, on the whole," Robert said. "What do you make of it?"

"What I should *like* to make of it," said the aesthete, with slow venom, "would be a *very nasty mess.*"

~~~~~~

· 7 ·

THE Wynns' home outside Aylesbury was in a countrified suburb; the kind of district where rows of semi-detached houses creep along the edge of the still unspoiled fields; selfconscious and aware that they are intruders, or smug and not caring, according to the character their builders have given them. The Wynns lived in one of the apologetic rows; a red-brick string of ramshackle dwellings that set Robert's teeth on edge; so raw they were, so crude, so hang-dog. But as he drove slowly up the road, looking for the appropriate number, he was won over by the love that had gone to the decoration of these regrettable objects. No love had gone to their building; only a reckoning. But to each owner, as he took over, the bare little house had represented his "sufficient beauty," and having found it he served it. The gardens were small miracles of loveliness; each succeeding one a fresh revelation of some unsuspected poet's heart.

Nevil really ought to be here to see, Robert thought, slowing down yet once more as a new perfection caught his eye; there was more poetry here than in a whole twelve months of his beloved *Watchman*. All his clichés were here: form, rhythm, colour, total gesture, design, impact . . .

Or would Nevil see only a row of suburban gardens? Only Meadowside Lane, Aylesbury, with some Woolworth plants in the gardens?

Probably.

Number 39 was the one with the plain green grass bordered by a rockery. It was also distinguished by the fact that its curtains were invisible. No genteel net was stretched across the window-pane, no cream casement cloth hung at the sides. The windows were bare to the sun, the air, and the human gaze. This surprised

Robert as much as it probably surprised the neighbours. It augured a nonconformity that he had not expected.

He rang the bell, wishing that he did not feel like a bagman. He was a suppliant; and that was a new role for Robert Blair.

Mrs. Wynn surprised him even more than her windows did. It was only when he had met her that he realised how complete a picture he had built in his mind of the woman who had adopted and mothered the child Betty Kane: the grey hair, the solid matronly comfortable figure, the plain broad sensible face; perhaps, even, an apron, or one of those flowered overalls that housewives wear. But Mrs. Wynn was not at all like that. She was slight and neat and young and modern and dark and pink-cheeked and still pretty, and had a pair of the most intelligent bright brown eyes Robert had ever seen.

When she saw a stranger she looked defensive, and made an involuntary closing movement with the door she was holding; but a second glance seemed to reassure her. Robert explained who he was, and she listened without interrupting him in a way he found quite admirable. Very few of his own clients listened without interrupting; male or female.

"You are under no obligation to talk to me," he finished, having explained his presence. "But I hope very much that you won't refuse. I have told Inspector Grant that I was going to see you this afternoon, on my clients' behalf."

"Oh, if the police know about it and don't mind——" She stepped back to let him come past her. "I expect you have to do your best for those people if you are their lawyer. And we have nothing to hide. But if it is really Betty you want to interview I'm afraid you can't. We have sent her into the country to friends for the day, to avoid all the fuss. Leslie meant well, but it was a stupid thing to do."

"Leslie?"

"My son. Sit down, won't you." She offered him one of the easy chairs in a pleasant, uncluttered sitting-room. "He was too angry about the police to think clearly—angry about their failure to do anything when it seemed so proved, I mean. He has always been devoted to Betty. Indeed until he got engaged they were inseparable."

Robert's ears pricked. This was the kind of thing he had come to hear.

"Engaged?"

"Yes. He got engaged just after the New Year to a very nice girl. We are all delighted."

"Was Betty delighted?"

"She wasn't jealous, if that is what you mean," she said, looking at him with her intelligent eyes. "I expect she missed not coming first with him as she used to, but she was very nice about it. She *is* a nice girl, Mr. Blair. Believe me. I was a schoolmistress before I married—not a very good one, that is why I got married at the first opportunity—and I know a lot about girls. Betty has never given me a moment's anxiety."

"Yes. I know. Everyone reports excellently of her. Is your son's fiancée a schoolfellow of hers?"

"No, she is a stranger. Her people have come to live near here and he met her at a dance."

"Does Betty go to dances?"

"Not grown-up dances. She is too young yet."

"So she had not met the fiancée?"

"To be honest, none of us had. He rather sprang her on us. But we liked her so much we didn't mind."

"He must be very young to be settling down?"

"Oh, the whole thing is absurd, of course. He is twenty and she is eighteen. But they are very sweet together. And I was very young myself when I married and I have been very happy. The only thing I lacked was a daughter, and Betty filled that gap."

"What does she want to do when she leaves school?"

"She doesn't know. She has no special talent for anything as far as I can see. I have a notion that she will marry early."

"Because of her attractiveness?"

"No, because——" she paused and apparently changed what she had been going to say. "Girls who have no particular bent fall easily into matrimony."

He wondered if what she had been going to say had any remote connection with slate-blue eyes.

"When Betty failed to turn up in time to go back to school, you thought she was just playing truant? Although she was a well-behaved child."

62

"Yes; she was growing bored with school; and she had always said—which is quite true—that the first day back at school is a wasted one. So we thought she was just 'taking advantage' for once, as they say. 'Trying it on' as Leslie said, when he heard that she hadn't turned up."

"I see. Was she wearing school clothes on her holiday?"

For the first time Mrs. Wynn looked doubtfully at him; uncertain of his motive in asking.

"No. No, she was wearing her week-end clothes. . . . You know that when she came back she was wearing only a frock and shoes?"

Robert nodded.

"I find it difficult to imagine women so depraved that they would treat a helpless child like that."

"If you could meet the women, Mrs. Wynn, you would find it still more difficult to imagine."

"But all the worst criminals look innocent and harmless, don't they?"

Robert let that pass. He wanted to know about the bruises on the girl's body. Were they fresh bruises?

"Oh, quite fresh. Most of them had not begun to 'turn' even."

This surprised Robert a little.

"But there were older bruises as well, I take it."

"If there were they had faded so much as to be unnoticeable among all the bad new ones."

"What did the new ones look like? A whipping?"

"Oh, no. She had actually been knocked about. Even her poor little face. One jaw was swollen, and there was a big bruise on the other temple."

"The police say that she grew hysterical when it was suggested that she should tell them her story."

"That was when she was still ill. Once we had got the story out of her and she had had a long rest, it was easy enough to persuade her to repeat it to the police."

"I know you will answer this frankly, Mrs. Wynn: Has there never been any suspicion in your mind that Betty's story might not be true? Even a momentary suspicion?"

"Not even a momentary one. Why should there be? She has always been a truthful child. Even if she hadn't, how could she invent a long circumstantial story like that without being found out? The police asked her all the questions they wanted to; there was never any suggestion of accepting her statement as it stood."

"When she first told her story to you, did she tell it all in a piece?"

"Oh, no; it was spread over a day or two. The outline, first. And then filling in the details as she remembered them. Things like the window in the attic being round."

"Her days of coma had not blurred her memory."

"I don't think they would in any case. I mean, with Betty's kind of brain. She has a photographic memory."

Has she indeed! thought Robert; both ears erect and wide open.

"Even as a small child she could look at the page of a book—a child's book, of course—and repeat most of the contents from the picture in her mind. And when we played the Kim game—you know? the objects on the tray—we had to put Betty out of the game because she invariably won. Oh, no, she would remember what she saw."

Well, there was another game in which the cry was "Growing warm!" Robert remembered.

"You say she was always a truthful child—and everyone supports you in that—but did she never indulge in romanticising her own life, as children sometimes do?"

"Never," said Mrs. Wynn firmly. The idea seemed faintly to amuse her. "She couldn't," she added. "Unless it was the real thing it was no use to Betty. Even playing dolls' tea-parties, she would never imagine the things on the plates as most children are quite happy to do; there had to be a real thing there, even if it was only a little cube of bread. Usually it was something nicer, of course; it was a good way to wangle an extra and she was always a little greedy."

Robert admired the detachment with which she considered her longed-for and much-loved daughter. The remains of a school-mistress's cynicism? So much more valuable, anyhow, for a child than a blind love. It was a pity that her intelligence and devotion had been so ill-rewarded.

"I don't want to keep on at a subject that must be unpleasant for you," Robert said. "But perhaps you could tell me something about the parents."

"Her parents?" Mrs. Wynn asked, surprised.

"Yes. Did you know them well? What were they like?"

"We didn't know them at all. We never even saw them."

"But you had Betty for—what was it?—nine months?—before her parents were killed, hadn't you?"

"Yes, but her mother wrote shortly after Betty came to us and said that to come to see her would only upset the child and make her unhappy and that the best thing for everyone would be to leave her to us until such times as she could go back to London. She said would I talk to Betty about her at least once every day."

Robert's heart contracted with pity for this unknown dead woman who had been willing to tear her own heart out for her only child. What treasure of love and care had been poured out in front of Betty Kane, child evacuee.

"Did she settle down easily when she came? Or did she cry for her mother?"

"She cried because she didn't like the food. I don't remember her ever crying for her mother. She fell in love with Leslie the first night—she was just a baby, you know—and I think her interest in him blotted out any grief she might have felt. And he, being four years older, was just the right age to feel protective. He still does—that is why we are in this mess today."

"How did this *Ack-Emma* affair happen? I know it was your son who went to the paper, but did you eventually come round to his——"

"Good heavens, no," Mrs. Wynn said indignantly. "It was all over before we could do anything about it. My husband and I were out when Leslie and the reporter came—they sent a man back with him when they heard his story, to get it first-hand from Betty—and when——"

"And Betty gave it quite willingly?"

"I don't know how willingly. I wasn't there. My husband and I knew nothing about it until this morning, when Leslie laid an *Ack-Emma* under our noses. A little defiantly, I may add. He is not feeling too good about it now that it is done. The *Ack-Emma*, I should like to assure you, Mr. Blair, is not normally my son's choice. If he had not been worked-up——"

"I know. I know exactly how it happened. And that tell-us-your-troubles-and-we'll-see-right-done is very insidious stuff." He

65

rose. "You have been very kind indeed, Mrs. Wynn, and I am exceedingly grateful to you."

His tone was evidently more heartfelt than she had expected and she looked doubtfully at him. What have I said to help you? she seemed to be asking, half-dismayed.

He asked where Betty's parents had lived in London, and she told him. "There is nothing there now," she added. "Just the open space. It is to be part of some new building scheme, so they have done nothing to it so far."

On the doorstep he ran into Leslie.

Leslie was an extraordinarily good-looking young man who seemed to be entirely unaware of the fact—a trait that endeared him to Robert, who was in no mood to look kindly on him. Robert had pictured him as the bull-in-a-china-shop type; but on the contrary he was a rather delicate, kind-looking boy with shy earnest eyes and untidy soft hair. He glared at Robert with frank enmity when his mother presented him and had explained his business there; but, as his mother had said, there was a shade of defiance in the glare; Leslie was obviously not very happy with his own conscience this evening.

"No one is going to beat my sister and get away with it," he said fiercely when Robert had mildly deplored his action.

"I sympathise with your point of view," Robert said, "but I personally would rather be beaten nightly for a fortnight than have my photograph on the front page of the *Ack-Emma*. Especially if I was a young girl."

"If you had been beaten every night for a fortnight and no one did anything about it you might be very glad to have your photograph published in any rag if it got you justice," Leslie observed pertinently and brushed past them into the house.

Mrs. Wynn turned to Robert with a small apologetic smile, and Robert, taking advantage of her softened moment, said: "Mrs. Wynn, if it ever occurs to you that anything in that story of Betty's does not ring true, I hope you won't decide that sleeping dogs are best left."

"Don't pin your faith to that hope, Mr. Blair."

"You would let sleeping dogs lie, and the innocent suffer?"

"Oh no; I didn't mean that. I meant the hope of my doubting

Betty's story. If I believed her at the beginning I am not likely to doubt her later."

"One never knows. Someday it may occur to you that this or that does not 'fit.' You have a naturally analytic mind; it may present you with a piece of subconscious when you least expect it. Something that has puzzled you deep down may refuse to be pushed down any more."

She had walked to the gate with him, and as he spoke the last sentence he turned to take farewell of her. To his surprise something moved behind her eyes at that light remark of his.

So she wasn't certain after all.

Somewhere, in the story, in the circumstances, there was some small thing that left a question in that sober analytical mind of hers.

What was it?

And then, with what he always remembered afterwards as the only perfect sample of telepathic communication in his experience, he paused as he was stepping into his car, and said: "Had she anything in her pockets when she came home?"

"She had only one pocket; the one in her dress."

"And was there anything in it?"

There was the faintest tightening of the muscles round her mouth. "Just a lipstick," she said, evenly.

"A lipstick! She is a little young for that, isn't she?"

"My dear Mr. Blair, they start experimenting with lipstick at the age of ten. As a wet-day amusement it has taken the place of dressing-up in Mother's things."

"Yes, probably; Woolworth is a great benefactor."

She smiled and said goodbye again and moved towards the house as he drove away.

What puzzled her about the lipstick? Robert wondered, as he turned from the uneven surface of Meadowside Lane on to the black smooth surface of the main Aylesbury-London road. Was it just the fact that the fiends at The Franchise should have left it with the girl? Was that what she found odd?

How amazing that the worry in her subconscious mind had communicated itself so instantly to him. He had not known that he was going to say that sentence about the girl's pockets until he heard himself saying it. It would never have occurred to him, left to himself, to wonder what was in the pocket of her frock. It would not occur to him that the frock might have a pocket at all.

So there was a lipstick.

And its presence was something that puzzled Mrs. Wynn.

Well; that was a straw that could be added to the little heap he had collected. To the fact that the girl had a photographic memory. To the fact that her nose had been put out of joint without warning only a month or two ago. To the fact that she was greedy. To the fact that she was bored with school. To the fact that she liked "reality."

To the fact—above all—that no one in that household, not even detached sensible Mrs. Wynn, knew what went on in Betty Kane's mind. It was quite unbelievable that a girl of fifteen who had been the centre of a young man's world could see herself supplanted overnight without reacting violently to the situation. But Betty had been "very nice about it."

Robert found this heartening. It was proof that that candid young face was no guide at all to the person who was Betty Kane.

~~~~~~

· 8 ·

ROBERT had decided to kill a great many birds with one stone by spending the night in London.

To begin with, he wanted to have his hand held. And in the circumstances no one would hold his hand to better purpose than his old school friend Kevin Macdermott. What Kevin did not know about crime was probably not so anyhow. And as a well-known defending counsel his knowledge of human nature was extensive, varied, and peculiar.

At the moment the betting was evens whether Macdermott would die of high blood-pressure before he was sixty, or grace the Woolsack when he was seventy. Robert hoped the latter. He was very fond of Kevin.

They had first gravitated towards each other at school because they were both "going in for Law," but they had become and re-mained friends because they were complementary. To the Irish-

68

man, Robert's equanimity was amusing, provocative, and—when he was tired—restful. To Robert, Kevin's Celt flamboyance was exotic and fascinating. It was typical that Robert's ambition was to go back to the little country town and continue life as it was; while Kevin's was to alter everything that was alterable in the Law and to make as much noise as possible in the doing of it.

So far Kevin had not altered much—though he had done his best where some judges' rulings were concerned—but he had made considerable noise in his effortless, slightly malicious, fashion. Already the presence of Kevin Macdermott in a case added fifty per cent to its newspaper value—and a good deal more than that to its cost.

He had married—advantageously but happily—had a pleasant house near Weybridge and three hardy sons, lean and dark and lively like their father. For town purposes he kept a small flat in St. Paul's Churchyard, where, as he pointed out, he "could afford to look down on Queen Anne." And whenever Robert was in town—which was not oftener than Robert could help—they dined together, either at the flat or at the latest place where Kevin had found good claret. Outside the Law, Kevin's interests were show hacks, claret, and the livelier films of Warner Brothers.

Kevin was to be at some Bar dinner tonight, so his secretary had said when Robert had tried to reach him from Milford; but he would be delighted to have a legitimate excuse for dodging the speeches, so would Robert go along to St. Paul's Churchyard after dinner, and wait for him.

That was a good thing; if Kevin came from a dinner he would be relaxed and prepared to settle down for the evening; not restless and with three-quarters of his mind still back in the courtroom as he sometimes was.

Meanwhile, he would ring up Grant at Scotland Yard and see if he could spare him some minutes tomorrow morning. He must get it clear in his mind how he stood in relation with Scotland Yard: fellow sufferers, but on opposite sides of the fence.

At the Fortescue, the Edwardian old place in Jermyn Street, where he had stayed ever since he was first allowed to go to London on his own, they greeted him like a nephew and gave him "the room he had last time"; a dim comfortable box with a

69

shoulder-high bed and a buttoned-plush settee; and brought him up a tray on which reposed an out-size brown kitchen teapot, a Georgian silver cream jug, about a pound of sugar lumps in a sixpenny glass dish, a Dresden cup with flowers and little castles, a red-and-gold Worcester plate made for "their Maj's" William IV and his Queen, and a much buckled kitchen knife with a stained brown handle.

Both the tea and the tray refreshed Robert. He went out into the evening streets feeling vaguely hopeful.

His search for the truth about Betty Kane brought him, only half consciously, to the vacant space where that block of flats had been; the spot where both her parents had died in one shattering burst of high explosive. It was a bare neat space, waiting its appointed part in some plan. Nothing was there to show that a building had ever stood on the spot. Round about, the unharmed houses stood with blank smug faces, like mentally deficient children too idiot to have understood the meaning of a disaster. It had passed them by and that was all they knew or cared about.

On the opposite side of the wide street, a row of small shops still stood as they had obviously stood for fifty years or more. Robert crossed to them and went into the tobacconist's to buy cigarettes; a tobacconist-and-newsagent knows everything.

"Were you here when that happened?" Robert asked, leaning his head towards the door.

"When what happened?" asked the rosy little man, so used to the blank space that he had long ago become unaware of it. "Oh, the incident? No, I was out on duty. Warden, I was."

Robert said that he had meant was he here in business at the time.

Oh, yes; yes, certainly he had the business then, and for long before it. Brought up in the neighbourhood, he was, and succeeded his father in the business.

"You would know the local people well, then. Do you remember the couple who were caretakers of the block of flats, by any chance?"

"The Kanes? Of course I do. Why wouldn't I remember them? They were in and out of this place all day. He for his paper in the morning, and then her for her cigarettes shortly after, and then back for his evening paper and her back for the third time

70

probably for cigarettes again, and then he and I used to have a pint at the local when my boy had finished his lessons and would take over for me here. You knew them, sir?"

"No. But I met someone the other day who spoke of them. How was the whole place wrecked?"

The little pink man sucked his teeth with a derisive sound.

"Jerry-built. That's what it was. Just jerry-built. The bomb fell in the area there—that's how the Kanes were killed, they were down in their basement feeling fairly safe—and the whole thing just settled down like a house of cards. Shocking." He straightened the edge of a pile of evening papers. "It was just her bad luck that the only evening in weeks that she was at home with her husband, a bomb had to come." He seemed to find a sardonic pleasure in the thought.

"Where was she usually, then?" Robert asked. "Did she work somewhere in the evenings?"

"Work!" said the little man, with vast scorn. "Her!" And then, recollecting: "Oh, I'm sorry, I'm sure. I forgot for the minute that they might be friends of——"

Robert hastened to assure him that his interest in the Kanes was purely academic. Someone had remembered them as caretakers of the block of flats, that was all. If Mrs. Kane was not out working in the evenings what was she out doing?

"Having a good time, of course. Oh, yes, people managed to have a good time even then—if they wanted it enough and looked hard enough for it. Kane, he wanted her to go away to the country with that little girl of theirs, but would she? Not her! Three days of the country would kill her she said. She didn't even go to see the little thing when they evacuated her. The authorities, that is. With the rest of the children. It's my opinion she was tickled to death to have the child off her hands so that she could go dancing at nights."

"Whom did she go dancing with?"

"Officers," the little man said succinctly. "A lot more exciting than watching the grass grow. I don't say there was any actual harm in it, mind you," he said hastily. "She's dead, and I wouldn't like to pin anything on her that she isn't here to unpin, if you take my meaning. But she was a bad mother and a bad wife, that's flat and no one ever said anything to the contrary."

"Was she pretty?" Robert asked, thinking of the good emotion he had wasted on Betty's mother.

"In a sulky sort of way, yes. She sort of smouldered. You wondered what she would be like when she was lit up. Excited, I mean; not tight. I never saw her tight. She didn't get her excitement that way."

"And her husband?"

"Ah, he was all right, Bert Kane was. Deserved better luck than that woman. One of the best, Bert was. Terribly fond of the little girl. Spoiled her, of course. She had only to want something and he got it for her; but she was a nice kid, for all that. Demure. Butter wouldn't melt in her little mouth. Yes, Bert deserved better out of life than a good-time wife and a cupboard-love kid. One of the best, Bert was. . . ." He looked over the roadway at the empty space, reflectively. "It took them the best part of a week to find him," he said.

Robert paid for his cigarettes and went out into the street both saddened and relieved. Sad for Bert Kane, who had deserved better; but glad that Betty Kane's mother was not the woman he had pictured. All the way to London his mind had grieved for that dead woman; the woman who had broken her heart for her child's good. It had seemed to him unbearable that the child she had so greatly loved should be Betty Kane. But now he was free of that grief. Betty Kane's mother was exactly the mother he would have chosen for her if he were God. And she on her part looked very like being her mother's daughter.

"A cupboard-love kid." Well, well. And what was it Mrs. Wynn had said? "She cried because she didn't like the food, but I don't remember her crying for her mother."

Nor for that father who so devotedly spoiled her, apparently.

When he got back to the hotel he took his copy of the *Ack-Emma* from his despatch case, and over his solitary dinner at the Fortescue considered at his leisure the story on Page Two. From its poster-simplicity opening—

"On a night in April a girl came back to her home clad in nothing but a frock and shoes. She had left home, a bright happy schoolgirl with not a . . ."

72

to its final fanfare of sobs, it was of its kind a small masterpiece. It did perfectly what it set out to do. And that was to appeal to the greatest number of readers with one and the same story. To those who wanted sex-interest it offered the girl's lack of clothes, to the sentimentalist her youth and charm, to the partisan her helpless condition, to the sadist the details of her beatings, to the sufferer from class-hatred a description of the big white house behind its high walls, and to the warm-hearted British public in general the impression that the police had been, if not "nobbled," then at least lax, and that Right had not been Done.

Yes. It was clever.

Of course the story was a gift for them—which is why they had sent a man back immediately with young Leslie Wynn. But Robert felt that, when really on their mettle, the *Ack-Emma* could probably make a good story of a broken connecting-rod.

It must be a dreary business catering exclusively for the human failings. He turned the pages over, observing how consistently each story was used to appeal to the regrettable in the reader. Even GAVE AWAY A MILLION, he noticed, was the story of a disgraceful old man unloading on his income-tax and not of a boy who had climbed out of a slum by his own courage and enterprise.

With a slight nausea he put the thing back in his case, and took the case with him to St. Paul's Churchyard. There he found the "daily" woman waiting for him with her hat on. Mr. Macdermott's secretary had telephoned to say that a friend of his was coming and that he was to be given the run of the house and left alone in it without scruple; she had stayed merely to let him in; she would now leave him to it; there was whisky on the little table by the fire, and there was another bottle in the cupboard, but it might, if you asked her, be wise not to remind Mr. Macdermott about it or he would stay up too late and she had great trouble getting him up in the morning.

"It's not the whisky," Blair said, smiling at her, "it's the Irish in him. All the Irish hate getting up."

This gave her pause on the doorstep; evidently struck by this new idea.

"I wouldn't wonder," she said. "My old man's the same, and

he's Irish. It's not whisky with him, just original sin. At least that's what I always thought. But perhaps it's just his misfortune in being a Murphy."

It was a pleasant little place; warm and friendly, and peaceful now that the roar of the city traffic was still. He poured himself a drink, went to the window to look down on Queen Anne, paused a moment to note once more how lightly the great bulk of the church floated on its base; so proportioned, so balanced, that it looked as if one could take it up on a palm and dandle it there; and then sat down and, for the first time since he had gone out that morning to see a maddening old woman who was changing her will again, relaxed.

He was half asleep when he heard Kevin's key in the lock, and his host was in the room before he could move.

Macdermott tweaked his neck in an evil pinch as he passed behind him to the decanters on the table. "It's beginning, old boy," he said, "it's beginning."

"What is?" Robert asked.

"The thickening of that handsome neck of yours."

Robert rubbed his neck lazily where it stung. "I do begin to notice draughts on the back of it, now you come to mention it," he said.

"Christ, Robert! does nothing distress you," Kevin said, his eyes pale and bright and mocking under their black brows, "even the imminent prospect of losing those good looks of yours?"

"I'm a little distressed at the moment, but it isn't my looks."

"Well, what with Blair, Hayward, and Bennet, it can't be bankruptcy; so I suppose it's a woman."

"Yes, but not the way you mean."

"Thinking of getting married? You ought to, Rob."

"You said that before."

"You want an heir for Blair, Hayward, and Bennet, don't you?" The calm certainty of Blair, Hayward, and Bennet had always pricked Kevin into small gibes, Robert remembered.

"There is no guarantee that it wouldn't be a girl. Anyhow, Nevil is taking care of that."

"The only thing that young woman of Nevil's will ever give birth to is a gramophone record. She was gracing a platform again

74

the other day, I hear. If she had to earn the money for her train fares she mightn't be so willing to dash about the country being the Vocal Minority." He sat down with his drink. "I needn't ask if you are up on business. Sometime you really ought to come up and see this town. I suppose you dash off again tomorrow after a 10 a.m. interview with someone's solicitors."

"No," Robert said. "With Scotland Yard."

Kevin paused with his glass half-way to his mouth. "Robert, you're slipping," he said. "What has the Yard to do with your Ivory Tower?"

"That's just it," Robert said equably, ignoring this additional flick at his Milford security. "It's there on the doorstep and I don't quite know how to deal with it. I want to listen to someone being intelligent about the situation. I don't know why I should unload it on you. You must be sick of problems. But you always did do my algebra for me."

"And you always reckoned the stocks and shares ones, if I remember rightly. I was always a fool about stocks. I still owe you something for saving me from a bad investment. Two bad investments," he added.

"Two?"

"Tamara, and Topeka Tin."

"I remember saving you from Topeka Tin, but I had nothing whatever to do with your breaking with Tamara."

"Oh, hadn't you, indeed! My good Robert, if you could have seen your face when I introduced you to her. Oh, no, not that way. Quite the contrary. The instantaneous *kindness* of your expression, that blasted English mask of courtesy and good breeding—it said everything. I saw myself going through life introducing Tamara to people and watching their faces being well-bred about it. It cured me of her in record time. I have never ceased to be grateful to you. So produce what is in the despatch case."

Nothing escaped Kevin, Robert thought, taking out his own copy of Betty Kane's statement to the police.

"This is a very short statement. I wish you would read it and tell me how it strikes you."

He wanted the impact on Kevin, without preliminaries to dull the edge of it.

75

Macdermott took it, read the first paragraph in one swift eye movement, and said: "This is the *Ack-Emma*'s protégée, I take it."

"I had no idea that you ever saw the *Ack-Emma*," Robert said, surprised.

"God love you, I feed on the *Ack-Emma*. No crime, no *causes célèbres*. No *causes célèbres*, no Kevin Macdermott. Or only a piece of him." He lapsed into utter silence. For four minutes his absorption was so complete that Robert felt alone in the room, as if his host had gone away. "Humph!" he said, coming out of it.

"Well?"

"I take it that your clients are the two women in the case, and not this girl?"

"Of course."

"Now you tell me your end," Kevin said, and listened.

Robert gave him the whole story. His reluctant visit, his growing partisanship as it became clear that it was a choice between Betty Kane and the two women, Scotland Yard's decision not to move on the available evidence, and Leslie Wynn's rash visit to the offices of the *Ack-Emma*.

"So tonight," Macdermott said, "the Yard is moving heaven and earth to find corroborative evidence that will back up the girl's story."

"I suppose so," said Robert, depressed. "But what I want to know is: Do you or do you not believe the girl's story?"

"I never believe anyone's story," Kevin pointed out with gentle malice. "What you want to know is: Do I find the girl's story believable? And of course I do."

"You do!"

"I do. Why not?"

"But it's an absurd story," Robert said, more hotly than he had intended.

"There is nothing absurd about it. Women who live lonely lives do insane things—especially if they are poor gentlewomen. Only the other day an elderly woman was found to have kept her sister chained up to a bed in a room no bigger than a good-sized cupboard. She had kept her like that for three years, and had fed her on the crusts and potato skins and the other scraps that she didn't want herself. She said, when it was discovered, that their money was going down too fast and this was her way of making ends meet. She had quite a good bank balance actually, but it was the fear induced by insecurity that had sent her crazy. That is a much more unbelievable—and from your point of view absurd—story than the girl's."

"Is it? It seems to me just an ordinary tale of insanity."

"Only because you know it happened. I mean, that someone had actually seen the thing. Suppose, on the contrary, that the rumour had merely gone round; that the crazy sister had heard it and released her victim before any investigation could be made; that the investigators found only two old ladies living an apparently normal life except for the invalidish nature of one of them. What then? Would you have believed the 'chained-up' tale? Or would you, more likely, have called it an 'absurd story'?"

Robert sank a little deeper into his depression.

"Here are two lonely and badly-dowered women saddled with a big house in the country; one of them too old to do much household work and the other loathing it. What is the most likely form for their mild insanity to take? The capture of a girl to be servant to them, of course."

Damn Kevin and his counsel's mind. He had thought that he had wanted Kevin's opinion, but what he had wanted was Kevin's backing for his own opinion.

"The girl they capture happens to be a blameless schoolgirl, conveniently far from her home. It is their bad luck that she is so blameless, because since she has never been caught out in a lie to date, everyone is going to take her word against theirs. If I were the police I would have risked it. It seems to me they are losing their nerve."

He shot an amused glance at Robert, sunk in his chair, glooming down his long legs at the fire. He sat for a moment or two enjoying his friend's discomfiture.

"Of course," he said, at length, "they may have remembered a parallel case, where everyone believed the girl's heart-rending story and were very thoroughly led up the garden."

"A parallel!" Robert said, folding his legs and sitting up. "When?"

"Seventeen-something. I forget the exact date."

"Oh," said Robert, dashed again.

"I don't know what is 'Oh' about it," Macdermott said mildly. "The nature of alibis has not changed much in two centuries."

"Alibis?"

"If the parallel case is any guide the girl's story is an alibi."

"Then you believe—I mean you find it believable—that the girl's story is all nonsense?"

"A complete invention from beginning to end."

"Kevin, you are maddening. You said you found it believable."

"So I do. I also find it believable that it is a tissue of lies. I am not briefed for either side. I can make a very good case out for either, at the shortest notice. On the whole I should prefer to be counsel for the young woman from Aylesbury. She would be wonderful in the witness box, and from what you tell me neither of the Sharpes would be much help, visually, to a counsel."

He got up to help himself to more whisky, holding out his other hand for Robert's glass. But Robert was in no mood for conviviality. He shook his head without lifting his gaze from the fire. He was tired and beginning to be out of temper with Kevin. He had been wrong to come. When a man had been a counsel in the criminal courts as long as Kevin had, his mind had only points of view, not convictions any more. He would wait until Kevin had half-finished the glass he was now sitting down with, and then make a movement to go. It would be good to put his head on a pillow and forget for a little that he was responsible for other people's problems. Or rather, for the solution of them.

"I wonder what she was doing all that month," Kevin said conversationally, taking a large gulp of practically neat whisky.

Robert's mouth opened to say: "Then you *do* believe the girl is a fake!" but he stopped himself in time. He rebelled against dancing any more this evening to Kevin's piping.

"If you drink so much whisky on top of claret, what *you* will be doing for a month is a cure, my lad," he said. And to his surprise Kevin lay back and laughed like a schoolboy.

"Oh, Rob, I love you," he said delightedly. "You are the very essence of England. Everything we admire and envy in you. You sit there so mild, so polite, and let people bait you, until they conclude that you are an old tabby and they can do what they like with you, and then just when they are beginning to preen themselves they go that short step too far and wham! out comes that business-like paw with the glove off!" He picked Robert's glass out of his hand without a by-your-leave and rose to fill it and Robert let him. He was feeling better.

~~~~~~

· 9 ·

THE London-Larborough road was a black straight ribbon in the sunshine, giving off diamond sparks as the crowded traffic caught the light and lost it again. Pretty soon both the air and the roads would be so full that no one could move in comfort and everyone would have to go back to the railways for quick travel. Progress, that was.

Kevin had pointed out last night that, what with present ease of communications, it was quite on the cards that Betty Kane had spent her month's vacation in Sydney, N.S.W. It was a daunting thought. She could be anywhere from Kamchatka to Peru, and all he, Blair, had to do was a little thing like proving she wasn't in a house on the Larborough-Milford road. If it were not a sunny morning, and if he were not sorry for Scotland Yard, and if he didn't have Kevin to hold his hand, and if he were not doing pretty well on his own so far, he might have felt depressed.

Feeling sorry for Scotland Yard was the last thing he had anticipated. But sorry he was. All Scotland Yard's energies were devoted to proving the Sharpes guilty and Betty Kane's story true; for the very good reason that they believed the Sharpes to be guilty. But what each one of them ached in his private soul to do was to push Betty Kane down the *Ack-Emma*'s throat; and they could only do that by proving her story nonsense. Yes, a really prize state of frustration existed in those large calm bodies at the Yard.

Grant had been charming in his quiet reasonable way—it had been rather like going to see a doctor, now he came to think of it —and had quite willingly agreed that Robert should be told about any letters that the *Ack-Emma* might provoke.

"Don't pin your hopes too firmly to that, will you," he had

79

said, in friendly warning. "For one letter that the Yard gets that has any worth it gets five thousand that are nonsense. Letterwriting is the natural outlet of the 'odds.' The busybodies, the idle, the perverted, the cranks, the feel-it-my-duties——"

" 'Pro Bono Publico'——"

"Him and 'Civis'," Grant said with a smile. "Also the plain depraved. They all write letters. It's their *safe* outlet, you see. They can be as interfering, as long-winded, as obscene, as pompous, as one-idea'd, as they like on paper, and no one can kick them for it. So they write. My God, how they write!"

"But there is a chance——"

"Oh, yes. There is a chance. And all these letters will have to be weeded out, however silly they are. Anything of importance will be passed on to you, I promise. But I do remind you that the ordinary intelligent citizen writes only one time in five thousand. He doesn't like what he thinks of as 'poking his nose in'—which is why he sits silent in a railway carriage and scandalises the Americans, who still have a hick interest in other folk—and anyhow he's a busy man, full of his own affairs, and sitting down to a letter to the police about something that doesn't concern him is against all his instincts."

So Robert had come away pleased with the Yard, and sorry for them. At least he, Robert, had a straight row to hoe. He wouldn't be glancing aside every now and then and wishing it was the next row he was hoeing. And moreover he had Kevin's approval of the row he had chosen.

"I mean it," Kevin had said, "when I say that if I were the police I should almost have risked it. They have a good enough case. And a nice little conviction is always a hitch up the ladder of promotion for someone. Unfortunately—or fortunately for the citizen—the man who decides whether there is a case or not is the chap higher up, and he's not interested in any subordinate's speedy promotion. Amazing that wisdom should be the by-product of office procedure."

Robert, mellow with whisky, had let the cynicism flow past him.

"But let them just get one spot of corroboration, and they'll have a warrant at the door of The Franchise quicker than you can lift a telephone receiver."

"They won't get any corroboration," said the mellow Robert. "Why should they? How could they? What we want to do is to disprove the girl's story ourselves, so that it doesn't damn the Sharpes' lives for as long as they live. Once I have seen the aunt and uncle tomorrow we may have enough general knowledge about the girl to justify a start on our own investigation."

Now he was speeding down the black shining Larborough road on the way to seeing Betty's relations in Mainshill; the people she had stayed with on the memorable holiday. A Mr. and Mrs. Tilsit, they were. Tilsit, 93 Cherrill Street, Mainshill, Larborough—and the husband was travelling agent for a firm of brush-makers in Larborough and they had no children. That was all Robert knew about them.

He paused for a moment as he turned off the main road in Mainshill. This was the corner where Betty Kane waited for her bus. Or said she waited. Over there on the other side, it must have been. There was no side turning on that side; nothing but the long stretch of unbroken pavement as far as one could see in either direction. A busy enough road at this time of day; but empty enough, Robert supposed, in the doldrum hour of the late afternoon.

Cherrill Street was one long series of angular bay windows in dirty red brick, their forward surface almost scraping the low red-brick wall that hemmed them in from the pavement. The sour soil on either side of the window that did duty for a garden had none of the virtues of the new-turned earth of Meadowside Lane, Aylesbury; it grew only thin London Pride, weedy wall-flowers, and moth-eaten forget-me-not. The same housewife's pride obtained in Cherrill Street as in Aylesbury, of course, and the same crisp curtains hung at the windows; but if there were poets in Cherrill Street they found other outlets for their soul than gardens.

When he had rung unavailingly, and then knocked, at 93—indistinguishable from the others as far as he could see except by its painted numerals—a woman flung up the bedroom window next door, leaned out and said:

"You looking for Mrs. Tilsit?"

Robert said that he was.

"She's gone to get her groceries. The shop at the corner."

"Oh, thanks. If that's all, I'll wait."

81

"Shouldn't wait if you want to see her soon. Should go and fetch her."

"Oh. Is she going somewhere else?"

"No, just the grocer's; it's the only shop round here. But she takes half a morning deciding between two brands of wheat flakes. You take one packet up right firm and put it in her bag and she'll be quite pleased."

Robert thanked her and began to walk away to the end of the street, when she hailed him again.

"Shouldn't leave your car. Take it with you."

"But it's quite a little way, isn't it?"

"Maybe, but it's Saturday."

"Saturday?"

"School's out."

"Oh, I see. But there's nothing in it——" "to steal," he was going to say but amended it to "Nothing in it that's movable."

"Movable! Huh! That's good. We had window-boxes once. Mrs. Laverty over the way had a gate. Mrs. Biddows had two fine wooden clothes posts and eighteen yards of clothes rope. They all thought they weren't movable. You leave your car there for ten minutes you'll be lucky to find the chassis!"

So Robert got obediently into the car, and drove down to the grocer's. And as he drove he remembered something, and the memory puzzled him. This was where Betty Kane had been so happy. This rather dreary, rather grimy street; one of a warren of streets very like itself. So happy that she had written to say that she was staying on for the rest of her holidays.

What had she found here that was so desirable?

He was still wondering as he walked into the grocer's and prepared to spot Mrs. Tilsit among the morning customers. But there was no need for any guesswork. There was only one woman in the shop, and one glance at the grocer's patient face and the cardboard packet in the woman's either hand, made it plain that she was Mrs. Tilsit.

"Can I get you something, sir," the grocer said detaching himself for a moment from the woman's ponderings—it wasn't wheat flakes this morning, it was powdered soap—and moving towards Robert.

"No, thank you," Robert said. "I am just waiting for this lady."

"For me?" the woman said. "If it's the gas, then——"

Robert said hastily that he wasn't the gas.

"I *have* a vacuum cleaner, and it's going fine," she offered, and prepared to go back to her problem.

Robert said that he had his car outside and would wait until she had finished, and was beating a hasty retreat; but she said: "A car! Oh. Well, you can drive me back, can't you, and save me carrying all those things. How much, Mr. Carr, please?"

Mr. Carr, who had taken a packet of soap-flakes from her during her interest in Robert and wedged it into her shopping-bag, took her money, gave her change, wished her a thankful good-day, and cast a pitiful glance at Robert as he followed the woman out to his car.

Robert had known that it was too much to hope for another woman with Mrs. Wynn's detachment and intelligence, but his heart sank as he considered Mrs. Tilsit. Mrs. Tilsit was one of those women whose minds are always on something else. They chat brightly with you, they agree with you, they admire what you are wearing, and they offer advice, but their real attention is concentrated on what to do with the fish, or what Florrie told them about Minnie's eldest, or where they have left the laundry book, or even just what a bad filling that is in your right front tooth; anything, everything, except the subject in hand.

She seemed impressed with the appearance of Robert's car, and asked him in to have a cup of tea—there being apparently no hour of the day when a cup of tea was not a possible article of diet. Robert felt that he could not drink with her—even a cup of tea—without making plain his position of opposing counsel, so to speak. He did his best, but it was doubtful if she understood; her mind was so plainly already deciding whether to offer him the Rich Tea or the Mixed Fancy biscuits with his tea. Mention of her niece made none of the expected stir in her emotions.

"A most extraordinary thing, that was, wasn't it?" she said. "Taking her away and beating her. What good did they think that was going to do them? Sit down, Mr. Blayne, come in and sit down. I'll just——"

A bloodcurdling scream echoed through the house. An urgent,

83

high-pitched, desperate screaming that went on and on, without even a pause for breath.

Mrs. Tilsit humped her parcels in a movement of exasperation. She leaned near enough to Robert to put her mouth within shouting distance of his ear. "My kettle," she yelled. "I'll be right back."

Robert sat down, and again considered the surroundings and wondered why Betty Kane had found them so good. Mrs. Wynn's front room had been a living-room; a sitting-room warm with human occupation and human traffic. But this was clearly a "best" room, kept for visitors who were not intimate enough to be admitted to the back regions; the real life of the house was in the poky room at the back. Either kitchen or kitchen-sitting-room. And yet Betty Kane had elected to stay. Had she found a friend? A girl-next-door? A boy-next-door?

Mrs. Tilsit came back in what seemed like two minutes, bearing a tray with tea. Robert wondered a little at this promptness of action until he saw the tray's contents. Mrs. Tilsit had not waited to make a decision; she had brought them both; Thin Wine and Sweet Shortbread. At least, he thought, watching her pour, that this woman explained one of the oddities in the affair: the fact that when the Wynns had written to have Betty sent home at once, her aunt had not flown to a telegraph office to break the news that Betty had left for home nearly a fortnight ago. The Betty who had gone a fortnight previously would be much less real in Mrs. Tilsit's mind than the jelly that was cooling on the back window-sill.

"I wasn't worried about her," Mrs. Tilsit said, as if in echo to his thoughts. "When they wrote from Aylesbury about her. I knew she would turn up. When Mr. Tilsit came home he was quite upset about it; he goes away for a week or ten days at a time you know; he's agent for Weekses; carried on like a mad thing, he did; but I just said you wait and she'll turn up all right, and she did. Well, nearly all right."

"She said she enjoyed her holiday here enormously."

"I suppose she did," she said vaguely, not looking gratified as Robert had expected. He glanced at her and realised that her mind was already on something else. The strength of his tea, if one was to judge by the direction of her eye.

84

"How did she pass her time? Did she make friends?"

"Oh, no, she was in Larborough most of the time."

"Larborough!"

"Oh, well, when I say most of the time, I do her an injustice. She helped with the house in the mornings, but in a house this size and me used to doing everything myself there isn't much to do. And she was here on holiday, wasn't she, poor thing, after all that school work. What good all that book work is to a young girl I don't know. Mrs. Harrap's daughter over the way could hardly write her name but she married the third son of a lord. Or perhaps it was the son of a third son," she said, looking doubtful. "I forget for the minute. She——"

"How did she spend her time in Larborough? Betty, I mean."

"Pictures, mostly."

"Pictures? Oh, the cinema. I see."

"You can do that from morning till night if you're given that way, in Larborough. The big ones open at half-past ten and they mostly change mid-week and there's about forty of them, so you can just go from one to another till it's time to go home."

"Is that what Betty did?"

"Oh, no. She's quite sensible, Betty is. She used to go in to the morning round because you get in cheaper before noon, and then she'd go bus-riding."

"Bus-riding. Where?"

"Oh, anywhere the fancy took her. Have another of these biscuits, Mr. Bain; they're fresh from the tin. She went to see the castle at Norton one day. Norton's the county town you know. Everyone imagines Larborough is because it's so big, but Norton's always been——"

"Did she not come home to lunch, then?"

"What? Oh, Betty. No, she'd have coffee lunch somewhere. We always have our real meal at night anyhow, you see, with Mr. Tilsit being out all day, so there was always a meal waiting when she came home. It's always been my pride to have a good nourishing sit-down meal ready for my——"

"What time would that be? Six?"

"No, Mr. Tilsit doesn't usually manage home before half-past seven."

"And I suppose Betty was home long before then?"

"Mostly she was. She was late once because she went to an afternoon show at the pictures, but Mr. Tilsit he created about it —though I'm sure he had no need to, what harm can you come to at the pictures?—and after that she was always home before him. When he was here, that is. She wasn't so careful when he was away."

So the girl had been her own mistress for a good fortnight. Free to come and go without question, and limited only by the amount of holiday money in her pocket. It was an innocent-sounding fortnight; and in the case of most girls of her age it undoubtedly would have been that. The cinema in the morning, or window gazing; a coffee lunch; a bus-ride into the country in the afternoon. A blissful holiday for an adolescent; the first taste of unsupervised freedom.

But Betty Kane was no normal adolescent. She was the girl who had told that long and circumstantial story to the police without a tremor. The girl with four weeks of her life unaccounted for. The girl that someone had ended by beating unmercifully. How, then, had Betty Kane spent her unsupervised freedom?

"Did she go to Milford on the bus, do you know?"

"No, *they* asked me that, of course, but I couldn't say yes or not."

"They?"

"The police."

Yes, of course; he had forgotten for the moment that the police would have checked Betty Kane's every sentence to the limit of their power.

"You're not police, I think you said."

"No," Robert said yet once again, "I'm a lawyer. I represent the two women who are supposed to have detained Betty."

"Oh, yes. You told me. I suppose they have to have a lawyer like anyone else, poor things. To ask questions for them. I hope I'm telling you the things you want to know, Mr. Blayne."

He had another cup of tea in the hope that sooner or later she would tell him something he wanted to know. But it was mere repetition now.

"Did the police know that Betty was away on her own all day?" he asked.

She really thought about that. "That I can't remember," she said. "They asked me how she passed her time and I said that mostly she went to pictures or bus-riding, and they said did I go with her and I said—well, I'll have to admit I told a white lie about it and said that I did now and then. I didn't want them to think that Betty went to places alone. Though of course there was no harm in it."

What a mind!

"Did she have letters while she was here?" he asked as he was taking his leave.

"Just from home. Oh, yes, I would know. I always took the letters in. In any case they wouldn't have written to her, would they?"

"Who?"

"Those women who kidnapped her."

It was with a feeling of escape that Robert drove in to Larborough. He wondered if Mr. Tilsit had always been away "ten days at a time" from his home, or if he had got the travelling job as an alternative to flight or suicide.

In Larborough, Blair sought out the main garage of the Larborough And District Motor Services. He knocked at the door of the small office that guarded one side of the entrance, and went in. A man in a bus inspector's uniform was going through papers on the desk. He glanced up at Robert and without asking his business continued his own affairs.

Robert said that he wanted to see someone who would know about the Milford bus service.

"Time table on the wall outside," the man said without looking up.

"I don't want to know about times. I know them. I live in Milford. I want to know if you ever run a double-decker bus on that route."

There was silence for a long time; a silence expertly calculated to end at the point where Robert was about to open his mouth again.

"No," said the man.

"Never?" Robert asked.

This time there was no answer at all. The inspector made it plain that he was finished with him.

"Listen," Robert said, "this is important. I am a partner in a firm of solicitors in Milford, and I——"

The man turned on him. "I don't care if you are the Shah of Persia; there are *no double-decker buses on the Milford run!* And what do *you* want?" he added as a small mechanic appeared behind Robert in the doorway.

The mechanic hesitated, as if the business he had come on had been upset by a newer interest. But he pulled himself together and began to state his business. "It's about those spares for Norton. Shall I——"

As Robert was edging past him out of the office he felt a tug on his coat and realised that the little mechanic wanted him to linger until he could talk to him. Robert went out and bent over his own car, and presently the mechanic appeared at his elbow.

"You asking about double-decker buses? I couldn't contradict him straight out, you know; in the mood he's in now it'd be as much as my job's worth. You want to *use* a double-decker, or just to know if they ever run at all? Because you can't *get* a double-decker on that route, not to travel in, because the buses on that run are all——"

"I know, I know. They are single-decks. What I wanted to know was whether there *ever* are two-deck buses on the Milford route."

"Well, there are not supposed to be, you understand, but once or twice this year we've had to use a double-decker when one of the old single ones broke down unexpected. Sooner or later they'll be all double-deck, but there isn't enough traffic on the Milford run to justify a double, so all the old crocks of singles eventually land on that route and a few more like it. And so——"

"You're a great help. Would it be possible to find out exactly when a double-decker did run on that route?"

"Oh, certainly," the mechanic said, with a shade of bitterness. "In this firm it's recorded every time you spit. But the records are in there," he tilted back his head to indicate the office, "and as long as *he's* there there's nothing doing."

Robert asked at what hour there would be something doing.

"Well: he goes off at the same time as me: six. But I could wait a few minutes and look up the schedules when he's gone if it's very important to you."

Robert did not know how he was going to wait through the hours till six o'clock, but six o'clock it would have to be.

"Righto. I'll meet you in the Bell, that's the pub at the end of the street, about a quarter past six. That do?"

That would do perfectly, Robert said. Perfectly.

And he went away to see what he could bribe the lounge waiter at the Midland into giving him out of hours.

~~~~~~~~~~~~~~

· 10 ·

"I suppose you know what you're doing, dear," Aunt Lin said, "but I can't help thinking it's very odd of you to defend people like that."

"I am not 'defending' them," Robert said patiently, "I am representing them. And there is no evidence whatever that they are 'people like that'."

"There is the girl's statement, Robert. She couldn't just have made all that up."

"Oh, couldn't she!"

"What advantage would it be to her to tell a lot of lies!" She was standing in his doorway passing her prayer-book from one hand to the other as she put on her white gloves. "What else could she have been doing if she wasn't at The Franchise?"

Robert bit back a "You'd be surprised!" It was always best with Aunt Lin to take the line of least resistance.

She smoothed her gloves into place. "If it's just that you're being noble, Robert dear, I must say you are just being wrong-headed. And do you have to go out to the *house*! Surely they could come to the office tomorrow. There's no hurry is there? It isn't as if someone was going to arrest them on the spot."

"It was my suggestion that I should go out to The Franchise. If someone accused *you* of stealing things off Woolworth's counter and you couldn't disprove it, I don't suppose you would enjoy walking down Milford High Street in broad daylight."

"I mightn't like it but I should most certainly do it, and give Mr. Hensell a piece of my mind."

"Who is Mr. Hensell?"

"The manager. Couldn't you come to church with me first and

89

then go out to The Franchise; it's such a long time since you've been, dear."

"If you stand there much longer you'll be late for the first time in ten years. You go and pray that my judgment may be perfected."

"I shall most certainly pray for you, dear. I always do. I shall also put up a little one for myself. All this is going to be very difficult for me."

"For you?"

"Now that you're acting for those people I shan't be able to talk about it to anyone. It is quite maddening, dear, to sit silent and hear everyone telling for gospel truth things you know for a fact are wrong. It's like wanting to be sick and having to postpone it. Oh, dear, the bells have stopped, haven't they? I'll just have to slip into the Bracketts' pew. They won't mind. You won't stay to lunch at that place, will you, dear."

"I don't suppose that I shall be invited."

But his welcome at The Franchise was so warm that he felt that he might very well be invited after all. He would say no, of course; not because Aunt Lin's chicken was waiting but because Marion Sharpe would have to do the washing up afterwards. When there was no one there they probably ate off trays. Or in the kitchen, for all anyone knew.

"I am sorry we refused to answer the telephone last night," Marion said, apologising again. "But after the fourth or fifth time it really was too much. And we didn't expect you to have news so soon. After all you had only set out on Friday afternoon."

"Your telephone callers: were they male or female?"

"One male, and four female, as far as I remember. When you rang this morning I thought it was beginning again, but they seem to be late-sleepers. Or perhaps they don't really get evil-minded much before evening. We certainly provided the Saturday evening's entertainment for the country youths. They congregated in a group inside the gate and cat-called. Then Nevil found a bar of wood in the out-house——"

"Nevil?"

"Yes, your nephew. I mean, your cousin. He came to pay what he called a visit of condolence, which was very nice of him. And he found a bar that could be wedged in the gateway to keep the thing shut; we have no key for it, you see. But of course that didn't stop them for long. They hoisted each other up on the wall, and sat there in a row being offensive until it was time for them to go to their beds."

"Lack of education," old Mrs. Sharpe said thoughtfully, "is an extraordinary handicap when one is being offensive. They had no resource at all."

"Neither have parrots," Robert said. "But they can be provocative enough. We must see what police protection we can claim. Meanwhile I can tell you something pleasanter about that wall. I know how the girl saw over it."

He told them about his visit to Mrs. Tilsit and his discovery that the girl amused herself by bus-riding (or said she did) and his subsequent visit to the Larborough And District Motor Services garage.

"In the fortnight that the girl was at Mainshill there were two breakdowns of single-deck buses due to go out on the Milford run; and each time a double-decker had to be substituted. There are only three services each way daily, you know. And each time the breakdown happened to the bus due to go out on the mid-day service. So there were at least two occasions in that fortnight when she could have seen the house, the courtyard, you two, and the car, all together."

"But could anyone passing on top of a bus take in so much?"

"Have you ever travelled on the upper deck of a country bus? Even when the bus is going at a steady thirty-five, the pace seems funeral. What you can see is so much further away, and you can see it so much longer. Down below, the hedges brush the window and the pace seems good because things are closer. That is one thing. The other is that she has a photographic memory." And he told them what Mrs. Wynn had said.

"Do we tell the police this?" Mrs. Sharpe asked.

"No. It doesn't prove anything; just solves the problem of how she knew about you. When she needed an alibi she remembered you, and risked your not being able to prove that you were somewhere else. When you bring your car to the door, by the way, which side of the car is nearest the door?"

"Whether I bring it round from the garage or in from the road the off side is next the door, because it's easier to get out of."

"Yes; so that the near side, with the darker paint on the front wheel, would be facing the gate," Robert said conclusively. "That is the picture she saw. The grass and the divided path, the car at the door with the odd wheel, two women—both individual—the round attic window in the roof. She had only to look at the picture in her mind and describe it. The day she was using the picture for—the day she was supposed to have been kidnapped—was more than a month away and it was a thousand to one against your being able to say what you had done or where you had been on that day."

"And I take it," Mrs. Sharpe said, "that the odds are very much greater against our being able to say what she has done or where she has been in that month."

"The odds are against us, yes. As my friend Kevin Macdermott pointed out last night, there is nothing to hinder her having been in Sydney, N.S.W. But somehow I am far more hopeful today than I was on Friday morning. We know so much more about the girl now." He told them of his interviews in Aylesbury and Mainshill.

"But if the police inquiries didn't unearth what she was doing that month——"

"The police inquiries were devoted to checking her statement. They didn't start, as we do, with the premise that her statement is untrue from beginning to end. They checked it and it checked. They had no particular reason to doubt it. She had a blameless reputation, and when they inquired from her aunt how she had spent her holiday time they found that it had consisted of innocent visits to the cinema and country bus-rides."

"And what do *you* think it consisted of?" Mrs. Sharpe asked.

"I think she met someone in Larborough. That, anyhow, is the obvious explanation. It's from that supposition that I think any inquiry of ours should start."

"And what do we do about engaging an agent?" asked Mrs. Sharpe. "Do you know of one?"

"Well," Robert said, hesitating, "it had crossed my mind that you might let me pursue my own inquiries a little further before we engage a professional. I know that——"

92

"Mr. Blair," the old woman said, interrupting him, "you have been called into this unpleasant case without warning, and it cannot have been very willingly; and you have been very kind in doing your best for us. But we cannot expect you to turn yourself into a private inquiry agent on our behalf. We are not rich—indeed we have very little to live on—but as long as we have any money at all we shall pay for what services are proper. And it is not proper that you should turn yourself into a—what is it?—a Sexton Blake for our benefit."

"It may not be proper but it is very much to my taste. Believe me, Mrs. Sharpe, I hadn't planned it with any conscious thought of saving your pocket. Coming home in the car last night, very pleased with what I had done so far, I realised how much I should hate giving up the search to someone else. It had become a personal hunt. Please don't discourage me from——"

"If Mr. Blair is willing to carry on a little longer," Marion interrupted, "I think we should thank him heartily and accept. I know just how he feels. I wish I could go hunting myself."

"There will no doubt come a time when I shall have to turn it over to a proper inquiry agent whether I want to or not. If the trail leads far from Larborough, for instance. I have too many other commitments to follow it far. But as long as the search is on our doorsteps I do want to be the one to pursue it."

"How had you planned to pursue it?" Marion asked, interested.

"Well, I had thought of beginning with the coffee-lunch places. In Larborough, I mean. For one thing, there can't be so very many of them. And for another, we do know that, at any rate at the beginning, that was the kind of lunch she had."

"Why do you say 'at the beginning'?" Marion asked.

"Once she had met the hypothetical X, she may have lunched anywhere. But up till then she paid for her own lunches, and they were 'coffee' ones. A girl of that age prefers a bun lunch anyhow, even if she has money for a two-course meal. So I concentrate on the coffee-places. I flourish the *Ack-Emma* at the waitresses and find out as tactfully as a country lawyer knows how whether they have ever seen the girl in their place. Does that sound like sense to you?"

"Very good sense," Marion said.

Robert turned to Mrs. Sharpe. "But if you think you will be

better served by a professional—and that is more than possible—then I shall bow out with——"

"I don't think we could be better served by anyone," Mrs. Sharpe said. "I have expressed my appreciation already of the trouble you have gone to on our behalf. If it would really please you to run down this—this——"

"Moppet," supplied Robert happily.

"Mopsy," Mrs. Sharpe amended, "then we can only agree and be grateful. But it seems to me likely to be a very long run."

"Why long?"

"There is a big gap, it seems to me, between meeting a hypothetical X in Larborough, and walking into a house near Aylesbury wearing nothing but a frock and shoes and well and truly beaten. Marion, there is still some of the Amontillado, I think."

In the silence that succeeded Marion's departure to fetch the sherry the quiet of the old house became apparent. There were no trees in the courtyard to make small noises in the wind and no birds to chatter. The silence was as absolute as the midnight silence of a small town. Was it peaceful, Robert wondered, after the crowded life of a boarding-house? Or was it lonely and a little frightening?

They had valued its privacy, old Mrs. Sharpe had said in his office on Friday morning. But was it a good life shut in behind the high walls in the perpetual silence?

"It seems to me," Mrs. Sharpe said, "that the girl took a great risk in choosing The Franchise, knowing nothing of the household or its circumstances."

"Of course she took a risk," Robert said. "She had to. But I don't think it was as big a gamble as you think."

"No?"

"No. What you are saying is that for all the girl knew there might be a large household of young people and three maid-servants at The Franchise."

"Yes."

"But I think she knew quite well that there was no such thing."

"How could she?"

"Either she gossiped with the bus-conductor, or—and I think this is the more likely—she overheard comment from her fellow-passengers. You know the kind of thing: 'There are the Sharpes. Fancy living alone in a big house like that, just the two of them. And no maids willing to stay in a lonely place so far from shops and the pictures——' and so on. It is very much a 'local' bus, that Larborough-Milford one. And it is a lonely route, with no wayside cottages, and no village other than Ham Green. The Franchise is the only spot of human interest for miles. It would be more than human nature is capable of to pass the combined interest of the house, the owners, and their car without comments of some kind."

"I see. Yes, that makes sense."

"I wish, in a way, it *had* been through chatting with the conductor that she learned about you. That way, he would be more likely to remember her. The girl says she was never in Milford and doesn't know where it is. If a conductor remembered her, we could at least shake her story to that extent."

"If I know anything of the young person she would open those childlike eyes of hers and say: 'Oh, was that Milford? I just got on a bus and went to the terminus and back.' "

"Yes. It wouldn't take us very far. But if I fail to pick up the girl's trail in Larborough, I'll try her picture on the local conductors. I do wish she was a more memorable creature."

The silence fell round them again while they contemplated the un-memorable nature of Betty Kane.

They were sitting in the drawing-room, facing the window, looking out on the green square of the courtyard and faded pink of the brick wall. And as they looked the gate was pushed open and a small group of seven or eight people appeared and stood at gaze. Entirely at their ease they were; pointing out to each other the salient points of interest—the favourite being apparently the round window in the roof. If last night The Franchise had provided the country youth with its Saturday evening entertainment, it was now, so it would seem, providing Sunday morning interest for Larborough. Certainly a couple of cars were waiting for them outside the gate, since the women of the party wore silly little shoes and indoor frocks.

Robert glanced across at Mrs. Sharpe, but except for a tightening of her always grim mouth she had not moved.

"Our public," she said at last, witheringly.

"Shall I go and move them on?" Robert said. "It's my fault for not putting back the wooden bar you left off for me."

"Let them be," she said. "They will go presently. This is what royalty puts up with daily; we can support it for a few moments."

But the visitors showed no sign of going. Indeed, one group moved round the house to inspect the out-buildings; and the rest were still there when Marion came back with the sherry. Robert apologised again for not having put up the bar. He was feeling small and inadequate. It went against the grain to stay there quietly and watch strangers prowling round as if they owned the place or were contemplating buying it. But if he went out and asked them to move on and they refused to, what power had he to make them go? And how would he look in the Sharpes' eyes if he had to beat a retreat to the house and leave these people in possession?

The group of explorers came back from their tour round the house and reported with laughter and gesticulation what they had seen. He heard Marion say something under her breath and wondered if she were cursing. She looked like a woman who would have a very fine line in curses. She had put down the sherry tray and had apparently forgotten about it; it was no moment for hospitality. He longed to do something decisive and spectacular to please her, just as he had longed to rescue his lady-love from burning buildings when he was fifteen. But alas, there was no surmounting the fact that he was forty-odd and had learned that it is wiser to wait for the fire-escape.

And while he hesitated, angry with himself and with those crude human creatures outside, the fire-escape arrived in the person of a tall young man in a regrettable tweed suit.

"Nevil," breathed Marion, watching the picture.

Nevil surveyed the group with his most insufferable air of superiority, and it seemed that they wilted slightly, but they were evidently determined to stand their ground. Indeed, the male with the sports jacket and the pin-striped trousers was clearly preparing to make an issue of it.

Nevil looked at them silently for a further few seconds and then fished in his inner pocket for something. At the first movement of his hand a strange difference came over the group. The outer members of it detached themselves and faded unobtrusively through the gate; the nearer ones lost their air of bravado, and became placatory. Finally the sports-jacket made small rejecting movements of surrender and joined the retreat through the gate.

Nevil banged the gate to behind them, levered the wooden bar into place, and strolled up the path to the door wiping his hands fastidiously on a really shocking handkerchief. And Marion ran out to the door to meet him.

"Nevil!" Robert heard her say. "How did you do it?"

"Do what?" Nevil asked.

"Get rid of those creatures."

"Oh, I just asked their names and addresses," Nevil said. "You've no idea how discreet people become if you take out a notebook and ask for their name and address. It's the modern equivalent to: 'Fly, all is discovered.' They don't wait to ask your credentials in case you may actually have some. Hello, Robert. Good morning, Mrs. Sharpe. I'm actually on my way to Larborough, but I saw the gate open and these two frightful cars outside so I stopped to investigate. I didn't know Robert was here."

This quite innocent implication that of course Robert was capable of dealing equally well with the situation was the unkindest cut of all. Robert could have brained him.

"Well, now that you are here and have so expertly rid us of the nuisance you must stay and drink a glass of sherry," Mrs. Sharpe said.

"Could I come in and drink it on my way home in the evening?" Nevil said. "You see, I'm on my way to lunch with my prospective father-in-law and it being Sunday there is a ritual. One must be there for the warming-up exercises."

"But of course come in on your way home," Marion said. "We shall be delighted. How shall we know it is you? For the gate, I mean." She was pouring sherry and handing it to Robert.

"Do you know morse?"

"Yes, but don't tell me you do."

"Why not?"

"You look a most unlikely morse addict."

"Oh, when I was fourteen I was going to sea, and I acquired in

97

the heat of my ambition a lot of incidental idiocies. Morse was one of them. I shall hoot the initials of your beautiful name on the horn, when I come. Two longs and three shorts. I must fly. The thought of talking to you tonight will support me through luncheon at the Palace."

"Won't Rosemary be any support?" Robert asked, overcome by his baser self.

"I shouldn't think so. On Sundays Rosemary is a daughter in her father's house. It is a role that does not become her. *Au revoir*, Mrs. Sharpe. Don't let Robert drink all the sherry."

"And when," Robert heard Marion ask as she went with him to the door, "did you decide not to go to sea?"

"When I was fifteen. I took up ballooning instead."

"Theoretical, I suppose."

"Well, I gassed about gases."

Why did they sound so friendly, so at ease, Robert wondered. As if they had known each other a long time. Why did she like that light-weight Nevil?

"And when you were sixteen?"

If she knew how many things Nevil had taken up and dropped in his time she might not be so pleased to be the latest of them.

"Is the sherry too dry for you, Mr. Blair," Mrs. Sharpe asked.

"No, oh no, thank you, it is excellent." Was it possible that he had been looking sour? Perish the thought.

He stole a cautious glance at the old lady and thought that she was looking faintly amused. And old Mrs. Sharpe being amused was no comfortable sight.

"I think I had better go before Miss Sharpe bars the gate behind Nevil," he said. "Otherwise she will have to come to the gate again with me."

"But won't you stay and have lunch with us? There is no ritual about it at The Franchise."

But Robert made his excuses. He didn't like the Robert Blair he was becoming. Petty and childish and inadequate. He would go back and have ordinary Sunday lunch with Aunt Lin and be again Robert Blair of Blair, Hayward, and Bennet, equable and tolerant and at peace with his world.

Nevil had gone by the time he reached the gate, in a flurry of sound that shattered the Sabbath quiet, and Marion was about to close the gate.

"I can't think that the Bishop approves of his future son-in-law's means of transport," she said looking after the roaring object as it streaked down the road.

"Exhausting," Robert said, still caustic.

She smiled at him. "I think that is the first witty pun I have ever heard anyone make," she said. "I hoped you would stay for lunch, but in a way I'm rather relieved that you aren't."

"Are you indeed?"

"I made a 'shape' but it didn't stand up. I'm a very bad cook. I do faithfully what it says in the book but it hardly ever works out. Indeed I'm surprised to death when it does. So you will be better off with your Aunt Lin's apple tart."

And Robert suddenly and illogically wished that he was staying, to share the "shape" that had not stood up and to be gently mocked by her along with her cooking.

"I'll let you know tomorrow night how I get on in Larborough," he said matter-of-factly. Since he was not on hens-and-Maupassant terms with her he would keep the conversation to practicalities. "And I'll ring up Inspector Hallam and see if one of their men can give a look round The Franchise once or twice a day; just to show the uniform, so to speak, and to discourage idlers."

"You are very kind, Mr. Blair," she said. "I can't imagine what it would be without you to lean on."

Well, if he couldn't be young and a poet, he could be a crutch. A dull thing, a thing resorted to only in emergencies, but useful; useful.

· 11 ·

By half-past ten on Monday morning he was sitting in front of a steaming cup of coffee in the Karena. He began with the Karena because when one thinks of coffee at all one thinks of a Karena, with the smell of the roasting coffee downstairs in the shop and the liquid version waiting upstairs among the little tables. And if he was going to have a surfeit of coffee he might as well have some good stuff while he could still taste it.

He was holding the *Ack-Emma* in his hand with the girl's photograph open to the gaze of the waitresses as they passed, hoping vaguely that his interest in it might cause one of them to say: "That girl used to come in here every morning." To his surprise the paper was gently removed from his grasp, and he looked up to see his waitress regarding him with a kind smile. "That is last Friday's," she said. "Here." And she proffered that morning's *Ack-Emma*.

He thanked her and said that while he would be glad to see this morning's paper he would like to keep the Friday one. Did this girl, this girl on the front page of Friday's, ever come in there for coffee?

"Oh, no, we'd have remembered her if she did. We were all discussing that case on Friday. Imagine beating her half to death like that."

"Then you think they did."

She looked puzzled. "The paper says they did."

"No, the paper reports what the girl said."

She obviously did not follow that. This was the democracy we deified.

"They wouldn't print a story like that if it wasn't true. It would be as much as their life's worth. You a detective?"

"Part time," Robert said.

"How much do you get an hour for that?"

"Not nearly enough."

"No, I suppose not. Haven't got a Union, I suppose. You don't get your rights in this world unless you have a Union."

"Too true," said Robert. "Let me have my bill, will you?"

"Your check, yes."

At the Palace, the biggest and newest of the cinemas, the restaurant occupied the floor behind the balcony and had carpets so deep that one tripped on them, and lighting so subdued that all the cloths looked dirty. A bored houri with gilt hair, an uneven hem to her skirt, and a wad of chewing gum in her right jaw, took his order without ever glancing at him, and fifteen minutes later put down a cup of washy liquid in front of him without letting her eyes stray even approximately in his direction. Since in the fifteen minutes Robert had discovered that the never-look-at-the-customers technique was universal—presumably they were all going to be film stars the year after next and could not be expected to take any interest in a provincial clientele—he paid for the untasted liquid and left.

At the Castle, the other big cinema, the restaurant did not open until afternoon.

At the Violet—royal purple everywhere and yellow curtains—no one had seen her. Robert, casting subtleties aside, asked them bluntly.

Upstairs at Griffon and Waldron's, the big store, it was rush hour and the waitress said: "Don't *bother* me!" The manageress, looking at him with absent-minded suspicion, said: "We never give information about our customers."

At the Old Oak—small and dark and friendly—the elderly waitresses discussed the case interestedly with him. "Poor love," they said. "What an experience for her. Such a nice face, too. Just a baby. Poor love."

At the Alençon—cream paint and old-rose couches against the walls—they made it plain that they had never heard of the *Ack-Emma* and could not possibly have a client whose photograph appeared in such a publication.

At the Heave Ho—marine frescos and waitresses in bell-bottomed trousers—the attendants gave it as their unanimous opinion that any girl who took a lift should expect to have to walk home.

At the Primrose—old polished tables with raffia mats and thin unprofessional waitresses in flowered smocks—they discussed the social implications of lack of domestic service and the vagaries of the adolescent mind.

At the Tea-Pot there was no table to be had, and no waitress willing to attend to him; but a second glance at the fly-blown place made him sure that, with the others to chose from, Betty Kane would not have come here.

At half-past twelve he staggered into the lounge of the Midland, and called for strong waters. As far as he knew he had covered all the likely eating-places in the centre of Larborough and in not one of them had anyone remembered seeing the girl. What was worse, everyone agreed that if she had been there they would have remembered her. They had pointed out, when Robert was sceptical of that, that a large proportion of their customers on any one day were regulars, so that the casuals stood out from the rest and were noted and remembered automatically.

As Albert, the tubby little lounge waiter, set his drink in front of him, Robert asked, more out of habit than volition: "I suppose you've never seen this girl in your place, Albert?"

Albert looked at the front page of the *Ack-Emma* and shook his head. "No, sir. Not that I recollect. Looks a little young, sir, if I may say so, for the lounge of the Midland."

"She mightn't look so young with a hat on," Robert said, considering it.

"A hat." Albert paused. "Now, wait a minute. A *hat*." Albert laid his little tray down and picked up the paper to consider it. "Yes, of course; that's the girl in the green hat!"

"You mean she came in here for coffee?"

"No, for tea."

"Tea!"

"Yes, of course, that's the girl. Fancy me not seeing that, and we had that paper in the pantry last Friday and chewed the rag over it for hours! Of course it's some time ago now, isn't it. About six weeks or so, it must be. She always came early; just about three, when we start serving teas."

So that is what she did. Fool that he was not to have seen that. She went into the morning round at the cinema in time to pay the cheaper price—just before noon, that was—and came out about three, and had tea, not coffee. But why the Midland, where the tea was the usual dowdy and expensive hotel exhibit, when she could wallow in cakes elsewhere?

"I noticed her because she always came alone. The first time she came I thought she was waiting for relations. That's the kind of kid she looked. You know: nice plain clothes and no airs."

"Can you remember what she wore?"

"Oh, yes. She always wore the same things. A green hat and a frock to match it under a pale grey coat. But she never met anyone. And then one day she picked up the man at the next table. You could have knocked me over with a feather."

"You mean: he picked her up."

"Don't you believe it! He hadn't even thought of her when he sat down there. I tell you, sir, she didn't look that sort. You'd expect an aunt or a mother to appear at any moment and say: 'So sorry to have kept you waiting, darling.' She just wouldn't occur to any man as a possible. Oh, no; it was the kid's doing. And as neat a piece of business, let me tell you, sir, as if she had spent a lifetime at it. Goodness, and to think that I didn't spot her again without her hat!" He gazed in wonder at the pictured face.

"What was the man like? Did you know him?"

"No, he wasn't one of our regulars. Dark. Youngish. Business gent, I should say. I remember being a little surprised at her taste, so I don't think he could have been up to much, now I come to think of it."

"You wouldn't know him again, then."

"I might, sir, I might. But not to swear to. You—er—planning any swearing to, sir?"

Robert had known Albert for nearly twenty years and had always found him of an excellent discretion. "It's like this, Albert," he said. "These people are my clients." He tapped the photograph of The Franchise, and Albert gave vent to a low whistle.

"A tough spot for you, Mr. Blair."

"Yes, as you say: a tough spot. But mostly for them. It is quite unbelievably tough for them. The girl comes out of the blue one day accompanied by the police, to whom she has told this fantastic story. Until then neither of the two women has ever set eyes on her. The police are very discreet, and decide that they haven't enough evidence to make it a good case. Then the *Ack-Emma* hears about it and makes capital out of it, and the story is all over Britain. The Franchise is wide open, of course. The police can't spare men to afford constant protection, so you can imagine the lives these women are leading. My young cousin, who looked in before dinner last night, says that from lunch-time on crowds of cars arrived from Larborough, and people stood on the roofs or hoisted themselves up on the wall to stare or take photographs. Nevil got in because he arrived at the same time as the policeman on the evening beat, but as soon as they left the cars were swarming again. The telephone went continually until they asked the Exchange not to put through any more calls."

"Have the police dropped it for good, then?"

"No, but they can't do anything to help *us*. What they are looking for is corroboration of the girl's story."

"Well, that's not very likely, is it? For them to get, I mean."

"No. But you see the spot we are in. Unless we can find out where the girl was during the weeks she says she was at The Franchise, the Sharpes will be in the position of being permanently convicted of a thing they haven't even been accused of!"

"Well, if it's the girl in the green hat—and I'm sure it is, sir— I'd say she was what is known as 'out on the tiles,' sir. A very cool customer she was for a girl that age. Butter wouldn't melt in her mouth."

"Butter wouldn't melt in her little mouth," the tobacconist had said of the child Betty.

And "on the tiles" was Stanley's verdict on the pictured face that was so like "the bint he had had in Egypt."

And the worldly little waiter had used both phrases in his estimate of her. The demure girl in the "good" clothes, who had come every day by herself to sit in the hotel lounge.

"Perhaps it was just a childish desire to be 'grand'," the nice side of him prompted; but his common sense refused it. She could have been grand at the Alençon, and eaten well, and seen smart clothes at the same time.

He went in to have lunch, and then spent a large part of the afternoon trying to reach Mrs. Wynn on the telephone. Mrs. Tilsit had no telephone and he had no intention of involving himself in a Tilsit conversation again if he could help it. When he failed he remembered that Scotland Yard would most certainly, in that painstaking way of theirs, have a description of the clothes the girl was wearing when she went missing. And in less than seven minutes, he had it. A green felt hat, a green wool frock to match, a pale grey cloth coat with large grey buttons, fawn-grey rayon stockings and black court shoes with medium heels.

Well, at last he had it, that setting-off place; that starting-point for inquiry. Jubilation filled him. He sat down in the lounge on his way out and wrote a note to tell Kevin Macdermott that the young woman from Aylesbury was not such an attractive brief as she had been on Friday night; and to let him know, of course,—

between the lines—that Blair, Hayward, and Bennet could get a move on when it was necessary.

"Did she ever come back?" he asked Albert, who was hovering. "I mean, after she had 'got her man'."

"I don't remember ever seeing either of them again, sir."

Well, the hypothetical X had ceased to be hypothetical. He had become plain X. He, Robert, could go back tonight to The Franchise in triumph. He had put forward a theory, and the theory had proved fact, and it was he who had proved it a fact. It was depressing, of course, that the letters received so far by Scotland Yard had all been merely anonymous revilings of the Yard for their "softness" to the "rich," and not claims to have seen Betty Kane. It was depressing that practically everyone he had interviewed that morning believed the girl's story without question; were, indeed, surprised and at a loss if asked to consider any other point of view. "The paper said so." But these were small things compared to the satisfaction of having arrived at that starting-point; of having unearthed X. He didn't believe that fate could be so cruel as to show that Betty Kane parted with her new acquaintance on the steps of the Midland and never saw him again. There *had* to be an extension of that incident in the lounge. The history of the following weeks demanded it.

But how did one follow up a young dark business gent who had tea in the lounge of the Midland about six weeks previously? Young dark business gents were the Midland's clientele; and as far as Blair could see all as like as two peas anyhow. He was very much afraid that this was where he bowed out and handed over to a professional bloodhound. He had no photograph this time to help him; no knowledge of X's character or habits as he had had in the case of the girl. It would be a long process of small inquiries; a job for an expert. All he could do at the moment, so far as he could see, was to get a list of residents at the Midland for the period in question.

For that he went to the Manager; a Frenchman who showed great delight and understanding in this *sub rosa* proceeding, was exquisitely sympathetic about the outraged ladies at The Franchise, and comfortingly cynical about smooth-faced young girls in good clothes who looked as if butter wouldn't melt in their mouths. He sent an underling to copy the entries from the great ledger, and entertained Robert to a *sirop* from his own cupboard. Robert had never subscribed to the French taste for small sweet mouthfuls of unidentifiable liquids drunk at odd times, but he swallowed the thing gratefully and pocketed the list the underling brought as one pockets a passport. Its actual value was probably nil, but it gave him a nice feeling to have it.

And if he had to turn over the business to a professional, the professional would have somewhere to start his burrowing. X had probably never stayed at the Midland in his life; he had probably just walked in for tea one day. On the other hand, his name might be among that list in his pocket; that horribly long list.

As he drove home he decided that he would not stop at The Franchise. It was unfair to bring Marion to the gate just to give her news that could be told over the telephone. He would tell the Exchange who he was, and the fact that the call was official, and they would answer it. Perhaps by tomorrow the first flood of interest in the house would have subsided, and it would be safe to unbar the gate again. Though he doubted it. Today's *Ack-Emma* had not been calculated to have an appeasing effect on the mob mind. True, there were no further front-page headlines; the Franchise affair had removed itself to the correspondence page. But the letters the *Ack-Emma* had chosen to print there—and two-thirds of them were about the Franchise affair—were not likely to prove oil on troubled waters. They were so much paraffin on a fire that was going quite nicely anyhow.

Threading his way out of the Larborough traffic, the silly phrases came back to him; and he marvelled all over again at the venom that these unknown women had roused in the writers' minds. Rage and hatred spilled over on to the paper; malice ran unchecked through the largely-illiterate sentences. It was an amazing exhibition. And one of the oddities of it was that the dearest wish of so many of those indignant protesters against violence was to flog the said women within an inch of their lives. Those who did not want to flog the women wanted to reform the police. One writer suggested that a fund should be opened for the poor young victim of police inefficiency and bias. Another suggested that every man of goodwill should write to his Member of Parliament about it, and make their lives a misery until something was done about this miscarriage of justice. Still another asked if anyone had noticed Betty Kane's marked resemblance to Saint Bernadette.

There was every sign, if today's correspondence page of the *Ack-Emma* was any criterion, of the birth of a Betty Kane cult. He hoped that its corollary would not be a Franchise vendetta.

As he neared the unhappy house, he grew anxious; wondering if Monday, too, had provided its quota of sightseers. It was a lovely evening, the low sun slanting great golden swathes of light over the spring fields; an evening to tempt even Larborough out to the midland dullness of Milford; it would be a miracle if, after the correspondence in the *Ack-Emma*, The Franchise was not the mecca of an evening pilgrimage. But when he came within sight of it he found the long stretch of road deserted; and as he came nearer he saw why. At the gate of The Franchise, solid and immobile and immaculate in the evening light, was the dark-blue-and-silver figure of a policeman.

Delighted that Hallam had been so generous with his scanty force, Robert slowed down to exchange greetings; but the greeting died on his lips. Along the full length of the tall brick wall, in letters nearly six feet high was splashed a slogan. "FASCISTS!" screamed the large white capitals. And again on the further side of the gate: "FASCISTS!"

"Move along, please," the Force said, approaching the staring Robert with slow, polite menace. "No stopping here."

Robert got slowly out of the car.

"Oh, Mr. Blair. Didn't recognise you, sir. Sorry."

"Is it whitewash?"

"No, sir; best quality paint."

"Great Heavens!"

"Some people never grow out of it."

"Out of what?"

"Writing things on walls. There's one thing: they might have written something worse."

"They wrote the worst insult they knew," said Robert wryly. "I suppose you haven't got the culprits?"

"No, sir. I just came along on my evening beat to clear away the usual gapers—oh, yes, there were dozens of them—and found it like that when I arrived. Two men in a car, if all reports are true."

"Do the Sharpes know about it?"

"Yes, I had to get in to telephone. We have a code now, us and the Franchise people. I tie my handkerchief on the end of my truncheon and wave it over the top of the gate when I want to speak to them. Do you want to go in, sir?"

"No. No, on the whole I think not. I'll get the Post Office to let me through on the telephone. No need to bring them to the gate. If this is going to continue they must get keys for the gate so that I can have a duplicate."

"Looks as though it's going to continue all right, sir. Did you see today's *Ack-Emma!*"

"I did."

"Strewth!" said the Force, losing his equanimity at the thought of the *Ack-Emma*, "you would think to listen to them we were nothing but a collection of itching palms! It's a holy wonder we're not, come to that. It would suit them better to agitate for more pay for us instead of slandering us right and left."

"You're in very good company, if it's any consolation to you," Robert said. "There can't be anything established, respectable, or praiseworthy that they haven't slandered at some time or other. I'll send someone either tonight or first thing in the morning to do something about this—obscenity. Are you staying here?"

"The sergeant said when I telephoned that I was to stay till dark."

"No one over-night?"

"No, sir. No spare men for that. Anyhow, they'll be all right once the light's gone. People go home. Especially the Larborough lot. They don't like the country once it gets dark."

Robert, who remembered how silent the lonely house could be, felt doubtful. Two women, alone in that big quiet house after dark, with hatred and violence just outside the wall—it was not a comfortable thought. The gate was barred, but if people could hoist themselves on to the wall for the purpose of sitting there and shouting insults, they could just as easily drop down the other side in the dark.

"Don't worry, sir," the Force said, watching his face. "Nothing's going to happen to them. This is England, after all."

"So is the *Ack-Emma* England," Robert reminded him. But he got back into the car again. After all, it *was* England; and the English countryside at that; famed for minding its own business. It was no country hand that had splashed that "FASCISTS!" on the wall. It was doubtful if the country had ever heard the term. The country, when it wanted insults, used older, Saxon words.

The Force was no doubt right; once the dark came everyone would go home.

· 12 ·

As Robert turned his car into the garage in Sin Lane and came to a halt, Stanley, who was shrugging off his overalls outside the office door, glanced at his face and said: "Down the drain again?"

"It isn't a bet," Robert said, "it's human nature."

"You start to be sorry about human nature and you won't have time for anything else. You been trying to reform someone?"

"No, I've been trying to get someone to take some paint off a wall."

"Oh, work!" Stanley's tone indicated that even to expect someone to do a job of work these days was being optimistic to the point of folly.

"I've been trying to get someone to wipe a slogan off the walls of The Franchise, but everyone is extraordinarily busy all of a sudden."

Stanley stopped his wriggling. "A slogan," he said. "What kind of slogan?" And Bill, hearing the exchange, oozed himself through the narrow office door to listen.

Robert told them. "In best quality white paint, so the policeman on the beat assures me."

Bill whistled. Stanley said nothing; he was standing with his overalls shrugged down to his waist and concertinaed about his legs.

"Who've you tried?" Bill asked.

Robert told them. "None of them can do anything tonight, and

109

tomorrow morning, it seems, all their men are going out early on important jobs."

"It's not to be believed," Bill said. "Don't tell me they're afraid of reprisals!"

"No, to do them justice I don't think it's that. I think, although they would never say so to me, that they think those women at The Franchise deserve it." There was silence for a moment.

"When I was in the Signals," Stanley said, beginning in a leisurely fashion to pull up his overalls and get into the top half again, "I was given a free tour of Italy. Nearly a year it took. And I escaped the malaria, and the Ities, and the Partisans, and the Yank transport, and most of the other little nuisances. But I got a phobia. I took a great dislike to slogans on walls."

"What'll we get it off with?" Bill asked.

"What's the good of owning the best equipped and most modern garage in Milford if we haven't something to take off a spot of paint?" Stanley said, zipping up his front.

"Will you really try to do something about it?" Robert asked, surprised and pleased.

Bill smiled his slow expansive smile. "The Signals, the R.E.M.E. and a couple of brooms. What more do you want?" he said.

"Bless you," Robert said. "Bless you both. I have only one ambition tonight; to get that slogan off the wall before breakfast tomorrow. I'll come along and help."

"Not in that Savile Row suit, you won't," Stanley said. "And we haven't a spare suit of——"

"I'll get something old on and come out after you."

"Look," Stanley said patiently, "we don't need any help for a little job like that. If we did we'd take Harry." Harry was the garage boy. "You haven't eaten yet and we have, and I've heard it said that Miss Bennet doesn't like her good meals spoiled. I suppose you don't mind if the wall looks smeary? We're just good-intentioned garage hands, not decorators."

The shops were shut as he walked down the High Street to his home at Number 10, and he looked at the place as a stranger walking through on a Sunday might. He had been so far from Milford during his day in Larborough that he felt that he had been away for years. The comfortable quiet of Number 10—so different from the dead silence of The Franchise—welcomed and soothed him. A faint smell of roasting apples escaped from the kitchen. The firelight flickered on the wall of the sitting-room, seen through its half-open door. Warmth and security and comfort rose up in a gentle tide and lapped over him.

Guilty at being the owner of this waiting peace, he picked up the telephone to talk to Marion.

"Oh, *you!* How nice," she said, when at last he had persuaded the Post Office that his intentions were honourable; and the warmth in her voice catching him unawares—his mind being still on white paint—caught him under the heart and left him breathless for a moment. "I'm so glad. I was wondering how we were going to talk to you; but I might have known that you would manage it. I suppose you just say you're Robert Blair and the Post Office gives you the freedom of the place."

How like her, he thought. The genuine gratitude of "I might have known that you would manage"; and then the faint amusement in the sentence that followed.

"I suppose you've seen our wall decoration?"

Robert said yes, but that no one ever would again, because by the time the sun rose it would have gone.

"Tomorrow!"

"The two men who own my garage have decided to obliterate it tonight."

"But—could seven maids with seven mops——?"

"I don't know; but if Stanley and Bill have set their minds on it, obliterated it will be. They were brought up in a school that doesn't tolerate frustrations."

"What school is that?"

"The British Army. And I have more good news for you: I have established the fact that X exists. She had tea with him one day. Picked him up at the Midland, in the lounge."

"Picked him up? But she is just a child, and so—— Oh, well, she told that story, of course. After that anything is possible. How did you find out that?"

He told her.

"You've had a bad day at The Franchise, haven't you," he said, when he had finished the saga of the coffee shops.

"Yes, I feel dirty all over. What was worse than the audience and the wall was the post. The postman gave it to the police to take in. It is not often that the police can be accused of disseminating obscene literature."

"Yes, I imagine it must have been pretty bad. That was only to be expected."

"Well, we have so few letters that we have decided that in future we shall burn everything without opening them, unless we recognise the writing. So don't use typescript if you write to us."

"But do you know my handwriting?"

"Oh, yes, you wrote us a note, you remember. The one Nevil brought that afternoon. Nice handwriting."

"Have you seen Nevil today?"

"No, but one of the letters was from him. At least, it wasn't a letter."

"A document of some kind?"

"No, a poem."

"Oh. Did you understand it?"

"No, but it made quite a nice sound."

"So do bicycle bells."

He thought she laughed a little. "It is nice to have poems made to one's eyebrows," she said. "But still nicer to have one's wall made clean. I do thank you for that—you and what's-their-names —Bill and Stanley. If you want to be very kind perhaps you would bring or send us some food tomorrow?"

"Food!" he said, horrified that he had not thought of that before; that was what happened when you lived a life where Aunt Lin put everything down in front of you, all but put the stuff in your mouth; you lost your capacity for imagination. "Yes, of course. I forgot that you would not be able to shop."

"It isn't only that. The grocer's van that calls on Monday didn't come today. Or perhaps," she added hastily, "it came and just couldn't call our attention. Anyhow, we should be so grateful for some things. Have you got a pencil there?"

She gave him a list of things, and then asked: "We didn't see today's *Ack-Emma*. Was there anything about us?"

"Some letters on the correspondence page, that is all."

"All anti, I suppose."

"I'm afraid so. I shall bring a copy out tomorrow morning when I bring the groceries, and you can see it for yourselves."

"I'm afraid we are taking up a great deal of your time."

"This has become a personal matter with me," he said.

"Personal?" She sounded doubtful.

"The one ambition of my life is to discredit Betty Kane."

"Oh; oh, I see." Her voice sounded half relieved, half—could it be?—disappointed. "Well, we shall look forward to seeing you tomorrow."

But she was to see him long before that.

He went to bed early, but lay long awake; rehearsing a telephone conversation that he planned to have with Kevin Macdermott; considering different approaches to the problem of X; wondering if Marion was asleep, in that silent old house, or lying awake listening for sounds.

His bedroom was over the street, and about midnight he heard a car drive up and stop, and presently through the open window he heard Bill's cautious call; not much more than a throaty whisper. "Mr. Blair! Hey, Mr. Blair!"

He was at the window almost before the second utterance of his name.

"Thank goodness," whispered Bill. "I was afraid the light might be Miss Bennet's."

"No, she sleeps at the back. What is it?"

"There's trouble at The Franchise. I've got to go for the police because the wire is cut. But I thought you'd want to be called, so I——"

"What kind of trouble?"

"Hooligans. I'll come in for you on my way back. In about four minutes."

"Is Stanley with them?" Robert asked, as Bill's great bulk merged with the car again.

"Yes, Stan's having his head bound up. Back in a minute." And the car fled away up the dark silent High Street.

Before Robert had got his clothes on he heard a soft "ssshush" go past his window, and realised that the police were already on their way. No screaming sirens in the night, no roaring exhausts; with no more sound than a summer wind makes among the leaves the Law was going about its business. As he opened the front door, cautiously so as not to wake Aunt Lin (nothing but the last trump was likely to wake Christina) Bill brought his car to a standstill at the pavement.

"Now tell me," Robert said, as they moved away.

"Well, we finished that little job by the light of the headlamps —not very professional, it isn't, but a lot better than it was when we got there—and then we switched off the heads, and began to put away our things. Sort of leisurely like; there was no hurry and it was a nice night. We'd just lit a cigarette and were thinking of pushing off when there was a crash of glass from the house. No one had got in our side while we were there, so we knew it must be round the sides or the back. Stan reached into the car and took out his torch—mine was lying on the seat because we'd been using it—and said: 'You go round that way and I'll go the other and we'll nip them between us.' "

"Can you get round?"

"Well, it was no end of a business. It's hedge up to the wall end. I wouldn't like to have done it in ordinary clothes, but in overalls you just push hard and hope for the best. It's all right for Stan; he's slim. But short of lying on the hedge till it falls down there's no way through for me. Anyhow we got through, one on each side, and through the one at the back corners, and met in the middle of the back without seeing a soul. Then we heard more crashing of glass, and realised that they were making a night of it. Stan said: 'Hoist me up, and I'll give you a hand after me.' Well, a hand would be no good to me, but it happens that the field level at the back comes fairly high up the wall—in fact I think it was probably cut away to build the wall—so that we got over fairly easily. Stan said had I anything to hit with besides my torch and I said yes, I had a spanner. Stan said: 'Forget your bloody spanner and use your ham fist; it's bigger.' "

"What was he going to use?"

"The old rugby tackle, so he said. Stan used to be quite a good stand-off half. Anyhow we went on in the dark towards the sound of the crashing glass. It seemed as if they were just having a breaking tour round the house. We caught up with them near the front corner again, and switched on our torches. I think there

114

were seven of them. Far more than we had expected, anyhow. We switched off at once, before they could see that we were only two, and grabbed the nearest. Stan said: 'You take that one, sergeant,' and I thought at the time he was giving me my rank out of old habit, but I realise now he was bluffing them we were police. Anyhow some of them beat it, because though there was a mix-up there couldn't have been anything like seven of them in it. Then, quite suddenly it seemed, there was quiet—we'd been making a lot of noise—and I realised that we were letting them get away, and Stan said from somewhere on the ground: 'Grab one, Bill, before they get over the wall!' And I went after them with my torch on. The last of them was just being helped over, and I grabbed his legs and hung on. But he kicked like a mule, and what with the torch in my hand he slipped from my hands like a trout and was over before I could grab him again. That finished me, be- cause from inside that wall at the back is even higher than it is at the front of the house. So I went back to Stan. He was still sitting on the ground. Someone had hit him a wallop over the head with what he said was a bottle and he was looking very cheap. And then Miss Sharpe came out to the top of the front steps, and said was someone hurt? She could see us in the torchlight. So we got Stan in—the old lady was there and the house was lit by this time —and I went to the phone, but Miss Sharpe said: 'That's no use. It's dead. We tried to call the police when they first arrived.' So I said I'd go and fetch them. And I said I'd better fetch you too. But Miss Sharpe said no, you'd had a very hard day and I wasn't to disturb you. But I thought you ought to be in on it."

"Quite right, Bill, I ought."

The gate was wide open as they drew up, the police car at the door, most of the front rooms lit, and the curtains waving gently in the night wind at the wrecked windows. In the drawing-room —which the Sharpes evidently used as a living-room—Stanley was having a cut above his eyebrow attended to by Marion, a sergeant of police was taking notes, and his henchman was laying out ex- hibits. The exhibits seemed to consist of half bricks, bottles, and pieces of paper with writing on them.

"Oh, Bill, I told you not to," Marion said as she looked up and saw Robert.

Robert noted how efficiently she was dealing with Stanley's injury; the woman who found cooking beyond her. He greeted the sergeant and bent to look at the exhibits. There was a large array of missiles but only four messages; which read, respectively: "Get out!" "Get out or we'll make you!" "Foreign bitches!" and "This is only a sample!"

"Well, we've collected them all, I think," the sergeant said. "Now we'll go and search the garden for footprints or whatever clues there may be." He glanced professionally at the soles that Bill and Stanley held up at his request, and went out with his aide to the garden, as Mrs. Sharpe came in with a steaming jug and cups.

"Ah, Mr. Blair," she said. "You still find us stimulating?"

She was fully dressed—in contrast to Marion who was looking quite human and un-Joan-of-Arc in an old dressing-gown—and apparently unmoved by these proceedings, and he wondered what kind of occasion would find Mrs. Sharpe at a disadvantage.

Bill appeared with sticks from the kitchen and lighted the dead fire, Mrs. Sharpe poured the hot liquid—it was coffee and Robert refused it, having seen enough coffee lately to lost interest in it—and the colour began to come back to Stan's face. By the time the policemen came back from the garden the room had acquired a family-party air, in spite of the waving curtains and the non-existent windows. Neither Stanley nor Bill, Robert noticed, appeared to find the Sharpes odd or difficult; on the contrary they seemed relaxed and at home. Perhaps it was that the Sharpes took them for granted; accepting this invasion of strangers as if it were an every-day occurrence. Anyhow, Bill came and went on his ploys as if he had lived in the house for years; and Stanley put out his cup for a second helping without waiting to be asked. Involuntarily, Robert thought that Aunt Lin in their place would have been kind and fussy and they would have sat on the edge of the chairs and remembered their dirty overalls.

Perhaps it was the same taking-for-granted that had attracted Nevil.

"Do you plan to stay on here, ma'am?" the sergeant asked as they came in again.

"Certainly," Mrs. Sharpe said, pouring coffee for them.

"No," Robert said. "You mustn't, you really must not. I'll find you a quiet hotel in Larborough, where——"

"I never heard anything more absurd. Of course we are going to stay here. What do a few broken windows matter?"

"It may not stop at broken windows," the sergeant said. "And you're a great responsibility to us as long as you are here; a responsibility we haven't really got the force to deal with."

"I'm truly sorry we are a nuisance to you, sergeant. We wouldn't have bricks flung at our windows if we could help it, believe me. But this is our home, and here we are staying. Quite apart from any question of ethics, how much of our home would be left to come back to if it was left empty? I take it if you are too short of men to guard human beings, you certainly have no men to guard empty property?"

The sergeant looked slightly abashed, as people so often did when Mrs. Sharpe dealt with them. "Well, there is that, ma'am," he acknowledged, with reluctance.

"And that, I think, disposes of any question of our leaving The Franchise. Sugar, sergeant?"

Robert returned to the subject when the police had taken their departure, and Bill had fetched a brush and shovel from the kitchen and was sweeping up the broken glass in room after room. Again he urged the wisdom of a hotel in Larborough, but neither his emotion nor his common sense was behind the words. He would not have gone if he had been in the Sharpes' place, and he could not expect them to; and in addition he acknowledged the wisdom of Mrs. Sharpe's view about the fate of the house left empty.

"What you want is a lodger," said Stanley, who had been refused permission to sweep up glass because he was classed as walking-wounded. "A lodger with a pistol. What d'you say I come and sleep here of nights? No meals, just sleeping night watchman. They all sleep anyhow, night watchmen do."

It was evident by their expressions that both the Sharpes appreciated the fact that this was an open declaration of allegiance in what amounted to a local war; but they did not embarrass him with thanks.

"Haven't you got a wife?" Marion asked.

"Not of my own," Stanley said demurely.

"Your wife—if you had one—might support your sleeping here," Mrs. Sharpe pointed out, "but I doubt if your business would, Mr.—er—Mr. Peters."

"My business?"

"I imagine that if your customers found that you had become night watchman at The Franchise they would take their custom elsewhere."

"Not them," Stanley said comfortably. "There's nowhere else to take it. Lynch is drunk five nights out of seven, and Biggins wouldn't know how to put on a bicycle chain. Anyhow, I don't let my customers tell me what I do in my spare time."

And when Bill returned, he backed Stanley up. Bill was a much married man and it was not contemplated that he would ever sleep anywhere except at home. But that Stanley should sleep at The Franchise seemed to both of them a natural solution of the problem.

Robert was mightily relieved.

"Well," Marion said, "if you are going to be our guest at nights you might as well begin now. I am sure that head feels like a very painful turnip. I'll go and make up a bed. Do you prefer a south view?"

"Yes," said Stanley gravely. "Well away from kitchen and wireless noises."

"I'll do what I can."

It was arranged that Bill should slip a note into the door of Stanley's lodgings to say that he would be in for lunch as usual. "She won't worry about me," Stanley said, referring to his landlady. "I've been out for nights before now." He caught Marion's eye, and added: "Ferrying cars for customers; you can do it in half the time at night."

They tacked down the curtains in all the ground-floor rooms to provide some protection for their contents if it rained before morning, and Robert promised to get glaziers out at the earliest possible moment. Deciding privately to go to a Larborough firm, and not risk another series of polite rebuffs in Milford.

"And I shall also do something about a key for the gate, so that I can have a duplicate," he said as Marion came out with them to bar the gate, "and save you from being gate-keeper as well as everything else."

She put out her hand, to Bill first. "I shall never forget what you three have done for us. When I remember tonight it won't be these clods that I shall remember," she tilted her head to the windowless house, "but you three."

"Those clods were local, I suppose you know," Bill said as they drove home through the quiet spring night.

"Yes," Robert agreed. "I realised that. They had no car, for one thing. And 'Foreign bitches!' smells of the conservative country, just as 'Fascists!' smells of the progressive town."

Bill said some things about progress.

"I was wrong to let myself be persuaded yesterday evening. The man on the beat was so sure that 'everyone would go home when it grew dark' that I let myself believe it. But I should have remembered a warning I got about witch-hunts."

Bill was not listening. "It's a funny thing how unsafe you feel in a house without windows," he said. "Take a house with the back blown clean off, and not a door that will shut; you can live quite happily in a front room provided it still has windows. But without windows even a whole undamaged house feels unsafe."

Which was not an observation that provided Robert with any comfort.

~~~~~~

· 13 ·

"I wonder if you would mind calling for the fish, dear," Aunt Lin said on the telephone on Tuesday afternoon. "Nevil is coming to dinner, and so we are going to have an extra course of what we were going to have for breakfast. I really don't see why we should have anything extra just for Nevil, but Christina says that it will keep him from making what she calls 'inroads' on the tart that is going to do again on her night-out tomorrow. So if you wouldn't mind, dear."

He was not looking forward greatly to an extra hour or two of Nevil's society, but he was feeling so pleased with himself that he was in a better humour to support it than usual. He had arranged with a Larborough firm for the replacement of the Franchise windows; he had miraculously unearthed a key that fitted the Franchise gate—and there would be two duplicates in existence by tomorrow; and he had personally taken out the groceries—together with an offering of the best flowers that Milford could supply. His welcome at The Franchise had been such that he had almost ceased to regret the lack of light exchanges on Nevil lines. There were, after all, other things than getting to Christian-name terms in the first half-hour.

In the lunch hour he had rung up Kevin Macdermott, and arranged with his secretary that when Kevin was free in the evening he would call him at 10 High Street. Things were getting out of hand, and he wanted Kevin's advice.

He had refused three invitations to golf, his excuse to his astounded cronies being that he had "no time to chase a piece of gutta-percha round a golf course."

He had gone to see an important client who had been trying to interview him since the previous Friday and who had been provoked into asking him on the telephone if "he still worked for Blair, Hayward, and Bennet."

He had got through his arrears of work with a mutely reproachful Mr. Heseltine; who, although he had allied himself on the Sharpe side, still obviously felt that the Franchise affair was not one for a firm like theirs to be mixed up in.

And he had been given tea by Miss Tuff out of the blue-patterned china on the lacquer tray covered by the fair white cloth and accompanied by two digestive biscuits on a plate.

It was lying on his desk now, the tea-tray; just as it had been a fortnight ago when the telephone had rung and he had lifted the receiver to hear Marion Sharpe's voice for the first time. Two short weeks ago. He had sat looking at it in its patch of sunlight, feeling uneasy about his comfortable life and conscious of time slipping past him. But today, the digestive biscuits held no reproach for him because he had stepped outside the routine they typified. He was on calling terms with Scotland Yard; he was agent for a pair of scandalous women; he had become an amateur sleuth; and he had been witness of mob violence. His whole world looked different. Even the people he met looked different. The dark skinny woman he used to see sometimes shopping in the High Street, for instance, had turned into Marion.

Well, one result of stepping out of a routined life was, of course, that you couldn't put on your hat and stroll home at four o'clock of an afternoon. He pushed the tea-tray out of his way, and went to work, and it was half-past six before he looked at the clock again, and seven before he opened the door of Number 10.

The sitting-room door was ajar as usual—like many doors in old houses it swung a little if left off the latch—and he could hear Nevil's voice in the room beyond.

"On the contrary, I think you are being extremely silly," Nevil was saying.

Robert recognised the tone at once. It was the cold rage with which a four-year-old Nevil had told a guest: "I am extremely sorry that I asked you to my party." Nevil must be very angry indeed about something.

With his coat half off Robert paused to listen.

"You are interfering in something you know nothing whatever about; you can hardly claim that is an intelligent proceeding."

There was no other voice, so he must be talking to someone on the telephone; probably keeping Kevin from getting through, the young idiot.

"I am not infatuated with anyone. I never *have* been infatuated with anyone. It is you who are infatuated—with ideas. You are being extremely silly, as I said before. . . . You are taking the part of an unbalanced adolescent in a case you know nothing about; I should have thought that was sufficient evidence of infatuation . . . You can tell your father from me that there is nothing Christian about it, just unwarranted interference. I'm not sure it isn't incitement to violence. . . . Yes, last night. . . . No, all their windows broken, and things painted on their walls. . . . If he is so interested in justice he might do something about that. But your lot are never interested in justice, are they? Only in injustice. . . . What do I mean by your lot? Just what I say. You and all your crowd who are for ever adopting good-for-nothings and championing them against the world. You wouldn't put out a finger to keep a hard-working little man from going down the drain, but let an old lag lack the price of a meal and your sobs can be heard in Antarctica. You make me sick. . . . Yes, I said you make me sick. . . . Cat-sick. Sick to my stomach. I retch!"

And the bang of the receiver on its rest indicated that the poet had said his say.

Robert hung up his coat in the cupboard and went in. Nevil with a face like thunder was pouring himself out a stiff whisky.

"I'll have one too," Robert said. "I couldn't help overhearing," he added. "That wasn't Rosemary, by any chance?"

"Who else? Is there anyone else in Britain capable of an ineffable silliness like that?"

"Like what?"

"Oh, didn't you hear that bit? She has taken up the cause of the persecuted Betty Kane." Nevil gulped some whisky, and glared at Robert as if Robert were responsible.

"Well, I don't suppose her stepping on the *Ack-Emma* bandwagon will have much effect one way or another."

"The *Ack-Emma!* It isn't the *Ack-Emma*. It's the *Watchman*. That mental deficient she calls father has written a letter about it for Friday's issue. Yes, you may well look squeamish. As if we weren't coping with enough without that highfalutin nugget of perverted sentimentality putting in its sixpenceworth!"

Remembering that the *Watchman* was the only paper ever to have published any of Nevil's poems, Robert thought this showed slight ingratitude. But he approved the description.

"Perhaps they won't print it," he said, less in hope than looking for comfort.

"You know very well they will print anything he chooses to send them. Whose money saved them just when they were going down for the third time? The Bishop's, of course."

"His wife's, you mean." The Bishop had married one of the two grand-daughters of Cowan's Cranberry Sauce.

"All right, his wife's. And the Bishop has the *Watchman* for a lay pulpit. And there isn't anything too silly for him to say in it, or too unlikely for them to print. Do you remember that girl who went round shooting taxi-drivers in cold blood for a profit of about seven-and-eleven a time? That girl was just his meat. He sobbed himself practically into a coma about her. He wrote a long heart-breaking letter about her in the *Watchman*, pointing out how under-privileged she had been, and how she had won a scholarship to a secondary school and hadn't been able to 'take it up' because her people were too poor to provide her with books or proper clothes, and so she had gone to blind-alley jobs and then to bad company—and so, it was inferred, to shooting taxi-drivers, though he didn't actually mention that little matter. Well, all the *Watchman* readers *lahved* that, of course; it was just their cup of tea; all criminals according to the *Watchman* readers are frustrated angels. And then the Chairman of the Board of Governors of the school—the school she was supposed to have won a scholarship to—wrote to point out that so far from winning anything was she that her name was 159th out of two hundred competitors; and that someone as interested in education as the Bishop was should have known that no one was prevented from accepting a scholarship through lack of money, since in needy cases books and money grants were forthcoming automatically. Well, you would have thought that that would shake him, wouldn't you? But not a bit. They printed the Chairman's letter on a back page, in small print; and in the very next issue the old boy was sobbing over some other case that he knew nothing about. And on Friday, so help me, he'll be sobbing over Betty Kane."

"I wonder—if I went over to see him tomorrow——"

"It goes to press tomorrow."

"Yes, so it does. Perhaps if I telephoned——"

"If you think that anyone or anything will make His Lordship keep back a finished composition from the public gaze, you're being naïve."

The telephone rang.

"If that's Rosemary, I'm in China," Nevil said.

But it was Kevin Macdermott.

"Well, sleuth," said Kevin. "My congratulations. But next time don't waste an afternoon trying to ring up civilians in Aylesbury, when you can get the same information from Scotland Yard by return."

Robert said that he was still sufficiently civilian not to think in terms of Scotland Yard at all; but that he was learning; rapidly.

He sketched the happenings of last night for Kevin's benefit, and said: "I can't afford to be leisurely about it any more. Something must be done as quickly as possible to clear them of this thing."

"You want me to give you the name of a private agent, is that it?"

"Yes, I suppose it has come to that. But I did wonder——"

"Wonder what?" Kevin asked, as he hesitated.

"Well, I did think of going to Grant at the Yard and saying quite frankly that I had found out how she could have known about the Sharpes and about the house; and that she had met a man in Larborough and that I had a witness of the meeting."

"So that they could do what?"

"So that they could investigate the girl's movements during that month instead of us."

"And you think they would?"

"Of course. Why not?"

"Because it wouldn't be worth their while. All they would do when they found out that she was not trustworthy would be to drop the case thankfully into oblivion. She has not sworn to anything so they could not prosecute her for perjury."

"They could proceed against her for having misled them."

"Yes, but it wouldn't be worth their while. It won't be easy to unearth her movements for that month, we may be sure. And on top of all that unnecessary investigation they would have the job of preparing and presenting a case. It's highly unlikely that an overworked department, with serious cases flooding in at their doors, are going to all that bother when they could quietly drop the thing on the spot."

"But it's supposed to be a department of Justice. It leaves the Sharpes——"

"No, a department of the Law. Justice begins in court. As you very well know. Besides, Rob, you haven't brought them any proof of anything. You don't know that she ever went to Milford. And the fact that she picked up a man at the Midland, and had tea with him, doesn't do anything to disprove her story that she was picked up by the Sharpes. In fact the only leg you have to stand on is Alec Ramsden, 5 Spring Gardens, Fulham, South West."

"Who is he?"

"Your private sleuth. And a very good one, take it from me. He has a flock of tame operators at call, so if he is busy himself he can supply you with a fairly good substitute. Tell him I gave you his name and he won't palm off a dud on you. Not that he would, anyhow. He's the salt of the earth. Pensioned from the Force because of a wound 'received in the course of duty.' He'll do you proud. I must go. If there's anything else I can do just give me a ring sometime. I wish I had time to come down and see The Franchise and your witches for myself. They grow on me. Goodbye."

Robert laid down the receiver, picked it up again, asked for Information, and obtained the telephone number of Alec Ramsden. There was no answer and he sent a telegram saying that he, Robert Blair, needed some work done urgently and that Kevin Macdermott had said that Ramsden was the man to do it.

"Robert," said Aunt Lin coming in pink and indignant, "did you know that you left the fish on the hall table and it has soaked through to the mahogany and Christina was waiting for it."

"Is the gravamen of the charge the mahogany or keeping Christina waiting?"

"Really, Robert, I hardly know what's come over you. Since you got involved in this Franchise affair you've changed entirely. A fortnight ago you would never have dreamed of putting a parcel of fish down on polished mahogany and forgetting all about it. And if you had you would be sorry about it and apologise."

"I do apologise, Aunt Lin; I am truly contrite. But it is not often I am saddled with a responsibility as serious as the present one and you must forgive me if I am a little jaded."

"I don't think you are jaded at all. On the contrary, I have never seen you so pleased with yourself. I think you are positively *relishing* this sordid affair. Only this morning Miss Truelove at the Anne Boleyn was condoling with me on your being mixed up in it."

"Was she indeed? Well, I condole with Miss Truelove's sister."

"Condole about what?"

"On having a sister like Miss Truelove. You *are* having a bad time, aren't you, Aunt Lin."

"Don't be sarcastic, dear. It is not pleasant for anyone in this town to see the notoriety that has overtaken it. It has always been a quiet and dignified little place."

"I don't like Milford as much as I did a fortnight ago," Robert said reflectively, "so I'll save my tears."

"No less than four separate charabancs arrived from Larborough at one time or another today, having come for nothing but to inspect The Franchise *en route*."

"And who catered for them?" Robert asked, knowing that coach traffic was not welcome in Milford.

"No one. They were simply furious."

"That will larn them to go poking their noses. There is nothing Larborough minds about as much as its stomach."

"The vicar's wife insists on being Christian about it, but I think that that is the wrong point of view."

"Christian?"

"Yes; 'reserving our judgment,' you know. That is merely feebleness, not Christianity. Of course I don't discuss the case, Robert dear; even with her. I am the soul of discretion. But of course she knows how I feel, and I know how she feels, so discussion is hardly necessary."

What was clearly a snort came from Nevil where he was sunk in an easy chair.

"Did you say something, Nevil dear?"

The nursery tone clearly intimidated Nevil. "No, Aunt Lin," he said meekly.

But he was not going to escape so easily; the snort had only too clearly been a snort. "I don't grudge you the drink, dear, but is that your *third* whisky? There is a Traminer for dinner, and you won't taste it at all after that strong stuff. You mustn't get into bad habits if you are going to marry a Bishop's daughter."

"I am not going to marry Rosemary."

Miss Bennet stared, aghast. "Not!"

"I would as soon marry a Public Assistance Board."

"But, Nevil!"

"I would as soon marry a radio set." Robert remembered Kevin's remark about Rosemary giving birth to nothing but a gramophone record. "I would as soon marry a crocodile." Since Rosemary was very pretty Robert supposed that "crocodile" had something to do with tears. "I would as soon marry a soap-box." Marble Arch, Robert supposed. "I would as soon marry the *Ack-Emma*." That seemed to be final.

"But Nevil, dear, *why!*"

"She is a very silly creature. Almost as silly as the *Watchman*." Robert heroically refrained from mentioning the fact that for the last six years the *Watchman* had been Nevil's bible.

"Oh, come, dear; you've had a tiff; all engaged couples do. It's a good thing to get the give-and-take business on a firm basis before marriage; those couples who never quarrel during their engagement lead surprisingly rowdy lives after marriage; so don't take a small disagreement too seriously. You can ring her up before you go home tonight——"

"It is a quite fundamental disagreement," Nevil said coldly. "And there is no prospect whatever of my ringing her up."

"But Nevil, dear, what——"

The three thin cracked notes of the gong floated through her protest and gave her pause. The drama of broken engagements gave place on the instant to more immediate concerns.

"That is the gong. I think you had better take your drink in with you, dear. Christina likes to serve the soup as soon as she has added the egg, and she is not in a very good mood tonight because of getting the fish so late. Though why that should make any difference to her I can't think. It is only grilled, and that doesn't take any time. It's not as if she had had to wipe the fish juice off the mahogany, because I did that myself."

· 14 ·

It further upset Aunt Lin that Robert should have breakfast next morning at 7.45 so that he could go early to the office. It was another sign of the degeneration that the Franchise affair was responsible for. To have early breakfast so that he might catch a train, or set out for a distant meet, or attend a client's funeral, was one thing. But to have early breakfast just so that he could arrive at work at an office-boy hour was a very odd proceeding, and unbefitting a Blair.

127

Robert smiled, walking up the sunny High Street still shuttered and quiet. He had always liked the early morning hours, and it was at this hour that Milford looked its best; its pinks and sepias and creams as delicate in the sunlight as a tinted drawing. Spring was merging into summer, and already the warmth of the pavement radiated into the cool air; the pollarded limes were full out. That would mean shorter nights for the lonely women at The Franchise, he remembered thankfully. But perhaps—with any luck —by the time the summer was actually here their vindication would be complete and their home no longer a beleaguered fortress.

Propped against the still closed door of the office was a long thin grey man who seemed to be all bones and to have no stomach at all.

"Good-morning," Robert said. "Did you want to see me?"

"No," said the grey man. "You wanted to see me."

"*I* did?"

"At least so your telegram said. I take it you're Mr. Blair?"

"But you can't be here already!" Robert said.

"It's not far," the man said laconically.

"Come in," said Robert trying to live up to Mr. Ramsden's standard of economy in comment.

In the office he asked as he unlocked his desk: "Have you had breakfast?"

"Yes, I had bacon and eggs at the White Hart."

"I am wonderfully relieved that you could come yourself."

"I had just finished a case. And Kevin Macdermott has done a lot for me."

Yes; Kevin, for all his surface malice and his overcrowded life, found the will and the time to help those who deserved help. In which he differed markedly from the Bishop of Larborough, who preferred the undeserving.

"Perhaps the best way would be for you to read this statement," he said, handing Ramsden the copy of Betty Kane's statement to the police, "and then we can go on with the story from there."

Ramsden took the typescript, sat down in the visitors' chair— folded up would be a more accurate description of his action—and withdrew himself from Robert's presence very much as Kevin had done in the room in St. Paul's Churchyard. Robert, taking out his own work, envied them their power of concentration.

"Yes, Mr. Blair?" he said presently; and Robert gave him the rest of the story: the girl's identification of the house and its inmates, Robert's own entrance into the affair, the police decision that they would not proceed on the available evidence, Leslie Wynn's resentment and its result in the *Ack-Emma* publicity, his own interviews with the girl's relations and what they revealed, his discovery that she went bus-riding and that a double-decker did run on the Milford bus-route during the relevant weeks, and his unearthing of X.

"To find out more about X is your job, Mr. Ramsden. The lounge waiter, Albert, knows what he looked like, and this is a list of residents for the period in question. It would be too great luck that he should be staying at the Midland, but one never knows. After that you're on your own. Tell Albert I sent you, by the way. I've known him a long time."

"Very good. I'll get over to Larborough now. I'll have a photograph of the girl by tomorrow, but perhaps you could lend me your *Ack-Emma* one for today."

"Certainly. How are you going to get a proper photograph of her?"

"Oh. Ways."

Robert deduced that Scotland Yard had been given one when the girl was reported missing, and that his old colleagues at Headquarters would not be too reluctant to give him a copy; so he left it at that.

"There's just a chance that the conductor of one of those double-decker buses may remember her," he said as Ramsden was going. "They are Larborough And District Motor Services buses. The garage is in Victoria Street."

At half-past nine the staff arrived—one of the first being Nevil; a change in routine which surprised Robert: Nevil was usually the last to arrive and the last to settle down. He would wander in, divest himself of his wrappings in his own small room at the back, wander into "the office" to say good morning, wander into the "waiting-room" at the back to say hello to Miss Tuff, and finally wander into Robert's room and stand there thumbing open the bound roll of one of the esoteric periodicals that came for him by post and commenting on the permanently deplorable state of affairs in England. Robert had grown quite used to running through his morning post to a Nevil obbligato. But today Nevil came in at the appointed time, went into his own room, shut the door firmly after him, and, if the pulling in and out of drawers was any evidence, settled down to work at once.

Miss Tuff came in with her notebook and her dazzling white peter-pan collar, and Robert's normal day had begun. Miss Tuff had worn peter-pan collars over her dark frock for twenty years, and would have looked undressed, almost indecent, without them now. A fresh one went on every morning; the previous day's having been laundered the night before and laid ready for putting on tomorrow. The only break in the routine was on Sundays. Robert had once met Miss Tuff on a Sunday and entirely failed to recognise her because she was wearing a jabot.

Until half-past ten Robert worked, and then realised that he had had breakfast at an abnormally early hour and was now in need of more sustenance than an office cup of tea. He would go out and have coffee and a sandwich at the Rose and Crown. You got the best coffee in Milford at the Anne Boleyn, but it was always full of shopping females ("*How* nice to see you, my dear! We *did* miss you so at Ronnie's party! And *have* you heard . . .") and that was an atmosphere he would not face for all the coffee in Brazil. He would go across to the Rose and Crown, and afterwards he would shop a little on behalf of the Franchise people, and after lunch he would go out and break to them gently the bad news about the *Watchman*. He could not do it on the telephone because they had no telephone now. The Larborough firm had come out with ladders and putty and recalcitrant sheets of glass and had replaced the windows without fuss or mess. But they, of course, were Private Enterprise. The Post Office, being a Government department, had taken the matter of the telephone into avizandum and would move in their own elephantine good time. So Robert planned to spend part of his afternoon telling the Sharpes the news he could not tell them by telephone.

It was still early for mid-morning snacks and the chintz and old oak of the Rose and Crown lounge was deserted except for Ben Carley, who was sitting by the gate-legged table at the window reading the *Ack-Emma*. Carley had never been Robert's cup-of-tea—any more than, he suspected, he was Carley's—but they had the bond of their profession (one of the strongest in human nature) and in a small place like Milford that made them very nearly bosom friends. So Robert sat down as a matter of course at Carley's table; remembering as he did so that he still owed Carley gratitude for that unheeded warning of his about the feeling in the countryside.

Carley lowered the *Ack-Emma* and regarded him with the too-lively dark eyes that were so alien in this English Midland serenity. "It seems to be dying down," he said. "Only one letter today; just to keep something in the kitty."

"The *Ack-Emma*, yes. But the *Watchman* is beginning a campaign of its own on Friday."

"The *Watchman!* What's *it* doing climbing into the *Ack-Emma's* bed?"

"It wouldn't be the first time," Robert said.

"No, I suppose not," Carley said, considering it. "Two sides of the same penny, when you come to think of it. Oh, well. That needn't worry you. The total circulation of the *Watchman* is about twenty thousand. If that."

"Perhaps. But practically every one of those twenty thousand has a second cousin in the permanent Civil Service in this country."

"So what? Has anyone ever known the permanent Civil Service to move a finger in any cause whatever outside their normal routine?"

"No, but they pass the buck. And sooner or later the buck drops into—into a—a——"

"A fertile spot," Carley offered, mixing the metaphor deliberately.

"Yes. Sooner or later some busybody or sentimentalist or egotist, with not enough to do, thinks that something should be done about this and begins to pull strings. And a string pulled in the Civil Service has the same effect as a string pulled in a peepshow. A whole series of figures is yanked into action, willy-nilly. Gerald obliges Tony, and Reggie obliges Gerald, and so on, to incalculable ends."

Carley was silent a moment. "It's a pity," he said. "Just when the *Ack-Emma* was losing way. Another two days and they would have dropped it for good. In fact they're two days over their normal schedule, as it is. I have never known them carry a subject longer than three issues. The response must have been terrific to warrant that amount of space."

"Yes," Robert agreed, gloomily.

"Of course, it was a gift for them. The beating of kidnapped girls is growing very rare. As a change of fare it was beyond price. When you have only three or four dishes, like the *Ack-Emma*, it's difficult to keep the customers' palates properly tickled. A tit-bit like the Franchise affair must have put up their circulation by thousands in the Larborough district alone."

"Their circulation will slack off. It's just a tide. But what I have to deal with is what's left on the beach."

"A particularly smelly beach, let me say," Carley observed. "Do you know that fat blonde with the mauve powder and the uplift brassiere who runs that Sports Wear shop next the Anne Boleyn? She's one of the things on your beach."

"How?"

"She lived at the same boarding-house in London as the Sharpes, it seems; and she has a lovely story as to how Marion Sharpe once beat a dog half to death in a rage. Her clients loved that story. So did the Anne Boleyn customers. She goes there for her morning coffee." He glanced wryly at the angry flush on Robert's face. "I needn't tell you that she has a dog of her own. It has never been corrected in its spoiled life, but it is rapidly dying of fatty degeneration through the indiscriminate feeding of morsels whenever the fat blonde is feeling gooey."

There were moments, Robert thought, when he could very nearly hug Ben Carley, striped suits and all.

"Ah, well, it will blow over," said Carley, with the pliant philosophy of a race long used to lying low and letting the storm blow past.

Robert looked surprised. Forty generations of protesting ancestors were surprised in his sole person. "I don't see that blowing over is any advantage," he said. "It won't help my clients at all."

"What can you do?"

"Fight, of course."

"Fight what? You wouldn't get a slander verdict, if that's what you're thinking of."

"No. I hadn't thought of slander. I propose to find out what the girl was really doing during those weeks."

Carley looked amused. "Just like that," he said, commenting on this simple statement of a tall order.

"It won't be easy and it will probably cost them all they have, but there is no alternative."

"They could go away from here. Sell the house and settle down somewhere else. A year from now no one outside the Milford district will remember anything about this affair."

"They would never do that; and I shouldn't advise them to, even if they would. You can't have a tin can tied to your tail and go through life pretending it isn't there. Besides, it is quite unthinkable that that girl should be allowed to get away with her tale. It's a matter of principle."

"You can pay too high a price for your damned principles. But I wish you luck, anyhow. Are you considering a private inquiry agent? Because if you are I know a very good——"

Robert said that he had got an agent and that he was already at work.

Carley's expressive face conveyed his amused congratulation at this swift action on the part of the conservative Blair, Hayward, and Bennet.

"The Yard had better look to its laurels," he said. His eyes went to the street beyond the leaded panes of the window, and the amusement in them faded to a fixed attention. He stared for a moment or two and then said softly: "Well! of all the nerve!"

It was an admiring phrase, not an indignant one; and Robert turned to see what was occasioning his admiration.

On the opposite side of the street was the Sharpes' battered old car; its odd front wheel well in evidence. And in the back, enthroned in her usual place and with her usual air of faint protest at this means of transport, was Mrs. Sharpe. The car was pulled up outside the grocer's, and Marion was presumably inside shopping. It could have been there only a few moments or Ben Carley would have noticed it before, but already two errand boys had paused to stare, leaning on their bicycles with voluptuous satisfaction in this free spectacle. And even while Robert took in the scene people came to the doors of neighbouring shops as the news flew from mouth to mouth.

"What incredible folly!" Robert said angrily.

"Folly nothing," said Carley, his eyes on the picture. "I wish they were clients of mine."

He fumbled in his pocket for change to pay for his coffee, and Robert fled from the room. He reached the near side of the car just as Marion came out on to the pavement at the other side. "Mrs. Sharpe," he said sternly, "this is an extraordinarily silly thing to do. You are only exacerbating——"

"Oh, good morning, Mr. Blair," she said, in polite social tones. "Have you had your morning coffee, or would you like to accompany us to the Anne Boleyn?"

"Miss Sharpe!" he said appealing to Marion, who was putting her packages down on the seat. "You must know that this is a silly thing to do."

"I honestly don't know whether it is or not," she said, "but it seems to be something that we must do. Perhaps we have grown childish with living too much to ourselves, but we found that neither of us could forget that snub at the Anne Boleyn. That condemnation without trial."

"We suffer from spiritual indigestion, Mr. Blair. And the only cure is a hair of the dog that bit us. To wit, a cup of Miss Truelove's excellent coffee."

"But it is so unnecessary! So——"

"We feel that at half-past ten in the morning there must be a large number of free tables at the Anne Boleyn," Mrs. Sharpe said tartly.

"Don't worry, Mr. Blair," Marion said. "It is a gesture only. Once we have drunk our token cup of coffee at the Anne Boleyn we shall never darken its doors again." She burlesqued the phrase in characteristic fashion.

"But it will merely provide Milford with a free——"

Mrs. Sharpe caught him up before he could utter the word. "Milford must get used to us as a spectacle," she said dryly, "since we have decided that living entirely within four walls is not something that we can contemplate."

"But——"

"They will soon grow used to seeing monsters and take us for granted again. If you see a giraffe once a year it remains a spectacle; if you see it daily it becomes part of the scenery. We propose to become part of the Milford scenery."

"Very well, you plan to become part of the scenery. But do one thing for me just now." Already the curtains of first-floor windows were being drawn aside and faces appearing. "Give up the Anne Boleyn plan—give it up for today at least—and have your coffee with me at the Rose and Crown."

"Mr. Blair, coffee with you at the Rose and Crown would be delightful, but it would do nothing to relieve my spiritual indigestion, which, in the popular phrase, 'is killing me'."

"Miss Sharpe, I appeal to you. You have said that you realise that you are probably being childish, and—well, as a personal obligation to me as your agent, I ask you not to go on with the Anne Boleyn plan."

"*That* is blackmail," Mrs. Sharpe remarked.

"It is unanswerable, anyhow," Marion said, smiling faintly at him. "We seem to be going to have coffee at the Rose and Crown." She sighed. "Just when I was all strung up for a gesture!"

"Well, of all the nerve!" came a voice from overhead. It was Carley's phrase over again but held none of Carley's admiration; it was loaded with indignation.

"You can't leave the car here," Robert said. "Quite apart from the traffic laws it is practically Exhibit A."

"Oh, we didn't intend to," Marion said. "We were taking it round to the garage so that Stanley can do something technical to its inside with some instrument he has there. He is exceedingly scornful about our car, Stanley is."

"I dare say. Well, I shall go round with you; and you had better step on it before we are run in for attracting a crowd."

"Poor Mr. Blair," Marion said, pressing the starter. "It must be horrid for you not to be part of the landscape any more, after all those years of comfortable merging."

She said it without malice—indeed there was genuine sympathy in her voice—but the sentence stuck in his mind and made a small tender place there as they drove round into Sin Lane, avoided five hacks and a pony that were trailing temperamentally out of the livery stable, and came to rest in the dimness of the garage.

Bill came out to meet them, wiping his hands on an oily rag. "Morning, Mrs. Sharpe. Glad to see you out. Morning, Miss Sharpe. That was a neat job you did on Stan's forehead. The edges closed as neat as if they had been stitched. You ought to have been a nurse."

"Not me. I have no patience with people's fads. But I might have been a surgeon. You can't be very faddy on the operating table."

Stanley appeared from the back, ignoring the two women who now ranked as intimates, and took over the car. "What time do you want this wreck?" he asked.

"An hour do?" Marion asked.

"A year wouldn't do, but I'll do all that can be done in an hour." His eye went on to Robert. "Anything for the Guineas?"

"I've had a good tip for Bali Boogie."

"Nonsense," old Mrs. Sharpe said. "None of that Hippocras blood were any good when it came to a struggle. Just turned it up."

The three men stared at her, astonished.

"You are interested in racing?" Robert said, unbelieving.

"No, in horseflesh. My brother bred thoroughbreds." Seeing their faces she gave her dry cackle of laughter, so like a hen's squawk. "Did you think I went to rest every afternoon with my Bible, Mr. Blair? Or perhaps with a book on black magic. No, indeed; I take the racing page of the daily paper. And Stanley would be well advised to save his money on Bali Boogie; if anything in horseflesh ever deserved so obscene a name that animal does."

"And what instead?" Stanley asked, with his usual economy.

"They say that horse sense is the instinct that keeps horses from

136

betting on men. But if you must do something as silly as betting, then you had better put your money on Kominsky."

"Kominsky!" Stanley said. "But it's at sixties!"

"You can of course lose your money at a shorter price if you like," she said dryly. "Shall we go, Mr. Blair?"

"All right," Stan said. "Kominsky it is; and you're on to a tenth of my stake."

They walked back to the Rose and Crown; and as they emerged from the comparative privacy of Sin Lane into the open street Robert had the exposed feeling that being out in a bad air-raid used to give him. All the attention and all the venom in the uneasy night seemed to be concentrated on his shrinking person. So now in the bright early-summer sunlight he crossed the street feeling naked and unprotected. He was ashamed to see how relaxed and seemingly indifferent Marion swung along at his side, and hoped that his self-consciousness was not apparent. He talked as naturally as he could, but he remembered how easily her mind had always read the contents of his, and felt that he was not making a very good job of it.

A solitary waiter was picking up the shilling that Ben Carley had left on the table, but otherwise the lounge was deserted. As they seated themselves round the bowl of wallflowers on the black oak table Marion said: "You heard that our windows are in again?"

"Yes; P. C. Newsam looked in on his way home last night to tell me. That was smart work."

"Did you bribe them?" Mrs. Sharpe asked.

"No. I just mentioned that it was the work of hooligans. If your missing windows had been the result of blast you would no doubt still be living with the elements. Blast ranks as misfortune, and therefore a thing to be put up with. But hooliganism is one of those things that Something Must Be Done About. Hence your new windows. I wish that it was all as easy as replacing windows."

He was unaware that there had been any change in his voice, but Marion searched his face and said: "Some new development?"

"I'm afraid there is. I was coming out this afternoon to tell you about it. It appears that just when the *Ack-Emma* is dropping the subject—there is only one letter today and that a mild one—just when the *Ack-Emma* has grown tired of Betty Kane's cause the *Watchman* is going to take it up."

"Excelsior!" said Marion. "The *Watchman* snatching the torch from the failing hands of the *Ack-Emma* is a charming picture."

"Climbing into the *Ack-Emma*'s bed," Ben Carley had called it; but the sentiment was the same.

"Have you spies in the *Watchman* office, Mr. Blair?" Mrs. Sharpe asked.

"No; it was Nevil who got wind of it. They are going to print a letter from his future father-in-law, the Bishop of Larborough."

"Hah!" said Mrs. Sharpe. "Toby Byrne."

"You know him?" asked Robert, thinking that the quality of her tone would peel the varnish off wood if spilt on it.

"He went to school with my nephew. The son of the horse-leech brother. Toby Byrne, indeed. He doesn't change."

"I gather that you didn't like him."

"I never knew him. He went home for the holidays once with my nephew but was never asked back."

"Oh?"

"He discovered for the first time that stable lads got up at the crack of dawn, and he was horrified. It was slavery, he said; and he went round the lads urging them to stand up for their rights. If they combined, he said, not a horse would go out of the stable before nine o'clock in the morning. The lads used to mimic him for years afterwards; but he was not asked back."

"Yes; he doesn't change," agreed Robert. "He has been using the same technique ever since, on everything from Kaffirs to crèches. The less he knows about a thing the more strongly he feels about it. Nevil was of the opinion that nothing could be done about the proposed letter, since the Bishop had already written it, and what the Bishop has written is not to be contemplated as waste-paper. But I couldn't just sit and do nothing about it; so I rang him up after dinner and pointed out as tactfully as I could that he was embracing a very doubtful cause, and at the same time doing harm to two possibly innocent people. But I might have saved my breath. He pointed out that the *Watchman* existed for the free expression of opinion, and inferred that I was trying to prevent such freedom. I ended up by asking him if he approved of lynching, because he was doing his best to bring one about. That was after I saw it was hopeless and had stopped being tactful." He took the cup of coffee that Mrs. Sharpe had poured out for him. "He's a sad come-down after his predecessor in the See; who was the terror of every evil-doer in five counties, and a scholar to boot."

"How did Toby Byrne achieve gaiters?" Mrs. Sharpe wondered.

"I assume that Cowan's Cranberry Sauce had no inconsiderable part in his translation."

"Ah, yes. His wife. I forgot. Sugar, Mr. Blair?"

"By the way, here are the two duplicate keys to the Franchise gate. I take it that I may keep one. The other you had better give to the police, I think, so that they can look round as they please. I also have to inform you that you now have a private agent in your employ." And he told them about Alec Ramsden, who appeared on doorsteps at half-past eight in the morning.

"No word of anyone recognising the *Ack-Emma* photograph and writing to Scotland Yard?" Marion asked. "I had pinned my faith to that."

"Not so far. But there is still hope."

"It is five days since the *Ack-Emma* printed it. If anyone was ever going to recognise it they would have by now."

"You don't make allowances for the discards. That is nearly always the way it happens. Someone spreads open their parcel of chips and says: 'Dear me, where did I see that face?' Or someone is using a bundle of newspapers to line drawers in a hotel. Or something like that. Don't lose hope, Miss Sharpe. Between the good Lord and Alec Ramsden, we'll triumph in the end."

She looked at him soberly. "You really believe that, don't you," she said as one noting a phenomenon.

"I do," he said.

"You believe in the ultimate triumph of Good."

"Yes."

"Why?"

"I don't know. I suppose because the other thing is unthinkable. Nothing more positive or more commendable than that."

"I should have a greater faith in a God who hadn't given Toby

139

Byrne a bishopric," Mrs. Sharpe said. "When does Toby's letter appear, by the way?"

"On Friday morning."

"I can hardly wait," said Mrs. Sharpe.

~~~~~~

· 15 ·

ROBERT was less sure about the ultimate triumph of good by Friday afternoon.

It was not the Bishop's letter which shook his faith. Indeed the events of Friday did much to take the wind out of the Bishop's sails; and if Robert had been told on Wednesday morning that he would bitterly regret anything that served to deflate the Bishop he would not have believed it.

His Lordship's letter had run very true to form. The *Watchman*, he said, had always set its face against violence and was not now, of course, proposing to condone it, but there were occasions when violence was but a symptom of a deep social unrest, resentment, and insecurity. As in the recent Nullahbad case, for instance. (The "unrest, resentment, and insecurity" in the Nullahbad case lay entirely in the bosoms of two thieves who could not find the opal bracelet they had come to steal and by way of reprisal killed the seven sleeping occupants of the bungalow in their beds.) There were undoubtedly times when the proletariat felt themselves helpless to redress a patent wrong, and it was not to be marvelled at that some of the more passionate spirits were moved to personal protest. (Robert thought that Bill and Stanley would hardly recognise the louts of Monday night under the guise of "passionate spirits"; and he held that "personal protest" was a slight understatement for the entire wrecking of the ground floor windows of The Franchise.) The people to be blamed for the unrest (the *Watchman* had a passion for euphemism: unrest, under-privileged, backward, unfortunate; where the rest of the world talked about violence, the poor, mentally deficient, and prostitutes; and one of the things that the *Ack-Emma* and the *Watchman* had in common, now he thought about it, was the belief that all prostitutes were hearts-of-gold who had taken the wrong turning)—the people to be blamed for the unrest were not those perhaps misguided persons who had demonstrated their resentment so unmistakably, but the powers whose weakness, ineptitude and lack of zeal had led to the injustice of a dropped case. It was part of the English heritage that justice should not only be done but that it should be shown to be done; and the place for that was in open court.

"What good does he think it would do anyone for the police to waste time preparing a case that they were foreordained to lose?" Robert asked Nevil, who was reading the letter over his shoulder.

"It would have done *us* a power of good," Nevil said. "He doesn't seem to have thought of that. If the Magistrate dismissed the case the suggestion that his poor bruised darling was telling fibs could hardly be avoided, could it! Have you come to the bruises?"

"No."

The bruises came near the end. The "poor bruised body" of this young and blameless girl, his lordship said, was a crying indictment of a law that had failed to protect her and now failed to vindicate her. The whole conduct of this case was one that demanded the most searching scrutiny.

"That must be making the Yard very happy this morning," Robert said.

"This afternoon," amended Nevil.

"Why this afternoon?"

"No one at the Yard would read a bogus publication like the *Watchman*. They won't see it until someone sends it to them this afternoon."

But they had seen it, as it turned out. Grant had read it in the train. He had picked it off the bookstall with three others; not because it was his choice but because it was a choice between that and coloured publications with bathing-belle covers.

Robert deserted the office and took the copy of the *Watchman* out to The Franchise together with that morning's *Ack-Emma*, which had quite definitely no further interest in the Franchise affair. Since the final, subdued letter on Wednesday it had ceased to mention the matter. It was a lovely day; the grass in the Franchise courtyard absurdly green, the dirty-white front of the house glorified by the sun into a semblance of grace, the reflected light from the rosy brick wall flooding the shabby drawing-room and giving it a smiling warmth. They had sat there, the three of them, in great contentment. The *Ack-Emma* had finished its undressing of them in public; the Bishop's letter was not after all as bad as it might have been; Alec Ramsden was busy on their behalf in Larborough and would without doubt unearth facts sooner or later that would be their salvation; the summer was here with its bright short nights; Stanley was proving himself "a great dear"; they had paid a second short visit to Milford yesterday in pursuance of their design to become part of the scenery, and nothing untoward had happened to them beyond stares, black looks, and a few audible remarks. Altogether, the feeling of the meeting was that it all might be worse.

"How much ice will this cut?" Mrs. Sharpe asked Robert, stabbing her skinny index finger at the correspondence page of the *Watchman*.

"Not much, I think. Even among the *Watchman* clique the Bishop is looked at slightly sideways nowadays, I understand. His championship of Mahoney didn't do him any good."

"Who was Mahoney?" Marion asked.

"Have you forgotten Mahoney? He was the Irish 'patriot' who put a bomb in a woman's bicycle basket in a busy English street and blew four people to pieces, including the woman, who was later identified by her wedding ring. The Bishop held that Mahoney was merely misguided, not a murderer; that he was fighting on behalf of a repressed minority—the Irish, believe it or not—and that we should not make him into a martyr. That was a little too much for even *Watchman* stomachs, and since then the Bishop's prestige is not what it was, I hear."

"Isn't it shocking how one forgets when it doesn't concern oneself," Marion said. "Did they hang Mahoney?"

"They did, I am glad to say—much to his own pained surprise. So many of his predecessors had benefited from the plea that we should not make martyrs, that murder had ceased to be reckoned in their minds as one of the dangerous trades. It was rapidly becoming as safe as banking."

"Talking of banking," Mrs. Sharpe said, "I think it would be best if our financial position were made clear to you, and for that you should get in touch with old Mr. Crowle's solicitors in London, who manage our affairs. I shall write to them explaining that you are to be given full details, so that you may know how much we have to come and go on, and can make corresponding arrangements for the spending of it in defence of our good name. It is not exactly the way we had planned to spend it."

"Let us be thankful we have it to spend," Marion said. "What does a penniless person do in a case like this?"

Robert quite frankly did not know.

He took the address of the Crowle solicitors and went home to lunch with Aunt Lin, feeling happier than he had at any time since he had first caught sight of the *Ack-Emma*'s front page on Bill's desk last Friday. He felt as one feels in a bad thunderstorm when the noise ceases to be directly overhead; it will still continue, and probably still be very unpleasant, but one can see a future through it, whereas but a moment ago there was nothing but the dreadful "now."

Even Aunt Lin seemed to have forgotten The Franchise for a spell and was at her woolly and endearing best—full of the birthday presents she was buying for Lettice's twins in Saskatchewan. She had provided his favourite lunch—cold ham, boiled potatoes, and brown-betty with thick cream—and moment by moment he was finding it more difficult to realise that this was the Friday morning he had dreaded because it would see the beginning of a *Watchman* campaign against them. It seemed to him that the Bishop of Larborough was very much what Lettice's husband used to call "a busted flush." He couldn't imagine now why he had wasted a thought on him.

It was in this mood that he went back to the office. And it was in this mood that he picked up the receiver to answer Hallam's call.

"Mr. Blair?" Hallam said. "I'm at the Rose and Crown. I'm afraid I've got bad news for you. Inspector Grant's here."

"At the Rose and Crown?"

"Yes. And he's got a warrant."

Robert's brain stopped functioning. "A search warrant?" he asked stupidly.

"No; a warrant to arrest."

143

"No!"

"I'm afraid so."

"But he *can't* have!"

"I expect it's a bit of a shock for you. I admit I hadn't anticipated it myself."

"You mean he has managed to get a witness—a corroborative
witness?"

"He has two of them. The case is sewn up and tied with ribbon."

"I can't believe it."

"Will you come over, or shall we go to you? I expect you'll
want to come out with us."

"Out where? Oh, yes. Yes, of course I shall. I'll come over to
the Rose and Crown now. Where are you? In the lounge?"

"No, in Grant's bedroom. Number Five. The one with the casement window on the street—over the bar."

"All right. I'm coming straight over. I say!"

"Yes?"

"A warrant for both?"

"Yes. For two."

"All right. Thank you. I'll be with you in a moment."

He sat for a moment getting back his breath, and trying to
orientate himself. Nevil was out on business, but Nevil was not
much of a moral support at any time. He got up, took his hat, and
went to the door of "the office."

"Mr. Heseltine, please," he said, in the polite formula always
used in the presence of the younger staff; and the old man followed him into the hall and out to the sunlit doorway.

"Timmy," Robert said. "We're in trouble. Inspector Grant is
here from Headquarters with a warrant to arrest the Franchise
people." Even as he said the words he could not believe that the
thing was really happening.

Neither could old Mr. Heseltine; that was obvious. He stared,
wordless; his pale old eyes aghast.

"It's a bit of a shock, isn't it, Timmy?" He shouldn't have hoped
for support from the frail old clerk.

But shocked as he was, and frail, and old, Mr. Heseltine was
nevertheless a law clerk, and the support was forthcoming. After

a lifetime among formulae his mind reacted automatically to the letter of the situation.

"A warrant," he said. "Why a *warrant?*"

"Because they can't arrest anyone without one," Robert said a trifle impatiently. Was old Timmy getting past his work?

"I don't mean that. I mean, it's a misdemeanour they're accused of, not a felony. They could surely make it a summons, Mr. Robert? They don't need to *arrest* them, surely? Not for a misdemeanour."

Robert had not thought of that. "A summons to appear," he said. "Yes, why not? Of course there's nothing to hinder them arresting them if they want to."

"But why should they want to? People like the Sharpes wouldn't run away. Nor do any further harm while they are waiting to appear. Who issued the warrant, did they say?"

"No, they didn't say. Many thanks, Timmy; you've been as good as a stiff drink. I must go over to the Rose and Crown now —Inspector Grant is there with Hallam—and face the music. There's no way of warning The Franchise because they have no telephone. I'll just have to go out there with Grant and Hallam hanging round my neck. And only this morning we were beginning to see daylight, so we thought. You might tell Nevil when he comes in, will you? And stop him doing anything foolish or impulsive."

"You know very well, Mr. Robert, I've never been able to stop Mr. Nevil doing anything he wanted to do. Though it has seemed to me that he has been surprisingly sober this last week. In the metaphorical sense, I mean."

"Long may it last," Robert said, stepping out into the sunlit street.

It was the dead period of the afternoon at the Rose and Crown and he passed through the hall and up the wide shallow stairs without meeting anyone, and knocked at the door of Number Five. Grant, calm and polite as always, let him in. Hallam, vaguely unhappy-looking, was leaning against the dressing-table in the window.

"I understand that you hadn't expected this, Mr. Blair," Grant said.

"No, I hadn't. To be frank, it is a great shock to me."

"Sit down," Grant said. "I don't want to hurry you."

"You have new evidence, Inspector Hallam says."

"Yes; what we think is conclusive evidence."

"May I know what it is?"

"Certainly. We have a man who saw Betty Kane being picked up by the car at the bus stop——"

"By *a* car," Robert said.

"Yes, if you like, by *a* car—but its description fits that of the Sharpes'."

"So do ten thousand others in Britain. And?"

"The girl from the farm, who went once a week to help clean The Franchise, will swear that she heard screams coming from the attic."

"*Went* once a week? Doesn't she go any longer?"

"Not since the Kane affair became common gossip."

"I see."

"Not very valuable pieces of evidence in themselves, but very valuable as proof of the girl's story. For instance she really did miss that Larborough-London coach. Our witness says that it passed him about half a mile down the road. When he came in sight of the bus-stop a few moments later the girl was there waiting. It is a long straight road, the main London road through Mainshill——"

"I know. I know it."

"Yes; well, when he was still some way from the girl he saw the car stop by her, saw her get in, and saw her driven away."

"But not who drove the car?"

"No. It was too far away for that."

"And this girl from the farm—did she volunteer the information about the screaming?"

"Not to us. She spoke about it to her friends, and we acted on information, and found her quite willing to repeat the story on oath."

"Did she speak about it to her friends before the gossip about Betty Kane's abduction got round?"

"Yes."

That was unexpected, and Robert was rocked back on his heels. If that was really true—that the girl had mentioned screaming

146

before there was any question of the Sharpes being in trouble—then the evidence would be damning. Robert got up and walked restlessly to the window and back. He thought enviously of Ben Carley. Ben wouldn't be hating this as he hated it, feeling inadequate and at a loss. Ben would be in his element; his mind delighting in the problem and in the hope of outwitting established authority. Robert was dimly aware that his own deep-seated respect for established authority was a handicap to him rather than an asset; he needed some of Ben's native belief that authority is there to be circumvented.

"Well, thank you for being so frank," he said at last. "Now, I'm not minimising the crime you are accusing these people of, but it *is* misdemeanour not felony, so why a warrant? Surely a summons would meet the case perfectly?"

"A summons would be in order certainly," Grant said smoothly. "But in cases where the crime is aggravated—and my superiors take a grave view of the present one—a warrant is issued."

Robert could not help wondering how much the gadfly attentions of the *Ack-Emma* had influenced the calm judgments at the Yard. He caught Grant's eye and knew that Grant had read his thought.

"The girl was missing for a whole month—all but a day or two," Grant said, "and had been very badly knocked about, very deliberately. It is not a case to be taken lightly."

"But what do you gain from arrest?" Robert asked, remembering Mr. Heseltine's point. "There is no question of these people not being there to answer the charge. Nor any question of a similar crime being committed by them in the interval. When did you want them to appear, by the way?"

"I planned to bring them up at the police court on Monday."

"Then I suggest that you serve them with a summons to appear."

"My superiors have decided on a warrant," Grant said, without emotion.

"But you could use your judgment. Your superiors can have no knowledge of local conditions, for instance. If The Franchise is left without occupants it will be a wreck in a week. Have your superiors thought of that? And if you arrest these women, you can only keep them in custody until Monday, when I shall ask for bail. It seems a pity to risk hooliganism at The Franchise just for the gesture of arrest. And I know Inspector Hallam has no men to spare for its protection."

This right-and-left gave them both pause. It was amazing how ingrained the respect for property was in the English soul; the first change in Grant's face had occurred at the mention of the possible wrecking of the house. Robert cast an unexpectedly kind thought to the louts who had provided the precedent, and so weighted his argument with example. As for Hallam, quite apart from his limited force he was not likely to look kindly on the prospect of fresh hooliganism in his district and fresh culprits to track down.

Into the long pause Hallam said tentatively: "There is something in what Mr. Blair says. Feeling in the countryside is very strong, and I doubt if they would leave the house untouched if it was empty. Especially if news of the arrest got about."

It took nearly half an hour to convince Grant, however. For some reason there was a personal element in the affair for Grant, and Robert could not imagine what it could be, or why it should be there.

"Well," the Inspector said at length, "you don't need me to serve a summons." It was as if a surgeon was contemptuous at being asked to open a boil, Robert thought, amused and vastly relieved. "I'll leave that to Hallam and get back to town. But I'll be in court on Monday. I understand that the Assizes are imminent, so if we avoid a remand the case can go straight on to the Assizes. Can you be ready with your defence by Monday, do you think?"

"Inspector, with all the defence my clients have we could be ready by tea-time," Robert said bitterly.

To his surprise, Grant turned to him with a broader smile than was usual with him; and it was a very kind smile. "Mr. Blair," he said, "you have done me out of an arrest this afternoon, but I don't hold it against you. On the contrary, I think your clients are luckier than they deserve in their solicitor. It will be my prayer that they are less lucky in their counsel! Otherwise I may find myself talked into voting them a testimonial."

So it was not with "Grant and Hallam hanging round his neck" that Robert went out to The Franchise; not with a warrant at all.

He went out in Hallam's familiar car with a summons sticking out of the pocket of it; and he was sick with relief when he thought of the escape they had had, and sick with apprehension when he thought of the fix they were in.

"Inspector Grant seemed to have a very personal interest in executing that warrant," he said to Hallam as they went along. "Is it that the *Ack-Emma* has been biting him, do you think?"

"Oh, no," Hallam said. "Grant's as nearly indifferent to that sort of thing as a human being can be."

"Then why?"

"Well, it's my belief—strictly between ourselves—that he can't forgive them for fooling him. The Sharpes, I mean. He's famous at the Yard for his good judgment of people, you see; and, again between ourselves, he didn't much care for the Kane girl *or* her story; and he liked them even less when he had seen the Franchise people, in spite of all the evidence. Now he thinks the wool was pulled over his eyes, and he's not taking it lightly. It would have given him a lot of pleasure, I imagine, to produce that warrant in their drawing-room."

As they pulled up by the Franchise gate and Robert took out his key, Hallam said: "If you open both sides I'll drive the car inside, even for the short time. No need to advertise the fact that we're here." And Robert, pushing open the solid iron leaves, thought that when visiting actresses said "Your policemen are wonderful" they didn't know the half of it. He got back into the car and Hallam drove up the short straight drive and round the circular path to the door. As Robert got out of the car Marion came round the corner of the house, wearing gardening gloves and a very old skirt. Where her hair was blown up from her forehead by the wind it changed from the heavy dark stuff that it was to a soft smoke. The first summer sun had darkened her skin and she looked more than ever like a gipsy. Coming on Robert unexpectedly she had not time to guard her expression, and the lighting of her whole face as she saw him made his heart turn over.

"How nice!" she said. "Mother is still resting but she will be down soon and we can have some tea. I——" Her glance went on to Hallam and her voice died away uncertainly. "Good afternoon, Inspector."

"Good afternoon, Miss Sharpe. I'm sorry to break into your mother's rest, but perhaps you would ask her to come down. It's important."

She paused a moment, and then led the way indoors. "Yes, certainly. Has there been some—some new development? Come in and sit down." She led them into the drawing-room that he knew so well by now—the lovely mirror, the dreadful fireplace, the bead-work chair, the good "pieces," the old pink carpet faded to a dirty grey—and stood there, searching their faces, savouring the new threat in the atmosphere.

"What is it?" she asked Robert.

But Hallam said: "I think it would be easier if you fetched Mrs. Sharpe and I told you both at the same time."

"Yes. Yes, of course," she agreed, and turned to go. But there was no need to go. Mrs. Sharpe came into the room, very much as she had on that previous occasion when Hallam and Robert had been there together: her short strands of white hair standing on end where they had been pushed up by her pillow, her seagull's eyes bright and inquiring.

"Only two kinds of people," she said, "arrive in noiseless cars. Millionaires and the police. Since we have no acquaintances among the former—and an ever-widening acquaintance with the latter— I deduced that some of *our* acquaintances had arrived."

"I'm afraid I'm even less welcome than usual, Mrs. Sharpe. I've come to serve a summons on you and Miss Sharpe."

"A summons?" Marion said, puzzled.

"A summons to appear at the police court on Monday morning to answer a charge of abduction and assault." It was obvious that Hallam was not happy.

"I don't believe it," Marion said slowly. "I don't believe it. You mean you are charging us with this thing?"

"Yes, Miss Sharpe."

"But how? Why now?" She turned to Robert.

"The police think they have the corroborative evidence they needed," Robert said.

"What evidence?" Mrs. Sharpe asked, reacting for the first time.

"I think the best plan would be for Inspector Hallam to serve you both with the summonses, and we can discuss the situation at greater length when he has gone."

"You mean, we have to accept them?" Marion said. "To appear in the public court—my mother too—to answer a—to be accused of a thing like that?"

"I'm afraid there is no alternative."

She seemed half intimidated by his shortness, half resentful at his lack of championship. And Hallam, as he handed the document to her, seemed to be aware of this last and to resent it in his turn.

"And I think I ought to tell you, in case he doesn't, that but for Mr. Blair here it wouldn't be a mere summons, it would be a warrant; and you would be sleeping tonight in a cell instead of in your own beds. Don't bother, Miss Sharpe: I'll let myself out."

And Robert, watching him go and remembering how Mrs. Sharpe had snubbed him on his first appearance in that room, thought that the score was now game all.

"Is that true?" Mrs. Sharpe asked.

"Perfectly true," Robert said; and told them about Grant's arrival to arrest them. "But it isn't me you have to thank for your escape: it is old Mr. Heseltine in the office." And he described how the old clerk's mind reacted automatically to stimulus of a legal sort.

"And what is this new evidence they think they have?"

"They have it all right," Robert said dryly. "There is no thinking about it." He told them about the girl being picked up on the London road through Mainshill. "That merely corroborates what we have always suspected: that when she left Cherrill Street, ostensibly on her way home, she was keeping an appointment. But the other piece of evidence is much more serious. You told me once that you had a woman—a girl—from the farm, who came in one day a week and cleaned for you."

"Rose Glyn, yes."

"I understand that since the gossip got round she doesn't come any more."

"Since the gossip——? You mean, the Betty Kane story? Oh, she was sacked before that ever came to light."

151

"*Sacked?*" Robert said sharply.

"Yes. Why do you look so surprised? In our experience of domestic workers sacking is not an unexpected occurrence."

"No, but in this case it might explain a lot. What did you sack her for?"

"Stealing," said old Mrs. Sharpe.

"She had always lifted a shilling or two from a purse if it was left around," supplemented Marion, "but because we needed help so badly we turned a blind eye and kept purses out of her way. Also any small liftable articles, like stockings. And then she took the watch I'd had for twenty years. I had taken it off to wash some things—the soapsuds rise up one's arms, you know—and when I went back to look for it it had gone. I asked her about it, but of course she 'hadn't seen it.' That was too much. That watch was part of me, as much a part of me as my hair or my fingernails. There was no recovering it, because we had no evidence at all that she had taken it. But after she had gone we talked it over and next morning we walked over to the farm, and just mentioned that we would not be needing her any more. That was a Tuesday —she always came on Mondays—and that afternoon after my mother had gone up to rest Inspector Grant arrived, with Betty Kane in the car."

"I see. Was anyone else there when you told the girl at the farm that she was sacked?"

"I don't remember. I don't think so. She doesn't belong to the farm—to Staples, I mean; they are delightful people. She is one of the labourer's daughters. And as far as I remember we met her outside their cottage and just mentioned the thing in passing."

"How did she take it?"

"She got very pink and flounced a bit."

"She grew beetroot red and bridled like a turkeycock," Mrs. Sharpe said. "Why do you ask?"

"Because she will say on oath that when she was working here she heard screams coming from your attic."

"Will she indeed," said Mrs. Sharpe, contemplatively.

"What is much worse, there is evidence that she mentioned the screams before there was any rumour of the Betty Kane trouble."

This produced a complete silence. Once more Robert was

aware how noiseless the house was, how dead. Even the French clock on the mantelpiece was silent. The curtain at the window moved inwards on a gust of air and fell back to its place as soundlessly as if it were moving in a film.

"That," said Marion at last, "is what is known as a facer."

"Yes. Definitely."

"A facer for you, too."

"For us, yes."

"I don't mean professionally."

"No? How then?"

"You are faced with the possibility that we have been lying."

"Really, Marion!" he said impatiently, using her name for the first time and not noticing that he had used it. "What I am faced with, if anything, is the choice between your word and the word of Rose Glyn's friends."

But she did not appear to be listening. "I wish," she said passionately, "oh, how I wish that we had one small, just one small piece of evidence on our side! She gets away—that girl gets away with everything, everything. We keep on saying 'It is not true,' but we have no way of *showing* that it is not true. It is all negative. All inconclusive. All feeble denial. Things combine to back up her lies, but nothing happens to help prove that we are telling the truth. Nothing!"

"Sit down, Marion," her mother said. "A tantrum won't improve the situation."

"I could kill that girl; I could kill her. My God, I could torture her twice a day for a year and then begin again on New Year's day. When I think what she has done to us I——"

"Don't think," Robert interrupted. "Think instead of the day when she is discredited in open court. If I know anything of human nature that will hurt Miss Kane a great deal worse than the beating someone gave her."

"You still believe that that is possible?" Marion said incredulous.

"Yes. I don't quite know how we shall bring it about. But that we shall bring it about I do believe."

"With not one tiny piece of evidence for us, not one; and evidence just—just *blossoming* for her?"

"Yes. Even then."

"Is that just native optimism, Mr. Blair," Mrs. Sharpe asked, "or your innate belief in the triumph of Good, or what?"

"I don't know. I think Truth has a validity of its own."

"Dreyfus didn't find it very valid; nor Slater; nor some others of whom there is record," she said dryly.

"They did in the end."

"Well, frankly, I don't look forward to a life in prison waiting for Truth to demonstrate its validity."

"I don't believe that it will come to that. Prison, I mean. You will have to appear on Monday, and since we have no adequate defence you will no doubt be sent for trial. But we shall ask for bail, and that means that you can go on staying here until the Assizes at Norton. And before that I hope that Alec Ramsden will have picked up the girl's trail. Remember we don't even have to know what she was doing for the rest of the month. All we have to show is that she did something else on the day she says you picked her up. Take away that first bit and her whole story collapses. And it is my ambition to take it away in public."

"To undress her in public the way the *Ack-Emma* has undressed us? Do you think she would mind?" Marion said. "Mind as we minded?"

"To have been the heroine of a newspaper sensation, to say nothing of the adored centre of a loving and sympathetic family, and then to be uncovered to the public gaze as a liar, a cheat and a wanton? I think she would mind. And there is one thing she would mind particularly. One result of her escapade was that she got back Leslie Wynn's attention; the attention she had lost when he became engaged. As long as she is a wronged heroine she is assured of that attention; once we show her up she has lost it for good."

"I never thought to see the milk of human kindness so curdled in your gentle veins, Mr. Blair," Mrs. Sharpe remarked.

"If she had broken out as a result of the boy's engagement— as she very well might—I should have nothing but pity for her. She is at an unstable age, and his engagement must have been a shock. But I don't think that had very much to do with it. I think she is her mother's daughter; and was merely setting out a little early on the road her mother took. As selfish, as self-indulgent, as

154

greedy, as plausible as the blood she came of. Now I must go. I said that I would be at home after five o'clock if Ramsden wanted to ring up to report. And I want to ring Kevin Macdermott and get his help about counsel and things."

"I'm afraid that we—that I, rather—have been rather ungracious about this," Marion said. "You have done, and are doing, so much for us. But it was such a shock. So entirely unexpected and out of the blue. You must forgive me if——"

"There is nothing to forgive. I think you have both taken it very well. Have you got someone in the place of the dishonest and about-to-commit-perjury Rose? You can't have this huge place entirely on your hands."

"Well, no one in the locality would come, of course. But Stanley—what would we do without Stanley?—Stanley knows a woman in Larborough who might be induced to come out by bus once a week. You know, when the thought of that girl becomes too much for me, I think of Stanley."

"Yes," Robert said, smiling. "The salt of the earth."

"He is even teaching me how to cook. I know how to turn eggs in the frying-pan without breaking them now. 'D'you have to go at them as if you were conducting the Philharmonic?' he asked me. And when I asked him how he got so neat-handed he said it was with 'cooking in a bivvy two feet square.'"

"How are you going to get back to Milford?" Mrs. Sharpe asked.

"The afternoon bus from Larborough will pick me up. No word of your telephone being repaired, I suppose?"

Both women took the question as comment not interrogation. Mrs. Sharpe took leave of him in the drawing-room, but Marion walked to the gate with him. As they crossed the circle of grass enclosed by the branching driveway, he remarked: "It's a good thing you haven't a large family or there would be a worn track across the grass to the door."

"There is that as it is," she said, looking at the darker line in the rough grass. "It is more than human nature could bear to walk round that unnecessary curve."

Small talk, he was thinking; small talk. Idle words to cover up a stark situation. He had sounded very brave and fine about the validity of Truth, but how much was mere sound? What were the odds on Ramsden's turning up evidence in time for the court on Monday? In time for the Assizes? Long odds against, wasn't it? And he had better grow used to the thought.

At half-past five Ramsden rang up to give him the promised report; and it was one of unqualified failure. It was the girl he was looking for, of course; having failed to identify the man as a resident at the Midland, and having therefore no information at all about him. But nowhere had he found even a trace of her. His own men had been given duplicates of the photograph and with them had made inquiries at the airports, the railway termini, travel agencies, and the more likely hotels. No one claimed to have seen her. He himself had combed Larborough, and was slightly cheered to find that the photograph he had been given was at least easily recognisable, since it had been readily identified at the places where Betty Kane had actually been. At the two main picture houses, for instance—where, according to the box-office girls' information, she had always been alone—and at the ladies' cloakroom of the bus-station. He had tried the garages, but had drawn blank.

"Yes," Robert said. "He picked her up at the bus-stop on the London road through Mainshill. Where she would normally have gone to catch her coach home." And he told Ramsden of the new developments. "So things really are urgent now. They are being brought up on Monday. If only we could prove what she did that first evening. That would bring her whole story crashing down."

"What kind of car was it?" Ramsden asked.

Robert described it, and Ramsden sighed audibly over the telephone.

"Yes," Robert agreed. "A rough ten thousand of them between London and Carlisle. Well, I'll leave you to it. I want to ring up Kevin Macdermott and tell him our woes."

Kevin was not in chambers, nor yet at the flat in St. Paul's Churchyard, and Robert eventually ran him to earth at his home near Weybridge. He sounded relaxed and amiable, and was instantly attentive when he heard the news that the police had got their evidence. He listened without remark while Robert poured out the story to him.

"So you see, Kevin," Robert finished, "we're in a frightful jam."

"A schoolboy description," Kevin said, "but exquisitely accurate. My advice to you is to 'give' them the police court, and concentrate on the Assizes."

"Kevin, couldn't you come down for the week-end, and let me talk about it to you? It's six years, Aunt Lin was saying yesterday, since you spent a night with us, so you're overdue anyhow. Couldn't you?"

"I promised Sean I'd take him over to Newbury on Sunday to choose a pony."

"But couldn't you postpone it? I'm sure Sean wouldn't mind if he knew it was in a good cause."

"Sean," said his doting parent, "has never taken the slightest interest in any cause that was not to his own immediate advantage. Being a chip off the old block. If I came would you introduce me to your witches?"

"But of course."

"And would Christina make me some butter tarts?"

"Assuredly."

"And could I have the room with the text in wools?"

"Kevin, you'll come?"

"Well, it's a damned dull country, Milford, except in the winter"—this was a reference to hunting, Kevin's only eye for country being from the back of a horse—"and I was looking forward to a Sunday riding on the downs. But a combination of witches, butter tarts, and a bedroom with a text in wools is no small draw."

As he was about to hang up, Kevin paused and said: "Oh, I say, Rob?"

"Yes?" Robert said, and waited.

"Have you considered the possibility that the police have the right of it?"

"You mean, that the girl's absurd tale may be true?"

"Yes. Are you keeping that in mind—as a possibility, I mean?"

"If I were I shouldn't——" Robert began angrily, and then laughed. "Come down and see them," he said.

"I come, I come," Kevin assured him, and hung up.

Robert called the garage, and when Bill answered asked if Stanley was still there.

"It's a wonder you can't hear him from where you are," Bill said.

"What's wrong?"

"We've just been rescuing that bay pony of Matt Ellis's from our inspection pit. Did you want Stan?"

"Not to speak to. Would you be very kind and ask him to pick up a note for Mrs. Sharpe on his way past tonight?"

"Yes, certainly. I say, Mr. Blair, is it true that there is fresh trouble coming about the Franchise affair—or shouldn't I ask that?"

Milford! thought Robert. How did they do it? A sort of information-pollen blown on the wind?

"Yes, I'm afraid there is," he said. "I expect they'll tell Stanley about it when he goes out tonight. Don't let him forget about the note, will you?"

"No, that's all right."

He wrote to The Franchise to say that Kevin Macdermott was coming down for Saturday night, and could he bring him out to see them on Sunday afternoon before he left to go back to town?

<hr />

· 16 ·

"Does Kevin Macdermott *have* to look like a tout when he comes to the country?" Nevil asked, the following evening as he and Robert waited for the guest to finish his ablutions and come down to dinner.

What Kevin in country clothes actually looked like, Robert considered, was a rather disreputable trainer of jumpers for the smaller meetings; but he refrained from saying that to Nevil. Remembering the clothes that Nevil had startled the countryside with for the last few years, he felt that Nevil was in no position to criticise anyone's taste. Nevil had turned up to dinner in a chaste dark grey suit of the most irreproachable orthodoxy, and seemed to think that his new conformity made him free to forget the experimentalism of his immediate past.

"I suppose Christina is in the usual lather of sentiment?"

"A lather of white of egg, as far as I have been able to judge."

158

Christina regarded Kevin as "Satan in person," and adored him. His Satanic qualities came not from his looks—though Kevin did indeed look a little like Satan—but from the fact that he "defended the wicked for the sake of worldly gain." And she adored him because he was good-looking, and a possibly reclaimable sinner, and because he praised her baking.

"I hope it's a soufflé, then, and not that meringue stuff. Do you think that Macdermott could be lured into coming down to defend them at Norton Assizes?"

"I think he is much too busy for that, even if he were interested. But I'm hoping that one of his dogs-bodies will come."

"Primed by Macdermott."

"That's the idea."

"I really don't see why Marion should have to slave to provide Macdermott with lunch. Does he realise that she has to prepare and clear away and wash up every single thing, to say nothing of carting them to and fro a day's journey to that antediluvian kitchen?"

"It was Marion's own idea that he should come to lunch with them. I take it that she considers the extra trouble worth while."

"Oh, you were always crazy about Kevin; and you simply don't know how to begin to appreciate a woman like Marion. It's—it's *obscene* that she should be wasting her vitality on household drudgery, a woman like that. She should be hacking her way through jungles, or scaling precipices, or ruling a barbarous race, or measuring the planets. Ten thousand nit-wit blondes dripping with mink have nothing to do but sit back and have the polish on their predatory nails changed, and Marion carts coal. Coal! *Marion!* And I suppose by the time this case is finished they won't have a penny to pay a maid even if they could get one."

"Let us hope that by the time this case is finished they are not doing hard labour by order."

"Robert, it *couldn't* come to that! It's unthinkable."

"Yes, it's unthinkable. I suppose it is always unbelievable that anyone one knows should go to prison."

"It's bad enough that they should go into the dock. Marion. Who never did a cruel, or underhand, or shabby thing in her life. And just because a—— Do you know. I had a lovely time the other night. I found a book on torture, and I stayed awake till two o'clock choosing which one I would use on the Kane."

"You should get together with Marion. That is her ambition too."

"And what would yours be?" There was a faint hint of scorn in the tone, as though it was understood that the mild Robert would have no strong feelings on the subject. "Or haven't you considered it?"

"I don't need to consider it," Robert said slowly. "I'm going to undress her in public."

"*What!*"

"Not that way. I'm going to strip her of every rag of pretence, in open court, so that everyone will see her for what she is."

Nevil looked curiously at him for a moment. "Amen," he said quietly. "I didn't know you felt like that about it, Robert." He was going to add something, but the door opened and Macdermott came in, and the evening had begun.

Eating solidly through Aunt Lin's superb dinner, Robert hoped that it was not going to be a mistake to take Kevin to Sunday lunch at The Franchise. He was desperately anxious that the Sharpes should make a success with Kevin; and there was no denying that Kevin was temperamental and the Sharpes not everyone's cup of tea. Was lunch at The Franchise likely to be an asset to their cause? A lunch cooked by Marion? For Kevin who was a gourmet? When he had first read the invitation—handed in by Stanley this morning—he was glad that they had made the gesture, but misgiving was slowly growing in him. And as one perfection succeeded the other in unhurried procession across Aunt Lin's shining mahogany, with Christina's large face hovering in eager benevolence beyond the candle-light, the misgiving swelled until it took entire possession of him. "Shapes that did not stand up" might fill his breast with a warm, protective affection; but they could hardly be expected to have the same effect on Kevin.

At least Kevin seemed glad to be here, he thought, listening to Macdermott making open love to Aunt Lin, with a word thrown to Christina every now and then to keep her happy and faithful. Dear Heaven, the Irish! Nevil was on his best behaviour, full of earnest attention, with a discreet "sir" thrown in now and again;

often enough to make Kevin feel superior but not often enough to make him feel old. The subtler English form of flattery, in fact. Aunt Lin was like a girl, pink-cheeked and radiant; absorbing flattery like a sponge, subjecting it to some chemical process, and pouring it out again as charm. Listening to her talk Robert was amused to find that the Sharpes had suffered a sea-change in her mind. By the mere fact of being in danger of imprisonment, they had been promoted from "these people" to "poor things." This had nothing to do with Kevin's presence; it was a combination of native kindness and woolly thinking.

It was odd, Robert thought, looking round the table, that this family party—so gay, so warm, so secure—should be occasioned by the dire need of two helpless women in that dark silent house set down among the endless fields.

He went to bed with the warm aura of the party still round him, but in his heart a chill anxiety and an ache. Were they asleep out there at The Franchise? How much sleep had they had lately?

He lay long awake, and wakened early; listening to the Sunday morning silence. Hoping that it would be a good day—The Franchise looked its worst in rain, when its dirty-white became almost grey—and that whatever Marion made for lunch would "stand up." Just before eight o'clock a car came in from the country and stopped below the window, and someone whistled a soft bugle call. A company call, it was. B Company. Stanley, presumably. He got up and put his head out of the window.

Stanley, hatless as usual—he had never seen Stanley in any kind of head covering—was sitting in the car regarding him with tolerant benevolence.

"You Sunday snoozers," said Stanley.

"Did you get me up just to sneer at me?"

"No. I have a message from Miss Sharpe. She says when you come out you're to take Betty Kane's statement with you, and you're on no account to forget it because it's of the first importance. I'll say it's important! She's going round looking as if she had unearthed a million."

"Looking happy!" Robert said, unbelieving.

"Like a bride. Indeed I haven't seen a woman look like that since my cousin Beulah married her Pole. A face like a scone, Beulah

161

has; and believe me that day she looked like Venus, Cleopatra, and Helen of Troy rolled into one."

"Do you know what it is that Miss Sharpe is so happy about?"

"No. I did cast out a few feelers, but she's saving it up, it seems. Anyhow, don't forget the copy of the statement, or the responses won't come right, or something. The pass-word's in the statement."

Stanley proceeded on his way up the street towards Sin Lane, and Robert took his towel and went to the bathroom greatly puzzled. While he waited for breakfast he looked out the statement from among the papers in his dispatch case, and read it through again with a new attention. What had Marion remembered or discovered that was making her so happy? Betty Kane had slipped somewhere, that was obvious. Marion was radiant, and Marion wanted him to bring the Kane statement when he came. That could only mean that somewhere in the statement was proof that Betty Kane was lying.

He reached the end of the statement without finding any likely sentence and began to hunt through it again. What could it be? That she had said it was raining, and that it—perhaps—had not been raining? But that would not have been vital, or even important to the credibility of her story. The Milford bus, then? The one she said she had passed, when being driven in the Sharpes' car. Were the times wrong? But they had checked the times long ago, and they fitted nearly enough. The "lighted sign" on the bus? Was the time too early for a sign to be lighted? But that would have been merely a slip of memory, not a discrediting factor in her statement.

He hoped passionately that Marion in her anxiety to obtain that "one small piece of evidence" on their side was not exaggerating some trifling discrepancy into proof of dishonesty. The descent from hope would be worse than no hope at all.

This real worry almost obliterated the social worry of the lunch from his mind, and he ceased to care greatly whether Kevin enjoyed his meal at The Franchise or not. When Aunt Lin said to him, covertly, as she set off for church: "What do you think they'll give you for lunch, dear? I'm quite sure they live on those toasted flake things out of packets, poor things," he said shortly: "They know good wine when they taste it; that should please Kevin."

"What has happened to young Bennet?" Kevin asked as they drove out to The Franchise.

"He wasn't asked to lunch," Robert said.

"I didn't mean that. What has happened to the strident suits and the superiority and the *Watchman* aggressiveness?"

"Oh, he has fallen out with the *Watchman* over this case."

"Ah!"

"For the first time he is in a position to have actual personal knowledge of a case the *Watchman* is pontificating about, and it has been a bit of a shock to him, I think."

"Is the reformation going to last?"

"Well, do you know, I shouldn't be a bit surprised if it did. Apart from the fact that he has got to an age when they normally give up childish things, and was due for a change, I think he has been doing some revision and wondering if any of the other *Watchman* white-headed boys were any more worthy of championing than Betty Kane. Kotovich, for instance."

"Hah! The patriot!" Kevin said expressively.

"Yes. Only last week he was holding forth on our duty to Kotovich; our duty to protect and cherish him—and eventually provide him with a British passport, I suppose. I doubt if today he would be quite so simple. He has grown up wonderfully in the last few days. I didn't know he even possessed a suit like the one he was wearing last night. It must be one he got to go to his school prize-giving in, for he certainly has worn nothing so sober since."

"I hope for your sake it lasts. He has brains, the boy; and once he got rid of his circus tricks would be an asset to the firm."

"Aunt Lin is distressed because he has split with Rosemary over the Franchise affair, and she is afraid he won't marry a Bishop's daughter after all."

"Hooray! More power to him. I begin to like the boy. You put a few wedges into that split, Rob—casual-like—and see that he marries some nice stupid English girl who will give him five children and give the rest of the neighbourhood tennis parties between showers on Saturday afternoons. It's a much nicer kind of stupidity than standing up on platforms and holding forth on subjects you don't know the first thing about. Is this the place?"

"Yes, this is The Franchise."

"A perfect 'mystery house'."

"It wasn't a mystery house when it was built. The gates, as you can see, were scroll work—rather nice work, too—so that the whole place was visible from the road. It was the simple operation of backing the gate with the iron sheeting that converted the house from something quite ordinary to something rather secret."

"A perfect house for Betty Kane's purpose anyhow. What a piece of luck for her that she remembered it."

Robert was to feel guilty afterwards that he had not had greater faith in Marion; both over the matter of Betty Kane's statement and over the lunch. He should have remembered how cool-minded she was, how analytic; and he should have remembered the Sharpe gift for taking people as they found them and its soothing effect on the persons concerned. The Sharpes had made no effort to live up to Aunt Lin's standard of hospitality; no effort to provide a formal dining-room lunch. They had set a table for four in the window of the drawing-room where the sun fell on it. It was a cherrywood table, very pleasant in grain but sadly needing polishing. The wine glasses, on the other hand, were polished to a diamond brilliance. (How like Marion, he thought, to concentrate on the thing that mattered and to ignore mere appearance.)

"The dining-room is an incredibly gloomy place," Mrs. Sharpe said. "Come and see it, Mr. Macdermott."

That too was typical. No sitting round with their sherry making small talk. Come and see our horrible dining-room. And the visitor was part of the household before he knew it.

"Tell me," Robert said to Marion as they were left alone, "what is this about the——"

"No, I am not going to talk about it until after lunch. It is to be your liqueur. It is a piece of the most astonishing luck that I should have thought of it last night, when Mr. Macdermott was coming to lunch today. It makes everything quite different. It

164

won't stop the case, I suppose, but it does make everything different for us. It is the 'small thing' that I was praying for to be evidence for *us*. Have you told Mr. Macdermott?"

"About your message. No, I haven't said anything. I thought it better—not to."

"Robert!" she said looking at him with a quizzical amusement. "You didn't trust me. You were afraid I was havering."

"I was afraid you might be building more on a small foundation than—than it would hold. I——"

"Don't be afraid," she said, reassuringly. "It will hold. Would you like to come to the kitchen and carry the tray of soup for me?"

They had even managed the service without fuss or flurry. Robert carried the tray with four flat bowls of soup, and Marion came after him with a large dish under a Sheffield plate cover, and that seemed to be all. When they had drunk their soup, Marion put the large dish in front of her mother, and a bottle of wine in front of Kevin. The dish was a pot-au-feu chicken with all its vegetables round it; and the wine was a Montrachet.

"A Montrachet!" Kevin said. "You wonderful woman."

"Robert told us you were a claret lover," Marion said, "but what is left in old Mr. Crowle's cellar is long past its best. So it was a choice between that and a very heavy red burgundy that is wonderful on winter evenings but not so good with one of the Staples' fowls on a summer day."

Kevin said something about how seldom it was that women were interested in anything that did not bubble, or alternatively explode.

"To be frank," Mrs. Sharpe said, "if these parcels had been saleable we should probably have sold them, but we were exceedingly glad that they were too scrappy and varied for that. I was brought up to appreciate wine. My husband had a fairly good cellar, though his palate was not as good as mine. But my brother at Lessways had a better one, and a fine palate to match."

"Lessways?" Kevin said, and looked at her as if searching for a resemblance. "You're not Charlie Meredith's sister, are you?"

"I am. Did you know Charles? But you couldn't. You are too young."

"The first pony I ever had of my own was bred by Charlie

Meredith," Kevin said. "I had him for seven years and he never put a foot wrong."

And after that, of course, both of them ceased to take any further interest in the others, and not over-much in the food.

Robert caught Marion's amused and congratulatory glance at him, and said: "You did yourself grave injustice when you said you couldn't cook."

"If you were a woman you would observe that I have not cooked anything. The soup I emptied out of a can, heated it, and added some sherry and flavouring; the fowl I put into a pot just as it came from Staples, poured some boiling water over it, added everything I could think of and left it on the stove with a prayer; the cream cheese also came from the farm."

"And the wonderful rolls to go with the cream cheese?"

"Stanley's landlady made those."

They laughed a little together, quietly.

Tomorrow she was going into the dock. Tomorrow she was going to be a public spectacle for the delight of Milford. But today her life was still her own, and she could share amusement with him; could be content with the hour. Or so it seemed if her shining eyes were any evidence.

They took the cheese plates from under the noses of the other two, who did not even pause in their conversation to remark the action, carried the trays of dirty dishes away to the kitchen and made the coffee there. It was a great gloomy place with a floor of stone slabs, and an old-fashioned sink that depressed him at sight.

"We put the range on only on Mondays when the scrubbing is done," Marion said, seeing his interest in the place. "Otherwise we cook on the little oil stove."

He thought of the hot water that ran so instantly into the shining bath when he turned the tap this morning, and was ashamed. He could hardly visualise, after his long years of soft living, an existence where one's bathing was done in water that was heated over an oil burner.

"Your friend is a charmer, isn't he," she said, pouring the hot coffee into its jug. "A little Mephistophelian—one would be terribly afraid of him as opposing counsel—but a charmer."

"It's the Irish," Robert said, gloomily. "It comes as natural to them as breathing. Us poor Saxons plod along our brutish way and wonder how they do it."

She had turned to give him the tray to carry, and so was facing him with their hands almost touching. "The Saxons have the two qualities that I value most in this world. Two qualities that explain why they have inherited the earth. Kindness and dependability—or tolerance and responsibility, if you prefer the terms. Two qualities the Celt never had; which is why the Irish have inherited nothing but squabbles. Oh damn, I forgot the cream. Wait a moment. It's keeping cold in the wash-house." She came back with the cream and said, mock rustic: "I have heard tell as how there's things called refrigerators in some folks' houses now, but we don't need none."

And as he carried the coffee to the sunlight of the drawing-room he visualised the bone-chilling cold of those kitchen quarters in winter with no roaring range as there had been in the palmy days of the house when a cook had lorded it over half a dozen servants and you ordered coal by the wagon load. He longed to take Marion away from the place. Where he would take her he did not quite know—his own home was filled with the aura of Aunt Lin. It would have to be a place where there was nothing to polish and nothing to carry and practically everything was done by pressing a button. He could not see Marion spending her old age in service to some pieces of mahogany.

As they drank their coffee he brought the conversation gently round to the possibility of their selling The Franchise at some time or other and buying a cottage somewhere.

"No one would buy the place," Marion said. "It is a white elephant. Not big enough for a school, too remote for flats, and too big for a family these days. It might make a good madhouse," she added, thoughtfully, her eyes on the high pink wall beyond the window; and Robert saw Kevin's glance flash over her and run away again. "It is quiet, at least. No trees to creak, or ivy to tap at the window-panes, or birds to go yap-yap-yap until you want to scream. It is a very peaceful place for tired nerves. Perhaps someone would consider it for that."

So she liked the silence; the stillness that had seemed to him so dead. It was perhaps what she had longed for in her London life of noise and elbowing and demands; her life of fret and cramped quarters. The big quiet ugly house had been a haven.

And now it was a haven no longer.

Some day—Oh-please-God-let-it-happen—some day he would strip Betty Kane for ever of credit and love.

"And now," Marion said, "you are invited to inspect the 'fatal attic'."

"Yes," Kevin said, "I should be greatly interested to see the things that the girl professed to identify. All her statements seemed to me the result of logical guesses. Like the harder carpet on the second flight of stairs. Or the wooden commode—something that you would almost certainly find in a country house. Or the flat-topped trunk."

"Yes, it was rather terrifying at the time, the way she kept hitting on things we had—and I hadn't had time to gather my wits —it was only afterwards I saw how little she really had identified in her statement. And she did make one complete bloomer, only no one thought of it until last night. Have you got the statement, Robert?"

"Yes." He took it out of his pocket.

They had climbed, she, and Robert and Macdermott, the last bare flight of stairs and she led them into the attic. "I came up here last night on my usual Saturday tour round the house with a mop. That is our solution to the housekeeping problem, in case you are interested. A good large mop well soaked in absorbent polish-stuff run over every floor once a week. It takes five minutes per room and keeps the dust at bay."

Kevin was poking round the room, and inspecting the view from the window. "So this is the view she described," he said.

"Yes," Marion said, "that is the view she described. And if I remember the words of her statement, as I remembered them last night, correctly, then she said something that she can't—Robert, would you read the bit where she describes the view from the window?"

Robert looked up the relevant passage, and began to read. Kevin was bending slightly forward staring out of the little round window, and Marion was standing behind him, smiling faintly like a sibyl.

168

" 'From the window of the attic,' " read Robert, " 'I could see a high brick wall with a big iron gate in the middle of it. There was a road on the further side of the wall, because I could see the telegraph posts. No, I couldn't see the traffic on it because the wall was too high. Just the tops of lorry loads sometimes. You couldn't see through the gate because it had sheets of iron on the inside. Inside the gate the carriage-way went straight for a little and then divided in two into a circle up to the door. No, it wasn't a garden, just——' "

"What!" yelled Kevin, straightening himself abruptly.

"What what?" Robert asked, startled.

"Read that last bit again, that bit about the carriage-way."

" 'Inside the gate the carriage-way went straight for a little and then divided in two into a circle up to the——.' "

Kevin's shout of laughter stopped him. It was an abrupt mono-syllable of amused triumph.

"You see?" Marion said into the sudden silence.

"Yes," Kevin said softly, his pale bright eyes gloating on the view. "That was something she didn't reckon with."

Robert moved over as Marion gave way to let him have her place, and so saw what they were talking about. The edge of the roof with its small parapet cut off the view of the courtyard be-fore the carriage-way branched at all. No one imprisoned in that room would know about the two half circles up to the doorway.

"You see," Marion said, "the Inspector read that description when we were all in the drawing-room. And all of us knew that the description was accurate. I mean, an accurate picture of what the courtyard is like; so we unconsciously treated it as something that was finished with. Even the Inspector. I remember his look-ing at the view from the window but it was quite an automatic gesture. It didn't occur to any of us that it would not have been as described. Indeed, except for one tiny detail it was as described."

"Except for one tiny detail," Kevin said. "She arrived in dark-ness and fled in darkness, and she says she was locked in the room all the time, so she could have known nothing of that branching drive. What does she say, again, about her arrival, Rob?"

Robert looked it up and read:

" 'The car stopped at last and the younger woman, the one with the black hair, got out and pushed open big double gates on to a drive. Then she got back in and drove the car up to a house. No, it was too dark to see what kind of a house, except that it had steps up to the door. No, I don't remember how many steps; four or five, I think. Yes, definitely a small flight of them.' And then she goes on about being taken to the kitchen for coffee."

"So," Kevin said. "And her account of her flight? What time of night was that?"

"Sometime after supper if I remember rightly," Robert said, shuffling through the pages. "After dark, anyhow. Here it is." And he read:

" 'When I got to the first landing, the one above the hall, I could hear them talking in the kitchen. There was no light in the hall. I went on down the last flight, expecting every moment that one of them would come out and catch me, and then made a dash for the door. It wasn't locked and I ran straight out and down the steps to the gate and out to the road. I ran along the road—yes, it was hard like a highroad—until I couldn't run any longer and I lay in the grass till I was feeling able to go on.' "

" 'It was hard, like a highroad,' " Kevin quoted. "The inference being that it was too dark to see the surface she was running on."

There was a short silence.

"My mother thinks that this is enough to discredit her," Marion said. She looked from Robert to Kevin, and back again, without much hope. "But you don't, do you." It was hardly a question.

"No," Kevin said. "No. Not alone. She might wriggle out of it with a clever counsel's help. Might say that she had deduced the circle from the swing of the car when she arrived. What she would normally have deduced, of course, would be the ordinary carriage sweep. No one would spontaneously think of anything as awkward as that circular drive. It makes a pretty pattern, that's all—which is probably why she remembered it. I think this tit-bit should be kept as make-weight for the Assizes."

"Yes, I thought you would say that," Marion said. "I'm not really disappointed. I was glad about it, not because I thought that it would free us of the charge, but because it frees us of the doubt that must have—must have——" She stammered unexpectedly, avoiding Robert's eyes.

"Must have muddied our crystal minds," finished Kevin, briskly; and cast a glance of pleased malice at Robert. "How did you think of this last night when you came to sweep?"

"I don't know. I stood looking out of the window, and at the view she described, and wishing that we might have just one small tiny microscopic piece of evidence on *our* side. And then, without thinking, I heard Inspector Grant's voice reading that bit in the drawing-room. Most of the story he told us in his own words, you know. But the bits that brought him to The Franchise he read in the girl's words. I heard his voice—it's a nice voice—saying the bit about the circular carriage-way, and from where I was at that moment there was no circular carriage-way. Perhaps it was an answer to unspoken prayer."

"So you still think that we had best 'give' them tomorrow and bank everything on the Assizes?" Robert said.

"Yes. It makes no difference actually to Miss Sharpe and her mother. An appearance in one place is very like an appearance in another—except that the Assizes at Norton will probably be less unpleasant than a police court in one's home town. And the shorter their appearance tomorrow the better from their point of view. You have no evidence to put before the court tomorrow, so it should be a very short and formal affair. A parade of *their* evidence, an announcement that you reserve your defence, an application for bail, and *voilà!*"

This suited Robert well enough. He did not want to prolong tomorrow's ordeal for them; he had more confidence in any case in a judgment framed outside Milford; and most of all he did not want, now that it had come to a case, a half-decision, a dismissal. That would not be sufficient for his purpose where Betty Kane was concerned. He wanted the whole story of that month told in open court, in Betty Kane's presence. And by the time the Assizes opened at Norton, he would, please God, have the story ready to tell.

"Whom can we get to defend them?" he asked Kevin as they drove home to tea.

Kevin reached into a pocket, and Robert took it for granted that what he was looking for was a list of addresses. But what he produced was obviously an engagement book.

"What is the date of the Assizes at Norton, do you know?" he asked.

Robert told him, and held his breath.

"It's just possible that I might be able to come down myself. Let me see, let me see."

Robert let him see in complete silence. One word, he felt, might ruin the magic.

"Yes," Kevin said. "I don't see why I shouldn't—short of the unforeseen. I like your witches. It would give me great pleasure to defend them against that very nasty piece of work. How odd that she should be old Charlie Meredith's sister. One of the best, the old boy was. About the only approximately honest horse-coper known in history. I have never ceased to be grateful to him for that pony. A boy's first horse is very important. It colours his whole after-life; not only his attitude to horse-flesh; everything else as well. There is something in the trust and friendship that exists between a boy and a good horse that——"

Robert listened, relaxed and amused. He had realised, with a gentle irony untinged with any bitterness, that Kevin had given up any thought of the Sharpes' guilt long before the evidence of that view from the window was presented to him. It was not possible that old Charlie Meredith's sister could have abducted anyone.

~~~~~~

· 17 ·

"It's a perpetual wonder to me," Ben Carley said, eyeing the well-populated benches in the little court, "how so many of the lieges have so little to do on a Monday morning. Though I must say it's some time since the gathering has had so much tone. Have you noticed the Sports Wear? Back row but one, in a yellow hat that doesn't go with her mauve powder *or* her hair. If she's left that little Godfrey girl in charge, she's going to be short of change tonight. I got that girl off when she was fifteen. She'd been swiping cash since she could walk and she's still swiping it. No female to be left alone with a till, believe me. And that Anne Boleyn woman. First time I've ever seen her in court. Though how she's

172

avoided it so long I don't know. Her sister's for ever paying out cheques to cover her R.D. ones. No one's ever discovered what she does with the money. Someone blackmailing her, perhaps. I wonder who. I wouldn't put it past Arthur Wallis, at the White Hart. Three different orders to pay every week, and another on the way, just won't come out of a potman's pay."

Robert let Carley burble on without listening to him. He was only too conscious that the audience in court was not the usual Monday morning collection of loafers putting off time until they opened. The news had gone round, by the mysterious Milford channels, and they had come to see the Sharpes charged. The normal drabness of the court was gay with women's clothes; and its normal drowsy silence sibilant with their chatter.

One face he saw which should have been hostile but was oddly friendly: that of Mrs. Wynn, whom he had last seen standing in her lovely little patch of garden in Meadowside Lane, Aylesbury. He could not think of Mrs. Wynn as an enemy. He liked her, admired her, and was sorry for her in advance. He would have liked to go over and say how d'you do to her, but the game had been laid out on the squares now and they were chequers of different colour.

Grant had not appeared so far, but Hallam was there, talking to the sergeant who had come to The Franchise the night the hooligans wrecked the windows.

"How's your sleuth doing?" Carley asked, during a pause in his running commentary.

"The sleuth's all right, but the problem is colossal," Robert said. "The proverbial needle just gives itself up by comparison."

"One girl against the world," mocked Ben. "I'm looking forward to seeing this floosie in the flesh. I suppose after all the fan mail she's had, and the offers of marriage, and the resemblance to Saint Bernadette, she'll think a country police court too small an arena for her. Did she have any stage offers?"

"I wouldn't know."

"I suppose Mama would repress them anyhow. That's her there with the brown suit, and she looks a very sensible woman to me. I can't think how she ever came to have a daughter like——. Oh, but she was adopted, wasn't she? An Awful Warning. It's a con-

173

stant wonder to me how little folk know about the people they live with. There was a woman over at Ham Green had a daughter that was never out of her sight as far as she knew, but daughter walked out in a pet one day and didn't come back and frantic mother goes howling to the police and police discover that the girl who has apparently never been away from mother for a night is a married woman with a child and has merely collected child and gone to live with husband. See police records if not believing Ben Carley. Ah, well, if you grow dissatisfied with your sleuth let me know and I'll give you the address of a very good one. Here we go."

He rose in deference to the Bench, while continuing a monologue on the Bench's complexion, possible temper, and probable occupation yesterday.

Three routine cases were disposed of; old offenders apparently so used to the procedure that they anticipated the drill, and Robert half expected someone to say "Wait for it, can't you!"

Then he saw Grant come in quietly and sit in an observer's position at the back of the Press bench, and he knew that the time had come.

They came in together when their names were called, and took their places in the horrid little pew as if they were merely taking their places in church. It *was* rather like that, he thought: the quiet, and observant eyes, and the suggestion of waiting for a performance to begin. But he suddenly realised what he would be feeling if it were Aunt Lin in Mrs. Sharpe's place, and was fully aware for the first time of what Marion must be suffering on her mother's behalf. Even if the Assizes saw them cleared of the charge, what would compensate them for what they had endured? What punishment fit Betty Kane's crime?

For Robert, being old-fashioned, believed in retribution. He might not go all the way with Moses—an eye was not always compensation for an eye—but he certainly agreed with Gilbert: the punishment should fit the crime. He certainly did not believe that a few quiet talks with the chaplain and a promise to reform made a criminal into a respect-worthy citizen. "Your true criminal," he remembered Kevin saying one night, after a long discussion on penal reform, "has two unvarying characteristics, and it is these two characteristics which make him a criminal. Monstrous vanity and colossal selfishness. And they are both as integral, as ineradicable, as the texture of the skin. You might as well talk of 'reforming' the colour of one's eyes."

"But," someone had objected, "there have been monsters of vanity and selfishness who were not criminal."

"Only because they have victimised their wives instead of their bank," Kevin had pointed out. "Tomes have been written trying to define the criminal, but it is a very simple definition after all. The criminal is a person who makes the satisfaction of his own immediate personal wants the mainspring of his actions. You can't cure him of his egotism, but you can make the indulgence of it not worth his while. Or almost not worth his while."

Kevin's idea of prison reform, Robert remembered, was deportation to a penal colony. An island community where everyone worked hard. This was not a reform for the benefit of the prisoners. It would be a nicer life for the warders, Kevin said; and would leave more room in this crowded island for good citizens' houses and gardens; and since most criminals hated hard work more than they hated anything in this world, it would be a better deterrent than the present plan which, in Kevin's estimation, was no more punitive than a third-rate public school.

Looking at the two figures in the dock Robert thought that in the "bad old days" only the guilty were put in the pillory. Nowadays, it was the untried who bore the pillory and the guilty went immediately into a safe obscurity. Something had gone wrong somewhere.

Old Mrs. Sharpe was wearing the flat black satin hat in which she had appeared at his office on the morning of the *Ack-Emma* irruption into their affairs, and looked academic, respectable, but odd. Marion too was wearing a hat—less, he supposed, out of deference to the court than as some protection against the public gaze. It was a country felt, with a short brim; and its orthodoxy lessened to some extent her normal air of being a law unto herself. With her black hair hidden and her brilliant eyes shadowed she looked no swarthier than a normal out-of-doors woman might. And though Robert missed the black hair and the brilliance he thought that it was all to the good that she should look as "ordinary" as possible. It might lessen the pecking-to-death instinct in her hostile fellows.

And then he saw Betty Kane.

It was the stir on the Press bench that told him she was in court. Normally the Press bench was occupied by two bored apprentices in the art of reporting: one for the *Milford Advertiser* (once weekly, on Fridays) and one combining the *Norton Courier* (twice weekly, Tuesdays and Fridays) with the *Larborough Times* and anyone else who would take the stuff. But today the Press bench was filled, and the faces there were neither young nor bored. They were the faces of men invited to a meal and quite ready for it.

And Betty Kane was two-thirds of what they had come for.

Robert had not seen her since she stood in the drawing-room at The Franchise in her dark blue school coat, and he was surprised all over again by her youth and her candid innocence. In the weeks since he had first seen her she had grown into a monster in his mind; he thought of her only as the perverted creature who had lied two human beings into the dock. Now, seeing the actual physical Betty Kane again, he was nonplussed. He *knew* that this girl and his monster were one, but he found it difficult to realise. And if he, who felt that he now knew Betty Kane so well, reacted like that to her presence, what effect would her child-like grace have on good men and true when the time came?

She was wearing "week-end" clothes, not her school things. A cloudy blue outfit that made one think of forget-me-nots and wood-smoke and bluebells and summer distances, and was further calculated to bedevil the judgment of sober men. Her young and simple and very-well-brought-up hat stood back from her face and showed the charming brow and the wide-set eyes. Robert absolved Mrs. Wynn, without even having to consider the matter, from any conscious dressing of the girl for the occasion, but was bitterly aware that if she had lain awake at nights devising the outfit it could not have served its purpose better.

When her name was called and she walked to the witness stand, he stole a glance at the faces of those who could see her clearly. With the sole exception of Ben Carley—who was looking at her with the interest one accords a museum exhibit—there was only one expression on the faces of the men: a sort of affectionate compassion. The women, he observed, had not surrendered so easily. The more motherly ones obviously yearned to her youth and her vulnerability, but the younger ones were merely avid; without emotion other than curiosity.

"I—don't—believe—it!" Ben said, *sotto voce*, while she was taking the oath. "You mean that child was on the loose for a month? I don't believe she's ever kissed anything but the book!"

"I'll bring witnesses to prove it," muttered Robert, angry that even the worldly and cynical Carley was succumbing.

"You could bring ten irreproachable witnesses and still not get a jury to believe it; and it's the jury who count, my friend."

Yes, what jury would believe any bad of her!

Watching her as she was led through her story, he reminded himself of Albert's account of her: the "nicely brought-up girl" whom no one would have thought of as a woman at all, and the cool expertness with which she attached the man she had chosen.

She had a very pleasant voice; young and light and clear; without accent or affectation. And she told her tale like a model witness; volunteering no extras, explicit in what she did say. The pressmen could hardly keep their eyes on their shorthand. The Bench was obviously doting. (God send there was something tougher at the Assizes!) The members of the police force were gently perspiring in sympathy. The body of the court breathless and motionless.

No actress had ever had a better reception.

She was quite calm, as far as anyone could see; and apparently unaware of the effect she was having. She made no effort to make a point, or to use a piece of information dramatically. And Robert found himself wondering whether the understatement was deliberate and whether she realised quite clearly how effective it was.

"And did you in fact mend the linen?"

"I was too stiff from the beating, that night. But I mended some later."

Just as if she were saying: "I was too busy playing bridge." It gave an extraordinary air of truth to what she said.

Nor was there any sign of triumph in the account of her vindication. She had said this and that about the place of her imprisonment, and this and that had proved to be so. But she showed no overt pleasure in the fact. When she was asked if she recognised the women in the dock, and if they were in fact the women who had detained and beaten her, she looked at them gravely for a moment of silence and then said that she did and they were.

"Do you want to examine, Mr. Blair?"

"No, sir. I have no questions."

This caused a slight stir of surprise and disappointment in the body of the court, who had looked forward to drama; but it was accepted by the initiates without remark; it was taken for granted that the case would go forward to another court.

Hallam had already given his statement, and the girl was now followed by the corroborative witnesses.

The man who had seen her picked up by the car proved to be a Post Office sorter called Piper. He worked on a postal van which the L.M.S. ran between Larborough and London, and he was dropped off at Mainshill station on the return journey because it was near his home. He was walking up the long straight London road through Mainshill, when he noticed that a young girl was waiting at the stop for the London coaches. He was still a long distance from her but he noticed her because the London coach had overtaken him about half a minute previously, before he had come within sight of the bus stop; and when he saw her waiting there he realised that she must just have missed it. While he was walking towards her but still some distance away, a car overtook him at a good pace. He did not even glance at it because his interest was concentrated on the girl and on whether when he came up with her he should stop and tell her that the London bus had passed. Then he saw the car slow down alongside the girl. She bent forward to talk to whoever was in it, and then got in herself and was driven away.

By this time he was near enough to describe the car but not to read the number. He had not thought of reading the number anyhow. He was merely glad that the girl had got a lift so quickly.

He would not take an oath that the girl in question was the girl he had seen give evidence, but he was certain in his own mind. She had worn a palish coat and hat—grey he thought—and black slippers.

Slippers?

Well, those shoes with no straps across the instep.

Court shoes.

Well, court shoes, but he called them slippers. (And had every intention, his tone made it clear, of going on calling them slippers.)

"Do you want to examine, Mr. Blair?"

"No, thank you, sir."

Then came Rose Glyn.

Robert's first impression was of the vulgar perfection of her teeth. They reminded him of a false set made by a not very clever dentist. There surely never had been, never could be, any natural teeth as flashily perfect as those Rose Glyn had produced as substitutes for her milk teeth.

The Bench did not like her teeth either, it seemed, and Rose soon stopped smiling. But her tale was lethal enough. She had been in the habit of going to The Franchise every Monday to clean the house. On a Monday in April she had been there as usual, and was preparing to leave in the evening when she heard screaming coming from upstairs somewhere. She thought something had happened to Mrs. or Miss Sharpe and ran to the foot of the stairs to see. The screaming seemed to be far away, as if it came from the attic. She was going to go upstairs, but Mrs. Sharpe came out of the drawing-room and asked her what she was doing. She said someone was screaming upstairs. Mrs. Sharpe said nonsense, that she was imagining things, and wasn't it time that she was going home. The screaming had stopped then, and while Mrs. Sharpe was talking Miss Sharpe came downstairs. Miss Sharpe went with Mrs. Sharpe into the drawing-room, and Mrs. Sharpe said something about "ought to be more careful." She was frightened, she did not quite know why, and went away to the kitchen and took her money from where it was always left for her on the kitchen mantelpiece, and ran from the house. The date was April the 15th. She remembered the date because she had decided that next time she went back, on the following Monday, she would give the Sharpes her week's notice; and she had in fact done that, and had not worked for the Sharpes since Monday April the 29th.

Robert was faintly cheered by the bad impression she was patently making on everyone. Her open delight in the dramatic,

179

her Christmas Supplement glossiness, her obvious malice, and her horrible clothes, were unhappily contrasted with the restraint and good sense and good taste of her predecessor in the witness box. From the expressions on the faces of her audience she was summed up as a slut and no one would trust her with sixpence.

But that did nothing to discount the evidence she had just given on oath.

Robert, letting her go, wondered if there was any way of pinning that watch on her, so to speak. Being a country girl, unversed in the ways of pawnshops, it was unlikely that she had stolen that watch to sell it; she had taken it to keep for herself. That being so, was there perhaps some way of convicting her of theft and so discrediting her evidence to that extent?

She was succeeded by her friend Gladys Rees. Gladys was as small and pale and skinny as her friend was opulent. She was scared and ill at ease, and took the oath hesitatingly. Her accent was so broad that even the Court found difficulty in following her, and the prosecution had several times to translate her wilder flights of English into something nearer common speech. But the gist of her evidence was clear. On the evening of Monday the 15th April she had gone walking with her friend, Rose Glyn. No, not anywhere special, just walking after supper. Up to High Wood and back. And Rose Glyn had told her that she was scared of The Franchise because she had heard someone screaming in an upstairs room, although there was supposed not to be anyone there. She, Gladys, knew that it was Monday the 15th that Rose had told her that, because Rose had said that when she went next week she was going to give notice. And she had given notice and had not worked for the Sharpes since Monday the 29th.

"I wonder what dear Rose has got on her," Carley said, as she left the witness box.

"What makes you think she has anything?"

"People don't come and perjure themselves for friendship; not even country morons like Gladys Rees. The poor silly little rat was frightened stiff. She would never have come voluntarily. No, that oleograph has a lever of some sort. Worth looking into if you're stuck, perhaps."

"Do you happen to know the number of your watch?" he

asked Marion as he was driving them back to The Franchise. "The one Rose Glyn stole."

"I didn't even know that watches had numbers," Marion said.

"Good ones do."

"Oh, mine was a good one, but I don't know anything about its number. It was very distinctive, though. It had a pale blue enamel face with gold figures."

"Roman figures?"

"Yes. Why do you ask? Even if I got it back I could never bear to wear it after that girl."

"It wasn't so much getting it back I thought of, as convicting her of having taken it."

"That would be nice."

"Ben Carley calls her 'the oleograph,' by the way."

"How lovely. That is just what she is like. Is that the little man you wanted to push us off on to, that first day?"

"That's the one."

"I am so glad that I refused to be pushed."

"I hope you will still be as glad when this case is over," Robert said, suddenly sober.

"We have not yet thanked you for standing surety for our bail," Mrs. Sharpe said from the back of the car.

"If we began to thank him for all we owe him," Marion said, "there would be no end to it."

Except, he thought, that he had enlisted Kevin Macdermott on their side—and that was an accident of friendship—what had he been able to do for them? They would go for trial at Norton little more than a fortnight hence, and they had no defence whatever.

* * *

· 18 ·

THE newspapers had a field-day on Tuesday.

Now that the Franchise affair was a court case, it could no longer provide a crusade for either the *Ack-Emma* or the *Watch-man*—though the *Ack-Emma* did not fail to remind its gratified readers that on such and such a date *they* had said so and so, a plain statement which was on the surface innocent and unexceptionable but was simply loaded with the forbidden comment; and Robert had no doubt that on Friday the *Watchman* would be taking similar credit to itself, with similar discretion. But the rest of the Press, who had not so far taken any interest in a case that the police had no intention of touching, woke with a glad shout to report a case that was news. Even the soberer dailies held accounts of the court appearance of the Sharpes, with headings like: EXTRAORDINARY CASE, and: UNUSUAL CHARGE. The less inhibited had full descriptions of the principal actors in the case, including Mrs. Sharpe's hat and Betty Kane's blue outfit, pictures of The Franchise, the High Street in Milford, a school friend of Betty Kane, and anything else that was even approximately relevant.

And Robert's heart sank. Both the *Ack-Emma* and the *Watchman*, in their different ways, had used the Franchise affair as a stunt. Something to be used for its momentary worth and dropped tomorrow. But now it was a national interest, reported by every kind of paper from Cornwall to Caithness; and showed signs of becoming a *cause célèbre*.

For the first time he had a feeling of desperation. Events were hounding him, and he had no refuge. The thing was beginning to pile up into a tremendous climax at Norton and he had nothing to contribute to that climax; nothing at all. He felt as a man might feel if he saw a stacked heap of loaded crates begin to lean over towards him and had neither retreat nor a prop to stay the avalanche.

Ramsden grew more and more monosyllabic on the telephone, and less and less encouraging. Ramsden was sore. "Baffled" was a word used in boys' detective stories; it had not until now had even the remotest connection with Alec Ramsden. So Ramsden was sore, monosyllabic, and dour.

The one bright spot in the days that followed the court at Milford was provided by Stanley, who tapped on his door on Thursday morning, poked his head in, and seeing that Robert was alone came in, pushing the door to with one hand and fishing in the pocket of his dungarees with the other.

"Morning," he said. "I think you ought to take charge of these. Those women at The Franchise have no sense at all. They keep pound notes in tea-pots and books and what not. If you're looking for a telephone number you're as likely as not to find a ten-shilling note marking the butcher's address." He fished out a roll of money and solemnly counted twelve ten-pound notes on to the desk under Robert's nose.

"A hundred and twenty," he said. "Nice, ain't it?"

"But what *is* it?" Robert asked, bewildered.

"Kominsky."

"Kominsky?"

"Don't tell me you didn't have anything on! After the old lady giving us the tip herself. Mean to say you *forgot* about it!"

"Stan, I haven't even remembered lately that there was such a thing as the Guineas. So you backed it?"

"At sixties. And that's the tenth I told her she was on to, for the tip."

"But—a tenth? You must have been plunging, Stan."

"Twenty pounds. Twice as much as my normal ceiling. Bill did a bit of good too. Going to give his missus a fur coat."

"So Kominsky won."

"Won by a length and a half on a tight rein; and was that a turn up for the book!"

"Well," Robert said, stacking the notes and banding them, "if the worst comes to the worst and they end up bankrupt, the old lady can always do a fair trade as a tipster."

Stanley eyed his face for a moment in silence, apparently not happy about something in his tone. "Things are pretty bad, 'm?" he said.

"Fierce," said Robert, using one of Stanley's own descriptions.

"Bill's missus went to the court," Stan said, after a pause. "She said she wouldn't believe that girl even if she told her there were twelve pennies in a shilling."

"Oh?" Robert said, surprised. "Why?"

"Much too good to be true, she said she was. She said no girl of fifteen was ever as good as that."

"She's sixteen now."

"All right, sixteen. She said she was fifteen once and so were all her girl friends, and that wide-eyed-wonder didn't fool her for a moment."

"I'm very much afraid it will fool a jury."

183

"Not if you had an all-woman jury. I suppose there's no way of wangling that?"

"Not short of Herod measures. Don't you want to give this money to Mrs. Sharpe yourself, by the way?"

"Not me. You'll be going out there sometime today, and you can give it to her if you like. But see you get it back and put it in the bank or they'll be picking it out of flower vases years hence and wondering when they put that there."

Robert smiled as he put the money away in his pocket to the sound of Stanley's departing feet. Endlessly unexpected, people were. He would have taken it for granted that Stan would have revelled in counting those notes out in front of the old lady. But instead he had turned shy. That tale of money in tea-pots was just a tale.

Robert took the money out to The Franchise in the afternoon, and for the first time saw tears in Marion's eyes. He told the tale as Stanley had told it—tea-pots and all—and finished: "So he made me his deputy"; and it was then that Marion's eyes had filled.

"Why did he mind about giving it to us?" she said, fingering the notes. "He's not usually so—so——"

"I think it may be that he considers that you need it now, and that that makes it a delicate affair instead of a matter-of-fact one. When you gave him the tip you were just the well-off Sharpes who lived at The Franchise, and he would have turned over the proceeds to you with éclat. But now you are two women out on bail of £200 each in your personal recognizances and of a similar sum by one surety on behalf of you each; to say nothing of having the expenses of a counsel to come; and are therefore, I think, in Stan's mind not people that one can hand over money to easily."

"Well," said Mrs. Sharpe, "not all my tips have had a margin of a length-and-a-half on the right side. But I don't deny that I am very glad to see the percentage. It was very kind of the boy."

"Should we keep as much as ten per cent?" Marion asked doubtfully.

"That was the arrangement," Mrs. Sharpe said equably. "If it hadn't been for me he would be short by the amount of a bet on Bali Boogie at this moment. What *is* a Bali Boogie, by the way?"

184

"I am glad you came," Marion said, ignoring her mother's quest for education, "because something unexpected has happened. My watch has come back."

"You mean you've found it?"

"No, oh, no. She sent it back through the post. Look!"

She produced a small, very dirty, white cardboard box, which contained her watch with the blue enamel face and the wrapping that had been round the watch. The wrapping was a square of pinkish tissue paper with a circular stamp reading SUN VALLEY, TRANSVAAL, and had evidently started life embracing an orange. On a torn piece of paper was printed: I DON'T WANT NONE OF IT. The capital I was dotted like a small letter, after the fashion of illiterates.

"Why do you think she turned squeamish about it?" Marion wondered.

"I don't for a moment think she did," Robert said. "I couldn't imagine that girl ever relinquishing anything that her hand had closed over."

"But she did. She sent it back."

"No. Someone sent it back. Someone who was frightened. Someone with a rudimentary conscience, too. If Rose Glyn had wanted to be rid of it she would have thrown it into a pond, without a second thought. But X wants to be rid of it and to make restitution at the same time. X has both a bad conscience and a frightened soul. Now who would have a bad conscience about you just now? Gladys Rees?"

"Yes, of course you are right about Rose. I should have thought of that. She never would have sent it back. She would have put her heel on it sooner. You think perhaps she gave it to Gladys Rees?"

"That might explain a lot. It might explain how Rose got her to court to back up that 'screaming' story. I mean, if she had been the receiver of stolen goods. When you come to think of it, Rose could have very little chance of wearing a watch that the Staples people must quite often have seen on your wrist. It is much more likely that she was 'large' with it in favour of her friend. 'A little thing I picked up.' Where does the Rees girl belong to?"

"I don't know where she belongs to; somewhere the other side of the county, I think. But she has come to work for that isolated farm beyond Staples."

"Long ago?"

"I don't know. I don't think so."

"So she could wear a new watch without question. Yes, I think it was Gladys who sent back your watch. If ever there was an unwilling witness it was Gladys on Monday. And if Gladys is shakeable to the point of sending back your property, a faint hope begins to dawn."

"But she has committed perjury," Mrs. Sharpe said. "Even a moron like Gladys Rees must have some glimmering of awareness that that is not well seen in a British court."

"She could plead that she was blackmailed into it. If someone suggested that course to her."

Mrs. Sharpe eyed him. "Isn't there anything in English law about tampering with a witness?" she asked.

"Plenty. But I don't propose to do any tampering."

"What do you propose to do?"

"I must think it over. It is a delicate situation."

"Mr. Blair, the intricacies of the Law have always been beyond me, and are always likely to be, but you won't get yourself put away for contempt of court, or something like that, will you? I can't imagine what the present situation would be like without your support."

Robert said that he had no intention of getting himself put away for anything. That he was a blameless solicitor of unblemished reputation and high moral principles and that she need have no fear either for herself or for him.

"If we could knock the prop of Gladys Rees from under Rose's story it would undermine their whole case," he said. "It's their most valuable piece of evidence: that Rose had mentioned the screaming before there was any suggestion of a charge against you. I suppose you couldn't see Grant's face when Rose was giving evidence? A fastidious mind must be a great handicap in the C.I.D. It must be sad to have your whole case depend on someone you would hate to touch with a barge-pole. Now I must be getting back. May I take the little cardboard box and the scrap of paper with the printing?"

186

"It was clever of you to have seen that Rose would not have sent it back," Marion said, putting the scrap of paper into the box and giving it to him. "You should have been a detective."

"Either that or a fortune-teller. Everything deduced from the egg-stain on the waistcoat. *Au revoir*."

Robert drove back to Milford with his mind full of this new possibility. It was no solution to their predicament, but it might be a lifeline.

In the office he found Mr. Ramsden waiting for him; long, grey, lean, and dour.

"I came to see you, Mr. Blair, because it wasn't a thing that could be said over the telephone very well."

"Well?"

"Mr. Blair, we're wasting your money. Do you happen to know what the white population of the world is?"

"No, I don't."

"Neither do I. But what you're asking me to do is to pick this girl out of the white population of the world. Five thousand men working for a year mightn't do it. One man might do it tomorrow. It's a matter of pure chance."

"But it always has been that."

"No. In the first days the chances were fair. We covered the obvious places. The ports, the airports, the travel places, the best known 'honeymoon' places. And I didn't waste your time or money in any travelling. I have contacts in all the big towns and in a lot of the smaller ones, and I just send them a request saying: 'Find out if such and such a person stayed at one of your hotels,' and the answer is back in a few hours. Answers from all over Britain. Well, that done, we are left with a small proposition called the rest of the world. And I don't like wasting your money, Mr. Blair. Because that is what it will amount to."

"Do I understand that you are giving up?"

"I don't put it like that, exactly."

"You think I should give you notice because you have failed."
Mr. Ramsden stiffened noticeably at the word "failed."

"It's throwing good money away on a long chance. It isn't a business proposition, Mr. Blair. It isn't even a good gamble."

"Well, I have something for your consideration that is definite

187

enough to please you, I think." He fished the little cardboard box out of his pocket. "One of the witnesses on Monday was a girl called Gladys Rees. Her role was to supply evidence that her friend Rose Glyn had talked to her about screams at The Franchise long before the police were interested in the place. Well, she supplied the evidence all right, but not *con amore*, as you might say. She was nervous, unwilling, and was obviously hating it—in contrast to her friend Rose who was having the time of her life. One of my local colleagues suggested that Rose had got her there by pressure, but that didn't seem very likely at the time. This morning, however, the watch that Rose stole from Miss Sharpe came back by post in this box, with the printed message enclosed. Now Rose would never have bothered to return the watch; she has no conscience at all. Nor would she have written the note; having no desire to repudiate anything. The conclusion is inescapable, that it was Gladys who received the watch—Rose could not have worn it without detection anyhow—and that that was how Rose got her to back up her lies."

He paused to let Ramsden comment. Mr. Ramsden nodded; but it was an interested nod.

"Now we can't approach Gladys with any kind of argument without being accused of intimidating witnesses. I mean, getting her to go back on her story before the Assizes is not possible. All we can do is to concentrate on breaking her down at the Assizes. Kevin Macdermott could probably do it by force of personality and persistent questions, but I doubt it; and anyhow the Court might stop him before he had achieved anything. They are apt to look sideways on him when he begins to ride a witness."

"They are?"

"What I want to do is to be able to put this printed scrap into court as evidence. To be able to say that it is Gladys Rees's writing. With the evidence that it was she who had the stolen watch, we make the suggestion that Rose used pressure on her to testify to what is not true, Macdermott assures her that if she was blackmailed into giving false evidence she will probably not be punished for it, and she breaks down and confesses."

"So you want another specimen of Gladys Rees's printing."

"Yes. And coming along just now I was thinking about it. I

have the impression that her present job is her first one, so it can't be very long since she left school. Perhaps her school could furnish one. Or anyhow, provide a starting-off place. It would be enormously to our advantage if we could come by a specimen without *provocateur* methods. Do you think you could do something about it?"

"I'll get you a specimen, yes," Ramsden said; as who should say: Give me any reasonable commission and it will be executed. "Did the Rees girl go to school here?"

"No, I understand she comes from the other side of the county."

"All right, I'll find out. Where is she working now?"

"At an isolated place called Bratt's Farm; over the fields from Staples, the place behind The Franchise."

"And about the search for the Kane girl——"

"Isn't there anything you could still do in Larborough itself? I can't teach you anything about your business, I know that, but she *was* in Larborough."

"Yes, and where she was we traced her. In public places. But X may *live* in Larborough, for all we know. She may just have gone to ground there. After all, a month—or practically a month—is an odd time for that sort of disappearance, Mr. Blair. That sort of thing usually ranges from a week-end to ten days but not longer. She may just have gone home with him."

"Do you think that is what happened?"

"No," Ramsden said slowly. "If you want my honest opinion, Mr. Blair, it is that we have missed her at one of the exits."

"Exits?"

"That she went out of the country, but looking so different that that butter-wouldn't-melt photograph didn't convey her at all."

"Why different?"

"Well, I don't suppose she was provided with a phoney passport, so she would presumably travel as his wife."

"Yes, of course. I took that for granted."

"And she couldn't do that looking as she does. But with her hair swept up and some make-up on, she would look quite different. You have no idea the difference sweeping-up hair-dressing makes to a woman. The first time I saw my wife with one I didn't recognise her. It made her so different, if you want to know, that

189

I felt quite shy with her; and we'd been married twenty years."

"So that's what you think happened. I expect you're right," Robert said sadly.

"That's why I don't want to waste any more of your money, Mr. Blair. Looking for the girl in the photograph is not much use, because the girl we're looking for didn't look a bit like that. When she *did* look like that, people recognised her at first glance. At the cinemas and what not. We traced her easily enough during her time on her own in Larborough. But from then on it's a complete blank. Her photograph doesn't convey her to anyone who saw her after she left Larborough."

Robert sat doodling on Miss Tuff's nice fresh blotting-paper. A herring-bone pattern; very neat and decorative. "You see what this means, don't you? We are sunk."

"But you have this," Ramsden protested, indicating the printed scrap of paper that had come with the watch.

"That merely destroys the police case. It doesn't disprove Betty Kane's story. If the Sharpes are ever to be rid of this thing the girl's story has to be shown to be nonsense. Our only chance of doing that is to find out where she was during those weeks."

"Yes. I see."

"I suppose you have checked on private owners?"

"Planes? Oh, yes. The same thing goes there. We have no photograph of the man, so he might be any one of the hundreds of private owners who went abroad with female companions in the specified time."

"Yes. Pretty well sunk. Not much wonder Ben Carley was amused."

"You're tired, Mr. Blair. You've been having a worrying time."

"Yes. It isn't very often a country solicitor has something like this dumped on his shoulders," Robert said wryly.

Ramsden regarded him with what amounted on the Ramsden visage to a smile. "For a country solicitor," he said, "it seems to me you're not doing badly, Mr. Blair. Not badly at all."

"Thanks," Robert said, really smiling. Coming from Alec Ramsden that was practically an O.M.

"I shouldn't let it get you down. You've got an insurance against the very worst happening—or will, when I get that printed evidence."

Robert flung down the pen he had been doodling with. "I'm not interested in insurance," he said with sudden heat. "I'm interested in justice. I have only one ambition in life at this moment. And that is to have Betty Kane's story disproved in open court. To have the full account of what she did during those weeks made public in her presence and duly backed up by irreproachable witnesses. What are our chances of that, do you think? And what —tell me—what have we left untried that could possibly help us?"

"I don't know," Mr. Ramsden said, seriously. "Prayer, perhaps."

~~~~~~

· 19 ·

THIS, oddly enough, was also Aunt Lin's reaction.

Aunt Lin had become gradually reconciled to Robert's connection with the Franchise affair as it moved from the provincial-unsavoury to the national-celebrated. It was, after all, no disgrace to be connected with a case that was reported in *The Times*. Aunt Lin did not, of course, read *The Times*, but her friends did. The vicar, and old Colonel Whittaker, and the girl at Boots and old Mrs. Warren from Weymouth (Swanage); and it was vaguely gratifying to think that Robert should be solicitor for the defence in a famous trial, even if the defence was against a charge of beating a helpless girl. And of course it had never even remotely shadowed her mind that Robert would not win the case. She had taken that quite placidly for granted. In the first place Robert himself was so clever; and in the second Blair, Hayward, and Bennet could not conceivably be connected with a failure. She had even regretted in her own mind, in passing, that his triumph would take place over at Norton and not in Milford where everyone might be there to see.

So that the first hint of doubt came as a surprise to her. Not a shock, since she still could not visualise the prospect of failure. But definitely as a new thought.

"But, Robert," she said, sweeping her foot round under the table in an effort to locate her footstool, "you don't suppose for a moment that you are going to *lose* the case, do you?"

"On the contrary," Robert said, "I don't suppose for a moment that we shall win it."

"Robert!"

"In trial by jury it is customary to have a case to put to the jury. So far we have no case. And I don't think that the jury is going to like that at all."

"You sound quite pettish, dear. I think you are allowing the thing to get on your nerves. Why don't you take tomorrow afternoon off and arrange a golf four? You have hardly golfed at all lately and it can't be good for your liver. Not golfing, I mean."

"I can't believe," Robert said wonderingly, "that I was ever interested in the fate of 'a piece of gutta-percha' on a golf course. That must have been in some other life."

"That is what I say, dear. You are losing your sense of proportion. Allowing this affair to worry you quite unnecessarily. After all, you have Kevin."

"That I take leave to doubt."

"What do you mean, dear?"

"I can't imagine Kevin taking time off and travelling down to Norton to defend a case that he is fore-ordained to lose. He has his quixotic moments, but they don't entirely obliterate his common sense."

"But Kevin promised to come."

"When he made that promise there was still time for a defence to materialise. Now we can almost count the days to the Assizes and still we have no evidence—and no prospect of any."

Miss Bennet eyed him over her soup spoon. "I don't think, you know, dear," she said, "that you have enough faith."

Robert refrained from saying that he had none at all. Not, anyhow, where divine intervention in the Franchise affair was concerned.

"Have faith, my dear," she said happily, "and it will all come right. You'll see." The charged silence that succeeded this evidently worried her a little, for she added: "If I had known you were doubtful or unhappy about the case, dear, I should have said extra prayers about it long ago. I am afraid I took it for granted

192

that you and Kevin would manage it between you." "It" being British justice. "But now that I know you are worrying about it I shall most certainly put up some special petitions."

The matter-of-fact application-for-relief tone with which this was uttered restored Robert's good humour.

"Thank you, darling," he said in his normal good-natured voice.

She laid the spoon down on her empty plate and sat back; and a small teasing smile appeared on her round pink face. "I know that tone," she said. "It means that you're humouring me. But there's no need to, you know. It's I who am right about this, and you are wrong. It says quite distinctly that faith will move mountains. The difficulty always is that it takes a quite colossal faith to move a mountain; and it is practically impossible to assemble so large a faith, so mountains are practically never moved. But in lesser cases—like the present one—it is possible to have enough faith for the occasion. So instead of being deliberately hopeless, dear, do *try* to have some confidence in the event. Meanwhile I shall go along to St. Matthew's this evening and spend a little time praying that you will be given a piece of evidence tomorrow morning. That will make you feel happier."

When Alec Ramsden walked into his room next morning with the piece of evidence, Robert's first thought was that nothing could prevent Aunt Lin taking credit for it. Nor was there any hope of his not mentioning it, since the first thing she would ask him at luncheon, in bright confident tones, would be: "Well, dear, did you get the evidence I prayed for?"

Ramsden was both pleased with himself and amused; so much could be translated, at any rate, from the Ramsden idiom into common knowledge.

"I had better confess frankly, Mr. Blair, that when you sent me to that school I had no great hopes. I went because it seemed to be as good a starting-place as any, and I might find out from the staff some good way of getting acquainted with Rees. Or rather, letting one of my boys get acquainted. I had even worked out how we could get printed letters from her without any fuss, once one of my boys got off with her. But you're a wonder, Mr. Blair. You had the right idea after all."

"You mean you've got what we wanted!"

"I saw her form mistress, and was quite frank about what we wanted and why. Well, as frank as need be. I said Gladys was suspected of perjury—a penal servitude affair—but that we thought she'd been blackmailed into giving her evidence, and to prove it was blackmail we needed a sample of any printed letters she ever wrote. Well, when you sent me there I took it for granted that she would not have printed a single letter since she left the kindergarten. But the form mistress—a Miss Baggaly—said to give her a minute to think. 'Of course,' she said, 'she was very good at drawing, and if I have nothing perhaps the visiting art-mistress might have something. We like to keep good work when our pupils produce it.' As a comfort for all the duds they have to put up with, I suppose, poor things. Well, I didn't have to see the art-mistress, because Miss Baggaly hunted through some things, and produced this."

He laid a sheet of paper down on the desk in front of Robert. It appeared to be a free-hand map of Canada, showing the principal divisions, towns and rivers. It was inaccurate but very neat. Across the bottom was printed DOMINION OF CAN-ADA. And in the right-hand corner was the signature: Gladys Rees.

"It seems that every summer, at breaking-up time, they have an exhibition of work, and they normally keep the exhibits until the next exhibition the following year. I suppose it would seem too callous just to toss them out the day after. Or perhaps they keep them to show to visiting big-wigs and inspectors. Anyhow, there were drawers full of the stuff. This," he indicated the map, "was a product of a competition—'Draw a map of any country from memory in twenty minutes'—and the three prize winners had their answers exhibited. This was a 'third equal'."

"I can hardly believe it," Robert said, feasting his eyes on Gladys Rees's handiwork.

"Miss Baggaly was right about her being good with her hands. Funny, when she stayed so illiterate. You can see where they corrected her dotted Capital I's."

You could indeed. Robert was gloating over the place.

"She has no mind, the girl, but a good eye," he said, considering Gladys's idea of Canada. "She remembered the shape of things but not the names. And the spelling is entirely her own. I suppose the 'third equal' was for the neat work."

"Neat work for us anyhow," Ramsden said, laying down the scrap of paper that had come with the watch. "Let us be thankful she didn't choose Alaska."

"Yes," Robert said. "A miracle." (Aunt Lin's miracle, his mind said.) "Who is the best man at this sort of thing?"

Ramsden told him.

"I'll take it up to town with me now, tonight, and have the report before morning, and I'll take it round to Mr. Macdermott at breakfast time, if that's all right with you."

"Right?" said Robert. "It's perfect."

"I think it might be a good idea to finger-print them too—and the little cardboard box. There *are* judges who don't like hand-writing experts, but the two together would convince even a judge."

"Well," Robert said, handing them over, "at least my clients are not going to be sentenced to hard labour."

"There's nothing like looking on the bright side," Ramsden commented dryly; and Robert laughed.

"You think I'm ungrateful for such a dispensation. I'm not. It's a terrific load off my mind. But the real load is still there. Proving that Rose Glyn is a thief, liar, and blackmailer—with perjury thrown in as a sideline—leaves Betty Kane's story still untouched. And it is Betty Kane's story that we set out to disprove."

"There's still time," Ramsden said; but half-heartedly.

"About all there is time for is a miracle."

"Well? Why not? They happen. Why shouldn't they happen to us? What time shall I telephone you tomorrow?"

But it was Kevin who telephoned on the morrow; full of congratulations and jubilation. "You're a marvel, Rob. I'll make mincemeat of them."

Yes, it would be a lovely little exercise in cat-and-mouse play for Kevin; and the Sharpes would walk out of the court "free." Free to go back to their haunted house and their haunted existence; two half-mad witches who had once threatened and beaten a girl.

"You don't sound very gay, Rob. Is it getting you down?"

Robert said what he was thinking; that the Sharpes saved from prison would still be in a prison of Betty Kane's making.

"Perhaps not, perhaps not," Kevin said. "I'll do my best with the Kane over that howler about the divided path. Indeed, if Miles Allison weren't prosecuting I could probably break her with it; but Miles will probably be quick enough to retrieve the situation. Cheer up, Rob. At the very least her credit will be seriously shaken."

But shaking Betty Kane's credit was not enough. He knew just how little effect that would have on the general public. He had had a large experience lately of the woman-in-the-street, and had been appalled by the general inability to analyse the simplest statement. Even if the newspapers were to report that small bit about the view from the window—and they would probably be much too busy reporting the more sensational matter of Rose Glyn's perjury—even if they reported it, it would have no effect on the average reader. "They tried to put her in the wrong but they were very quickly put in their place." That is all it would convey to them.

Kevin might successfully shake Betty Kane's credit with the Court, the reporters, the officials, and any critical minds who happened to be present; but on the present evidence he could do nothing to alter the strong feeling of partisanship that Betty Kane's case had aroused throughout the country. The Sharpes would stay condemned.

And Betty Kane would "get away with it."

That to Robert was a thought that was even worse than the prospect of the Sharpes' haunted life. Betty Kane would go on being the centre of an adoring family; secure, loved, hero-worshipped. The once easy-going Robert grew homicidal at the thought.

He had had to confess to Aunt Lin that a piece of evidence had turned up at the time specified in her prayers, but had pusillanimously refrained from telling her that the said evidence was good enough to destroy the police case. She would call that winning the case; and "winning," to Robert, meant something very different.

To Nevil too, it seemed. And for the first time since young

Bennet came to occupy the back room that used to be his, Robert thought of him as an ally; a communal spirit. To Nevil, too, it was unthinkable that Betty Kane should "get away with it." And Robert was surprised all over again at the murderous rage that fills the pacifist-minded when their indignation is roused. Nevil had a special way of saying "Betty Kane": as if the syllables were some poison he had put in his mouth by mistake and he was spitting it out. "Poisonous," too, was his favourite epithet for her. "That poisonous creature." Robert found him very comforting.

But there was little comfort in the situation. The Sharpes had accepted the news of their probable escape from a prison sentence with the same dignity that had characterised their acceptance of everything, from Betty Kane's first accusation to the serving of a summons and an appearance in the dock. But they, too, realised that the thing would be escape but not vindication. The police case would break down, and they would get their verdict. But they would get it because in English law there was no middle course. In a Scots court the verdict would be Not Proven. And that, in fact, would be what the result of the Assizes verdict next week would amount to. Merely that the police had not had good enough evidence to prove their case. Not that the case was necessarily a bad one.

It was when the Assizes were only four days away that he confessed to Aunt Lin that the evidence did suffice to defeat the charge. The growing worry on that round pink face was too much for him. He had meant merely to give her that sop and leave the matter there; but instead he found himself pouring it all out to her as he had poured out his troubles as a small boy; in the days when Aunt Lin was an omniscient and omnipotent angel and not just kind, silly Aunt Lin. She listened to this unexpected torrent of words—so different from the normal phrases of their meal-time intercourse—in surprised silence, her jewel-blue eyes attentive and concerned.

"Don't you see, Aunt Lin, it isn't victory; it's defeat," he finished. "It's a travesty of justice. It isn't a verdict we're fighting for; it's justice. And we have no hope of getting it. Not a ghost of a hope!"

"But why didn't you tell me all this, dear? Did you think I would not understand, or agree, or something?"

"Well, you didn't feel as I did about——"

"Just because I didn't much like the look of those people at The Franchise—and I must confess, dear, even now, that they aren't the kind of people I naturally take to—just because I didn't much like them doesn't mean that I am indifferent to seeing justice done, surely?"

"No, of course not; but you said quite frankly that you found Betty Kane's story believable, and so——"

"That," said Aunt Lin calmly, "was before the police court."

"The court? But you weren't at the court."

"No, dear, but Colonel Whittaker was, and he didn't like the girl at all."

"Didn't he, indeed."

"No. He was quite eloquent about it. He said he had once had a—a what-do-you-call-it—a lance-corporal in his regiment, or battalion or something, who was exactly like Betty Kane. He said he was an injured innocent who set the whole battalion by the ears and was more trouble than a dozen hard-cases. Such a nice expression: hard-cases, isn't it. He finished up in the greenhouse, Colonel Whittaker said."

"The glasshouse."

"Well, something like that. And as for the Glyn girl from Staples, he said that one glance at her and you automatically began to reckon the number of lies there would be per sentence. He didn't like the Glyn girl either. So you see, dear, you needn't have thought that I would be unsympathetic about your worry. I am just as interested in abstract justice as you are, I assure you. And I shall redouble my prayers for your success. I was going over to the Gleasons' garden party this afternoon, but I shall go along to St. Matthew's instead and spend a quiet hour there. I think it is going to rain in any case. It always does rain at the Gleasons' garden party, poor things."

"Well, Aunt Lin, I don't deny we need your prayers. Nothing short of a miracle can save us now."

"Well, I shall pray for the miracle."

"A last-minute reprieve with the rope round the hero's neck?

198

That happens only in detective stories and the last few minutes of horse-operas."

"Not at all. It happens every day, somewhere in the world. If there was some way of finding out and adding up the times it happens you would no doubt be surprised. Providence does take a hand, you know, when other methods fail. You haven't enough faith, my dear, as I pointed out before."

"I don't believe that an angel of the Lord is going to appear in my office with an account of what Betty Kane was doing for that month, if that is what you mean," Robert said.

"The trouble with you, dear, is that you think of an angel of the Lord as a creature with wings, whereas he is probably a scruffy little man in a bowler hat. Anyhow, I shall pray very hard this afternoon, and tonight too, of course; and by tomorrow perhaps help will be sent."

~~~~~~

· 20 ·

The angel of the Lord was not a scruffy little man, as it turned out; and his hat was a regrettably continental affair of felt with a tightly rolled brim turned up all round. He arrived at Blair, Hayward, and Bennet's about half-past eleven the following morning.

"Mr. Robert," old Mr. Heseltine said, putting his head in at Robert's door, "there's a Mr. Lange in the office to see you. He——"

Robert, who was busy, and not expecting angels of the Lord, and quite used to strangers turning up in the office and wanting to see him, said: "What does he want? I'm busy."

"He didn't say. He just said he would like to see you if you were not too busy."

"Well, I'm scandalously busy. Find out tactfully what he wants, will you? If it is nothing important Nevil can deal with it."

"Yes, I'll find out; but his English is very thick, and he doesn't seem very willing to——"

"English? You mean, he has a lisp?"

"No, I mean his pronunciation of English isn't very good. He——"

"The man's a foreigner, you mean?"

"Yes. He comes from Copenhagen."

"Copenhagen! Why didn't you tell me that before!"

"You didn't give me a chance, Mr. Robert."

"Show him in, Timmy, show him in. Oh, merciful Heaven, do fairy-tales come true?"

Mr. Lange was rather like one of the Norman pillars of Notre Dame. Just as round, just as high, just as solid and just as dependable-looking. Far away at the top of this great round solid erect pillar his face shone with friendly rectitude.

"Mr. Blair?" he said. "My name is Lange. I apologise for bothering you"—he failed to manage the TH—"but it was important. Important to you, I mean. At least, yes I think."

"Sit down, Mr. Lange."

"Thank you, thank you. It is warm, is it not? This is perhaps the day you have your summer?" He smiled on Robert. "That is an idiom of the English, that joke about one-day summer. I am greatly interested in the English idiom. It is because of my interest in English idiom that I come to see you."

Robert's heart sank to his heels with the plummet swoop of an express lift. Fairy-tales, indeed. No; fairy-tales stay fairy-tales.

"Yes?" he said encouragingly.

"I keep a hotel in Copenhagen, Mr. Blair. The hotel of the Red Shoes it is called. Not, of course, because anyone wears red shoes there but because of a tale of Andersen, which you perhaps may——"

"Yes, yes," Robert said. "It has become one of our tales too."

"Ah, so! Yes. A great man, Andersen. So simple a man and now so international. It is a thing to marvel at. But I waste your time, Mr. Blair, I waste your time. What was I saying?"

"About English idiom."

"Ah, yes. To study English is my hubby."

"Hobby," Robert said, involuntarily.

"Hobby. Thank you. For my bread and butter I keep a hotel—and because my father and his father kept one before me—but for a hub . . . a hobby? yes; thank you—for a hobby I study the idiomatic English. So every day the newspapers that they leave about are brought to me."

"They?"

"The English visitors."

"Ah, yes."

"In the evening, when they have retired, the page collects the English papers and leaves them in my office. I am busy, often, and I do not have time to look at them, and so they go into the pile and when I have leisure I pick one up and study it. Do I make myself clear, Mr. Blair?"

"Perfectly, perfectly, Mr. Lange." A faint hope was rising again. Newspapers?

"So it goes on. A few moments of leisure, a little reading in an English paper, a new idiom—perhaps two—all very without excitement. How do you say that?"

"Placid."

"So. Placid. And then one day I take this paper from the pile, just as I might take any of the others, and I forget all about idiom." He took from his capacious pocket a once-folded copy of the *Ack-Emma*, and spread it in front of Robert on the desk. It was the issue of Friday, May the 10th, with the photograph of Betty Kane occupying two-thirds of the page. "I look at this photograph. Then I look inside and read the story. Then I say to myself that this is most extraordinary. Most extraordinary it is. The paper say this is the photograph of Betty Kann. Kann?"

"Kane."

"Ah. So. Betty Kane. But it is also the photograph of Mrs. Chadwick, who stay at my hotel with her husband."

"What!"

Mr. Lange looked pleased. "You are interested? I so hoped you might be. I did so hope."

"Go on. Tell me."

"A fortnight they stayed with me. And it was most extraordinary, Mr. Blair, because while that poor girl was being beaten and starved in an English attic, Mrs. Chadwick was eating like a young wolf at my hotel—the cream that girl could eat, Mr. Blair, even I, a Dane, was surprised—and enjoying herself very much."

"Yes?"

"Well, I said to myself: It is after all a photograph. And although it is just the way she looked when she let down her hair to come to the ball——"

"Let it down!"

"Yes. She wore her hair brushed up, you see. But we had a ball with costume—Costume?"

"Yes. Fancy dress."

"Ah. So. Fancy dress. And for her fancy dress she lets her hair hang down. Just like that there." He tapped the photograph. "So I say to myself: It is a photograph, after all. How often has one seen a photograph that does not in the least resemble the real person. And what has this girl in the paper to do, possibly, with little Mrs. Chadwick who is here with her husband during that time! So I am reasonable to myself. But I do not throw away the paper. No. I keep it. And now and then I look at it. And each time I look at it I think: But that *is* Mrs. Chadwick. So I am still puzzled, and going to sleep I think about it when I should be thinking about tomorrow's marketing. I seek explanation from myself. Twins, perhaps? But no; the Betty girl is an only child. Cousins. Coincidence. Doubles. I think of them all. At night they satisfy me, and I turn over and go to sleep. But in the morning I look at the photograph, and all comes to pieces again. I think: But certainly beyond a doubt that is Mrs. Chadwick. You see my dilemma?"

"Perfectly."

"So when I am coming to England on business, I put the newspaper with the Arabic name——"

"Arabic? Oh, yes, I see. I didn't mean to interrupt."

"I put it into my bag, and after dinner one night I take it out and show it to my friend where I am staying. I am staying with a compatriot of mine in Bayswater, London. And my friend is instantly very excited and say: But it is now a police affair, and these women say that never have they seen the girl before. They have been arrested for what they are supposed to have done to this girl and they are about to be tried for it. And he calls to his wife: 'Rita! Rita! Where is the paper of a week last Tuesday?' It is the kind of household, my friend's, where there is always a paper of a week last Tuesday. And his wife come with it and he shows me the account of the trial—no, the—the——"

"Court appearance."

"Yes. The appearance in court of the two women. And I read how the trial is to be at some place in the country in a little more

202

than a fortnight. Well, by now, that would be in a very few days. So my friend say: How sure are you, Einar, that that girl and your Mrs. Chadwick are one? And I say: Very sure indeed I am. So he say: Here in the paper is the name of the solicitor for the women. There is no address but this Milford is a very small place and he will be easy to find. We shall have coffee early tomorrow —that is breakfast—and you will go down to this Milford and tell what you think to this Mr. Blair. So here I am, Mr. Blair. And you are interested in what I say?"

Robert sat back, took out his handkerchief, and mopped his forehead. "Do you believe in miracles, Mr. Lange?"

"But of course. I am a Christian. Indeed, although I am not yet very old I have myself seen two."

"Well, you have just taken part in a third."

"So?" Mr. Lange beamed. "That makes me very content."

"You have saved our bacon."

"Bacon?"

"An English idiom. You have not only saved our bacon. You have practically saved our lives."

"You think, then, as I think, that they are one person, that girl and my guest at the Red Shoes?"

"I haven't a doubt of it. Tell me, have you the dates of her stay with you."

"Oh, yes, indeed. Here they are. She and her husband arrived by air on Friday the 29th of March, and they left—again by air, I think, though of that I am not so certain—on the 15th of April, a Monday."

"Thank you. And her 'husband,' what did he look like?"

"Young. Dark. Good-looking. A little—now, what is the word? Too-bright. Gaudy? No."

"Flashy?"

"Ah. There is it. Flashy. A little flashy, I think. I observe that he was not greatly approved of by the other Englishmen who came and went."

"Was he just on holiday?"

"No, oh, no. He was in Copenhagen on business."

"What kind of business?"

"That I do not know, I regret."

"Can't you even make a guess? What would he be most likely to be interested in in Copenhagen?"

"That depends, Mr. Blair, on whether he was interested in buying or selling."

"What was his address in England?"

"London."

"Beautifully explicit. Will you forgive me a moment while I telephone? Do you smoke?" He opened the cigarette box and pushed it towards Mr. Lange.

"Milford 195. You will do me the honour of having lunch with me, Mr. Lange, won't you? Aunt Lin? I have to go to London directly after lunch. . . . Yes, for the night. Will you be an angel and pack a small bag for me? . . . Thank you, darling. And would it be all right if I brought someone back to take pot-luck for lunch today? . . . Oh, good. . . . Yes, I'll ask him." He covered the mouthpiece, and said: "My aunt, who is actually my cousin, wants to know if you eat pastry?"

"Mr. Blair!" Mr. Lange said, with a wide smile and a wide gesture for his girth. "And you ask a Dane?"

"He loves it," Robert said into the telephone. "And I say, Aunt Lin. Were you doing anything important this afternoon? . . . Because what I think you ought to do is to go to St. Matthew's and give thanks . . . Your angel of the Lord has arrived."

Even Mr. Lange could hear Aunt Lin's delighted: *"Robert!* No, not really!"

"In the flesh. . . . No, not a bit scruffy . . . Very tall and beautiful and altogether perfect for the part. . . . You'll give him a good lunch, won't you? . . . Yes, that's who is coming to lunch. An angel of the Lord."

He put down the telephone and looked up at the amused Mr. Lange.

"And now, Mr. Lange, let us go over to the Rose and Crown and have some bad beer."

WHEN Robert went out to The Franchise, three days later, to drive the Sharpes over to Norton for the Assizes on the morrow,

he found an almost bridal atmosphere about the place. Two absurd tubs of yellow wallflowers stood at the top of the steps; and
the dark hall gleamed with flowers like a church decorated for a
wedding.

"Nevil!" Marion said, with an explanatory wave of her hand to
the massed glory. "He said the house should be *en fête*."

"I wish that I had thought of it," Robert said.

"After the last few days, it surprises me that you can think at
all. If it were not for you, it is not rejoicing we should be today!"

"If it weren't for a man called Bell, you mean."

"Bell?"

"Alexander Bell. He invented the telephone. If it weren't for
that invention we should still be groping in the dark. It will be
months before I can look at a telephone without blenching."

"Did you take turn about?"

"Oh, no. We each had our own. Kevin and his clerk at his
chambers, me at his little place in St. Paul's Churchyard, Alec
Ramsden and three of his men at his office and wherever they
could find a telephone that they could use uninterruptedly."

"That was six of you."

"Seven of us with six telephones. And we needed them!"

"Poor Robert!"

"At first it was fun. We were filled with the exhilaration of the
hunt, of knowing that we were on the right track. Success was
practically in our laps. But by the time we had made sure that
none of the Chadwicks in the London telephone book had any
connection with a Chadwick who had flown to Copenhagen on
the 29th of March, and that all the Air line knew about him was
that two seats had been booked from Larborough on the 27th,
we had lost any feeling of fun we had started with. The Larborough information cheered us, of course. But after that it was
pure slog. We found out what we sold to Denmark and what she
bought from us, and we divided them up between us."

"The merchandise?"

"No, the buyers and sellers. The Danish tourist office was a
god-send. They just poured information at us. Kevin, his clerk,
and I took the exports, and Ramsden and his men took the im-
ports. From then on it was a tedious business of being put through

to managers and asking: 'Have you a man called Bernard Chadwick working for you?' The number of firms who *haven't* got a Bernard Chadwick working for them is unbelievable. But I know a lot more about our exports to Denmark than I did before."

"I have no doubt of it!"

"I was so sick of the telephone that when it rang at my end I nearly didn't pick it up. I had almost forgotten that telephones were two-way. A telephone was just a sort of quiz instrument that I could plug into offices all over the country. I stared at it for quite a while before I realised that it was after all a mutual affair and that someone was trying to call me for a change."

"And it was Ramsden."

"Yes, it was Alec Ramsden. He said: 'We've got him. He buys porcelain and stuff for Brayne, Havard and Co.' "

"I am glad it was Ramsden who unearthed him. It will comfort him for his failure to run down the girl."

"Yes, he's feeling better about it now. After that it was a rush to interview the people we needed and to obtain subpoenas and what not. But the whole lovely result will be waiting for us in the court at Norton tomorrow. Kevin can hardly wait. His mouth waters at the prospect."

"If it was ever in my power to be sorry for that girl," Mrs. Sharpe said, coming in with an over-night bag and dumping it on a mahogany wall-table in a way that would have turned Aunt Lin faint, "it would be in a witness-box facing a hostile Kevin Macdermott." Robert noticed that the bag, which had originally been a very elegant and expensive one—a relic of her prosperous early married life, perhaps—was now deplorably shabby. He decided that when he married Marion his present to the bride's mother would be a dressing-case; small, light, elegant and expensive.

"It will never be in my power," Marion said, "to have even a passing sensation of sorrow for that girl. I would swat her off the earth's face as I would swat a moth in a cupboard—except that I am always sorry about the moth."

"What had the girl intended to do?" Mrs. Sharpe asked. "Had she intended to go back to her people at all?"

"I don't think so," Robert said. "I think she was still filled with rage and resentment at ceasing to be the centre of interest at 39

Meadowside Lane. It is as Kevin said long ago: crime begins in egotism; inordinate vanity. A normal girl, even an emotional adolescent, might be heart-broken that her adopted brother no longer considered her the most important thing in his life; but she would work it out in sobs, or sulks, or being difficult, or deciding that she was going to renounce the world and go into a convent, or half a dozen other methods that the adolescent uses in the process of adjustment. But with an egotism like Betty Kane's there is no adjustment. She expects the world to adjust itself to her. The criminal always does, by the way. There was never a criminal who didn't consider himself ill-done-by."

"A charming creature," Mrs. Sharpe said.

"Yes. Even the Bishop of Larborough would find some difficulty in thinking up a case for her. His usual 'environment' hobby-horse is no good this time. Betty Kane had everything that he recommends for the cure of the criminal: love, freedom to develop her talents, education, security. It's quite a poser for his lordship when you come to consider it, because he doesn't believe in heredity. He thinks that criminals are made, and therefore can be unmade. 'Bad blood' is just an old superstition, in the Bishop's estimation."

"Toby Byrne," Mrs. Sharpe said with a snort. "You should have heard Charles's stable lads on him."

"I've heard Nevil," Robert said. "I doubt if anyone could improve on Nevil's version of the subject."

"Is the engagement definitely broken, then?" Marion asked.

"Definitely. Aunt Lin has hopes of the eldest Whittaker girl. She is a niece of Lady Mountleven, and a grand-daughter of Karr's Krisps."

Marion laughed with him. "Is she nice, the Whittaker girl?" she asked.

"Yes. Fair, pretty, well-brought-up, musical but doesn't sing."

"I should like Nevil to get a nice wife. All he needs is some permanent interest of his own. A focus for his energies and his emotions."

"At the moment the focus for both is The Franchise."

"I know. He has been a dear to us. Well, I suppose it is time that we were going. If anyone had told me last week that I should

207

be leaving The Franchise to go to a triumph at Norton I wouldn't have believed it. Poor Stanley can sleep in his own bed from now on, instead of guarding a couple of hags in a lonely house."

"Isn't he sleeping here tonight?" Robert asked.

"No. Why should he?"

"I don't know. I don't like the idea of the house being left entirely empty."

"The policeman will be round as usual on his beat. Anyhow, no one has even tried to do anything since the night they smashed our windows. It is only for tonight. Tomorrow we shall be home again."

"I know. But I don't much like it. Couldn't Stanley stay one more night? Until the case is over."

"If they want to wreck our windows again," Mrs. Sharpe said, "I don't suppose Stanley's being here will deter them."

"No, I suppose not. I'll remind Hallam, anyhow, that the house is empty tonight," Robert said, and left it there.

Marion locked the door behind them, and they walked to the gate, where Robert's car was waiting. At the gate Marion paused to look back at the house. "It's an ugly old place," she said, "but it has one virtue. It looks the same all the year round. At midsummer the grass gets a little burnt and tired-looking, but otherwise it doesn't change. Most houses have a 'best' time; rhododendrons, or herbaceous borders, or virginia creeper, or almond blossom, or something. But The Franchise is always the same. It has no frills. What are you laughing at, Mother?"

"I was thinking how *bedizened* the poor thing looks with those tubs of wallflower."

They stood there for a moment, laughing at the forbidding, dirty-white house with its incongruous decoration of frivolity; and laughing, shut the gate on it.

But Robert did not forget; and before having dinner with Kevin at The Feathers in Norton he called the police station at Milford and reminded them that the Sharpes' house would be empty for that one night.

"All right, Mr. Blair," the sergeant said, "I'll tell the man on the beat to open the gate and look round. Yes, we still have a key. That'll be all right."

Robert did not quite see what that would achieve; but then he did not see what protection could be afforded in any case. Mrs. Sharpe had said, if anyone was minded to break windows then the windows would inevitably be broken. He decided that he was being fussy, and joined Kevin and his law friends with relief.

The Law talks well, and it was late before Robert went to bed in one of the dark panelled rooms that made The Feathers famous. The Feathers—one of the "musts" of American visitors to Britain—was not only famous but up to date. Pipes had been led through the linen-fold oak, wires through the beamed ceilings, and a telephone line through the oak planks of the floor. The Feathers had been providing comfort for the travelling public since 1480, and saw no reason why it should stop.

Robert fell asleep as soon as his head touched the pillow and the telephone at his ear had been ringing for some moments before he became aware of it.

"Well?" he said, still half-asleep. And became instantly wide awake.

It was Stanley. Could he come back to Milford? The Franchise was on fire.

"Badly?"

"It's got a good hold, but they think they can save it."

"I'll be over as soon as I can make it."

He made the twenty miles in a door-to-door time that the Robert Blair of a month ago would have considered reprehensible in the achievement of another, and quite inconceivable as an achievement of his own. As he tore past his own home at the lower end of Milford High Street and out into the country beyond, he saw the glow against the horizon, like the rising of a full moon. But the moon hung in the sky, a young silver moon in the pale summer night. And the glow of the burning Franchise wavered in sickening gusts that tightened Robert's heart with remembered horror.

At least there was no one in the building. He wondered if anyone had been there in time to rescue what was valuable from the house. Would there be anyone there who could distinguish what was valuable from what was worthless?

The gates were wide open and the courtyard—bright in the

flames—was crowded with the men and machines of the Fire Service. The first thing he saw, incongruous on the grass, was the bead-work chair from the drawing-room; and a wave of hysteria rose in him. Someone had saved that, anyhow.

An almost unrecognisable Stanley grabbed his sleeve and said: "There you are. I thought you ought to know, somehow." Sweat trickled down his blackened face, leaving clear rivulets behind them, so that his young face looked seamed and old. "There isn't enough water. We've got quite a lot of the stuff out. All the drawing-room stuff that they used every day. I thought that's what they'd want, if it had to be a choice. And we flung out some of the upstairs stuff but all the heavy stuff has gone up."

Mattresses and bed-linen were piled on the grass out of the way of the firemen's boots. The furniture stood about the grass as it had been set down, looking surprised and lost.

"Let's take the furniture further away," Stanley said. "It's not safe where it is. Either some lighted bits will fall on it or one of those bastards will use it to stand on." The bastards were the Fire Service, doing their sweating and efficient best.

So Robert found himself prosaically carting furniture through a fantastic scene; miserably identifying pieces that he had known in their proper sphere. The chair that Mrs. Sharpe had considered Inspector Grant too heavy for; the cherry-wood table they had given Kevin luncheon at; the wall-table that Mrs. Sharpe had dumped her bag down on only a few hours ago. The roar and crackle of the flames, the shoutings of the firemen, the odd mixture of moonlight, head-lights, and wavering flame, the mad juxtaposition and irrelevance of the bits of furniture, reminded him of how it felt to be coming round from an anaesthetic.

And then two things happened together. The first floor fell in with a crash. And as the new spout of flame lit the faces round him he saw two youths alongside whose countenances were alive with gloating. At the same moment he became aware that Stanley had seen them too. He saw Stanley's fist catch the further one under the chin with a crack that could be heard even over the noise of the flames, and the gloating face disappeared into the darkness of the trampled grass.

Robert had not hit anyone since he gave up boxing when he left school, and he had no intention of hitting anyone now. His left arm seemed to do all that was necessary of its own accord. And the second leering face went down into obscurity.

"Neat," remarked Stanley, sucking his broken knuckles. And then, "Look!" he said.

The roof crumpled like a child's face when it is beginning to cry; like a melting negative. The little round window, so famous and so ill-reputed, leaned forward a little and sank slowly inwards. A tongue of flame leapt up and fell again. Then the whole roof collapsed into the seething mass below, falling two floors to join the red wreck of the rest of the interior. The men moved back from the furnace heat. The fire roared in unrestricted triumph into the summer night.

When at last it died away Robert noticed with a vague surprise that the dawn had come. A calm, grey dawn, full of promise. Quiet had come too; the roar and the shoutings had faded to the soft hiss of water on the smoking skeleton. Only the four walls stood, blurred and grimy, in the middle of the trampled grass. The four walls and the flight of steps with their warped iron railing. On either side of the doorway stood what remained of Nevil's gay little tubs, the soaked and blackened flowers hanging in unrecognisable shreds over their edges. Between them the square opening yawned into a black emptiness.

"Well," said Stanley, standing beside him, "that seems to be that."

"How did it begin?" asked Bill, who had arrived too late to see anything but the wreck that was left.

"No one knows. It was well alight when P.C. Newsam arrived on his beat," Robert said. "What became of those two chaps, by the way?"

"The two we corrected?" Stanley said. "They went home."

"It's a pity that expression is no evidence."

"Yes," Stanley said. "They won't get anyone for this any more than they got anyone for the window-breaking. And I still owe someone for a crack on the head."

"You nearly broke that creature's neck tonight. That ought to be some kind of compensation to you."

"How are you going to tell them?" Stanley said. This obviously referred to the Sharpes.

"God knows," Robert said. "Am I to tell them first and let it spoil their triumph in court for them; or am I to let them have their triumph and face the awful come-down afterwards?"

"Let them have their triumph," Stanley said. "Nothing that happens afterwards can take that away from them. Don't mess it up."

"Perhaps you are right, Stan. I wish I knew. I had better book rooms at the Rose and Crown for them."

"They wouldn't like that," Stan said.

"Perhaps not," Robert said, a shade impatiently. "But they have no choice. Whatever they decide to do they will want to stay here a night or two to arrange about things, I expect. And the Rose and Crown is the best available."

"Well," Stanley said, "I've been thinking. And I'm sure my landlady would be glad to have them. She's always been on their side, and she has a spare room, and they could have that sitting-room in front that she never uses, and it's very quiet down there, that last row of Council houses facing on the Meadows. I'm sure they'd rather have that than a hotel where they would be stared at."

"They would indeed, Stan. I should never have thought of it. You think your landlady would be willing?"

"I don't think; I'm sure. They're her greatest interest in life at the moment. It would be like royalty coming to stay."

"Well, find out definitely, would you, and telephone me a message to Norton. To The Feathers at Norton."

~~~~~~

· 22 ·

It seemed to Robert that at least half Milford had managed to pack itself into the Court at Norton. Certainly a great many citizens of Norton were milling round the outer doors, vocal and frustrated; furious that when a case of national interest was being decided at "their" Assizes they should be done out of their right to witness it by an influx of foreigners from Milford. Wily and deceitful foreigners, too, who had suborned the Norton youth to keep places in the queue for them; a piece of forethought which had not occurred to Norton adults.

It was very warm, and the packed court stirred uneasily

throughout the preliminaries and through most of Miles Allison's account of the crime. Allison was the antithesis of Kevin Macdermott; his fair, delicate face that of a type rather than a person. His light dry voice was unemotional, his method matter-of-fact. And since the story he was telling was one which they had all read about and discussed until it was threadbare, they withheld their attention from him and amused themselves by identifying friends in court.

Robert sat turning over and over in his pocket the little oblong of pasteboard that Christina had pressed into his hand on his departure yesterday, and rehearsing phrases for afterwards. The pasteboard was a bright Reckitt's blue and bore in gold letters the words: NOT A SPARROW SHALL FALL, and a picture in the right upper corner of a robin with an out-size red breast. How, wondered Robert, turning the little text over and over in his fingers, did you tell someone that they had no home any more?

The sudden movement of a hundred bodies and the subsequent silence brought him back to the court-room, and he realised that Betty Kane was taking the oath preparatory to giving evidence. "Never kissed anything but the book," Ben Carley had said of her appearance on a similar occasion. And that is what she looked like today. The blue outfit still made one think of youth and innocence; speedwell, and camp-fire smoke, and harebells in the grass. The tilted-back brim of her hat still showed the childish forehead with its charming hair line. And Robert, who knew now all about her life in the weeks she was missing, found himself being surprised all over again at sight of her. Plausibility was one of the first endowments of the criminal; but up to now such plausibility as he had had to deal with was of the old-soldier-ten-bob-note kind. Easily recognised for what it was. The work of amateurs at the job. It occurred to him that for the first time he was seeing the real thing at work.

Once again she gave her evidence in model fashion; her clear young voice audible to everyone in court. Once again she had her audience breathless and motionless. The only difference this time was that the Bench was not doting. The Bench, indeed, if one was to judge by the expression on the face of Mr. Justice Saye, was very far from doting. And Robert wondered how much the judge's critical gaze was due to natural distaste for the subject, and how much to the conclusion that Kevin Macdermott would not be sitting there ready to defend the two women in the dock unless they had a thundering good defence.

The girl's own account of her sufferings did what her counsel's had not done: roused the audience to an emotional reaction. More than once they had given vent to a united sigh, a murmur of indignation; never overt enough to rank as a demonstration, and so bring down the Court's rebuke, but audible enough to show which way their sympathies lay. So that it was in a charged atmosphere that Kevin rose to cross-examine.

"Miss Kane," began Kevin in his gentlest drawl, "you say that it was dark when you arrived at The Franchise. Was it *really* so dark?"

This question, with its coaxing tone, made her think that he did not want it to be dark, and she reacted as he intended.

"Yes. Quite dark," she said.

"Too dark to see the outside of the house?"

"Yes, much too dark."

He appeared to give that up and try a new tack.

"Then the night you escaped. Perhaps that was not quite dark?"

"Oh, yes. That was even darker, if possible."

"So that you could not possibly have seen the outside of the house on some occasion?"

"Never."

"Never. Well, having settled that point, let us consider what you say you could see from the window of your prison in the attic. You said in your statement to the police, when you were describing this unknown place where you were imprisoned, that the carriage-way from the gate to the door 'went straight for a little and then divided in two into a circle up to the door'."

"Yes."

"How did you know it did that?"

"How did I know it? I could see it."

"From where?"

"From the window in the attic. It looked out on the courtyard in front of the house."

"But from the window in the attic it is possible to see only the straight part of the carriage-way. The edge of the roof cuts off the rest. How did you know that the carriage-way divided in two and made a circle up to the door?"

"I saw it!"

"How?"

"From that window."

"You want us to understand that you see on a different principle from ordinary beings? On the principle of the Irishman's gun that shoots round corners. Or is it all done by mirrors?"

"It is the way I described!"

"Certainly it is the way you described; but what you described was the view of the courtyard as seen by, let us say, someone looking over the wall at it; not by someone looking at it from the window in the attic. Which you assure us was your only view of it."

"I take it," said the Court, "that you have a witness to the extent of the view from the window."

"Two, my lord."

"One with normal vision will be sufficient," said the Court dryly.

"So you cannot explain how, speaking to the police that day in Aylesbury, you described a peculiarity that you could not possibly have known about, if your story was true. Have you ever been abroad, Miss Kane?"

"Abroad?" she said, surprised by the change of subject. "No."

"Never?"

"No, never."

"You have not, for instance, been to Denmark lately? To Copenhagen, for instance."

"No." There was no change in her expression but Robert thought that there was the faintest uncertainty in her voice.

"Do you know a man called Bernard Chadwick?"

She was suddenly wary. Robert was reminded of the subtle change in an animal that has been relaxed and becomes attentive. There is no alteration in pose; no actual physical change. On the contrary, there is only an added stillness; an awareness.

"No." The tone was colourless; uninterested.

"He is not a friend of yours."

"No."

"You did not, for instance, stay with him at a hotel in Copenhagen?"

"No."

"Have you stayed with anyone in Copenhagen?"

"No, I have never been abroad at all."

"So that if I were to suggest that you spent those missing weeks in a hotel in Copenhagen and not in an attic at The Franchise, I should be mistaken."

"Quite mistaken."

"Thank you."

Miles Allison, as Kevin had anticipated, rose to retrieve the situation.

"Miss Kane," he said, "you arrived at The Franchise by car."

"Yes."

"And that car, you say in your statement, was driven up to the door of the house. Now, if it was dark, as you say, there must have been side-lights on the car, if not head-lights; which would illuminate not only the carriage-way but most of the courtyard."

"Yes," she broke in, before he could put it to her, "yes, of course I must have seen the circle then. I knew I had seen it. I knew it." She glanced at Kevin for a moment, and Robert was reminded of her face when she saw that she had guessed correctly about the suitcases in the cupboard, that first day at The Franchise. If she knew what Kevin had waiting for her, Robert thought, she would have no spare thought for a passing triumph.

She was succeeded in the witness-box by Carley's "oleograph"; who had bought both a new frock and a new hat for her appearance at Norton—a tomato-red frock and a puce hat with a cobalt ribbon and a pink rose—and looked more luscious and more revolting than ever. Again Robert was interested to note how her relish of her part discounted, even with this more emotional audience, the effect of what she said. They didn't like her, and in spite of their *parti pris* attitude their English distrust of malice cooled their minds towards her. When Kevin, cross-examining, suggested that she had in fact been dismissed and had not "given in her notice" at all, there was a So-that's-it! expression on every second face in court. Apart from an attempt to shake her credit, there was not much that Kevin could do with her, and he let her go. He was waiting for her poor stooge.

The stooge, when she arrived, looked even less happy than she had looked in the police court at Milford. The much more impressive array of robes and wigs clearly shook her. Police uniforms were bad enough, but in retrospect they seemed positively home-like compared with this solemn atmosphere, this ritual. If she was out of her depth in Milford, she was obviously drowning here. Robert saw Kevin's considering eye on her, analysing and understanding; deciding on his approach. She had been scared stiff by Miles Allison, in spite of his patient quietness; evidently regarding anything in a wig and gown as hostile and a potential dispenser of penalties. So Kevin became her wooer and protector.

It was positively indecent, the caress that Kevin could get into his voice, Robert thought, listening to his first sentences to her. The soft unhurried syllables reassured her. She listened for a moment and then began to relax. Robert saw the small skinny hands that had been clutched so tightly together on the rail of the box slacken and spread slowly to a prone position. He was asking about her school. The fright had faded from her eyes and she was answering quite calmly. Here, she quite obviously felt, was a friend.

"Now, Gladys, I am going to suggest to you that you did not want to come here today and give evidence against these two people at The Franchise."

"No, I didn't. Indeed I didn't!"

"But you came," he said; not accusing, just making the statement.

"Yes," she said; shamefaced.

"Why? Because you thought it was your duty?"

"No, oh no."

"Was it because someone forced you to come?"

Robert saw the judge's instant reaction to this, but so out of the tail of his eye did Kevin. "Someone who held something over your head?" finished Kevin smoothly, and his lordship paused. "Someone who said: 'You say what I tell you to say or I'll tell about you'?"

217

She looked half-hopeful, half-bewildered. "I don't know," she said, falling back on the escape of the illiterate.

"Because if anyone made you tell lies by threatening what they would do to you if you didn't, they can be punished for it."

This was clearly a new idea to her.

"This court, all these people you see here, have come here to-day to find out the truth about something. And His Lordship up there would deal very sternly with anyone who had used threats to make you come here and say something that was not true. What is more, there is a very heavy punishment for persons who take an oath to speak truth and tell what is not true; but if it so happened that they had been frightened into telling lies by some-one threatening them, then the person who would be punished most would be the person who made the threats. Do you understand that?"

"Yes," she said in a whisper.

"Now I am going to suggest to you what really happened, and you will tell me whether I am right." He waited for her agreement, but she said nothing, so he went on. "Someone—a friend of yours, perhaps—took something from The Franchise—let us say, a watch. She did not want the watch herself, perhaps, and so she handed it on to you. It may be that you did not want to take it, but your friend is perhaps a domineering person and you did not like to refuse her gift. So you took it. Now I suggest that presently that friend proposed to you that you should back up a story she was going to tell in court and you, being averse to telling lies, said no. And that she then said to you: 'If you don't back me up I shall say that you took that watch from The Franchise one day when you came to see me'—or some other threat of that sort."

He paused a moment but she merely looked bewildered.

"Now, I suggest that because of those threats you did actually go to a police court and did actually back up your friend's untrue story, but that when you got home you were sorry and ashamed. So sorry and ashamed that the thought of keeping that watch any longer was unbearable to you. And that you then wrapped up the watch, and sent it back to The Franchise by post with a note saying: 'I don't want none of it'." He paused. "I suggest to you, Gladys, that that is what really happened."

218

But she had had time to take fright. "No," she said. "No, I never had that watch."

He ignored the admission, and said smoothly: "I am quite wrong about that?"

"Yes. It wasn't me sent back the watch."

He picked up a paper and said, still mildly: "When you were at that school we were talking about, you were very good at drawing. So good that you had things put up for show at the school exhibition."

"Yes."

"I have here a map of Canada—a very neat map—which was one of your exhibits and which indeed won you a prize. You have signed it here in the right-hand corner, and I have no doubt that you were proud to sign such a neat piece of work. I expect you will remember it."

It was taken across the court to her, while Kevin added:

"Ladies and Gentlemen of the Jury, it is a map of Canada which Gladys Rees made in her last year at school. When his lordship has inspected it he will no doubt pass it on to you." And then, to Gladys: "You made that map yourself?"

"Yes."

"And wrote your name in the corner."

"Yes."

"And printed DOMINION OF CANADA across the bottom?"

"Yes."

"You printed those letters across the bottom that read: DOMINION OF CANADA. Good. Now, I have here the scrap of paper on which someone wrote the words: I DON'T WANT NONE OF IT. This scrap of paper, with its printed letters, was enclosed with the watch that was sent back to The Franchise. The watch that had gone missing while Rose Glyn was working there. And I suggest that the printing of I DON'T WANT NONE is the same as the printing of DOMINION OF CAN-ADA. That it was written by the same hand. And that that hand was yours."

"No," she said, taking the scrap of paper as it was handed to her and putting it hastily down on the ledge as though it might sting her. "I never. I never sent back no watch."

"You didn't print those letters that read: I DON'T WANT NONE OF IT?"

"No."

"But you did print those letters that read DOMINION OF CANADA?"

"Yes."

"Well, later in this case I shall bring evidence that these two printings are by the same hand. In the meantime the jury can inspect them at their leisure and arrive at their own conclusions. Thank you."

"My learned friend has suggested to you," said Miles Allison, "that pressure was brought on you to come here. Is there any truth in that suggestion?"

"No."

"You did not come here because you were frightened of what might happen to you if you didn't?"

She took some time to think over this, evidently disentangling it in her mind. "No," she ventured at last.

"What you said in the witness-box at the police court, and what you have said today, is the truth?"

"Yes."

"Not something that someone suggested you might say?"

"No."

But the impression that was left with the jury was just that: that she was an unwilling witness repeating a story that was someone else's invention.

That ended the evidence for the prosecution and Kevin went straight on with the matter of Gladys Rees; on the housewife principle of "getting his feet clear" before he began the real work of the day.

A handwriting expert gave evidence that the two samples of printing which had been put into court were by the same hand. Not only had he no doubt about it, but he had rarely been given an easier task. Not only were letters duplicated in the two samples but combinations of letters were similarly duplicated, combinations such as DO and AN and ON. As it was evident that the jury had already made up their minds for themselves on this point— no one who saw the two samples could doubt that they were by the same hand—Allison's suggestion that experts could be wrong was automatic and half-hearted. Kevin demolished it by producing his fingerprint witness, who deponed that the same fingerprints were to be found on each. And Allison's suggestion that the fingerprints might not be those of Gladys Rees was a last-stand effort. He had no wish that the Court might put it to the test.

Now that he had established the fact that Gladys Rees had, when she made her first declaration, been in possession of a watch stolen from The Franchise and had returned it immediately after that declaration, with a conscience-stricken note, Kevin was free to deal with Betty Kane's story. Rose Glyn and her story had been sufficiently discredited for the police to be already laying their heads together. He could safely leave Rose to the police.

When Bernard William Chadwick was called, there was a craning forward and a murmur of interrogation. This was a name that the newspaper readers did not recognise. What could he be doing in the case? What was he here to say?

He was here to say that he was a buyer of porcelain, fine china, and fancy goods of various kinds for a wholesale firm in London. That he was married and lived with his wife in a house in Ealing.

"You travel for your firm," Kevin said.

"Yes."

"In March of this year did you pay a visit to Larborough?"

"Yes."

"While you were in Larborough did you meet Betty Kane?"

"Yes."

"How did you meet her?"

"She picked me up."

There was an instant and concerted protest from the body of the court. Whatever discrediting Rose Glyn and her ally had suffered, Betty Kane was still sacrosanct. Betty Kane, who looked so much like Bernadette, was not to be spoken of lightly.

The judge rebuked them for the demonstration, involuntary though it had been. He also rebuked witness. He was not quite clear, he inferred, what "picking up" involved and would be grateful if the witness would confine himself to standard English in his replies.

"Will you tell the Court just how you did meet her," Kevin said.

"I had dropped into the Midland lounge for tea one day, and she—er—began to talk to me. She was having tea there."

"Alone?"

"Quite alone."

"You did not speak to her first?"

"I didn't even notice her."

"How did she call attention to her presence, then?"

"She smiled, and I smiled back and went on with my papers. I was busy. Then she spoke to me. Asked what the papers were, and so on."

"So the acquaintance progressed."

"Yes. She said she was going to the flicks—to the pictures—and wouldn't I come too? Well, I was finished for the day and she was a cute kid so I said yes, if she liked. The result was that she met me next day and went out to the country in my car with me."

"On your business trips, you mean."

"Yes; she came for the ride, and we would have a meal somewhere in the country and tea before she went home to her aunt's place."

"Did she talk about her people to you?"

"Yes, she said how unhappy she was at home, where no one took any notice of her. She had a long string of complaints about her home, but I didn't take much notice of them. She looked a pretty sleek little outfit to me."

"A what?" asked the judge.

"A well-cared for young girl, my lord."

"Yes?" Kevin said. "And how long did this idyll in Larborough persist?"

"It turned out that we were leaving Larborough on the same day. She was going back to her people because her holiday was over—she had already extended it so that she could run about with me—and I was due to fly to Copenhagen on business. She then said she had no intention of going home and asked me to take her with me. I said nothing doing. I didn't think she was so much of an innocent child as she seemed in the lounge at the Midland—I knew her better by that time—but I still thought she was inexperienced. She was only sixteen, after all."

"She told you she was sixteen."

"She had her sixteenth birthday in Larborough," Chadwick said with a wry twist of the mouth under the small dark moustache. "It cost me a gold lip-stick."

Robert looked across at Mrs. Wynn and saw her cover her face with her hands. Leslie Wynn, sitting beside her, looked unbelieving and blank.

"You had no idea that actually she was still fifteen."

"No. Not until the other day."

"So when she made the suggestion that she should go with you you considered her an inexperienced child of sixteen."

"Yes."

"Why did you change your mind about her?"

"She—convinced me that she wasn't."

"Wasn't what?"

"Inexperienced."

"So after that you had no qualms about taking her with you on the trip abroad?"

"I had qualms in plenty, but by then I had learned—what fun she could be, and I couldn't have left her behind if I had wanted to."

"So you took her abroad with you."

"Yes."

"As your wife?"

"Yes, as my wife."

"You had no qualms about any anxiety her people might suffer?"

"No. She said she still had a fortnight's holiday to come, and that her people would take it for granted that she was still with her aunt in Larborough. She had told her aunt that she was going home, but had told her people that she was staying on. And as they never wrote to each other it was unlikely that her not being in Larborough would become known to her people."

"Do you remember the date on which you left Larborough?"

"Yes; I picked her up at a coach stop in Mainshill on the afternoon of March the 28th. That was where she would normally have got her bus home."

Kevin left a pause after this piece of information, so that its full significance should have a chance. Robert, listening to the momentary quiet, thought that if the court-room were empty the silence could not be more absolute.

"So you took her with you to Copenhagen. Where did you stay?"

"At the Red Shoes Hotel."

"For how long?"

"A fortnight."

There was a faint murmur of comment or surprise at that.

"And then?"

"We came back to England together on the 15th of April. She had told me that she was due home on the 16th. But on the way over she told me that she had actually been due back on the 11th and would now have been missing for four days."

"She misled you deliberately?"

"Yes."

"Did she say why she had misled you?"

"Yes. So that it would be impossible for her to go back. She said she was going to write to her people and say that she had a job and was quite happy and that they were not to look for her or worry about her."

"She had no compunction about the suffering that would cause parents who had been devoted to her?"

"No. She said her home bored her so much she could scream."

Against his will, Robert's eyes went to Mrs. Wynn, and came away again at once. It was crucifixion.

"What was your reaction to the new situation?"

"I was angry to begin with. It put me in a spot."

"Were you worried about the girl?"

"No, not particularly."

"Why?"

"By that time I had learned that she was very well able to take care of herself."

"What exactly do you mean by that?"

"I mean: whoever was going to suffer in any situation she created, it wouldn't be Betty Kane."

The mention of her name suddenly reminded the audience that the girl they had just been hearing about was "the" Betty Kane.

"Their" Betty Kane. The one like Bernadette. And there was a small uneasy movement; a taking of breath.

"So?"

"After a lot of rag-chewing——"

"Of what?" said his lordship.

"A lot of discussion, my lord."

"Go on," said his lordship, "but do confine yourself to English, standard or basic."

"After a lot of talk I decided the best thing to do would be to take her down to my bungalow on the river near Bourne End. We used it for weekends in the summer and for summer holidays, but only rarely for the rest of the year."

"When you say 'we,' you mean your wife and you."

"Yes. She agreed to that quite readily, and I drove her down."

"Did you stay there with her that night?"

"Yes."

"And on the following nights?"

"The following night I spent at home."

"In Ealing."

"Yes."

"And afterwards?"

"For a week after that I spent most nights at the bungalow."

"Was your wife not surprised that you did not sleep at home?"

"Not unbearably."

"And how did the situation at Bourne End disintegrate?"

"I went down one night and found that she had gone."

"What did you think had happened to her?"

"Well she had been growing very bored for the last day or two —she found housekeeping fun for about three days but not more, and there wasn't much to do down there—so when I found she had gone I took it that she was tired of me and had found someone or something more exciting."

"You learned later where she had gone, and why?"

"Yes."

"You heard the girl Betty Kane give evidence today?"

"I did."

"Evidence that she had been forcibly detained in a house near Milford."

225

"Yes."

"That is the girl who went with you to Copenhagen, stayed there for a fortnight with you, and subsequently lived with you in a bungalow near Bourne End?"

"Yes, that is the girl."

"You have no doubt about it?"

"No."

"Thank you."

There was a great sigh from the crowd as Kevin sat down and Bernard Chadwick waited for Miles Allison. Robert wondered if Betty Kane's face was capable of showing any emotion other than fear and triumph. Twice he had seen it pulse with triumph and once—when old Mrs. Sharpe crossed the drawing-room towards her that first day—he had seen it show fear. But for all the emotion it showed just now she might have been listening to a reading of Fat Stock prices. Its effect of inward calm, he decided, must be the result of physical construction. The result of wide-set eyes, and placid brow, and inexpensive small mouth always set in the same childish pout. It was that physical construction that had hidden, all those years, the real Betty Kane even from her intimates. A perfect camouflage, it had been. A façade behind which she could be what she liked. There it was now, the mask, as childlike and calm as when he had first seen it above her school coat in the drawing-room at The Franchise; although behind it its owner must be seething with unnameable emotions.

"Mr. Chadwick," Miles Allison said, "this is a very *belated* story, isn't it?"

"Belated?"

"Yes. This case has been a matter for press-report and public comment for the past three weeks, or thereabouts. You must have known that two women were being wrongfully accused—if your story was true. If, as you say, Betty Kane was with you during those weeks, and not, as she says, in the house of these two women, why did you not go straight to the police and tell them so?"

"Because I didn't know anything about it."

"About what?"

"About the prosecution of these women. Or about the story that Betty Kane had told."

226

"How was that?"

"Because I have been abroad again for my firm. I knew nothing about this case until a couple of days ago."

"I see. You have heard the girl give evidence; and you have heard the doctor's evidence as to the condition in which she arrived home. Does anything in your story explain that?"

"No."

"It was not you who beat the girl?"

"No."

"You say you went down one night and found her gone."

"Yes."

"She had packed up and gone?"

"Yes; so it seemed at the time."

"That is to say, all her belongings and the luggage that contained them had disappeared with her."

"Yes."

"And yet she arrived home without belongings of any sort, and wearing only a dress and shoes."

"I didn't know that till much later."

"You want us to understand that when you went down to the bungalow you found it tidy and deserted, with no sign of any hasty departure."

"Yes. That's how I found it."

When Mary Frances Chadwick was summoned to give evidence there was what amounted to a sensation in court, even before she appeared. It was obvious that this was "the wife"; and this was fare that not even the most optimistic queuer outside the court had anticipated.

Frances Chadwick was a tallish good-looking woman; a natural blonde with the clothes and figure of a girl who has "modelled" clothes; but growing a little plump now, and, if one was to judge from the good-natured face, not much caring.

She said that she was indeed married to the previous witness, and lived with him in Ealing. They had no children. She still worked in the clothes trade now and then. Not because she needed to, but for pocket-money and because she liked it. Yes, she remembered her husband's going to Larborough and his subsequent trip to Copenhagen. He arrived back from Copenhagen a day

227

later than he had promised, and spent that night with her. During the following week she began to suspect that her husband had developed an interest elsewhere. The suspicion was confirmed when a friend told her that her husband had a guest at their bungalow on the river.

"Did you speak to your husband about it?" Kevin asked.

"No. That wouldn't have been any solution. He attracts them like flies."

"What did you do, then? Or plan to do?"

"What I always do with flies."

"What is that?"

"I swat them."

"So you proceeded to the bungalow with the intention of swatting whatever fly was there."

"That's it."

"And what did you find at the bungalow?"

"I went late in the evening hoping I would catch Barney there too——"

"Barney is your husband?"

"And how. I mean, yes," she added hastily, catching the judge's eye.

"Well?"

"The door was unlocked so I walked straight in and into the sitting-room. A woman's voice called from the bedroom: 'Is that you, Barney? I've been so lonely for you.' I went in and found her lying on the bed in the kind of negligée you used to see in vamp films about ten years ago. She looked a mess, and I was a bit surprised at Barney. She was eating chocolates out of an enormous box that was lying on the bed alongside her. Terribly nineteen-thirty, the whole set-up."

"Please confine your story to the essentials, Mrs. Chadwick."

"Yes. Sorry. Well, we had the usual exchange——"

"The usual?"

"Yes. The what-are-you-doing-here stuff. The wronged-wife and the light-of-love, you know. But for some reason or other she got in my hair. I don't know why. I had never cared very much on other occasions. I mean, we just had a good row without any real hard feelings on either side. But there was something about this little tramp that turned my stomach. So——"

"Please, Mrs. Chadwick!"

"All right. Sorry. But you did say tell it in my own words. Well, there came a point where I couldn't stand this floo—— I mean, I got to a stage when she riled me past bearing. I pulled her off the bed and gave her a smack on the side of the head. She looked so surprised it was funny. It would seem no one had ever hit her in her life. She said: 'You hit me!' just like that; and I said: 'A lot of people are going to hit you from now on, my poppet,' and gave her another one. Well, from then on it was just a fight. I own quite frankly that the odds were all on my side. I was bigger for one thing and in a flaming temper. I tore that silly negligée off her, and it was ding-dong till she tripped over one of her mules that was lying on the floor and went sprawling. I waited for her to get up, but she didn't, and I thought she had passed out. I went into the bathroom to get a cold wet cloth and mopped her face. And then I went into the kitchen to make some coffee. I had cooled off by then and thought she would be glad of something when she had cooled off too. I brewed the coffee and left it to stand. But when I got back to the bedroom I found that the faint had been all an act. The little—the girl had lit out. She had had time to dress, so I took it for granted that she had dressed in a hurry and gone."

"And did you go too?"

"I waited for an hour, thinking Barney might come. My husband. All the girl's things were lying about, so I slung them all into her suitcase and put it in the cupboard under the stairs to the attic. And I opened all the windows. She must have put her scent on with a ladle. And then when Barney didn't come I went away. I must just have missed him, because he did go down that night. But a couple of days later I told him what I had done."

"And what was his reaction?"

"He said it was a pity her mother hadn't done the same thing ten years ago."

"He was not worried as to what had become of her?"

"No. I was, a bit, until he told me her home was only over at

Aylesbury. She could quite easily cadge a lift that distance."

"So he took it for granted that she had gone home?"

"Yes. I said, hadn't he better make sure. After all, she was a kid."

"And what did he say in answer to that?"

"He said: 'Frankie, my girl, that "kid" knows more about self-preservation than a chameleon.' "

"So you dismissed the affair from your mind."

"Yes."

"But it must have come to your mind again when you read accounts of the Franchise affair?"

"No, it didn't."

"Why was that?"

"For one thing, I never knew the girl's name. Barney called her Liz. And I just didn't connect a fifteen-year-old schoolgirl who was kidnapped and beaten somewhere in the Midlands with Barney's bit. I mean, with the girl who was eating chocolates on my bed."

"If you had realised that the girls were identical, you would have told the police what you knew about her?"

"Certainly."

"You would not have hesitated owing to the fact that it was you who had administered the beating?"

"No. I would administer another tomorrow if I got the chance."

"I will save my learned friend a question and ask you: Do you intend to divorce your husband?"

"No. Certainly not."

"This evidence of yours and his is not a neat piece of public collusion?"

"No. I wouldn't need collusion. But I have no intention of divorcing Barney. He's fun, and he's a good provider. What more do you want in a husband?"

"I wouldn't know," Robert heard Kevin murmur. Then in his normal voice he asked her to state that the girl she had been talking about was the girl who had given evidence; the girl who was now sitting in court. And so thanked her and sat down.

But Miles Allison made no attempt to cross-examine. And Kevin moved to call his next witness. But the foreman of the jury was before him.

The jury, the foreman said, would like his lordship to know that they had all the evidence they required.

"What was this witness that you were about to call, Mr. Macdermott?" the judge asked.

"He is the owner of the hotel in Copenhagen, my lord. To speak to their having stayed there over the relevant period."

The judge turned inquiringly to the foreman.

The foreman consulted the jury.

"No, my lord; we don't think it is necessary, subject to your lordship's correction, to hear the witness."

"If you are satisfied that you have heard enough to arrive at a true verdict—and I cannot myself see that any further evidence would greatly clarify the subject—then so be it. Would you like to hear counsel for the defence?"

"No, my lord, thank you. We have reached our verdict already."

"In that case, any summing-up by me would be markedly redundant. Do you want to retire?"

"No, my lord. We are unanimous."

~~~~~~

· 23 ·

"WE had better wait until the crowd thins out," Robert said. "Then they'll let us out the back way."

He was wondering why Marion looked so grave; so unrejoicing. Almost as if she were suffering from shock. Had the strain been as bad as all that?

As if aware of his puzzlement, she said: "That woman. That poor woman. I can't think of anything else."

"Who?" Robert said, stupidly.

"The girl's mother. Can you imagine anything more frightful? To have lost the roof over one's head is bad—— Oh, yes, Robert my dear, you don't have to tell us——" She held out a late edition of the *Larborough Times* with a Stop Press paragraph reading: THE FRANCHISE, HOUSE MADE FAMOUS BY MILFORD ABDUCTION CASE, BURNT TO THE GROUND LAST NIGHT. "Yesterday that would have seemed to me an enormous tragedy. But compared with that woman's calvary it seems an incident. What *can* be more shattering than to find that the person you have lived with and loved all those years not only doesn't exist but has never existed? That the person you have so much loved not only doesn't love you but doesn't care two hoots about you and never did? What is there *left* for someone like that? She can never again take a step on to green grass without wondering if it is bog."

"Yes," Kevin said, "I couldn't bear to look at her. It was indecent, what she was suffering."

"She has a charming son," Mrs. Sharpe said. "I hope he will be a comfort to her."

"But don't you *see*," Marion said. "She *hasn't* got her son. She has nothing now. She thought she had Betty. She loved her and was as sure of her as she loved and was sure of her son. Now the very foundations of her life have given way. How is she to judge, any longer, if appearances can be so deceptive? No, she has nothing. Just a desolation. I am bleeding inside for her."

Kevin slipped an arm into hers and said: "You have had sufficient trouble of your own lately without saddling yourself with another's. Come; they'll let us go now, I think. Did it please you to see the police converging in that polite casual way of theirs on the perjurers?"

"No, I could think of nothing but that woman's crucifixion." So she too had thought of it as that.

Kevin ignored her. "And the indecent scramble for a telephone that the Press indulged in the moment his lordship's red tail was through the door? You will be vindicated at great length in every newspaper in Britain, I promise you. It will be the most public vindication since Dreyfus. Wait here for me, while I get out of these. I shan't be a moment."

"I suppose we had best go to a hotel for a night or two?" Mrs. Sharpe said. "Have we any belongings at all?"

"Yes, quite a few, I'm glad to say," Robert told her; and described what had been saved. "But there is an alternative to the hotel." And he told them of Stanley's suggestion.

So it was to the little house on the outer rim of the "new" town that Marion and her mother came back; and it was in the front room at Miss Sim's that they sat down to celebrate; a sober little group: Marion, her mother, Robert, and Stanley. Kevin had had to go back to town. There was a large bunch of garden flowers on the table which had come with one of Aunt Lin's best notes. Aunt Lin's warm and gracious little notes had as little actual meaning as her "Have you had a busy day, dear?" but they had the same cushioning effect on life. Stanley had come in with a copy of the *Larborough Evening News* which carried on its front page the first report of the trial. The report was printed under a heading which read: ANANIAS ALSO RAN.

"Will you golf with me tomorrow afternoon?" Robert asked Marion. "You have been cooped up too long. We can start early, before the two-rounders have finished their lunch and have the course to ourselves."

"Yes, I should like that," she said. "I suppose tomorrow life will begin again and be just the usual mixture of good and bad. But tonight it is just a place where dreadful things can happen to one."

When he called for her on the morrow, however, all seemed well with life. "You can't imagine what bliss it is," she said. "Living in this house, I mean. You just turn a tap and hot water comes out."

"It is also very educational," Mrs. Sharpe said.

"Educational?"

"You can hear every word that is said next door."

"Oh, come, Mother! Not every word!"

"Every third word," amended Mrs. Sharpe.

So they drove out to the golf course in high spirits, and Robert decided that he would ask her to marry him when they were having tea in the club-house afterwards. Or would there be too many people interrupting there, with their kind words on the result of the trial? Perhaps on the way home again?

He had decided that the best plan was to leave Aunt Lin in possession of the old house—the place was so much hers that it was unthinkable that she should not live there until she died—and to find a small place for Marion and himself somewhere else in Milford. It would not be easy, these days, but if the worst came to the worst they could make a tiny flat on the top floor of Blair, Hayward, and Bennet's. It would mean removing the records of

233

two hundred years or so; but the records were rapidly arriving at museum quality and should be moved in any case.

Yes, he would ask her on the way home again.

This resolution lasted until he found that the thought of what was to come was spoiling his game. So on the ninth green he suddenly stopped waggling his putter at the ball, and said: "I want you to marry me, Marion."

"Do you, Robert?" She picked her own putter out of her bag, and dropped the bag at the edge of the green.

"You will, won't you?"

"No, Robert dear, I won't."

"But Marion! Why? Why not, I mean."

"Oh—as the children say, 'because'."

"Because why?"

"Half a dozen reasons, any one of them good by themselves. For one, if a man is not married by the time he is forty, then marriage is not one of the things he wants out of life. Just something that has overtaken him; like flu and rheumatism and income-tax demands. I don't want to be just something that has overtaken you."

"But that is——"

"Then, I don't think that I should be in the least an asset to Blair, Hayward, and Bennet. Even——"

"I'm not asking you to marry Blair, Hayward, and Bennet."

"Even the proof that I didn't beat Betty Kane won't free me of being 'the woman in the Kane case'; an uncomfortable sort of wife for the senior partner. It wouldn't do you any good, Robert, believe me."

"Marion, for heaven's sake! Stop——"

"Then, you have Aunt Lin and I have my mother. We couldn't just park them like pieces of chewing-gum. I not only love my mother, I *like* her. I admire her and enjoy living with her. You, on the other hand, are used to being spoiled by Aunt Lin—— Oh, yes, you are!—and would miss far more than you know all the creature comforts and the cosseting that I wouldn't know how to give you—and wouldn't give you if I knew how," she added, flashing a smile at him.

"Marion, it is *because* you don't cosset me that I want to marry you. Because you have an adult mind and a——"

"An adult mind is very nice to go to dinner with once a week, but after a lifetime with Aunt Lin you would find it a very poor exchange for good pastry in an uncritical atmosphere."

"There is one thing you haven't even mentioned," Robert said.

"What is that?"

"Do you care for me at all?"

"Yes. I care for you a great deal. More than I have ever cared for anyone, I think. That is, partly, why I won't marry you. The other reason has to do with myself."

"With you?"

"You see, I am *not* a marrying woman. I don't want to have to put up with someone else's crochets, someone else's demands, someone else's colds in the head. Mother and I suit each other perfectly because we make no demands on each other. If one of us has a cold in the head she retires to her room without fuss and doses her disgusting self until she is fit for human society again. But no husband would do that. He would expect sympathy—even though he brought on the cold himself by pulling off clothes when he grew warm instead of waiting sensibly to get cool—sympathy and attention and feeding. No, Robert. There are a hundred thousand women just panting to look after some man's cold; why pick on me?"

"Because you are that one woman in a hundred thousand, and I love you."

She looked slightly penitent. "I sound flippant, don't I? But what I say is good sound sense."

"But, Marion, it is a lonely life——"

"A 'full' life in my experience is usually full only of other people's demands."

"—and you will not have your mother for ever."

"Knowing Mother as I do, I have no doubt that she will outlive me with perfect ease. You had better hole out: I see old Colonel Whittaker's four on the horizon."

Automatically he pushed his ball into the hole. "But what will you do?" he asked.

"If I don't marry you?"

He ground his teeth. She was right: perhaps her mocking habit of mind would not be a comfort to live with.

"What had you and your mother thought of doing now that you have lost The Franchise?"

She delayed over her answer, as if it were difficult to say. Fussing with her bag, and keeping her back to him.

"We are going to Canada," she said.

"Going away!"

She still had her back to him. "Yes."

He was aghast. "But Marion, you can't. And why to Canada?"

"I have a cousin who is a professor at McGill. A son of Mother's only sister. He wrote some time ago to ask Mother if we would go out to keep house for him, but by that time we had inherited The Franchise and were very happy in England. So we said no. But the offer is still open. And we—we both will be glad to go now."

"I see."

"Don't look so downcast. You don't know what an escape you are having, my dear."

They finished the round in a business-like silence.

But driving back to Sin Lane after having dropped Marion at Miss Sim's, Robert smiled wryly to think that to all the new experiences that knowing the Sharpes had brought to him was now added that of being a rejected suitor. The final, and perhaps the most surprising, one.

Three days later, having sold to a local dealer what had been saved of their furniture, and to Stanley the car he so much despised, they left Milford by train. By the odd toy train that ran from Milford to the junction at Norton. And Robert came to the junction with them to see them on to the fast train.

"I always had a passion for travelling light," Marion said, referring to their scanty luggage, "but I never imagined it would be indulged to the extent of travelling with an over-night case to Canada."

But Robert could not think of small-talk. He was filled with a misery and desolation that he had not known since his small soul was filled with woe at going back to school. The blossom foamed

236

along the line side, the fields were burnished with buttercups, but the world for Robert was grey ash and drizzle.

He watched the London train bear them away, and went home wondering how he could support Milford without the hope of seeing Marion's thin brown face at least once a day.

But on the whole he supported it very well. He took to golfing of an afternoon again; and although a ball would always in the future be for him a "piece of gutta-percha," his form had not seriously deteriorated. He rejoiced Mr. Heseltine's heart by taking an interest in work. He suggested to Nevil that between them they might sort and catalogue the records in the attic and perhaps make a book of them. By the time Marion's goodbye letter from London came, three weeks later, the soft folds of life in Milford were already closing round him.

MY VERY DEAR ROBERT (wrote Marion).

This is a hasty *au revoir* note, just to let you know that we are both thinking of you. We leave on the morning plane to Montreal the day after tomorrow. Now that the moment is almost here we have discovered that what we both remember are the good and lovely things, and that the rest fades to comparative insignificance. This may be only nostalgia in advance. I don't know. I only know that it will always be happiness to remember you. And Stanley, and Bill—and England.

Our united love to you, and our gratitude

MARION SHARPE.

He laid the letter down on his brass and mahogany desk. Laid it down in the afternoon patch of sunlight.

Tomorrow at this time Marion would no longer be in England.

It was a desolating thought, but there was nothing to do but be sensible about it. What, indeed, was there to do about it?

And then three things happened at once.

Mr. Heseltine came in to say that Mrs. Lomax wanted to alter her will again, and would he go out to the farm immediately.

Aunt Lin rang up and asked him to call for the fish on his way home.

And Miss Tuff brought in his tea.

He looked for a long moment at the two digestive biscuits on the plate. Then, with a gentle finality, he pushed the tray out of his way and reached for the telephone.

$\sim\sim\sim\sim\sim\sim\sim\sim\sim\sim\sim\sim\sim\sim\sim$

· 24 ·

THE summer rain beat on the air-field with a dreary persistence. Every now and then the wind would lift it and sweep the terminus buildings with it in one long brush-stroke. The covered way to the Montreal plane was open on either side and the passengers bent their heads against the weather as they filed slowly into it. Robert, moving up at the tail of the queue, could see Mrs. Sharpe's flat black satin hat, and the short strands of white hair being blown about.

By the time he boarded the plane they were seated, and Mrs. Sharpe was already burrowing in her bag. As he walked up the aisle between the seats Marion looked up and saw him. Her face lighted with welcome and surprise.

"Robert!" she said. "Have you come to see us off?"

"No," Robert said. "I'm travelling by this plane."

"Travelling!" she said, staring. "*You* are?"

"It's a public conveyance, you know."

"I know, but—you're going to Canada?"

"I am."

"What for?"

"To see my sister in Saskatchewan," Robert said demurely. "A much better pretext than a cousin at McGill."

She began to laugh; softly and consumedly.

"Oh, Robert, my dear," she said, "you can't imagine how revolting you are when you look smug!"

238

Brat Farrar

1

"AUNT BEE," said Jane, breathing heavily into her soup, "was Noah a cleverer back-room boy than Ulysses, or was Ulysses a cleverer back-room boy than Noah?"

"Don't eat out of the point of your spoon, Jane."

"I can't mobilise the strings out of the side."

"Ruth does."

Jane looked across at her twin, negotiating the vermicelli with smug neatness.

"She has a stronger suck than I have."

"Aunt Bee has a face like a very expensive cat," Ruth said, eyeing her aunt sideways.

Bee privately thought that this was a very good description, but wished that Ruth would not be quaint.

"No, but which was the cleverest?" said Jane, who never departed from a path once her feet were on it.

"Clever-*er*," said Ruth.

"Was it Noah or Ulysses? Simon, which was it, do you think?"

"Ulysses," said her brother, not looking up from his paper.

It was so like Simon, Bee thought, to be reading the list of runners at Newmarket, peppering his soup, and listening to the conversation at one and the same time.

"Why, Simon? Why Ulysses?"

"He hadn't Noah's good Met. service. Whereabouts was Firelight in the Free Handicap, do you remember?"

"Oh, away down," Bee said.

"A coming-of-age is a little like a wedding, isn't it, Simon?" This was Ruth.

"Better on the whole."

"Is it?"

"You can stay and dance at your own coming of age. Which you can't at your wedding."

"I shall stay and dance at *my* wedding."

"I wouldn't put it past you."

1

Oh, dear, thought Bee, I suppose there are families that have *conversation* at meals, but I don't know how they manage it. Perhaps I haven't been strict enough.

She looked down the table at the three bent heads, and Eleanor's still vacant place, and wondered if she had done right by them. Would Bill and Nora be pleased with what she had made of their children? If by some miracle they could walk in now, young and fine-looking and gay as they had gone to their deaths, would they say: "Ah, yes, that is just how we pictured them; even to Jane's ragamuffin look."

Bee's eyes smiled as they rested on Jane.

The twins were nine-going-on-ten and identical. Identical, that is to say, in the technical sense. In spite of their physical resemblance there was never any doubt as to which was Jane and which was Ruth. They had the same straight flaxen hair, the same small-boned face and pale skin, the same direct gaze with a challenge in it; but there the identity stopped. Jane was wearing rather grubby jodhpurs and a shapeless jersey festooned with pulled ends of wool. Her hair was pushed back without aid of mirror and held in the uncompromising clasp of a kirby-grip so old that it had reverted to its original steel colour, as old hairpins do. She was slightly astigmatic and, when in the presence of Authority, was in the habit of wearing horn-rimmed spectacles. Normally they lived in the hip pocket of her breeches, and they had been lain-upon, leant-upon, and sat-upon so often that she lived in a permanent state of bankruptcy: breakages over the yearly allowance having to be paid for out of her money-box. She rode to and fro to lessons at the Rectory on Fourposter, the old white pony; her short legs sticking out on either side of him like straws. Fourposter had long ago become a conveyance rather than a ride, so it did not matter that his great barrel was as manageable as a feather-bed and almost as wide.

Ruth, on the other hand, wore a pink cotton frock, as fresh as when she had set off on her bicycle that morning for the Rectory. Her hands were clean and the nails unbroken, and somewhere she had found a pink ribbon and had tied the two side-pieces of her hair in a bow on the top of her head.

Eight years, Bee was thinking. Eight years of contriving, conserving, and planning. And in six weeks' time her stewardship would come to an end. In little more than a month Simon would be twenty-

2

one, and would inherit his mother's fortune and the lean years would be over. The Ashbys had never been rich but while her brother lived there was ample to keep Latchetts—the house and the three farms on the estate—as it should be kept. Only his sudden death had accounted for the near-poverty of those eight years. And only Bee's own resolution accounted for the fact that her sister-in-law's money would, next month, come to her son intact. There had been no borrowing on the strength of that future inheritance. Not even when Mr. Sandal, of Cosset, Thring and Noble, had been prepared to countenance it. Latchetts must pay its way, Bee had said. And Latchetts, after eight years, was still self-supporting and solvent.

Beyond her nephew's fair head she could see, through the window, the white rails of the south paddock, and the flick of old Regina's tail in the sunlight. It was the horses that had saved them. The horses that had been her brother's hobby had proved the salvation of his house. Year after year, in spite of all the ills, accidents, and sheer cussedness that afflict horseflesh, the horses had shown a profit. The swings had always paid a little more than the roundabouts. When the original small stud that had been her brother's delight seemed likely to be a doubtful prop, Bee had added the small hardy children's ponies to occupy the colder pastures half-way up the down. Eleanor had schooled doubtful hacks into "safe rides for a lady," and had sold them at a profit. And now that the manor was a boarding-school she was teaching others to ride, at a very respectable price per hour.

"Eleanor is very late, isn't she?"

"Is she out with La Parslow?" Simon asked.

"The Parslow girl, yes."

"The unhappy horse has probably dropped dead."

Simon got up to take away the soup plates, and to help out the meat course from the sideboard, and Bee watched him with critical approval. At least she had managed not to spoil Simon; and that, given Simon's selfish charm, was no small achievement. Simon had an air of appealing dependence that was quite fallacious, but it had fooled all and sundry since he was in the nursery. Bee had watched the fooling process with amusement and something that was like a reluctant admiration; if she herself had been gifted with Simon's particular brand of charm, she felt, she would in all likelihood have made it work for her as Simon did. But she had seen to it that it did not work with her.

3

"It would be nice if a coming-of-age had something like brides-maids," Ruth observed, turning over her helping with a fastidious fork.

This fell on stony ground.

"The Rector says that Ulysses was probably a frightful nuisance round the house," said the undeviating Jane.

"Oh!" said Bee, interested in this sidelight on the classics. "Why?"

"He said he was 'without doubt a—a gadget-contriver,' and that Penelope was probably very glad to be rid of him for a bit. I wish liver wasn't so *smooth*."

Eleanor came in and helped herself from the sideboard in her usual silent fashion.

"Pah!" said Ruth. "What a smell of stables."

"You're late, Nell," Bee said, inquiring.

"She'll never ride," Eleanor said. "She can't even bump the saddle yet."

"Perhaps loony people can't ride," Ruth suggested.

"Ruth," Bee said, with vigour. "The pupils at the Manor are not lunatic. They are not even mentally deficient. They are just 'difficult.'"

"Ill-adjusted is the technical description," Simon said.

"Well, they *behave* like lunatics. If you behave like a lunatic how is anyone to tell that you're not one?"

Since no one had an answer to this, silence fell over the Ashby luncheon table. Eleanor ate with the swift purposefulness of a hungry schoolboy, not lifting her eyes from her plate. Simon took out a pencil and reckoned odds on the margin of his paper. Ruth, who had stolen three biscuits from the jar on the Rectory sideboard and eaten them in the lavatory, made a castle of her food with a moat of gravy round it. Jane consumed hers with industrious pleasure. And Bee sat with her eyes on the view beyond the window.

Over that far ridge the land sloped in chequered miles to the sea and the clustered roofs of Westover. But here, in this high valley, shut off from the Channel gales and open to the sun, the trees stood up in the bright air with a midland serenity: with an air, almost, of enchantment. The scene had the bright perfection and stillness of an apparition.

A fine inheritance; a fine rich inheritance. She hoped that Simon would do well by it. There were times when she had—no, not been afraid. Times perhaps when she had wondered. Simon had far too

4

many sides to him; a quicksilver quality that did not go with a yeoman inheritance. Only Latchetts, of all the surrounding estates, still sheltered a local family and Bee hoped that it would go on sheltering Ashbys for centuries to come. Fair, small-boned, long-headed Ashbys like the ones round the table.

"Jane, must you splash fruit juice round like that?"

"I don't like rhubarb in inches, Aunt Bee, I like it in mush."

"Well, mush it more carefully."

When she had been Jane's age she had mushed up her rhubarb too, and at this same table. At this same table had eaten Ashbys who had died of fever in India, of wounds in the Crimea, of starvation in Queensland, of typhoid at the Cape, and of cirrhosis of the liver in the Straits Settlements. But always there had been an Ashby at Latchetts; and they had done well by the land. Here and there came a ne'er-do-well—like her cousin Walter—but Providence had seen to it that the worthless quality had been confined to younger sons, who could practise their waywardness on subjects remote from Latchetts.

No queens had come to Latchetts to dine; no cavaliers to hide. For three hundred years it had stood in its meadows very much as it stood now; a yeoman's dwelling. And for nearly two of those three hundred years Ashbys had lived in it.

"Simon, dear, see to the cona."

Perhaps its simplicity had saved it. It had pretended to nothing; had aspired to nothing. Its goodness had been dug back into the earth; its sap had returned to its roots. Across the valley the long white house of Clare stood in its park, gracious as a vicereine, but there were no Ledinghams there now. The Ledinghams had been prodigal of their talents and their riches; using Clare as a background, as a purse, as a decoration, as a refuge, but not as a home. For centuries they had peacocked over the world: as pro-consuls, explorers, court jesters, rakes, and revolutionaries; and Clare had supported their extravagances. Now only their portraits remained. And the great house in the park was a boarding-school for the unmanageable children of parents with progressive ideas and large bank accounts.

But the Ashbys stayed at Latchetts.

2

As Bee poured the coffee the twins disappeared on ploys of their own, this being their half-holiday; and Eleanor drank hers hastily and went back to the stables.

"Do you want the car this afternoon?" Simon asked. "I half promised old Gates that I would bring a calf out from Westover in one of our trailers. His own has collapsed."

"No, I don't need it," Bee said, wondering what had prompted Simon to so dull a chore. She hoped it was not the Gates daughter; who was very pretty, very silly, and very commonplace. Gates was the tenant of Wigsell, the smallest of the three farms; and Simon was not normally tolerant of his opportunism.

"If you really want to know," Simon said as he got up, "I want to see June Kaye's new picture. It's at the Empire."

The disarming frankness of this would have delighted anyone but Beatrice Ashby, who knew very well her nephew's habit of throwing up two balls to divert your attention from the third.

"Can I fetch you anything?"

"You might get one of the new bus timetables from the Westover and District offices if you have time. Eleanor says they have a new Clare service that goes round by Guessgate."

"Bee," said a voice in the hall. "Are you there, Bee?"

"Mrs. Peck," Simon said, going out to meet her.

"Come in, Nancy," Bee called. "Come and have coffee with me. The others have finished."

And the Rector's wife came into the room, put her empty basket on the sideboard, and sat down with a pleased sigh. "I could do with some," she said.

When people mentioned Mrs. Peck's name they still added: "Nancy Ledingham that was, you know;" although it was a decade since she had stunned the social world by marrying George Peck and burying herself in a country rectory. Nancy Ledingham had been more than the "débutante of her year;" she had been a national possession. The penny Press had done for her what the penny post-

6

card had done for Lily Langtry: her beauty was common property. If the public did not stand on chairs to see her pass they certainly stopped the traffic; her appearance as bridesmaid at a wedding was enough to give the authorities palpitations for a week beforehand. She had that serene unquestionable loveliness that defeats even a willing detractor. Indeed the only question seemed to be whether the ultimate coronet would have strawberry leaves or not. More than once the popular Press had supplied her with a crown, but this was generally considered mere wishful thinking; her public would settle for strawberry leaves.

And then, quite suddenly—between a *Tatler* and a *Tatler*, so to speak—she had married George Peck. The shattered Press, doing the best they could for a shattered public, had pulled out the *vox humana* stop and quavered about romance, but George had defeated them. He was a tall, thin man with the face of a very intelligent and rather nice ape. Besides, as the society editor of the *Clarion* said: "A clergyman! I ask you! I could get more romance out of a cement-mixer!"

So the public let her go, into her chosen oblivion. Her aunt, who had been responsible for her coming-out, disinherited her. Her father died in a welter of chagrin and debts. And her old home, the great white house in the park, had become a school.

But after thirteen years of rectory life Nancy Peck was still serenely and unquestionably beautiful; and people still said: "Nancy Ledingham that was, you know."

"I've come for the eggs," she said, "but there's no hurry, is there? It's wonderful to sit and do nothing."

Bee's eyes slid sideways at her in a smile.

"You have such a nice face, Bee."

"Thank you. Ruth says it is a face like a very expensive cat."

"Nonsense. At least—not the furry kind. Oh, I know what she means! The long-necked, short-haired kind that show their small chins. Heraldic cats. Yes, Bee, darling, you have a face like a heraldic cat. Especially when you keep your head still and slide your eyes at people." She put her cup down and sighed again with pleasure. "I can't think how the Nonconformists have failed to discover coffee."

"Discover it?"

"Yes. As a snare. It does far more for one than drink. And yet no one preaches about it, or signs pledges about it. Five mouthfuls and the world looks rosy."

7

"Was it very grey before?"

"A sort of mud colour. I was so happy this week because it was the first week this year that we hadn't needed sitting-room fires and I had no fires to do and no fireplaces to clean. But nothing—I repeat, nothing—will stop George from throwing his used matches into the fireplace. And as he takes fifteen matches to light one pipe——! The room swarms with waste-paper baskets and ash trays, but no, George must use the fireplace. He doesn't even *aim*, blast him. A fine careless flick of the wrist and the match lands anywhere from the fender to the farthest coal. And they have all got to be picked out again."

"And he says: why don't you leave them."

"He does. However, now that I've had some Latchetts coffee I have decided not to take a chopper to him after all."

"Poor Nan. These Christians."

"How are the coming-of-age preparations getting on?"

"The invitations are about to go to the printers; which is a nice definite stage to have arrived at. A dinner for intimates, here; and a dance for everyone in the barn. What is Alec's address, by the way?"

"I can't remember his latest one off-hand. I'll look it up for you. He has a different one almost every time he writes. I think he gets heaved out when he can't pay his rent. Not that I hear from him often, of course. He has never forgiven me for not marrying well, so that I could keep my only brother in the state to which he had been accustomed."

"Is he playing just now?"

"I don't know. He had a part in that silly comedy at the Savoy but it ran only a few weeks. He is so much a type that his parts are necessarily limited."

"Yes, I suppose so."

"No one could cast Alec as anything but Alec. You don't know how lucky you are, Bee, to have Ashbys to deal with. The incidence of rakes in the Ashby family is singularly low."

"There was Walter."

"A lone wolf crying in the wilderness. What became of Cousin Walter?"

"Oh, he died."

"In an odour of sanctity?"

"No. Carbolic. A workhouse ward, I think."

8

"Even Walter wasn't bad, you know. He just liked drink and hadn't the head for it. But when a Ledingham is a rake he is plain bad."

They sat together in a comfortable silence, considering their respective families. Bee was several years older than her friend: almost a generation older. But neither could remember a time when the other was not there; and the Ledingham children had gone in and out of Latchetts as if it were their home, as familiar with it as the Ashbys were with Clare.

"I have been thinking so often lately of Bill and Nora," Nancy said. "This would have been such a happy time for them."

"Yes," Bee said, reflectively; her eyes on the window. It was at that view she had been looking when it happened. On a day very like this and at this time of the year. Standing in the sitting-room window, thinking how lovely everything looked and if they would think that nothing they had seen in Europe was half as lovely. Wondering if Nora would look well again; she had been very pulled down after the twins' birth. Hoping she had been a good deputy for them, and yet a little pleased to be resuming her own life in London to-morrow.

The twins had been asleep, and the older children upstairs grooming themselves for the welcome and for the dinner they were to be allowed to stay up for. In half an hour or so the car would swing out from the avenue of lime trees and come to rest at the door and there they would be; in a flurry of laughter and embracing and present-giving and well-being.

The turning on of the wireless had been so absent-minded a gesture that she did not know that she had done it. "The two o'clock plane from Paris to London," said the cool voice, "with nine passengers and a crew of three crashed this afternoon just after crossing the Kent coast. There were no survivors."

No. There had been no survivors.

"They were so wrapped up in the children," Nancy said. "They have been so much in my mind lately, now that Simon is going to be twenty-one."

"And Patrick has been in mine."

"Patrick?" Nancy sounded at a loss. "Oh, yes, of course. Poor Pat."

Bee looked at her curiously. "You had almost forgotten, hadn't you?"

9

"Well, it is a long time ago, Bee. And—well, I suppose one's mind tidies away the things it can't bear to remember. Bill and Nora—that was frightful, but it *was* something that happened to people. I mean, it was part of the ordinary risks of life. But Pat—that was different." She sat silent for a moment. "I have pushed it so far down in my mind that I can't even remember what he looked like any more. Was he as like Simon as Ruth is like Jane?"

"Oh, no. They weren't identical twins. Not much more alike than some brothers are. Though oddly enough they were much more in each other's pockets than Ruth and Jane are."

"Simon seems to have got over it. Do you think he remembers it often?"

"He must have remembered it very often lately."

"Yes. But it is a long way between thirteen and twenty-one. I expect even a twin grows shadowy at that distance."

This gave Bee pause. How shadowy was he to her: the kind solemn little boy who should have been coming into his inheritance next month? She tried to call up his face in front of her but there was only a blur. He had been small and immature for his age, but otherwise he was just an Ashby. Less an individual than a family resemblance. All she really remembered, now she thought about it, was that he was solemn and kind.

Kindness was not a common trait in small boys.

Simon had a careless generosity when it did not cost him inconvenience; but Patrick had had that inner kindness that not only gives but gives up.

"I still wonder," Bee said unhappily, "whether we should have allowed the body that was found on the Castleton beach to be buried over there. A pauper's burial, it was."

"But, Bee! It had been months in the water, hadn't it? They couldn't even tell what sex it was; could they? And Castleton is miles away. And they get all the corpses from the Atlantic founderings, anyhow. I mean, the nearer ones. It is not sense to worry over—to identify it with——" Her dismayed voice died into silence.

"No, of course it isn't!" Bee said briskly. "I am just being morbid. Have some more coffee."

And as she poured the coffee she decided that when Nancy had gone she would unlock the private drawer of her desk and burn that pitiful note of Patrick's. It was morbid to keep it, even if she had not

10

looked at it for years. She had never had the heart to tear it up because it had seemed part of Patrick. But of course that was absurd. It was no more part of Patrick than was the despair that had filled him when he wrote: "I'm sorry, but I can't bear it any longer. Don't be angry with me. Patrick." She would take it out and burn it. Burning it would not blot it from her mind, of course, but there was nothing she could do about that. The round schoolboy letters were printed there for always. Round, careful letters written with the stylograph that he had been so attached to. It was so like Patrick to apologise for taking his own life.

Nancy, watching her friend's face, proffered what she considered to be consolation. "They say, you know, that when you throw yourself from a high place you lose consciousness almost at once."

"I don't think he did it that way, Nan."

"No!" Nancy sounded staggered. "But that was where the note was found. I mean, the coat with the note in the pocket. On the cliff-top."

"Yes, but by the path. By the path down the Gap to the shore."

"Then what do you——?"

"I think he swam out."

"Till he couldn't come back, you mean?"

"Yes. When I was *in loco parentis* that time, when Bill and Nora were on holiday, we went several times to the Gap, the children and I; to swim and have a picnic. And once when we were there Patrick said that the best way to die—I think he called it the lovely way— would be to swim out until you were too tired to go any farther. He said it quite matter-of-factly, of course. In those days it was—a mere academic matter. When I pointed out that drowning would still be drowning, he said: 'But you would be so tired, you see; you wouldn't care any more. The water would just take you.' He loved the water."

She was silent for a little and then blurted out the thing that had been her private nightmare for years.

"I've always been afraid that when it was too late to come back he may have regretted."

"Oh, Bee, no!"

Bee's sidelong glance went to Nancy's beautiful, protesting face.

"Morbid. I know. Forget I said it."

"I don't know now how I *could* have forgotten," Nancy said, wondering. "The worst of pushing horrible things down into one's sub-

11

conscious is that when they pop up again they are as fresh as if they had been in a refrigerator. You haven't allowed time to get at them to—to mould them over a little."

"I think a great many people have almost forgotten that Simon had a twin," Bee said, excusing. "Or that he has not always been the heir. Certainly no one has mentioned Patrick to me since the coming-of-age celebrations have been in the air."

"Why was Patrick so inconsolable about his parents' death?"

"I didn't know he was. None of us did. All the children were wild with grief to begin with, of course. Sick with it. But none more than another. Patrick seemed bewildered rather than inconsolable. 'You mean: Latchetts belongs to me now?' I remember him saying, as if it were some strange idea, difficult to understand. Simon was impatient with him, I remember. Simon was always the brilliant one. I think that it was all too much for Patrick; too strange. The adrift feeling of being suddenly without his father and mother, and the weight of Latchetts on his shoulders. It was too much for him and he was so unhappy that he—took a way out."

"Poor Pat. Poor darling. It was wrong of me to forget him."

"Come; let us go and get those eggs. You won't forget to let me have Alec's address, will you? A Ledingham must have an invitation."

"No, I'll look it up when I go back, and telephone it to you. Can your latest moron take a telephone message?"

"Just."

"Well, I'll stick to basic. You won't forget that he is Alec Loding on the stage, will you?" She picked up her basket from the sideboard. "I wonder if he would come. It is a long time since he has been to Clare. A country life is not Alec's idea of amusement. But an Ashby coming-of-age is surely something that would interest him."

3

But Alec Loding's main interest in the Ashby coming-of-age was to blow the celebrations sky-high. Indeed, he was at this moment actively engaged in pulling strings to that end.

12

Or, rather, trying to pull strings. The strings weren't pulling very well.

He was sitting in the back room at the Green Man, the remains of lunch spread before him, and beside him sat a young man. A boy, one would have said, but for something controlled and still that did not go with adolescence. Loding poured coffee for himself and sugared it liberally; casting a glance now and then at his companion, who was turning an almost empty beer glass round and round on the table. The movement was so deliberate that it hardly came under the heading of fidgeting.

"Well?" said Loding at last.

"No."

Loding took a mouthful of coffee.

"Squeamish?"

"I'm not an actor."

Something in the unaccented phrase seemed to sting Loding and he flushed a little.

"You're not asked to be emotional, if that is what you mean. There is no filial devotion to be simulated, you know. Only dutiful affection for an aunt you haven't seen for nearly ten years—which one would expect to be more dutiful than affectionate."

"No."

"You young idiot, I'm offering you a fortune."

"Half a fortune. And you're not offering me anything."

"If I'm not offering it to you, what am I doing?"

"Propositioning me," said the young man. He had not raised his eyes from his slowly-turning beer.

"Very well, I'm propositioning you, to use your barbarous idiom. What is wrong with the proposition?"

"It's crazy."

"What is crazy about it, given the initial advantage of your existence?"

"No one could bring it off."

"It is not so long since a famous general whose face was a household word—if you will forgive the metaphor—was impersonated quite successfully by an actor in broad daylight and in full view of the multitude."

"That is quite different."

"I agree. You aren't asked to impersonate anyone. Just to be yourself. A much easier task."

"No," said the young man.

Loding kept his temper with a visible effort. He had a pink, collapsed face that reminded one of the underside of fresh mushrooms. The flesh hung away from his good Ledingham bones with a discouraged slackness, and the incipient pouches under his eyes detracted from their undoubted intelligence. Managers who had once cast him for gay young rakes now offered him nothing but discredited roués.

"My God!" he said suddenly. "Your teeth!"

Even that did not startle the young man's face into any expression. He lifted his eyes for the first time, resting them incuriously on Loding. "What's the matter with my teeth?" he asked.

"It's how they identify people nowadays. A dentist keeps a record of work, you know. I wonder where those kids went. Something would have to be done about that. Are those front teeth your own?"

"The two middle ones are caps. They were kicked out."

"They went to someone here in town, I remember that much. There was a London trip to see the dentist twice a year; once before Christmas and once in the summer. They went to the dentist in the morning and to a show in the afternoon: pantomime in the winter and the Tournament at Olympia in the summer. These are the kind of things you would have to know, by the way."

"Yes?"

The gentle monosyllable maddened Loding.

"Look, Farrar, what are you frightened of? A strawberry mark? I bathed with that kid in the buff many a time and he hadn't as much as a mole on him. He was so ordinary that you could order him by the dozen from any prep. school in England. You are more like his brother at this moment than that kid ever was, twins though they were. I tell you, I thought for a moment that you *were* young Ashby. Isn't that good enough for you? You come and live with me for a fortnight and by the end of it there won't be anything you don't know about the village of Clare and its inhabitants. Nor anything about Latchetts. I know every last pantry in it. Nor anything about the Ashbys. Can you swim, by the way?"

The young man nodded. He had gone back to his glass of beer.

"Swim well?"

"Yes."

"Don't you ever qualify a statement?"

"Not unless it needs it."

"The kid could swim like an eel. There's the matter of ears, too. Yours look ordinary enough, and his must have been ordinary too or I should remember. Anyone who has worked in a life-class notices ears. But I must see what photographs of him exist. Front ones wouldn't matter, but a real close-up of an ear might be a give-away. I think I must take a trip to Clare and do some prospecting."

"Don't bother on my account."

Loding was silent for a moment. Then he said, reasonably: "Tell me, do you believe my story at all?"

"Your story?"

"Do you believe that I am who I say I am, and that I come from a village called Clare, where there is someone who is practically your double? Do you believe that? Or do you think that this is just a way of getting you to come home with me?"

"No, I didn't think it was that. I believe your story."

"Well, thank heaven for that, at least," Loding said with a quirk of his eyebrow. "I know that my looks are not what they were, but I should be shattered to find that they suggested the predatory. Well, then. That settled, do you believe that you are as like young Ashby as I say?"

For a whole turn of the glass there was no answer. "I doubt it."

"Why?"

"On your own showing it is some time since you saw him."

"But you don't have to be young Ashby. Just look like him. And believe me you do! My God, how you do! It's something I wouldn't have believed unless I saw it with my own eyes; something I have imagined only happened in books. And it is worth a fortune to you. You have only to put out your hand and take it."

"Oh, no, I haven't."

"Metaphorically speaking. Do you realise that except for the first year or so your story would be truth? It would be your own story; able to stand up to any amount of checking." His voice twisted into a comedy note. "Or—would it?"

"Oh, yes, it would check."

"Well, then. You have only to stow away on the *Ira Jones* out of Westover instead of going for a day trip to Dieppe, *et voilà!*"

15

"How do you know there was a ship called the *Ira Jones* at West-over about then?"

"'About then'! You do me scant justice, *amigo*. There was a ship of that repellent title at Westover the day the boy disappeared. I know because I spent most of the day painting her. On canvas, not on her plates, you understand. And the old scow went out before I had finished; bound for the Channel Islands. All my ships go out before I have finished painting them."

There was silence for a little.

"It's in your lap, Farrar."

"So is my table napkin."

"A fortune. A charming small estate. Security. A——"

"*Security,* did you say?"

"After the initial gamble, of course," Loding said smoothly.

The light eyes that looked at him for a moment held a faint amusement.

"Hadn't it occurred to you at all, Mr. Loding, that the gamble was yours?"

"Mine?"

"You're offering me the sweetest chance for a double-cross that I ever heard. of. I take your coaching, pass the exam, and forget about you. And you wouldn't be able to do a thing about it. How did you figure to keep tabs on me?"

"I hadn't. No one with your Ashby looks could be a double-crosser. The Ashbys are monsters of rectitude."

The boy pushed away the glass.

"Which must be why I don't take kindly to the idea of being a phoney. Thank you for my lunch, Mr. Loding. If I had known what you had in mind when you asked me to lunch with you, I wouldn't have——"

"All right, all right. Don't apologise. And don't run away; we'll go together. You don't like my proposition: very good: so be it. But you, on the other hand, fascinate me. I can hardly take my eyes off you, or believe that anything so unique exists. And since you are sure that my improper proposal to you has nothing of the personal in it, there is nothing against our walking as far as the Underground together."

Loding paid for their lunch, and as they walked out of the Green Man he said: "I won't ask where you are living in case you think

I want to hound you. But I shall give you my address in the hope that you will come to see me. Oh, no; not about the proposition. If it isn't your cup of tea then it isn't your cup of tea; and if you felt like that you certainly wouldn't make a success of it. No, not about the proposition. I have something in my rooms that I think would interest you."

He paused artistically while they negotiated a street crossing.

"When my old home, Clare, was sold—after my father's death—Nancy bundled together all the personal things in my room and sent them to me. A whole trunkful of rubbish, which I have never had the energy to get rid of, and a large proportion of it consists of snapshots and photographs of the companions of my youth. I think you would find it very interesting."

He glanced sideways at the uncommunicative profile of his companion.

"Tell me," he said as they stopped at the entrance to the Underground, "do you play cards?"

"Not with strangers," said the young man pleasantly.

"I just wondered. I had never met the perfect poker face until now, and I should be sorry if it was being wasted on some nonconformist abstainer. Ah, well. Here is my address. If by any chance I have fled from there the *Spotlight* will find me. I am truly sorry I couldn't sell you the idea of being an Ashby. You would have made an excellent master of Latchetts, I feel. Someone who was at home with horses, and used to an outdoor life."

The young man, who had made a gesture of farewell and was in the act of turning away, paused. "Horses?" he said.

"Yes," Loding said, vaguely surprised. "It's a stud, you know. Very well thought of, I understand."

"Oh." He paused a moment longer, and then turned away.

Loding watched him as he went down the street. "I missed something," he was thinking. "There was some bait he would have risen to, and I missed it. Why should he have nibbled at the word horse? He must be sick of them."

Ah, well; perhaps he would come to see what his double looked like.

4

Tʜᴇ boy lay on his bed in the dark, fully dressed, and stared at the ceiling.

There were no street lamps outside to illuminate this back room under the slates; but the faint haze of light that hangs over London at night, emanation from a million arcs and gas-lights and paraffin lamps, shone ghost-like on the ceiling so that its cracks and stains showed like a world map.

The boy was looking at a map of the world too, but it was not on the ceiling. He was examining his odyssey; conducting a private inventory. That meeting to-day had shaken him. Somewhere, it seemed, there was another fellow so like him that for a moment they could be mistaken for each other. To one who had been very much alone all his life that was an amazing thought.

Indeed, it was the most surprising thing that had happened to him in all his twenty-one years. In a way it was as if all those years that had seemed so full and exciting at the time had been merely leading up to that moment when the actor chap had caught himself short in the street and said: "Hello, Simon."

"Oh! Sorry!" he had said at once. "Thought you were a friend of——" And then he had stopped and stared.

"Can I do something for you?" the boy had asked at last, since the man showed no sign of moving on.

"Yes. You could come and have lunch with me."

"Why?"

"It's lunch-time, and that's my favourite pub behind you."

"But why me?"

"Because you interest me. You are so like a friend of mine. My name is Loding, by the way. Alec Loding. I act a bad part in a bad farce at that very bad old theatre over there." He had nodded across the street. "But Equity, God bless them, has ordained a minimum fee for my labours, so the hire is considerably better than the part, I rejoice to say. Do you mind telling me your name?"

"Farrar."

"Farrell?"

"No. Farrar."

"Oh." The amused, considering look was still in his eye. "Is it long since you came back to England?"

"How did you know I had been out of it?"

"Your clothes, my boy. Clothes are my business. I have dressed too many parts not to recognise American tailoring when I see it. Even the admirably conservative tailoring that you so rightly wear."

"Then what makes you think I'm not American?"

At that the man had smiled quite broadly. "Ah, *that*," he said, "is the eternal mystery of the English. You watch a procession of monks in Italy and your eye singles out one and you say: 'Ha! An English-man.' You come across five hoboes wrapped in gunny sacks sheltering from the rain in Wisconsin, and you notice the fifth and think: 'Dear goodness, that chap's English.' You see ten men stripped to the buff for the Foreign Legion doctor to pass judgement on, and you say—— But come to lunch and we can explore the subject at leisure."

So he had gone to lunch, and the man had talked and been charming. But always behind the lively puffy eyes there had been that quizzical, amused, almost unbelieving look. That look was more eloquent than any of his subsequent argument. Truly he, Brat Farrar, *must* be like that other fellow to bring that look of half-incredulous amusement into someone's eyes.

He lay on the bed and thought about it. This sudden identification in an unbelonging life. He had a great desire to see this twin of his; this Ashby boy. Ashby. It was a nice name: a good English name. He would like to see the place too: this Latchetts, where his twin had grown up in belonging quiet while he had bucketed round the world, all the way from the orphanage to that moment in a London street, belonging nowhere.

The orphanage. It was no fault of the orphanage that he had not belonged. It was a very good orphanage; a great deal happier than many a home he had seen in passing since. The children had loved it. They had wept when they left and had come back for visits; they had sent contributions to the funds; they had invited the staff to their marriages, and brought their subsequent children for the matron's approval. There was never a day when some old girl or boy was not cluttering up the front door. Then why had he not felt like that?

Because he was a foundling? Was that why? Because no visitors ever came for him; no parcels or letters or invitations? But they had been very wise about that; very determined to prop his self-esteem. If anything he had been privileged beyond the other children by his foundling status. His Christmas present from Matron, he remembered, had been looked upon with envy by children whose only present came from an aunt or uncle; a mere relation, as it were. It was Matron who had taken him off the doorstep; and who saw to it that he heard how well-dressed and cared-for he had been. (He heard about this at judicious intervals for fifteen years but he had never been able to feel any satisfaction about it.) It was Matron who had determined his name with the aid of a pin and the telephone directory. The pin had come down on the word Farrell. Which had pleased Matron considerably; her pin had once, long ago, come down on the word Coffin, and she had had to cheat and try again.

There had never been any doubt about his first name, since he had arrived on the doorstep on St. Bartholomew's day. He had been Bart from the beginning. But the older children had changed that to Brat, and presently even the staff used the more familiar name (another device of Matron's to prevent his feeling "different"?) and the name had followed him to the grammar school.

The grammar school. Why had he not "belonged" there, then?

Because his clothes were subtly different? Surely not. He had not been thin-skinned as a child; merely detached. Because he was a scholarship boy? Certainly not: half his form were scholarship boys. Then why had he decided that the school was not for him? Decided with such un-boylike finality that all Matron's arguments had died into ultimate silence, and she had countenanced his going to work.

There was no mystery about his not liking the work, of course. The office job had been fifty miles away, and since no ordinary lodgings could be paid for out of his salary he had had to stay in the local "boys' home." He had not known how good the orphanage was until he had sampled the boys' home. He could have supported either the job or the home, but not the two simultaneously. And of the two the office was by far the worse. It was, as a job, comfortable, leisurely, and graced with certain, if far-off, prospects; but to him it had been a prison. He was continually aware of time running past him; time that he was wasting. This was not what he wanted.

20

He had said good-bye to his office life almost accidentally; certainly without premeditation. "DAY RETURN TO DIEPPE" a bill had said, plastered against the glass of a newsagent's window; and the price, in large red figures, was exactly the amount of his savings to the nearest half-crown. Even so, he would have done nothing about it if it had not been for old Mr. Hendren's funeral. Mr. Hendren was the "retired" partner, and on the day of his funeral the office shut down "out of respect." And so, with a week's pay in his pocket and a whole week-day free, he had taken his savings and gone to see "abroad." He had had a grand time in Dieppe, where his first-year French was no deterrent to enjoyment, but it had not even crossed his mind to stay there until he was on his way home. He had reached the harbour before the shocking idea took hold of him.

Was it native honesty, he thought, staring at the Pimlico ceiling, or his good orphanage training that had made his unpaid laundry bill bulk so large in the subsequent mental struggle? A boy who had no money and no bed for the night should hardly have been concerned with the ethics of bilking a laundry of two-and-threepence.

The camion, rolling up from the harbour, had been his salvation. He had held up his thumb, and the brown, sweaty brigand at the wheel had grinned at this international gesture and slowed as he passed. He had run at the moving cliff-face, snatched and clung, and been hauled aboard. And all his old life was behind him.

He had planned to stay and work in France. Debated with himself during the long run to Havre, when gesture had given out and the driver's patois proved unintelligible, how best he might earn enough to eat. It was his neighbour in the Havre *bistro* who enlightened him. "My young friend," the man had said, fixing him with melancholy spaniel's eyes, "it is not sufficient to be a man in France in order to work. One has also to have papers."

"And where," he had asked, "does one not have papers? I mean, in what country? I can go anywhere." He was suddenly conscious of the world, and that he was free of it.

"God knows," the man had said. "Mankind grows every day more like sheep. Go to the harbour and take a ship."

"Which ship?"

"It is immaterial. Have you in English a game that——" He made descriptive gestures.

"A counting-out game? Oh, yes. Eenie, meenie, minie, moe."

21

"Good. Go to the harbour and do 'Eenie, meenie, minie, moe. And when you go aboard 'moe' see that no one is looking. On ships they have a passion for papers that amounts to a madness."

"Moe" was the *Barfleur,* and he had not needed papers after all. He was the gift from heaven that the *Barfleur's* cook had been looking for for years.

Good old *Barfleur;* with her filthy pea-green galley smelling of over-used olive oil, and the grey seas combing up mountains high, and the continuous miracle of their harmless passing, and the cook's weekly drunk that left him acting unpaid cook, and learning to play a mouth-organ, and the odd literature in the fo'c'sle. Good old *Barfleur!*

He had taken a lot away with him when he left her, but most important of all he took a new name. When he had written his name for the Captain, old Bourdet had taken the final double-L to be an R, and copied the name Farrar. And he had kept it so. Farrell came out of a telephone directory; and Farrar out of a tramp skipper's mistake. It was all one.

And then what?

Tampico and the smell of tallow. And the tally-man who had said: "You Englishman? You want shore job?"

He had gone to inspect the "job," expecting dish-washing.

Odd to think that he might still be living in that great quiet house with the tiled patio, and the bright scentless flowers, and the bare shadowed rooms with the beautiful furniture. Living in luxury, instead of lying on a broken-down bedstead in Pimlico. The old man had liked him, had wanted to adopt him; but he had not "belonged." He had enjoyed reading the English newspaper to him twice a day, the old man following with a slender yellow forefinger on his own copy; but it was not the life he was looking for. ("If he doesn't understand English, what's the good of reading English to him?" he had asked when the job was first explained to him; and they had made him understand that the old man knew "reading" English, having taught himself from a dictionary, but did not know how to pronounce it. He wanted to listen to it spoken by an Englishman.)

No, it had not been for him. It had been like living in a film set.

So he had gone as cook to a collection of botanists. And as he was packing to go the butler had said consolingly: "Better you go, after all. If you stay his mistress poison you."

It was the first he had heard of a mistress.

He had cooked his way steadily to the New Mexico border. That was the easy way into the States: where there was no river to stop you. He enjoyed this absurd, brilliant, angular country but, like the old aristocrat's home near Tampico, it was not what he was looking for.

After that it had been a slow crescendo of satisfaction.

Assistant cook for that outfit at Las Cruces. Their intolerance of any variation from the food they knew, and their delight in his accent. ("Say it again, Limey." And then their laughter and their delighted "Whaddya know!")

Cook to the Snake River round-up. And his discovery of horses. And the feeling it gave him of having come home.

Riding herd for the Santa Clara. And the discovery that "ornery" horses were less ornery when ridden by the limey kid.

A spell with the shoesmith at the Wilson ranch. He had had his first girl there, but it hadn't been half as exciting as seeing what he could do with the "hopeless lot" in the corral. "Nothing but shooting for them," the boss had said. And when he had suggested trying to do something about them, the boss had said unenthusiastically: "Go ahead; but don't expect me to pay hospital bills. You're hired as help to the farrier."

It was from that lot that Smoky came: his beautiful Smoky. The boss gave it him as a reward for what he had done with the hard cases. And when he went to the Lazy Y he took Smoky with him.

Breaking horses for the Lazy Y. That had been happiness. That had been happiness full up and running over. Nearly two years of it.

And then. That momentary slowness on his part; drowsy with heat or dazzled by the sun. And seeing the writhing brown back turning over on him. And hearing his thighbone crack.

The hospital at Edgemont. It had not been at all like the hospitals in films. There were no pretty nurses and no handsome internes. The ward had sage-green walls, the fittings were old and dingy, and the nurses overworked. They alternately spoiled and ignored him.

The sudden stoppage of letters from the boys.

The sweat-making business of learning to walk again, and the slow realisation that his leg had mended "short." That he was going to be permanently lame.

The letter from the boss that put an end to the Lazy Y.

23

Oil. They had struck oil. The first derrick was already going up not two hundred yards from the bunk house. The enclosed cheque would look after Brat till he was well again. Meanwhile, what should be done with Smoky?

What would a lame man do with a horse in an oil field?

He had cried about Smoky; lying in the dark of the ward. It was the first time he had cried about anyone.

Well, he might be too slow to break horses any more, but he would be no servant to oil. There were other ways of living with horseflesh.

The dude ranch. That had not been like the films either.

Ungainly women in unseemly clothes punishing the saddles of broken-spirited horses until he wondered that they didn't break in two.

The woman who had wanted to marry him.

She had been not at all the kind of woman you'd imagine would want a "kept man." Not fat or silly or amorous. She was thin, and tired-looking, and rather nice; and she had owned the place up the hill from the dude ranch. She would get his leg put right for him, she said. That was the bait she had offered.

The one good thing about the dude ranch was that you made money at it. He had never had so much money in his life as when he finished there. He planned to go East and spend it. And then something had happened to him. The smaller, greener country in the East, the smell of spring gardens, woke in him a nostalgia for England that dismayed him. He had no intention of going back to England for years yet.

For several restless weeks he fought the longing—it was a baby thing to want to go back—and then quite suddenly gave in. After all, he had never seen London. Going to see London was quite a legitimate reason for going to England.

And so to the back room in Pimlico and that meeting in the street.

5

He got up and took his cigarettes from the pocket of the coat that was hanging on the back of the door.

Why hadn't he been more shocked when Loding made his suggestion?

Because he had guessed that a proposition would be coming? Because the man's face had been warning enough that his interests would be shady? Because it quite simply had nothing to do with him, was not anything that he was likely to touch?

He had not been indignant with the man; had not said: "You swine, to think of cheating your friend out of his inheritance!" or words to that effect. But then he had never been interested in other people's concerns: their sins, their griefs, or their happiness. And anyhow, you couldn't be righteous with a man whose food you were eating.

He moved over to the window and stood looking out at the dim frieze of chimney-pots against the luminous haze. He was not broke yet but he had got the length of prospecting for a job, and the prospects were anything but encouraging. It seemed that there were far more people interested in stable jobs in England than stables to accommodate them. The horse world contracted as the horse lovers expanded. All those men who had lost their main interest in living when the cavalry was put down were still hale and active, and besieged stable entrances at the mere whiff of a vacancy.

Besides, he didn't want just to "do his two a day." If road engineering interested you you didn't pine to spend your days putting tar on the surface.

He had tried a few contacts, but none of the good places was interested in a lame stranger without references. Why should they be? They had their pick of England's best. And when he had mentioned that his experience of breaking had been in the States, that seemed to settle it. "Oh, cattle horses!" they said. They said it quite kindly and politely—he had forgotten until he came back how polite his countrymen were—but they had inferred in one way or another

25

that Western kill-or-cure methods were not theirs. Since they never said so openly he could not explain that they were not his either. And anyhow, it wouldn't have been any good. They wanted to know something about you before they took you to work with them in this country. In America, where a man moved on every so often, it was different; but here a job was for life, and what you were mattered almost as much as what you could do.

The solution, of course, was to leave the country. But the real, the insurmountable trouble was that he didn't want to go. Now that he was back he realised that what he had thought of as free, purposeless wandering had merely been a long way round on the way back to England. He had come back, not via Dieppe, but via Las Cruces and points east; that was all. He had found what he wanted when he found horses; but he had no more sense of "belonging" in New Mexico than he had had at the grammar school. He had liked New Mexico better, that was all.

And better still, now that he looked at it, he liked England. He wanted to work with English horses in an English greenness on English turf.

In any case, it was much more difficult to get out of this country than to get into it, if you were broke. He had shared a table at the Coventry Street Lyons one day with a man who had been trying for eighteen months to work his passage somewhere or other. "Cards!" the little man had snarled. "That's all they ever say. Where is your card? If you don't happen to belong to the Amalgamated Union of Table-napkin Folders you can't as much as help a steward set a table. I'm just waiting to see them let a ship sink under them because no one aboard has the right card for manning a pump with."

He had looked at the Englishman's furious blue eyes and remembered the man in the Havre *bistro*. "One has also to have papers." Yes, the world was cluttered up with paper.

It was a pity that Loding's proposition was so very criminal.

Would he have listened to it with any more interest if Loding had mentioned the horses earlier?

No, of course not; that was absurd. The thing was criminal and he wouldn't touch it.

"It would be quite safe, you know," said a voice in him. "They wouldn't prosecute you even if they found out, because of the scandal. Loding said that."

"Shut up," he said. "The thing's criminal."

It might be amusing to go and see Loding act, one night. He had never met an actor before. It would be a new sensation to sit and watch the performance of someone you knew "off." How would Loding be as a partner?

"A very clever partner, believe me," said the voice.

"A plain bad lot," he said. "I don't want any part of him."

"You don't need any part of any of it," said the voice. "You have only to go to Latchetts and say: Take a look at me. Do I remind you of anyone? I was left on a doorstep on such-and-such a date, and as from to-day I want a job."

"Blackmail, 'm? And how much do you think I'd enjoy a job I'd blackmailed out of anyone? Don't be silly."

"They owe you something, don't they?"

"No, they don't. Not a bean."

"Oh, come off it! You're an Ashby and you know it."

"I don't know it. There have been doubles before. Hitler had several. *Lots* of famous people have doubles. The papers are for ever printing photographs of the humble doubles of great men. They all look like the great men with the character sponged out."

"Bunk. You're an Ashby. Where did you get your way with horses?"

"Lots of people have a way with horses."

"There were sixty-two kids at that orphanage, and did any of them go about spurning good jobs, and adoption by rich parents, so that they could find their way to horses?"

"I didn't know I was looking for horses."

"Of course you didn't know. Your Ashby blood knew."

"Oh, shut up."

To-morrow he would go down to Lewes and have a go at that jumping stable. He might be lame but he could still ride anything on four legs. They might be interested in someone who could ride at ten stone and didn't mind risking his neck.

"Risk your neck when you might be living in clover?"

"If it was clover I wanted I could have had it long ago."

"Ah, but not clover with horses in it."

"Shut up. You're wasting your time."

He began to undress, as if movement might put an end to the voice. Yes: he would go down to Lewes. It was a little too near his calf country, but no one would recognise him after those six years.

27

It wouldn't really matter, of course, if they did; but he didn't want to go backwards.

"You could always say: Sorry, my name is Ashby," mocked the voice.

"Will you be quiet!"

As he hung his jacket over the back of the chair he thought about that young Ashby who had bowed out. With everything in the world to live for he had gone and thrown himself off a cliff. It didn't make sense. Did parents matter all that much?

"No, he was a poor thing, and you'd make a much better job of Latchetts in his place."

He poured cold water into the basin and washed vigorously; an orphanage training being almost as lasting as a Regular Service one. And as he towelled himself on the thin turkish—so old that it was limp-wet before he was dry—he thought: "I wouldn't like it, anyhow. Butlers, and things." His idea of English middle-class life being derived from American films.

Anyhow, the thing was unthinkable.

And he'd better stop thinking about it.

Someone had said that if you thought about the unthinkable long enough it became quite reasonable.

But he would go some time and see those photographs of Loding's. There was no harm in that.

He must see what his "twin" looked like.

He didn't like Loding much, but just going to see him could do no harm, and he did want to see photographs of Latchetts.

Yes, he would go to see Loding.

The day after to-morrow perhaps; after he had been to Lewes.

Or even to-morrow.

6

Mr. Sandal, of Cosset, Thring and Noble, was nearing the end of his afternoon's work and his mind was beginning its daily debate as to whether it should be the 4.55 or the 5.15 that should bear him home. This was almost the only debate that ever exercised

Mr. Sandal's mind. The clients of Cosset, Thring and Noble were of two kinds only: those who made up their own minds about a problem and told their solicitors in firm tones what they wanted done, and those who had no problems. The even pulse of the Georgian office in the shadow of the plane trees was never quickened by unexpected news or untoward happenings. Even the death of a client was not news: clients were expected to die; the appropriate will would be in the appropriate deed-box and things would go on as before.

Family solicitors; that is what Cosset, Thring and Noble were. Keepers of wills and protectors of secrets; but not wrestlers with problems. Which is why Mr. Sandal was by no means the best person to take what was coming to him.

"Is that all, Mercer?" he said to his clerk, who had been showing a visitor out.

"There's one client in the waiting-room, sir. Young Mr. Ashby."

"Ashby? Of Latchetts?"

"Yes, sir."

"Oh, good; good. Bring in a pot of tea, Mercer, will you?"

"Yes, sir." And to the client: "Will you come in, sir?"

The young man came in.

"Ah, Simon, my dear boy," Mr. Sandal said, shaking hands with him, "I am delighted to see you. Are you up on business, or are you just——"

His voice died away uncertainly, and he stared, the gesture of his arm towards a chair arrested mid-way.

"God bless my soul," he said, "you are not Simon."

"No. I am not Simon."

"But—but you *are* an Ashby."

"If you think that, it makes things a whole lot easier for me."

"Yes? Do forgive me if I am a little confused. I didn't know that there were Ashby cousins."

"There aren't, as far as I know."

"No? Then—forgive me—which Ashby are you?"

"Patrick."

Mr. Sandal's neat mouth opened and shut like a goldfish's.

He stopped being a green thought in a green shade and became a very worried and staggered little lawyer.

For a long moment he looked into the light Ashby eyes so near

29

his own without finding any words that seemed adequate to the occasion.

"I think we had better both sit down," he said at last. He indicated the visitors' chair, and subsided into his own with an air of being glad of an anchorage in a world suddenly at sea.

"Now, let us clarify the situation," he said. "The only Patrick Ashby died at the age of thirteen, some—let me see—eight years ago, it must be."

"What makes you think he died?"

"He committed suicide, and left a farewell note."

"Did the note mention suicide?"

"I am afraid I cannot recall the wording."

"Nor can I, exactly. But I can give you the sense of it. It said: 'I can't stand it any longer. Don't be angry with me.'"

"Yes. Yes, that was the tenor of the message."

"And where in that is the mention of suicide?"

"The suggestion surely is—One would naturally infer—The letter was found on the cliff-top with the boy's coat."

"The cliff path is the short cut to the harbour."

"The harbour? You mean——"

"It was a running-away note; not a suicide one."

"But—but the coat?"

"You can't leave a note on the open down. The only way to leave it is in the pocket of something."

"Are you seriously suggesting that—that—that you are Patrick Ashby, and that you never committed suicide at all?"

The young man looked at him with those unrevealing eyes of his. "When I came in," he said, "you took me for my brother."

"Yes. They were twins. Not identical twins, but of course very——" The full implication of what he was saying came home to him. "God bless my soul, so I did. So I did."

He sat for a moment or two staring in a helpless fashion. And while he stared Mercer came in with the tea.

"Do you take tea?" Mr. Sandal asked, the question being merely a reflex conditioned by the presence of the tea-tray.

"Thank you," said the young man. "No sugar."

"You do realise, don't you," Mr. Sandal said, half-appealingly, "that such a very startling and—and serious claim must be investigated? One cannot, you understand, merely accept your statement."

30

"I don't expect you to."

"Good. That is good. Very sensible of you. At some later date it may be possible—the fatted calf—but just now we have to be sensible about it. You do see that. Milk?"

"Thank you."

"For instance: you ran away, you say. Ran away to sea, I take it."

"Yes."

"On what ship?"

"The *Ira Jones*. She was lying in Westover harbour."

"You stowed away, of course."

"Yes."

"And where did the ship take you?" asked Mr. Sandal, making notes and beginning to feel that he wasn't doing so badly after all. This was quite the worst situation he had ever been in, and there was no question of catching the 5.15 now.

"The Channel Islands. St. Helier."

"Were you discovered on board?"

"No."

"You disembarked at St. Helier, undiscovered."

"Yes."

"And there?"

"I got the boat to St. Malo."

"You stowed away again?"

"No, I paid my fare."

"You remember what the boat was called?"

"No; it was the regular ferry service."

"I see. And then?"

"I went bus-riding. Buses always seemed to me more exciting than that old station wagon at Latchetts, but I never had a chance of riding in them."

"The station wagon. Ah, yes," said Mr. Sandal; and wrote: "Remembers car." "And then?"

"Let me see. I was garage-boy for a while at an hotel in a place called Villedieu."

"You remember the name of the hotel, perhaps?"

"The Dauphin, I think. From there I went across country and fetched up in Havre. In Havre I got a job as galley boy on a tramp steamer."

"The name? You remember it?"

31

"I'll never forget it! She was called the *Barfleur*. I joined her as Farrar. F-a-r-r-a-r. I stayed with her until I left her in Tampico. From there I worked my way north to the States. Would you like me to write down for you the places I worked at in the States?"

"That would be very kind of you. Here is—ah, you have a pen. If you would just write them here, in a list. Thank you. And you came back to England——?"

"On the 2nd of last month. On the *Philadelphia*. As a passenger. I took a room in London and have lived there ever since. I'll write the address for you; you'll want to check that too."

"Yes. Thank you. Yes." Mr. Sandal had an odd feeling that it was this young man—who after all was on trial, so to speak—who was dominating the situation and not, as it certainly should be, himself. He pulled himself together.

"Have you attempted to communicate with your—I mean, with Miss Ashby?"

"No, is it difficult?" said the young man gently.

"What I mean is——"

"I've done nothing about my family, if that is what you mean. I thought this was the best way."

"Very wise. Very wise." There he was again, being forced into the position of chorus. "I shall get in touch with Miss Ashby at once, and inform her of your visit."

"Tell her that I'm alive, yes."

"Yes. Quite so." Was the young man making fun of him? Surely not.

"Meanwhile you will go on living at this address?"

"Yes, I shall be there." The young man got up, again taking the initiative from him.

"If your credentials prove to be good," Mr. Sandal said with an attempt at severity, "I shall be the first to welcome you back to England and to your home. In spite of the fact that your desertion of it has caused deep grief to all concerned. I find it inexplicable that you should not have communicated with your people before now."

"Perhaps I liked being dead."

"Being dead!"

"Anyhow you never did find me very explicable, did you?"

"Didn't I?"

32

"You thought it was because I was afraid that I cried, that day at Olympia, didn't you?"

"Olympia?"

"It wasn't you know. It was because the horses were so beautiful."

"Olympia! You mean . . . But that was . . . You remember, then——"

"I expect you'll let me know, Mr. Sandal, when you have checked my statements."

"What? Oh, yes; yes, certainly." Good heavens, even he himself had forgotten that children's party at the Tournament. Perhaps he had been altogether too cautious. If this young man—the owner of Latchetts—dear me! Perhaps he should not have been so——

"I hope you don't think——" he began.

But the young man was gone, letting himself out with cool decision and a brief nod to Mercer.

Mr. Sandal sat down in the inner office and mopped his brow.

And Brat, walking down the street, was shocked to find himself exhilarated. He had expected to be nervous and a little ashamed. And it had not been in the least like that. It had been one of the most exciting things he had ever done. A wonderful, tight-rope sort of thing. He had sat there and lied and not even been conscious that he was lying, it had been so thrilling. It was like riding a rogue; you had the same wary, strung-up feeling; the same satisfaction in avoiding an unexpected movement to destroy you. But nothing he had ever ridden had given him the mental excitement, the subsequent glow of achievement, that this had given him. He was drunk with it.

And greatly surprised.

So this, he thought, was what sent criminals back to their old ways when there was no material need. This breathless, step-picking excitement; this subsequent intoxication of achievement.

He went to have tea, according to Loding's instructions; but he could not eat. He felt as if he had already had food and drink. No previous experience of his had had this oddly satisfying effect. Normally, after the exciting things of life—riding, love-making, rescue, close calls—he was ravenously hungry. But now he just sat and looked at the food in front of him in a daze of content. The glow inside him left no room for food.

No one had followed him into the restaurant, and no one seemed to be taking any interest in him.

He paid his bill and went out. No one was loitering anywhere; the pavement was one long stream of hurrying people. He went to a telephone at Victoria.

"Well?" said Loding. "How did it go?"

"Wonderful."

"Have you been drinking?"

"No. Why?"

"That is the first time I have ever heard you use a superlative."

"I'm just pleased."

"My God, you must be. Does it show?"

"Show?"

"Is there any faint change in that poker face of yours?"

"How should I know? Don't you want to know about this afternoon?"

"I already know the most important thing."

"What is that?"

"You haven't been given in charge."

"Did you expect me to be?"

"There was always the chance. But I didn't really expect it. Not with our combined intelligences."

"Thanks."

"Did the old boy fall on your neck?"

"No. He nearly fell over. He's being very correct."

"Everything to be verified."

"Yes."

"How did he receive you?"

"He took me for Simon."

He heard Loding's amused laughter.

"Did you manage to use his Tournament party?"

"Yes."

"Oh, my God, don't go monosyllabic on me. You didn't have to rake it up, did you?"

"No. It fitted very neatly."

"Was he impressed?"

"It had him on the ropes."

"It didn't convince him, though?"

"I didn't wait to see. I was on my way out."

"You mean, that was your exit line? My boy, I take off my hat to you. You're a perishing marvel. After living in your pocket for

34

the last fortnight I thought I was beginning to know you. But you're still surprising me to death."

"I surprise myself, if it's any consolation to you."

"I don't detect any bitterness in that line, do I?"

"No. Just surprise. Neat."

"Ah, well; we shall not be meeting for some time to come. It has been a privilege to know you, my boy. I shall never hear Kew Gardens mentioned without thinking tenderly of you. And I look forward, of course, to further privileges from knowing you in the future. Meanwhile, don't ring me up unless there is absolutely no alternative. You are as well briefed as I can make you. From now on you're on your own."

Loding was right: it had been a wonderful briefing. For a whole fortnight, from early morning till seven in the evening, rain or shine, they had sat in Kew Gardens and rehearsed the ways of Latchetts and Clare, the histories of Ashbys and Ledinghams, the lie of a land he had never seen. And that too had been exciting. He had always been what they called "good at exams"; and had always come to an examination paper with the same faint pleasure that an addict brings to a quiz party. And those fourteen days in Kew Gardens had been one glorified quiz party. Indeed, the last few days had had some of the tight-rope excitement that had characterised this afternoon. "Which arm did you bowl with?" "Go to the stables from the side door." "Did you sing?" "Could you play the piano?" "Who lived in the lodge at Clare?" "What colour was your mother's hair?" "How did your father make his money, apart from the estate?" "What was the name of his firm?" "What was your favourite food?" "The name of the tuck-shop owner in the village?" "Where is the Ashby pew in the church?" "Go from the great drawing-room to the butler's pantry in Clare." "What was the housekeeper's name?" "Could you ride a bicycle?" "What do you see from the south window in the attic?" Loding fired the questions at him through the long days, and it had been first amusing and then exciting to avoid being stumped.

Kew had been Loding's idea. "Your life since you came to London must be subject to the most searching scrutiny, if you will forgive the cliché. So you can't come and live with me as I suggested. You can't even be seen with me by anyone we know. Nor can I come to your Pimlico place. You must go on being unvisited there as you have been up till now." So the Kew scheme had been evolved. Kew

Gardens, Loding said, had perfect cover and a wonderful field of fire. There was nowhere in London where you could see approaching figures at such a distance and still be unnoticed yourself. Nowhere in London that offered the variety of meeting-places, the undisturbed quiet, that Kew did.

So each morning they had arrived separately, by different gates; had met at a new point and gone to a different region; and there for a fortnight Loding had primed him with photographs, maps, plans, drawings, and pencilled diagrams. He had begun with a one-inch Ordnance Survey map of Clare and its surroundings, progressed to a larger size, and thence to plans of the house; so that it was rather like coming down from above in a plane. First the lie of the country, then the details of fields and gardens, and then the close-up of the house so that the thing was whole in his mind from the beginning, and the details had merely to be pointed on a picture already etched. It was methodical, careful teaching, and Brat appreciated it.

But the highlight, of course, was provided by the photographs. And it was not, oddly enough, the photograph of his "twin" that held his attention once he had seen them all. Simon, of course, was extraordinarily like him; and it gave him a strange, almost embarrassed, feeling to look at the pictured face so like his own. But it was not Simon who held his interest; it was the child who had not lived to grow up; the boy whose place he was going to take. He had an odd feeling of identity with Patrick.

Even he himself noticed this, and found it strange. He should have been filled with guilt when he considered Patrick. But his only emotion was one of partisanship; almost of alliance.

Crossing the courtyard at Victoria after telephoning, he wondered what had prompted him to say that about Patrick crying. Loding had told him merely that Patrick had cried for no known reason (he was seven then) and that old Sandal had been disgusted and had never taken the children out again. Loding had left the story with him to be used as and when he thought fit. What had prompted him to say that Patrick had cried because the horses were so beautiful? Was that, perhaps, why Patrick *had* cried?

Well, there was no going back now, whether he wanted to or not. That insistent voice that had talked to him in the dark of his room had fought for its head and got it. All he could do was sit in the saddle and hope for the best. But at least it would be a breath-taking ride; a unique, heart-stopping ride. Danger to life and limb he was used to; but far more exciting was this new mental danger, this pitting of wits.

This danger to his immortal soul, the orphanage would call it. But he had never believed in his immortal soul.

He couldn't go to Latchetts as a blackmailer, he wouldn't go as a suppliant, he would damn well go as an invader.

7

The telegraph wires swooped and the earth whirled round the carriage window; and Bee's mind swooped and whirled with them.

"I would have come down to see you, of course," Mr. Sandal had said on the telephone. "It is against all my principles to deal with such grave matters by telephone. But I was afraid that my presence might suggest to the children that there was something serious afoot. And it would be a pity to upset them if there is a chance that—that the trouble is temporary."

Poor dear old Sandal. He had been very kind; had asked her if she were sitting down, before he broke the news; and had said: "You're not feeling faint, are you, Miss Ashby?" when his shock had been administered.

She had not fainted. She had sat for a long time letting her knees get back their strength, and then she had gone to her room and looked for photographs of Patrick. Except for a studio group taken when Simon and Patrick were ten and Eleanor nine, she seemed to have nothing. She was not a snapshot-keeper.

Nora had been a passionate collector of her children's photographs, but she had spurned photograph albums, which she held to be "a great waste of time and space." (Nora had never wasted anything; it had been as if she was half conscious that her allotted time was short.) She had kept them all in a tattered and bursting manila envelope with O.H.M.S. on it, and the envelope went everywhere with her. It had gone to Europe on that holiday with her, and had made part of that blaze on the Kent coast.

Balked of photographs, Bee went up to the old nursery, as if there she would get nearer to the child Patrick, although she knew very well that nothing of Patrick's remained there. Simon had burned them all. It was the only sign he had given that his twin's death was more than he could well bear. Simon had gone away to school after Patrick's death, and when he came back for the summer holidays he had behaved normally, if one took it for granted that not mentioning Patrick was in the circumstances normal enough. And then one day Bee had come on him tending a bonfire where the children had made their "Red Indian" and campfires, beyond the shrubbery, and on the fire were Patrick's toys and other small belongings. Even exercise books, she noticed, had been brought down to feed the flames. Books and childish paintings and the silly horse that had hung at the end of his bed; Simon was burning them all.

He had been furious when he saw her. He had moved between her and the fire, standing at bay, as it were, and glared at her.

"I don't want them around," he had said, almost shouting.

"I understand, Simon," she had said, and had gone away.

So there was nothing of Patrick in the old nursery under the eaves; and not very much of the other children, after all. When this had been Bee's own nursery it had been ugly and individual and furnished largely with rejections from the other parts of the house. It had patterned linoleum, and a rag rug, and a cuckoo clock, and crazy basket chairs, and a clothes-horse, and a deal table covered with a red rep tablecloth trimmed with bobbles and marked with ink-stains; and coloured prints of "Bubbles" and similar masterpieces hung against a cabbage-rose wallpaper. But Nora had done it over, so that it became an illustration from a homemaker magazine, in powder-blue and white, with a wallpaper of nursery-rhyme characters. Only the cuckoo clock had stayed.

The children had been happy there, but had left no mark on it. Now that it was empty and tidy, it looked just like something in a furniture shop window.

She had gone back to her own room, baffled and sick at heart, and had packed a small bag for her use in the morning. To-morrow she must go up to town and face this new emergency in the history of the Ashbys.

"Do you believe, yourself, that it is Patrick?" she had asked.

But Mr. Sandal could give her no assurance.

"He has not the air of a pretender," he allowed. "And if he is not Patrick, then who is he? The Ashby family resemblance has always been abnormally strong. And there is no other son of this generation."

"But Patrick would have written," she said.

That is the thought she always went back to. Patrick would never have left her in grief and doubt all those years. Patrick would have written. It couldn't be Patrick.

Then if it wasn't Patrick, who *was* it?

Round and round went her mind, swooping and whirling.

"You will be the best judge," Mr. Sandal had said. "Of those now living you are the one who knew the boy best."

"There is Simon," she had said.

"But Simon was a boy at the time and boys forget, don't they? You were grown up."

So the onus was being put upon her. But how was *she* to know? She who had loved Patrick but now could hardly remember what he looked like at thirteen. What test would there be?

Or would she know at once when she saw him that he was Patrick? Or that he—wasn't?

And if he wasn't and yet insisted that he was, what would happen? Would he bring a claim? Make a court action of it? Drag them all through the publicity of the daily Press?

And if he was Patrick, what of Simon? How would he take the resurrection of a brother he had not seen for eight years? The loss of a fortune. Would he be glad about it, fortune or no, or would he hate his brother?

The coming-of-age celebrations would have to be postponed, that was clear. They were much too close now for anything to be decided by that time. What excuse should they make?

But oh, if it *could*, by some miracle, be Patrick, she would be free of that haunting horror, that thought of the boy who regretted too late to come back.

Her mind was still swooping and swirling as she climbed the stairs to the offices of Cosset, Thring and Noble.

"Ah, Miss Ashby," Mr. Sandal said. "This is a shocking dilemma. A most unprecedented—— Do sit down. You must be exhausted. A dreadful ordeal for you. Sit down, sit down. Mercer, some tea for Miss Ashby."

39

"Did he say why he didn't write, all those years?" she asked; this being the all-important thing in her mind.

"He said something about 'perhaps preferring to be dead'."

"Oh."

"A psychological difficulty, no doubt," Mr. Sandal said, proffering comfort.

"Then you believe it *is* Patrick?"

"I mean, if it is Patrick, his 'preferring to be dead' would no doubt arise from the same psychological difficulty as did his running away."

"Yes. I see. I suppose so. Only—it is so unlike Patrick. Not to write, I mean."

"It was unlike Patrick to run away."

"Yes; there is that. He certainly wasn't a runner-away by nature. He was a sensitive child but very brave. Something must have gone very wrong." She sat silent for a moment. "And now he is back."

"We hope so; we hope so."

"Did he seem quite normal to you?"

"Excessively," said Mr. Sandal, with a hint of dryness in his tone.

"I looked for photographs of Patrick, but there is nothing later than this." She produced the studio group. "The children had studio portraits taken regularly every three years, from the time they were babies. This was the last of them. The new one would have been taken in the summer of the year that Bill and Nora were killed; the year Patrick—disappeared. Patrick is ten there."

She watched while Mr. Sundal studied the small immature face.

"No," he said at last. "It is impossible to say anything from so early a photograph. As I said before, the family likeness is very strong. At that age they are just young Ashbys, aren't they? Without any great individuality." He looked up from studying the photograph and went on: "I am hoping that when you yourself see the boy—the young man—you will have no doubt one way or another. After all, it is not entirely a matter of likeness, this recognition, is it? There is an aura of—of personality."

"But—but if I am not sure? What is to happen if I am not sure?"

"About that: I think I have found a way out. I dined last night with my young friend Kevin Macdermott."

"The K.C.?"

"Yes. I was greatly distressed, of course, and told him of my difficulty, and he comforted me greatly by assuring me that identification would be a quite simple matter. It was merely an affair of teeth."

"Teeth? But Patrick had quite ordinary teeth."

"Yes, yes. But he had no doubt been to a dentist, and dentists have records. Indeed, most dentists have a sort of visual memory, I understand, of mouths they have treated—a very grim thought—and would almost recognise one at sight. But the record will certainly show——" He caught the look on Bee's face and paused. "What is the matter?"

"The children went to Hammond."

"Hammond? Well? That is simple, isn't it? If you don't definitely identify the boy as Patrick, we have only to——" He broke off. "Hammond!" he said quietly. "Oh!"

"Yes," Bee said, agreeing with the tone of the monosyllable.

"Dear me, how unfortunate. How very unfortunate."

Into the subsequent silence Mr. Sandal said miserably: "I think I ought to tell you that Kevin Macdermott thinks the boy is lying."

"What could Mr. Macdermott possibly know about it," said Bee angrily. "He has not even seen him!" And as Mr. Sandal went on sitting in miserable silence, "Well?"

"It was only Kevin's opinion on the hypothesis."

"I know, but why did he think that?"

"He said it was a—a 'phoney thing to come straight to a lawyer'."

"What nonsense! It was a very sensible thing to do."

"Yes. That was his point. It was too sensible. Too pat. Everything, Kevin said, was too pat for his liking. He said a boy coming home after years away would go home."

"Then he doesn't know Patrick. That is just what Patrick would have done: broken it gently by going to the family lawyer first. He was always the most thoughtful and unselfish of creatures. I don't think much of the clever Mr. Macdermott's analysis."

"I felt it only right to tell you everything," Mr. Sandal said, still miserably.

"Yes, of course," Bee said kindly, recovering her temper. "Did you tell Mr. Macdermott that Patrick—that the boy had remembered crying at Olympia? I mean, that he had volunteered the information."

"I did; yes."

"And he still thought the boy was lying?"

"That was part of the 'patness' he professed not to like."

41

Bee gave a small snort. "What a mind!" she said. "I suppose that is what a court practice does."

"It is a detached mind, that is all. One not emotionally engaged in the matter, as we are. It behooves us to keep our minds detached."

"Yes, of course," Bee said, sobered. "Well, now that poor old Hammond is to be no help to us—they never found him, did you know? Everything was just blown to dust."

"Yes. Yes, so I heard; poor fellow."

"Now that we have no physical evidence, I suppose we have to rely on the boy's own story. I mean, on checking it. I suppose that can be done."

"Oh, quite easily. It is all quite straightforward, with dates and places. That is what Kevin found so—— Yes. Yes. Of course it can be checked. And of course I am sure that it *will* check. He would not have offered us information which would be proved nonsense."

"So really there is nothing to wait for."

"No, I—— No."

Bee braced herself.

"Then how soon can you arrange for me to meet him?"

"Well—I have been thinking about it, and I don't think, you know, that it should be arranged at all."

"What?"

"What I should like to do—with your permission and co-operation—would be to, as it were, walk in on him. Go and see him unannounced. So that you would see him as he is and not as he wants you to see him. If we made an appointment here at the office, he would——"

"Yes, I see. I understand. I agree to that. Can we go now?"

"I don't see why not. I really don't see why not," Mr. Sandal said in that regretful tone that lawyers use when they cannot see any reason why not. "There is, of course, the chance that he may be out. But we can at least go and see. Ah, here is your tea! Will you drink it while Mercer asks Simspon to ask Willett to get us a taxi?"

"You haven't got anything stronger, have you?" Bee asked.

"I'm afraid not; I'm afraid not. I have never succumbed to the transatlantic custom of the bottle in the office. But Willett will get you anything you may——"

"Oh, no, thank you; it's all right. I'll drink the tea. They say the effects are much more lasting, anyway."

Mr. Sandal looked as though he would like to pat her encouragingly on the shoulder, but could not make up his mind to it. He was really a very kind little man, she thought, but just—just not much of a *prop*.

"Did he explain why he chose the name Farrar?" she asked, when they were seated in the taxi.

"He didn't explain anything," Mr. Sandal said, falling back on his dry tone.

"Did you gather that he was badly off?"

"He did not mention money, but he seemed very well-dressed in a slightly un-English fashion."

"There was no suggestion of a loan?"

"Oh, no. Oh, dear me, no."

"Then he hasn't come back just because he is broke," Bee said, and felt somehow pleased. She sat back and relaxed a little. Perhaps everything was going to be all right.

"I have never quite understood why Pimlico descended so rapidly in the social scale," said Mr. Sandal, breaking the silence as they travelled down the avenues of pretentious porches. "It has fine wide streets, and little through-traffic, and no more smuts than its neighbours. Why should the well-to-do have deserted it and yet stayed in Belgravia? Very puzzling."

"There is a sort of suction about desertion," Bee said, trying to meet him on the small-talk level. "The local Lady Almighty occasions the draught by leaving, and the rest, in descending order of importance, follow in her wake. And the poorer people flood in from either side to fill the vacuum. Is this the place?"

Her dismay took possession of her again as she looked at the dismal front of the house; at the peeling paint and the stained stucco, the variety of drab curtains at the windows, the unswept doorway and the rubbed-out house-number on the horrible pillar.

The front door was open and they walked in.

A different card on each door in the hallway proclaimed the fact that the house was let out in single rooms.

"The address is 59K," Mr. Sandal said. "I take it that K is the number of the room."

"They begin on the ground floor and work upwards," Bee said. "This is B on my side." So they mounted.

"H," said Bee, peering at a first-floor door. "It's up the next flight."

The second floor was also the top one. They stood together on the dark landing listening to the silence. He is out, she thought, he is out, and I shall have to go through all this again.

"Have you a match?" she said.

"I and J," she read, on the two front-room doors.

Then it was the back one.

They stood in the dark for a moment, staring at it. Then Mr. Sandal moved purposively forward and knocked.

"Come in!" said a voice. It was a deep, boy's voice; quite unlike Simon's light sophisticated tones.

Bee, being half a head taller than Mr. Sandal, could see over his shoulder; and her first feeling was one of shock that he should be so much more like Simon than Patrick ever was. Her mind had been filled with images of Patrick: vague, blurred images that she strove to make clear so that she could compare them with the adult reality. Her whole being had been obsessed with Patrick for the last twenty-four hours.

And now here was someone just like Simon.

The boy got up from where he had been sitting on the edge of the bed, and with no haste or embarrassment pulled from off his left hand the sock he had been darning. She couldn't imagine Simon darning a sock.

"Good morning," he said.

"Good morning," said Mr. Sandal. "I hope you don't mind: I've brought you a visitor." He moved aside to let Bee come in. "Do you know who this is?"

Bee's heart hammered on her ribs as she met the boy's light calm gaze and watched him identify her.

"You do your hair differently," he said.

Yes, of course; hairdressing had changed completely in those eight years; of course he would see a difference.

"You recognise her, then?" Mr. Sandal said.

"Yes, of course. It's Aunt Bee."

She waited for him to come forward to greet her, but he made no move to. After a moment's pause he turned to find a seat for her.

"I'm afraid there is only one chair. It is all right if you don't lean back on it," he said, picking up one of those hard chairs with a black curved back and a tan seat with small holes in it. Bee was glad to sit down on it.

44

"Do you mind the bed?" he said to Mr. Sandal.

"I'll stand, thank you, I'll stand," Mr. Sandal said hastily.

The details of the face were not at all like Simon's, she thought; watching the boy stick the needle carefully in the sock. It was the general impression that was the same; once you really looked at him the startling resemblance vanished, and only the family likeness remained.

"Miss Ashby could not wait for a meeting at my office, so I brought her here," Mr. Sandal said. "You don't seem particularly——" He allowed the sentence to speak for itself.

The boy looked at her in a friendly unsmiling way and said: "I'm not very sure of my welcome."

It was a curiously immobile face. A face like a child's drawing, now she came to think of it. Everything in the right place and with the right proportions, but without animation. Even the mouth had the straight uncompromising line that is a child's version of a mouth.

He moved over to lay the socks on the dressing-table, and she saw that he was lame.

"Have you hurt your leg?" she asked.

"I broke it. Over in the States."

"But should you be walking about on it if it is still tender?"

"Oh, it doesn't hurt," he said. "It's just short."

"Short! You mean, permanently short?"

"It looks like it."

They were sensitive lips, she noticed, for all their thinness; they gave him away when he said that.

"But something can be done about that," she said. "It just means that it was mended badly. I expect you didn't have a very good surgeon."

"I don't remember a surgeon. Perhaps I passed out. They did all the correct things: hung weights on the end of it, and all that."

"But Pat——" she began, and failed to finish his name.

Into the hiatus he said: "You don't have to call me anything until you are sure."

"They do miracles in surgery nowadays," she said, covering her break. "How long ago is it since it happened?"

"I'd have to think. About a couple of years now, I think."

Except for the flat American *a*, his speech was without peculiarity.

"Well, we must see what can be done about it. A horse, was it?"

"Yes. I wasn't quick enough. How did you know it was a horse?"

"You told Mr. Sandal that you had worked with horses. Did you enjoy that?" Just like railway-carriage small-talk, she thought.

"It's the only life I do enjoy."

She forgot about small-talk. "Really?" she said, pleased. "Were they good horses, those western ones?"

"Most of them were commoners, of course. Very good stuff for their work—which, after all, is being a good horse, I suppose. But every now and then you come across one with blood. Some of those are beauties. More—more individual than I ever remember English horses being."

"Perhaps in England we 'manner' the individuality out of them. I hadn't thought of it. Did you have a horse of your own at all?"

"Yes, I had one. Smoky."

She noticed the change in his voice when he said it. As audible as the flat note in the cracked bell of a chime.

"A grey?"

"Yes, a dark grey with black points. Not that hard, iron colour, you know. A soft, smoky colour. When he had a tantrum he was just a whirling cloud of smoke."

A whirling cloud of smoke. She could see it. He must love horses to be able to see them like that. He must particularly have loved his Smoky.

"What happened to Smoky?"

"I sold him."

No trespassers. Very well, she would not trespass. He had probably had to sell the horse when he broke his leg.

She began to hope very strenuously that this was Patrick.

The thought recalled her to the situation which she had begun to lose sight of. She looked doubtfully at Mr. Sandal.

Catching the appeal in her glance, Mr. Sandal said: "Miss Ashby is no doubt prepared to vouch for you, but you will understand that the matter needs more clarification. If it were a simple matter of a prodigal's homecoming, your aunt's acceptance of you would no doubt be sufficient to restore you to the bosom of your family. But in the present instance it is a matter of property. Of the ultimate destination of a fortune. And the law will require incontrovertible

46

evidence of your identity before you could be allowed to succeed to anything that was Patrick Ashby's. I hope you understand our position."

"I understand perfectly. I shall, of course, stay here until you have made your inquiries and are satisfied."

"But you can't stay *here*," Bee said, looking with loathing at the room and the forest of chimney-pots beyond the window.

"I have stayed in a great many worse places."

"Perhaps. That is no reason for staying here. If you need money we can give you some, you know."

"I'll stay here, thanks."

"Are you just being independent?"

"No. It's quiet here. And handy. And bung full of privacy. When you have lived in bunk houses you put a high value on privacy."

"Very well, you stay here. Is there anything else we can—can stake you to?"

"I could do with another suit."

"Very well. Mr. Sandal will advance whatever you need for that." She suddenly remembered that if he went to the Ashby tailor there would be a sensation. So she added: "And he will give you the address of his tailor."

"Why not Walters?" said the boy.

For a moment she could not speak.

"Aren't they there any more?"

"Oh, yes; but there would be too many explanations if you went to Walters." She must keep a hold on herself. Anyone could find out who the Ashby tailor had been.

"Oh, yes. I see."

She fell back on small-talk and began to take her leave.

"We have not told the family about you," she said, as she prepared to go. "We thought it better not to, until things are—are what Mr. Sandal calls clarified."

A flash of amusement showed in his eyes at that. For a moment they were allied in a secret laughter.

"I understand."

She turned at the door to say good-bye. He was standing in the middle of the room watching her go, leaving Mr. Sandal to shepherd her out. He looked remote and lonely. And she thought: "If this *is* Patrick, Patrick come home again, and I am leaving him like this, as if he were a casual acquaintance——" It was more than she could bear, the thought of the boy's loneliness.

She went back to him, took his face lightly in her gloved hand, and kissed his cheek. "Welcome back, my dear," she said.

8

So Cosset, Thring and Noble began their investigations, and Bee went back to Latchetts to deal with the problem of postponing the coming-of-age celebrations.

Was she to tell the children now, before the thing was certain? And if not, what excuse could she possibly put forward for not celebrating at the proper time?

Mr. Sandal was against telling the children yet. The unknown Kevin's verdict had left a mark on him, it seemed; and he was entirely prepared to find a flaw in the so-complete dossier that had been handed to them. It would be inadvisable, he thought, to bring the children into this until the claim had been sifted through the finest mesh.

With that she agreed. If this thing passed—if that boy in the back room in Pimlico was not Patrick—they need never know anything about it. Simon would probably have to be told, so that he could be warned against future attempts at fraud, but by that time it would be of no more than academic interest; a quite impersonal affair. Her present difficulty was how to reconcile the children's ignorance with the postponing of the celebrations.

The person who rescued her from this dilemma was Great-uncle Charles, who cabled to announce his (long overdue) retirement, and his hope to be present at his great-nephew's coming-of-age party. He was on his way home from the Far East, and, since he refused to fly, his home-coming was likely to be a protracted one, but he hoped Simon would keep the champagne corked till he came.

Great-uncles do not normally cut much ice in the families in which they survive, but to the Ashbys Great-uncle Charles was much more than a great-uncle: he was a household word. Every birthday had been made iridescent and every Christmas a tingling expectation

48

by the thought of Great-uncle Charles's present. There were reasonable bounds to the possible presents of parents; and Father Christmas's were merely the answer to indents.

But neither reason nor bounds had any connection with presents from Great-uncle Charles. Once he had sent a set of chopsticks, which upset nursery discipline for a week. And once it had been the skin of a snake; the glory of owning the skin of a snake had made Simon dizzy for days. And Eleanor still ran to and from her bath in a pair of odd-smelling leather slippers that had come on her twelfth birthday. At least four times every year Great-uncle Charles became the most important factor in the Ashby family; and when you have been of first importance four times a year for twenty years your importance is pretty considerable. Simon might grumble and the others protest a little, but they would without doubt wait for Great-uncle Charles.

Besides, she had a shrewd idea that Simon would not be willing to offend the last-surviving Ashby of his generation. Charles was not rich—he had been far too liberal a giver all his life—but he was comfortably off; and Simon, for all his careless good nature and easy charm, was an exceedingly practical person.

So the postponement was taken by the family with resignation, and by Clare with equanimity. It was held to be a very proper thing that the Ashbys should wait until the old boy could be present. Bee spent her after-dinner leisure altering the date on the invitation cards, and thanking heaven for the mercifulness of chance.

Bee was at odds with herself these days. She wanted this boy to be Patrick; but it would be so much better for all concerned, she felt, if he proved not to be Patrick. Seven-eighths of her wanted Patrick back; warm, and alive, and dear; wanted it passionately. The other eighth shrank from the upheaval of the happy Ashby world that his return would bring with it. When she caught this renegade eighth at its work she reproved it and was suitably ashamed of herself; but she could not destroy it. And so she was distrait and short-tempered, and Ruth, commenting on it to Jane, said:

"Do you think she can have a Secret Sorrow?"

"I expect the books won't balance," Jane said. "She's a very bad adder-up."

Mr. Sandal reported from time to time on the progress of the investigations, and the reports were uniform and monotonous. Everything seemed to confirm the boy's story.

"The most heartening thing, using the word in its sense of reassurance," Mr. Sandal said, "is that the young man seems to have no contacts since he came to England. He has lived at that address since the *Philadelphia's* arrival, and he has had neither letters nor visitors. The woman who owns the house occupies one of the front rooms on the ground floor. She is one of those women who has nothing to do but sit back and watch her neighbours. The lives of her tenants seem to be an open book to the good lady. She is also accustomed to waiting for the postman and collecting the letters he drops. Nothing escapes her. Her description of myself was, I understand, hardly flattering but quite touching in its fidelity. The young man could therefore have hardly had visitors without her being aware of it. He was out all day, of course; as any young man in London would be. But there is no trace of that intimacy which would suggest connivance. He had no friends."

The young man came willingly to the office and answered questions freely. With Bee's consent, Kevin Macdermott had "sat in" at one of these office conferences, and even Kevin had been shaken. "What shakes me," Kevin had said, "is not the fellow's knowledge of the subject—all good con. men are glib—but the general cut of his jib. He's quite frankly not what I expected. After a little while in my job you develop a smell for a wrong 'un. This chap has me baffled. He doesn't smell like a crook to me, and yet the set-up stinks."

So the day came when Mr. Sandal announced to Bee that Cosset, Thring and Noble were now prepared to accept the claimant as Patrick Ashby, the eldest son of William Ashby of Latchetts, and to hand over to him everything that was due to him. There would be legal formalities, of course, since the fact of his death eight years ago had been presumed; but they would be automatic. As far as they, Cosset, Thring and Noble, were concerned, Patrick Ashby was free to go home whenever he pleased.

So the moment had come, and Bee was faced with breaking the news to the family.

Her instinct was to tell Simon first, privately; but she felt that anything that set him apart from the others in this matter of welcoming back his brother was to be avoided. It would be better to take for granted that for Simon, as for the others, the news would be a matter for unqualified happiness.

It was after lunch on a Sunday that she told them.

"I have something to tell you that will be rather a shock to you. But a nice kind of shock," she said. And went on from there. Patrick had not committed suicide, as they had thought. He had merely run away. And now he had come back. He had been living for a little in London because, of course, he had to prove to the lawyers that he was Patrick. But he had had no difficulty in doing that. And now he was going to come home.

She had avoided looking at their faces as she talked; it was easier just to talk into space, impersonally. But in the startled silence that followed her story she looked across at Simon; and for a moment did not recognise him. The shrunk white face with the blazing eyes had no resemblance to the Simon she knew. She looked away hastily.

"Does it mean that this new brother will get all the money that is Simon's?" asked Jane, with her usual lack of finesse.

"Well, I think it was a horrible thing to do," Eleanor said bluntly.

"What was?"

"Running away and leaving us all thinking he was dead."

"He didn't know that, of course. I mean: that we would take his note to mean that he was going to kill himself."

"Even so. He left us all without a word for—for—how long is it? Seven years? Nearly eight years. And then comes back one day without warning, and expects us to welcome him."

"Is he nice?" asked Ruth.

"What do you mean by nice?" Bee asked, glad for once of Ruth's interest in the personal.

"Is he nice to look at? And does he talk nicely or has he a frightful accent?"

"He is exceedingly nice to look at, and he has no accent whatsoever."

"Where has he been all this time?" Eleanor asked.

"Mexico and the States, mostly."

"Mexico!" said Ruth. "How romantic! Does he wear a black sailor hat?"

"A what? No, of course he doesn't. He wears a hat like anyone else."

"How often have you seen him, Aunt Bee?" Eleanor asked.

"Just once. A few weeks ago."

"Why didn't you tell us about it then?"

51

"It seemed better to wait until the lawyers were finished with him and he was ready to come home. You couldn't all go rushing up to London to see him."

"No, I suppose not. But I expect Simon would have liked to go up and see him, wouldn't you, Simon, and we wouldn't have minded? After all, Patrick was his twin."

"I don't believe for one moment that it is Patrick," Simon said, in a tight, careful voice that was worse than shouting.

"But, Simon!" Eleanor said.

Bee sat in a dismayed silence. This was worse than she had anticipated.

"But, Simon! Aunt Bee has seen him. She must know."

"Aunt Bee seems to have adopted him."

Much worse than she had anticipated.

"The people who *have* adopted him, Simon, are Cosset, Thring and Noble. A not very emotional firm, I think you'll agree. If there had been the faintest doubt of his being Patrick, Cosset, Thring and Noble would have discovered it during those weeks. They have left no part of his life since he left England unaccounted for."

"Of *course* whoever it is has had a life that can be checked! What did they expect? But what possible reason can they have for believing that he is Patrick?"

"Well, for one thing, he is your double."

This was clearly unexpected. "My double?" he said vaguely.

"Yes. He is even more like you than when he went away."

The colour had come back to Simon's face and the stuff on the bones had begun to look like flesh again; but now he looked stupid, like a boxer who is taking too much punishment.

"Believe me, Simon dear," she said, "it *is* Patrick!"

"It isn't. I know it isn't. You are all being fooled!"

"But, Simon!" Eleanor said. "Why should you think that? I know it won't be easy for you to have Patrick back—it won't be easy for any of us—but there's no use making a fuss about it. The thing is there and we just have to accept it. You are only making things worse by trying to push it away."

"How did this—this creature who says he is Patrick, how did he get to Mexico? How did he leave England? And when? And where?"

"He left from Westover in a ship called the *Ira Jones*."

"Westover! Who says so?"

"He does. And according to the harbourmaster, a ship of that name did leave Westover on the night that Patrick went missing."

Since this seemed to leave Simon without speech, she went on: "And everything he did from then on has been checked. The hotel he worked at in Normandy is no longer there, but they have found the ship he sailed from Havre in—it's a tramp, but it belongs to a firm in Brest—and people have been shown photographs and identified him. And so on, all the way back to England. Till the day he walked into Mr. Sandal's office."

"Is that how he came back?" Eleanor asked. "Went to see old Mr. Sandal?"

"Yes."

"Well, I should say that proves that he is Patrick, if anyone is in any doubt about it. But I don't know why there should be doubt at all. After all, it would be very easy to catch him out if he wasn't Patrick, wouldn't it? All the family things he wouldn't know . . ."

"It *isn't* Patrick."

"It is a shock for you, Simon, my dear," Bee said, "and, as Eleanor says, it won't be easy for you. But I think it will be easier when you see him. Easier to accept him, I mean. He is so undeniably an Ashby, and so very like you."

"Patrick *wasn't* very like me."

Eleanor saved Bee from having to reply to that. "He was, Simon. Of course he was. He was your twin."

"If *I* ran away for years and years, would you believe I was me, Jane?" Ruth asked.

"You wouldn't stay away for years and years, anyhow," Jane said.

"What makes you think I wouldn't?"

"You'd come home in no time at all."

"Why would I come home?"

"To see how everyone was taking your running away."

"When is he coming, Aunt Bee?" Eleanor asked.

"On Tuesday. At least that is what we had arranged. But if you would like to put it off a little—until you grow more used to the idea, I mean . . ." She glanced at Simon, who was looking sick and baffled. In her most apprehensive moments she had never pictured a reaction as serious as this.

"If you flatter yourself that I shall grow used to the idea, you are wrong," Simon said. "It makes no difference to me when the fellow

53

comes. As far as I'm concerned he is not Patrick and he never will be."

And he walked out of the room. Walking, Bee noticed, not very steadily, as if he were drunk.

"I've never known Simon like that before," Eleanor said, puzzled. "I should have broken it to him differently. I'm afraid it is my fault. I just—didn't want to make him different from anyone else."

"But he loved Patrick, didn't he? Why shouldn't he be glad about it? Even a *little* glad!"

"I think it is horrid that someone can come and take Simon's place, without warning, like that," Jane said. "Simply horrid. And I don't wonder that Simon is angry."

"Aunt Bee," said Ruth, "can I wear my blue on Tuesday when Patrick comes?"

9

BEE waited till Evensong would be over, and then walked across the fields to the Rectory. Ostensibly, she was going to tell them the news; actually she was going to pour out her troubles to George Peck. When George could withdraw his mind sufficiently from the classic world to focus it on the present one, he was a comfortable person to talk to. Unemotional and unshockable. Bee supposed that an intimate acquaintance with classic on-goings, topped-off with a cure of souls in a country parish, had so conditioned him to shocks that he had long ago become immune from further attack. Neither ancient iniquity nor modern English back-sliding surprised him. So it was not to Nancy, her friend, that she was taking her unquiet heart, but to the Rector. Nancy would wrap her round with warm affection and sympathy, but it was not sympathy she needed; it was support. Besides, if she was to find understanding it would not be with Nancy, who had forgotten Patrick's very existence, but with George Peck, who would most certainly remember the boy he had taught.

So she walked in the sunlight over the fields, through the church-yard, and into the Rectory garden through the little iron gate that had caused that terrific row in 1723. Very peaceful it all was to-night,

54

and very peaceful were the rival smiths, sleeping within twelve feet of each other over there in the corner in good Clare earth. Some day quite soon, she thought, pausing with her hand on the delicate iron scroll, my trouble too will be just an old song; one must try to keep things in proportion. But it was her head talking to her heart, and her heart would not listen.

She found the Rector where she knew he would be. Always after Evensong it was his habit to go and stare at something in the garden; usually at something at the farther end of the garden from which he could not be too easily recalled to the trivialities of social obligation. This evening he was staring at a purple lilac and polluting the fragrant air with a pipe that smelt like a damp bonfire. "There should be a by-law against pipes like George's," his wife had said, and the present sample was no exception. It depressed Bee still further.

He glanced up as she came down the path and went back to staring at the lilac. "Wonderful colour, isn't it," he said. "Odd to think that it is just an optical illusion. What colour is a lilac when you are not looking at it, I wonder?"

Bee remembered that the Rector had once broken it to the twins that a clock does not tick if no one is in the room. She had found Ruth being surreptitious in the hall, and Ruth, when asked what this noiseless progress was occasioned by, had said that she was "trying to sneak up on the drawing-room clock." She wanted to catch it not ticking.

Bee stood by the Rector in silence for a little, looking at the glory and trying to arrange her thoughts. But they would not arrange.

"George," she said at length, "you remember Patrick, don't you?"

"Pat Ashby? Of course." He turned to look at her.

"Well, he didn't die at all. He just ran away. That is what the note meant. And he is coming back. And Simon isn't pleased." A great round shameless tear slipped out of her eye and ran down her cheek. She brushed it off her chin and went on staring at the lilac.

George extended a bony forefinger and gently speared the front of her shoulder with it.

"Sit down," he said.

She sat down on the seat behind her, under the arch of the young green honeysuckle, and the Rector sat down beside her. "Now, tell me," he said; and she told him. All the bewildering story, in the proper order and with full detail; Mr. Sandal's telephone call, the journey to town, the top-floor-back in Pimlico, the investigations of Cosset, Thring and Noble, the rescue by Great-uncle Charles, the ultimate facing of the facts and announcing them to the family, the family reaction.

"Eleanor is a little cold about it, but reasonable as she always is. The thing is there and she is going to make the best of it. Jane, of course, is partisan, and sorry for Simon, but she will get over that when she meets her brother in the flesh. She is a friendly soul by nature."

"And Ruth?"

"Ruth is planning her wardrobe for Tuesday," Bee said tartly.

The Rector smiled a little. "The happy ones of the earth, the Ruths."

"But Simon . . . How can one account for Simon?"

"I don't think that that is very difficult, you know. Simon would have had to be a saint to welcome back a brother who was going to supplant him. A brother, moreover, who has been dead to him since the age of thirteen."

"But, George, his twin! They were inseparable."

"I think that thirteen is further removed from twenty-one than almost any other equidistant points in life. It is a whole lifetime away. An association that ended at thirteen has little but sentimental value for the boy of twenty-one. Latchetts has been Simon's for—what is it?—eight years; he has known for eight years that he would come into his mother's money at twenty-one: to be deprived of all that without warning would upset a stronger character than Simon's."

"I expect I did it badly," Bee said. "The way I told them, I mean. I should have told Simon first, privately. But I did so want to keep them all on the same level. To pretend that they would all be equally glad. Taking Simon apart and telling him before the others would have—would have——"

"Anticipated the trouble."

"Yes. Something like that, I suppose. I suppose I had known quite well that his reaction would be—different from the others. And I just wanted to minimise the difference. I had never imagined for a moment, you see, that his reaction would be so violent. That he would go to the length of denying that Patrick was alive."

"That is only his method of pushing the unwelcome fact away from him."

"Unwelcome," Bee murmured.

"Yes, unwelcome. And very naturally unwelcome. You make things difficult for yourself if you don't accept that fundamental fact. *You* remember Patrick with your adult mind, and are rejoiced that he is still alive." He turned his head to look at her. "Or—are you?"

"Of *course* I am!" she said, a shade too emphatically. But he let it go.

"Simon doesn't remember him with an adult mind or adult emotions. To Simon he is a remembered emotion; not a present one. He has no present love to fight his present—hatred with."

"Oh, George."

"Yes; it is best to face it. It would take an almost divine love to combat the resentment that Simon must be feeling now; and there has never been anything in the least divine about Simon. Poor Simon. It is a wretched thing to have happened to him."

"And at the very worst moment. When we were all ready for celebration."

"At least this is the answer to something that has puzzled me for eight years."

"What is that?"

"The fact of Patrick's suicide. I could never reconcile it with the Patrick I knew. Patrick was a sensitive child, but he had a tremendous fund of good common sense; a balance. A far better equilibrium, for instance, than the less sensitive but more brilliant Simon. He had also, moreover, a great sense of obligation. If Latchetts was suddenly and unaccountably his he might be overwhelmed to the point of running away, but not unbalanced to the point of taking his life."

"Why did we all so unquestioningly accept the suicide theory?"

"The coat on the cliff-top. The note—which did read like a suicide one, undoubtedly. The complete lack of anyone who had seen him after old Abel met him between Tanbitches and the cliff. The persistence with which suicides use that particular part of the coast for their taking-off. It was the natural conclusion to come to. I don't remember that we ever questioned it. But it had always stayed in my mind as an unaccountable thing. Not the method, but the fact that Patrick should have taken his own life. It was unlike everything I knew about Patrick. And now we find that, after all, he did no such thing."

"I shut my eyes and the lilac is no colour; I open them and it is purple," Bee was saying to herself; which was her way of keeping her tears at bay. Just as she counted objects when in danger of crying at a play.

"Tell me, are you pleased with this adult Patrick who has come back?"

"Yes. Yes, I am pleased. He is in some ways very like the Patrick who went away. Very quiet. Self-contained. Very considerate. Do you remember how Patrick used to turn and say: "Are you all right?" before he began whatever he was planning to do on his own? He still thinks of the other person. Didn't try to—rush me, or take his welcome for granted. And he still keeps his bad times to himself. Simon always came flying to one with his griefs and grievances, but Patrick dealt with his own. He seems still to be able to deal with his own."

"Has he had a bad time, then, do you think?"

"I gather it hasn't been a bed of roses. I forgot to tell you that he is lame."

"Lame!"

"Yes. Just a little. Some accident with a horse. He is still mad about horses."

"That will make you happy," George said. He said it a little wryly, being no horseman.

"Yes," agreed Bee with a faint smile for the wryness. "It is good that Latchetts should go to a real lover."

"You rate Simon as a poor lover?"

"Not poor. Indifferent, perhaps. To Simon horses are a means of providing excitement. Of enhancing his prestige. A medium for trade; for profitable dickering. I doubt if it goes further than that. For horses as—people, if you know what I mean, he has little feeling. Their sicknesses bore him. Eleanor will stay up for nights on end with a horse that is ill, sharing the nursing fifty-fifty with Gregg. The only time Simon loses sleep is when a horse he wants to ride, or jump, or hunt, has a 'leg'."

"Poor Simon," the Rector said reflectively. "Not the temperament to make a successful fight against jealousy. A very destructive emotion indeed, jealousy."

58

Before Bee could answer, Nancy appeared.

"Bee! How nice," she said. "Were you at Evensong, and did you see the latest contingent from our local school for scandalisers? Two adolescents who are 'studying the prevalent English superstitions': to wit, the Church of England. A boy, very hairy for fourteen, it seemed to me; and a girl with eleven combs keeping up her not very abundant wisps. What would you say a passion for combs was an indication of? A sense of insecurity?"

"Beatrice has come with a very wonderful piece of news," the Rector said.

"Don't tell me Simon has got himself engaged."

"No. It is not about Simon. It's about Patrick."

"Patrick?" Nancy said uncertainly.

"He is alive." And he told her how.

"Oh, Bee, my dear," Nancy said, putting her arms round her friend, "how glorious for you. Now you won't have to wonder any more."

That Nancy's first reaction was to remember that private nightmare of hers broke Bee down altogether.

"You need a drink," Nancy said, briskly. "Come along in and we'll finish what's left in the sherry bottle."

"A deplorable reason for drinking sherry," the Rector said.

"What is?"

"That one 'needs a drink'."

"An even more deplorable reason is that if we don't drink it Mrs. Godkin will. She has had most of the rest of the bottle. Come along."

So Bee drank the Rectory sherry and listened while George enlightened Nancy on the details of Patrick Ashby's return. Now that her weight of knowledge was shared with her own generation, the burden was suddenly lighter. Whatever difficulties lay ahead, there would be George and Nancy to support and comfort her.

"When is Patrick coming?" Nancy asked; and the Rector turned to Bee.

"On Tuesday," Bee told them. "What I can't decide is the best way of spreading the news in the district."

"That's easy," Nancy said. "Just tell Mrs. Gloom."

Mrs. Gloom kept the sweets-tobacco-and-newspaper shop in the village. Her real name was Bloom, but her relish for disaster caused her to be known, first by the Ledingham and Ashby children, and later by all and sundry, as Mrs. Gloom.

"Or you could send yourself a postcard. The post office is almost as good. That is what Jim Bowden did when he jilted the Heywood girl. Sent his mother a telegram announcing his wedding. The fuss was all over before he came back."

"I'm afraid we are going to be at the exact centre of the fuss until the nine days' wonder is over," Bee said. "One must just put up with it."

"Ah, well, my dear, it's a *nice* sort of fuss," Nancy said, comforting.

"Yes. But the situation is so—so incalculable. It's like—like——"

"I know," Nancy said, agreeing. "Like walking on jelly."

"I was going to say picking one's way over a bog, but I think the jelly is a better description."

"Or one of those uneven floors at fun fairs," the Rector said unexpectedly, as Bee took her leave.

"How do you know about fun fairs, George?" his wife asked.

"They had one at the Westover Carnival a year or two ago, I seem to remember. A most interesting study in masochism."

"You see now why I have stuck to George," Nancy said, as she walked with Bee to the garden gate. "After thirteen years I am still finding out things about him. I wouldn't have believed that he even knew what a fun fair was. Can you picture George lost in contemplation of the Giant Racer?"

But it was not of Nancy's George that she was thinking as she walked away through the churchyard, but of the fun-fair floor that she was doomed to walk in the days ahead. She turned in at the south porch of the church and found the great oak door still unlocked. The light of the sunset flooded the grey vault with warmth, and the whole building held peace as a cup holds water. She sat down on a bench by the door and listened to the silence. A companionable silence which she shared with the figures on the tombs, the tattered banners, the names on the wall, the Legion's garish Union Jack, and the slow ticking of a clock. The tombs were all Ledingham ones: from the simple dignity of the Crusader to the marble family that wept with ostentatious opulence over the eighteenth-century politician. The Ashbys had no crusaders and no opulence. Their memorials were tablets on the wall. Bee sat there and read them for the

60

thousandth time. "Of Latchetts" was the refrain. "Of Latchetts in this parish." No field-marshals, no chancellors, no poets, no reformers. Just the yeoman simplicity of Latchetts; the small-squire sufficiency of Latchetts.

And now Latchetts belonged to this unknown boy from half a world away.

"A great sense of obligation," the Rector had said, speaking of the Patrick he remembered. And that had been the Patrick that she, too, remembered. And that Patrick would have written to them.

Always she came back to that in her mind. The Patrick they knew would never have left them in grief and doubt for eight years.

"Some psychological difficulty," Mr. Sandal had said. And after all, he *had* run away. A sufficiently unlikely thing for Patrick to do. Perhaps he had been overcome by shame when he came to himself. And yet. And yet.

That kind child who so automatically asked: "Are you all right?" That child with the "great sense of obligation"?

10

AND while Bee sat and stared at the Ashby tablets in the church at Clare, Brat Farrar was standing in the back room in Pimlico in a brand-new suit and a state of panic.

How had he got himself into this? What could he have been thinking of? He, Brat Farrar. How did he ever think that he could go through with it? How had he ever in the first place consented to lend himself to such a plan?

It was the suit that had shocked him into realisation. The suit was wrong-doing made concrete and manifest. It was a wonderful suit. The kind of suit that he had dreamed of possessing; so unremarkable, so unmistakable once you had remarked it: English tailoring at its unobtrusive best. But he stood looking at himself in the mirror in a kind of horror.

He couldn't do it, that was all. He just couldn't do it.

He would duck, before it was too late.

He would send back the goddamned suit to the tailor, and send a letter to that woman who had been so nice, and just duck out of sight.

"What!" said the voice. "And pass up the greatest adventure of your life? The greatest adventure that has happened to any man within living memory?"

"Adventure my foot. It's plain false pretences."

They wouldn't bother to look for him. They would be too relieved to have him out of their hair. He could duck without leaving a ripple.

"And leave a fortune behind?" said the voice.

"*Yes*, and leave a fortune behind. Who wants a fortune, anyhow?"

They would have his letter to insure them against any further nuisance from his side, and they would just let him go. He would write to that woman who, because she was kind, had kissed him before she was sure, and confess, and say he was sorry, and that would be that.

"And pass up the chance of owning a stud?"

"Who wants a stud? The world's lousy with horses."

"And you are going to own some, perhaps?"

"I may, some day. I may."

"Pigs may fly."

"Shut up."

He would write to Loding and tell him that he would be no party to his criminal schemes.

"And waste all that knowledge? All that training?"

"I should never have started it."

"But you did start it. You finished it. You are primed to the gills with knowledge worth a fortune. You can't waste it, surely!"

Loding would have to whistle for that fifty per cent. How could he ever have thought of letting himself be an instrument in the hands of a crook like Loding!

"A very amusing and intelligent crook. On the highest level of crookery. Nothing to be ashamed of, believe me."

He would go to a travel agency to-morrow morning and get a berth out of the country. Anywhere out of the country.

"I thought you wanted to stay in England?"

He would put the sea between him and temptation.

"Did you say temptation? Don't tell me that you're still wavering!"

He hadn't enough left for a fare to America, but he had enough to take him quite a distance. The travel agency would offer him a choice of places. The world was wide and there was a lot of fun left in it. By Tuesday morning he would be out of England, and this time he would stay out.

"And never see Latchetts at all?"

He would find some—— "What did you say?"

"I said: And never see Latchetts at all?"

He tried to think of an answer.

"Stumped you, haven't I!"

There must be an answer.

"Money, and horses, and fun, and adventure are common change. You can have them anywhere in the world. But if you pass up Latchetts now you pass it up for good. There won't be any going back."

"But what has Latchetts to do with me?"

"You ask that? You, with your Ashby face, and your Ashby bones, and your Ashby tastes, and your Ashby colouring, and your Ashby blood."

"I haven't any evidence at all that——"

"And your Ashby blood, I said. Why, you poor little brute of a foundling, Latchetts is your belonging-place, and you have the immortal gall to pretend that you don't care a rap about it!"

"I didn't say I didn't care. Of course I care."

"But you'll walk out of this country to-morrow, and leave Latchetts behind? For always? Because that is what it amounts to, my boy. That is the choice before you. Take the road of high adventure and on Tuesday morning you will see Latchetts. Duck, and you will never see it at all."

"But I'm not a crook! I can't do something that is criminal."

"Can't you? You've been giving a pretty good imitation of it these last few weeks. And enjoying it too. Remember how you enjoyed that tight-rope business on that first visit to old Sandal? How you enjoyed all the others? Even with a K.C. sitting across the table and doing a sort of mental X-ray on you. You loved it. All that is wrong with you just now is cold feet. Nerves. You want to see Latchetts as you have never wanted anything before. You want to live at Latchetts as an Ashby. You want horses. You want adventure. You want a life in England. Go to Latchetts on Tuesday and they are all yours."

"But——"

"You came half across the world to that meeting with Loding. Was

63

that just chance? Of course not. It was all meant. Your destiny is at Latchetts. Your destiny. What you were born for. Your destiny. At Latchetts. You're an Ashby. Half across a world to a place you never heard of. Destiny. You can't pass up destiny. . . ."

Brat got slowly out of the brand-new suit, and hung it up with orphanage neatness on its fine new hanger. Then he sat down on the edge of his bed and buried his face in his hands.

He was still sitting there when the darkness came.

11

IT was a beautiful day, the day that Brat Farrar came to Latchetts, but a restless little wind kept turning the leaves over so that in spite of the sunlight and the bright air the world was filled with a vague unease and a promise of storm.

"Much too shiny!" thought Bee, looking at the landscape from her bedroom window after breakfast. "'Tears before night,' as Nanny used to say of too exuberant children. However. At least he will arrive in sunshine."

She had been greatly exercised in her mind over that arrival. It was to be as informal as possible; that was a thing that was agreed to by all concerned. Someone would meet him at the station and bring him home, and there would be luncheon with only the family present. The question was: Who was to meet him? The twins had held that the whole family should go to the station, but that, of course, was not to be thought of. The prodigal could hardly be welcomed publicly on the platform at Guessgate for the entertainment of the railway staff and casual travellers between Westover and Bures. She herself could not go without giving the returning Patrick an air of being her protégé; which was something to be avoided at all costs. She had not forgotten Simon's sneer about her "adoption" of Patrick. Simon—the obvious choice for the role of welcomer—was not available; since her announcement on Sunday he had slept at home but had not otherwise taken part in Latchetts activities, and Bee's attempt to talk to him in his room late on Monday night had been futile.

So she had been relieved when Eleanor offered to drive the four miles to the station at Guessgate and bring Patrick back.

The present load on her mind was that family meal after his arrival. If Simon did not turn up how was his absence to be explained? And if he did turn up what was that lunch going to be like?

She turned to go down for one more rehearsal with the cook—their third cook in the last twelve months—when she was waylaid by Lana, their "help." Lana came from the village, and had gilt hair and varnished fingernails and the local version of the current make-up. She "obliged" only because her "boy-friend" worked in the stables. She would sweep and dust, she explained when she first came, because that was "all right," but she would not wait at table because that was "menial." Bee had longed to tell her that no one with her hands, or her breath, or her scent, or her manners, would ever be allowed to hand an Ashby a plate; but she had learned to be politic. She explained that there was, in any case, no question of waiting at table; the Ashbys always waited on themselves.

Lana had come to say that the "vacuum was vomiting instead of swallowing," and domestic worries closed once more over Bee's head and swamped domestic drama. She came to the surface in time to see Eleanor getting into her little two-seater.

"Aren't you taking the car?" she asked. "The car" was the family vehicle, Eleanor's disreputable little conveyance being known as "the bug."

"No. He'll have to take us as we are," Eleanor said.

Bee noticed that she had not bothered to change into a dress. She was wearing the breeches and gaiters in which she had begun the morning.

"Oh, take me, take me!" Ruth said, precipitating herself down the steps and on to the car, but taking good care, Bee noticed, to keep "her blue" away from the bug's dusty metal.

"No," Eleanor said firmly.

"I'm sure he would like me to be there. One of my generation, I mean. After all, he knows you. It won't be exciting for him to see you the way it would be for him to see——"

"No. And keep off if you don't want that dazzling outfit of yours to be mucked up."

"I do think it is selfish of Eleanor," Ruth said, dusting her palms

65

as she watched the car grow small between the lime trees. "She just wants to keep the excitement to herself."

"Nonsense. It was arranged that you and Jane should wait here. Where is Jane, by the way?"

"In the stables, I think. She isn't interested in Patrick."

"I hope she comes in in good time for lunch."

"Oh, she will. She may not be interested in Patrick, but she is always ready for her meals. Is Simon going to be there, at lunch?"

"I hope so."

"What do you think he will say to Patrick?"

If the peace and happiness of Latchetts was going to break down into a welter of discord the twins must go away to school. They would be going to school in a year or two, anyhow; they had much better go now than live in an atmosphere of strain and hatred.

"Do you think there will be a scene?" Ruth asked, hopefully.

"Of course not, Ruth. I wish you wouldn't dramatise things."

But she wished, too, that she could count on there being no scene. And Eleanor, on her way to the station, was wishing the same thing. She was a little nervous of meeting this new brother, and annoyed with herself for being nervous. Her everyday clothes were her protest against her own excitement: a pretence that nothing of real moment was about to happen.

Guessgate, which served three villages but no town, was a small wayside station with a fairly heavy goods business but little passenger traffic, so that when Brat climbed down from his carriage there was no one on the platform but a fat countrywoman, a sweating porter, the ticket-collector, and Eleanor.

"Hullo," she said. "You are very like Simon." And she shook hands with him. He noticed that she wore no make-up. A little powdering of freckles went over the bridge of her nose.

"Eleanor," he said, identifying her.

"Yes. What about your luggage? I have just the small car but the dickey holds quite a lot."

"I have just this," he said, indicating his "grip."

"Is the rest coming later?"

"No, this is all I possess."

"Oh." She smiled just a little. "No moss."

"No," he said, "no moss," and began to like her very much.

66

"The car is out in the yard. Through this way."

"Been away, Mr. Ashby?" the ticket-collector said, accepting his piece of pasteboard.

"Yes, I've been away."

At the sound of his voice the ticket-collector looked up, puzzled.

"He took you for Simon," Eleanor said, as they got into the car; and smiled properly. Her two front teeth crossed just a little; which gave her face an endearing childishness. It was a cool, determined, small face when she was serious. "You couldn't have come home at a better time of the year," she said, as they scrunched over the gravel of the station yard and fled away into the landscape.

"Home," he thought. Her hair was the colour of corn so ripe that it was nearly white. Pale, silky stuff, very fine. It was brushed back into a knot, as if she could not be bothered to do anything else with it.

"The blossom is just beginning. And the first foals are here."

The knees in their worn whipcord were just like a boy's. But the bare arms protruding from the jacket she wore slung over her shoulders were delicately round.

"Honey has a filly foal that is going to make history. Wait till you see it. You won't know Honey, of course. She was after your time. Her real name is Greek Honey. By Hymettus out of a mare called Money For Jam. I hope you will be impressed with our horses."

"I expect to be," he said.

"Aunt Bee says that you're still interested in them. Horses, I mean."

"I haven't done much on the breeding side, of course. Just preparing horses for work."

They came to the village.

So this was Clare. This warm, living, smiling entity was what those little flat squares on the map had stood for. There was the White Hart; there was the Bell. And up there behind, on its knoll, was the church where the Ashby tablets hung.

"The village is looking nice, isn't it?" Eleanor said. "Not changed a bit since I can remember. Not changed since the Flood, if it comes to that. The names of the people in the houses come in the same order down the street as they did in the time of Richard the Second. But of course you know that! I keep thinking of you as a visitor."

Beyond the village, he knew, were the great gates of Clare Park.

He waited, mildly curious, to see the entrance to what had been Alec Loding's home. It proved to be a sweeping curve of iron lace flanked by two enormous pillars bearing on each a lion passant. Astride the farther lion was a small boy clad in a leopard-skin rug with green baize edging, a seaside pail worn helmet-wise, and nothing else that was visible. A very long brass poker stood up lance-wise from its rest on his bare foot.

"It's all right," Eleanor said. "You did see it."

"That comforts me quite a bit."

"Did you know that Clare was a school nowadays?"

He had nearly said yes, when he remembered that this was merely one of the things Loding had told him, not one of the things that he was supposed to know.

"What kind of school?"

"A school for dodgers."

"Dodgers?"

"Yes. Anyone who loathes hard work and has a parent with enough money to pay the fees makes a bee-line for Clare. No one is forced to learn anything at Clare. Not even the multiplication table. The theory is that one day you'll feel the need of the multiplication table and be seized with a mad desire to acquire the nine-times. Of course, it doesn't work out like that at all."

"Doesn't it?"

"Of course not. No one who could get out of the nine-times would ever dream of acquiring it voluntarily."

"And if they don't do lessons what do they do all day?"

"Express their personalities. They draw things; or make things; or whitewash the coach-house; or dress up, like Antony Toselli. That was Tony on the lion. I teach some of them to ride. They like that. Riding, I mean. I think they are so bored with easy things that they find something a little difficult simply fascinating. But of course it has to be something out of the ordinary. The difficult thing, I mean. If it was a difficulty that everyone was supposed to overcome they wouldn't be interested. That would bring them down to the common level of you and me. They wouldn't be 'different' any longer."

"Nice people."

"Very profitable to Latchetts, anyhow. And here *is* Latchetts."

Brat's heart rose up into his throat. Eleanor turned slowly into the white gateway between the limes.

It was just as well that she was going slowly, for she had no sooner entered the green tunnel than something like a giant blue butterfly shot out from the boles of the trees and danced wildly in front of the car.

Eleanor braked and swore simultaneously.

"Hullo! Hullo!" shouted the butterfly, dancing to Brat's side of the car.

"You little idiot," Eleanor said. "You deserve to be killed. Don't you know that a driver doesn't see well coming into the avenue out of the sunlight?"

"Hullo! Hullo, Patrick! It's me! Ruth. How d'you do. I came to ride up with you. To the house, you know. Can I sit on your knee? There isn't very much room in that awful old car of Eleanor's, and I don't want to crush my dress. I hope you like my dress. It is put on specially for your coming home. You're very good-looking, aren't you? Am I what you expected?"

She waited for an answer to that, so Brat said that he hadn't really thought about it.

"Oh," said Ruth, much dashed. "We thought about you," she said reprovingly. "No one has talked about anything else for days."

"Ah well," Brat said, "when *you* have run away for years and years people will talk about *you.*"

"I shouldn't dream of doing anything so *outré,*" Ruth said, unforgiving.

"Where did you get that word?" Eleanor asked.

"It's a very good word. Mrs. Peck uses it."

Brat felt that he ought to paint in a little local colour by saying: "How are the Pecks, by the way?" But he had no mind to spare for artifice. He was waiting for the moment when the limes would thin out and he would see Latchetts.

For the moment when he would be face to face with his "twin."

"Simon hasn't come back yet," he heard Ruth say; and saw her sideways glance at Eleanor. The glance, even more than the information, shook him.

So Simon wasn't waiting on the doorstep for him. Simon was "away" somewhere and the family was uneasy about it.

Alec Loding had disabused him of the idea that a feudal staff reception would await him at Latchetts; that there would be a line of servants, headed by the butler and descending in strict order to the latest tweeny, to welcome the Young Master to the ancestral home. That, Loding had said, had gone out with bustles, and Latchetts had never had a butler, anyhow. And he had known, too, that there would be no array of relations. The children's father had been an only son with one sister, Aunt Bee. The children's mother had been an only daughter with two brothers: both of them killed by the Germans before they were twenty. The only near Ashby relation was Great-uncle Charles, reported by Loding to be now nearing Singapore.

But it had not occurred to him that all the available Ashbys might not be there. That there might be dissenters. The ease of his meeting with Eleanor had fooled him. Metaphorically speaking, he picked up the reins that had been lying on his neck.

The car ran out of the thin spring green of the avenue into the wide sweep in front of the house, and there in the too-bright gusty sunlight stood Latchetts; very quiet, very friendly, very sure of itself. The gabled front of the original building had been altered by some eighteenth-century Ashby to conform with the times, so that only the tiled roof showed its age and origin. Built in the last days of Elizabeth, it was now blandly "Queen Anne." It stood there in its grasslands, undecorated and sufficient; needing no garden for its enhancement. The green of the small park flowered at its heart into the house itself, and any other flowering would have been redundant.

As Eleanor swept round towards the house, Brat saw Beatrice Ashby come out on to the doorstep, and a sudden panic seized him; a mad desire to blurt out the truth to her and back out there and then; before he had put foot over the doorstep; before he was definitely "on" in the scene. It was going to be a damnably difficult and awkward scene and he had no idea how to play it.

It was Ruth who saved him from the worst moment of awkwardness. Before the car had come to a halt she was piping her triumph to the world, so that Brat's arrival somehow took second place to her own achievement.

"I met him after all, Aunt Bee! I met him after all. I came up from the gate with them. You don't mind, do you? I just strolled down as far as the gate and when I got there I saw them coming, and they stopped and gave me a lift and here we are and so I met him after all."

She linked her arm through Brat's and tumbled with him out of the car, dragging him behind her as if he were a find of her own. So that it was with a mutual shrug for this display of personality that Brat and Bee greeted each other. They were united for the moment in a rueful amusement, and by the time the amusement had passed so had the moment.

Before awkwardness could come flooding back, there was a second distraction. Jane came riding round the corner of the house on Fourposter on her way to the stables. The instant check of her hands on the reins when she saw the group at the door made it obvious that she had not planned on being one of that group. But it was too late now to back out, even if backing out had been possible. It was never possible to back away from anything that Fourposter might happen to be interested in; he had no mouth and an insatiable curiosity. So forward came the reluctant Jane on a highly interested pony. As Fourposter came to a halt she slid politely to the ground and stood there shy and defensive. When Bee introduced her she laid a small limp hand in Brat's and after a moment withdrew it.

"What is your pony's name?" Brat asked, aware of her antagonism.

"That's Fourposter," Ruth said, appropriating Jane's mount. "The Rector calls him the Equine Omnibus."

Brat put out his hand to the pony, who refused the advance by withdrawing a pace and looking contemptuously down his Roman nose. As a gesture it was pure burlesque; a Victorian gesture of repudiation from a Victorian drama.

"A comedian," remarked Brat; and Bee, delighted with his perception, laughed.

"He doesn't like people," Jane said, half-repressive, half-defending her friend.

But Brat kept his hand out, and presently Fourposter's curiosity overcame his stand-offishness and he dropped his head to the waiting hand. Brat made much of him, till Fourposter capitulated entirely and nuzzled him with elephantine playfulness.

"Well!" said Ruth, watching. "He never does that to *anyone!*"

Brat looked down into the small tight face by his elbow, at the small grubby hands clutching the reins so tightly.

"I expect he does to Jane when no one is around," he said.

"Jane, it is time you were cleaned up for lunch," Bee said, and turned to lead the way indoors.

And Brat followed her, over the threshold.

12

"I HAVE put you in the old night nursery," Bee said. "I hope you don't mind. Simon has the room that he used to share with—that you used to share with him." Oh, dear, what a gaffe, she thought; shall I ever be able to think of him as Patrick? "And to give you one of the spare rooms was to treat you like a visitor."

Brat said that he would be glad to have the night nursery.

"Will you go up now, or will you have a drink first?"

"I'll go up now," Brat said, and turned to the stairway.

He knew that she had been waiting for this moment; waiting for the moment when he must show knowledge of the house. So he turned from her and led the way upstairs; up to the big first landing and down the narrow corridor to the north wing, and to the children's rooms facing west from it. He opened the third of the four doors and stood in the room that Nora Ashby had arranged for her children when they were small. One window looked west over the paddocks and the other north to the rise of the down. It was on the quiet side of the house, away from the stables and the approach from the road. He stood at the window looking at the soft blue English distances, thinking of the brilliant mountains beyond the whirling dust of the West, and very conscious of Bee Ashby behind him.

There was something else that he must take the initiative about.

"Where is Simon?" he said, and turned to face her.

"He is like Jane," she said. "Late for lunch. But he'll be in at any moment."

It was smoothly done, but he had seen her shy at his unheralded question, as if he had flicked a whip. Simon had not come to meet him; Simon had not been at Latchetts to greet him; Simon, it was to be deduced, was being difficult.

Before he could pursue the subject she took the initiative from him.

"You can have the nursery bathroom all to yourself, but *do* go slow on the hot water, will you? Fuel is a dreadful problem. Now wash and come down at once. The Pecks sent over some of the Rectory sherry."

"Aren't they coming to lunch?"

"No, they're coming to dinner to-night. Lunch is for family only."

She watched him turn to the fourth door, which he knew to be the bathroom of the nursery wing, and went away looking comforted. He knew why she was comforted: because he had known his way about the house. And he felt guilty and ill at ease. Fooling Mr. Sandal—with a K.C. sitting opposite you and gimletting holes in you with cynical Irish eyes—had been one thing; fooling Mr. Sandal had been fun. But fooling Bee Ashby was another thing altogether.

He washed absentmindedly, turning the soap in his hands with his eyes on the line of the down. There was the turf he had wanted to ride on; the turf he had sold his soul for. Presently he would get a horse and go up there and ride in the quiet, away from human relationships and this fantastic game of human poker, and up there it would once more seem right and worth while.

He went back to his room and found a brassy blonde in tight flowered rayon tweaking the wallflower in the bowl on the window-sill.

"Hullo," said the blonde. "Welcome home, and all that."

"Thanks," Brat said. Was this someone that he should know? Surely not!

"You're very like your brother, aren't you?"

"I suppose so." He took his brushes from his "grip" and put them on the dressing-table; it was a symbolical taking-possession.

"You won't know me, of course. I'm Lana Adams from the village. Adams the joiner was my father. I oblige because my boy-friend works in the stables."

So that is what she was: the help. He looked at her and was sorry for the boy-friend.

"You look a lot older than your brother, don't you? I suppose it's knocking about the world that does it. Having to look out for yourself, and all that. Not being spoilt like your brother. You'll excuse me saying it but spoilt he is. That's why he's made all this

73

to-do about you coming back. Silly, I call it. You've only to look at you to know that you're an Ashby. Not much point in saying you're not, I should think. But you take my tip and stand up to him. He can't stand being stood up to. Been humoured all his life, I should say. Don't let it get you down."

As Brat went silently on with his unpacking, she paused; and before she could resume Eleanor's cool voice said from the doorway:

"Have you everything you want?"

The blonde said hastily: "I was just welcoming Mr. Patrick back," and, having flung Brat a radiant smile, made a hip-swing exit from the room.

Brat wondered how much Eleanor had heard.

"It's a nice room this," Eleanor said, "except that it doesn't get the morning sun. That bed is from Clare Park. Aunt Bee sold the little ones and bought that one at the Clare sale. It's nice, isn't it? It was the one in Alec Ledingham's room. Except for that the room is just the same."

"Yes; the old wallpaper, I notice."

"Robinson Crusoe and company. Yes. I had a great weakness for Hereward the Wake. He had such an enchanting profile." She pointed to Hereward's place in the pattern of fictional heroes that Nora had chosen for her children's nightly entertainment.

"Is the nursery-rhyme paper still next door?"

"Yes, of course. Come and see."

He went with her, but while she rehearsed the pictured tales his mind was busy with the village girl's revelation about Simon and with the ironic fact that he was to sleep in Alec Loding's bed.

So Simon had refused to believe that he was Patrick. "Not much point in saying you're not, I should think." That could only mean that Simon, in the face of all the evidence, refused to accept him. Why?

He followed Eleanor downstairs, still wondering.

Eleanor led him into a big sunny sitting-room where Bee was pouring sherry, and Ruth was picking out a tune on a piano.

"Would you like to hear me play?" Ruth asked, inevitably.

"No," Eleanor said, "he wouldn't. We've been looking at the old wallpapers," she said to Bee. "I'd forgotten how in love with Hereward I used to be. It's just as well that I was removed from him in time or he might have become a fixation or something."

74

"*I* never *liked* that baby stuff on the walls," Ruth said.

"*You* never *read*, so you couldn't know anything about them," Eleanor said.

"We gave up using the nursery wing when the twins ceased to have a Nanny," Bee said. "It was too far away from the rest of the house."

"It was a day's march to call the twins in the morning," Eleanor said, "and as Ruth always needed calling several times we had to move them into the normal family orbit."

"Delicate people need more sleep," Ruth said.

"Since when have you been delicate?" asked Eleanor.

"It's not that I'm delicate but that Jane's more robust, aren't you, Jane?" she said, appealing to Jane, who sidled into the room, the hair at her temples still damp from her hasty ablutions.

But Jane's eyes were on Bee.

"Simon is here," she said in a small voice; and crossed the room to stand near Bee as if for reassurance.

There was an instant of complete silence. In the moment of suspended animation only Ruth moved. Ruth sat up and sparkled with anticipation.

Then Bee's hand moved again and went on filling the glasses. "That is very nice," she said. "We needn't keep luncheon back after all."

It was so beautifully done that Brat, knowing what he knew now, felt like applauding.

"Where is Simon?" Eleanor asked casually.

"He was coming downstairs," Jane said; and her eyes went back to Bee.

The door opened and Simon Ashby came in.

He paused a moment, looking across at Brat, before closing the door behind him. "So you've come," he said.

There was no emphasis on the words; no apparent emotion in the tone.

He walked slowly across the room until he was standing face to face with Brat by the window. He had abnormally clear grey eyes with a darker rim to the iris, but they had no expression in them. Nor had his pale features any expression. He was so tightly strung, Brat thought, that if you plucked him with a finger he would twang.

And then quite suddenly the tightness went.

75

He stood for a moment searching Brat's face; and his own was suddenly slack with relief.

"They won't have told you?" he said, drawling a little, "but I was prepared to deny with my last breath that you were Patrick. Now that I've seen you I take all that back. Of course you are Patrick." He put out his hand. "Welcome home."

The stillness behind them broke in a flurry of movement and competing voices. There was a babble of mutual congratulation, of chinking glasses and laughter. Even Ruth, it seemed, stifled her disappointment at being done out of melodrama, and devoted her talents to wheedling a little more sherry into her glass than the "sip" that was the twins' allowance for health-drinking.

But Brat, drinking the golden liquid and thanking heaven that the moment was over, was puzzled. Why *relief?* he was thinking. What had Ashby expected? What had he been afraid of?

He had denied the possibility of Brat's being Patrick. Had that been just a defence against hope; an insurance against ultimate disappointment? Had he said to himself: I won't believe that Patrick is alive, and so when it is proved that he isn't I won't have hoped for nothing? And was that overwhelming relief a moment ago due merely to the realisation that he was after all Patrick?

It didn't fit.

He watched Simon being the life of the party, and wondered about him. A few moments ago Ashby had been steeled to face something, and now it seemed he had been—let off. That was it. That was what that sudden relief had been. The reaction of some-one steeled to face the worst and suddenly reprieved.

Why should he feel reprieved?

He took the small puzzle into luncheon with him, and it lay at the back of his mind while he dealt with the problems of Ashby conversation and answered their crowding questions.

"You're in!" gloated the voice inside him. "You're in! You're sitting as of right at the Ashby table, and they're all tickled to death about it."

Well, perhaps not all. Jane, loyal to Simon, was a small silent oasis in the right talk. And it was not to be expected that Simon himself, for all his capitulation, was tickled to any great extent. But Bee, entirely uncritical of that capitulation, was radiant: and Eleanor melted moment by moment from conversational politeness to a frank interest.

76

"But a Comanche bridle is a kind of twitch, isn't it?"

"No; just a gag. The rope goes through the mouth the way a bit does. It's best for a led horse. He'll follow to lessen the pull."

Ruth, having quite forgiven his lack of speculation about her looks, paid assiduous court to him; and she was the only one who called him Patrick.

This became more noticeable as the meal went on, and her continual interjection of "Patrick!" as she claimed his attention contrasted with the others' half-conscious avoidance of the name. Brat wished that his sole "follower" had proved to be Jane and not Ruth. If he had ever had a small sister he would have liked her to be just like Jane. It annoyed him that he had difficulty in meeting Jane's eyes. It cost him the same effort to meet her regard with equanimity as it did to meet the eyes of the portrait behind her. The dining-room was positivly papered with portraits, and the one behind Jane was of William Ashby the Seventh, wearing the uniform of the Westover Fencibles, in which he had proposed to resist the invasion of Napoleon the First. Brat had learned those portraits off by heart, sitting under the pagoda in Kew Gardens, and every time he lifted his eyes to those of William Ashby the Seventh he was plagued by the ridiculous notion that William knew all about the pagoda.

One thing helped him enormously, however, in this first difficult meeting with the Ashbys. The tale he had to tell, as Loding had pointed out during that meal at the Green Man, was, except for its beginnings, true; it was the tale of his own life. And since the whole family with one accord avoided any reference to the events which had catapulted him into that life, the conversational ground he moved on was firm. There was need for neither side-stepping nor manoeuvre.

Nor was there any need for him to "mind his manners"; and for that too Alec Loding had given loud thanks. It seemed that, short of a first-class and very strict Nanny, there was no more rigorous training in the civilised consumption of food than was to be had at a first-class orphanage. "My God," Loding had said, "if I ever have any change from a round of drinks I'll send it to that caravanserai of yours, as a mark of my gratitude that you were not brought up in some genteel suburb. Gentility is practically ineradicable, my boy. And whatever Pat Ashby might conceivably do, it is quite inconceivable that he should ever stick out his little finger when he drank."

So Brat had no social habits to unlearn. Indeed, his orthodoxy slightly disappointed Ruth, always on the lookout for the flamboyant.

"You don't eat with your fork," she said; and when he looked puzzled, added: "The way they do in American pictures; they cut things up with their knives and forks and then they change the fork over to their other hand and eat with it."

"I don't chew gum either," he pointed out.

"I wonder how that very elaborate method of dealing with their food arose," Bee said.

"Perhaps knives were scarce in the early days," Eleanor suggested.

"Knives were far too useful to be scarce in a pioneer society," Simon said. "It's much more likely that they lived so long on hash that when they got things in slices their instinct was to make hash of it as soon as possible."

Brat thought, listening to them, how very English it all was. Here he was, back from the dead, and they were calmly discussing American table manners. There was no backslapping, congratulatory insistence on the situation as there would be in a transatlantic household. They avoided the do-you-remember theme as determinedly as Americans would have wallowed in it. Remembering his friends of the Lazy Y, he thought what a fine exhibition of Limey snootiness this would be from the point of view of Pete, and Hank, and Lefty.

But perhaps the happiness on Bee's face would have impressed even Lefty.

"Do you smoke?" Bee asked, when she had poured the coffee; and she pushed the cigarette box over to him. But Brat, who liked his own brand, took out his case and offered the contents to her.

"I've given them up," Bee said. "I have a bank balance instead." So Brat offered the case to Eleanor.

Eleanor paused with her fingers touching the cigarettes, and bent forward to read something engraved on the inside of the case.

"Brat Farrar," she said. "Who is that?"

"Me," said Brat.

"You? Oh, yes; Farrar, of course. But why Brat?"

"I don't know."

"Did they call you that? Brat, I mean?"

"Yes."

"Why Brat?"

"I don't know. Because I was small, I guess."

78

"Brat!" Ruth said delighted. "Do you mind if I call you Brat? Do you?"

"No. I haven't been called anything else for a large part of my life."

The door opened and Lana appeared to say that a young man had called to see Miss Ashby and she had put him in the library.

"Oh, what a nuisance," Bee said. "What does he want, do you know?"

"He says he's a reporter," Lana said, "but he doesn't look like a reporter to me. Quite tidy and clean and polite." Lana's experience of the Press, like Brat's knowledge of middle-class life, was derived solely from films.

"Oh, *no!*" Bee said. "Not the Press. Not already."

"The *Westover Times* he says he is."

"Did he say why he had come?"

"Come about Mr. Patrick, of course," Lana said, turning her thumb in Patrick's direction.

"Oh, God," Simon groaned, "and the fatted calf not half-way down our gullets. I suppose it had to come sooner or later!"

Bee drank the remains of her coffee. "Come on, Brat!" she said, putting out her hand and pulling him to his feet. "We might as well go and get it over. You too, Simon." She led Brat out of the room, laughing at him, and still hand in hand with him. The warm friendliness of her clasp sent a rush of emotion through him that he could not identify. It was like nothing he had so far experienced in life. And he was too busy with thoughts of the reporter to pause to analyse it.

The library was the dark room at the back of the house where Bee kept her roll-top desk, her accounts, and her reference books. A small young man in a neat blue suit was puzzling over a stud book. At their entrance he dropped the book and said in a rich Glasgow accent: "Miss Ashby? My name is Macallan. I'm working on the *Westover Times*. I'm awfully sorry about barging in like this, but I thought you'd have finished eating this long time."

"Well, we began late, and I'm afraid we lingered over things," Bee said.

"Uh-huh," said Mr. Macallan understandingly. "A very special occasion. I've no right to be spoiling it for you, but 'the first with the latest' is my motto, and just this minute you're the latest."

"I suppose you mean my nephew's homecoming."

"Just that."

"And how did you find out about it so soon, Mr. Macallan?"

"One of my contacts heard about it in one of the Clare pubs."

"A deplorable word," said Bee.

"Pub?" Mr. Macallan said, puzzled.

"No. Contact."

"Och, well, one of my stooges, if you like that better," Mr. Macallan said agreeably. "Which of these young gentlemen is the returned prodigal, may I ask?"

Bee introduced Brat and Simon. Some of the cold tightness had come back to Simon's face; but Brat, who had been around when Nat Zucco had cut his throat in the kitchen of his ex-wife's eating-house and had witnessed the activities of the American Press on that occasion, was entranced by this glimpse of news-gathering in Britain. He answered the obvious questions put to him by Mr. Macallan and wondered if there would be any suggestion of a photograph. If so, he must get out of it somehow.

But it was Bee who saved him from that. No photograph, said Bee. No; positively *no* photograph. All the information he liked to ask for, but no photograph.

Mr. Macallan accepted this, but reluctantly. "The story of the missing twin won't be half so good without a photograph," he complained.

"You're not going to call it 'The Missing Twin,' are you?" Bee said.

"No; he's going to call it 'Back From The Dead'," Simon said, speaking for the first time. His cool drawl fell on the room like a shadow.

Mr. Macallan's pale blue eyes went to him, rested a moment on him consideringly, and then came back to Bee. "I *had* thought of 'Sensation at Clare'," he said, "but I doubt the *Westover Times* won't stand for it. A very conservative organ. But I expect the *Daily Clarion* will do better."

"The *Clarion*!" Bee said. "A London paper! But—but I hope there is no question of that. This is an entirely local—an entirely family matter."

"So was that affair in Hilldrop Crescent," Mr. Macallan said.

"What affair?"

80

"Crippen was the name. The world's Press is composed of family affairs, Miss Ashby."

"But this is of no possible interest to anyone but ourselves. When my nephew—disappeared, eight years ago, the *Westover Times* reported it quite—quite incidentally."

"Ay, I know. I looked it up. A small paragraph at the bottom of page three."

"I fail to see why my nephew's return should be of any more interest than his disappearance."

"It's the man-bites-dog affair over again. People go to their deaths every day, but the amount of people who come back from the dead is very small indeed, Miss Ashby. Coming back from the dead, in spite of the advances of modern science, is still a sensation. And that's why the *Daily Clarion* is going to be interested."

"But how should they hear about it?"

"Hear about it!" Mr. Macallan said, genuinely horrified. "Miss Ashby, this is my own *scoop*, don't you see."

"You mean you are going to send the story to the *Clarion?*"

"Assuredly."

"Mr. Macallan, you mustn't; you really must not."

"Listen, Miss Ashby," Mr. Macallan said patiently, "I agreed about the no-photographs prohibition, and I respect the agreement —I won't go sneaking around the countryside trying to snap the young gentlemen unawares, or anything like that—but you can't ask me to give up a scoop like this. Not a scoop of 'London daily' dimensions." And as Bee, caught in the toils of her natural desire to be fair, hesitated, he added: "Even if I didn't send them the story, there's nothing to hinder a sub-editor lifting the story from the *Westover Times* and making it front-page news. You wouldn't be a scrap better off and I'd have lost my chance of doing a bit of good for myself."

"Oh, dear," Bee said, tacitly acknowledging that he was right, "I suppose that means swarms of newspaper men from London."

"Och, no. Only the *Clarion*. If it's the *Clarion's* story none of the rest will bother. And whoever they send down you don't have to worry. They're all Balliol men, I understand."

With which flip at the English Press, Mr. Macallan looked round for his hat and made motions of departure.

"I'm very grateful to you, and to you, Mr. Ashby, for being so accommodating in the matter of information. I won't keep you any longer. May I offer you my congratulations on your happiness"—for a second the pale blue eyes rested in mild benevolence on Simon— "and my thanks for your kindness."

"You're a long way from home, aren't you, Mr. Macallan?" Bee said conversationally as she went to the front door with him.

"Home?"

"Scotland."

"Oh, I see. How did you know I was Scots? Oh, my name, of course. Ay, it's a far cry to Glasgow; but this is just the long way round to London, so to speak. If I'm going to work on an English paper it's as well to know something of the—the——"

"Aborigines?" suggested Bee.

"Local conditions, I *was* going to say," Mr. Macallan said solemnly.

"Haven't you a car?" Bee said, looking at the empty sweep in front of the door.

"I left it parked at the end of your drive there. I've never got used to sweeping up to strange houses as if I owned them."

With which startling exhibition of modesty the little man bowed, put on his hat, and walked away.

13

In the library, as the voices of Bee and Mr. Macallan faded down the hall and into the out-of-doors, there was silence. Brat, uncertain of the quality of that silence, turned to the shelves and began to consider the books.

"Well," said Simon, lounging in the window, "another hazard safely negotiated."

Brat waited, trying to analyse the sound of the words while they still hung in the air.

"Hazard?" he said at length.

"The snags and bunkers in the difficult business of coming back. It must have taken some nerve, all things considered. What moved you to it, Brat—homesickness?"

This was the first frank question he had been asked, and he suddenly liked Ashby the better for it.

"Not exactly. A realisation that my place was here, after all." He felt that that had a self-righteous sound, and added: "I mean, that my place in the world was here."

This was succeeded by another silence. Brat went on looking at books and hoped that he was not going to like young Ashby. That would be an unforeseen complication. It was bad enough not to be able to face the person he was supplanting, now that he was left alone in a room with him; but to find himself liking that person would make the situation intolerable.

It was Bee who broke the silence.

"I think we should have offered the poor little man a drink," she said, coming in. "However, it's too late now. He can get one from his 'contact' at the White Hart."

"The Bell, I suspect," Simon said.

"Why the Bell?"

"Our Lana frequents that in preference to the White Hart."

"Ah, well. The sooner everyone knows the sooner the fuss will be over." She smiled at Brat to take any sting from the words. "Let's go and look at the horses, shall we? Have you any riding clothes with you, Brat?"

"Not any that Latchetts would recognise as riding clothes," Brat said, noticing how thankfully she seized on the excuse not to call him Patrick.

"Come up with me," Simon said, "and I'll find you something."

"Good," said Bee, looking pleased with him. "I'll collect Eleanor."

"Did you like being given the old night nursery?" Simon asked, preceding Brat upstairs.

"Very much."

"Same old paper, I suppose you noticed."

"Yes."

"Do you remember the night we had an Ivanhoe-Hereward battle?"

"No; I don't remember that."

"No. Of course you wouldn't."

Again the words hung on the silence, teasing Brat's ear with an echo of their tone.

He followed young Ashby into the room he had shared with his brother, and noticed that there was no suggestion in the room that it had ever been shared by another person. It was, on the contrary, very much Simon's own room; being furnished with his possessions to an extent that made it as much a sitting-room as a bedroom. Shelves of books, rows of silver cups, framed sketches of horses on the walls, easy chairs, and a small desk with a telephone extension on it.

Brat moved over to the window while Simon rummaged among his clothes for appropriate garments. The window, as he knew, looked over the stables, but a green hedge of lilac and laburnum trees hid the buildings from view. Above them, in the middle distance, rose the tower of Clare church. On Sunday, he supposed, he would be taken to service there. Another hazard. Hazard had been an odd word for young Ashby to choose, surely?

Simon emerged from the cupboard with breeches and a tweed coat.

"I think these ought to do," he said, throwing them on the bed. "I'll find you a shirt." He opened a drawer of the chest which held his dressing mirror and toilet things. The chest stood by the window, and Brat, still uneasy in Ashby's vicinity, moved over to the fireplace and began to look at the silver cups on the mantelpiece. All of them were prizes for horsemanship, and they ranged from a hurdle race at the local point-to-point to Olympia. All of them except one were of a date too late to have concerned Patrick Ashby; the exception being a small and humble chalice that had been awarded to Simon Ashby on "Patience" for being the winner of the juvenile jumping class at the Bures Agricultural Show in the year before Patrick Ashby committed suicide.

Simon, looking round and seeing the small cup in Brat's hand, smiled and said: "I took that from you, if you remember."

"From me?" Brat said, unprepared.

"You would have won on Old Harry if I hadn't done you out of it by doing a perfect second round."

"Oh, yes," Brat said. And to lay a new scent: "You seem to have done well for yourself since."

"Not badly," Simon said, his attention going back to his shirt drawer. "But I'm going to do a lot better. Ballsbridge and all stops to Olympia." It was said absentmindedly, but with confidence; as if the money to buy good horseflesh would automatically be available.

Brat wondered a little, but felt that this was no moment for discussing the financial future.

"Do you remember the object that used to hang at the end of your bed?" Simon asked casually, pushing the shirt drawer shut.

"The little horse?" Brat said. "Yes, of course. Travesty," he added, giving its name and mock breeding. "By Irish Peasant out of Bog Oak."

He turned from the exhibits on the mantelpiece, meaning to collect the clothes that Ashby had looked out for him; but as he turned he saw Ashby's face in the mirror, and the naked shock on that face stopped him in his tracks. Simon had been in the act of pushing the drawer shut, but the action was arrested half-way. It was, thought Brat, exactly the reaction of someone who has heard a telephone ring; the involuntary pause and then the resumed movement.

Simon turned to face him, slowly, the shirt hanging over his left forearm. "I think you'll find that all right," he said, taking the shirt in his right hand and holding it out to Brat but keeping his eyes on Brat's face. His expression was no longer shocked; he merely looked blank, as if his mind were elsewhere. As if, Brat thought, he were doing sums in his head.

Brat took the shirt, collected the rest of the clothes, expressed his thanks, and made for the door.

"Come down when you're ready," Simon said, still staring at him in that blank way. "We'll be waiting for you."

And Brat, making his way round the landing to his own room in the opposite wing, was shocked in his turn. Ashby hadn't expected him to know that. Ashby had been so certain, indeed, that he would not know about the toy horse that he had been rocked back on his heels when it was clear that he did know about it.

And that meant?

It could mean only one thing.

It meant that young Ashby had not believed for a moment that he was Patrick.

Brat shut the door of the peaceful old night nursery behind him and stood leaning against it, the clothes cascading slowly to the ground from his slackened arm.

Simon had not been fooled. That touching little scene over the sherry glasses had been only an act.

It was a staggering thought.

Why had Simon bothered to pretend?

Why had he not said at once, "You are not Patrick and nothing will make me believe that you are!"?

That had been his original line, if Lana's report and the family atmosphere meant anything. Up to the last moment they had been unsure of his reaction to Brat's arrival; and he had gratified them all by a frank and charming capitulation.

Why the gratuitous capitulation?

Was it—was it a trap of some sort? Were the welcome and the charm merely the grass and green leaves laid over a pit he had prepared?

But he could not have known until the actual face-to-face meeting that he, Brat, was not Patrick. And he had apparently known instantly that the person he was facing was not his brother. Why then should he . . .

Brat stooped to pick up the clothes from the floor and straightened himself abruptly. He had remembered something. He had remembered that odd relaxing on Simon's part the moment he had had a good look at himself. That suggestion of relief. Of being "let off."

So that was it!

Simon had been afraid that it *was* Patrick.

When he found that he was faced with a mere impostor he must have had difficulty in refraining from embracing him.

But that still did not explain the capitulation.

Perhaps it was a mere postponement; a setting to partners. It might be that he planned a more dramatic *dénouement*; a more public discrediting.

If that were so, Brat thought, there were a few surprises in store for young Mr. Ashby. The more he thought about the surprises the better he began to feel about things. As he changed into riding clothes he recalled with something like pleasure that shocked face in the mirror. Simon had been unaware that he, Brat, had passed any "family" tests. He had not been present when Brat passed the searching test of knowing his way about the house; and he had not had any chance of being told about it. All that he knew was that Brat had satisfied the lawyers of his identity. Having been faced with, to him, an obvious impostor he must have looked forward with a delighted malice to baiting the pretender.

Yes; all ready to pull the wings off flies was young Mr. Ashby.

The first tentative pull had been about the Ivanhoe-Hereward battle. Something that only Patrick would know about. But something, too, that he might easily have forgotten.

The little wooden horse was something that only Patrick would know about and something that Patrick could in no circumstances have forgotten.

And Brat had known about it.

Not much wonder that Ashby had been shocked. Shocked and at sea. Not much wonder that he looked as if he were doing sums in his head.

Brat spared a kind thought for that master tutor, Alec Loding. Loding had missed his vocation; as a coach he was superb. Sometime, somewhere, something was going to turn up that Alec Loding had either forgotten to tell him about or had not himself known; and the moment was going to be a very sticky one; but so far he had known his lines. So far he was word perfect.

Even to the point of Travesty.

A little object of black bog oak, it had been. "Rudimentary and surrealist," Loding had said, "but recognisable as a horse." It had originally been yoked to a jaunting car, the whole turn-out being one of those bog-oak souvenirs that tourists brought back from Ireland in the days before it was more advisable to bring home the bacon. The small car, being made of bits and pieces, soon went the way of all nursery objects; but the little horse, chunky and solid, had survived and had become Patrick's halidom and fetish. It was Alec Loding who had been responsible for its naming; one winter evening over nursery tea. He and Nancy had looked in at Latchetts on their way home from some pony races, hoping for a drink; but finding no one at home except Nora, who was having tea upstairs with her children, they had joined the nursery party. And there, while they made toast, they had sought a name for Patrick's talisman. Patrick, who always referred to the object as "my little Irish horse," and was conscious of no need for a more particular description, rejected all suggestions.

"What would you call it, Alec?" his mother asked Loding, who had been too busy consuming buttered toast to care what a toy was called.

"Travesty," Alec had said, eyeing the thing. "By Irish Peasant out of Bog Oak."

The grown-ups had laughed, but Patrick, who was too young to know the meaning of the word, thought that Travesty was a fine, proud-sounding name. A name filled with the tramplings and prancings and curvettings of war horses, and worthy therefore of the little black object of his love.

"He kept it in a pocket," Loding had said in Queen Adelaide's sitting-room (it was raining that morning) "but when he grew too big for that it hung on a frayed Stewart tartan ribbon off a box of Edinburgh rock at the end of his bed."

Yes: not much wonder that Simon had been shaken to the core. No stranger to the Ashby family could have known about Travesty.

Brat, buttoning himself into Ashby garments and noticing how a well-cut article adapts itself even to an alien figure, wondered what Simon was making of the problem. He had no doubt learned by now that the "impostor" not only knew about the existence of Travesty but had walked about the house with the confidence of long acquaintance. A faint flare of excitement woke in Brat. The same excitement that had made those interviews with old Mr. Sandal so enjoyable. For the last couple of hours—ever since his arrival at Guessgate station—he had been received with kindness and welcome, and the result had been a faint queasiness, a sort of spiritual indigestion. What had been a dice game for dangerous stakes had become a mere taking candy from a baby. Now that Simon was his opponent, the thing was once more a contest.

Not dice, thought Brat, considering himself in the mirror. Chequers rather. A matter of cautious moves, of anticipating attack, of blocking an unforeseen thrust. Yes; chequers.

Brat went downstairs buoyed up with a new anticipation. He would not any more have to stand with his back to young Ashby because he was unable to face him. The pieces were laid out on the board and they faced each other across it.

Through the wide-open door of the hall he could see the Ashbys grouped in the sunlight on the steps and went forward to join them. Ruth, with her chronically roving eye, was the first to see him.

"Oh, doesn't he look nice," said Ruth, still paying court.

Brat was aware that he looked "nice" but wished that Ruth had not called attention to his borrowed finery. He wondered if anyone had ever smacked Ruth Ashby.

"You must get some riding clothes from Walters as soon as may be," Bee said. "These are almost a good enough fit to do as a pattern. Which would save you having to go to town for measurements only."

"Those breeches aren't Walters'," Simon said, eyeing the clothes lazily. "They're Gore and Bowen's. Walters never made a good pair of breeches in his life."

He was draped against the wall by the doorway, relaxed and apparently at peace with the world. His eyes travelled slowly up from Brat's boots to his shirt, and came to rest, with the same detached interest on his face.

"Well," he said amiably, pushing himself off the wall, "let's go and look at some horses."

Not chequers, thought Brat. No, not chequers. Poker.

"We'll show you the stables this afternoon," Bee said, "and leave the mares until after tea."

She ran an arm through Brat's and gathered Simon in with her other one, so that they went towards the stables arm-in-arm like old friends; Eleanor and the twins tailing along behind.

"Gregg is all agog to see you," she said. "Not that you'll notice any agogness, of course. His face doesn't permit anything like that. You'll just have to believe me that he is excited inside."

"What happened to old Malpas?" Brat asked, although he had heard all about old Malpas one afternoon outside the Orangery.

"He became very astigmatic," Bee said. "Figuratively speaking. We could never see eye to eye. He didn't really like taking orders from a woman. So he retired about eighteen months after I took over, and we've had Gregg ever since. He's a misanthropist, and a misogynist, and he has his perks, of course; but he doesn't let any of them interfere with the running of the stables. There was a noted drop in the fodder bills after old Malpas left. And the local people like Gregg better because he buys his hay direct from the farmers and not through a contractor. And I think on the whole he's a better horsemaster than Malpas was. Cleverer at getting a poor horse into condition. And a genius at doctoring a sick one."

Why doesn't he relax? she was thinking, feeling the boy's arm rigid under her fingers. The ordeal is over now, surely. Why doesn't he relax?

And Brat for his part was conscious of her fingers clasping his forearm as he had never been conscious before of a woman's hand. He was experiencing again that surge of an unrecognised emotion that had filled him when Bee had taken his hand to lead him to the interview with Mr. Macallan.

But his first sight of the stables distracted his attention from both emotional and ethical problems.

His reaction to the stable yard at Latchetts was very much the reaction of a merchant seaman to his first acquaintance with one of His Majesty's ships. A sort of contemptuous but kindly amusement. A wonder that the thing wasn't finished off with ribbons. Only the fact that several horses' heads protruded inquisitively from the loose boxes convinced him that the place was seriously used as a stable at all. It was like nothing so much as one of the toy models he had seen in expensive toy shops. He had always imagined that those gay little affairs with their bright paint and their flowers in tubs had been manufactured to a child's taste. But apparently they had been authentic copies of an actual article. He was looking at one of the articles at this moment, and being very much surprised.

Not even the dude ranch had prepared him for this. There was paint galore at the dude ranch, but there was also a tradition of toughness. The dude ranch would never have thought of mowing the bit of grass in the middle until it looked like a square of green baize, so neat-edged and trim that it looked as if you could roll it up and take it away. At the dude ranch there was still a suggestion of the mud, dung, sweat, and flies which are inseparable from a life alongside horseflesh.

The little building on the left of the yard entrance was the saddle room, and in the saddle-room door was the stud-groom, Gregg. Gregg had in the highest degree that disillusioned air common to those who make their living out of horses. He had also the horseman's quality of agelessness. He was probably fifty, but it would not be surprising to be told that he was thirty-five.

He took two paces forward and waited for them to come up to him. The two paces were his concession to good manners, and the waiting emphasised the fact that he was receiving them on his own ground. His clear blue eyes ran over Brat as Bee introduced them, but his expression remained polite and inscrutable. He gave Brat a conventional welcome and a crushing hand-clasp.

"I hear you've been riding horses in America," he said.

"Only western ones," Brat said. "Working horses."

"Oh, these work," Gregg said, inclining his head towards the boxes. Don't be in any doubt about it, the tone said. It was as if he had understood Brat's distrust of the spit and polish. His eyes went past Brat to Eleanor standing behind and he said: "Have you seen what's in the saddle room, Miss Eleanor?"

From the gloom of the saddle room there materialised as if in answer to his question the figure of a small boy. He materialised rather reluctantly as if uncertain of his welcome. In spite of a change of costume Brat recognised him as the rider of the stone lion at the gates of Clare. His present apparel, though less startling, was hardly more orthodox than his leopard-skin outfit. He was wearing a striped football jersey that clung to his tadpole body, a pair of jodhpurs so large that they hung in a fold above each skinny knee, a steeple-chasing jockey cap with the crash-lining showing at the back, and a pair of grubby red moccasins.

"Tony!" said Eleanor. "Tony, what are you doing here?"

"I've come for my ride," said Tony, his eyes darting to and fro among the group like lizards.

"But this isn't the day for your ride."

"Isn't it, Eleanor? I thought it was."

"You know quite well that you don't ride on a Tuesday."

"I thought this was Wednesday."

"You're a dreadful little liar, Tony," Eleanor said dispassionately. "You knew quite well this wasn't Wednesday. You just saw me in a car with a stranger and so you came along to find out who the stranger was."

"Eleanor," murmured Bee, deprecating.

"You don't know him," Eleanor said, as if the subject of discussion was not present. "His curiosity amounts to a mania. It's almost his only human attribute."

"If you take him to-day you won't have to take him to-morrow," Simon said, eyeing the Toselli child with distaste.

"He can't come and expect to ride just when he feels like it!" Eleanor said. "Besides, I said I wouldn't take him out again in these things. I told you to get a pair of boots, Tony."

The black eyes stopped being lizards and became two brimming pools of grief. "My father can't afford boots for me," said Tony with a catch in his alto, guaranteed to draw blood from a stone.

"Your father has £12,000 a year free of income tax," Eleanor said briskly.

"If you took him to-day, Nell," Bee said, "you'd be free to help me to-morrow when half the countryside comes dropping in to have a look at Brat." And, as Eleanor hesitated: "You might as well get it over now that he's here."

"And he'll still be wearing moccasins to-morrow," Simon drawled.

"Indian riders wear moccasins," Tony observed mildly, "and they are very good riders."

"I don't think your destitute father would be very pleased if you turned up with moccasins in the Row. You get a pair of boots. And if I take you this afternoon, Tony, you are not to think that you can make a habit of this."

"Oh, no, Eleanor."

"If you come on the wrong day again you'll just have to go away without a ride."

"Yes, Eleanor." The eyes were lizards again, darting and sliding.

"All right. Go and ask Arthur to saddle Spuds for you."

"Yes, Eleanor."

"No thanks, you'll observe," Eleanor said, watching him go.

"What is the crash helmet for?" Simon asked.

"His skull is as thin as cellophane, he says, and must be protected. I don't know how he got one that size. Out of a circus, I should imagine. What with his Indian longings I suppose I should be thankful that he doesn't turn up in a headband and a single feather."

"He will one day, when it occurs to him," Simon said.

"Oh, well, I suppose I'd better go and saddle Buster. I'm sorry, Brat," she said, smiling a little at him, "but it is really one of those blessings in disguise. The pony he rides will be a lot less fresh with him to-day than he would be to-morrow, after a day in the stable. And you don't really need three people to show you round. I'll go round the paddocks with you after tea."

14

BRAT's tendency to be patronising about spit and polish died painlessly and permanently somewhere between the fourth and fifth boxes. The pampered darlings that he had been prepared to find in these boxes did not exist. Thoroughbred, half-bred, cob, or pony, the shine on their coats came from condition and grooming and not from coddling in warm stables; Brat had lived long enough with horses to recognise that. The only ribbons that had ever been tied on these animals were rosettes of red or blue or yellow; and the rosettes were quite properly in the saddle room.

Bee did the honours, with Gregg as assistant; but since it is not possible for four horsemen to consider any given horse without entering into a discussion, the occasion soon lost the slight formality of its beginnings and degenerated into a friendly free-for-all. And presently Brat, always a little detached from his surroundings, noticed that Bee was leaving the discussion more and more to Simon. That it was Simon instead of Bee who said: "This is a throwout from a racing stable that Eleanor is schooling into a hack," or, "Do you remember old Thora? This is a son of hers by Cold Steel." That Bee was quite deliberately edging herself out.

The twins had soon grown tired and evaporated; Ruth because horses bored her, and Jane because she knew all that was to be known about the horses and did not like the thought that they belonged to a person she did not know. And Gregg, congenitally taciturn, fell more and more into the background with Bee. So that in no time at all it was Simon's occasion; Simon's and Brat's.

Simon behaved as if he had not a care in the world. As if this were just another afternoon and Brat just another visitor. A rather privileged and knowledgeable visitor; unquestionably welcome. Brat, coming to the surface every now and then from his beguilement with the horses, would listen to the light drawl discussing pedigree, conformation, character, or prospects; would watch the cool untroubled profile, and wonder. "A bit light in front," the cool voice would be saying, and the untroubled eyes would be running over the animal as if no more important matter clouded the sun. "Nice, though, don't you think?" or "This one should really be turned out: he's been hunted all the winter; but I'm going pot-hunting on him this summer. And anyhow Bee's awfully stingy with her pasture."

And Bee would put in her tuppenceworth and fade out again.

It was Bee who "ran" Latchetts, but the various interests involved were divided between the three Ashbys. Eleanor's chief concerns were the hacks and hunters, Simon's were hunters and show jumpers, and Bee's were the mares and the Shetland ponies. During Bill

Ashby's lifetime, when Latchetts was purely a breeding establishment, the hacks and hunters in the stables had been there for family use and amusement. Occasionally, when there happened to be an extra-good horse in the stable, Bee, who was a better horsewoman than her brother, would come down from London for a week or two to school it and afterwards show it for him. It was good advertisement for Latchetts; not because Latchetts ever dealt in made horses but because the simple repetition of a name is of value in the commercial world, as the writers of advertisements have discovered. Nowadays the younger Ashbys, under Bee's supervision, had turned the stables into a profitable rival to the brood mares.

"Mr. Gates is asking if he can speak to you, sir," said the stable-man to Gregg. And Gregg excused himself and went back to the saddle room.

Fourposter came to the door of his box, stared coldly at Brat for a moment, and then nudged him jocosely with his Roman nose.

"Has he always been Jane's?" Brat asked.

"No," Bee said, "he was bought for Simon's fourteenth birthday. But Simon grew so fast that in a year or so he had outgrown him, and Jane at four was already clamouring to ride a 'real' horse instead of a Shetland. So she fell heir to him. If he ever had any manners he has forgotten them, but he and Jane seem to understand each other."

Gregg came back to say that it was Miss Ashby that Gates wanted to see. It was about the fencing.

"All right, I'll come," Bee said. And as Gregg went away: "What he really wants to see is Brat, but he'll just wait till to-morrow like the rest of the countryside. It's so like Gates to try to steal a march. Opportunism is his middle name. If you two go trying out any of the horses, do be back for tea. I want to go round the paddocks with Brat before it gets dark."

"Do you remember Gates?" Simon asked, opening the door of another box.

"No, I don't think so."

"He's the tenant of Wigsell."

"What became of Vidler, then?"

"He died. This man was married to his daughter and had a small farm the other side of Bures."

Well, Simon had dealt him the cards he needed that time. He

94

looked at Simon to see how he had taken it, but Simon's whole interest seemed to be in the horse he was leading out of the box.

"These last three boxes are all new acquisitions, bought with an eye on the show ring. But this is the pick of the bunch. He's a four-year-old by High Wood out of a mare called Shout Aloud. His name is Timber."

Timber was a black without a brown hair in him. He had a rudimentary white star, and a ring of white on each coronet; and he was quite the handsomest thing in horseflesh that Brat had ever been at close quarters with. He came out of his box with an air of benevolent condescension, as if aware of his good looks and pleased that they should be the subject of tribute. There was something oddly demure about him, Brat thought, watching him. Perhaps it was just the way he was standing, with his forefeet close together. Whatever it was it didn't go with the self-confident, considering eye.

"Difficult to fault, isn't he?" Simon said.

Brat, lost in admiration of his physical conformation, was still puzzled by what he thought of as the butter-wouldn't-melt air.

"He has one of the best-looking heads I've ever seen on a horse," Simon said. "And just look at the bone." He led the horse round. "And a sweet mover, too," he said.

Brat went on looking in silence, admiring and puzzled.

"Well?" Simon said, waiting for Brat's comment.

"Isn't he *conceited*!" said Brat.

Simon laughed.

"Yes, I suppose he is. But not without cause."

"No. He's a good-looker all right."

"He is more than that. He's a lovely ride. And he can jump anything you can see the sky over."

Brat moved forward to the horse and made friendly overtures. Timber accepted the gesture without responding. He looked gratified but faintly bored.

"He should have been a tenor," Brat said.

"A tenor?" Simon said. "Oh, I see. The conceit." He considered the horse afresh. "I suppose he is rather pleased with himself. I hadn't thought about it before. Would you like to try him out, by the way?"

"I certainly would."

"He ought to have some exercise to-day and he hasn't had it so

95

far." He hailed a stable-man. "Arthur, bring a saddle for Timber."

"Yes, sir. A double bridle, sir?"

"No; a snaffle." And, as the man went, to Brat: "He has a mouth like a glove."

Brat wondered if he was merely reluctant to submit that tender mouth to the ham hands of a Westerner with a curb rein at his disposal.

While Timber was being saddled they inspected the two remaining "acquisitions." They were a long-backed bay mare with a good head and quarters ("Two good ends make up for a middle," as Simon said) who was called Scapa; and Chevron, a bright chestnut of great quality with a nervous eye.

"What are you riding?" Brat asked, as Simon led Chevron back to his box.

Simon bolted the half-door and turned to face him.

"I thought you might like to have a look round by yourself," he said. And as Brat, surprised by this piece of luck, was momentarily wordless: "Don't let him get lit-up too much, will you, or he'll break out again when he has been dried."

"No, I'll bring him back cool," Brat said; and flung his leg across his first English horse.

He took one of the two whips that Arthur was holding out for his choosing, and turned the horse to the inner end of the yard.

"Where are you going?" Simon asked, as if surprised.

"Up to the down, I think," Brat said, as if Simon's question had applied to his choice of a place to ride in.

If that gate at the north-west corner of the yard didn't still lead to the short-cut to the downs, then Simon would have to tell him. If it still did lead there, Simon would have one more item to worry about.

"You haven't chosen a very good whip for shutting gates with," Simon said smoothly. "Or are you going to jump everything you come to?" You rodeo artist, the tone said.

"I'll shut the gates," Brat said equably.

He began to walk Timber to the corner of the yard.

"He has his tricks, so look out for him," Simon said, as an afterthought.

"I'll look out for him," Brat said, and rode away to the inner gate which Arthur was waiting to open for him.

96

Arthur grinned at him in a friendly fashion and said admiringly: "He's a fly one, that, sir."

As he turned to his right into the little lane he considered the implication of that very English adjective. It was a long time since he had heard anything called fly. "Fly" was "cute"—in the English sense, not in the American. Fly was something on the side. A fly cup. Something sly with a hint of cleverness in it.

A fly one, Timber was.

The fly one walked composedly up the track between the green banks netted with violets, his ears erect in anticipation of the turf ahead of them. As they came in sight of the gate at the far end he danced a little. "No," said Brat's hands, and he desisted at once. Someone had left the gate open, but since there was a notice saying PLEASE SHUT THE GATE neatly painted in the middle of it, Brat manoeuvred Timber into the appropriate position for closing it. Timber seemed as well acquainted with gates and their uses as a cow pony was with a rope, but never before had Brat had so delicate and so well-oiled a mechanism under him. Timber obeyed the slightest indication of hand or heel with a lack of questioning and a confidence that was new in Brat's experience. Surprised and delighted, Brat experimented with this new adaptability. And Timber, even with the turf in front of him, with the turf practically under his feet, moved sweetly and obediently under his hands.

"You wonder!" said Brat softly.

The ears flicked at him.

"You perishing marvel," he said, and closed his knees as he turned to face the down. Timber broke into a slow canter, headed for the clumps of gorse and juniper bushes that marked the skyline.

So this was what riding a good English horse was like, he thought. This communion, this being one half of a whole. This effortlessness. This magic.

The close, fine turf slipped by under them, and it was odd to see no little spurt of dust coming up as the shoes struck. England, England, England, said the shoes as they struck. A soft drum on the English turf.

I don't care, he thought, I don't care. I'm a criminal, and a heel, but I've got what I wanted, and it's worth it. By God, it's worth it. If I died to-morrow, it's worth it.

They came to the level top of the down and faced the double

row of bushes that made a rough natural avenue, about fifty yards wide, along the crest. This was something that Alec Loding had forgotten to tell him about, and something that had not appeared on a map. Even the Ordnance Survey can hardly take note of juniper growths. He pulled up to consider it. But Timber was in no considering mood. Timber knew all about that level stretch of down between the rows of bushes.

"All right," said Brat, "let's see what you can do," and let him go.

Brat had ridden flyers before. Dozens of them. He had ridden sprinters and won money with them. He had been bolted with at the speed of jet propulsion. Mere speed no longer surprised him. What surprised him was the smoothness of the progress. It was like being carried through the air on a horse suspended to a merry-go-round.

The soft air parted round his face and tickled his ears and fled away behind them, smelling of grass with the sun on it and leather and gorse. Who cares, who cares, who cares! said the galloping feet. Who cares, who cares, who cares! said the blood in Brat's veins.

If he died to-morrow it was all the same to him.

As they came to the end of the stretch Timber began to pull up of his own accord, but it was against Brat's instincts to let a horse make the decisions, so he kept him going, turned him round the south end of the green corridor, and cantered him gently to a walk, and Timber responded without question.

"Brother," said Brat, running his fingers up the dark crest, "are there more like you in England, or do you rate special?"

Timber bent his head to the caress, still with the air of one receiving his due.

But as they walked back on the south side of the irregular green hedge Brat's attention and interest went to the countryside spread below them. Except that he was looking at it upside down, as it were—from the north, instead of from the south as one looks normally at a map—this was Clare as he had first become acquainted with it. All laid out below his eye in Ordnance Survey clarity and precision.

Down below him, a little to his left, were the crimson roofs of Latchetts, set in the neat squares of paddock. Farther to the left was the church, on its own small rise; and left of it again, the village of

Clare, a huddle of roofs in pale green trees. Where the land sloped up from the village to make the south side of the small valley stood Clare Park, a long white house sheltered from the south-west Channel gales by the slope behind it.

Directly opposite him that slope rose into a smaller and tamer version of the down he was sitting on; a low green hill called Tanbitches. It was an open stretch of grazing, marked half-way up with the green scar of an old quarry, and crowned by the beeches that had given it its name. There were only seven beeches now instead of ten, but the clump made a decorative and satisfying climax to the southern side of the valley.

The other side of the Tanbitches hill, as he knew from the maps, ran away in a gentle slope for a mile and a half to the cliffs. To the cliffs where Patrick Ashby had put an end to his life. Behind the lower rise of the valley, on the reverse slope of Clare Park, were farms that merged imperceptibly in a mile or two into the suburbs of Westover. In the slight hollow that marked the Clare Park slope from Tanbitches hill was a path that led to the coast. The path that Patrick Ashby had taken on that day eight years ago.

It was suddenly more real to him than it had ever been so far: this tragedy which he was using to his advantage. More real even than it had been in the rooms that Patrick had lived in. In the house there had been other associations besides Patrick: associations more present and alive. There had been the distractions of human intercourse and of his own need to be constantly wary. Out here in the open and alone it had a reality that it had never had before. Up that straggling path on the other side of the valley a boy had gone, so loaded with misery that this neat green English world had meant nothing to him. He had had horses like Timber, and friends and family, and a belonging-place, and it had all meant nothing to him.

For the first time in his detached existence Brat was personally aware of another's tragedy. When Loding had first told him the story, in that London pub, he had had nothing but contempt for the boy who had had so much and could not do without that little extra. A poor thing, he had thought. Then Loding had brought those photographs to Kew, and had shown him Patrick, and he had had that odd feeling of identification, of partisanship.

99

"That is Pat Ashby. He was about eleven there," Loding had said, his feet propped comfortably on the railings of the park, and had passed him the piece of paper. It was a snapshot taken with a Brownie 2A, and Brat had accepted it with a curiosity that was active but not urgent.

But Pat Ashby had not been the anonymous "poor thing" that he had so far held in his mind. He had been a real person. A likeable real person. A person who would have been, Brat felt, very much his cup of tea. From being vaguely anti-Patrick he had become Patrick's champion.

It was not, however, until this moment of quiet above Latchetts that he had been moved to sorrow for him.

Clink—clink! came the faint sound from the valley; and Brat's eyes travelled down from Tanbitches to the cottage at its foot. The blacksmith's, that was. A quarter of a mile west of the village. A tiny black square by the roadside it had been on the map; now it was a small building with a black chimney and an occupant who made musical sounds with a hammer.

The whole scene was very like the picture from which he had acquired his first-year French. *Voilà le forgeron.* It needed only a curé coming from the church. And a postman on a bicycle between the forge and the village.

Brat slid from Timber's back, from long habit loosened the girths as if he saddled up hours ago, and sat down with his back to the gorse and juniper to feast his eyes on this primer of the English countryside.

15

THE great clouds sailed up and past, the sunlight flickered and ran, the uncertain soft wind edged in and out of the junipers and made soft scufflings in the grass. Timber made small sounds with his bit, and cropped turf in a tentative and superior fashion. Brat sank into a daze of pleasure and ceased altogether from conscious thought.

He was roused by the swift fling-up of Timber's head, and almost
100

at the same moment a female voice behind him said, as if it were a chant and rhymed:

> "Don't look,
> Don't move,
> Shut your eyes
> And guess who."

It was a slightly Cockney voice, and it dripped with archness.

Like anyone else in the circumstances Brat disobeyed the injunction automatically. He looked round into the face of a girl of sixteen or so. She was a large, plumpish girl, with bright auburn hair and prominent blue eyes. The eyes were remarkable in that they managed to be at once avid and sleepy. As they met Brat's they almost popped out altogether.

"Oh!" said the girl, in a half-shriek. "I thought you were Simon. You're not!"

"No," agreed Brat, beginning to get to his feet.

But before he could move she had dropped to the grass beside him.

"My, you gave me a shock. I bet I know who you are. You're the long-lost brother, aren't you? You must be; you're so like Simon. That's who you are, isn't it?"

Brat said that it was.

"You even wear the same kind of clothes."

Brat said that they were Simon's clothes. "You know Simon?"

"Of course I know Simon. I'm Sheila Parslow. I'm a boarder at Clare Park."

"Oh." The school for dodgers, Eleanor had called it. The place where no one had to learn the nine-times.

"I'm doing my best to have an *affaire* with Simon, but it's uphill work."

Brat did not know the correct rejoinder to this, but she did not need conversational encouragement.

"I have to do something to put some pep into life at Clare Park. You can't imagine the screaming boredom of it. You simply can't imagine. There is nothing, but I mean *nothing*, that you are forbidden to do. I once got so desperate I took off all my clothes and walked into Cedric's office—Cedric is our Leader, he doesn't like being called the Head, but that's what he is, of course—I walked in with nothing on, not a stitch, and all he said was: 'Have you ever

301

thought of going on a diet, Sheila dear?' Just took a look at me and said: 'Have you ever thought of going on a diet?' and then went on with looking up *Who's Who*. He's always looking up *Who's Who*. You don't really stand much of a chance of fetching up at Clare Park unless your father is in *Who's Who*. Or your mother, of course. My father's not in it, but he has millions, my father, and that makes a very good substitute. Millions are a very good introduction, aren't they?"

Brat said that he supposed they were.

"I flapped Father's millions in front of Simon; Simon has a great respect for a good investment and I hoped it would weight my charms, so to speak; but he's a frightful snob, Simon, isn't he?"

"Is he?"

"Don't you *know*?"

"I've only met him to-day."

"Oh, of course. You've just come back. How exciting for you. I can understand Simon not being overjoyed, of course, but it must be exciting for you to put his nose out of joint."

Brat wondered if she, too, pulled the wings off flies.

"I may have more chance with Simon now that you've taken his fortune from him. I'll have to waylay him somewhere and see. I thought I was waylaying him now, when I saw Timber. He often comes up here because it's his favourite place for exercising the horses. He hates Tanbitches." She jerked her chin at the opposite side of the valley. "And this is a good place for getting him alone. So I came up here on spec, and then I saw that black brute, and I thought I had him cold. But it was only you."

"I'm sorry," Brat said meekly.

She considered him.

"I suppose it's no good my trying to seduce you instead?" she said.

"I'm afraid not."

"Is it that I'm not your type, or is it not your line?"

"Not much in my line, I'm afraid."

"No, I suppose not," she said, agreeing with him. "You have a face like a monk. Funny you should look so like Simon and yet look so different. Simon's no monk; as that Gates girl over at Wigsell could tell you. I make images of that Gates girl and stick pins in them, but it doesn't do any good. She goes on blooming like a blasted peony and fascinating him like fly-paper."

192

She was rather like a well-blown peony herself, he thought, looking at her wet red mouth and the buttons straining the cloth across her ample bust. A rather drooping and disappointed peony at the moment.

"Does Simon know that you are fond of him?" Brat asked.

"Fond of him? I'm not fond of him. I don't think I like him at all. I just want to have an *affaire* with him to brighten up the term a bit. Until I can leave this boring place."

"If you can do anything you like, why can't you leave now?" Brat asked reasonably.

"Well, I don't want to look too much of a fool, you know. I went to school at Ling Abbey, you see, and I made the place a hell so that my people would take me away and send me here. I thought I was going to have the time of my life here, with no lessons and no timetable and no rules or anything. I had no idea it would be so boring. I could weep with boredom."

"Isn't there anyone at Clare Park you could substitute for Simon? I mean, someone who would be more—accommodating?"

"No, I had a look at them first. Skinny and hairy and intellectual. Have you ever noticed how the intellect runs to hair? Some people get a kick out of disgust, but not me. I like them good-looking. And you have to admit Simon is very good-looking. There was an under-gardener at Ling Abbey that was almost as handsome, but he hadn't that lovely God-damn-you look that Simon has."

"Didn't the under-gardener keep you at the Abbey place?"

"Oh, no, they sacked him. It was easier than expelling me and having a scandal. But they had to expel me in any case, so they might as well have kept poor Albert. He was much better with his lobelias than he was with girls. But of course they couldn't be expected to know that. I suppose you wouldn't put in a good word for me with Simon? It would be such a pity to waste all the agony I've gone through trying to interest him."

"Agony?"

"You don't suppose I endure hours on those horrible quadrupeds just for *fun*, do you? With that cold stick of a sister of his looking down her nose at me. Oh, I forgot: she's your sister too, isn't she? But perhaps you've been away so long that you don't think of her the way a boy thinks of his sister."

"I certainly don't," Brat said; but she was not listening.

"I suppose you've ridden horses since you could crawl, so you have no idea what it is like to be bumped about on a great shapeless mountain of a thing that's far too high from the ground and has nothing to hold on to. It looks so easy when Simon does it. The horse looks so nice and *narrow* when you're standing on the ground. You think you could ride it the way you ride a bicycle. It's only when you get up you find that its back is simply acres across and you can make no impression on it at all. You just sit there and are bumped about, and your legs slip backwards and forwards instead of staying still like Simon's, and you get large blisters and can't sit down in the bath for weeks. You don't look quite so like a monk when you smile a bit."

Brat suggested that surely there were better ways of attracting favourable notice than being a tyro at something that the object of one's pursuit already did to perfection.

"Oh, I didn't think that I'd attract him that way. It just gave me an excuse for being round the stables. That sister of—your sister doesn't stand any hanging round if you haven't got business."

"Your sister," he thought, and liked the sound of it.

He had three sisters now, and at least two of them were the kind he would have indented for. Presently he must go down and make their further acquaintance.

"I'm afraid I must go," he said, getting up and putting the reins over Timber's head.

"I wish you didn't have to," she said, watching him tighten the girth. "You are quite the nicest person I have talked to since I came to Clare. It's a pity you aren't interested in women. You might cut Simon out with the Gates girl, and then I'd have more chance. Do you know the Gates girl?"

"No," Brat said, getting up on Timber.

"Well, have a look at her. She's very pretty."

"I'll do that," Brat said.

"Now that you're home, I'll be running across you in the stables, I suppose."

"I expect so."

"You wouldn't like to give me one of my lessons instead of your sister, would you?"

"I'm afraid that's not my department."

"Oh, well." She sounded resigned. "You look very nice on that

104

brute. I suppose *his* back is acres across too. They all are. It's a conspiracy."

"Good-bye," said Brat.

"Do you know, I don't know your name. Someone told me, of course, but I forget. What is it?"

"Patrick."

And as he said the word his mind went back to the path across the valley, and he forgot Miss Parslow almost instantly. He cantered back along the top of the down until he came level with Latchetts, and then began to walk Timber down. Below him, a green ride led through the paddocks to the west of the house and so to the sweep of gravel in front of it. It was by that way that Jane had come this morning, when she had become mixed up with his reception at the front door. The gate to the ride stood open, the gate lying flat against the stout paddock rails that bordered the ride. Brat rode down until the steepness of the down gave way to a gentle slope and then pressed Timber into a canter. The green tunnel of the ride with its soft floor was open before them, and he was not going to spoil it by stopping to shut another gate that someone else had left open.

It was due to no good riding on Brat's part that his left leg was still whole five seconds later. It was due entirely to the years of rough-riding that had made his physical reactions quicker than conscious thought. The swerve was so sudden and so wholehearted that the white rail was scraping along the saddle where his leg should have been before he realised that his leg was not there. That he had taken it away before he had had time to think about it.

As Timber came away from the rails he settled back into the saddle and pulled the horse to a stop. Timber stopped obediently.

"Whew!" said Brat, expelling his pent breath. He looked down at Timber standing innocent and demure in the exact centre of the ride.

"You ornery thing, you," he said, amused.

Timber went on looking demure but the ears listened to him. A trifle apprehensively, Brat thought.

"I know men who'd beat the bejasus out of you for that," Brat said, and turned the horse's nose to the down again. Timber retraced his steps obediently, but was obviously not easy in his mind. When he was far enough away from the gate Brat took him into a canter once more and down to the opening. He had neither spurs nor curb but he was curious to see what Timber would do this time. Timber, as he had expected, swept good-manneredly into the ride, bisecting the distance from either rail with mathematical precision.

"What, me!" he seemed to be saying. "Do a thing like that on purpose? Me, with my perfect manners? Of course not. I just lost my balance for a moment, coming into the ride there. It can happen to the best of us."

"Well, well," thought Brat, pulling him to a walk. "Think you're smart, don't you," he said aloud, walking him down the ride. "Far smarter horses than you have tried to brush me off, take it from me. I've been brushed off horses that would make you look like five-cents worth of candy."

The black ears flickered, listening to him, analysing the sound of his voice, its tone; puzzled.

The mares came to the rails to watch them pass, pleased with this small event in their placid lives; and the foals ran round and round in a self-induced excitement. But Timber took no notice of them. He had lost any active interest in mares at a very early age, and just now his whole interest seemed to be in the fact that he had been outwitted, and that the outwitting one made sounds which he did not understand. His ears, which should have been pricked at the thought of his nearing stable, were restless and enquiring.

Brat rode round the front of the house, as Jane had that morning, but he saw no one. He went on to the stables and found Eleanor just riding in with a led horse, having given Tony his lesson and left him at Clare Park.

"Hullo!" she said, "have you been out on Timber?" She sounded a little surprised. "I hope Simon warned you about him."

"Yes, thank you, he warned me."

"One of my bad buys," she said ruefully, eyeing Timber as they rode side by side towards the yard.

"Yours?" he said.

"Yes. Didn't Simon tell you about that?"

"No."

"That was nice of him. I expect he didn't want you to find out too soon what a fool of a sister you have." She smiled a little at him, as if she were glad to be his sister. "I bought him at the Lerridge Hunt sale. It was Timber who killed old Felix. Old Felix Hunstanton, the Master, you know. Did Simon tell you?"

"No. No, he just told me about his tricks."

"Old Felix had some good horses, and when they were being sold I went over to see what I could pick up. None of the Lerridge Hunt regulars was bidding for Timber, but I thought it was because of sentiment, perhaps. I thought they probably didn't want to own the horse the Master was killed on. As if there was ever any sentiment about horse-dealing! I oughtn't to be let out alone. Even so, I ought to have wondered why I was getting him so cheap; with his looks and his breeding and his performance. It was only afterwards that we found that he had done the same thing to the huntsman a few days later, only the branches were small and broke, instead of braining him or sweeping him off."

"I see," said Brat, who was beginning to.

"Not that anyone needed convincing, apparently. No one who was there when Felix was killed believed it was an accident. It was a Lerridge Castle meet, and they had found in one of the Lerridge woods and gone away over the park. Good open galloping country with the trees isolated. And yet Timber took Felix under an oak, going an awful bat, and he was dead before he hit the ground. But of course we heard about all that later. All I knew when I was bidding for him was that Felix had hit his head on a branch during the hunt. Which is something that has been happening to people ever since William Rufus."

"Did anyone actually see it happen?"

"No, I don't think so. Everyone just knew that with the whole park to choose from Felix wouldn't have ridden under the oak. And when he tried the same thing on Samms, the huntsman, there was no doubt. So he is put into the sale with the rest of the lot and all the Lerridge regulars sit around in silence and watch Eleanor Ashby from over Clare way buying a pup."

"He's a very elegant pup, there's no denying," Brat said, rubbing Timber's neck.

"He's beautiful," Eleanor said. "And a faultless jumper. Did you jump him at all to-day? No? You must next time. He is safest jumping because his mind is distracted. He hasn't time to think up mischief. It's odd, isn't it; he doesn't *look* untrustworthy," she added, still eyeing her bad bargain with a puzzled eye.

"No."

She caught the tone and said: "You don't sound too sure."

"Well, I must allow he is the most conceited animal I've ever met."

This seemed to be as new an idea to Eleanor as it had been to Simon.

"Vain, is he? Yes, I suppose he is. I expect *I'd* be conceited if I were a horse and I had been clever enough to kill a man. Did he try any tricks to-day?"

"He swerved at the entrance to the ride, but that was all." He did not say: He took advantage of the first good stout piece of timber to mash my leg against. That was something between the horse and himself. He and Timber had a long acquaintanceship in front of them, and a lot to say to each other.

"He behaves like an angel most of the time," Eleanor said. "That is what is so lethal about him. We have all ridden him; Simon and Gregg and Arthur and me, and he has only twice played up. Once with Simon and once with Arthur. But of course," she added with a grin, "we have always given trees a wide berth."

"He'd be a great success in the desert. Not a rail or a limb in a day's journey."

Eleanor looked sadly at the black horse as Brat drew up to let her precede him into the yard. "He'd think up something else, I expect."

And Brat, thinking it over, agreed with her. Timber was that rare thing in horses: a deliberate and intelligent rogue. Balked of his normal fun, he would think up something new. There was nothing small-time about Timber.

Nor was Simon exactly small-time. Simon had sent him out on a notorious rogue, with a light remark about the horse "having its tricks." As neat a piece of vicarious manslaughter as anyone ever thought up.

16

BEATRICE ASHBY looked down the dining-table at her nephew Patrick and thought how well he was doing it. The occasion must be an extraordinarily difficult one for him, but he was carrying it off beautifully. He was neither awkward nor exuberant. He brought to the situation the same quiet detachment that he had shown on

108

their first meeting in that Pimlico room. It was a very adult quality, and a little surprising in a boy not yet twenty-one. He had great dignity this Patrick Ashby, she thought, watching him dealing with the Rector. Surely never before can anyone have been so silent by habit without appearing either stiff or stupid.

It was she who had brought Simon up, and she was pleased with the result. But this boy had brought himself up, and the result was even better, it seemed. Perhaps it was a case of "giving the first seven years" and the rest followed automatically. Or perhaps it was that the goodness in Patrick had been so innate that he had needed no other guidance. He had followed his own lights, and the result was this quiet, adult young man with the still face.

It was a mask of a face; a sad mask, on the whole. It was such a contrast to the similar set of features in Simon's mobile countenance that they reminded one of those reversible comedy-tragedy masks that are used to decorate the title-pages of plays.

Simon was being particularly gay to-night, and Bee's heart ached for him. He too was doing it well, and to-night she loved him almost without reservation. Simon was abdicating, and doing it with a grace and spontaneity that she would not have believed possible. She felt a little guilty that she had underrated him. She had not credited the selfish, acquisitive Simon with such a power of renunciation.

They were choosing a name for Honey's filly foal, and the conversation was growing ribald. Nancy was insisting that "honey" was an endearment, and should be translated as "poppet," and Eleanor said that no thoroughbred as good as Honey's present foal should be damned by a name like Poppet. If Eleanor had refused to dress especially for Patrick's arrival, she had now made up for it. It was a long time since Bee had seen her looking so well or so pretty. Eleanor belonged to a type which did not glow easily.

"Brat is in love with Honey," Eleanor said.

"I suppose Bee dragged you round the paddocks before you were well over the doorstep," said Nancy. "Were you impressed, Brat?"

She too had adopted the nickname. Only the Rector called him Patrick.

"I'm in love with the whole bunch," Brat said. "And I found an old friend."

"Oh? Who was that?"

"Regina."

"Oh, yes, of course. Poor old Regina. She must be about twenty!" Nancy said.

"Not so much of the 'poor'," said Simon. "Regina has kept us shod and clothed for a whole generation. We ought to pay her a dividend."

"She takes her dividends out in pasture," Eleanor said. "She was always a greedy eater."

"When you drop foals like Regina year after year without a break, you're entitled to an appetite," Simon said.

Simon was drinking a great deal more than usual, but it seemed to be having little effect on him. Bee thought that the Rector looked at him now and then with pity in his eyes.

And Brat, too, at the other end of the table, was watching Simon, but without pity. Pity was not an emotion that Brat indulged in very often: like everyone who despises self-pity he did not readily pity others; but it was not because of his native disinclination to pity that he withheld sympathy from Simon Ashby. It was not even because Simon was his declared enemy; he had admired enemies before now. It was because there was something about Simon Ashby that repelled him. There was something unaccountable about Simon. There he sat, being light-hearted and charming, and there sat his relations and friends silently applauding his nobility and his courage. They were applauding an "act," but they would all be staggered to know what an act Simon was really putting on for their benefit.

Watching him as he displayed his graces, Brat felt that Simon reminded him of someone that he had met quite lately. Someone who had just that air of breeding, and excellent good manners, and good looks, and that—unaccountability. Who could that have been?

He was maddened by that tip-of-the-tongue feeling. In one more second he would remember. Loding? No. Someone on the ship coming over? Not very likely. That lawyer chap: the K.C. chap, Macdermott? No. Then who could it——

"Don't you think so, Patrick?"

It was the Rector again. He must be careful with the old boy. He had been more afraid of meeting George Peck than of anyone but Simon. After a twin brother there is no one who is liable to remember so much about you or to remember that much so well as the man who taught you. There would be a score of small things that George Peck would know about Patrick Ashby that not even Patrick Ashby's

110

mother would know. But the meeting had gone off very well. Nancy Peck had kissed him on both cheeks and said: "Oh, dear, you've got very grown-up and serious, haven't you!"

"Patrick always was," the Rector had said, and had shaken hands.

He had looked consideringly at Brat, but no more consideringly than was normal in a man examining an old pupil met after a decade of absence. And Brat, who had no love for the Cloth, found himself liking the Rector. He was still wary of him, but the wariness was due not to the Rector's calling but to his knowledge of Pat Ashby, and to the intelligence and penetration of the eyes in his simian face.

Considering that intelligence, Brat was glad that he was particularly well primed in the matter of Pat Ashby's schooling. The Rector was Alec Loding's brother-in-law, and Loding had had what he called a front-stall view of the Ashby twins' education.

As for Alec Loding's sister, she was the most beautiful woman that Brat had ever seen. He had never heard of the famous Nancy Ledingham, but her brother had been eloquent about her. "Could have had anyone in the world; any man would have been delighted to keep her just to look at; but she had to choose George Peck." He had been shown Nancy in every kind of garment, from a swimming suit to her court presentation gown, but none of the photographs had done justice to her serene beauty, her gaiety, her general niceness. He felt that George Peck must be all right if Nancy had married him.

"Was that the Toselli child you had out with you?" she was saying to Eleanor. "That object I met you with this afternoon?"

"That was Tony," Eleanor said.

"How he brought back the days of my youth!"

"Tony did? How?"

"You won't remember it, but there used to be things called cavalry regiments. And every regiment had a trick-riding team. And every trick-riding team had a "comedy" member. And every "comedy" member of a trick-riding team looked just like Tony."

"So they did!" Bee said, delighted. "That was what he reminded me of this afternoon and I couldn't think of it at the time. That masterly irrelevance. The completely unrelated garments."

"You may wonder why I took him out at all," Eleanor remarked. "But after Sheila Parslow he's a positive holiday. He'll ride quite well some day, Tony."

111

"To the prospective horseman all things are forgiven, are they?" the Rector said, mocking mildly.

"Doesn't La Parslow get any better?" Simon asked.

"She will never get any better. She skates about in the saddle like a block of ice on a plate. I could weep for the horse all the time we are out. Luckily Cherrypicker has an indestructible frame and practically no feelings."

The move from the dining-room to the living-room produced an anti-climax. The talk ceased to flow and ran into aimless trickles. Brat was suddenly so tired that he could hardly stand up. He hoped that no one would spring anything on him now; his normally hard head was muzzy with unaccustomed wine, and his thoughts fumbled and stuck. The twins said good night and went upstairs. Bee poured the coffee which had been placed in readiness for them on a low table by the fire, and it was not as hot as it should have been. Bee made despairing grimaces at Nancy.

"Our Lana, is it?" Nancy asked, sympathetic.

"Yes. I suppose she had to meet our Arthur and couldn't wait another ten minutes."

Simon, too, fell silent, as if the effort he had been making seemed suddenly not worth while. Only Eleanor seemed to have brought from the dining-room the warmth and happiness that had made dinner a success. In the moments of silence between the slow spurts of talk the rain fell against the tall windows with a soft shush.

"You were right about the weather, Aunt Bee," Eleanor said. "She said this morning that it was that too-bright kind that would bring rain before night."

"Bee is perennially right," the Rector said, giving her a look that was half a smile, half a benediction.

"It sounds loathsome," Bee said.

Nancy waited until they had lingered properly over their coffee and then said: "It has been a very full day for Brat, Bee; and I expect you are all tired. We won't stay now, but you'll come over and see us when you can crawl out from under the crush, won't you, Brat?"

Simon fetched her wraps and they all went out to the doorstep to see their guests off. On the doorstep Nancy took off her evening shoes, tucked them under her arm, and stepped into a pair of wellingtons that she had left behind the door. Then she tucked her other arm under her husband's, huddled close to him under their single umbrella, and walked away with him into the night.

"Good old Nancy," Simon said. "You can't keep a Ledingham down." He sounded just a little drunk.

"Dear Nan," Bee said softly. She moved into the living-room and surveyed it in an absent fashion.

"I think Nan is right," she said. "It is time we all went to bed. It has been an exciting day for all of us."

"We don't want it to end so soon, do we?" Eleanor said.

"You have La Parslow at nine-thirty to-morrow," Simon reminded her. "I saw it in the book."

"What were *you* doing with the riding book?"

"I like to see that you're not cheating on your income tax."

"Oh, yes, let's go to bed," Eleanor said, with a wide happy yawn. "It's been a wonderful day."

She turned to Brat to say good night, became suddenly shy, gave him her hand and said: "Good night then, Brat. Sleep well," and went away upstairs.

Brat turned to Bee, but she said: "I shall come in to see you on my way up." So he turned back to face Simon.

"Good night, Simon." He met the clear cold eyes levelly.

"Good night to you—Patrick," Simon said, looking faintly amused. He had managed to make the name sound like a provocation.

"Are you coming up now?" Brat heard Bee ask him as he climbed the stairs.

"Not quite yet."

"Will you see that the lights are out, then? And make sure of the locks?"

"Yes, of course I'll do that. Good night, Bee darling."

As Brat turned on to the landing he saw Bee's arms go round Simon. And he was stabbed by a hot despairing jealousy that shocked him. What had it to do with him?

Bee followed him into the old night nursery in a few moments. She looked with a practised eye at the bed and said: "That moron promised to put in a hot-water bottle and she has forgotten to do it."

"Don't worry," Brat said. "I'd only have put it out again. I don't use the things."

"You must think us a crowd of soft-livers," she said.

"I think you're a nice crowd," he said.

She looked at him and smiled.

"Tired?"

"Yes."

"Too tired for breakfast at eight-thirty?"

"That sounds luxuriously late to me."

"Did you enjoy it, that hard life—Brat?"

"Sure."

"I think you're nice too," she said, and kissed him lightly. "I wish you hadn't stayed away from us so long, but we are glad to have you back. Good night, my dear." And as she went out: "It's no use ringing a bell, of course, because no one will answer. But if you have a mad desire for fried shrimps, or iced water, or a copy of the *Pilgrim's Progress* or something, come along to my room. It is still the right-hand one in front."

"Good night," he said.

She stood for a moment outside his room, the door-knob still in her hand, and then moved away to Eleanor's door. She knocked and went in. For the last year or so Eleanor had been a great comfort to her. She had been so long alone in her need for judgment and resolution that it was refreshing to have the companionship of her own kind; to have Eleanor's unemotional good sense on tap when she wanted it.

"Hullo, Bee," Eleanor said, looking up through the hair she was brushing. She was beginning to drop the "aunt," as Simon did.

Bee sank into a chair and said: "Well, that's over."

"It turned out to be quite a success, didn't it," Eleanor said. "Simon behaved beautifully. Poor Simon."

"Yes. Poor Simon."

"Perhaps Brat—Patrick—will offer him some kind of partnership. Do you think? After all, Simon helped to make the stable. It wouldn't be fair to walk in and grab the lot after taking no interest for years and years."

"No. I don't know. I hope so."

"You sound tired."

"Aren't we all?"

"D'you know, Bee, I must confess I have the greatest difficulty in connecting the two."

"The two? Simon and Patrick?"

"No. Patrick and Brat."

114

There was a moment's silence, filled with the soft sound of the rain and the strokes of Eleanor's brush.

"You mean you—don't think he is Patrick?"

Eleanor stopped brushing and looked up, her eyes wide with surprise. "Of course he's Patrick," she said, astonished. "Who else would he be?" She put down the brush and began to tie up her hair in a blue ribbon. "It's just that I have no feeling of ever having met him before. Odd, isn't it? When we spent nearly twelve years of our lives together. I like him; don't you?"

"Yes," Bee said. "I like him." She, too, had no feeling of ever having met him before, and she too did not see "who else he could be."

"Did Patrick not smile very often?"

"No; he was a serious child."

"When Brat smiles I want to cry."

"Good heavens, Eleanor."

"You can 'good heavens' all you like, but I expect you know what I mean."

Bee thought that she did.

"Did he tell you why he didn't write to us all those years?"

"No. There wasn't much opportunity for confidences."

"I thought you might have asked him when you were going round the paddocks with him this evening."

"No. He was too interested in the horses."

"Why do *you* think he didn't take any interest in us after he left?"

"Perhaps he took what old Nannie used to call a 'scunner' to us. It's not so surprising, in a way, as the fact that he ran away in the first place. The urge to put Latchetts behind him must have been overwhelming."

"Yes. I suppose so. But he was such a kind person: Pat. And so fond of us all. He mightn't have wanted to come back, but you would have thought he'd want to let us know that he was safe."

Since this was her own private stumbling-block, Bee had no help to offer.

"It must have been difficult to come back," Eleanor said, running the comb through her brush. "He looked so tired to-night that he looked like a *dead* man. It's not a very lively face at the best of times, is it? If you chopped it off behind the ears and hung it on a wall, no one would know the difference."

115

Bee knew Eleanor well enough, and agreed with her sufficiently, to translate this successfully.

"You don't think he'll want to sheer off again once the excitement of coming home has worn off?"

"Oh, no, I'm quite sure he won't."

"You think he is here for keeps?"

"Of course I do."

But Brat, standing in the dark before the open window of his room and looking at the curve of the down in the wet starlight, was wondering about that very matter. The thing had succeeded beyond Loding's most extravagant promises, and now?

Where did he go from here? How long would it be before Simon had him cold? And if Simon failed, how long could he go on living a life where at any moment someone might spring a mine?

That is what he had set out to do, of course. But somehow he had not really looked beyond the first stages. In his heart he had been unable to believe that he would succeed. Now that success was his he felt rather like someone who has climbed a pinnacle and can't get down again. Elated but misgiving.

He turned from the window and switched the lamp on. His land-lady in Pimlico used to say that she "was so tired that she felt as if she'd been through a mangle"; he knew now how good a description that had been. That was exactly how he felt. Wrung out and empty. So limp that it was an effort to lift a hand to undress. He pulled off his nice new suit—the suit that had made him feel so guilty in that other life way back in London—and made himself hang it up. He peeled off his underclothes and stumbled into his faded old pyjamas. He wondered for a moment whether they would mind if the rain came in and marked the carpet, but decided to risk it. So he left the window wide open and got into bed.

He lay for a long time listening to the quiet sound of the rain and looking at the room. Now was the time for Pat Ashby's ghost to come and chill that room. He waited for the ghost but it did not come. The room was warm and welcoming. The figures on the wallpaper, the figures that those children had grown up with, looked friendly and alive. He turned his head to look at the groups by the bedside. To look for the one Eleanor had been in love with. The chap with the profile. He wondered if she was in love with anyone now.

His eyes went on to the wood of the bedstead, and he remembered

116

that this was Alec Loding's bed, and was pleased once more by the irony of it all. It was fantastically right that he should come to Latchetts only to sleep in Alec Loding's bed. He must tell him one day. It was the kind of thing that Loding would appreciate.

He wondered whether it was Eleanor or Bee who had put the flowers in the bowl. Flowers to welcome him—home.

Latchetts, he said to himself, looking at the room. This is Latchetts. I'm here. This is Latchetts.

The sound of the word was a soporific; like the swing of a hammock. He put out his hand and switched off the light. In the dark the rain suddenly sounded louder.

This morning he had got up and dressed in that back room under the slates, with the crowding chimney-pots beyond the window. And here he was, going to sleep in Latchetts, with the sweet cold smell of the down blowing in on the damp air from the window.

As sleep drew him under he had an odd feeling of reassurance. A feeling that Pat Ashby didn't mind his being there; that he was on the contrary pleased about it all.

The unlikeliness of this roused him a little, and his thoughts, running on approval and disapproval, went to Bee. What was it that he had felt when Bee took his hand to lead him to the interview this afternoon? What was different from any other of the thousand handclasps he had experienced in his time? Why the surge of warmth under his heart, and what kind of emotion was it anyway? He had suffered the same obscure gratification when Bee had thrust her arm through his on the way to the stables. What was so remarkable about a woman putting her hand on your arm? A woman, moreover, that you were not in love with, and were never likely to be in love with.

It *was* because she was a woman, of course, but the thing that made it remarkable was something else again. It had something to do with being taken for granted by her. No one else had taken his hand in just that way. Casual but—no, not possessive. Quite a few had been possessive with him, and he had not been gratified in the least. Casual but—what? Belonging. It had something to do with belonging. The hand had taken him for granted because he belonged. It was the unthinking friendliness of a woman to one of her family. Was it because he had never "belonged" before, that made that commonplace gesture into a benediction?

He went on thinking of Bee as he fell asleep. Her sidelong glance when she was considering something; her courage; the way she had braced herself to meet him that day in the back room in Pimlico; the way she had kissed him before she was sure, just in case he was Patrick; the way she had dealt with the suspense of Simon's absence when he arrived to-day.

She was a lovely woman, Beatrice Ashby, and he loved her.

He had reached the toppling-over place of sleep when he was yanked of a sudden wide awake.

He had remembered something.

He knew now who it was that Simon Ashby reminded him of.

It was Timber.

17

ON Wednesday morning Bee took him to call on the tenants of the three farms: Frenchland, Upacres, and Wigsell. "Gates last; just to larn him," Bee said. Gates was last also in importance, since Wigsell was the smallest of the three farms. It had originally been the home farm of Latchetts and lay just beyond the Rectory, on the slope north of the village. It was almost too small a farm to be self-supporting, but Gates also ran the butcher's shop in the village (open twice a week) and was not dependent on what he made from Wigsell.

"Do you drive, Brat?" Bee asked, as they prepared to get into the car.

"Yes, but I'd rather you did. You know the"—"road" he had almost said—"the car better."

"Nice of you to call it a car. I expect you're used to a left-hand drive."

"Yes."

"I'm sorry it had to be the bug. It isn't often the car goes wrong on us. Jameson has all its inside out on the garage floor, and is conducting a post-mortem in a silent fury."

"I like the bug. I came from the station in it yesterday."

"So you did. What a very long time ago that seems. Does it seem like that to you?"

"Yes." It seemed years away to him.

118

"Have you heard that we've been saved from the *Clarion*?" she asked, as they sped down the avenue to the accompaniment of the bug's sewing-machine song.

"No?"

"Are you not a consumer of the Press at breakfast?" asked Bee, who had breakfasted at eight o'clock.

"I never lived where we had papers to read at breakfast. We just switched on the radio."

"Oh, lord, yes. I forget that your generation doesn't have to read."

"How have we been saved?"

"We have been rescued by three people we never heard of, and are never likely to meet. The fourth wife of a Manchester dentist, the husband of a principal boy, and the owner of a black leather trunk." She pressed the horn and turned slowly to the right out of the avenue. "The owner of the trunk left it at Charing Cross with someone's arms and legs in it. Or, of course, it may be the owner's arms and legs. That is a question which will occupy the *Clarion* for some time to come, I expect. The husband of the principal boy is suing for alienation of affection, and none of the three people concerned has ever been bothered with an inhibition, which is very nice for the *Clarion*. Since the reports of divorce cases have been pruned the *Clarion* has been suffering from frustration, and a suit for alienation of affection is a gift from heaven. Especially when it is Tattie Thacker's affections." She looked with pleasure at the morning. "I do like a morning after rain."

"You've still one to come?"

"What?"

"The fourth wife of the Manchester dentist."

"Oh. Yes. She, poor wretch, has just been exhumed from a very expensive and elaborate tomb and found to be loaded with arsenic. Her husband is found to be missing."

"And you think that the *Clarion* will be too busy to bother about —us?"

"I'm sure of it. They haven't room as it is for all they want to do with Tattie. She had a whole page to herself this morning. If they ever bothered about the Ashbys they would print the report in a tiny paragraph at the bottom of a page, and five million people would read it and not be able to tell you two minutes later what was in it.

119

I think we are quite safe. The *Westover Times* will have one of their usual discreet paragraphs this morning, and that will be the end of the matter."

Well, that was another snag out of the way. In the meantime he must keep his wits alive for the visits to Frenchland and Upacres. He was supposed to know these people.

Frenchland was farmed by a tall rosy old man and his tall sallow sister. "Everyone was terrified of Miss Hassell," Loding had said. "She had a face like a witch, and a tongue that took the skin off you. She didn't talk; just made one remark and you found that you were raw."

"Well, this is an honour," old Mr. Hassell said, coming to the garden gate and seeing whom Bee had with her. "Mr. Patrick, I'm glad to see you. I'm tarnation glad to see you." He took Brat's hand in his gnarled old fist and closed on it with his other one. There was no doubt that he was glad to see Patrick Ashby again.

It was difficult to know whether Miss Hassell was glad or not. She eyed Brat while she shook hands with him and said: "This is an unexpected pleasure." Her dry use of the conventional phrase and its wicked appropriateness amused Brat.

"Foreign parts don't seem to have changed you much," she said, as she set out glasses in the crowded little parlour.

"I've changed in one way," Brat said.

"You have?" She wasn't going to gratify him by asking in what way.

"I'm not frightened of you any more."

Old Mr. Hassell laughed.

"You beat me there, son. She still puts the fear of God in me. If I'm half an hour late getting home from market I creep up the lane with my tail down like I was a sheep-stealer."

Miss Hassell said nothing, but Brat thought there was a new interest in her glance; almost as if she were pleased with him. And she went away and fetched some shortbread from the kitchen which she had obviously had no intention of producing before.

They drank a liquid called White Port Wine Type, and discussed Rhode Island Reds.

At Upacres there was only plump Mrs. Docket, and she was busy making butter in the dairy at the back.

"Come in, whoever you are!" she called, and they went down the

120

cool tiled passage from the open front door, and turned into the chill of the dairy.

"I can't stop this," she said, looking round at them. "The butter is just—Oh, goodness, I didn't know! I just thought it was someone passing. The children are all at school and Carrie is out in the barn and——Goodness! To think of it!"

Bee automatically took her place at the churn while she shook hands with Brat.

"Well, well," said kind plump Mrs. Docket, "a fine, good-looking Ashby you are. You're more like Mr. Simon than ever you were."

Brat thought that Bee looked up with interest when she said that.

"It's a happy day for us all, Miss Ashby, isn't it? I could hardly believe it. I just said to Joe, I don't believe it, I said. It's the kind of thing that happens in books. And in pictures and plays. Not the kind of thing that would happen to quiet folk like us in a quiet place like Clare, I said. And yet here you are and it's really happened. My, Mr. Patrick, it's nice to see you again, and looking so well and bonny."

"Can I have a shot at that?" Brat asked, indicating the churn. "I've never handled one of those things."

"But of course you have!" Mrs. Docket said, looking taken aback. "You used to come in special on Saturday mornings to have a go at it."

Brat's heart missed a beat. "Did I?" he said. "I've forgotten that."

Always say quite frankly that you don't remember, Loding had advised. No one can deny that you don't remember, but they will certainly jump on you if you try to make-believe about anything.

"I thought you did this by electricity now," he heard Bee say as she made way for him at the churn.

"Oh, we do everything else by electricity, of course," Mrs. Docket said. "But I can't believe it makes good butter. No more home-made taste to it than you'd get at the International in Westover. Sometimes when I'm rushed I switch on the electricity, but I'm always sorry afterwards. Awful *mechanical*, it is. No artfulness about it."

They drank hot black tea and ate light floury scones and discussed the children's schooling.

"She's a darling, Mrs. Docket," Bee said as they drove away. "I think she is still of the opinion in her heart of hearts that electricity is an invention of the devil."

121

But Brat was thoughtful. He must stop himself from volunteering remarks. It was not important about the churn, but it quite easily might have been something vital. He must be less forthcoming.

"About Friday, Brat," Bee said, as they made their way back to Clare and to Wigsell.

"What is on Friday?" said Brat, out of his absorption.

Bee looked round and smiled at him. "Your birthday," she said.

Of course. He was now the possessor of a birthday.

"Had you forgotten that you are going to be twenty-one on Friday?" she asked.

"I had, almost." He caught her sidelong look at him. After a pause she said: "You came of age a long time ago, didn't you." She said it without smiling and it was not a question.

"About Friday," she went on. "I thought that since we have postponed the celebrations for Uncle Charles's benefit, we wouldn't have a party on Friday. Mr. Sandal will be coming down with the papers he wants you to sign, so we shall have him to lunch, and make it just a quiet family party."

Papers to sign. Yes, he had known that there would be papers to sign sooner or later. He had even learned to make his capital letters the way Patrick did, thanks to an old exercise book that Loding had unearthed and filched from the Rectory. And, after all, signing a paper didn't make him any more of a heel than he was being at this moment. It just put him more surely in the Law's reverence, made the thing irrevocable.

"Is that how you would like it?"

"What? Oh, the birthday. Yes, of course. I don't want a party. I don't want a celebration, if it comes to that. Can't we just take this coming-of-age for granted?"

"I don't think the neighbourhood would be very pleased if we did. They are all looking forward to some kind of party. I think we shall have to give them one. Even the invitation cards are all ready. I altered the date to a fortnight after Charles's arrival. He is due in about twenty-three days. So you'll have to 'thole' it, as old Nannie used to say."

Yes, he would have to thole it. Anyhow, he could sit back now and relax for a little. He was not supposed to know the Gates family.

They were coming back to the village now; the white rails of the south paddocks on their left. It was a washed and shining morning, but it had an uneasy glitter. The sky was metallic, and the light had a silver edge to it.

As they passed the entrance to the Rectory Bee said: "Alec Loding came down for the week-end not long ago."

"Oh? What is he doing now?"

"Still playing roué parts in dreadful little comedies and farces. You know: four characters, five doors, and one bed. I didn't see him, but Nancy said he had improved."

"In what way?"

"Oh, more interested in other people. Kindlier. He even made efforts to get on with George. Nancy thought age was beginning to tell. He was quite happy to sit for hours with a book in George's study when George was out. And when George was in they would yarn quite happily. Nancy was delighted. She has always been fond of Alec, but she used to dread his visits. The country bored him and George bored him even more, and he never bothered to hide it. So it was a pleasant change."

Half-way through the village they turned into the lane that led to Wigsell.

"You don't remember Emmy Vidler, do you?" she asked Brat. "She was brought up at Wigsell, and married Gates when he had a farm the other side of Bures. When her father died, Gates put a bailiff into his farm and took over Wigsell. And, of course, the butcher's shop. So they are very comfortably off. The boy couldn't stand his father, and got himself a job in the Midlands somewhere; engineering. But the girl lives at home, and is the apple of her father's eye. She went to an expensive boarding school, where I understand she was known as Margot. Her name is Peggy."

They swung into the farm entrance and came to rest on the small old cobbles of the yard. Two dogs rushed at them in wild self-importance, yelling their arrival to the world.

"I do wish Gates would train his dogs," said Bee, whose dogs were as well-trained as her horses.

The clamour brought Mrs. Gates to the front door. She was a faded and subdued little woman who must once have been very pretty.

"Glen! Joy! Be quiet!" she called, ineffectually, and came forward to greet them. But before she reached them Gates came round the corner of the house, and in a few strides had anticipated her. His pompous welcome drowned her more genuine pleasure, and she stood smiling gently at Brat while her husband trumpeted forth their satisfaction in seeing Patrick Ashby on their doorstep again.

Gates was a large, coarse individual, but Brat supposed that once he had had the youthful vigour and assurance that appealed to pretty, fragile little women like Emmy Vidler.

"They tell me that you've been making money in horses over there," he said to Brat.

"I've earned my living from them," Brat said.

"You come and see what I've got in *my* stable." He began to lead the way to the back of the house.

"But Harry, they must come in and sit down for a little," his wife protested.

"They'll sit down presently. They'd much rather look at a piece of good horseflesh than at your gewgaws. Come along, Mr. Patrick. Come along, Miss Ashby. Alfred!" he bellowed as they went down the yard. "Turn out that new horse for Miss Ashby to see."

Mrs. Gates, tailing along behind, found herself side by side with Brat. "I am so happy about this," she said quietly. "So happy about your coming back. I remember you when you were little; when I lived here in my father's day. Except for my own son I've never been so fond of a small boy as I was of you."

"Now then, Mr. Patrick, have a look at this here, have a look at this! Tell me if that doesn't fill the eye for you."

Gates swept his great limb of an arm at the stable door where Alfred was leading out a brown horse that looked oddly out of place in the small farmyard, even in a region where every small farmer kept a mount that would carry him across country in the winter. There was no denying it, the brown horse was something exceptional.

"There! what do you think of that, eh? What do you think of that?"

Bee, having looked, said: "But that, surely, is the horse that Dick Pope won the jumping on at the Bath Show last year."

"That's the horse," Gates said complacently. "And not only the jumping. The cup for the best riding horse in the show. Cost me a pretty penny, that did, but I can afford it and nothing's too good for my girl. Oh ah! It's for Peggy I bought it. That wouldn't carry me, that wouldn't." He gave an abrupt shout of laughter; at least Brat supposed it was laughter. "But my girl, now, she's a feather in

124

the saddle. I don't have to tell you, Miss Ashby; you've seen her. There's no one in the county deserves a good horse better than my Peggy, and I don't grudge the money for it."

"You've certainly got a good horse, Mr. Gates," Bee said, with an enthusiasm in her voice that surprised Brat. He looked across at her and wondered why she was looking so pleased. After all, this brown horse was a potential rival to Timber, and all the other Latchetts' animals.

"Got a vet's certificate with it, I need hardly say. I don't buy pigs in pokes."

"Is Peggy going to show it this year?"

"Of course she is, of course she is. What did I buy it for but for her to show?"

Bee's face was positively blissful. "How nice!" she said, and she sounded rapturous.

"Do you like it, Miss Ashby?" Peggy Gates said, appearing at Brat's side.

Peggy was a very pretty creature. Pink and white and gold. Brat thought that if it were possible to cross Miss Parslow and Eleanor the result would probably be Peggy Gates. She accepted her introduction to Brat with composure, but managed to convey the impression that it was personally delightful to her to have Patrick home again. Her small hand lay in his with a soft pressure that was intimate rather than friendly. Brat shook it heartily and resisted a temptation to wipe his palm down his hip.

She accepted Bee's congratulations on her possession of the horse, allowed a decent interval for further contemplation of it, and then with an admirable display of social dexterity, lifted the whole family from the yard into the drawing-room of the house. It was called the drawing-room, and was furnished as such, but Bee, who remembered it as old Mrs. Vidler's parlour, thought the water-colours and wistaria wallpaper a poor exchange for the lustre jugs and framed engravings of Mrs. Vidler's day.

They drank very good madeira and talked about the Bures Agricultural Show.

And they drove home with Bee still looking as if someone had left her a fortune. She caught Brat's considering look at her and said: "Well?"

"You look like a cat that has been given cream," he said.

She gave him her sideways, amused glance. "Cream and fish and liver," she said; but did not tell him the translation.

"When all the fuss of Friday is over, Brat," she said, "you must go up to town and get yourself a wardrobe. Walters will take weeks to make your evening things, and you'll need them for the celebration when Uncle Charles comes home."

"What shall I get?" he asked, at a loss for the first time.

"I should leave it to Walters, if I were you."

"Outfit for a young English gentleman," Brat said.

And she looked sideways again, surprised by the twist in his voice.

18

ELEANOR came into the sitting-room as Bee was opening the midday post, and said: "She bumped!"

Bee looked up hazily, her mind still on the contents of her mail.

"She bumped, I tell you. For a whole fifty yards she bumped like a good 'un."

"The Parslow girl? Oh, congratulations, Nell, dear."

"I never thought I'd live to see this day. Is no one having sherry?"

"Brat and I have drunk sufficient strange liquids this morning to last us for the rest of the week."

"How did it go, Brat?" Eleanor asked, pouring herself some sherry.

"Not as badly as I'd been prepared for," Brat said, watching her thin capable hand manipulating the glasses. That hand wouldn't lie soft and confidential and insinuating in one's own.

"Did Docket tell you how he got his wound?"

"Docket was at market," Bee said. "But we had hot buttered scones from Mrs. Docket."

"Dear Mrs. Docket. What did Miss Hassell give you?"

"Shortbread. She wasn't going to give us that, but she succumbed to Brat's charms." So Bee had noticed that.

"I'm not surprised," Eleanor said, looking at Brat over her glass. "And Wigsell?"

126

"Do you remember that brown horse of Dick Pope's? The one he swept the board with at Bath last year?"

"Certainly."

"Gates has bought it for Peggy."

Eleanor stopped sipping sherry and thought about this in silence for a moment or two.

"For Peggy to show."

"Yes."

"Well, well!" said Eleanor slowly: and she looked amused and thoughtful. She looked at Bee, met Bee's glance, and looked away again. "Well, well!" she said again, and went on sipping sherry. After an interval broken only by the rip of paper as Bee opened envelopes, she said: "I don't know that that was such a very good move."

"No," said Bee, not looking up.

"I'm going to wash. What is for lunch?"

"Goulash."

"As made by our Mrs. Betts, that is just stew."

The twins came in from lessons at the Rectory, and Simon from the stables, and they went in to lunch.

Simon had come down so late to breakfast that Brat's only intercourse with him to-day had been to wish him good morning. He seemed amiable and relaxed, and inquired with what appeared to be genuine interest about the success of the morning. Bee provided an account, with periodic confirmation from Brat. When she came to Wigsell, Eleanor interrupted her to say:

"Did you know that Gates has bought Peggy a new horse?"

"No," Simon said, looking up with mild interest.

"He has bought her that brown horse of Dick Pope's."

"Riding Light?"

"Yes. Riding Light. She is going to show it this year."

For the first time since he had met him Brat saw Simon Ashby flush. He paused for a moment, and then went on with his lunch. The flush slowly died, and the cool pale profile resumed its normal calm. Both Eleanor and Bee had avoided looking at him while he absorbed the news, but Ruth studied him with interest.

And Brat, eating Mrs. Betts's goulash, studied him with his mind. Simon Ashby was reputedly crazy about the Gates girl. But was he glad that the girl had been given a good horse? No. He was furious. And what was more, his womenfolk had known that he would be furious. They had known beforehand that he would find Peggy's entry as a rival unforgivable. They had, understandably, not wanted the Gates affair to last or to become serious; and they had recognised instantly, both of them, that Peggy's possession of Riding Light had saved them. What kind of creature was this Simon Ashby, who could not bear to be beaten by the girl he was in love with?

He remembered Bee's inordinate pleasure in the brown horse. He saw again Eleanor's slow amusement at the news. They had known at once that that was the end of the Peggy affair. Gates had bought that horse to be "upsides" with Latchetts; to give his daughter a mount as good as any owned by the man he hoped she would marry. And all he had done was to destroy any chance that Peggy ever had of being mistress of Latchetts.

Well, Simon was no longer master of Latchetts, so it would not matter to the Gates family that Simon resented Peggy's possession of the horse. But what kind of heel was Simon that he could not love a rival?

"What is Brat going to ride at the Bures Show," he heard Eleanor say, and brought his attention back to the lunch table.

"All of them," Simon said. And as Eleanor looked her question: "They are his horses."

This was the kind of thing that the English did not say. Simon must be very angry to desert the habit of a lifetime.

"I'm not going to 'show' any horses, if that is what you mean," Brat said. "That requires technique, and I haven't got it."

"But you used to be very good," Bee said.

"Did I? Oh, well, that is a long time ago. I certainly don't want to show any horses in the ring at Bures."

"The show isn't for nearly three weeks yet," Eleanor said. "Bee could coach you for a day or two, and you'd be as good as ever."

But Brat was not to be moved. It would have been fun to see what he could do against English horsemen; fun especially to jump the Latchetts horses and perhaps win with them; but he was not going to make any public appearance as Patrick Ashby of Latchetts if he could help it.

"Brat could ride in the races," Ruth said. "The races they end up with. He could beat everyone on Timber, couldn't he?"

"Timber is not going to be knocked about in any country bumpkins'
128

race if I still have any say in the matter," Simon said, speaking into his plate. "He is going to Olympia, which is his proper place."

"I agree," Brat said. And the atmosphere ceased to be tense. Jane wanted to know why fractions were vulgar, and Ruth wanted a new bicycle tire, and the conversation became the normal family conversation of any meal-time in any home.

Before lunch was over the first of the visitors arrived; and the steady stream went on, from after-luncheon coffee, through tea, to six o'clock drinks. They had all come to inspect Brat, but he noticed that those who had known Patrick Ashby came with a genuine pleasure in welcoming him back. Each of them had some small memory of him to recount, and all of them had kept the memory green because they had liked Pat Ashby and grieved for him. And Brat caught himself being gratified in an absurd and proprietorial way, as if some protégé of his own was being praised. The light that had been shed on Simon this morning made him more than ever Patrick's champion. It was all wrong that Latchetts should have been Simon's all those years. It was Patrick's inheritance and it was all wrong that Patrick should not be here to inherit it. Patrick was all right. Patrick would not have gone sick with rage because his best girl had a better horse than he had. Patrick was all right.

So he accepted the small verbal gifts on Patrick's behalf and was pleased and gratified.

About the time when tea-cups were being mixed up with cocktail glasses the local doctor appeared, and Brat ceased to be gratified, and became interested in Eleanor's reactions to the doctor. Eleanor seemed to like the doctor very much, and Brat, knowing nothing whatever about him, was straightway convinced that he was not good enough for her. The only guests left now were Colonel Smollett, the Chief Constable for the county; the two Misses Byrne, who occupied the Jacobean house at the far end of the village and, according to Bee, had their walls hung with "plates and warming-pans, and other kitchen utensils"; and Dr. Spence. Dr. Spence was young and red-haired and bony, and he had freckles and a friendly manner. He was the successor of the old country doctor who had brought the whole Ashby family up, and he was, so Bee confided in an interval of tea-pouring, "much too brilliant to stay in a country practice." Brat wondered if he stayed for Eleanor's sake; he seemed to like Eleanor very much.

"You caused us a lot of trouble, young man," Colonel Smollett
129

had said, greeting him; and Brat, after the polite evasions he had experienced so far, was glad of his frankness. Just as his notions of English middle-class had been derived from American films, so his idea of a colonel had been derived from the English Press, and was equally erroneous. Colonel Smollett was a small, thin man with a beaked nose and a self-effacing manner. What one noticed about him was his extraordinary neatness and his gay blue eyes.

The Colonel gave the Misses Byrne a lift in his car, but the doctor lingered, and it was only when Bee asked him to stay for dinner that he pulled himself together and went.

"Poor Dr. Spence," Bee said at dinner. "I'm sorry he wouldn't stay. I'm sure that landlady of his starves him."

"Nonsense," said Simon, who had recovered his good temper and had been very bright all the afternoon; "that lean, red-haired type always look underfed. Besides, he wouldn't have eaten, anyhow. All he wants is to sit and look at Eleanor."

Which confirmed Brat's worst fears.

But all Eleanor said was: "Don't be absurd"; and she said it without heat and without interest.

They were all tired by dinner-time, and it was a quiet meal. The excitement of having Brat there had died into acceptance, and they no longer treated him as a newcomer. Even the unforthcoming Jane had stopped accusing him with her eyes. He was part of the landscape. It was wonderfully restful to be part of the landscape again. For the first time since he came to Latchetts he was hungry.

But as he got ready for bed he puzzled over the problem of Simon. Simon, who was quite sure that he was not Patrick, but had no intention of saying so. (Why? Because he would not be believed, and his protest would be put down to resentment at his brother's return? Because he had plans for a dramatic unveiling? Because he had some better way of dealing with an impostor who would not be unveiled?) Simon, who was so good a dissembler that he could fool his own family about his inmost feelings. Simon, who was so self-centred, so vain, that to come between him and the sun was to insult him. Simon, who had charm enough for ten men, and an appealing air of vulnerability. Simon, who was like Timber.

He stood again at the open window in the dark, looking at the curve of the down against the sky. Perhaps because he was less tired to-night he was no longer so afraid; but the incalculable factor in this life that he was due to lead was still Simon.

If Simon so resented Peggy Gates's owning a better horse than his, what, wondered Brat, could have been his reaction to Patrick's sudden succession to Latchetts?

He considered this a long time, staring into the dark.

And as he turned at last to put the light on, a voice in his mind said: I wonder where Simon was when Patrick went over the cliff.

But he noticed the heinousness of this at once, of course. What was he suggesting? Murder? In Latchetts? In Clare? By a boy of thirteen? He was letting his antipathy to Simon run away with his common sense.

The suicide of Patrick Ashby had been a police affair. An affair of inquest and evidence. The thing had been investigated, and the police had been satisfied that it was in truth suicide.

Satisfied? Or just without a case?

Where would that coroner's report be now? In the police records he supposed. And it was not easy for a civilian to persuade the police to satisfy an idle curiosity; they were busy people.

But the thing must have been reported in the local Press. It must have been a local sensation. Somewhere in the files there would be an account of that inquest, and he, Brat Farrar, would unearth it at the first opportunity.

Antipathy or no antipathy, common sense or no common sense, he wanted to know where Simon Ashby was when his twin went over the Westover cliffs.

19

Mr. Sandal was to come on Thursday night and stay over till after luncheon on Friday.

On Thursday morning Bee said that she was going into Westover to do some special shopping for Mr. Sandal's meals, and what would Brat like to do with his day?

Brat said that he would like to come with her and see Westover again, and Bee looked pleased.

"We can stop on the way through the village," she said, "and let Mrs. Gloom run her eye over you. It will be one less for you to meet after church on Sunday."

So they stopped at the newsagent's, and Brat was exhibited, and Mrs. Gloom sucked the last ounce of satisfaction out of the drama of his return, and they laughed together about her as they sped away to the sea.

"People who can't sing are horribly frustrated," Bee said, after a little.

Brat considered this *non sequitur*. "The highest mountain in Britain is Ben Nevis," he said, proffering one in his turn.

Bee laughed at that and said: "No, I just meant that I should like to sing at the top of my voice, but I can only croak. Can you sing?"

"No. I croak too. We could croak together."

"I doubt if it is legal to croak in a built-up area. One never knows nowadays. And anyhow, there is that." She waved her hand at a large sign which read:

MOTORISTS. PLEASE REFRAIN FROM USING YOUR HORN.
THIS IS A HOSPITAL.

Brat glanced up at the building, set on the slope above the town, and remarked that it was uncommonly pretty for a hospital.

"Yes; much less terrifying than the normal place. It is a great pity that *that* was allowed to happen." She jerked her chin at the row of cheap shops on the opposite side of the road; some of them not much better than shacks. Dingy cafés, a cobbler's, a bicycle "depot," a seller of wreaths and crosses, a rival seller of flowers, a greengrocer's, and anonymous businesses with windows painted half-way up and odd bills tacked in the window.

They were running down the slope into the town, and this miscellaneous strip of roadside commerce was the last petering-out of the poorer suburbs. Beyond was Westover proper: clean and neat and shining in the reflected light from the sea.

As Bee turned into the car park she said: "You don't want to tail round looking at 'sea-food' for Mr. Sandal's consumption. Go away and amuse yourself, and we'll meet for lunch at the Angel about a quarter to one."

He was some distance away when she called him back. "I forgot to ask if you were short of money. I can lend you some if you——"

"Oh, no, thanks; I still have some of what Cosset, Thring and what-you-may-call-'em advanced me."

He went first to the harbour to see the place that he was supposed

132

to have set out from eight years ago. It was filled with coastwise shipping and fishing boats, very gay in the dancing light. He leaned against the warm stones of the breakwater and contemplated it. It was here that Alec Loding had sat painting his "old scow" on the last day of Pat Ashby's life. It was over those cliffs away to the right that Pat Ashby had fallen to his death.

He pushed himself off the breakwater and went to look for the office of the *Westover Times*. It took him some time to find it because, although every citizen of Westover read the local paper, very few of them had occasion to seek it out in its home. Its home was a stone's-throw from the harbour, in a small old house in a small old street which still had its original cobbles. The entrance was so low that Brat instinctively ducked his head as he went in. Beyond, after the bright sunlight outside, there was blackness. But out of the blackness the unmistakable adolescent voice of an office boy said: "Yes?"

Brat said that he would like to see Mr. Macallan.

The voice said that Mr. Macallan was out.

"I suppose you couldn't tell me where I could find him?"

"The fourth table on the left upstairs at the Blue Bird."

"That's explicit."

"Can't help it; that's where he is. That's where he always is, this time of day."

The Blue Bird, it seemed, was a coffee-shop round the corner on the harbour front. And Mr. Macallan was indeed sitting at the fourth table on the left upstairs, which was the one by the far window. Mr. Macallan was sitting with a half-drunk cup of coffee in front of him, glowering down on the bright front. He greeted Brat amiably, however, as one old friend to another, and pulled out a chair for him.

"I'm afraid I haven't been much good to you," Brat said.

"The only way I'll ever get myself on to the front page of the *Clarion* is in a trunk," Mr. Macallan said.

"A trunk?"

"In sections. And I can't help feeling that would be a wee bit drastic." He spread out that morning's *Clarion* so that the shrieking black print screamed up from the table. The trunk murder was still front-page news after three days, it having been discovered that the legs in the case belonged to two different persons; a complication which put the present case *hors concurs* in the trunk-murder class.

133

"What's horrible about murder," Mr. Macallan said reflectively, "is not that it happens, but that it happens to your Aunt Agnes, if you follow me. Hi! *Miss!* A cup of coffee for my friend here. Brother Johnny goes to the war and gets killed and it is all very sad, but no one is shocked—civilisation being what it is. But if someone bumps Aunt Agnes off on her way home one night that *is* a shock. That sort of thing just doesn't happen to people you know."

"It must be worse when someone you know bumps off someone's Aunt Agnes."

"Ay," said Mr. Macallan, shooting an extra spoonful of sugar into his half-cold coffee and stirring it vigorously. "I've seen some of that. Families, you know. It's always the same: they just can't believe it. *Their* Johnny. That is the horror in murder. The domesticity of it." He took out his cigarette case and offered it. "And how do you like being Clare's white-headed boy? Are you glad to be back?"

"You can't imagine how glad."

"After that fine free life in Arizona or Texas or wherever it was? You mean you actually prefer this?" Mr. Macallan jerked his head at the Westover front filled with placid shoppers. And, as Brat nodded: "Mercy-be-here! I can hardly credit it."

"Why? Don't you like the place?"

Mr. Macallan looked down at the southern English walking about in their southern English sunshine, and metaphorically spat. "They're so satisfied with themselves I can't take my eyes off them," he said.

"Satisfied with their lot, you mean? Why not?"

"Nothing in this world came out of satisfaction."

"Except the human race," said Brat.

Mr. Macallan grinned. "I'll allow you that." But he went on glowering down at the bright harbour scene. "I look at them and think: 'These people kept Scotland fighting for four hundred years,' and I can't find the answer."

"The answer, of course, is that they didn't."

"No? Let me tell you that my country——"

"They've been much too busy for the last thousand years keeping the shores of England. But for them your Scotland would be part of Spain to-day."

This was apparently a new idea to Mr. Macallan. He decided to let it ride.

134

"You weren't looking for me, were you? When you came to the Blue Bird?"

"Yes. I went to the office first and they told me you would be here. There's something I want and I thought that you might help me to it."

"Not publicity, I take it," Mr. Macallan said dryly.

"No, I want to read my obituary."

"Man, who doesn't! You're a privileged person, Mr. Ashby, a very privileged person."

"I suppose the *Westover Times* keeps back numbers."

"Och, yes, back to June the 18th, 1827. Or is it June the 28th? I forget. So you want to look at the files. Well, there's not very much, but you'll find it very interesting of course. One's own death must be a fascinating subject to read about."

"You've read about it, then?"

"Och, yes. Before I went out to Latchetts on Tuesday, I naturally looked you up."

So it was that, when they stumbled down the dark stairs to the cellar of the *Westover Times* offices, Mr. Macallan was able to put his hand on the required copy without delay and without raising the dust of a hundred and fifty years about their ears.

"I'll leave you to it," Mr. Macallan said, spreading the volume open under the naked light above the old-fashioned sloping desk. "Have a good time. If there is anything else I can do for you, just let me know. And drop in when you feel like it."

He trotted up the stone stairs, and the scuffling sound of his shoes faded upwards into the world of men, and Brat was left alone with the past.

The *Westover Times* appeared twice a week: on Wednesdays and Saturdays. Patrick Ashby's death had occurred on a Saturday, so that a single Wednesday issue carried both the announcement of his death and the report of the inquest. As well as the usual announcement inserted by the family in the list of deaths, there was a short news item on the middle page. The *Westover Times* had been owned and run by a Westover family since its founding, and it still kept the stateliness, the good manners, and the reticence of an early Edwardian doctor's brougham plying between Harley Street and Knightsbridge. The paper announced the sad occurrence and offered its sympathy to the family in this great trial which had come to them so soon after the tragic deaths of Mr. and Mrs. Ashby in a flying accident. It offered no information beyond the fact that on Saturday afternoon or evening Patrick Ashby had met his death by falling over the cliffs to the west of the town. An account of the inquest would be found on page five.

On page five there was a whole column on the inquest. A column was not enough, of course, to do justice to the inquest in detail, but all the salient facts were there, and now and then a piece of evidence was reported verbatim.

Saturday afternoon was a holiday for the Ashby children and they were accustomed in the summer to take a "piece" with them and pursue their various interests in the countryside until it was time to come home to their evening meal. No alarm had been raised about Patrick's non-appearance in the evening until he had been missing for several hours. It was taken for granted that he had gone farther than he had intended in his latest hobby of bird-watching, and that he was merely late. When darkness closed down and he still had not come home, telephoned inquiries were sent all round the country-side in an effort to find someone who had seen him, so that if an accident had overtaken him rescue might be directed to the proper locality. When these inquiries proved barren, a search-party was organised to beat all the likely places for the missing boy. The search was conducted both on horse and on foot, and along the roads by car, without success.

In the first light of early morning the boy's jacket was found by a coastguard patrolling along the cliffs. Albert Potticary, the coast-guard in question, gave evidence that the coat was lying about fifty yards from the cliff-edge, just where the path from Tanbitches began to descend through the gap to the harbour at Westover. It was lying a few yards off the path on the side nearer the cliff, and was weighted in its place by a stone. It was wet with dew when he picked it up, and the pockets were empty except for a note written in thin ink. The note was the one now shown him. He telephoned the news to the police and at once instituted a search for a body on the beach. No body was found. High tide the previous night had been at seven-twenty-nine, and if the boy had fallen into the water, or if he had fallen before high-water so that his body was taken out by the tide, it would not be washed up again at Westover. No one drowned in the Westover district had ever been washed up nearer than Castleton, away to the west; and most of them farther west than that. He was therefore not hopeful of finding any body when he instituted the search. It was merely routine.

The last person to see Patrick Ashby turned out to be Abel Tusk, the shepherd. He had met the boy in the early afternoon, about half-way between Tanbitches and the cliff.

Q. What was he doing?

A. He was lying on his belly in the grass.

Q. Doing what?

A. Waiting for a lark.

Q. What kind of lark?

A. An English lark.

Q. Ah, you mean he was bird-watching. Did he appear his normal self?

Yes, Abel said, as far as he could judge Pat Ashby had looked much as usual. Never very "gabby" at any time. A quiet boy? Yes, a nice quiet boy. They discussed birds for a little and then parted. He, Abel Tusk, was on his way into Westover by the cliff path, it being also his own half-holiday. He did not get back until late at night and did not hear about the search for the boy until Sunday morning.

Asked if many people used that cliff path he said no. There were buses from the village that got you into Westover in a tenth of the time, but he didn't care for buses. It was rough walking, the cliff part of the path, and not suitable for the kind of shoes that people going to town would be wearing. So no one but someone like himself who was already on the sea side of Tanbitches hill would think of going to Westover that way.

Bee gave evidence that his parents' deaths had been a great shock to the boy, but that he had taken it well and had seemed to be recovering. She had no reason to think that he contemplated taking his own life. The children separated on Saturday afternoons because their interests were different, so that it was not unusual for Patrick to be alone.

Q. His twin did not accompany him?

A. No. Patrick was fascinated by birds, but Simon's tastes are mechanical.

Q. You have seen the note found in the boy's coat, and you recognise it as the handwriting of your nephew Patrick?

137

A. Oh, yes. Patrick had a very individual way of making his capital letters. And he was the only person I know who wrote with a stylograph.

She explained the nature of a stylograph. The one Patrick owned had been black vulcanite with a thin yellow spiral down the barrel. Yes, it was missing. He carried it always with him; it was one of his pet possessions.

Q. Can you think of any reason why this sudden desire to take his own life should overcome him, when he seemed to his friend, the shepherd, to be normally happy in the afternoon?

A. I can only suggest that he *was* normally happy during the afternoon, but that when it was time to turn homeward the thought of going back to a house empty of so much that had made life fine for him was suddenly too much, and that he was overcome by an impulse born of a moment's despair.

And that was the verdict of the court, too. That the boy had succumbed to a passing impulse at a moment when the balance of his mind had been disturbed.

That was the end of the column and that was the end of Patrick Ashby. Brat turned over the pages of the next issue, filled with the small importances of summer-time Westover: shows, bowling competitions, tennis tournaments, council meetings, trade outings; but there was no mention of Pat Ashby. Pat Ashby already belonged to the past.

Brat sat back in the dead quiet of the cellar and thought about it all. The boy lying in the summer grass waiting for his beloved larks to drop out of the sky. And the night coming. And no boy coming home across Tanbitches hill.

Mechanical interests, Bee had said, describing Simon's way of spending his half-holiday. That meant the internal combustion engine, he supposed. It was about the age of thirteen that one did begin to be interested in cars. Simon had probably been innocently tinkering in the garage at Latchetts. Certainly there was no suggestion at the inquest, as reported in the Press, that his whereabouts had been a matter for question.

When he joined Bee for lunch at the Angel he longed to ask her bluntly where Simon had been that afternoon. But of course one could not say: "Where was Simon the afternoon I ran away from home?" It was an utterly pointless question. He must think up some other way of bringing the subject into the conversation. He was distracted by the old head-waiter at the Angel, who had known all the Ashby children and was shaken to the core, apparently, by Patrick's unexpected return. His old hands trembled as they laid the various dishes in front of him, and each dish was accompanied by a quavered "Mr. Patrick, sir," as if he was glad to use the name. But the climax came with the sweet course. The sweet was fruit tart, and he had already served both Bee and Brat, but he returned immediately and with great empressment laid a large meringue on a silver dish in front of Brat's place. Brat gazed at it in surprise and then looked up to find the old man waiting for his comment with a proud smile and tears in his eyes. His mind was so full of Simon that he was not quick enough, and it was Bee who saved the situation.

"How wonderful of Daniel to remember that you always had that!" she said, and Brat followed her lead and the old man went away pleased and moved, mopping his eyes on a dazzling white handkerchief that looked as large as a sheet.

"Thanks," Brat said to Bee. "I hadn't remembered that."

"Dear old Daniel. I think it is almost like seeing his own son coming back. He had three, you know. They all died in one war, and his grandsons all died in the following one. He was very fond of you children, so I expect it is very wonderful for him to see anyone he has loved come back from the dead. What have you been doing with your morning?"

"Reading my obituary."

"How morbid of you. Or, no, of course, it isn't. It is what we all want to do. Did you see little Mr. Macallan?"

"I did. He sent his best respects to you. Aunt Bee——"

"You are too old to begin calling me aunt."

"Bee, what were Simon's 'mechanical interests'?"

"Simon never had any mechanical interests as far as I know."

"You said at the inquest that he had."

"I did? I can't imagine what they could have been. What was it apropos of?"

"To explain why we didn't do things together on a Saturday afternoon. What did Simon do when I went bird-watching?" He tried to make it sound like someone trying to remember an old way of life.

"Pottered about, I expect. Simon was always a potterer. His hobbies never lasted longer than a fortnight at the outside."

"So you don't remember what Simon was using for a hobby the day I ran away?"

"It's absurd of me, my dear, but I don't. I don't even remember where he was that day. When something dreadful happens, you know, you push it down in your mind and never bring it up again if you can help it. I do remember that he spent all night out on his pony looking frantically for you. Poor Simon. You did him a bad turn, Brat. I don't know if you realise it. Simon changed after you went. I don't know whether it was the shock of your going or the lack of your sober companionship, but he was a different person afterwards."

Since Brat had no answer to this he ate in silence, and presently she said: "And you did me a bad turn in never writing to me. Why didn't you, Brat?"

This was the weak spot in the whole structure, as Loding had continually pointed out.

"I don't *know*," he said. "Honestly, I don't *know!*"

The exasperation and desperation of his tone had an appropriateness that he had not foreseen.

"All right," she said. "I won't worry you, my dear. I didn't mean to. It is just something that has puzzled me. I was so very fond of you when you were small, and we were such very good friends. It was not like you to live a life of your own without once glancing back."

He raked up an offering from the depths of his own experience. "It's easier than you'd think to drop the past behind you when you are fourteen. If you are continually meeting fresh experience, I mean. The past has no greater reality than something you saw in a cinema. No personal reality, I mean."

"I must try running away one day," she said lightly. "There is a lot of the past I should like to drop behind me."

And Daniel came with the cheese, and they talked about other things.

20

Brat had not been prepared to find birthday presents by his plate on Friday morning. He had not, in fact, reckoned with a birthday at all. "All celebration has been postponed until Mr. Charles Ashby comes back to this country," Mr. Sandal had said to him in London, and it was not until Bee had drawn his attention to it that he had remembered that, celebration apart, there would inevitably be a day on which he would become twenty-one. He had had so little experience of birthdays that he had taken it for granted that a postponement of celebration meant a simple verbal congratulation from each member of the family, and he was dismayed by the pile of parcels by his breakfast plate. He quailed at the thought of having to open them in public.

The sardonic light in Simon's eye braced him to the task. He had a suspicion that Simon's punctuality at breakfast this morning was due less to the presence of Mr. Sandal than to the prospect of enjoying his embarrassment over those presents.

"Happy birthday, Brat!" they said, as they came in. "Happy birthday, Brat!" One after another. So that the light benedictions fell round him like confetti.

He wished he didn't feel so bad about it. He wished that they were really his family, and that these were his presents by his plate, and that it was his birthday. It was a very nice thing, a family birthday.

"Are you an opener-before-breakfast or an opener-after, Brat?" Eleanor asked.

"After," he said promptly, and won a breathing-space.

After several cups of strong coffee he might feel braver.

Simon had, as well as presents, a pile of telegrams from the still large numbers of his acquaintances who had not heard of his twin's return, and he opened them as he ate and shared the contents. Having read each message aloud he added a postscript of comment.

"An exact shilling, the cheeseparing adding-machine! And I gave her a wonderful lunch last time I was in town. . . . What do you imagine Bobby is doing in Skye? He loathes mountains and is a martyr to midges. . . . Gore and Bowen. I suppose that's to remind me to pay my bill. . . . I'm sure I don't know anyone called Bert Burt. Do you think he can be a bookie?"

When eventually Brat could no longer postpone the opening of his parcels, his task was made easier by the fact that his presents were for the most part replicas of those Simon was pulling out of his own pile. Mr. Sandal's Georgian sugar-sifter, Bee's silver flask, Eleanor's whip, and the twins' pocket-book, were all duplicated. Only the present from the Rectory was individual. It was a small wooden box that played a tune when the lid was opened. Brat had never seen or heard of such a thing before, and was so delighted with it that he forgot to be self-conscious and became absorbed in it.

"That came from Clare Park," Bee said.

And at that reminder of Loding he came back to reality and shut down the lid on the sweet frail melody.

This morning he was going to sign his soul away. It was no time for tinkling little tunes.

This signing-away was also the subject of surprise. He had imagined in his innocence that various papers would be put in front of him and he would sign them, and that would be that. A matter of twenty minutes at the most. But it proved to be a matter of hours. He and Mr. Sandal sat side by side at the big table in the library, and the whole economic history of Latchetts was laid open for his inspection. Cosset, Thring and Noble were accounting to their young client for the years of his minority.

Brat, a little bewildered but interested, toiled after Mr. Sandal in his progress through the years, and admired the way the old man handled this legal and mathematical exploration.

"Your dear mother's fortune is not what it was in the prosperous days when she inherited it, of course; but it will be sufficient to ensure that you may live at Latchetts in the future without anxiety. As you have observed, the margin of safety has often been very small during the years of your minority, but it was Miss Ashby's wish that there should be no borrowing on the strength of your inheritance from your mother. She was determined that that should come to you intact when you were twenty-one."

He went on laying statements in front of Brat, and for the first time Brat was aware of the struggle and the insecurity that lay behind the assured contentment that Latchetts presented to the eye.

"What happened that year?" he asked, putting his finger on a particularly black record.

Mr. Sandal flipped over some papers. "Ah, yes. I remember. That was a bad year. A very bad year. One of the mares died and two were barren, and a very fine foal broke a leg. A heart-breaking year. It is a precarious way of making a living. That year, for instance," his thin dry finger pointed out another unsatisfactory report, "everything went swimmingly at Latchetts but it happened to be a year when no one was buying and none of the yearlings made their reserve price at the sales. A matter of luck. Merely luck. You will observe that some of the years were exceedingly lucky ones, so that the losses were overtaken."

He left the stables and went on to the farms: the conditions of lease, the improvements, the standing of the tenants, the nature of the crops. Eventually he came to the matter of personal income.

"Your father made a very good income in his profession of consulting engineer, and there seemed, of course, nothing to prevent him making that large yearly sum for a lifetime to come. He therefore spent generously on Latchetts and on the horses that were his hobby. Bought expensive and finely-bred mares, and so on, so that when he died his investments were not very extensive, and death duties had of course to be paid, so the investments had to go."

He slipped another sheet in front of Brat's eye, showing how the duty had been paid without mortgaging Latchetts.

"Miss Ashby has her own income and has never taken an allowance from the Latchetts estate. Except a house-keeping one, that is. The two elder children have had increasing allowances as they grew up. With the exception of some personal possessions—the children's ponies, for instance—the horses in the stable belong to the estate. When the children went to sales to buy for re-selling they were given money by Miss Ashby, and any profit on the improved horses went towards the expenses of Latchetts. I understand, however, that Simon has lately bought one or two with the result of profitable bets, and Eleanor with the result of her efforts as an instructress in the art of riding. Miss Ashby will no doubt tell you which these are. They do not appear in the relevant papers. The Shetland ponies were

143

Miss Ashby's own venture, and are her own property. I hope that is all clear?"

Brat said that it was.

"Now about the future. It is the Bank's advice that the money left you by your mother should stay invested as it is now. Have you any objection to that?"

"I don't want any lump sum," Loding had said. "I should only blue it, in the first place. And in the second place, it would cause a shocking amount of heart-searching at the bank. We don't want any heart-searching once you're in the saddle. All I want is a cosy little weekly allowance for the rest of my life, so that I can thumb my nose at Equity, and managements, and producers who say that I'm always late for rehearsals. *And* landladies. Riches, my boy, don't consist in having things, but in not having to do something you don't want to do. And don't you forget it. Riches is being able to thumb your nose."

"What income would that bring me, as it is?" Brat asked Mr. Sandal, and Mr. Sandal told him.

That was all right. He could peel Loding's cut off that and still have enough to meet his obligations at Latchetts.

"These are the children's present allowances. The twins, of course, will be going away to school presently, and that will be a charge on the estate for a few years."

He was surprised by the smallness of the allowances. Why, he thought, I made more than that in three months at the dude ranch. It subtly altered his attitude to Simon that Simon in the matter of spending money should have been so much his inferior.

"They're not very big, are they?" he said to Mr. Sandal, and the old man looked taken aback.

"They are in accordance with the size of the estate," he said dryly.

"Well, I think they ought to be stepped up a bit now."

"Yes; that would be quite in order. But you cannot expect to carry two adults as passengers on the estate. It would not be just to the estate. They are both capable of earning their own living."

"What do you suggest, then?"

"I would suggest that Eleanor be given a slightly increased allowance while she lives at Latchetts, or until she marries."

"Is she thinking of getting married?"

"My dear boy, all young ladies think of getting married, especially

144

when they are as pleasant to look upon as your sister. I am not aware, however, that she has so far exhibited any specific interest in the matter."

"Oh. And Simon?"

"Simon's case is difficult. Until a few weeks ago he looked upon Latchetts as his. He is not likely to remain long at Latchetts now, but the slightly increased allowance you suggest could be paid to him while he gives you his services here."

"I don't think that is good enough," said Brat, who was surprised by Mr. Sandal's assumption that Simon would go. Simon showed no signs of going. "I think a bit of the estate is owing to him."

"Morally owing, you mean?"

"Yes, I suppose so."

"No doubt you are right, but it is a dangerous assumption which you cannot expect me to countenance. One cannot hand out bits of a financial estate and still keep the said estate in good heart. An allowance is one thing: it comes out of income. But the giving away of the fabric of the thing is to damage its whole structure."

"Well, I suggest that if Simon wants to go away and begin somewhere on his own that the money to start should be lent to him out of the estate at a nominal rate of interest. I suppose if I say without interest you'll jump down my throat."

The old man smiled on him, quite kindly. "I think there is nothing against that. I am looking forward to a period of great prosperity for Latchetts now that the lean years are over. I don't suppose a loan to Simon would greatly incommode the estate. There would be the saving of the allowance to balance it. Now, about the increase in the present allowances——"

They settled the amounts of that.

"Lastly," said Mr. Sandal, "the pensioners."

"Pensioners?"

"Yes. The various dependents of the family who have become too old to work."

For the fourth time that morning Brat was surprised. He looked at the long list and wondered if all established English families had this drain on their income. Mr. Sandal seemed to take it as a matter of course; as much a commonplace of honourable practice as paying one's income tax. Mr. Sandal had frowned on any extravagance where the family was concerned: able-bodied Ashbys must earn their own living. The obligation to support the aged and infirm retainers of the family he took for granted. There was Nannie, who was now ninety-two and lived in a place called New Deer in Scotland; there was an old groom of eighty-nine who lived in the village, and another at Guessgate; there was a cook who had cooked for them until she was sixty-eight and now lived with a daughter of sixty-nine in Horsham; and so on.

He thought of the brassy blonde in the flowered rayon who had bade him welcome to Latchetts. Who would pension her? The country, he supposed. For long and honourable service?

Brat agreed to the continuance of the pensions, and then Simon was called in to do his share of signing. It pleased Brat, who had found it a depressing morning, to notice the sudden widening of Simon's eye as it lighted on his own signature. It was nearly a decade since Simon had set eyes on those capital letters of Patrick's, and here they were blandly confronting him on the library table. That would "larn" him to be sardonic over Brat's efforts to carry off a birthday that was not his.

Then Bee came in, and Mr. Sandal explained the increased provisions in the matter of allowances and the plan for providing for Simon's future. When Simon heard of the plan he eyed Brat thoughtfully; and Brat could read quite plainly what the look said. "Bribery, is that it? Well, it won't work. I'm damned well staying here and you will damned well pay me that allowance." Whatever plans Simon had, they centred round Latchetts.

Bee seemed pleased, however. She put her arm through his to lead him to lunch, and squeezed it. "Dear Brat!" she said.

"I congratulated you both and gave you my good wishes at breakfast," Mr. Sandal said, picking up his glass of claret, "but I should like now to drink a toast." He lifted his glass to Brat. "To Patrick, who has not only succeeded to his inheritance but has accepted its obligations."

"To Patrick!" they said. "To Patrick!"

"To Patrick!" said Jane, last.

He looked at her and found that she was smiling at him.

21

Simon took Mr. Sandal to the station in the afternoon, and when they had gone Bee said: "If you want to avoid the social life this afternoon I'll hold the fort for you. I have the books to do, anyhow. Perhaps you would like to take out one of the horses with Eleanor. She has gone back to the stables, I think."

There were few things in life that Brat would have liked so much as to go riding with Eleanor, but there was one thing that he wanted to do more. He wanted, on this day when Pat Ashby should have come into his inheritance, to walk over Tanbitches hill by the path that Pat had taken on the last day of his life.

"I want to go with Brat," Ruth said; and he noticed that Jane lingered to hear the result of this proposition, as if she too might have come. But Bee quashed the suggestion. Brat had had enough of his family for a little, she said.

"But he is going with Eleanor!" protested Ruth.

But Brat said no. He was going walking by himself.

He avoided the avenue, in case that he might meet visitors bound for the house, and went down through the paddocks to the road. In one of the paddocks that bordered the avenue Eleanor was lunging a bay colt. He stood under the trees and watched her; her unruffled patience, her mastery of the puzzled and resentful youngster; the way she managed, even at the end of a long rein, to reassure him. He wondered if that doctor fellow knew anything about horses.

The turf on Tanbitches delighted him. He had not had turf like that underfoot since he was a child. He walked slowly upward, smelling the grassy smell and watching the great cloud shadows flying before the wind. He bore away from the path towards the crown of beeches on the hill-top. If he went up there he would be able to see the whole slope of the countryside to the cliff edge; the country-side that Pat Ashby had shared with the larks.

As he came level with the green clump of bushes and young trees that marked the old quarry, he found an old man sitting in its shelter eating solid slabs of bread and jam, and gave him a greeting as he passed.

"Proud, a'nt yu!" said the old man tartly.

Brat swung on his heel and stared.

"Wonderful dentical and Frenchy furrin parts makes folks, surely."

He took another large bite and surveyed Brat from under the battered felt of his hat.

"Dunnamany nests you'd never seen but fur me."

"Abel!" said Brat.

"Well, that's summat," said the old man grudgingly.

"Abel!" said Brat, and sat down beside him. "Am I glad to see you!"

"Adone do!" Abel said to his dog, who came out from under the spread of his coat to sniff at the newcomer.

"Abel!" He could hardly believe that yesterday's occupant of a newspaper morgue was here in the flesh.

Abel began to exhibit signs of gratification at this undoubted enthusiasm for his society, and allowed that he had recognised him afar off. "Lame, are yu?"

"Just a bit."

"Bruck?"

"Yes."

"Weren't never one to make a pucker," Abel said, approving his laconic acceptance of bad luck.

Brat propped his back against the stout wooden fencing that kept the sheep from the quarry face, took out his cigarette case, and settled down for the afternoon.

In the hour that followed he learned a great deal about Pat Ashby, but nothing that helped to explain his suicide. Like everyone else, old Abel had been shocked and surprised by the boy's death, and now felt that his disbelief in a suicidal Patrick had been vindicated.

Patrick "weren't never one to make a pucker," no matter how "tedious bad" things were.

The old shepherd walked with him to the beeches, and Brat stayed there and watched man and dog grow small in the distance. Long after they were indistinguishable he stayed there, soothed by the loneliness and the great "hush" of the wind in the beech trees. Then he followed them down into the green plain until he came to the path, and let it lead him back over the hill to Clare.

As he came down the north slope to the road, a familiar "clink-clink" came up to him on the wind. For a moment he was back on the Wilson ranch, with the forge glowing in the thin mountain air and—what was her name?—Cora waiting for him beyond the barn when he was tidied up after supper. Then he remembered where the forge was: in that cottage at the foot of the hill. It was early yet. He would go and see what an English smithy looked like.

It looked very like the Wilson one, when at last he stood in the doorway, except that the roof was a good deal lower. The smith was alone, his mate being no doubt an employee and subject to a rationing of labour, and he was fashioning horse-shoes. He looked up as Brat darkened the doorway, and gave him a greeting without pausing in his work. Brat watched him for a little in a companionable quiet, and then moved over to work the bellows for him. The man looked up and smiled. He finished what he was doing at the moment and then said: "I didn't know you against the light. I'm unaccountable glad to see you in my place again, Mr. Patrick."

"Thanks, Mr. Pilbeam."

"You're a deal handier with that thing than you used to be."

"I've earned my living at it since I saw you last."

"You have? Well, I'll be——!" He took a half-made shoe red-hot from the furnace and was about to resume work when he changed his mind and held it out with a grin to Brat. Brat accepted the challenge and made a good job of it, Mr. Pilbeam acting as mate with critical approval.

"Funny," he said, as Brat plunged the shoe into the water, "if any Ashby was to earn his living at this job it ought to have been your brother."

"Why?"

"You never showed much interest."

"And did Simon?"

"There was a time when I couldn't keep him out of this place. There wasn't anything he wasn't going to make, from a candlestick to gates for the avenue at Latchetts. Far as I remember, all he ever made was a sheep-crook, and that not over-well. But he was always round the place. It was a craze of his for the whole of a summer."

"Which summer was that?"

"Summer you left us, it was. I'd misremember about it, only he was here seeing us put an iron on a cartwheel the day you ran away. I had to shoo him home for his supper."

Brat considered the shoe he had made, while Mr. Pilbeam made ready to call it a day.

"I ought to hang that up," Mr. Pilbeam said, nodding at Brat's handiwork, "and label it: Made by Patrick Ashby of Latchetts. And I couldn't make a better one myself," he added handsomely.

"Give it to old Abel to nail on his door."

"Bless you, old Abel wouldn't have cold iron on his threshold. Keep his visitors away."

"Oh. Friendly with 'them,' is he?"

"Do all his washing up and keep his house clean, if you'd believe all you hear."

"I wouldn't put it past him," Brat said. And set out for Latchetts.

So Simon had an alibi. Simon had been nowhere near the cliffs that afternoon. He had never been out of the Clare valley.

And so that was that.

On his way home up the ride between the paddocks he met Jane. Jane had every appearance of "hanging around," and he wondered if it was to intercept him that she lingered there. She was talking to Honey and her foal, and made no effort to efface herself as she had done hitherto at his approach.

"Hullo, Jane," he said, and joined in the intercourse with Honey to give her time. Her small pale face had flushed, and she was evidently struggling with a quite unusual emotion.

"It's about time we were going home to wash up," he suggested at last, as she seemed no nearer speech.

She dropped her hand from Honey's head and turned to face him, braced for effort.

"I wanted to say something to you. Do you mind?"

"Something you want me to do for you?"

"Oh, no. Nothing like that. It's just that I wasn't very nice to you when you came home from America, and I want to apologise."

"Oh, Jane," he said, wanting to take the small brave figure in his arms.

"It wasn't because I *wanted* to be horrid to you," she said, anxious that he should understand. "It was because—it was because——"

"I know why it was."

"Do you?"

"Yes, of course. It was a very natural thing to feel."

"Was it?"

"In fact, all things considered, it does you credit."

"Then you'll accept my apology?"

750

"I accept your apology," Brat said gravely, and they shook hands.

She did not immediately put her arm through his as Ruth would have done. She walked beside him in a grown-up fashion, talking politely about the chances of Honey's foal in the market, and what it should be called. The matter of the name was such an absorbing and exciting one that presently she forgot her self-consciousness, so that by the time they reached the house she was chattering unreservedly.

As they crossed the wide gravel sweep, Bee came to the door and stood there watching them come.

"You are going to be late for dinner, you two," she said.

22

So BRAT took possession of Latchetts and of everyone in it, with the exception of Simon.

He went to church on Sunday and submitted to being stared at for an hour and a half with time off for prayers. The only people not in Clare Church that morning were the Nonconformists and three children who had measles. Indeed, there were, as Bee pointed out, several members of the congregation whose normal place of Sunday worship was the blue brick barn at the other end of the village, and who had decided to put up with ritual and prelacy this once in order to share in the sensation of his appearance. As for the orthodox flock, there were individuals there, Bee said, who had not entered a church since their last child was christened. There was even Lana Adams who, as far as anyone knew, had not been in any church since her own baptism in the blue brick barn some twenty years ago.

Brat sat between Bee and Eleanor, and Simon on the other side of Bee. The twins were beyond Eleanor; Ruth wallowing in the drama and singing hymns loudly with a rapt expression, and Jane looking at the congregation with stony disapproval. Brat read the Ashby tablets over and over again, and listened to the Rector's unemphatic voice providing the inhabitants of Clare with their weekly ration of the abstract. The Rector did not preach, in the accepted

151

meaning of the term. He sounded as if he were arguing the matter out for himself; so that, if you shut your eyes, you could be in a chair at the other side of the Rectory fireplace listening to him talk. Brat thought of the fine variety of preachers who had come to take Sunday service at the orphanage: the shouters, the between-you-and-me-ers, the drama merchants who varied their tones and dropped their voices like amateur reciters, the hearties, the mincing aesthetes; and he thought that George Peck came very well out of the comparison. George Peck really did look as if he were not thinking about himself at all; as if he might conceivably have become a clergyman even if there had been no such inducement as public appearances in a pulpit.

After service Brat went to Sunday lunch at the Rectory, but not until he had run the gamut of village good wishes. Bee had come out of church at his side ready to pilot him through the ordeal, but she was accosted by Mrs. Gloom, and he was left defenceless. He looked in panic at the first of these unknowns bearing down on him: a big apple-cheeked woman with pink roses in a crinoline hat. How was he going to pretend to remember her? Or all the others who were obviously lingering?

"You remember Sarah Godwin, who used to come on washing days," a voice said, and there was Eleanor at his elbow. She moved him on from one group to another as expertly as a social secretary, briefing him quickly in a muttered phrase as each new face loomed up. "Harry Watts. Used to mend our bicycles." "Miss Marchant. Village school." "Mrs. Stapley. Midwife." "Tommy Fitt. Used to be the gardener's boy." "Mrs. Stack. Rural industries."

She saw him safely to the little iron gate that led into the Rectory garden, opened it, pushed him through, and said: "Now you're safe. That's 'coolee'."

"That's what?"

"Don't tell me you have forgotten that. In our hide-and-seek games a safe hide was always a 'coolee'."

Some day, Brat Farrar, he thought as he walked down the path to the Rectory, you are going to be faced with something that you *couldn't possibly* have forgotten.

At luncheon he and his host sat in relaxed silence while Nancy entertained them, and afterwards he walked in the garden with the Rector and answered his questions about the life he had been leading

152

these last eight years. One of George Peck's charms was that he listened to what was said to him.

On Monday he went to London and sat in a chair while rolls of cloth were exhibited several yards away from him, and were then brought forward to touching distance so that he might gauge the weight, texture, and wearing qualities of the cloth. He was fitted by Gore and Bowen, and measured by Walters, and assured by both that in record time he would have an outfit that no Englishman would blush to own. It was a revelation to him that shirts were made to measure. He had been pleased that he could present himself to the Ashby tailors in a suit as respect-worthy as that made for him by Mr. Sandal's tailor, and it was a shock to him to be sympathised with about the nice clean blue American shirt that he was wearing under it. However, when in Rome . . . So he was measured for shirts too.

He lunched with Mr. Sandal, who took him to meet the manager of his bank. He cashed a cheque at the bank, bought a registered envelope, and sent a fat wad of notes to Alec Loding. That had been the arrangement; "notes and no note," Loding had said. No telephones either. There must never be any communication between them again beyond the anonymous notes in the registered envelope.

This first payment to his partner in crime left a taste in his mouth that was not entirely due to the gum on the envelope that he had licked. He went and had a beer to wash it away, but it was still there. So he got on a 24 bus and went to have a look at his late lodgings in Pimlico, and immediately felt better.

He caught the 4.10 down, and Eleanor was waiting in the bug at Guessgate to meet him. His heart was no longer in his mouth, and Eleanor was no longer an abstraction and an enemy.

"It seemed a shame to let you wait for the bus when I was free to come to meet you," she said, and he got in beside her and she drove him home.

"Now you won't have to go away again for a long time," she said.

"No. Except for a fitting, and to the dentist."

"Yes; just up for the day. And perhaps Uncle Charles will expect someone to go up to meet him. But until then we can settle down and be quiet."

So he settled down.

He exercised the horses in the mornings, or schooled them over the jumps in the paddock. He rode out with Eleanor and the children from Clare Park; and so satisfied Antony Toselli's romantic soul that he arrived for his lesson one morning in a complete "child's riding outfit," to obtain which he had sent telegrams of a length and fluency that made history in the life of the Clare post office. He lunged the yearling for Eleanor, and watched while she taught a young thoroughbred from a racing stable to walk collected and carry his head like a gentleman. Nearly all his days were spent with Eleanor, and when they came in in the evenings it was to plan for to-morrow's task.

Bee watched this companionship with pleasure, but wished that Simon had more share in it. Simon found more and more excuses to be away from home from breakfast to dinner. He would school Timber or Scapa in the morning, and then find some excuse for going into Westover for lunch. Occasionally when he came home for dinner after being out all day Bee wondered whether he was quite sober. But except for the fact that he now took two drinks where once he would have taken one, he drank little at home, and so she decided that she must be mistaken. His alternate fits of moodiness and gaiety were nothing new: Simon had always been mercurial. She took it that his absence was his way of reducing the strain of a difficult situation, and hoped that presently he would make a third in the partnership that was blossoming so happily between Eleanor and Patrick.

"You'll have to do *something* at the Bures Show," Eleanor said one day as they came in tired from the stables. "Otherwise people will think it very odd."

"I could ride in a race, as Ruth suggested."

"But that is just fun. I mean, no one takes that seriously. You ought to show one of the horses. Your own riding things will be here in time, so there's no reason why you shouldn't."

"No."

"I'm getting to know that monosyllable of yours."

"It's no monopoly of mine."

"No. Just your speciality."

"What could I ride in the races?"

"Well, after Timber, Chevron is the fastest we have."

"But Chevron is Simon's."

"Oh, no. Chevron was bought by Bee with stable money. Have you ridden races at all?"

154

"Oh, yes. Often. Local ones, of course. For small stakes."

"Well, I think Bee plans to show Chevron as a hack, but that's no reason she shouldn't be entered for the races at the end of the day. She's very nervous and excitable, but she jumps clean and she's very fast."

They put the proposition to Bee at dinner, and Bee agreed to it. "What do you ride at, Brat?"

"Nine stone thirteen."

Bee looked at him reflectively as he ate his dinner. He was too fine-drawn. None of the Ashbys of the last two generations had run to weight, but there was a used-up look about the boy; especially at the end of the day. Presently, when the business of the celebration was all over, they must do something about his leg. Perhaps that accounted for the strung look that marked his spareness. Both physically and psychologically it must be a drag on him. She must ask Peter Spence about a good surgeon to consult.

Bee had been delighted to find that Brat had what Simon so conspicuously lacked: an interest in the genus horse in the abstract. Simon was knowledgeable about breeding in so far as it concerned his own particular interests, but his theoretical study of the matter was confined to *Racing Up to Date*. Brat, on the other hand, took to stud books as some people take to detection. She had gone in one evening to turn off a light that someone had evidently left on in the library, and found Brat poring over a stud book. He was trying to work back on Honey's pedigree, he said.

"You've got the wrong book," she said, and provided him with the right one. She was busy with some W.R.I. matter and so she left him to it and forgot him. But nearly two hours later she noticed the light still there and went in to find Brat surrounded by tomes of all kinds and so dead to the world that he did not hear her come in.

"It's fascinating, Bee," he said. He was mooning over a photograph of Bend Or, and had propped various other volumes open at photographs that gave him particular pleasure, so that the big table looked like some second-hand bookstall with the plates exhibited to entice the purchaser.

"You haven't got my favourite in your collection," she said, having examined his choice, and brought another tome from the shelves. And then, finding that he was totally ignorant, she took him back to the beginning and showed him the foundations—Arab, Barb, and Turk—of the finished product. By midnight there were more books on the floor than there were on the shelves but they had both had a marvellous time.

After that if Brat was missing from the normal orbit, one could always find him in the library, either working out something in a stud book or going slowly through the photographs of remarkable horses.

He sat openly at Gregg's feet, with the result that in a week Gregg was according him a respect that he had never paid to Simon. Bee noticed that where he addressed Simon as "Mr. Simon," Brat was "Mr. Patrick, sir." There was never any trace of the defensive attitude of a stud-groom faced with a newcomer who was also his master. Gregg recognised an enthusiast who did not think that he already knew it all, and so Brat was "Mr. Patrick, sir." Bee would smile as she passed the saddle room and heard the long monotone of Gregg's speech punctuated by Brat's monosyllables.

"Shoot him, I said, I'll do nothing of the kind, that horse'll walk out of here like a Christian inside a month, your blasted hounds can starve, I said, before they get their jaws on as good a piece of horseflesh as ever looked through a bridle, so what do you think I did?"

"What?"

Bee was humbly grateful to fate not only for her nephew's return but for the form in which he had returned. Rehearsing in her mind all the shapes that Patrick might have reappeared in, she was filled with wonder that the actual one should be so cut-to-measure, so according to her own prescription. Brat was what she would have indented for if she could have chosen. He was too silent, of course; too reticent. One felt at peace in his company without having any feeling of knowing him. But his unchanging front was surely easier to deal with than Simon's fluidity.

She wrote a long letter to Uncle Charles, to meet him at Marseilles, describing this new nephew to him, and saying all that could not be said in the initial cables. It would not impress Charles, of course, that Brat was useful with horses, since Charles loathed horses; which he held to be animals of an invincible stupidity, uncontrolled imagination, and faulty deduction. Indeed, Charles claimed that a three-months-old child not actually suffering from encephalitis or

156

other congenital incapacity was more capable of drawing a correct deduction than the most intelligent and most impeccably bred thoroughbred. Charles liked cats; and if ever against his better judgement he was lured within smell of a stable, he made friends with the stable cat and retired with it to some quiet corner until the process of horse exhibition was finished. He was rather like a cat himself; a large soft man with a soft round face that creased only sufficiently to hold an eyeglass; in either eye, according to which hand Charles had free at the moment. And although he was over six feet tall, he padded as lightly on his large feet as though he were partly filled with air.

Charles was devoted to his old home and to his family, but was fond of declaring himself a throw-back to a more virile age when a horse was simply a means of transport, capable of carrying a respectable weight, and it was not necessary for a man to develop bones that would disgrace a chicken so that brittle thoroughbreds should be induced to surmount unnecessary and unwarrantable obstacles.

A half-starved cat could out-jump any horse anyhow; and no one had to teach it to, either.

But his brother's grandchildren were the apple of his eye, and he loved every brittle bone of them. And it was to this Charles that Bee commended his new nephew.

"In the short two weeks that he has been here, he has passed from being a complete stranger to being so much part of Latchetts that one doesn't notice him. He has a peculiar trick of being part of the landscape, of course, but it is not just that he is self-effacing. It is that he has dropped into place. I notice that even the country people, to whom he ought still to be strange and a matter for sideways-looking, treat him as if he had been here all along. He is very silent, and rarely volunteers a remark, but his mind is extraordinarily alive, and his comment when he makes one would be blistering sometimes if it were not uttered so gently. He speaks very correct American—which, dear Uncle Charles, is very correct English with a flat A—and drawls a little. It is quite a different drawl from Simon's. I mean, from the drawl Simon uses when he drawls. It is not a comment; just a method of production.

"His greatest conquest was Jane, who resented his coming bitterly, on Simon's behalf. She made a wide sweep round him for days, and then capitulated. Ruth made a tremendous fuss of him, but got little encouragement—I think he felt her disloyalty to Simon—and she is now a little 'off' him.

"George Peck seems pleased with him, but I think finds it hard to forgive his silence all those years. I do too, of course. I find it inexplicable. One can only try to understand the immensity of the upheaval that sent him away from us.

"Simon has been beyond praise. He has taken his relegation to second place with a fortitude and a grace that is touching. I think he is very unhappy, and finds it difficult to join up this new Patrick with the old one. The greatest wrong Pat did in keeping silence was the wrong to Simon. I can only suppose that he intended never to come back at all. I have tried to sound him about it, but he is not an easy person to talk to. He was a reserved child and he is even more reserved to-day. Perhaps he will talk to you when you come.

"We are busy preparing for the Bures Show—which, you will be glad to hear, occurs at least three days before you are even due to arrive in England—and have hopes of a little successful publicity for Latchetts. We have three new horses that are well above average, and we are hoping that at least two of them are of Olympia standard. We shall see what their ring manners are like when we take them to Bures. Patrick has refused to take any part in this year's showings, leaving all the kudos to Simon and Eleanor—to whom, of course, it belongs. I think that, more than anything, describes this Patrick who has come home to us."

23

BECAUSE it was Simon who would show Timber and jump him, Brat left his schooling entirely to him, and shared his attentions between the other horses. But there were days, especially now that Simon absented himself more and more, when someone else had to exercise Timber, and Brat looked forward to those days more than he acknowledged even to himself. He liked most of the Latchetts horses, despised a few, and had an affection for the lively Chevron, the kind, sensible Scapa, and Eleanor's aged hack, Buster: a disillusioned but lovable old gentleman. But Timber was something else again. Timber was challenge, and excitement, and satisfaction; Timber was question and glory.

He planned to cure Timber of brushing people off his back, but he would do nothing yet a while. It was important, if he was going to be jumped at Bures, that nothing should be done to damage his self-confidence. Some day, if Brat had anything to do with it, Timber was going to feel very small indeed, but meanwhile let Simon have at his command every jot of that lordly assurance. So Brat exercised him mildly, and as he rode round the countryside kept his eyes open for a likely curing-place for Timber when the time came. The beeches on Tanbitches had no branches low enough for his purpose, and there was no room on that hill-top to get up the necessary speed. He wanted some open country with isolated or bunched trees with their lowest branches the right height from the ground to tempt Timber to his undoing. He remembered that Timber's most spectacular exploit had been in Lerridge Park and over there was Clare Park, with its surrounding stretch of turf and trees.

"Do the Clare Park people mind if we ride through the park?" he asked Eleanor one day when there was still seven days before the Bures Show.

Eleanor said no, provided they kept away from the playing fields. "They don't play anything because organised games are dreadful unless they are organised by Russians in Russia, but they keep the playing fields because they look well in the prospectus."

So Brat took Timber to the other side of the valley, and cantered him gently on the centuries-old turf of Clare Park, keeping well away from the trees. Then he walked him round the various clumps, gauging the height of the lowest limbs from the ground. The manoeuvre was received by Timber with a puzzled but passionate interest. One could almost see him trying to work it out. What was this for? What did the man come and look at large trees for? With a horse's abnormal memory, he was well aware that large trees were associated with private delights of his own, but, being a horse, he was also incapable of drawing any reasonable deduction from his rider's interest in the same kind of trees.

He walked up to each clump with a mannerly grace, until they approached the large oak which had been for five hundred years the pride of Clare Park. As they came within its flung shadow Timber

159

propped himself suddenly on his forelegs and snorted with fright. Brat was puzzled. What did he remember about the oak that would cause a reaction as strong as that? He looked at the ears that were sticking up as stiff as horns. Perhaps it wasn't a memory. Perhaps there was something in the grass.

"Do you always sneak up on girls under trees?" said a voice from the shadows, and from the grass there emerged the seal-like form of Miss Parslow. She propped herself on an elbow and surveyed the pair. Brat was a little surprised that she was alone. "Don't you ever ride anything but that black brute?"

Brat said that he did, quite often.

"I suppose it would be too much to expect that you were looking for me when you came over to the park to ride?"

Brat said that he was looking for a place to teach Timber manners.

"What's the matter with his manners?"

"He has a habit of diving suddenly under a tree so that he scrapes his rider off."

Miss Parslow propped herself a little farther up and looked with new interest at the horse. "You don't say! I never thought the brutes had that much sense. How are you going to stop him?"

"I'm going to make riding under trees a painful experience for him."

"You mean you'll beat him when he tries to do it?"

"Oh, no. That wouldn't do much good."

"After he has actually done it, then?"

"No. He mightn't associate the beating with a tree at all." He rubbed his whip up Timber's dark crest, and Timber bowed. "You'd be surprised at the odd things they associate."

"Nothing would surprise me to any extent about horses. How are you going to do it then?"

"Let him go full bat near a nice tempting tree, and when he swerves under it give him a cut on the belly that he'll remember all his life."

"Oh, no, that's too bad. The poor brute."

"It will be just too bad if I don't time my slip sideways on the saddle properly," Brat said dryly.

"And will that cure him?"

"I hope so. Next time he sees a likely tree he'll remember that it hurt like the blazes last time he tried it."

160

"But he'll hate you."

Brat smiled. "I'd be very surprised if he associated me with the business at all. I'd be surprised if he even associated it with the whip. Horses don't think like humans."

"What will he think hurt him, then?"

"The tree, more than likely."

"I always *thought* they were awfully silly animals."

It occurred to Brat that she had not made one of those riding parties on which he had accompanied Eleanor. Nor had he seen her about the stables lately. He asked how her riding was getting on.

"I've given it up."

"Altogether?"

"Uh-huh."

"But you were getting on well, weren't you? Eleanor said you had learned to bump."

"It was a very slithery bump, and it hurt me far more than it hurt the horse." She pulled a long grass and began to chew it, eyeing him with a sly amusement. "I don't have to hang around the stables any more. If I want to see Simon I know where to find him nowadays."

"Where?" said Brat before he could stop himself.

"The upstairs bar at the Angel."

"In Westover? But are you allowed to go to Westover when you like?"

"I'm attending a Westover dentist." She giggled. "Or rather, I was. The school made the first appointment for me, of course, but after that I just told them when I had to go next. I've reckoned that I have about thirty teeth, which should last me till the end of term quite nicely." She opened her red mouth wide and laughed. They were excellent teeth. "That's what I'm doing at the moment. Putting off time till the Westover bus is due. I could have gone with the earlier one but there is a very good-looking conductor on this one. He's got the length of asking me to the pictures one night next week. If Simon was going on the way he has been all those months, not knowing I'm alive, I'd maybe have done something about the conductor boy—he has lashes about an inch long—but now that Simon has stopped looking down his nose I think I'll give the conductor boy a miss." She chewed the stalk provocatively. "Got quite matey, Simon has."

"Oh."

"Have you been seducing the Gates girl from him, like I suggested?"

"I have not."

"That's funny. He's distinctly off her. And he's not awfully enamoured of you, if it comes to that. So I thought you'd been cutting him out with that Peggy woman. But I suppose it's just that you cut him out of Latchetts."

"You're going to miss your bus, aren't you?"

"You can be just as squashing as Simon, in your own way."

"I was only pointing out that the bus is almost at the smithy. It will be at the Park gates in——"

"What!" she shrieked, exploding to her feet in one enormous convulsion, so that Timber whirled in alarm from the wild eruption. "Oh, great heavens! Oh, for the love of . . .! Oh! Oh!"

She fled down the park to the avenue gates, screaming her distress as she went. Brat watched the green bus skim along the road past the white gates of Latchetts and slow down as it came to the gates of Clare Park. She was going to catch it after all, and her day would not be wasted. She would find Simon. At the Angel. In the upstairs bar.

That Simon should spend his time in Westover in the Angel bar was distressing but not, in the circumstances, surprising. What was surprising was the emergence of a Simon who was "matey" with Sheila Parslow. In Simon's eyes the Parslow girl had always been something beneath contempt; a lower form of life. He dismissed her with a gibe when her name was mentioned and in her presence was, as she had said herself, unaware that she was alive. What had happened to Simon that he was not only resigned to her companionship, but was "matey"? The girl was not lying about it. If her glowing self-satisfaction was not sufficient evidence, there was the obvious fact that Simon could avoid her by changing his drinking place. There was no lack of pubs in Westover; most of them more exclusively masculine haunts than the very social and female-ridden Angel.

Brat tried to imagine Simon with Sheila Parslow and failed.

What had come over Simon—the fastidious, critical Simon—that he found it possible to endure her? To spend hours in her company?

Was it a sort of "larning" his family for the disappointment he had been caused? A sort of you-don't-like-me-therefore-I'll-take-up-with-Sheila-Parslow? A sorry-when-I'm-dead reaction? There was a very childish side to Simon.

There was also, Brat thought from all he had heard, a very practical

162

side, and Sheila Parslow had money, and Simon needed it. But somehow Brat could not believe that Simon, even in his most deplorable moments, would ever consider pawning his life to a nymphomaniacal moron.

As he walked Timber home he considered yet once more the general oddity of Simon, but as usual came to no conclusion.

He handed Timber over to Arthur to be rubbed down, and went down with Eleanor to inspect Regina's new foal.

"She's an old marvel, isn't she," Eleanor said, watching the new arrival stagger about on its out-of-proportion legs. "It's another good one. Not much wonder that she looks complacent. People have been coming to admire her foals for practically a lifetime, the old duchess. I think foals to her are just a means of achieving this annual homage. She doesn't care a rap about the foal."

"It's not any better than Honey's," Brat said, looking at the foal without enthusiasm.

"You and your Honey!"

"And you wait and see what Honey will produce next year with this new mating. A foal that will make history."

"Your enthusiasm for Honey borders on the indecent."

"You heard Bee say that."

"How do you know?"

"I heard her too."

They laughed a little, and she said: "It's so nice to have you here, Brat." He noticed that she did not say: It is so nice to have you back, Patrick; but he realised that she herself was unaware of any oddity in the form she used.

"Is that doctor chap going over to Bures for the show?"

"I shouldn't think so. He's much too busy. What made you think of him?"

Brat did not know.

They pottered round the paddocks for so long that they came in for tea very late, and had it by themselves. Jane was pounding her way through a Chopin valse with conscientious accuracy, and stopped with undisguised relief when they came in.

"Could I say twenty-five minutes was half an hour, Eleanor?" she asked. "It's twenty-five-and-a-half minutes, really."

"You can say anything you like as long as we don't have to listen to that valse while we eat."

So Jane slid off the piano-stool, removed the glasses that gave her such an owl-like look, pushed them into her breeches pocket, and disappeared thankfully into the out-of-doors.

"Ruth puts in all the tiddley bits and the expression and doesn't mind how many wrong notes she strikes, but with Jane it is accuracy or nothing. I don't know which Chopin would have hated more," Eleanor said, folding bread and butter into a thickness that would match her appetite.

Brat watched her pour the tea with a delight in her clean un-hurried movements. Some day the foundation of the life he was living here would give way; Simon would achieve the plan he was devising to undo him, or some incautious word of his own would bring the whole structure crashing down; and then there would be no more Eleanor.

It was not the least of his fears for the future.

They ate in a friendly silence, dropping unrelated remarks into the quiet as they happened to occur to them.

Presently Eleanor said: "Did you ask Bee about colours for the race next week?"

Brat said that he had forgotten.

"Let's go and look them out now. They are in that locker in the saddle room."

So they went back to the stables. The saddle room was empty; Gregg had gone home to his supper; but Eleanor knew where the key was.

"They are practically in ribbons, they are so old," she said as she spread the colours on the table. "They were actually made for Father, and then they were taken in a bit for Simon to wear at point-to-points when he was narrower than he is now. And then let out again when he grew. So they are just hanging together. Perhaps now we'll be able to afford——" She pulled herself up.

"Yes. We'll have a new set."

"I think violet and primrose are nice colours, don't you; but they do fade an unattractive shade. Simon goes blue with cold in the winter, and he says the colours were designed to tone with his face."

They rummaged in the chest, turning up souvenirs of old races. They moved round the saddle room studying the long row of ribbon rosettes, each with its tab under it telling where and how it had been won.

At last Eleanor shut the chest, saying: "It is time we got ready

164

for dinner." She locked the chest and hung up the key. "We'll take the colours with us. I expect they'll fit you all right, since Simon was the last to wear them. But they'll have to be pressed."

She took the colours in her arms, and together they walked out of the saddle-room door and came face to face with Simon.

"Oh, you're back, Simon," Eleanor was beginning, when she caught sight of his face.

"*Who had Timber out?*" he said, furious.

"I had," Brat said.

"Timber is my business and you have no right to have him out when my back is turned."

"Someone had to exercise him to-day," Brat said mildly.

"*No one* exercises Timber but me. *No one.* If I'm going to be responsible for jumping him, then I say when he is to be exercised, and *I* do the exercising."

"But, Simon," Eleanor said, "that is absurd. There are——"

"Shut up!" he said, through his teeth.

"I will *not* shut up! The horses are Brat's, and if anyone says who does what, and when, then it is——"

"Shut up, I tell you. I won't have a ham-handed lout from the backwoods ruining a good piece of horseflesh like Timber."

"Simon! *Really!*"

"Coming from nowhere and interfering in the stables as if he had lived here all his life!"

"You must be drunk, Simon, to talk like that about your own brother."

"My brother! *That!* Why, you poor little fool, he isn't even an Ashby. God knows what he is. Somebody's groom, I have no doubt. And that is what he should be doing. Sweeping out stables. Not lording it round the countryside on my best horses. After this, you damned little upstart, you leave the horses I intend to ride in their stable unless I say they are to be taken out, and if I say they are to be taken out it is not you who will ride them. We have plenty of other stablemen."

His chin was sticking out about two feet from Brat's face, and Brat could have brought one from the ground that would have lifted him half over the saddle room. He longed to do it, but not with Eleanor there. And not now, perhaps. Better not do anything that he could not foresee the consequences of.

165

"Well? Did you hear me?" shouted Simon, maddened by his silence.

"I heard you," Brat said.

"Well, see that you remember what I said. Timber is my business, and you don't put a leg across him again until I say so."

And he flung away from them towards the house.

Eleanor looked stricken.

"Oh, Brat, I'm sorry. I'm so sorry. He had that mad notion about your not being Patrick before he ever saw you, and now that he has been drinking I suppose it came from the back of his mind and he said it because he was angry. He always did say a lot of things he didn't mean when he was in a temper, you know."

It was Brat's experience that, on the contrary, it was only when a person was in a temper that they said exactly what they did mean. But he refrained from telling Eleanor that.

"He *has* been drinking, you know," she went on. "I know he doesn't look as if he has, but I can tell from his eyes. And he would never have behaved like that when he was sober, even in a temper. I do apologise for him."

Brat said that everyone made a fool of themselves some time or other when they had "drink taken," and she was not to bother about it.

They followed Simon to the house soberly, the happiness of their long afternoon together vanished as if it had not been.

As he changed into what he still thought of as "his good suit" Brat thought that if the cracks that were showing in Simon widened sufficiently he might one day show his hand, and he would find out what Simon's plans for him were. He wondered if Simon would be sober enough to behave normally at dinner.

But there was no Simon at dinner, and when Eleanor asked where he was, Bee said that he had gone over to the pub at Guessgate to meet a friend who was staying there. Someone had telephoned just before dinner, it appeared.

Bee looked equable, and Brat decided that Simon had seemed normal to her and that she had believed his story of the friend staying the night at the Guessgate inn.

And in the morning Simon came down to breakfast his usual sunny self.

166

"I'm afraid I was tight last night," he said. "And very objectionable, I'm afraid. I apologise unreservedly."

He regarded Brat and Eleanor, the only other people at the table, with friendly confidence. "I ought never to drink gin," he said. "It obscures the judgement and destroys the soul."

"You were quite horrible," Eleanor said coldly.

But the atmosphere cleared, and the day was just another day. Bee came in from out-of-doors for her second cup of coffee; Jane arrived clutching to her stomach the bowl of porridge which she had fetched from the kitchen for herself, according to Latchetts routine; Ruth came flying in very late with a "diamond" clasp in her hair and was sent back to take the thing off.

"Where did she get that loathsome object," Bee said, when Ruth had disappeared with wild cries that Bee was going to make her late for lessons.

"She bought it at Woolworth's last time we were in Westover," Jane said. "They're not real diamonds, you know, but it seemed a bargain for one-and-sixpence."

"Why didn't you buy one then, Jane?" Bee asked, looking at the aged kirby-grip that kept Jane's hair off her face.

"Oh, I don't think I'm the diamond type," Jane said.

So the Ashby household settled back to its normal placidity, and to its preparations for that day at Bures that was to alter all their lives.

24

BURES was a little market town, set north of Westover and almost in the middle of the county. It was like almost every other little market town in the south of England, except perhaps that it stood in slightly richer and more unspoiled country than most. For which reason the Bures Agricultural Show, although a small country affair, had a standing and reputation considerably greater than its size alone would warrant. Every year animals would appear at the Bures Show on their way to more mature triumphs elsewhere, and it was common for someone, watching an exhibit at one of the great shows, to say: "I remember that when it was a novice at Bures three years ago."

It was a pleasant, civilised little town, with a minister, some fine old inns, a High Street both broad and gay, and no self-consciousness whatsoever. The farmers who brought their wares to its markets would have annoyed Mr. Macallan exceedingly by their content with their lot, and their evident unawareness that there were other worlds to conquer. An air of well-being came off the Bures pavements like reflected sunlight. Bad years there might be, for both tradespeople and farmers, but that was a risk that was incidental in a life that was satisfying and good.

The annual show, in the early summer, was a social reunion as well as a business affair, and the day ended with a "ball" in the assembly room of the Chequers, at which farmers' wives who hadn't seen each other since New Year swopped gossip, and young blades who had not met since the Combined Hunts Ball swopped horses. The combined hunts, between them, embraced the town; the Lerridge to the south and the Kenley Vale to the north; and did much to ensure that the horses exhibited at Bures should be worth more than a passing glance. And since almost every farmer well enough off to own both a horse and a tractor belonged to one or other of the hunts, there was never any lack of competition.

In the early days of the show, when transport was still by horse and slow, it was the custom to stay overnight at Bures; and the Chequers, the Rose and Crown, the Wellington, and the Kenley Arms packed them in three to a bed. But with the coming of the motor all that changed. It was more fun to go home nine-to-a-car in the summer dawn than to sleep three-to-a-bed in the Wellington. It was not always a successful method of getting home, of course, and more than one young farmer had spent his summer months in hospital after the Bures Show, but to the younger generation it was inconceivable that they should sleep in an inn when their home was less than forty miles away. So only the older exhibitors, who clung to tradition, or those who lived at an inconvenient distance from Bures, or could not, owing to difficult communications, get their animals away on the evening of the show, still stayed overnight at Bures. And of these most stayed at the Chequers.

The Ashbys had had the same bedrooms at the Chequers for the

168

night of the Bures Show since the days of William Ashby the Seventh: he who had joined the Westover Fencibles to resist the expected invasion of Napoleon the First. They were not the best bedrooms, because in those days the best bedrooms went to the Ledinghams of Clare, who also, of course, had a yearly reservation for the night of the show. What the Ledinghams left went to the Shirleys of Penbury and the Hallands of Hallands House. The Hallands, on whose lands on the outskirts of the town the show was held, had used the bedrooms only for their overflow of guests, but a Hallands guest rated a great deal higher, of course, than any Ashby in the flesh.

Penbury was now the possession of the nation in the shape of the National Trust; a shillingsworth of uplift for coachloads who didn't know Gibbons from Adam and wanted their tea. Hallands House was also the possession of the nation, in the shape of a Government department. No one quite knew what this alien community did. Mrs. Thrale, who ran the Singing Kettle tea-rooms out on the Westover road, once boldly asked a young Government employee who was drinking her coffee what her task was at the moment, and was told that it was "arranging the translation of *Tom Jones* into Turkish"; but this was held to be merely a misunderstanding on Mrs. Thrale's part, and no one had the heart to question the aliens further. They kept themselves to themselves very determinedly, and it was no longer possible for the people of Bures to walk through Hallands Park.

It would have been possible long ago for the Ashbys on their annual visit to have some of the finer bedrooms at the Chequers, but no such idea ever crossed an Ashby mind. The difference between Number 3 and Number 17 was not that one was a fine room with a pleasant outlook and good furniture and the other a back room looking on to the roof of the assembly room, but that one wasn't "their" room and the other was. So they still had the three little rooms in the older wing, which, since the bathroom had been added at the end of the passage, made it practically an Ashby apartment.

Gregg took the horses over to Bures on Tuesday evening. Arthur followed on Wednesday morning with the ponies and Eleanor's hack, Buster, who hated any box but his own, and was liable to kick a strange stable to pieces. Simon and the twins went in the car with Bee; and Brat shared the bug with Eleanor and Tony Toselli, who had insisted on being allowed to compete in the Best Child Rider class. ("My father will commit suicide if I am not allowed to try.")

169

Brat wished that this tadpole creature was not sitting between himself and Eleanor. The feeling that his time with Eleanor was short was constantly with him, making each indifferent moment a matter of consequence. But Eleanor seemed happy enough to feel charitable even to Tony Toselli.

"It's going to be perfect weather," she said, looking at the high arch of the sky with no cloud in it. "I can remember only one real soaker at Bures and that's years ago. They've always been awfully lucky. Did I put my string gloves in the locker?"

"Yes."

"What are you going to do all the morning? Look at Mrs. Godwin's jam exhibit?"

"I'm going to walk the course."

"Canny Brat," she said, approving. "How right you are."

"The other fellows probably know every inch of it."

"Oh, yes. For most of them it is an annual. In fact, if you started the horses off they'd probably go round by themselves, they are so used to it. Did Bee remember to give you your stand ticket?"

"Yes."

"And have you got it with you?"

"I have."

"I sound a fusser this morning, don't I? You are a nice reassuring person to be with. Do you never get excited, Brat?"

"Oh, yes."

"Inside-churning excited?"

"Inside turning over and over."

"That's interesting. It just doesn't show, I suppose."

"I suppose not."

"It's an extraordinarily useful sort of face to have. Mine goes a dull unhealthy pink, as you can see."

He thought the warm childish flush on her normally cool features touching and endearing.

"I hear that Peggy Gates has a new outfit for the occasion. Have you ever seen her on a horse? I can't remember."

"No."

"She looks nice," Eleanor said approvingly. "She rides very well. I think she will do justice to that horse of Dick Pope's."

It was typical of Eleanor that her judgement was independent of her emotions.

The High Street of Bures glittered in the low morning sunlight. Large Motoring Association signs encouraged the traveller, and fluttering advertisements cajoled him. "Carr's Meal for Calves," said a banner. "Saffo, the Safe Disinfectant!" screamed a chimney-to-chimney pendant. "Pett's Dip," said a placard quietly, taking it for granted that the Dip was sufficiently famous to explain itself.

In the dim hall of the Chequers Bee was waiting for them. Simon had gone round to the stables, she said.

"The rooms are Numbers 17, 18, and 19, Brat. You are sharing 17 with Simon, Nell and I have 18, and the twins are in the connecting one, 19."

Sharing a room with Simon was something he had not reckoned with, but there was nothing he could do about it. He picked up Eleanor's bag and his own and went upstairs with them, since the hall was a flurry of arriving guests. Eleanor came with him and showed him where the rooms were.

"The first time I came here and was allowed to stay the night I thought life had nothing left to offer," she said. "Put it down there, Brat, thank you, and I'll unpack it at once or my frock will be ruined."

In Number 17 Simon's things were already strewn all over the room, including the second bed. It was odd how these inanimate belongings of Simon's had, even in his absence, a kind of arrogance.

Brat cleared his own bed and unpacked, hanging his new evening things carefully in the still empty wardrobe. To-night for the first time in his life he would wear evening clothes.

"In case you get lost, Brat," Bee said to him when he came down, "lunch is at twelve-thirty in the luncheon tent. The last table to your left as you come in. What do you plan to do this morning? Poke the pigs?"

"No, he is going to walk the course," Eleanor said.

"All right. Don't stray off it into any Government holy-of-holies and get yourself arrested, will you?"

Tony was handed over to Mrs. Stack, who, being interested solely in rural industries, represented a Fixed Point in the flux of an agricultural show.

"If he tells you that his father is dying and he is urgently wanted at home, don't believe him," Eleanor said.

"Is his father ill, then?"

171

"No, but Tony may grow bored before half-past twelve. I'll come and fetch him for lunch."

Brat walked into the High Street of Bures with a feeling of escape. For the first time for nearly a month he was his own master, free to be himself. He had forgotten what it was like to walk about without care. For nearly three hours he could go where he liked, ask what he wanted, and answer without a curb on his tongue.

"Hallands Park," said the direction sign on a bus, so he got on the bus and went there. He had never been to a country show before, and he went round the exhibits with an interest that was at once fresh and critical, comparing all he saw with similar things seen elsewhere. Homespuns in Arizona, farm implements in Normandy, rams in Zacatecas, Herefords after American air, pottery in New Mexico. Occasionally someone looked at him curiously, and more than one hand was half lifted in salutation only to fall again. He was too like an Ashby ever to be completely free in Bures. But, speaking generally, people were too absorbed in the exhibits and in their own cares at that hour of the morning to take much interest in the passer-by.

Having exhausted the exhibition, he walked out into the park, where the red flags marked out the temporary race-course. It was a straight, fast-galloping course over hurdles for the first half-mile through the park, then it went out into the country in a wide curve of a mile or more, came back to the park about half a mile from the stands, and from then on was another series of hurdles up to the finish in front of the stands. Except for the sharp turns and a few very blind fences in the country, it was not a difficult course. The hurdles in the park stretches were regulation racing ones, and the turf was wonderful. Brat's heart lifted.

It was very peaceful out there in the country, and he came back to the show with a sense of reluctance. But he was surprised to find how glad he was to see the familiar faces round the table in the luncheon tent when he got there; how glad he was to sink into the place kept for him, and be part of this family again.

People came up to their table to welcome him back to Bures Show, to England. People who had known Bill and Nora Ashby, and Bill's father before him. None of them expected him to remember them, and he had merely to be polite.

172

25

"I THINK I'm going to be sick," Ruth said, when she and Brat were left alone in the stand.

"I don't wonder," said Brat.

"Why?" she was surprised into saying, this being not at all the reaction she expected.

"Three ices on top of dressed crab."

"It is not anything I *ate*," she said, repressive. "It's that I have a delicate nervous system. Excitement makes me feel ill. I get sick with it."

"I should go and get it over," Brat advised.

"Be sick, you mean!"

"Yes. It's a wonderful feeling."

"If I sit very still I may feel better," Ruth said, giving up.

Ruth was feeling her lack of importance to-day. She avoided horses too consistently for the rest of the year to claim any right to exhibit any on this one day at Bures, so she sat in the stand in her neat grey flannel and looked on. It was to her credit that she did not grudge her twin her well-earned place in the sun, and was passionately anxious that Jane should come first in her class.

"There's Roger Clint with Eleanor."

Brat looked for the couple and found them.

"Who is Roger Clint?"

"He has a big farm near here."

Roger Clint was a black-browed young man, and he was being old-friendly with Eleanor.

"He's in love with Eleanor," said Ruth, having failed with one try for drama.

"A very good person to be in love with," Brat said, but his heart contracted.

"It would be a very good thing if she married him. He has lots of money and a lovely big house and simply scads of horses."

Against his will Brat asked if Eleanor were thinking of it.

173

Ruth considered the pros and cons of this as they fitted into her dramatic framework.

"She is making him serve his seven years for her. You know: like Jacob. He is simply frantic about it, poor Roger, but she is La Belle Dame Sans Merci."

La Belle Dame Sans Merci bade Mr. Clint a temporary farewell and came up to join them in the stands as the Novices under Ten filed into the ring.

"Do you know that Tony scraped into this by the skin of his teeth," she said, sitting down by Brat. "He is going to be ten the day after to-morrow."

There were eleven novices, the youngest being a fat child of four in a black velvet jockey cap, who bounced about on a solid pony of which she had no control whatever.

"Well, at least Tony never looked as awful as that, even in his bad days," Eleanor said.

"Tony looks wonderful," Ruth said, and Tony did indeed look wonderful. As Eleanor had said on an earlier occasion, Tony had the root of the matter in him.

The novices walked, and trotted, and cantered, under the lenient eye of the judges, and presently the seeding began. Even from the stand the fanatic determination in Tony's snail-black eyes was plain to see. He was going to be in the money or die in the attempt. From being six possibles they were narrowed down to four, but these four kept the judges puzzled. Again and again they were sent out to canter and brought back for inspection, and sent out to canter again. There were only three prizes and one must go.

It was at this stage that Tony played what he evidently considered his ace. As he cantered along in front of the stand he got to his knees in the saddle and with a slight scramble stood up in it, straight and proud.

"Oh, God," said Eleanor reverently and with feeling.

A ripple of laughter went through the stand. But Tony had another shot in his locker. He slipped to his knees, grabbed the front edge of the saddle, and stood on his head, his thin spider-legs waving rather uncertainly in the air.

At that a gale of laughter and applause broke out, and Tony, much gratified, resumed his seat and urged his astonished pony, who had slowed to a trot, into a canter again.

174

That of course settled the matter very nicely for the judges, and Tony had the mortification of seeing the three rosettes handed to his rivals. But his mortification was nothing to the mortification he had already inflicted on his preceptress.

"I hope I don't see that child until I cool off," she said, "or I am liable to take an axe to him."

But Tony, having handed his pony over to Arthur, came blithely to the stands to find her.

"Tony, you little *idiot*," she said, "what made you do a thing like that?"

"I wanted to show how I could ride, Eleanor."

"And where did you learn to do those circus tricks?"

"I practised on the pony that mows the lawn. At school, you know. He has a much broader back than Muffet, and that's why I wasn't so steady to-day. I don't think these people appreciate good riding," he added, nodding his head at the offending judges.

Eleanor was speechless.

Brat presented him with a coin and told him to go and buy himself an ice.

"If I didn't want to see Jane ride," Eleanor said, "I would go and bury my shame in the ladies' room. I'm *curdled* with humiliation."

Jane, on Rajah, in her best riding things, was a pleasant sight. Brat had never seen her in anything but the shabby jodhpurs and shapeless jersey that she wore at home, and was surprised by this trim little figure.

"Jane has the best seat of all the Ashbys," Eleanor said affectionately, watching the serious and efficient Jane making Rajah change his leg to order. "That is her only rival: that tall girl on the grey."

The tall girl was fifteen and the grey very handsome, but the judges preferred Jane and Rajah. Jane might have lost for all the emotion she showed, but Ruth was rapturous.

"Good old Jane," Simon said, appearing beside them. "A veteran at nine."

"Oh, Simon, did you *see!*" Eleanor said, in agony again as she remembered.

"Cheer up, Nell," he said, dropping a commiserating hand on her shoulder. "It might have been worse."

"How *could* it be worse?"

"He didn't yodel," Simon said.

At that she began to laugh, and went on laughing. "Oh, I suppose it is very funny," she said, wiping her eyes, "and I expect I shall laugh over it for years, but at the moment I just wish I could be in Australia for the rest of the afternoon."

"Come on, Nell," he said. "It's time to collect the horses," and they went away together as Jane came to sit in the stand.

"This is the exciting class coming now. It isn't very much to win a Fifteen and Under," was her answer to Brat's congratulations. "Some day I'll be down there with *them*. With Aunt Bee, and Eleanor, and Simon, and Peggy, and Roger Clint, and all of them."

Yes, there was Roger Clint. Eleanor was riding the long-backed bay mare Scapa, and Roger Clint was standing next to her on a chestnut with four of the longest and whitest stockings Brat had ever seen. While the judges walked down the row he and Eleanor talked quietly together.

"Who do you think will be first?" Jane asked.

Brat took his eyes from Eleanor and Clint and forced himself to consider the entry. The judge had sent Bee out to canter Chevron, the chestnut he was going to race this afternoon, and she was coming down in front of the stands now. He had never seen Bee in formal riding clothes, and was surprised again, as he had been with Jane. It was a new, serious, rather intimidating Bee.

"Who do you think, Brat?" Jane said again.

"Timber, of course."

"Not Peggy's horse? The one Dick Pope had?"

"Riding Light? No. He may win the jumping, but not this."

And he was right. This was the judges' first sight of Timber and they were too much impressed to be seduced even by the looks and reputation of Riding Light.

And it was a popular verdict. As Simon cantered Timber down in front of the stands after accepting the rosette the applause broke into cheering.

"Isn't that the brute that killed old Felix?" a voice behind said. "They ought to shoot it instead of giving it prizes."

Second was Peggy on Riding Light, looking flushed and pleased; her father's extravagance had been justified. Third, rather unexpectedly, was Bee on Chevron.

"The Ashbys cleaning up as usual," the voice said, and was instantly shushed, and the proximity of the Ashbys presumably indicated.

It was when the Open Jumping Class began that the real excitement of the day was reached, and Bee came to sit in the stand and share it with them.

"Number One, please," said the loud-speaker, and Eleanor came into the ring on Scapa. Scapa was a careful and unemotional jumper, but could never be persuaded into standing away from her fences. By dint of patient schooling with a guard rail, Eleanor hoped that she had now persuaded her into better ways. And for half a round it worked, until Scapa noticed that there was no plaguey obstruction to beware of at the foot of these jumps, and began to go close in again, with the inevitable result. Nothing Eleanor could do would make her take off in time. She jumped "fit to hit the moon," but came down in the wrong place, and the little battens of white-painted wood came down with her.

"Poor Nell," said Bee. "After all her schooling."

Number Two and Number Three did not appear to have been schooled at all.

"Number Four, please," said the loud-speaker, and Riding Light appeared. Peggy's "new outfit" consisted of a dark snuff-coloured coat a little too tight in the waist, and a pair of buff breeches a little too pale in the buff, but she looked well on the brown horse and handled him beautifully. Or rather, she sat still and let Riding Light do his stuff. He was a finished jumper who took the obstacles in his stride, propelling himself into the air in a long effortless curve and tucking his hind feet after him like a cat. He went out having done a perfect round.

"Number Five, please," said the loud-speaker.

Number Five was Roger Clint's mount with the long white stockings. "Do you know what he calls it?" Bee said. "Operation Stockings."

"It's very ugly," Brat said. "Looks as if he had walked through a trough of whitewash."

"He can jump, though."

He could certainly jump, but he had phobia about water.

"Poor Roger," laughed Bee, watching Stockings refuse the water. "He has been jumping him backwards and forwards across the duck pond at home in the hope of curing him, and now he does this!"

177

Stockings continued to refuse, and Clint had to take him out, in a burst of sympathetic applause.

Numbers Six and Seven had one fault each.

Number Eight was Simon on Timber.

The black horse came into the ring exactly as he had come out of his box on the day Brat first saw him, pleased with himself and ready for homage. His excited, flickering ears pricked into attention as he caught sight of the jumps. Simon took him into a canter and moved down to the first one. Even from where he was sitting, Brat could feel the smoothness of that action. The smoothness that had astonished him that first day at Latchetts when he had ridden on the top of the down. Smoothly the black horse rose into the air and came down on the far side of the jump, and a murmur of admiration came from the crowd at the almost feline beauty of it. Brat, with the most wholehearted respect, watched Simon's body swing with the black horse's rise and fall as though he were part of it. It was right that Simon should ride it. He would never attain that perfection if he lived to be a hundred. A great silence settled on the crowd as one by one the jumps fled away behind Timber. It would be monstrous if this beauty were to fail or be faulted. It was so quiet when he faced the water jump that the voice of a paper-seller far away at the main gate was the only sound to be heard. And when he landed smoothly and neatly on the far bank, a great sigh went up from them. They had seen a perfect thing. They had not been cheated of it after all.

So moved were they that Simon was almost out of the ring before the applause broke out.

The last three entries had been scratched, and Simon was the final performer, so the second round began as soon as he had left.

Eleanor came back on Scapa, and by dint of voice and spur managed to make the unwilling mare take off at the proper place, and so did something to retrieve her self-respect. The crowd, appreciating what had been wrong in the first place and what she had now suc-ceeded in doing, gave her credit for it.

Number Two did a wild but lucky round, and Number Three a wild and unlucky one; and then came Peggy again, still flushed from the pleasure of her perfect round.

Again she had the sense to sit still while Riding Light heaved her into the air with the thrust of his tremendous quarters, sailed

178

over the jump, and made for the next one with his ears erect and confident. It seemed that there was nothing to hinder the brown horse doing this all day. There was an air of routine about the business that somehow detracted from his performance; he made it look too easy. There seemed little doubt that he would do another perfect round. His judgement of distance was faultless. He never had to stop and put in a short one to bring him to the proper taking-off point; he arrived at the taking-off point by some computing of his own, taking the jumps in his stride as if they were hurdles. He was coming up to the wall now, and they waited to see if he would treat that, too, like a hurdle.

"Thump! Thump! Thump!" said the drum of the Bures Silver Band, as the preliminary to *Colonel Bogey* and their entry into the front gate of the show for their afternoon performance. Riding Light's ears flickered in question, in doubt. His mind was distracted from that rapidly nearing wall. His ears shot forward again in alarm as he saw it almost upon him. He shortened his stride, trying to fit it into the remaining space, but he had misjudged it. He rose at it with determination and landed on the other side, flinging his quarters upwards in a successful effort to avoid hitting the fence that was now too close under him. But the shoe of his near fore had touched the wall as he rose to it, and a billet slid out of place, wavered a moment on the edge, and then dropped to the ground.

"A-a-ah!" said the crowd in quick sympathy, and Peggy looked back to see what had happened. She saw the little gap in the top of the wall, but it did not rattle her. She collected Riding Light, patted him encouragingly on the neck, and headed him for the next.

"Good girl, Peggy!" murmured Bee.

The distant band was now playing *Colonel Bogey*, and Riding Light took no further notice of it; he knew all about bands. Bands had been the accompaniment to some of his best performances. He settled down again to his routine, and finished by taking the water jump with a margin that made the crowd gasp.

"Simon will never beat that," Bee said. "That perfect round of Timber's was a miracle in the first place."

The four long stockings of Roger Clint's mount flashed round the ring in a brisk and willing fashion until they came to the water. Faced with the long distance to the last jump, Stockings stopped and

179

pondered. Clint argued amiably with him, but Stockings would have none of it. "I know what is behind that hedge quite well, and I *don't like* it!" he seemed to be saying. And then, with that perennial unreasonableness of horses, he decided to have a go at it. Of his own accord he turned towards the jump and began to canter. Roger sat down and drove him at it, and Stockings went flying down to it with purpose in every line of him. In the last half-second he changed his mind just as suddenly as he had made it up, stuck both toes in hard, and skidded to a stop up against the fence.

The crowd laughed, and so did Roger Clint. He hauled himself back into the saddle from his position round his mount's neck. He took Stockings round to the other side of the fence and showed him the water. He took him up to it and let him inspect it at close quarters. He walked him round it and let him look at the other edge. And then he took him back to the far end of the ring and turned him to the jump. With an air of "Oh, well, let's get this thing over with" Stockings jumped off his haunches, tore down the ring, and fled over the water with a yard or two to spare.

The crowd laughed delightedly, and the white teeth showed in Clint's brown face. He lifted his hat to the applause without looking at them, as a cricketer lifts his cap, and rode out of the ring, well satisfied to have ignored the judge's disqualifying eye long enough to have induced Stockings to cross the hated obstacle.

Number Six had two faults. Number Seven two-and-a-half.

"Number Eight, please," said the loud-speaker, and Jane shivered and put her hand in Bee's. For once Ruth did not have to manufacture drama to suit her; her mouth was open with suspense and she was entirely oblivious of Ruth Ashby.

Timber had neither the experience nor the machine-like power of Riding Light. He had to be ridden. It rested as much on Simon's judgement as on Timber's powers whether they could beat the almost faultless performance of Peggy Gates's horse. Brat thought that Simon looked very white about the mouth. There was more in this for Simon than winning a cup at a small country show. He had to take that prize from the girl who had tried to be upsides with him by introducing a made winner to beat his own untried horses.

Timber came in looking puzzled. It was as if he said: "I've *done* this." His ears pricked at the sight of the jumps and then flickered in question. There was no eagerness to go at them as there had been

180

when it was a new experience. But he went good-manneredly down to the first and cleared it in his effortless fluid fashion. Brat thought that he could hear the Ashby hearts thumping alongside him. He could certainly hear his own; it was making a noise like the Bures Silver Band's drum. Simon was half-way round. Ruth had shut her mouth and her eyes and looked as if she were praying. She opened her eyes in time to see Timber clear the gate; a smooth river of black pouring over the white barrier. "Oh, thank you, God," said Ruth. There was only the wall and the water left.

As Timber turned at the far end of the ring to come back to the wall a gust of wind lifted Simon's hat from his head and sent it bowling along the ground behind him. Brat was of the opinion that Simon was not even aware of it. Not even Tony Toselli had shown a concentration like Simon's. For Simon there quite patently existed nothing in this world but himself, the black horse, and the jumps. No one, *no one*, was going to come between Simon Ashby and the sun and get away with it.

Everything that Simon knew of riding, everything he had learned since he first sat on a pony at the age of two, was devoted to getting Timber safely over the wall. Timber did not like hard bare obstacles.

He had started his canter to the wall when a shrieking white terrier shot out from the stand in pursuit of the distant hat, streaking across in front of the advancing Timber like a hard-kicked ball, and yelling its excitement as only a terrier can.

Timber swerved from this terror and broke into a sweat.

Ruth shut her eyes again and resorted to further prayer. Simon soothed Timber patiently, cantering him round and making much of him while someone retrieved the dog and brought it back to its owner. (Who said: "Poor darling Scottie, he might have been killed!") Patiently, while the unforgiving seconds ticked on, Simon worked to reassure Timber. He must know that time was running out, that the dog incident was now officially over and each additional second's delay piling up against him.

Brat had marvelled often at Simon's powers of self-control, but he had never seen a more remarkable sample of it. The temptation to take Timber to the jump as he was must be enormous. But Simon was taking no chances with Timber. He was pawning time to gain a little better odds for Timber.

And then, having apparently calculated his time to the nearest possible margin, he brought Timber, still sweating but collected, to the wall again. Just before he came to the fence Timber hesitated a little.

And Simon sat still.

If it had been possible for Brat to like Simon Ashby he would have liked him at that moment.

The horse, undistracted from the task in front of him, gathered himself together and catapulted himself over the hated obstacle. And then, relieved to have it behind him, he raced on delightedly to the water and rocketed across it like a blackbird.

Simon had done it.

Jane took her hand out of Bee's, and wiped her palms on a screwed-up ball of handkerchief.

Bee slipped her arm through Brat's and squeezed it.

The great burst of cheering made speech inaudible.

In the quiet that succeeded it Ruth said, as one remembering an awkward engagement: "Oh, dear! I've pawned my month's allowance."

"To whom?" asked her aunt.

"God," said Ruth.

26

BRAT surveyed himself in the small cracked mirror of the Gent's Temporary Dressing-room and decided that primrose and violet did not become him any better than they became Simon. It would take Roger Clint's dark face to do justice to those springtime glories. Roger Clint would probably look dashing in them. He was in no mood to look favourably on Roger Clint. Whenever he had caught sight of Eleanor this afternoon it seemed that she was in the company of Mr. Clint, and what is more, seemed to be enjoying the company.

Brat tugged the yellow visor a little farther over his eyes. A sick misery burned in him; a spiritual heartburn.

"What's it got to do with you?" said a voice in him. "You're her brother: remember?"

"Shut up!"

"Can't have your cake and eat it, you know."

"*Shut up!*"

He walked out of the almost deserted dressing-room and went to find Chevron. The serious business of the day was over and there was an air of relaxation. In the shade of the trees competitors who had taken part in the sober events were now walking ponies and coffeehousing while they waited for the bending race. Alone for the moment, on a solid dun pony, was Peggy Gates, her eyes roving over the crowd in search of someone. She looked tired and discouraged. As Brat came level with her he paused and said:

"That was very bad luck."

"Oh, hullo, Mr. Ashby! What was?"

"The big drum."

"Oh, that!" she said, and smiled at him. "Oh, that was just one of those things."

She sounded quite philosophical about it, and yet Brat could have sworn that when he came up she had tears in her eyes.

"Good luck to the race," she said.

Brat thanked her and was moving away when she said: "Mr. Ashby, have I done anything to offend Simon, do you know?"

Brat said no, not that he knew.

"Oh. It's just that he seems to be avoiding me lately, and I'm not aware of having done anything—anything that he wouldn't——"

There were undoubted tears in her eyes now.

"Oh, you *know*," she said, tried a smile, didn't manage it very well, and moved away with a wave of her hand.

So it had not been a desire to be mistress of Latchetts that had moved pretty Peggy; it was devotion to Simon. Poor Peggy. Simon would never forgive her for Riding Light.

Eleanor was waiting under the trees on Buster, but stirrup to stirrup with her was Roger Clint, who had also found a pony for the bending race. Roger was pouring out a long story and Eleanor was nodding sympathetically; Brat gave them a wide berth and betook himself to the stables. In the stables he found Bee and Gregg. Gregg saw him weighed out and saddled Chevron, who was nervous and unhappy.

"It's the sound of the crowd that worries her," Gregg said. "Something she hears and can't understand. If I were you, Mr. Patrick, sir,

I'd take her out and walk her. Take her out and show her the crowds and she'll be so interested she'll forget her nerves."

So Brat took the dithering chestnut out into the park, and she became gradually quieter, as Gregg had known she would. Presently Simon found him and suggested that it was time to be going down to the start.

"Did you remember to sign the book?" he asked.

"Book?" said Brat. "Sign for what?"

"To show that you consent to your horse running."

"I never heard of anyone signing a book. The horse was entered, wasn't it?"

"Yes, but in previous years they had trouble with gate-crashers. Some bright sparks who took out horses that didn't belong to them, when their owners didn't intend to run them. Had a free jaunt on them, and in at least one case broke the already tired horse down."

"All right. Where is the book?"

"In the weighing-room place. I'll look after Chevron till you come back. No need to take her into that mêlée."

In the little office, sitting behind the desk, was Colonel Smollett.

"Well, young Ashby, your family has been doing very well to-day, eh? Three firsts, no less. Are you going to add a fourth? Book? What book? Oh, the paper. Yes, yes. Here it is."

Brat, signing the single sheet of paper that was presented to him, said that he had never heard of this procedure.

Probably not. Never heard of it myself. But it does insure the show against loss to a certain extent. That fellow whose horse was ridden unbeknownst to him last year, he sued the Show for damages. Very nearly got them, too. So your brother suggested this method of insurance."

"My brother? Simon suggested it?"

"Yes. Got a head on him, Simon. Now no one can say that his horse was pulled out without his permission."

"I see."

He went back and retrieved Chevron from Arthur's custody.

"Mr. Simon said he couldn't wait, Mr. Patrick, but he said to wish you luck. He's gone back to the stands with the rest of the family to watch the finish."

"All right, Arthur; thanks."

"Would you like me to come to the start with you, sir?"

184

"Oh, no, thanks."

"In that case, I'll go and see about getting myself a place to see from. Good luck, sir. We're betting on you."

And he hurried off through the crowd.

Brat put the reins over Chevron's head and was just about to mount when he thought that he would take one more look at the girth. He had already tightened it, but perhaps he had made it too tight.

But someone had loosened the girth.

Brat stood holding up the flap with his hand and stared. Someone had loosened it since he left the mare with Simon. He put his hand under the girth and tested its degree of slackness. He reckoned that it would have got him out of the park into the country and would have lasted perhaps another two fences. After that, the saddle would have slipped round on the highly excitable Chevron and she would have gone crazy.

Arthur? No, not Arthur. Simon almost certainly.

He tightened the girth and made for the start. As he arrived he was overtaken by Roger Clint in white and scarlet on Operation Stockings.

"You're Patrick Ashby, aren't you?" he said. "My name is Roger Clint." He leaned over and shook hands. "Very nice to have you at Bures again."

"Who won the bending race?" Brat asked.

"I did. By a short head from Nell."

"Nell" indeed!

"She won it last year on Buster, so it is just as well that the thing should go round. And I wanted a silver cup, anyway."

Brat had no time to ask why he had this longing for a silver cup. They were lining up, and he was Number Five, and Roger Clint was away on the outside. There were fourteen runners and a considerable amount of jostling. There was no gate, of course, the start being by flag.

Brat was in no hurry at the start. He let the others lead him so that he could gauge the opposition. At least five, he decided, were horses that had been ridden so much to-day that they were of no consequence and were merely cluttering up the course and spoiling things for their betters. Three more he had seen jumped in a junior competition, and had no belief that they would ever get round the course. That left five possibles, and of these three were dangerous: a bay charger ridden by his officer owner; a great raking brown youngster ridden by a young farmer; and Roger Clint's mount.

They took the hurdles at a tearing pace, and two of the overworked lot, fighting for position, struck into each other and rolled into a third. One of the "junior" jumpers came a frightful purler over the first fence going into the country, and brought down the other two over-tired animals. Which cleared the field very happily.

Chevron liked seeing her horses in front of her, and was patently enjoying herself. She loved jumping and was taking her fences with an off-handed confidence. One could almost hear her humming. She watched the other two "junior" jumpers fail to get over a blind fence and flicked her heels in their faces.

The field was thinning out very nicely.

Brat began to move up.

He passed the fifth of the possibles without effort. The fourth was making a noise like a pipe band but seemed good for a little yet. In front of him at the farthest point of the course were the soldier on the bay charger, the farmer on the big young brown horse, and Roger Clint on the chestnut with the white stockings. Apart from his own Chevron, Clint's was probably the best quality horse in the race, but like the soldier was riding like a veteran, and the farmer like someone who has no respect for his neck.

It was a right-handed course, and the farmer's young horse jumped consistently to the right, so that no one could with any safety come up on the inside of him as long as he hugged the turns tightly. And since no one wanted to go wider than they need at the turns they dallied a little behind the big brown until they could come into the straight and pass him without disadvantage. It was going to be a race when they came back to that last half-mile of park.

Gradually the pipe band that had been so long at his left ear faded backwards into the distance, and when they came back to the park there were only four of them in it: the soldier, the farmer, Clint, and himself. He didn't mind about the other two, but he wanted very much to beat Roger Clint.

Clint had a look round as they left the country behind, and flashed a friendly smile to him. After that there was no time for courtesies. The pace was turned on with the suddenness of a tap, and the four of them pounded down the green avenue between the fluttering red flags as if classic honours were waiting for them at the other end. The big young brown horse began to sprawl; and the charger, though steady as a rock and apparently tireless, seemed to have no turn of speed to finish with. Brat decided to keep Chevron's nose level with the chestnut's quarters and see what transpired. Together they forged ahead of the bay and the brown. The farmer was using his whip and his horse sprawled more at every lift of it. The soldier was sitting still on the bay and evidently hoping that stamina would tell in the end.

Brat had a good look at Stockings and decided that he was tiring rapidly and that Clint, from the careful way he was riding him, knew it. There were two hurdles to go. He had no idea how much speed or stamina Chevron might have left, so he decided that the safest method was to try to trick Clint out of it. He shook Chevron up and took her up level with Stockings as if he were making his effort. Clint increased his speed to match, and together they crossed the last two obstacles, Brat still by his own choice a little in the rear, and therefore out of Clint's vision. Then Brat eased the pressure momentarily, and Clint, taking it for granted that a falling back so near the post argued failing stamina, was glad that he would not have to ask his mount for the last ounce and relaxed a little. Brat gathered Chevron together with all his strength and came like a rocket from behind him. Clint looked, startled, and set Stockings alight again, but it was too late. They were far too near the post for that, as Brat had reckoned. He had stolen the race.

"Of all the 'old soldier' tricks to fall for!" laughed Clint, as they walked their horses together to the weighing-room. "I ought to have my head examined."

And Brat felt that whether Eleanor was going to marry him or not he really did like Roger Clint quite a lot.

27

BRAT had expected that Simon's success would have shored up his disintegrating spiritual structure and that the cracks would have disappeared. But it seemed that the very opposite had happened.

'The strain of the afternoon followed by the triumph of having beaten a performer like Riding Light had eaten away a little more of the foundation and shaken his equilibrium still further.

"I've never seen Simon so cock-a-hoop," Eleanor said, watching Simon over Brat's shoulder as they danced together that night. She said it as one making an apology. "He is usually so off-hand about his triumphs."

Brat said that it was probably the champagne, and turned her away from her view of Simon.

He had looked forward all day to dancing with Eleanor, but it was with Bee that he had danced first. Just as he had given up his first chance of a ride with Eleanor to walk on Tanbitches with the ghost of Pat Ashby, so when faced with the moment of his first dance with Eleanor he had found something else that he wanted more. He had crossed the room to Bee and said: "Will you dance with me?" They had danced together in a happy quiet, her only remark being: "Who taught you to cheat someone out of a race like that?"

"I didn't have to be taught. It's original sin."

She laughed a little and patted him with the hand that was lying on his shoulder. She was a lovely woman, Bee Ashby, and he loved her. The only other person he had ever loved was a horse called Smoky.

"I haven't seen much of you this afternoon since that awful exhibition of Tony's," Eleanor said.

Brat said that he had wanted to talk to her before the race but that she was in deep conversation with Roger Clint.

"Oh, yes. I remember. His uncle wants him to give up the farm and go and live in Ulster. His uncle is Tim Connell, you know, who has the Kilbarty stud. Tim wants to retire, and would lease the place to Roger, but Roger doesn't want to leave England."

Understandably, Brat thought. England and Eleanor together was heaven enough. "I don't see him here to-night?"

"No, he didn't stay for the dance. He just came to get a silver cup to take home to his wife."

"His *wife*!"

"Yes, she had their first baby last week, and she sent him to the show to get a christening mug for it. What is the matter?" she asked.

"Remind me sometime to break Ruth's neck," he said, beginning to dance again.

She looked amused and said: "Has Ruth been romancing?"

"She said he wanted to marry you."

"Oh, well, he did have an idea like that but it's a long time ago. And of course he wasn't married last year, so Ruth probably didn't know about it. Are you going to be all patriarchal and supervise my marriage plans?"

"Have you any?"

"None at all."

As the night wore on and he danced more and more with Eleanor, she said: "You really must dance with someone else, Brat."

"I have."

"Only with Peggy Gates."

"So you've been keeping track of me. Am I keeping you from dancing with someone you want to dance with?"

"No. I love dancing with you."

"All right, then."

This was perhaps the first and the last night he would ever dance with Eleanor. A little before midnight they went up together to the buffet, filled their plates, and took them to one of the little tables in the balcony. The buffet was part of the actual hotel building, and the balcony, a piece of Regency ironwork, looked down on the little garden at the side of the hotel. Chinese lanterns hung in the garden and above the tables in the balcony.

"I'm too happy to eat," Eleanor said, and drank her champagne in a dreamy silence. "You look very nice in your evening things, Brat."

"Thank you."

"Do you like my frock?"

"It's the most beautiful frock I ever saw."

"I did hope you would like it."

"Have you had supper already to-night?"

"No. Only some drinks and a sandwich."

"Better eat, then."

She ate in an uninterested fashion that was new in Eleanor.

"It has been an Ashby occasion, hasn't it, the Seventy-fourth Annual Show of the Bures Agricultural . . . Stay still for a moment, you have a gnat crawling down your collar."

She leant over and struck the back of his neck lightly. "Oh, it's going down!" In a rough sisterly fashion she bent his head aside with one hand while she retrieved the insect with the other.

"Got it?" he said.

But she was silent, and he looked up at her.

"You're *not* my brother!" she said. "I couldn't feel the way I——"
She stopped, horrified.

In the silence the beat of the distant drums came up from the
assembly room.

"Oh, Brat, I'm sorry! I didn't mean that! I think I must have
drunk too much." She began to sob. "Oh, Brat, I'm sorry!" She
gathered up her bag from the table and stumbled from the dim
balcony into the buffet room. "I'll go and lie down and get sober."

Brat let her go and sought counsel in the bar. There was some
sort of stunt in the assembly room at midnight, and the bar was
deserted except for Simon, all by himself with a bottle of champagne
at a table in the far corner.

"Ah! My big brother," said Simon. "Are you not interested in
the lottery drawing? Have a drink."

"Thanks. I'll buy my own."

He bought a drink at the bar and carried it down the long room
to Simon's table.

"I suppose lottery odds are too long for you," Simon said. "You
want the table rigged before you bet."

Brat ignored that. "I haven't had a chance of congratulating you
on your win with Timber."

"I don't need praise from you."

Simon was certainly drunk.

"That was very rude of me, wasn't it?" he said like a pleased child.
"But I enjoy being rude. I'm behaving very badly to-night, aren't I?
I seem to be slipping. Have a drink."

"I've got one."

"You don't like me, do you?" He looked pleased by Brat's dislike.

"Not much."

"Why not?"

"I suppose because you are the only one who doesn't believe that
I am Patrick."

"You mean, don't you, that I'm the only one who *knows* you're
not?"

There was a long silence while Brat searched the shining eyes
with their odd dark rim.

"You killed him," he said, suddenly sure of it.

"Of course I did." He leaned forward and looked delightedly at

190

Brat. "But you'll never be able to say so, will you? Because of course Patrick isn't dead at all. He's alive, and I'm talking to him."

"How did you do it?"

"You'd like to know, wouldn't you? Well, I'll tell you. It's very simple." He leaned still closer and said in a mock-confidential undertone: "You see, I'm a witch. I can be in two places at once."

He sat back and enjoyed Brat's discomfiture.

"You must think that I'm a lot drunker than I am, my friend," he said. "I've told you about Patrick, because you are my posthumous accomplice. A wonderful epithet, that, and I managed it very well. But if you think that I am going to make you free of the details, you are mistaken."

"Then, why did you do it?"

"He was a very stupid little boy," he said in his airy "Simon" tone, "and not worthy of Latchetts." Then he added, without façade: "I hated him, if you want to know."

He poured himself another glass of the Ayala, and drank it. He laughed under his breath, and said: "It's a wonderful spiritual twinship, isn't it? I can't tell about you and you can't tell about me!"

"You have the advantage of me, though."

"I have? How?"

"You have no scruples."

"Yes; I suppose it is an advantage."

"I have to put up with you, but you have no intention of putting up with me, have you? You did your best to kill me this afternoon."

"Not my best."

"You'll improve on it, I take it?"

"I'll improve."

"I expect you will. A person who can be in two places at once can do better than a loosened girth."

"Oh, much better. But one has to accept the means to hand."

"I see."

"I suppose you wouldn't like, in return for my confidences, to tell *me* something?"

"Tell you what?"

"Who you are?"

Brat sat looking at him for a long time.

"Don't you recognise me?" he said.

"No. Who are you?"

"Retribution," said Brat, and finished his drink.

He walked out of the bar and hung for a little over the banisters until his inside settled down and his breath came more easily. He tried to think of some place where he could be alone to think this thing out. There was nowhere in the hotel; even in his bedroom Simon might join him at any moment; he would have to go out.

He went to get his coat from Number 17, and on the way back again he met Bee.

"Has everyone gone crazy?" Bee said angrily. "Eleanor is upstairs crying, Simon is getting drunk in the bar, and now you look as if you had seen a ghost. What is the matter with everyone? Have you had a quarrel?"

"A quarrel? No. Eleanor and Simon have had a wearing day, I expect."

"And what makes *you* so white about the gills?"

"Ballroom air. I'm from the wide open spaces: remember?"

"I've always understood that the wide open spaces were just seething with dance halls."

"Do you mind if I take the car, Bee?"

"Take it where?"

"I want to see the sun rise over Kenley Vale."

"Alone?"

"Definitely alone."

"Put on your coat," she said. "It's cold out."

At the top of the rise looking over Kenley Vale he stopped the car and shut off the engine. It was still dark and would be dark for some time yet. He got out and stood on the grass verge, leaning against the bonnet, and listened to the silence. The earth and grass smelt strong in the cool damp after the sun of yesterday. The air was motionless. Far away across the Vale a train whistled.

He had a cigarette, and his stomach felt better. But the turmoil had merely moved up. The turmoil was now in his head.

He had been right about Simon. He had been right in seeing the resemblance to Timber: the well-bred creature with the beautiful manners who was also a rogue. Simon had told the truth, back there in the bar. He had been glad to tell him the truth. They said all killers wanted to boast about their killings; Simon must have longed often to tell someone how clever he had been. But he could never tell until now; when he had a "safe" listener.

He, Brat Farrar, was the "safe" listener.

He, Brat Farrar, owned Latchetts, and Simon took it for granted that he would keep what he had taken. That he would keep it as Simon's accessory.

But that, of course, was not possible. The unholy alliance with Loding was one thing; but the alliance that Simon took so mockingly for granted was not possible. It was monstrous. Unthinkable.

And that being that, what was he going to do about it?

Go to the police and say: Look, I'm not Patrick Ashby at all. Patrick Ashby was killed by his brother eight years ago. I know, because he told me so when he was a little drunk.

And then they would point out that in the course of their investigation into the death of Patrick Ashby it was proved that Simon Ashby had spent the relevant hours in the smith's company in Clare.

He could tell them the truth about himself, but nothing would be changed except his own life. Patrick Ashby would remain a suicide.

How had Simon done it?

"One has to accept the means at hand," he had said, about his slackening of the girth.

What "means at hand" had there been that day eight years ago?

The slackening of the girth had been a combination of planning and improvisation. The "signing the book" suggestion had been a long shot. If it worked successfully to get him out of the way, then Simon was free to complete the rest of his plan. If it did not work, then no harm was done. The set-up was innocent to the observer's eye.

That was the way Simon's mind had worked about the girth, and that was the way it had worked eight years ago, undoubtedly. The set-up that was innocent and unquestionable. The using of the means at hand.

How, eight years ago, had Simon used an innocent set of circumstances to provide him with the chance he wanted?

Brat's mind was still toiling round and round the problem when the first sigh of the stirring air told him that the dawn was coming. Presently the wind came again, lifting the leaves this time and ruffling the grass, and the east was grey. He watched the light come. The first bird notes dropped into the quiet.

He had been there for hours and he was no nearer a solution of the problem that faced him.

A policeman came along at leisure, pushing a bicycle, and paused to ask if he were in trouble. Brat said that he was getting some fresh air after a dance.

The policeman looked at his starched linen and accepted his explanation without remark. He looked at the interior of the car and said: "First time I ever saw a young gentleman getting fresh air alone after a dance. You haven't made away with her, by any chance, have you, sir?"

Brat wondered what he would say if he said: "No, but I'm accessory after the fact to another murder."

"She turned me down," he said.

"Ah. I see. Nursing your grief. Take it from me, sir, a week from now you'll be so thankful you'll feel like dancing in the street."

And he pushed his bicycle away along the ridge.

Brat began to shiver.

He got into the car and headed after the policeman. Where could he get something hot, he asked?

There was an all-night café at the main crossroads two miles ahead, the policeman said.

At the café, warm and bright and mundane after the grey spaces of the dawn, he drank scalding coffee. A buxom woman was frying sausages for two lorry-drivers, and a third was trying his luck at a penny-in-the-slot game in the corner. They glanced incuriously at his dance clothes, but beyond exchanging greetings with him they left him alone.

He came back to Bures at breakfast time, and put the car in the garage. The Chequers vestibule had a littered look; it was still only half-past seven, and show people notoriously made a night of it. He went up to Number 17 and found Simon fast asleep, with all his clothes in one single heap on the floor just as he had peeled them off. He changed into his day clothes, quietly at first and then less carefully as he realised that only long shaking would awaken Simon in his present condition. He looked down at Simon and marvelled. He slept quietly, like a child. Had he grown so used to the thing after eight years that it no longer troubled him, or was it that it never had been a monstrous thing in his estimation?

It was a charming face, except perhaps for the pettish mouth. A delightful face; delicately made and proportioned. There was no more suggestion of wrong-doing about it than there was in the beauty that was Timber.

194

He went downstairs and washed, wishing that he had thought in time of having a bath. He had been too obsessed by the desire to change clothes without having to talk to Simon.

When he came into the dining-room he found Bee and the twins having breakfast, and joined them.

"Nell and Simon are still asleep," Bee said. "You'd better come back with me and the twins in the car, and let Eleanor take Simon when they waken."

"What about Tony?"

"Oh, he went back yesterday with Mrs. Stack."

It was a relief to know that he could go back to Latchetts with Bee in peace.

The twins began to talk about Tony's exploit, which was patently going to be part of Latchetts history, and he did not have to make conversation. Bee asked if the dawn had come up to expectation, and remarked that he was looking the better of it.

Through the green early-morning countryside they drove home to Clare, and Brat caught himself looking at it with the emotions of someone who has only a short time to live. He looked at things with a that-will-still-be-there attitude.

He would never come to Bures. He might never even drive with Bee again.

Whatever else Simon's confession meant, it meant the end of his life at Latchetts.

28

It was Thursday morning and on Sunday Charles Ashby would come sailing up Southampton Water, and nothing would stop the subsequent celebrations. He followed Bee into the hall at Latchetts feeling desperate.

"Do you mind if I desert you and go into Westover?" he asked Bee.

"No, I think you are due a little rest from the family. Simon is for ever running away."

So he took the bus into Westover and waited until it was time for Mr. Macallan to be having his mid-morning coffee. He went to the *Westover Times* office and asked to see the files. The office boy, who showed no sign of ever having seen him before, took him to the cellar and showed him where they were. Brat read the report of the inquest all over again, but could find no help there.

Perhaps in the full report there would be something?

He went out and looked up Colonel Smollett in the telephone book. Where, he asked the Colonel, would the report of the inquest on himself be now? With the police? Well, would he make it easy for him to see it?

The Colonel would, but he considered it a most morbid and undesirable ambition, and implored young Ashby to think again.

So armed with the Colonel's telephoned introduction, he went to see a highly amused police force, who sat him down in a leather armchair and offered him cigarettes, and set before him the coroner's report of eight years ago with the empressment of a conjurer who has produced the rabbit from the hat.

He read it all through several times. It was merely the *Westover Times'* report in greater detail.

He thanked the police, offered them cigarettes in his turn, and went away as empty of suggestion as he had come. He went down to the harbour and hung over the wall, staring westward at the cliffs.

He had a fixed point, anyhow. A fixed point that could not be altered. Simon Ashby was in Clare that day. That was held to by a man who had no reason for lying, and no suspicion that the fact was of any importance. Simon had never been long enough away from Mr. Pilbeam's vicinity to make his absence felt.

Pat Ashby must have been killed between the time that old Abel met him in the early afternoon and the moment when Mr. Pilbeam had to chase Simon home for six o'clock supper.

Well, there was that old saying about Mahomet and the mountain.

He thought the Mahomet theory over, but was stumped by the coat on the cliff-top. It was Simon who had written that note, but Simon was never out of Clare.

It was two o'clock when he came to himself, and he went to have lunch at a small pub in the harbour. They had nothing much left, but it did not matter because he sat staring at his plate until they put the bill in front of him.

He went back to Latchetts and without going to the house went to the stables and took out one of the horses that had not been at Bures. There was no one about but Arthur, who reported that all the horses were safely back and all well except that Buster had an overreach.

"Taking him out like that, sir?" Arthur asked, nodding at Brat's tweed suit. And Brat said that he was.

He turned up to the down as he had that first morning when he took out Timber, and did again what he had done on Timber's back. But all the glory was gone. The whole world looked sick. Life itself tasted bad.

He dismounted and sat down where he had sat that morning a month ago, looking out over the small green valley. It had seemed paradise to him then. Even that silly girl who had come and talked to him had not sufficed to spoil it for him. He remembered how her eyes had popped when she found he was not Simon. She had come there sure of seeing Simon because it was his favourite place for exercising the horses. Because he . . .

The horse by his side threw up his head as Brat's sudden movement jerked the bit in his mouth.

Because he . . .?

He listened to the girl's voice in his mind. Then he got slowly to his feet and stood a long time staring across the valley.

He knew now how Simon had done it. And he also knew the answer to something that had puzzled him. He knew why Simon had been afraid that, by some miracle, it was the real Patrick who had come back.

He got on the horse and went back to the stables. The great clouds were racing up from the south-west and it was beginning to rain. In the saddle room he took a sheet of writing paper from the desk and wrote on it: "Out for dinner. Leave the front door on the latch for me, and don't worry if I am late." He put it in an envelope, addressed it to Bee, and asked Arthur to hand it in at the house when he was passing. He took his burberry from the back of the saddle-room door, and went out into the rain, away from Latchetts. He had the knowledge now. What was he going to do with it?

He walked without conscious purpose, unaware of anything but the dreadful question to be answered. He came to the smithy where Mr. Pilbeam was still working, and greeted him, and exchanged opinions on the work in hand and on the weather to come, without having for a moment ceased to battle with the thing in his mind.

He walked up the path to Tanbitches and up the hill over the wet

grass to the crown of beeches, and walked there to and fro among
the great boles of the trees, distracted and stricken.

How could he bring this thing on Bee?

On Eleanor? On Latchetts?

Had he not already done Latchetts sufficient harm?

Would it matter so much if Simon were left in possession as he
had been for eight years?

Who had been harmed by that? Only one person: Patrick.

If Simon was to be brought to justice for Patrick's death, it would
mean horror beyond horror for Bee and the rest.

He didn't have to do it at all. He could go away; stage a suicide.
After all, Simon had staged Patrick's suicide, and it had passed a
police investigation. If a boy of thirteen could do that he could do
it. He could just drop out, and things would be as they were a
month ago.

And—Pat Ashby?

But Pat, if he could choose, would not want justice on Simon
at the cost of his family's ruin. Not Pat, who had been kind and
always thought first of others.

And Simon?

Was he to make good Simon's monstrous supposition that he would
do nothing? Was Simon to spend a long life as the owner of Latchetts?
Were Simon's children to inherit Latchetts?

But they would still be Ashbys. If Simon were brought to justice
there would be no more Ashbys at Latchetts.

And how would it advantage Latchetts to have its inheritance
made safe by the condoning of murder?

Was it not, perhaps, to uncover that murder that he had come
by such strange ways to Latchetts?

He had come half across a world to that meeting with Loding in
the street, and he had said to himself that so strange a chance must
be destiny. But he had not imagined it to be an important destiny.
Now, it would seem, it was an all-important one.

What was he to do? Who could advise him? Decide for him? It was
not fair that this should be put on his shoulders. He had not the
wisdom, the experience, to deal with a thing of this magnitude.

"I am retribution," he had said to Simon, and meant it. But that
was before he had the weapon of retribution in his hand.

What was he to do?

198

Go to the police to-night? To-morrow?

Do nothing, and let the celebrations begin when Charles Ashby came home?

What was he to do?

It was late that night that George Peck, sitting in his study and conscious every now and then even from his distant vantage point in Thebes of the lashing rain on the window of the Rectory in Clare, heard a tapping at that window, and came back from Thebes and went to the front door. It was by no means the first time that people had tapped on that window late at night.

In the light from the hall he saw one of the Ashbys, he could not tell which because the soaked hat almost obscured the face.

"Rector, may I come in and talk to you?"

"Of course, Patrick. Come in."

Brat stood on the step, the rain sluicing from his coat.

"I'm afraid I'm very wet," he said vaguely.

The Rector looked down and saw that the grey tweed of his trousers was black, and his shoes an oozing pulp. His eyes went sharply to the boy's face. Brat had taken off his limp hat and the rain-water from his soaked hair was running down his face.

"Take off your coat and leave it here," the Rector said. "I'll give you another one when you are ready to go." He went to the hall cloakroom and came back with a towel. "Rub your head with that."

Brat did as he was told, with the obedient air and fumbling movements of a child. The Rector went through to the empty kitchen and brought a kettle of water.

"Come in," he said. "Just drop the towel where your wet coat is." He led the way into his study and put the kettle on an electric ring. "That will be hot in no time. I often make tea for myself when I sit up late. What was it you wanted to talk to me about?"

"A pit in Dothan."

"What?"

"I'm sorry. My mind has stopped working. Have you a drink of any kind?"

The Rector had meant to put the whisky in the tea, as a toddy, but he poured a stiff one now and Brat drank it.

"Thank you. I am sorry to come and worry you like this, but I had to talk to you. I hope you don't mind."

"I am here to be talked to. Some more whisky?"

"No, thanks."

"Then let me give you some dry shoes."

"Oh, no, thank you. I'm used to being wet, you know. Rector, I want your advice about something very important, but can I talk to you as if—as if it were confessional? I mean, without your feeling that you must do something about it."

"Whatever you say I shall treat as confession, certainly."

"Well, first I have to tell you something. I am not Patrick Ashby."

"No," agreed the Rector. And Brat stared.

"You mean—you mean, you *knew* I wasn't Patrick?"

"I rather thought that you weren't."

"Why?"

"There is more to any person than a physical presence; there is an aura, a personality, a being. And I was almost sure the first time I met you that I had never met you before. There was nothing in you that I recognised, although you have many things in common with Patrick as well as your appearance."

"And you did nothing about it!"

"What do you suggest that I should have done? Your lawyer, your family, and your friends had all accepted and welcomed you. I had no evidence to show that you were not Patrick. Nothing but my own belief that you weren't. What good would it have done to express my disbelief? It did not seem to me that it would be long before the situation resolved itself without my interference."

"You mean: that I should be found out."

"No. I mean that you did not seem to me someone who would be happy in the life you had chosen. Judging by your visit to-night, I was right."

"But I didn't come here to-night just to confess to not being Patrick."

"No?"

"No, that is only—I had to tell you that because it was the only way you could understand what has—I wish my mind was clearer. I've been walking about trying to get things straight."

"Perhaps if you told me first how you came to Latchetts at all, it would at least clear *my* mind."

"I—I met someone in America who had lived in Clare. They—she thought I looked like an Ashby, and suggested that I should pretend to be Patrick."

200

"And you were to pay her a share of the proceeds of the deception."

"Yes."

"I can only say that she earned her percentage whatever it was. As a tutor she must be remarkable. I have never seen a better piece of coaching. Are you American, then?"

"No," said Brat, and the Rector smiled faintly at the emphasis. "I was brought up in an orphanage. I was left on its doorstep."

And he sketched for the Rector the story of his life.

"I have heard of your orphanage," the Rector said, when he had finished. "It explains one thing that puzzled me: your good upbringing." He poured tea, and added whisky. "Would you like something more substantial than biscuits, by the way? No? Then have the oatmeal ones; they are very filling."

"I had to tell you all this because of something I found out. Patrick didn't commit suicide. He was murdered."

The Rector set down the cup he was holding. For the first time he looked startled.

"Murdered? By whom?"

"His brother."

"*Simon?*"

"Yes."

"But, Patrick! That—— What is your name, by the way?"

"You forget. I haven't got one. I've always been called Brat. It was a corruption of Bartholomew."

"But my dear fellow, that is absurd. What evidence have you of anything so incredible?"

"I have Simon's word for it."

"*Simon* told you?"

"He boasted about it. He said that I could never do anything about it because it would mean giving myself away. He knew as soon as he saw me that I wasn't Patrick, you see."

"When did this extraordinary conversation take place?"

"Last night, at the Bures ball. It wasn't as sudden as it sounds. I began to wonder about Simon long before that, and I challenged him about it because of something he said about *knowing* I wasn't Patrick, and he laughed and boasted about it."

"I think that the setting of this scene does a lot to explain it."

"You mean you think we were drunk?"

"Not exactly. Elated, shall we say. And you challenged Simon on the subject, and Simon with his perverted sense of mischief provided you with what you expected from him."

"Do you really believe I have as little intelligence as that?" Brat asked quietly.

"It surprises me, I must admit. I have always considered you to be highly intelligent."

"Then believe me, I am not here because of a piece of fooling on Simon's part. Patrick didn't commit suicide. Simon killed him. Deliberately. And what is more, I know how he did it."

And he told him.

"But Brat, you have no evidence even now. That is theory, what you have just told me. An ingenious and likely theory, I admit. It has the merit of simplicity. But you have no evidence whatsoever."

"We can get the evidence, if the police once know the truth. But that isn't what I want to know. What I want advice about is—well, whether to let sleeping dogs lie."

And he explained his dilemma.

But the Rector, rather surprisingly in view of his silence about his doubts of Brat's identity, had no doubts on the subject at all. If murder had been done, then the law must be invoked. Anything else was anarchy.

His point was that Brat had no case against Simon. His mind had run on murder, he had taunted Simon with it, Simon had one of his well-known impish moments and confessed, and Brat after long thought had found a theory to fit the alleged confession.

"And you think that I've been walking about in the rain since four o'clock because of a little joke of Simon's? You think that I came here to-night and confessed to not being Patrick because of a little joke of Simon's?" The Rector was silent. "Tell me, Rector, were you surprised when Pat committed suicide?"

"Exceedingly."

"Do you know anyone who wasn't surprised?"

"No. But suicide *is* a surprising thing."

"I give up," Brat said.

In the contemplative silence that followed, the Rector said: "I see what you meant by the pit in Dothan. That was an excellent upbringing at the orphanage."

"It was a very thoroughly Biblical one, if that is what you mean. Simon knows that story, too, by the way."

"I expect so, but how do you happen to know?"

"When he heard that Patrick had come back he couldn't help, in spite of his denials, a fear that it might be true. There had been that other case, you see. That time the victim had survived by a miracle. He was afraid that by some miracle Patrick had survived. I know, because he came into that room, the first day I was there, strung up to face something dreadful. And his relief when he saw me was almost funny."

He drank down the rest of his tea and looked quizzically at the Rector. In spite of himself he was beginning to feel better.

"Another of Simon's little jokes was to send me out that first day on Timber, without telling me he was a rogue. But I suppose that was just his 'perverted sense of mischief.' And still another of his little jokes was to loosen my girth yesterday before I started a race on Chevron. But I suppose that was just one of his 'well-known impish moments'."

The Rector's deep eyes considered Brat.

"I am not defending Simon—he has never been an admirable character—but tricks played on an interloper, a pretender—even dangerous tricks, are one thing, and the murder of a well-loved brother is quite another. Why, by the way, did Simon not denounce you at once if he did not believe you were his brother?"

"For the same reason that you didn't."

"I see. He would merely be held to be—difficult."

"And of course, having got rid of one Patrick with impunity, he looked forward with confidence to getting rid of another."

"Brat, I wish I could convince you that this is a figment of your imagination."

"You must have a great respect for my imaginative powers."

"If you look back, critically and honestly, you must see how the thing grew in your mind from quite small beginnings. An edifice of your own making."

And that, when Brat took his leave towards two o'clock in the morning, was still the Rector's opinion.

He offered Brat a bed, but Brat compromised on the loan of a waterproof and a torch, and found his way back to Latchetts by the soaking field-path with the rain still pouring hopelessly down.

"Come and see me again before you decide anything," the Rector had said; but he had at least been helpful in one direction. He had answered Brat's main question. If it was a choice between love and justice, the choice had to be justice.

He found the front door of Latchetts unlocked, a note from Bee on the hall table, saying: "Soup on the ring in the pantry," and a silver cup on an ebony stand bearing a card in Eleanor's writing which said: "You forgot this, you blasé rodeo hound!"

He put out the lights and crept up through the silent house to his bed in the old night nursery. Someone had put a hot-water bottle in his bed. He was asleep almost before his head touched the pillow.

29

On Friday morning Simon came bright and cheerful to breakfast and greeted Brat with pleasure. He commented on the process of the "trunk" murder investigations, the character of Tattie Thacker (whose value had been estimated by the court at one half-penny) and the iniquity of poisoning as a means of ridding oneself of a human encumbrance. Except for an occasional gleam in his eye he showed no awareness of their changed relationship. He was taking their "spiritual twinship" for granted.

Eleanor too seemed to be back on the old footing, although she seemed shy, like someone who has made a social gaffe. She suggested that in the afternoon they should take the four silver cups into Westover and give instructions for their engraving.

"It will be nice to have 'Patrick Ashby' on a cup again," she said.

"Yes, won't it!" Simon said.

Simon evidently looked forward to years of baiting his spiritual twin. But when Brat said, in answer to Bee, that he had talked late with the Rector, Simon's head came up as if he had heard a warning. And after that Brat caught Simon's glance at him every now and then.

When Eleanor and Brat were setting off for Westover in the afternoon, he appeared and insisted on making a third in the bug's scanty space. One of the cups was his own unaided work, he said, and he had a right to say what was to go on it, and whether it should be in Roman, Arabic, Hebrew, Greek or Cyrillic script, or mere shorthand.

So powerful was Simon's indifferent charm that even Brat found himself on the verge of wondering whether the Rector had been right and he had built his story out of whole cloth. But he remembered the horse that Farmer Gates had bought for his daughter Peggy, and concluded that that was a more reliable guide to Simon than anything Simon himself might provide.

When they had decided on the lettering for the names on the cups, Simon and Eleanor went to tea, but Brat said that he had some shopping to do. Brat had decided what he had to do in the present impasse. He could not go to the police with his story in its present form with any more hope of being believed than he had been by the Rector. If the Rector, who knew Simon's weaknesses, refused to believe without concrete evidence, how much more would the police refuse to believe, when Simon to them was not a wayward boy but Mr. Ashby of Latchetts?

Brat therefore proposed to provide them with the evidence.

He went down to the harbour and sought a chandler's, and there, after some consultation and a deal of choosing, bought two hundred feet of rope. The rope was so thin that it was not much thicker than stout string, but its breaking-point under tension was very much that of steel. He asked them to pack it in a cardboard box and deliver it to the Angel garage, where the bug was. He received it at the garage and packed it away in the luggage compartment.

When the others arrived to go home he was waiting innocently in the car with an evening paper.

They had packed themselves into the bug and were preparing to go when Simon said: "Whoa! We've forgotten to leave that old tire with them," and he got out and opened the rear compartment to get the tire.

"What is in the box, Nell?"

"I didn't put any box there," Eleanor said, not moving. "It can't be for us."

"It's mine," Brat said.

"What is it?"

"Secret."

"James Fryer and Son, Ship Chandlers," said Simon's voice.

Oh, God! There was a label on the box that he had not noticed.

Simon shut the luggage compartment with a bang and came back to his seat. "What have you been buying, Brat? One of those ships in a bottle? No, it is a little too large for that. One of those ships not in a bottle. One of those full-sailed galleons that sit on suburban sideboards to delight the heart of our Island Race and comfort it for being sick on the trip to Margate."

"Don't be a fool, Simon. What is it, Brat? Is it really a secret?"

If Simon wanted to find out what was in the box he most certainly would, by one method or another. And to make a mystery of it was to call attention to it. Far better to be apparently frank about it.

"If you must know, I'm afraid I'll lose the knack of spinning a rope, so I've bought some to practise on."

Eleanor was delighted. Brat must show them some spinning that very evening.

"No. Not till I've tried it out in camera first."

"You'll teach me how, won't you?"

Yes, he would teach her how to throw a rope. She was going to hate him one day soon, if that rope did what it was bought for.

When they arrived back at Latchetts he took the rope out and left it openly in the hall. Bee asked about it, and accepted the explanation of its presence, and no one took any more notice of it. He wished that his last short time at Latchetts did not have to be spent in lying. It was odd that, having spent his whole time at Latchetts lying like a Levantine, he should mind so much about this smaller deception.

There was still time to do nothing about it. To leave the rope there, and not ask it to answer any question. It was the wrong kind of rope for throwing, but he could change it for the right kind.

But when night came, and he was alone in his room, he knew that he had no choice. This was what he had come half across a world to do, and he was going to do it.

The household went early to bed, still tired from their excitements at Bures, and he gave them till half-past twelve, and then prospected. There seemed to be no light anywhere. There was certainly no sound. He went downstairs and took the rope from its corner. He unlatched the dining-room window, stepped over the sill into the night, and drew it gently down again behind him. He waited for any reaction, but there was none.

He made his way softly over the gravel to the grass, sat down in the shelter of the first paddock trees, out of the range of the windows, and without need of any light, deftly knotted footholds at intervals down the length of rope. It was a pleasant reassuring thing to feel the familiar touch of rope after so long. It was a well-bred rope and answered sweetly to his demands. He felt grateful to James Fryer and Son.

He wound the rope and put the coil of it over his shoulder. In half an hour the moon would be up. It was a young moon, and not much of a lamp, but he had two good torches in his pocket and he did not very much desire a full moon's frankness to-night.

Every five minutes he stopped and waited to see if he had been followed. But nothing at all moved in the night. Not even a cat.

The grey light of the coming moon greeted him as he came towards the foot of Tanbitches, and he found the path to Westover without having to flick a torch. He followed it up a little and then, when he could see the beech-crown of the hill against the sky, he struck off it until he reached the thicket on the upper side of the old quarry. There he sat down and waited. But again there was no sound in all the sleeping countryside except the sudden cry of a sheep on the hill. He tied the rope round the bole of the largest of the young beeches that had seeded themselves there, and let it uncoil itself until it fell over the edge of the quarry into the green thickness below. This was the steep side of the quarry. The lower side had had a narrow entrance, but it had long ago fallen together and become overgrown with an impenetrable denseness of briars. Old Abel had told him all about it the day they had sat there and talked of Patrick. Abel knew all about the quarry because he had once rescued a sheep from it. It was much easier to go down the sheer face, Abel said, than in at the lower side. In fact, to go in at the lower side, or any other side, was plumb impossible. No, there was no water in it; at least there wasn't any twenty years ago, which was when last he went down after a sheep; the water all drained away under the hill to the sea.

Brat tested the rope several times, and felt for it fraying. But the bole of the tree was smooth, and where it went over the lip of the quarry he had padded it. He slid over the edge and felt for his first toe-hold. Now that he was level with the ground he was more aware of the brightness of the sky. He could see the dark shape of the low thicket against it, and the larger darkness of the tree above him.

He had found his first foothold in the rope now, but his hands were still on the rope where it lay taut on the turf.

"I should hate," said Simon's voice in its most "Simon" drawl, "to let you go without an appropriate farewell. I mean, I could just cut the rope and let you think, if you had time to think at all, that it had broken. But that wouldn't be any fun, would it?"

Brat could see his bulk against the sky. From the shape of it, he was half-kneeling on the edge, by the rope. Brat could touch him by putting out a hand.

Fool that he had been to underrate Simon. Simon had taken no chances. He hadn't even taken the chance of following him. He had come first and waited.

"Cutting the rope won't do much good," he said. "I'll only land in the branches of some tree farther down, and yell my head off until someone comes."

"I know better than that. A personal acquaintance of mine, this quarry is. Almost a relation, one might say." He expelled his breath in a whispered laugh. "A sheer drop to the ground, half a hillside away."

Brat wondered if he had time to slide down the rope in one swift rush before Simon cut it. The footholds had been for coming up again. He could just ignore them and slide. Would he be near enough the bottom before Simon realised what he had done?

Or would it be better——? Yes. His hand tightened on the rope and he pressed on his toe-hold and lifted himself until he had almost got one knee on the turf again. But Simon must have his hand on the rope somewhere. He had felt the movement.

"Oh, no, you don't!" he said, and brought his heel down on Brat's hand. Brat grabbed the foot with his other hand and hung on, his fingers in the opening of the shoe. Simon brought his knife down on Brat's wrist and Brat yelled, but continued to hang on. He dragged his right hand from under Simon's shoe and caught him round the back of the ankle. He was covering with his body the rope in front of Simon and as long as he held on Simon could not turn to cut the rope behind him. It is very upsetting to have one's foot grasped from below when one is standing on the very edge of a precipice.

"Let go!" said Simon, stabbing frantically.

"If you don't stop that," panted Brat, "I'll drag you over with me."

"Let go! Let go!" Simon said, hitting wildly in blind panic and not listening.

Brat removed the hand that was holding on to the edge of the
208

shoe and caught the knife-hand as it came down. He now had his right hand round Simon's left ankle, and his left hand was clutching Simon's right wrist.

Simon screamed and pulled away, but Brat hung his weight on the wrist. He had the confidence of a toe-hold, but Simon had nothing to brace himself against. Simon tore at the hand that was hanging on to his knife-wrist, and Brat, with a great heave, took his right hand from Simon's foot and caught Simon's left hand with it. He had now got Simon by both wrists, and Simon was bent over like a bow above him.

"Drop that knife!" he said.

As he said it he felt the turf at the quarry edge settle a little and slide forward. It made no difference to him, except to press him out a little from the face of the cliff. But to Simon, already bent over by the weight of Brat's arms and body, it was fatal.

Horrified, Brat saw the dark mass come forward on top of him. It struck him from his toe-hold, and he fell down with it into darkness.

A great light exploded in his head, and he ceased to know anything.

30

BEE sat in the dingy café with a cup of slopped coffee in front of her and read the sign on the other side of the road for the hundredth time in the last forty-eight hours. The sign said: MOTORISTS. PLEASE REFRAIN FROM USING YOUR HORN. THIS IS A HOSPITAL. It was only seven o'clock in the morning, but the café opened at six, and there was always at least one other customer having a meal as she sat there. She did not notice them. She just sat with a cup of coffee in front of her and stared at the hospital wall opposite. She was an old inhabitant of the café by now. "Better go out and have a meal," they would say kindly, and she would cross the road and sit for a little with a cup of coffee in front of her and then go back again.

Her life had narrowed down to this pendulum existence between the hospital and café. She found it difficult to remember a past, and quite impossible to visualise a future. There was only the "now," a

dreary half-world of grey misery. Last night they had given her a
cot in one of the sisters' rooms, and the night before that she had
spent in the hospital waiting-room. There were two phrases that they
used to her, and they were as sickeningly familiar as the sign on
their wall: "No, no change," they would say, or, "Better go out
and get a meal."

The slatternly girl came and pushed a fresh cup of coffee in front
of her and took away the one she had. "That one's cold," said the
slatternly girl, "and you haven't even touched it." The fresh cup
was slopped over, too. She was grateful to the slatternly girl but felt
outraged by her sympathy. She was enjoying the vicarious drama
of her presence in the café, and its implications.

MOTORISTS. PLEASE REFRAIN FROM USING—— She must stop reading that thing. Must look at something else. The blue checked pattern
of the plastic tablecloth, perhaps. One, two, three, four, five, six——
Oh, no. Not counting things.

The door opened and Dr. Spence came in, his red hair tumbled
and his chin unshaved. He said "Coffee!" to the girl, and slid into
the seat beside her.

"Well?" she said.

"Still alive."

"Conscious?"

"No. But there are better indications. I mean, of a chance of
his regaining consciousness, not necessarily of—his living."

"I see."

"We know about the skull fracture, but there are no means of
telling what other injuries there may be."

"No."

"You oughtn't to be living on cups of coffee. That's all you've
been having, isn't it?"

"She hasn't been having that," said the slatternly girl, putting
down his full cup. "She just sits and looks at them."

A wave of weary anger rose in her at the slatternly girl's appropria-
tion of her concerns.

"Better let me take you downtown and give you a meal."

"No. No, thank you."

"The Angel is only a mile away, and you can rest properly there
and——"

210

"No. No, I can't go as far away as that. I'll drink this cup. It's nice and hot."

Spence gulped down his coffee and paid for it. He hesitated a moment as if reluctant to leave her. "I have to go back to Clare now. You know I shouldn't leave him if he wasn't in good hands, don't you? They'll do more for him than I ever could."

"You've done wonders for all of us," she said. "I shall never forget it."

Now that she had begun drinking the coffee she went on drinking it, and did not look up when the door opened again. It would not be another message from the hospital already, and nothing had any importance for her that was not a message from the hospital. She was surprised when George Peck sat down beside her.

"Spence told me I should find you here."

"George!" she said. "What are you doing in Westover at this hour of the morning?"

"I have come to bring you comfort that Simon is dead."

"Comfort?"

"Yes."

He took something from an envelope and laid it in front of her on the table. It was weatherworn but recognisable. It was a slender black stylograph with a decoration consisting of a thin yellow spiral.

She looked at it a long time without touching it, then looked up at the Rector.

"Then they have found—it?"

"Yes. It was there. Do you want to talk about it here? Wouldn't you prefer to go back to the hospital?"

"What difference does it make? They are both just places where one waits."

"Coffee?" said the slatternly girl, appearing at George's shoulder.

"No; no, thank you."

"Righteeo!"

"What—what is there? I mean, what—what is left? What did they find?"

"Just bones, my dear. A skeleton. Under three feet of leaf mould. And some shreds of cloth."

"And his pen?"

211

"That was separate," he said carefully.

"You mean, it—had been—that it had been thrown down after?"

"Not necessarily, but—probably."

"I see."

"I don't know whether you will find it comforting or not—I think it is—but the police surgeon is of the opinion that he was not alive—or perhaps it would be more accurate to say not conscious—when he——"

"When he was thrown over," Bee said for him.

"Yes. The nature of the skull injury, I understand, leads him to that conclusion."

"Yes. Yes, I am glad, of course. He probably knew nothing about it. Just ended quite happy on a summer afternoon."

"There were some small objects in the cloth. Things that he probably had in his trousers pockets. But the police have kept these. Colonel Smollett gave me this," he picked up the stylograph and put it back in its envelope, "and asked me to show it you so that you might identify it. What news from the hospital? Spence was driving away when I saw him."

"None. He is not conscious."

"I blame myself greatly for that, you know," the Rector said. "If I had listened with understanding he would not have been driven to this *sub rosa* proceeding, to that crazy night-time search."

"George, we must do something to find out who he is."

"But I understand that the orphanage——"

"Oh, I know. They made the usual inquiries. But I don't suppose they were very persistent ones. We could do much better, surely."

"Starting from the pre-supposition that he has Ashby blood in him?"

"Yes. I can't believe that a resemblance like that could exist without it. The coincidence would be too great."

"Very well, my dear. Do you want it put in hand—now?"

"Yes. Especially now. Time may be precious."

"I'll speak to Colonel Smollett about it. He'll know how to go about it. I talked to him about the inquest, and he thinks it may be possible to manage without your appearing. Nancy told me to ask you if you would like her to come in to Westover to be with you, or if it would only worry you to have someone around."

"Dear Nan. Say it is easier alone, will you? But thank her. Tell

212

her to stand by Eleanor, rather. It must be dreadful for Nell, having to toil with unimportant things in the stables."

"I think it must be a soothing thing to have to devote oneself to the routine demands of the animal world."

"Did you break the news to her, as you promised? The news that Brat was not Patrick?"

"Yes. I dreaded it, Bee, I confess frankly. You had given me one of the hardest tasks of my life. She was still fresh from the shock of knowing that Simon had been killed. I dreaded it. But the event was surprising."

"What did she do?"

"She kissed me."

The door opened, and a probationer, flushed and young and pretty, and looking in her lilac print and spreading white linen like a visitor from another world, stood in the dim opening. She saw Bee and came over to her.

"Are you Miss Ashby, please?"

"Yes?" said Bee, half rising.

"Miss *Beatrice* Ashby? Oh, that's nice. Your nephew is conscious now, but he doesn't recognise anyone or where he is; he just keeps talking about someone called Bee, and we thought it might be you. So Sister sent me across to see if I could find you. I'm sorry to interrupt you, and you haven't finished your coffee, have you, but you see——"

"Yes, yes," said Bee, already at the door.

"He may be quieter, you see, if you are there," the probationer said, following her out. "They often are, when someone they know is there, even if they don't actually recognise them. It's funny. It's as if they could see them through their skin. I've noticed it often. They'll say, Eileen?—or whoever it is. And Eileen says, Yes. And then they're quiet for a bit. But if anyone else says yes, nine times out of ten they're not fooled at all, and get restless and fractious. It's very strange."

What really was strange was to hear that steady stream of words from the lips of the normally silent Brat. For a day and a night and a day again she sat by his bed and listened to that restless torrent of talk. "Bee?" he would say, just as the little probationer had recounted to her. And she would say: "Yes, I'm here," and he would go back reassured to whatever world he was wandering in.

213

His most constant belief was that this was the time he had broken his leg, and this the same hospital; and he was torn with anxiety about it. "I'll be able to ride again, won't I? There's nothing really wrong with my leg, is there? They won't take it off, will they?"

"No," she would say, "everything is all right."

And once, when he was quieter: "Are you very angry with me, Bee?"

"No, I'm not angry with you. Go to sleep."

The world went on outside the hospital; ships arrived in South-ampton Water, inquests were held, bodies were consigned to the earth, but for Bee the world had narrowed to the room where Brat was and her cot in the Sister's room.

On Wednesday morning Charles Ashby arrived at the hospital, padding lightly down the polished corridors on his large noiseless feet. Bee went down to receive him and took him up to Brat's room. He had hugged her as he used to when she was a little girl, and she felt warm and comforted.

"Dear Uncle Charles. I'm so glad you were fifteen years younger than Father, or you wouldn't be here to be a comfort to us all."

"The great point in being fifteen years younger than your brother is that you don't have to wear his cast-offs," Charles said.

"He's asleep just now," she said, pausing outside Brat's room, "so you'll be very quiet, won't you?"

Charles took one look at the young face with the slack jaw, the blue shadows under the closed eyes, and the grey haze of stubble, and said: "Walter."

"His name is Brat."

"I know. I wasn't addressing him. I was merely pointing out the resemblance to Walter. That is exactly what Walter used to look like, at his age, when he had a hangover."

Bee came nearer and looked. "Walter's son?"

"Undoubtedly."

"I don't see any resemblance, somehow. He doesn't look like any-one but himself, now."

"You never saw Walter sleeping it off." He looked at the boy a little longer. "A better face than Walter's, though. A good face." He followed her into the corridor. "I hear you all liked him."

"We loved him," she said.

214

"Well, it's all very sad, very sad. Who was his accomplice, do you know?"

"Someone in America."

"Yes, so George Peck told me. But who would that be? Who went to America from Clare?"

"The Willett family went to Canada. And they had daughters. It was a woman, you know. Perhaps they finished up in the States."

"If it was a woman I'll eat my hat."

"I feel that way too."

"Do you? Good girl. You're an admirably intelligent woman, Bee. Nice-looking, too. What are we going to do about the boy? For the future, I mean."

"We don't know yet if he has a future," she said.

31

ONLY the Rector, Bee, Charles, Eleanor, and the firm of Cosset, Thring and Noble knew, so far, that Brat was not Patrick Ashby.

And the police.

The police, that is, at what is known as "the highest level."

The police had been told everything, and they were now engaged in their own admirable fashion in smoothing out the mess to the best of their ability without breaking any of the laws which they were engaged to uphold. Simon Ashby was dead. It was to no one's advantage to uncover the story of his crime. By a process of not saying too much, the ritual of the Law might be complied with, leaving unwanted truths still buried; a harrow dragging over earth that held below its surface unexploded bombs.

The coroner sat on the poor bones found in the quarry, and adjourned the inquest *sine die*. No one in the neighbourhood had ever been reported missing. Tanbitches, on the other hand, was a favourite camping ground for gipsies, who were not given to reporting accidents to the police. Nothing remained of the clothing but a few scraps of unrecognisable cloth. The objects found in the vicinity of

215

the bones were unidentifiable; they consisted of a corroded piece of metal that might once have been a whistle, another corroded piece still recognisable as a knife, and several coins of small denominations.

"George!" said Bee. "What became of the pen?"

"The stylograph? I lost it."

"George!"

"Someone had to lose it, my dear. Colonel Smollett couldn't; he's a soldier, with a soldier's sense of duty. The police couldn't; they have their self-respect and their duty to the public to consider. But my conscience is between me and my God. I think they were touchingly grateful to me in their tacit way."

The adjourned inquest on Simon Ashby came later, since it had been postponed until Brat was capable of being interviewed in hospital. The policeman who had interviewed him reported that Mr. Ashby could remember nothing about the accident, or why he should have gone there with his brother at that hour to climb down into the quarry. He had an idea that it was the result of a bet. Something about whether there was water in the old quarry or not, he thought; but could not take his oath on it since his recollection was vague. He had serious head injuries and was still very ill. He did know, however, that he had found out from Abel Tusk that there was no water there; and Simon probably had said that that was highly unlikely, and so the contest may have arisen.

Abel Tusk corroborated the fact that Patrick Ashby had asked him about water in the quarry, and that it was an unusual thing to find the floor of an old quarry dry. It was Abel Tusk who had given the first alarm of the accident. He had been out on the hill with his sheep and had heard what he took to be cries for help from the direction of the quarry, and had gone there as fast as he could and found the undamaged rope, and had gone down to the blacksmith's and used his telephone to call the police.

Bee, replying to the coroner, agreed that she would most certainly have taken steps to put an end to any such plan had she heard about it. And the coroner expressed his opinion that it was for that reason that the thing had been done *sub rosa*.

The verdict was death by misadventure, and the coroner expressed his sympathy with the family on the loss of this high-spirited young man.

So the problem of Simon was settled. Simon who, before he was fourteen, had killed his brother, calmly written a note on that brother's behalf, tossed the pen into the abyss after his brother's body, and gone home calmly to six o'clock supper when he was chased out of the smithy. Who had joined the night search for his brother on his pony, and some time during that long night had taken his brother's coat to the cliff-top and left it there with the note in the pocket. Who was now to be mourned by the countryside as a high-spirited young man of memorable charm.

The problem of Brat remained.

Not the problem of who he was, but of the problem of his future. The doctors had decided that, having against all probability lived so long, he was likely to go on living. He would need long care, however, and a peaceful life if he was to recover properly.

"Uncle Charles came to see you one day when you were ill," Bee said to him when he was well enough to keep his attention on a subject. "He was astonished by your resemblance to Walter Ashby. My cousin."

"Yes?" said Brat. He was not interested. What did it matter now?

"We began inquiries about you."

"The police did that," he said wearily. "Years ago."

"Yes, but they had very little to come and go on. Only that a young girl had arrived by train with a baby, and gone away by train without one. The train had come from the crowded Birmingham district with all its ramifications. We started at the other end. Walter's end. We went back to where Walter was, somewhere about twenty-two years ago, and began from there. Walter was a rolling stone, so it wasn't easy, but we did find out that, among his other jobs, he was in charge of a stable in Gloucestershire for a couple of months while the owner was away having an operation. The household was a housekeeper and a young girl who cooked. She was a very good cook, but her real ambition was to be a hospital nurse. The housekeeper liked her and so did the owner, and when they found she was going to have a baby they let her stay on, and she had her baby in the local maternity home. The housekeeper always believed that it was Walter's child, but the girl would not say. She did not want to get married; she wanted to be a nurse. She said that she was taking the baby home for the christening—she came from Evesham way—and she didn't come back. But the housekeeper had a letter from her long afterwards, thanking her for her goodness and

217

telling her that the girl had realised her ambition and was a nurse. "No one knows about my baby," she said, "but I have seen that he is well looked after."

She glanced at Brat. He was lying with his eyes on the ceiling, but he appeared to be listening.

"Her name was Mary Woodward. She was an even better nurse than she was a cook. She was killed during the war, taking patients out of a ward to safety in a shelter."

There was a long silence.

"I seem to have inherited my cooking talents too," he said; and she could not tell whether the words were bitter or not.

"I was very fond of Walter. He was a dear; very kind. He had only one fault; he had no head for drink, and he liked drink very much. I don't believe for a moment that Walter knew about the girl. He was the kind who would have rushed to marry her. I think she didn't want him to know."

She had another look at Brat. Perhaps she had told him all this too soon; before he was strong enough to be interested. But she had hoped that it would give him an interest in life.

"I'm afraid that is as near as we can get, Brat. But none of us have any doubt about it. Charles took one look at you and said, 'Walter.' And I think myself you look a little like your mother. That is Mary Woodward. It was taken in her second year at St. Luke's."

She gave him the photograph, and left it with him.

A week or two later she said to Eleanor: "Nell, I'm going to leave you. I've taken a lease of Tim Connell's stud at Kilbarty."

"Oh, Bee!"

"Not immediately, but when Brat is able to travel."

"You're taking Brat there? Oh, yes, of course you must go! Oh, that is a wonderful idea, Bee. It solves such a lot of problems, doesn't it? But can you afford it? Shall I lend you money for it?"

"No, Uncle Charles is doing that. Lovely to think of Charles supporting horses, isn't it? You'll need all you have to pay death duty, my dear. Mr. Sandal has broken it to the Bank that the place belonged to Simon all the time."

"What shall we do about letting people know about Brat? I mean, about his not being Patrick."

"I don't think we'll have to do anything about it. The facts will inevitably *ooze*. They always do. I think we just do nothing to

218

prevent the leak. The fact that we are making him part of the family instead of starting prosecutions and things will take a lot of the fun out of it for the scandal-mongers. We'll survive, Nell. And so will he."

"Of course we will. And the first time someone mentions it boldly to me, I shall say: "My cousin? Yes, he did pretend to be my brother. He *is* very like Patrick, isn't he? As if we were discussing cream-cakes." She paused a moment and then added: "But I should like the news to get round before I'm too old to marry him."

"Are you thinking of it?" Bee said, taken aback.

"I'm set on it."

Bee hesitated; and then decided to let the future take care of itself.

"Don't worry. It will get round," she said.

"Now that Uncle Charles is here, and is going to settle down at Latchetts," she said later to Brat, "I can go back to having a life of my own somewhere else."

His eyes came away from the ceiling, and watched her.

"There's a place in Ulster I have my eye on. Tim Connell's place at Kilbarty."

She saw his fingers begin to play with the sheet, unhappily.

"Are you going away to Ulster, then?" he asked.

"Only if you will come with me, and run the stable for me."

The easy tears of the newly-convalescent rose in his eyes and ran down his cheek.

"Oh, Bee!" he said.

"I take it that means that my offer is accepted," she said.